NAGUIB MAHFOUZ

Midaq Alley
The Thief and
the Dogs
Miramar

NAGUIB MAHFOUZ

MIDAQ ALLEY
Translated from the Arabic by Trevor Le Gassick

THE THIEF AND THE DOGS
Translated from the Arabic by Trevor Le Gassick
and M. M. Badawi
Revised by John Rodenbeck

MIRAMAR
Translated by Fatma Moussa Mahmoud
Edited and revised by Maged el Kommos
and John Rodenbeck
Notes by Omar el Qudsy

Introduction by John Fowles

Quality Paperback Book Club
New York

CONTENTS

MIDAQ
ALLEY

INTRODUCTION

he novel and short story, not truly traditional forms of Arabic literary expression, have developed great popularity over the past century in most countries of the Middle East. Cairo, the cosmopolitan capital of the most populous country of the area, has throughout the period been its cultural and literary center. There, in 1911 in the Gamaliyya section of the old city, Naguib Mahfouz was born. Despite his full-time career in responsible positions in various departments of the Egyptian civil service, he was to develop a dedication to literature that would later give him international prominence as his country's leading author. He has received honorary degrees from France, the Soviet Union and Denmark and his works have been translated into many languages. In 1970 he received Egypt's prestigious National Prize for Letters and in 1972 he was awarded the Collar of the Republic, his nation's highest honor.

Mahfouz' parents were of the middle-class Muslim merchant class of Cairo and in his sixth year they moved away from the crowded

and conservative ancient quarter where he was born to the modern
European-style inner suburb of Abbasiyyah. Naguib grew up and went
to school there and later attended Cairo University where he obtained
his bachelor's degree in philosophy in 1934. After graduation he
joined the university's administration for a short period and then
embarked on his long career with the Ministry of Waqf Pious Foundations and later other administrative branches of the Egyptian
government.

He began writing even before completing his university education, publishing occasional short stories in literary journals. Though
merely awkward little sketches of contemporary life and not popular
today, they give the impression of a sober young man particularly
sensitive to areas of conflict and tragedy in the lives of others; they are
highly reminiscent of the works of Mustafā al-Manfalūtī, to whose
influence Mahfouz readily gives acknowledgement. It is clear that
even then, unlike so many of his contemporaries who still despised
prose fiction as a literary form, Mahfouz saw his stories as a means
to bring enlightenment and reform to his society. The same sense
of high morality and interest in the thoughts and motivations of
others apparent in these early stories have marked all his later works
as well, and contributed greatly to the broad range of respect he
enjoys.

Also in the thirties he published a translation from English of a
work dealing with life in ancient Egypt. This subject had then, after
the sensational archaeological discoveries at Luxor and particularly
the uncovering of the tomb of Tutankhamen, come to fascinate many
of his countrymen. Following publication of a volume of further short
stories set in modern Egypt, his attention again reverted to ancient
times. In the middle and late thirties he wrote three novels depicting
aspects of life in ancient Egypt that had obvious significance for his
countrymen still living under forms of British control and a somewhat tyrannical King Farouk. Two of the novels deal with the struggle
of the people of Egypt against despotic monarchs; the third shows
how the Egyptians cast off the rule of the Hyksos invaders.

Mahfouz has said that his intention at that time was to write a
lengthy series of historical novels set in ancient Egypt, but by the

early forties his attention had in fact come to focus firmly once more on life in his contemporary society. A series of four novels of the period demonstrate the instability of family life in Cairo and the corruption pervasive in the governmental and party-political structure of the country. They stress in particular how dependent morality is on a secure material base and on simple good fortune. In these stories we see the Cairo of the Second World War, living under the pressures of the presence of a Britain at war and in the expectations of a Nazi invasion. The social consequences of the German air raids are a common theme of Egyptian literature of the time and in Mahfouz' novels too we see how barriers of class, age and sex dissolve as people are forced to crowd together in the air-raid shelters. In his novels *Khān al-Khalīlī* and *Zuqāq al-Midaq* (*Midaq Alley*), both named after streets in the Azhar quarter of the ancient city, the author turned his attention away from the comparative sophistication of his middle-class and suburban characters to those of an area similar to that of his own birth. How he is charmed and intrigued by the richly colorful life of these people is apparent in all his major work for the next decade. Whatever his central themes, the novels crowd with minor characters depicted with keen perception and great humor.

During the late forties he busied himself with construction of his 1500-page *Trilogy*, each part named after a street near the great and revered mosque of Husain in the same quarter of Cairo. Covering the fortunes of a large Muslim merchant family, perhaps like his own, over the first half of this century, it provides fascinating insight into the panorama of Egyptian life of the period. The cast of characters is rich and their interpersonal and societal relationships are examined in precise detail and authenticity. Time and change is a recurring theme of Mahfouz' work and in the *Trilogy* he has ample room to develop it to the full. He shows how traditional Muslim views of, for example, the marriage relationship developed in the space of only fifty years from one of absolute subservience of the wife to one of near equality. The social and political conflicts of the turbulent period are seen to influence every aspect of Egyptian life, as controversies rage between individual members of the family over their allegiance to conflicting systems of belief and behavior. Support and opposition to the monarchy and the various political factions, the Muslim Brethren or the Marxists, and devotion or indifference to the constant struggle with the British, are seen as dominant and explosive issues.

The *Trilogy* went through the usual pattern of Mahfouz' works—first serialization and later publication in book form. It achieved growing popularity through the fifties and its success drew new attention to his earlier works, many of which originally had appeared almost unnoticed; they were consequently republished several times. But for seven years following the 1952 Free Officers' Revolution under Colonel Nasser, Naguib Mahfouz wrote nothing more. His silence was broken only in 1959 with publication of his *Awlād Ḥāritnā* (*Children of Our Quarter*), an allegorical novel offering an essentially pessimistic view of man's struggle for existence. His treatment of the subject proved unpopular with Egypt's religious establishment and he felt best advised to refrain from publishing it in book form within Egypt, although it has since become available from a Lebanese publisher. Clearly discouraged by the work's mixed reception, Mahfouz published no further novels for several years and his 1962 *al-Liṣṣ wa al-Kilāb* (*The Thief and the Dogs*) deals in a circumspect way with a less complex and controversial issue. And now his style had changed from realist to impressionist and he used the stream of consciousness technique to pursue the thoughts and motivations of his central character, a convicted burglar seeking vengeance on his release from jail against the individuals and society that he thinks have corrupted and destroyed him. It is a powerful and fast-moving work, a drama in which the killing of the hero is inevitable but tragic.

Again, then, the view is pessimistic and the later novels of the sixties pursue similar themes. In *al-Ṭarīq* (*The Road*) the central figure (modern Egypt?), the son of a prostitute, is involved in a fruitless and tragic search for his father and his honor. In *al-Summān wa al-Kharīf* (*Quails and the Fall*), Mahfouz pursues a politically sensitive theme; a bright young star of the Wafdist old regime loses his position, self-respect and fiancée in the early purges of Nasser's Revolution. His utter demoralization and the waste of his talents, for all his obvious faults, is shown as a national as well as personal tragedy. The novel expresses obvious regret at the Revolutionary government's failure to rehabilitate earlier intellectuals and others of such importance to Egypt.

His other novels of the middle sixties were equally courageous in their frank portrayal of the distress of many intellectuals living within the tight confines of Nasser's Egypt. In *al-Shaḥḥādh* (*The Beggar*) the reader witnesses the trauma of a successful lawyer coming close to insanity as he grows to realize the extent to which the Revolution is failing to achieve the high hopes for a new morality of those who, like himself, had worked under the Egyptian monarchy for political and social reform. Mahfouz' next novel, *Thartharah fawqa al-Nīl* (*Small-talk on the Nile*), is full of outright ridicule of life under Nasser's regime. The total absurdity of the bureaucratic structure is revealed in the novel's opening scene, when the central character is asked by his department head the whereabouts of a requested report. Pointing to the finished report on his superior's desk, the civil servant is amazed to discover that his pen must have dried out while he was writing, after only the first few lines! Yet he fails to see any justification for his superior's anger; after all, the indentations on the paper remained, proof that he had written it as requested! In a series of brilliant scenes set on a houseboat on the Nile, the novel's characters, all important members of Cairo's intelligentsia, drown their depression in drugs and express the utmost disgust and derision for the values and structures of their society. In this novel and in *Mīrāmār* that closely followed it, Mahfouz argued that it was the cowardice and irresponsibility of the intellectuals themselves that had led their society to its sorry state.

By the late fifties Naguib Mahfouz was achieving recognition as his country's most gifted novelist and publication of his recent works have been covered by all the country's information media and soon adapted for television, theater and film presentation. As a consequence his reputation is unrivalled throughout the Arabic-speaking world. His work has been a careful and deliberate reflection of the moods and frequently the malaise of his country. And so deep was the national depression after the Arabs' disastrous defeat in the 1967 war with Israel and the subsequent invasion of Sinai, loss of the Suez

Canal and the destruction and evacuation of the major towns along its banks, that Mahfouz, like the other major fiction writers of Arabic, has been in no mood for sustained literary production. In recent years his output has been largely restricted to allegorical and philosophical short stories and playlets. His latest novel, *al-Ḥubb taḥta al-Maṭar* (*Love in the Rain*), published in 1973, reflects the new sense of freedom then briefly being enjoyed by Egyptian writers and since heavily curtailed. Its subject matter was particularly sensitive at the time; it shows and by implication criticizes the carefree and dissolute life continuing in Cairo while troops suffer and wait on the front lines for a renewal of conflict with Israel.

Midaq Alley, then, belongs to the earlier period of Mahfouz' work. Although written and set in the early forties, it provides glimpses of unusual intimacy into Egypt in a period of fast transition that is still today in progress. The past thirty years have seen enormous changes in every area of Egyptian life, yet much there has remained the same. Many of the tourists in Cairo's great hotels who buy the recently republished pocket edition of E. W. Lane's famous *Manners and Customs of the Modern Egyptians* must fail to notice, as they view the colorful scene around them, that the book was first published in 1836!

Both the locale and the events of this novel should certainly not be viewed within a narrow framework of time. In *Midaq Alley* we see how characters are enticed away from the roles natural to their birth and upbringing by the hope of material gains chiefly through work with the British Army; nowadays it is the factories of semi-industrial Africa and the Arab world that draw people away from their traditional roles in village and town. The universal problems of behavior and morality the novel examines remain, of course, the same; Kirsha's drug addiction and homosexuality and Hamida's ambitions, Alwan's middle-aged fantasies and Husain's dissatisfaction, are restricted neither to time nor place. And the views expressed in eternal optimism by Radwan Husaini, and the attitudes of his neighbors towards him, remind one of the place of men of religion in all societies today.

In this, as in many of Mahfouz' works, we perceive time, here personified in the ageless Alley, to be the novel's central focus. The aspirations and tragedies of its inhabitants are witnessed with total indifference by the Alley within which the circle of life and death is forever run again. In this it is a view in close focus of the human drama at large, selected by a literary craftsman of impressive skills. And in *Midaq Alley*, as in life itself, there is much gaiety, color and excitement to enliven the passing scene.

NOTE ON THIS TRANSLATION

Arabic is, of course, a language far different in syntax and sounds from English and gives expression to a highly distinctive people and a complex culture. The translator has, then, an almost limitless range of choices and dilemmas over vocabulary and arrangement when attempting to convey the spirit of a work of fiction. The present translation offers an approximation of how Mahfouz might have expressed himself had English been his native tongue.

Very little deliberate editing was, however, in fact found necessary; some phrases and short passages that tended to be repetitious have been dropped or condensed and the names of characters and places have been simplified, while left in recognizable form. The changes made have been kept as insignificant as possible consistent with a text that should move easily and naturally for an English-speaking readership. A few words, relating to aspects of Egyptian national and Muslim cultural life for which we have no parallel, have been given brief descriptive definitions within the text where essential. The only alternative, a glossary and notations, would seem unfortunate in a work of creative fiction, a cumbersome and largely unnecessary barrier between the work and its readers.

Trevor Le Gassick

1

any things combine to
show that Midaq Alley is
one of the gems of times
gone by and that it once
shone forth like a flashing star in the history of Cairo. Which Cairo do
I mean? That of the Fatimids, the Mamluks or the Sultans? Only God
and the archaeologists know the answer to that, but in any case, the
alley is certainly an ancient relic and a precious one. How could it be
otherwise with its stone-paved surface leading directly to the historic
Sanadiqiyya Street? And then there is its coffee-shop known as
"Kirsha's." Its walls decorated with multicolored arabesques, now
crumbling, give off strong odors from the medicines of olden times,
smells which have now become the spices and folk-cures of today and
tomorrow . . .

Although Midaq Alley lives in almost complete isolation from all
surrounding activity, it clamors with a distinctive and personal life of
its own. Fundamentally and basically, its roots connect with life as a
whole and yet, at the same time, it retains a number of the secrets of a
world now past.

The sun began to set and Midaq Alley was veiled in the brown hues of the glow. The darkness was all the greater because it was enclosed like a trap between three walls. It rose unevenly from Sana-diqiyya Street. One of its sides consisted of a shop, a café and a bakery, the other of another shop and an office. It ends abruptly, just as its ancient glory did, with two adjoining houses, each of three stories.

The noises of daytime life had quieted now and those of the evening began to be heard, a whisper here and a whisper there: "Good evening, everyone." "Come on in; it's time for the evening get-together." "Wake up, Uncle Kamil, and close your shop!" "Change the water in the hookah, Sankir!" "Put out the oven, Jaada!" "This hashish hurts my chest." "If we've been suffering terrors of blackouts and air raids for five years it's only due to our own wickedness!"

Two shops, however, Uncle Kamil's, the sweets seller to the right of the alley entrance and the barber's shop on the left, remain open until shortly after sunset. It is Uncle Kamil's habit, even his right, to place a chair on the threshold of his shop and drop off to sleep with a fly-whisk resting in his lap. He will remain there until customers either call out to him or Abbas the barber teasingly wakes him. He is a hulk of a man, his cloak revealing legs like tree trunks and his behind large and rounded like the dome of a mosque, its central portion resting on the chair and the remainder spilling over the sides. He has a belly like a barrel, great projecting breasts, and he seems scarcely to have any neck at all. Between his shoulders lies his rounded face, so puffed and blood-flecked that his breathing makes its furrows disappear. Consequently, scarcely a single line can be seen on the surface and he seems to have neither nose nor eyes. His head topping all this is small, bald and no different in color from his pale yet florid skin. He is always panting and out of breath, as if he has just run a race, and he can scarcely complete the sale of a sweet before he is overcome by a desire for sleep. People are always telling him he will die suddenly because of the masses of fat pressing round his heart. He always agrees with them. But how will death harm him when his life is merely a prolonged sleep?

The barber's shop, although small, is considered in the alley to be rather special. It has a mirror and an armchair, as well as the usual instruments of a barber. The barber is a man of medium height, pallid complexion and slightly heavy build. His eyes project slightly and his wavy hair is yellowish, despite the brown color of his skin. He wears a suit and never goes without an apron; perhaps in imitation of more fashionable hairdressers.

These two individuals remain in their shops while the large company office next to the barber closes its doors and its employees go home. The last to leave is its owner, Salim Alwan. He struts off, dressed in his flowing robe and cloak and goes to the carriage waiting for him at the street's entrance. He climbs in sedately and fills the seat with his well-built person, his large Circassian moustaches standing out before him. The driver kicks the bell with his foot and it rings out loudly. The carriage, drawn by one horse, moves off towards Ghouriyya on its way to Hilmiyya.

The two houses at the end of the street have closed their shutters against the cold, and lantern-light shines through their cracks. Midaq Alley would be completely silent now, were it not for Kirsha's coffee-shop, light streaming from its electric lamps, their wires covered with flies.

The café is beginning to fill with customers. It is a square room, somewhat dilapidated. However, in spite of its dinginess, its walls are covered with arabesques. The only things which suggest a past glory are its extreme age and a few couches placed here and there. In the café entrance a workman is setting up a second-hand radio on a wall. A few men are scattered about on the couches smoking and drinking tea.

Not far from the entrance, on a couch, sits a man in his fifties dressed in a cloak with sleeves, wearing a necktie usually worn by those who affect Western dress. On his nose perches a pair of expensive-looking gold-rimmed spectacles. He has removed his wooden sandals and left them lying near his feet. He sits as stiffly as a statue, as silent as a corpse. He looks neither to the right nor to the left, as though lost in a world all his own.

A senile old man is now approaching the café. He is so old that the passing of time has left him with not a single sound limb. A boy leads him by his left hand and under his right arm he carries a two-stringed fiddle and a book. The old man greets all those present and makes his way to the couch in the middle of the room. He climbs up with the help of the boy, who sits beside him. He places the instrument and the book between them and looks hard into the faces of the men present, as though searching for their reaction to his coming there. His dull and inflamed eyes, filled with expectation and apprehension, settle on the café's young waiter, Sankir. Having sat patiently waiting for some time and having observed the youth's studied disregard for himself, he breaks his silence, saying thickly:

"Coffee, Sankir."

The youth faces slightly towards him and after a slight hesitation turns his back on him again without saying a word, completely disregarding the request. The old man realizes the youth will go on ignoring him and, indeed, he expected nothing more. Just then help came, as though from the heavens, with the entry of someone who heard the old man's shout and saw the youth ignore him. The newcomer shouted imperiously to the waiter:

"Bring the poet's coffee, lad!"

The old poet gazed gratefully at the newcomer and said somewhat sadly:

"Thanks be to God, Dr. Bushi."

The "doctor" greeted him and sat down beside him. Dressed incongruously in a cloak, a skull cap and wooden clogs, he was a dentist who learned his profession from life, having had no medical or any other schooling. Bushi began his professional life as assistant to a dentist in the Gamaliyya district. He learned by observing the dentist's skill and so became proficient himself. He was well-known for the effectiveness of his prescriptions, although he generally preferred extraction as the best cure! His roving dental surgery would no doubt have been considered unbearably painful were it not for the fact that his fees were so low. He charged one piaster for the poor and two for the rich (the rich of Midaq Alley, of course!). If there were serious loss of blood, as frequently happened, he generally considered it the work of God. He relied on God, too, to prevent the blood from flowing! Moreover, he had made a set of gold teeth for Kirsha, the café owner, for only two guineas. In Midaq Alley and the surrounding area, he was addressed as "doctor." He was, perhaps, the very first doctor to receive his title from his patients.

Sankir brought the coffee for the poet, as the "doctor" requested. The old man raised the cup to his lips, blowing into it to cool the drink. He then sipped it and continued to do so until it was finished. He placed the cup to one side and only then recalled the ill-mannered behavior of the waiter towards him. Gazing at the youth with apparent disdain, he muttered indignantly:

"Ill-mannered fellow . . ."

He picked up his instrument and began to pluck its strings, avoiding the angry looks Sankir gave him. He played a few introductory notes just as the coffee-house had heard him play every evening for twenty years or more. His frail body swayed in time with the music. Then he cleared his throat, spat, and said: "In the name of God." Crying out in his harsh-sounding voice, he continued:

"We are going to begin today by saying a prayer for the Prophet. An Arab Prophet, the chosen son of the people of Adnan. Abu Saada, the Zanati, says that . . ." He was interrupted by someone who entered at that point and said roughly:

"Shut up! Don't say a single word more!"

The old man lifted his failing eyes from his instrument and saw the sleepy, gloomy eyes of Kirsha, the tall, thin, dark-faced café owner looking down at him. He stared at him glumly and hesitated a moment as though unable to believe his ears. Trying to ignore Kirsha's unpleasantness, he began reciting again:

"Abu Saada, the Zanati, says that . . ."

The café owner shouted in angry exasperation:

"Are you going to force your recitations on us? That's the end — the end! Didn't I warn you last week?"

A look of disappointment came into the poet's face and he commented critically:

"I can see you have been living fast lately. Can't you take it out on someone else?"

Even more exasperated, Kirsha shouted again:

"I know what I said and what I want, you imbecile. Do you think I am going to allow you to perform in my café if you are going to slander me with your vile tongue?"

The old poet sweetened his tone a little as he tried to soothe the angry man and said:

"This is my café too. Haven't I been reciting here for the last twenty years?"

The café owner took his usual seat behind the till and replied:

"We know all the stories you tell by heart and we don't need to run through them again. People today don't want a poet. They keep asking me for a radio and there's one over there being installed now. So go away and leave us alone and may God provide for you . . ."

The old man's face clouded and he remembered sadly that Kirsha's café was the only one left to him and, indeed, his last source of livelihood and one which had done him well. Only the day before the "Castle" café had sent him away. Old as he was, and now with his living cut off, what was he to do with his life? What was the point of teaching his poor son this profession when it had died like this? What could the future hold for him and how could he provide for his son? A feeling of despair seized him and increased in intensity when he saw the look of regretful determination on Kirsha's face. The old man pleaded:

"Slowly, slowly, Mr. Kirsha. Public reciters still have an appeal which won't disappear. The radio will never replace us."

Firmly and decisively, however, the café owner replied:

"That is what you say, but it is not what my customers say and you are not going to ruin my business. Everything has changed!"

In despair, the old man insisted:

"Haven't people listened to these stories without being bored since the days of the Prophet, peace be upon him?"

Kirsha brought his hand down hard on the till and shouted:

"I said everything has changed!"

At this the absentminded and statuesque man wearing the gold-rimmed spectacles and the necktie moved for the first time. He turned his gaze to the café's roof and sighed so deeply that his friends almost expected pieces of flesh to come up with the passage of air. In a dreamy tone, he said:

"Yes, everything has changed. Yes, indeed, everything has changed, my lady. Everything has changed except my heart and it still loves the people of the house of Amir."

He lowered his head slowly, moving it to the left and to the right as he did so, with movements gradually decreasing in extent until he at last returned to his previous immobile position. Once again he sank into oblivion. None of those present, accustomed as they were to his peculiarities, had so much as turned towards him, with the exception of the old reciter who looked at him and said appealingly:

"Sheikh Darwish, does this please you?"

The other man remained, however, as though lost to the world and said nothing. Just then another person arrived who was greeted with looks of admiration and affection, and they all responded enthusiastically to his greeting.

Radwan Husaini was a man of impressive appearance, both broad and tall, a flowing black cloak covering his ample form, his face large and whitish with tinges of red. He wore a reddish-colored beard. His forehead seemed to shine with light and its surface gleamed with happiness, tolerance and deep faith. He walked slowly, with his head slightly bent, and a smile on his lips announced his love for both people and life.

He chose a seat next to the poet's sofa and, as soon as he did so, the old man began to complain to him. Radwan Husaini listened good-naturedly, although he knew well what the trouble was. Indeed, on a number of occasions he had tried to dissuade the café owner, Kirsha, from his intention to dispense with the reciter but he had always been unsuccessful. When the old man finished his complaint, Husaini did what he could to console him and promised to help him find a job for the poet's son. He then generously placed some coins in his hand and whispered in his ear:

"We are all sons of Adam. If poverty descends on you then seek help from your brother. Man's provider is God and it is to God that any excess is due."

As he said this, his fine face was filled with even greater radiance, just as all noble men, doing the good they love, become happier and more handsome through their actions. He had always taken care that not a single day should pass without doing some good deed or receiving in his home some abused or unfortunate person. From his love of goodness and his generosity he appeared to be richly endowed with wealth and property, but the fact was that he owned nothing except the house on the right hand side of Midaq Alley and a few acres of land in Marj. The people who lived in his house—Kirsha on the third floor, and Uncle Kamil and Abbas the barber on the first—had found him a kind and fair landlord. He had ignored the rights the special military edict had given him to raise the rent of first-floor tenants, out of compassion for the occupants of modest means. He was, in fact, in all his actions wherever he went, a man of compassion and sympathy.

His life, especially in its earlier stages, had been filled with disappointment and pain. The period he had spent studying at the University of al-Azhar had ended in failure. He had spent a considerable portion of his life within its cloisters and yet had not succeeded in obtaining a degree. Besides, he had been afflicted with the loss of his children and now none remained, although he had had several. He had tasted the bitterness of disappointment so much that his heart almost overflowed with a despair that nearly choked him . . .

His faith rescued him from the gloom of his sorrows to the light of love, and his heart now no longer held grief or anxiety. He was filled with an all-embracing love, goodness and wonderful patience. He stepped lightly over the sorrows of the world, his heart soaring heavenwards as he embraced everyone with his love.

As time brought him added tragedies, so had he increased in his patience and love. One day people saw him laying one of his sons in his last resting place while he recited the Koran, his face filled with happiness. They gathered around him comforting and consoling him, but he had only smiled and, pointing to the sky, said:

"He gave and He has taken back; all things are at His command and all things belong to Him. It would be blasphemous to sorrow."

Thus he gave consolation to others. So it was that Dr. Bushi once said: "If you are sick, then go to Mr. Husaini for a cure. If you are despairing, then gaze at the light of his innocence to teach you hope. If you are sorrowing, then listen to him and he will make you happy again." His face was a true picture of his inner self; he was the picture of grace in its most radiant form. As for the poet he was already somewhat cheered and consoled. He left the couch, the boy following him carrying the fiddle and the book. The old man heartily shook Radwan Husaini's hand and said goodbye to the other men in the café, pretending to ignore its owner, Kirsha. He threw a scornful look at the radio which the workmen had almost finished installing, gave his hand to the lad and drew him outside. They walked out of sight.

Life stirred once again in Sheikh Darwish and he turned his head towards the direction in which they had disappeared, mumbling: "The poet has gone and the radio has come. This is the way of God in His creation. Long ago it was told in *tarikh* which in English means 'history' and is spelled, H-I-S-T-O-R-Y."

Before he finished spelling out the word, Kamil and Abbas arrived, having just closed their shops. Abbas came first; he had washed his face and combed his fair hair. Uncle Kamil followed, swaying like a palanquin, picking his feet up laboriously and deliberately as he walked. They greeted the company present, sat down and ordered tea. They no sooner arrived before they filled the air with gossip. Abbas spoke first:

"Listen everyone. My friend Uncle Kamil here has been complaining to me that he is likely to die any minute and, if he does, he won't have enough money to be properly buried."

One of the men present muttered sarcastically:

"All's well with Muhammad's people!"

Some of the others commented that Uncle Kamil's profits from his sales of sweets would probably suffice to bury an entire nation. Dr. Bushi laughed and addressed Uncle Kamil:

"Are you still harping on dying? By God, you'll probably bury the lot of us with your own hands!"

Uncle Kamil, his voice high-pitched and innocent as a child's, replied:

"Be careful what you say and put your trust in God, my friend, I am a poor man . . ."

Abbas continued:

"I was upset by what Uncle Kamil told me. After all, his sweets have done us a lot of good and that can't be denied. So I have bought him a nice shroud as a precaution and put it away in a safe place until the inevitable time comes." He turned to Uncle Kamil and went on: "This is a secret I have been keeping from you deliberately. Now you can see I have made it known to everyone here, so that they can bear witness."

Many of the men in the café expressed delight, trying to appear serious so that Uncle Kamil, who was famous for his gullibility, would believe the story. They praised the thoughtfulness and generosity of Abbas and said that what he had done was a worthy deed and one most appropriate towards the man he liked so well and with whom he shared a flat and indeed his life, just as if they were of the same flesh and blood. Even Radwan Husaini smiled delightedly, and Uncle Kamil gazed at his friend in innocent amazement and asked:

"Is it true what you said, Abbas?"

Dr. Bushi replied for him, saying:

"Don't doubt it for a minute, Uncle Kamil. I can vouch for what your friend says and I have seen the shroud with my own eyes. It's a very fine one indeed and I would be delighted to have one just like it."

Sheikh Darwish moved for the third time and said:

"Good luck to you! Shrouds are the veils of the after-life. Enjoy your shroud, Uncle Kamil, before it enjoys you! You will be wholesome food for the worms. The reptiles will feed off your tender flesh as though it were a sweet. Why, the worms will grow so fat they will be like *dafaadi*. The meaning of this word in English is 'frogs' and it is spelled F-R-O-G-S."

Uncle Kamil believed all now and he asked Abbas what type of shroud it was, its color and size. Then he invoked a long blessing on his friend, smiled broadly and gave praise to God. Just then the voice of a young man entering from the street was heard to say:

"Good evening."

He passed by on his way to Radwan Husaini's house. Husain Kirsha was the son of the café owner. He was in his twenties and had the near-black skin of his father. Husain was slight of build, however, and his delicate features indicated his youth, fitness and vitality. Dressed in a blue woollen shirt, khaki trousers, a hat and heavy boots, he had the satisfied, well-off look of all those who worked with the British Army. This was the usual time for him to return home from the camp. Many men in the café stared after him in both admiration and envy. His friend Abbas invited him into the café but he thanked him and moved on.

Darkness now completely enveloped the street and the only light came from lanterns in the café; they drew a square of light which was reflected on the ground and extended up the walls of the office. The lights which had shone dimly from behind the window shutters of the street's two houses disappeared one after the other. The men in the coffee-house were all playing dominoes or cards, except for Sheikh Darwish, quite lost in his usual stupor, and Uncle Kamil, who had laid his head on his chest and sunk into a deep sleep. Sankir, the waiter, was as busy as ever, bringing orders and putting money-tokens into the till. Kirsha, the café owner, followed him with his heavy eyes, enjoying the numbing stream from hashish flowing into his stomach and giving himself over to its delicious power. It was very late now and Radwan Husaini left the café for his house. Dr. Bushi soon left for his flat on the first floor of the alley's second house. The next to leave were Abbas and Uncle Kamil.

The other seats began to empty too, until at midnight only three remained in the café: Kirsha its owner, the young waiter Sankir and Sheikh Darwish. Then another group of men arrived, all peers of the café owner Kirsha, and they went with him up to a wooden hut built on the roof of Radwan Husaini's house, where they sat around a lighted brazier. There they started a small party which would not end until the dawn gave enough light to distinguish "a black from a white thread."

Sankir the waiter now spoke gently to Sheikh Darwish, telling him that midnight had come. The old man looked up at the sound of his voice, took off his spectacles quietly and polished them with a corner of his shirt. He then put them on again, straightened his necktie and rose, placing his feet in his wooden clogs. He left the café without uttering a word, shattering the silence with the noise of his clogs striking the stones of the street. All was silent outside, the darkness heavy and the streets and alleys somber and empty. He let his feet lead him where they wished, for he had no home and no purpose. He walked off into the darkness.

In his youth, Sheikh Darwish had been a teacher in one of the religious foundation schools. He had, moreover, been a teacher of the English language. He had been known for his energetic diligence; and fortune, too, had been good to him and he had been the head of a happy family. When the religious foundation schools merged with the Ministry of Education, his position changed as did that of many of his associates, who, like him, lacked high qualifications. He became a clerk in the Ministry of Religious Endowments and went down from the sixth to the eighth grade, his salary adjusted accordingly. It was only natural that he was hurt by what happened to him and he began a continuous rebellion.

Occasionally he rebelled openly; at other times he felt defeated and concealed his rebellion. He had tried every method, drawing up petitions, appealing to his superiors and complaining about his poverty and the size of his family. All without success. At last he gave way to despair, his nerves almost in shreds. His case became famous in his ministry and he became notorious as a rebel, always complaining, extremely stubborn and obstinate, and very quick-tempered. Scarcely a day went by without his becoming involved in an argument or quarrel.

He was renowned for his self-assertive manner and defiance towards everyone. When a dispute flared up between him and another person, as often happened, he would address his adversary in English. If the man should complain at his using a foreign language unnecessarily, Darwish would shout in great scorn:

"Go off and learn something before you argue with me!"

Eventually reports of his bad disposition reached his superiors but they were always lenient out of sympathy and out of fear of his temper. Therefore he was able to carry on without severe consequences, except for a few warnings and the loss of one or two days salary. As time went on, however, his blustering egotism increased. One day he decided to write all his official correspondence in English. His explanation for this was that he was an artistic man, not like the other clerks.

He now neglected his work to such a degree that his supervisor decided to deal with him in a firm and severe manner. Fate, however, was quicker than the supervisor for he insisted on seeing the Deputy Minister himself. Darwish "Effendi," as he was then still known, entered the Deputy Minister's office looking very serious and respectful, greeted him in a man-to-man fashion and addressed him in a manner filled with confidence and self-assurance:

"God has chosen his man, sir!"

The Deputy Minister asked him to explain what he meant and Darwish continued respectfully and with dignity:

"I am a messenger to you from God and I bring you a new mission!"

Thus his career at the ministry ended, as did his connections with friends and relations who had been close to him. He deserted his family, friends and acquaintances and wandered off into the world of God, as it is called. The only memento he now had of his past life were his gold-rimmed spectacles. He had passed into his new life without a friend, money, or a home. His life showed that some people can live in this world, festering as it is with its bitter troubles, without either home, money or friends, and know neither worry, grief nor need. Never for a day did he hunger; he never went without clothing, nor was he ever driven away.

He had moved into a state of peace, contentment, and beatitude such as he had never known before. Even though he had lost his house, the whole world had become his home. Even though he had lost his salary, gone, too, was his dependence on money. Though he had lost his own family and friends, everyone he met became his family. If his gown wore out, someone would bring him a new one; if his tie became ragged, someone brought him a new one of those too. Everywhere he went people made him welcome and even Kirsha, despite his apparent absentmindedness, would miss him if he should be absent for a day from the café. He could not, despite what simple folk said, perform miracles nor predict the future. He was either distracted and silent or extremely talkative without ever knowing particularly what he was saying.

Loved and honored, everyone always welcomed his presence amongst them as a good sign and said that he was a fine and holy man of God, to whom revelation came in two languages, Arabic and English!

2

She gazed into the mirror with uncritical eyes, or rather with eyes gleaming with delight. The mirror reflected a long, thin face; cosmetics had indeed done wonders with her eyelashes, eyebrows, eyes and lips. She turned her face to the right and to the left while her fingers stroked her braided hair. She muttered almost inaudibly, "Not bad. Very nice. Yes, by God, very nice!" The fact was, her face had gazed upon the world for close to fifty years and nature never leaves a face unharmed for over half a century. The body was slim, even thin, as the women of the alley described it and her bust meager, although her nice dress hid it from sight.

This lady was Mrs. Saniya Afifi, the owner of the alley's second house, on the first floor of which lived Dr. Bushi. She had got herself ready on this particular day to visit the middle flat of her house, where Umm Hamida lived. She was not accustomed to visiting tenants and, indeed, probably the only times she had been in the flat were at the beginning of each month to collect the rent. Now, however, a new and deep impulse made visiting Hamida's mother an absolute necessity.

She walked out of the flat and down the stairs, mumbling hopefully to herself, "Oh God, please fulfil my wishes."

She knocked on the door with a perspiring hand and Hamida opened it. The girl gave her an insincere smile of welcome, led her into the sitting room and then left to call her mother.

The room was small, with two old-fashioned sofas facing one another and a battered table on which rested an ashtray. On the floor was a straw mat. The visitor did not wait long; soon Hamida's mother rushed in, having just changed from her housecoat. The two women greeted one another warmly, exchanged kisses and sat down. Umm Hamida said:

"Welcome, welcome. Why, it's as though the Prophet himself had come to visit us, Mrs. Afifi!"

Umm Hamida was a well-built woman of medium stature, in her mid-sixties. Still fit and healthy, with protruding eyes and pock-marked cheeks, she had a rough and resonant voice. When she talked she almost screamed. Indeed her voice was her most effective weapon in the frequent quarrels between her and her neighbors. She was, of course, not at all pleased with the visit, as any visit from the landlady could have unfortunate consequences and might even spell real trouble. However, she had accustomed herself to be ready at all times for any eventuality, whether good or bad, and she was able to deal with both with complete equanimity.

By profession she was a bath-attendant and a marriage broker, and was both shrewd and talkative. To be sure, her tongue was hardly ever still and she scarcely missed a single report or scandal concerning anyone or any house in the neighborhood. She was both a herald and historian of bad news of all kinds and a veritable encyclopedia of woes.

As usual, she went to great pains to make her visitor feel welcome, praising her extravagantly. She gave her a resumé of the news of the alley and the surroundings. Had she heard of Kirsha's new scandal? It was just like the previous ones and the news got back to his wife who had a fight with him and tore his cloak. Husniya, the baker's wife, the day before struck her husband so hard that blood had flowed from his forehead. Radwan Husaini, that good and pious man, had rebuked his wife most strongly and why should he treat her in this way, the good man that he was, if she were not a vile and wicked hussy! Dr. Bushi had interfered with a little girl in the shelter in the last air raid and some upright citizen had struck him for it. The wife of Mawardi the wood merchant had run off with her servant and her father had informed the police. Tabuna Kafawi was secretly selling bread made of pure flour—and so on.

Mrs. Afifi listened with disinterest to all this, her mind busy with the matter about which she had come. She was determined, no matter what the effort cost her, to broach the subject which had been simmering within her for so long. She let the woman talk on until the right opportunity came, as it did when Umm Hamida asked:

"And how are you, Mrs. Afifi?"

She frowned a little and replied:

"The truth is that I am tired out, Umm Hamida!"

The older woman arched her eyebrows as though really troubled:

"Tired? May God lighten your load!"

Mrs. Afifi made no reply while Hamida, her tenant's daughter, who had just come into the room, placed a tray with coffee on the table and left again. Then she said indignantly:

"Yes, I am tired, Umm Hamida. Don't you think it's exhausting, collecting the rent from the shops? Imagine a woman like me standing in front of strange men asking for rent . . ."

Umm Hamida's heart had missed a beat at the mention of the rents, but she said sympathetically:

"Yes, you are quite right. May God come to your aid."

Umm Hamida wondered to herself why Mrs. Afifi should keep making these complaints. This was the second or third time her landlady had visited her recently and it was still not the beginning of the month. All at once an astonishing idea struck her. Could the visits be connected with her own profession? In such matters her powers of deduction were unparalleled and she determined to quietly plumb by degrees the depths of her visitor. Maliciously, she said:

"This is one of the evils of being alone. You are a woman all by yourself, Mrs. Afifi. In your house you are alone, in the street alone, and in your bed you are alone. Isn't loneliness terrible?"

Mrs. Afifi was pleased with the woman's comments, which corresponded exactly with her own thoughts. Hiding her delight, she replied:

"What can I do? My relatives all have families and I am only happy in my own home. Yet thanks be to God for making me quite independent."

Umm Hamida watched her cunningly and then said, coming to the point:

"Thanks be to God a thousand times; but tell me honestly, why have you remained single so long?"

Mrs. Afifi's heart beat faster and she found herself just where she wanted to be. Nevertheless, she sighed and murmured in feigned disgust:

"No more of the bitterness of marriage for me!"

In her youth, Mrs. Afifi had married the owner of a perfume shop, but it was an unsuccessful marriage. Her husband treated her badly, made her life miserable and spent all her savings. He left her a widow ten years ago and she had remained single all this time because, as she said, she had no taste for married life.

In saying this, she was not merely trying to hide the indifference of the other sex towards her. She had genuinely disliked married life and was delighted when she regained her peace and freedom. For a long time now, she had remained averse to marriage and happy in her freedom. Gradually, however, she forgot this prejudice and would not have hesitated had anyone asked for her hand in marriage. From time to time she lived in hope, but as the years passed, she had begun to despair. She refused to allow herself to entertain further false hopes, and she had accustomed herself to satisfaction with her life just as it was.

Her pastimes were not, fortunately, those that would lead to criticism of a widowed lady like herself. Her only passions were a fondness for coffee, cigarettes and hoarding banknotes. She kept her new banknotes in a small ivory casket hidden in the depths of her clothes closet and arranged them in packages of fives and tens, delighting herself by looking at them, counting and rearranging them. Because the banknotes, unlike metal coins, made no noise, the money was safe and none of the alley's clever people, despite their great sensitivity, knew of its existence. She had always inclined towards avarice and was one of the earliest contributors to the savings bank.

Mrs. Afifi found great consolation in her financial activities, seeing in them a compensation for her unmarried state. She would tell herself that any husband would be likely to plunder her funds, just as her dead husband had done, and that he would squander in the twinkle of an eye the fruits of long years of savings. Despite all this, the idea of marriage had gradually taken root and all her excuses and fears had been wiped out.

It was really Umm Hamida who was responsible for this strange change in her, whether intentionally or not. She had told her how she had arranged a marriage for an elderly widow and she had begun thinking the same might be possible for her. Very soon the idea had quite taken possession of her and she now felt compelled to follow it through. She had once thought that she had forgotten marriage and, all of a sudden, marriage was her ambition and hope and no amount of money, coffee, cigarettes or new banknotes could dissuade her from the idea. Mrs. Afifi had begun wondering despondently how she had wasted her life in vain and how she had spent ten years, until she was now approaching fifty, quite alone. She decided that it had been simple madness, laid the responsibility on her dead husband and determined that she would be unfaithful to his memory as soon as possible.

The match-maker listened with shrewd contempt to her fake disgust at the idea of marriage and told herself: "I can see through your cunning, Mrs. Afifi." She reproached her visitor:

"Don't exaggerate, Mrs. Afifi. Even if your luck was bad the first time, there are very many happy marriages indeed."

Replacing her coffee cup on the tray and thanking her hostess, Mrs. Afifi replied:

"No sensible person would persist in trying her luck if it looked bad."

Umm Hamida disagreed:

"What talk is this for a sensible woman like yourself? You have had enough, quite enough, of being alone."

The widow struck her meager breast with the palm of her left hand and said in mock disbelief:

"What? Do you want people to think that I am mad?"

"What people do you mean? Women older than yourself get married every day."

Mrs. Afifi was annoyed at this phrase "older than yourself" and she said quietly:

"I am not as old as you may think, God curse the idea!"

"I didn't mean that, Mrs. Afifi, and I am sure you are still within the bounds of youth. I thought it might be some excuse behind which you were hiding yourself."

The lady was pleased at this, but she was still determined to act the part of someone who might be ready to accept marriage, but who had no clear intention or desire for marriage. After a little hesitation, she asked:

"Wouldn't it be wrong for me to get married now, after this long period of being unmarried?"

Umm Hamida said to herself: "Then why, woman, did you come to talk to me?" But out loud she said:

"Why should it be wrong to do something both lawful and right? You are a respectable and sensible person, as everyone knows. Why, my dear, 'Marriage is one half of religion.' Our Lord in his wisdom made it lawful and it was prescribed by the Prophet, peace and blessings upon him!"

Mrs. Afifi echoed piously:

"Peace and blessings upon him!"

"Why not, my dear? Both God and the Arab Prophet love the faithful!"

Mrs. Afifi's face had grown red beneath its covering of rouge and her heart was filled with delight. She took out two cigarettes from her case and said:

"Whoever would want to marry me?"

Umm Hamida bent her forefinger and drew it to her forehead in a gesture of disbelief, saying:

"A thousand and one men!"

The lady laughed heartily and said:

"One man will suffice!"

Umm Hamida now declared with conviction:

"Deep down all men like marriage and it's only married men who complain about marriage. What a lot of bachelors there are who want to get married. I have only to say to one of them: 'I have a bride for you' and a look of interest comes into their eyes as they smile and ask in unconcealable passion: 'Really—who is it—who?' Men, even though they might be completely senile, always want women and this is part of the wisdom of our Lord."

Mrs. Afifi nodded her head happily in agreement and commented:

"Glory be to His wisdom!"

"Yes, Mrs. Afifi, it was for that God created the world. It was within His power to fill it with men alone or women alone but He created male and female and gave us the intelligence to understand His wish. There is no avoiding marriage."

Mrs. Saniya Afifi smiled again:

"Your words are as sweet as sugar, Umm Hamida."

"May God sweeten your whole life and delight your heart with a perfect marriage."

Now thoroughly encouraged, the visitor agreed:

"If God wishes and with your help."

"I am, and thanks be to God, a very fortunate woman. Marriages I arrange never break up. How many of my couples have gone off and set up homes, produced children and been very happy. Put your trust in God, and in me!"

"I will never be able to reward you enough with money."

At this, however, Umm Hamida said to herself, "Oh no you don't, my woman. You will have to reward me well enough with money and a great deal of it. We will go to the savings bank together, and you won't be stingy." She then said out loud and in the serious, determined tone of a businessman who, having finished the preliminaries, was about to get down to the really important matters:

"I take it you would prefer a man well advanced in years?"

The widow did not know how to reply. She did not want to marry a youth who would be an unsuitable husband for her and yet she was not pleased at the expression "well advanced in years." The way the conversation had developed had made her feel a little more at ease with Umm Hamida and she was able to say, laughing to hide her embarrassment:

"What, 'break a fast by eating an onion'?!"

Umm Hamida let out a raucous, throaty laugh, increasing in confidence that the deal she was about to make would be lucrative indeed. She went on drily:

"You are quite right, Mrs. Afifi. The truth is that experience has shown me that the happiest marriages are those in which the wife is older than the husband. A man of thirty or just a little older would suit you well."

Her visitor asked anxiously:

"Would one agree?"

"Certainly one would agree. You are good-looking and wealthy."

"May you be safe from all evil!"

Her pock-marked face having taken on a serious and conscientious look, Umm Hamida then said:

"I will tell him you are a lady of middle age, with no children, no mother-in-law, well-mannered and wholesome and have two shops in Hamzawi and a two-story house in Midaq Alley."

The lady smiled and said, to correct what she considered an error:

"No, the house has three stories."

Umm Hamida, however, could not agree to this and said:

"Only two, because you are not going to take any rent for the third floor where I am for as long as I am alive!"

Mrs. Afifi agreed happily:

"All right, I give my word, Umm Hamida."

"Your word is taken then. May our Lord work things out for the best!"

Her visitor shook her head as though amazed and said:

"What an astonishing thing! I just came to visit you and look where our talk has got us. How has it happened that I am leaving you as good as married?"

Umm Hamida joined in her laughter as though she too was surprised, although she said under her breath: "Shame on you, woman. Do you think your cunning has fooled me?" Out loud she commented:

"The will of our Lord, don't you think? Is not everything in His hands?"

And so Mrs. Saniya Afifi returned to her own flat well pleased, although she thought to herself: "Rent of the flat for the rest of her life! What a greedy woman she is!"

3

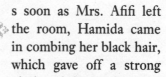s soon as Mrs. Afifi left the room, Hamida came in combing her black hair, which gave off a strong smell of kerosene. Her mother gazed at her dark and shining hair, the ends of which nearly reached to the girl's knees, and said sadly:

"What a pity! Fancy letting lice live in that lovely hair!"

The girl's black eyes, framed with mascara, flashed angrily and took on a determined and intent look.

"What lice? I swear by the Prophet that my comb found only two lice!"

"Have you forgotten that I combed your hair two weeks ago and squashed twenty lice for you?"

The girl answered indifferently:

"Well, I hadn't washed my hair for two months . . ."

She sat down at her mother's side and continued combing her hair vigorously.

Hamida was in her twenties, of medium stature and with a slim figure. Her skin was bronze-colored and her face a little elongated,

34

unmarked and pretty. Her most remarkable features were her black, beautiful eyes, the pupils and whites of which contrasted in a most striking and attractive way. When, however, she set her delicate lips and narrowed her eyes she could take on an appearance of strength and determination which was most unfeminine. Her temper had always, even in Midaq Alley itself, been something no one could ignore.

Even her mother, famous for her roughness, did her best to avoid crossing her. One day when they had quarreled her mother cried out to her: "God will never find you a husband; what man would want to embrace a burning firebrand like you?" On other occasions she had said that a real madness overcame her daughter when she got angry and she nicknamed her tempers the *khamsin*, after the vicious and unpredictable summer winds.

Despite all this, she was really very fond of Hamida, even though she was only her foster mother. The girl's real mother had been her partner in making and selling sweet and fattening potions. She was eventually compelled by her poverty to share Umm Hamida's flat in Midaq Alley and had died there, leaving her daughter still a baby. Umm Hamida had adopted her and placed her under the care of the wife of Kirsha, the café owner, who had suckled her along with her son Husain Kirsha, who was therefore a sort of foster brother to the girl Hamida.

She went on combing her black hair, waiting for her mother to comment as usual on the visit and visitor. When the silence remained unbroken unusually long, she asked:

"It was a long visit. What were you talking about?"

Her mother laughed sardonically and murmured:

"You guess!"

The girl, now even more interested, asked:

"She wants to raise the rent?"

"If she had done that, she would have left here carried by ambulance men! No, she wants to lower the rent!"

"Have you gone mad?" Hamida exclaimed.

"Yes, I have gone mad. But guess . . ."

The girl sighed and said:

"You've tired me out!"

Umm Hamida twitched her eyebrows and announced, winking an eye:

"Her ladyship wants to get married!"

The girl was overcome with astonishment and gasped:

"Married?"

"That's right and she wants a young husband. How sorry I am for an unlucky young woman like you who can't find anyone to ask for her hand!"

Hamida gazed at her derisively and commented, now braiding her hair:

"Oh yes, I could find many, but the fact is that you are a rotten match-maker who merely wants to hide her failure. What's wrong with me? Just as I said, you are a failure and you only go to prove the saying: 'It's always the carpenter's door that's falling apart.'"

Her foster mother smiled and said:

"If Mrs. Saniya Afifi can get married, then no woman at all should despair."

The girl stared at her furiously and said:

"I am not the one who is chasing marriage, but marriage is chasing me. I will give it a good run, too!"

"Of course you will, a princess like yourself, a daughter of royalty."

The girl ignored her mother's sarcasm and went on in the same severe tone:

"Is there anyone here in Midaq Alley who is worth considering?"

In fact, Umm Hamida had no fear that her daughter would be left on the shelf and she had no doubts about the girl's beauty. Nevertheless, she frequently felt resentful about her vanity and conceit and she now said bitingly:

"Don't slander the alley like that. The people who live here are the best in the world!"

"You're the best in the world yourself, I don't think! They are all nonentities. Only one of them has a spark of life and you had to go and make him my foster brother!"

She was referring to Husain Kirsha with whom she had been suckled. This remark annoyed her mother and she objected angrily: "How can you say such a thing? I didn't make him your brother. No one can make you a brother or a sister. He is your brother because you both suckled the same woman just as God ordained."

A spirit of devilment seemed to take possession of the girl. She said jokingly:

"Couldn't he have always sucked from one breast and me from the other?"

At this her mother punched her hard in the back and snorted: "May God punish you for saying that."

The girl replied by muttering:

"Nothing Alley!"

"You deserve to marry some really important civil servant, I suppose?"

"Is a civil servant a god?" retorted Hamida defiantly.

Her mother sighed deeply and said:

"If only you would stop being so conceited . . ."

The girl mimicked Umm Hamida's voice and replied:

"If you would only be reasonable for once in your life."

"You eat and drink my food but you are never grateful. Do you remember all that fuss you made about a dress?"

Hamida asked in astonishment:

"And is a dress something of no importance? What's the point of living if one can't have new clothes? Don't you think it would be better for a girl to have been buried alive rather than have no nice clothes to make herself look pretty?"

Her voice filled with sadness as she went on:

"If only you had seen the factory girls! You should just see those Jewish girls who go to work. They all go about in nice clothes. Well, what is the point of life then if we can't wear what we want?"

Her foster mother replied cuttingly:

"Watching the factory girls and the Jewish women has made you lose your senses. If only you would stop worrying about all this."

The girl took no notice of what Umm Hamida said. She had now finished braiding her hair and she took a small mirror from her pocket and propped it up on the back of the sofa. She then stood in front of it, bending down slightly to see her reflection. In a wondering voice, she said:

"Oh what a shame, Hamida. What are you doing living in this alley? And why should your mother be this woman who can't tell the difference between dust and gold-dust?"

She leaned out of the room's only window, which overlooked the street, and stretched her arms out to the open shutters, drawing them together so that only a couple of inches of space was left between them. She then sat resting on her elbows placed on the window sill and gazed out into the street, moving her attention from place to place and saying as though to herself:

"Hello, street of bliss! Long life to you and all your fine inhabitants. What a pretty view and see how handsome the people are! I can see Husniya, the baker's wife, sitting like a big sack before the oven with one eye on the loaves and one on Jaada, her husband. He works only because he is afraid of her beatings and blows. Over there sits Kirsha, the café owner, his head bowed as if in a deep sleep, but he is not really. Uncle Kamil is fast asleep, of course, while the flies swarm over his tray of unprotected sweets. Look there! That's Abbas Hilu peeping up at my window, preening himself. I'm sure he thinks that the power of his look will throw me down at his feet. You're not for me, Abbas! Well now, Mr. Salim Alwan, the company owner, has just lifted up his eyes, lowered them and raised them once again. We'll say the first time was an accident, but the second, Mr. Alwan? Sir? Watch now, he's just started a third time! What do you want, you senile and shameless old man? You want a rendezvous with me every day at this time? If only you weren't a married man and a father, I'd give you look for look and say welcome and welcome again! Well, there they all are. That is the alley and why shouldn't Hamida neglect her hair until it gets lice? Oh, yes, and there's Sheikh Darwish plodding along with his wooden clogs striking the pavement like a gong."

At this point her mother interrupted:

"Who would make a better husband for you than Sheikh Darwish?"

Hamida remained looking out the window, and, with a shake of her behind, she replied:

"What a powerful man he must have been! He says he has spent a hundred thousand pounds on his love for our lady Zainab. Do you think he would have been too mean to give me ten thousand?"

She drew back suddenly, as though bored with her survey. Now she moved in front of the mirror and gazing into it searchingly, she sighed and said:

"Oh, what a pity, Hamida, what a shame and a waste."

4

I n the early morning Midaq Alley is dreary and cold. The sun can only reach it after climbing high into the sky. However, life begins to stir early in the morning in parts of the street. Sankir, the café waiter, begins activity by arranging the chairs and lighting the spirit stove. Then the workmen in the company office start coming in ones and twos. Presently Jaada appears carrying the wood for baking the bread. Even Uncle Kamil is busy at this early hour, opening his shop and then having his nap before breakfast. Uncle Kamil and Abbas the barber always have breakfast together from a tray placed between them containing plates of cooked beans, onion salad, and pickled gherkins.

They each approach their food in a different manner. Abbas devours his roll of bread in a few seconds. Uncle Kamil, on the other hand, is slow and chews each piece of food laboriously until it almost dissolves in his mouth. He often says: "Good food should first be digested in the mouth." So it is that Abbas will have finished eating his food, sipping his tea and smoking his pipe while his friend is still

slowly munching his onions. Kamil, therefore, prevents Abbas from
taking any of his share by always dividing the food into two separate
sections.

In spite of his portly build, Uncle Kamil could not be considered a
glutton, although he was very fond of sweets and extremely clever at
making them. His artistry was completely fulfilled in making orders
for people like Salim Alwan, Radwan Husaini and Kirsha the café
owner. His reputation was widely known and had even crossed the
boundaries of the alley to the quarters of Sanadiqiyya, Ghouriyya and
Sagha. However his means were modest and he had not lied when he
complained to Abbas that after his death there would be no money to
bury him. That very morning he said to Abbas after they finished
breakfast:

"You said you bought me a burial shroud. Now that really is
something that calls for thanks and blessings. Why don't you give it to
me now?"

Abbas, the typical liar, had forgotten all about the shroud. He
asked:

"Why do you want it now?"

His friend answered him in his high-pitched adolescent voice:

"I could do with what it's worth. Haven't you heard that the price
of cloth is going up?"

Abbas chuckled:

"You are really a shrewd one in spite of your fake simplicity. Only
yesterday you were complaining that you hadn't enough money for a
proper burial. Now that I have a shroud for you, you want to sell it and
use the money! No, this time you won't get your way. I bought your
shroud to honor your body after a long life, if God wills."

Uncle Kamil smiled in embarrassment and shifted his chair
nervously:

"Suppose my life lasts so long that things get back to the way they
were before the war? Then we'll have lost the value of an expensive
shroud, don't you agree?"

"And suppose you die tomorrow?"

"I hope to God not!"

This made Abbas roar with laughter:

"It's useless to try to change my mind. The shroud will stay in a safe place with me until God works His will . . ."

He laughed again so loudly that his friend joined in. The barber now spoke teasingly:

"You're completely without profit for me. Have I ever managed to make a penny out of you in your whole life? No! Your chin and upper lip simply don't sprout and your head's quite bald. On all that vast world you call your body there's not a single hair for me to cut. God forgive you!"

"It's a fine clean body which no one would mind washing down," said Uncle Kamil with a mock seriousness.

The sound of someone yelling interrupted them. Down the street they saw Husniya beating her husband Jaada the baker with her slippers. The man collapsed in front of her, offering no defence at all. His wails reverberated from each side of the alley and the two men laughed uproariously.

"Have forgiveness and mercy on him, madam!" shouted Abbas loudly.

The woman continued pummelling him until Jaada lay at her feet weeping and begging forgiveness.

"Those slippers could do your body some good," said Abbas turning to Uncle Kamil. "They'd soon melt that fat away!"

Just then Husain Kirsha appeared; he was dressed in trousers, a white shirt and straw hat. He made an ostentatious show of looking at his gold wrist watch, his small darting eyes filled with pride of possession. He greeted his friend the barber in a friendly fashion and seated himself in a chair. It was his day off and he wanted his hair cut.

The two friends had grown up together in Midaq Alley. Indeed they had been born in the same house, that of Radwan Husaini, Abbas three years before Husain. Abbas lived with his parents fifteen years before he and Uncle Kamil met and decided to share a flat and had remained close friends with Husain until their work separated them. Abbas went to work as a barber's assistant near New Street, and Husain took a job in a bicycle repair shop in Gamaliyya.

From the first, they were of entirely different character: perhaps it was this dissimilarity which strengthened their mutual affection.

Abbas was gentle, good-natured, and inclined towards peace, tolerance and kindness. He was content to fill his leisure time with card playing and idle gossip with his friends at the coffee-house. He avoided participation in quarrels and all unpleasantness by waving both aside with a smile and a kind word for the contestants. He conscientiously performed the prayers and fasted and never missed Friday prayers in Husain Mosque. Lately he had tended to neglect some religious duties, not from indifference, but rather out of laziness. However, he still attended Friday prayers and faithfully fasted during the month of Ramadan. Sometimes disputes occurred between him and Husain Kirsha, but whenever his friend became too excited Abbas yielded and thus avoided a serious quarrel.

He was known to be easily satisfied and he was often rebuked because he continued to work as a barber's helper for ten years. He had only opened his own little shop five years ago. In that time he thought that he had prospered as well as could be expected. This spirit of satisfaction with his lot was reflected in his quiet eyes, his healthy and vital body and his perpetually even disposition.

It was agreed that Husain Kirsha was one of the cleverest people in the alley. He was known for his energy, intelligence and courage, and he could be most aggressive at times. He had begun by working in his father's café, but because their personalities conflicted he had left to work in a bicycle shop. He remained there until the war broke out and then went to work in a British Army camp. His daily wages were now thirty piasters compared to the three piasters in his first job. All this was apart from what he made by applying his philosophy that: "For a decent living you need a nice quick hand!" Thus his standard of living and his finances had increased.

His new wealth afforded him undreamed-of luxuries. He bought new clothes, frequented restaurants and delighted in eating meat, which he considered a luxury reserved especially for the rich. He attended cinemas and cabarets and found pleasure in wine and the company of women. Frequently his drinking kindled his hospitality and he would invite his friends to the roof of his house where he would offer them food, wine and hashish. On one occasion when he was a little drunk he said to his guests: "In England they call those who enjoy my easy life 'large.'" For some time after this his jealous rivals called him "Husain Kirsha the Large"; later this became corrupted to "Husain Kirsha the Garage."

Abbas began to tidy up carefully and quickly the back and sides of Husain's head. He did not disturb the thick mass of wavy hair on top. Meetings with his old friend now usually had a sad effect on him. They were still friends, but life had changed and Abbas missed those evenings when Husain used to work in his father's café. Now they met only rarely. Then too, Abbas was aware that envy was a part of the wide gulf that now separated them. However, like all his emotions, this new one was under careful control. He never said an unkind word about his friend and he hoped for the same in return. Sometimes, to ease the gnawing envy, he would say to himself: "Soon the war will end and Husain will return to the alley as penniless as when he left."

Husain Kirsha, in his usual prattling manner, began telling the barber about life in the Depot, about the workers, their good wages, the thefts, about his adventures with the British, and the affection and admiration the soldiers showed him.

"Corporal Julian," he related proudly, "once told me that the only difference between me and the British is that of color. He tells me to be careful with my money but an arm" — and here he waved wildly — "which can make money during the war can make double that in times of peace. When do you think the war will be over? Don't let the Italian defeat fool you, they didn't matter anyway. Hitler will fight for twenty years! Corporal Julian is impressed with my bravery and has a blind faith in me. He trusts me so much that he has let me in on his big trade in tobacco, cigarettes, chocolate, knives, bedcovers, socks and shoes! Nice, isn't it?"

"Yes, very," Abbas muttered in reply.

Husain peered at himself carefully in the mirror and asked Abbas:

"Do you know where I'm going now? To the zoo. Do you know who with? With a girl as sweet as cream and honey." He kissed the air noisily: "I'm going to take her to see the monkeys."

Roaring with laughter he continued:

"I bet you wonder why the monkeys? That's just what one would expect from someone like you who has only seen trained monkeys. You must learn, you fool, that the zoo monkeys live in groups in the cages. They're just like humans in their actions. You can see them making love or fighting, right in public! When I take this girl there, she'll have as good as opened up the doors for me!"

"Very good," muttered Abbas without interrupting his work.

"Women are an extensive study and one doesn't succeed with wavy hair alone."

"I'm just a poor ignorant fellow," laughed Abbas in reply, looking at his hair in the mirror.

Husain threw a sharp glance at his reflection in the mirror and asked:

"And Hamida?"

The barber's heart skipped a beat. He had not expected to hear her name mentioned. Her image rose before him and he flushed red:

"Hamida?"

"Yes. Hamida, the daughter of Umm Hamida."

Abbas took refuge in silence, a look of confusion on his face, while his friend went on:

"What a bashful simpleton you are! Your body is asleep, your shop is asleep, your whole life is sleeping. Why should I tire myself out trying to wake you up? You're a dead man. How can this dreary life of yours ever fulfil your hopes? Never! No matter how much you try, you'll only make a bare living."

The barber's pensiveness showed in his eyes as he said half-aloud:

"It's God who chooses for us."

His young friend said scornfully:

"Uncle Kamil, Kirsha's coffee-house, smoking a water pipe, playing cards!"

The barber, now really perplexed, asked:

"Why do you make fun of this life?"

"Is it a life at all? Everyone in this alley is half dead, and if you live here long, you won't need burying. God have mercy on you!"

Abbas hesitated, then asked, although he could anticipate the reply:

"What do you want me to do?"

"The many times I've told you," shouted Husain. "The times I've given you my advice. Shake off this miserable life, close up your shop, leave this filthy alley behind. Rest your eyes from looking at Uncle Kamil's carcass. Work for the British Army. It's a gold-mine that will never be exhausted. Why, it's exactly like the treasure of Hassan al-Basari! This war isn't the disaster that fools say it is. It's a blessing! God sent it to us to rescue us from our poverty and misery. Those air raids are throwing gold down on us!

"I'm still telling you to join the British Army. Italy is finished but Germany isn't defeated and Japan is behind her. The war will last at least another twenty years. I'm telling you for the last time, there are jobs to be had in Tell al-Kabir. Go and get one!"

The barber was so excited he had difficulty in finishing his job. Abbas had a lazy dislike for change, dreaded anything new, hated travelling, and if he were left to himself he would make no choice other than the alley. If he spent the rest of his life there, he would be quite happy. The truth was he loved it.

Now, however, the image of Hamida rose before him. His hopes and desires and her image formed one indivisible whole. Despite all this, he feared to reveal his true feelings. He knew he must have time to plan and to think. He said aloud, feigning disinterest:

"Oh, travelling is such a bore."

Husain stamped his foot and shouted:

"You're the real bore! Going anywhere is much better than Midaq Alley, and better than Uncle Kamil. Go and put your trust in God. You've never lived. What have you eaten? What have you drunk? What have you seen? Believe me, you haven't been born yet. . . . Look at your dreary clothes . . ."

"It's a pity I wasn't born rich."

"It's a pity you weren't born a girl! If you were born a girl, you'd be one of Midaq Alley's many old maids. Your life revolves only around the house. You never even go to the zoo, or to Mouski Street. Do you know that Hamida walks there every afternoon?"

Mention of her name redoubled his confusion and it hurt him that his friend should talk to him so insultingly.

"Your sister Hamida is a girl of fine character. There's nothing wrong with her strolling occasionally along the Mouski."

"All right, but she's an ambitious girl, and you'll never win her unless you change your life . . ."

Abbas' face burned with outrage. He had finished cutting the young man's hair and he set about combing it silently, his thoughts in a turmoil. Eventually Husain Kirsha rose and paid him, but before he left the saloon he discovered that he had forgotten his handkerchief and he hurried back home for it.

Abbas stood watching him and was struck by how purposeful and happy Husain seemed. It was just as though he was witnessing these things for the first time. "You'll never win her unless you change your life." Surely Husain was right. His life was mere drudgery. Each day's work scarcely paid for that day's expenses. If he wanted to save in these hard times, it was clear he must try something new. How long could he continue to feed on hopes and dreams? Why shouldn't he try his luck like the others? "An ambitious girl." That's what Husain had said and he was certainly in a position to know. If the girl he loved were ambitious, then he must acquire ambitions himself. Perhaps tomorrow Husain would think — and he smiled at the thought — that it was he who had awakened him from his stupor. He knew better, however. He realized that were it not for Hamida, nothing could stir him from this life. Abbas now marvelled at the strength of love, its power and its strange magic. He thought it right that God had created mankind capable of love and then left the task of developing life to the fertility of love.

The young man asked himself why he should not leave. He had lived in the alley almost a quarter of a century. What had it done for him? It was a place that did not treat its inhabitants fairly. It did not reward them in proportion to their love for it. It tended to smile on those who abused it and abused those who smiled on it. For example, it had barely kept him alive, while it rained wealth on Salim Alwan. There was Salim, a short distance away, piling up banknotes so high that Abbas could almost detect their seductive smell, whereas this palm clutched at what was scarcely the price of bread. Why shouldn't he leave in search of a better life?

These thoughts ran their jagged course as he stood before his shop, gazing at Uncle Kamil, who was snoring loudly, a fly-whisk in his lap. He heard steps coming from the top of the alley, and he turned to see Husain Kirsha striding back down again. He looked at him as a gambler beholds a turning roulette wheel. Husain approached and almost passed; just then Abbas put his hand on his shoulder:

"Husain, I want to talk to you about something important . . ."

5

ate afternoon . . .

The alley returned once more to that hour of murky shadows. Hamida set out, wrapping her cloak around her and listening to the clack of her shoes on the stairs as she made her way to the street. She walked slowly, conscious of both her gait and her appearance, for she was aware that four eyes were examining her closely. The eyes belonged to Salim Alwan, the company owner, and to Abbas, the barber. She was well aware of her attire; a faded cotton dress, an old cloak and shoes with time-worn soles. Nevertheless she draped her cloak in such a way that it emphasized her ample hips and her full and rounded breasts. The cloak revealed her trim ankles on which she wore a bangle; it also exposed her black hair and attractive bronze face.

She was determined to take no notice of anything, simply to make her way from Sanadiqiyya to Mouski Street. As soon as she was beyond the range of the penetrating eyes, her lips parted in a smile, her beautiful eyes quickly surveyed the activity in the bustling street. For a girl of uncertain origins she never lost her spirit of self-confidence. Perhaps her beauty contributed to her self-assurance, but this was not the only factor.

She was by nature strong, and this strength had never once deserted her. Sometimes her eyes revealed this inner strength; some thought it detracted from her beauty, others that it enhanced it. She was constantly beset by a desire to fight and conquer. This she showed in her pleasure in attracting men and also in her efforts to dominate her mother.

It also revealed itself in quarrels which were always flaring up between her and other women of the alley. As a consequence, they all hated her and said nothing but unkind things about her. Perhaps the most commonly said thing about her was that she hated children and that this unnatural trait made her wild and totally lacking in the virtues of femininity. It was this that made Mrs. Kirsha, the café owner's wife, who had nursed her, hope to God to see her a mother too, suckling children under the care of a tyrannical husband who beat her unmercifully!

Hamida continued on her way, enjoying her daily promenade and looking in the shop windows, one after the other. The luxurious clothes stirred in her greedy and ambitious mind bewitching dreams of power and influence. Anyone could have told her that her yearning for power centered around her love for money. She was convinced that it was the magic key to the entire world. All she knew about herself was that she dreamed constantly of wealth; of riches which would bring her every luxury her heart had ever desired.

In spite of her fantasies of wealth, she was not unaware of her situation. Indeed, she remembered a girl in Sanadiqiyya Street who was even poorer than she. Then fortune sent a rich contractor who transported her from her miserable hovel to a fairy-tale life. What was to prevent good fortune from smiling twice in their quarter? This ambition of hers, however, was limited to her familiar world which ended at Queen Farida Square. She knew nothing of life beyond it.

In the distance, she saw some of the factory girls approaching her. She hurried towards them; her unpleasant thoughts were now replaced by a smile on her face. In the midst of their greetings and chattering, Hamida gazed searchingly at their faces and clothes, envying them their freedom and obvious prosperity. They were girls from the Darasa district, who, taking advantage of wartime employment opportunities, ignored custom and tradition and now worked in public places just like the Jewish women. They had gone into factory work exhausted, emaciated and destitute. Soon remarkable changes were noticeable: their once undernourished bodies filled out and seemed to radiate a healthy pride and vitality. They imitated the Jewish girls by paying attention to their appearance and in keeping slim. Some even used unaccustomed language and did not hesitate to walk arm-in-arm and stroll about the streets of illicit love. They exuded an air of boldness and secret knowledge.

As for Hamida, her age and ignorance had deprived her of their opportunities. She joined their laughter with a false sincerity, all the while envy nibbling at her. She did not hesitate to criticize them, even though in fun. This girl's frock, for instance, was too short and immodest, while that one's was simply in bad taste. A third girl was too obvious, the way she stared at men, while she remembered the fourth one from the days when lice crawled about her neck like ants. No doubt these encounters were one of the roots of her constant rebelliousness, but they were also her main source of diversion in the long days filled with boredom and quarrels. So it was that one day she had said to her mother:

"The Jewish girls have the only real life here."

"You must have been conceived by devils!" her mother shouted. "None of my blood is in you."

"Maybe I'm a pasha's daughter, even if illegitimately."

The woman shook her head and moaned:

"May God have mercy on your father, a poor vegetable seller in Margush!"

She walked along with her companions, proud in the knowledge of her beauty, impregnable in the armour of her sharp tongue and pleased that the eyes of passers-by settled on her more than on the others.

When they reached the middle of Mouski, she saw Abbas lagging behind them a little, gazing at her with his customary expression. She wondered why he had left his shop at this time of day. Was he following her on purpose? Couldn't he read the message in her eyes? She had to admit that despite his poverty he was presentable looking, as were all those in his trade. Yes, his appearance pleased her. She told herself that not one of her friends could hope to marry anyone better than Abbas.

Her feelings towards him were strange and complicated. On the one hand, he was the only young man in the alley who would make a suitable husband for her while she, on the other hand, dreamed of a husband like the rich contractor her neighbor had married. The truth was she neither loved nor wanted him; at the same time she could not dismiss him. Perhaps his passionate glances pleased her.

It was her custom to walk with the girls as far as the end of Darasa and then return alone to the alley. She continued with them, stealing an occasional glance at Abbas. She no longer doubted he was following her intentionally and that he wanted to break his long silence. She was not mistaken. She had scarcely said goodbye to the girls and turned around when he made his way towards her. In a few quick steps he was at her side.

"Good evening, Hamida . . ." he said awkwardly.

She turned suddenly and pretended to be surprised by his appearance. Then she scowled and lengthened her stride without saying a word. His face reddened, but he caught her up and said in a hurt voice:

"Good evening, Hamida . . ."

She was afraid that if she kept silent and continued to hurry they would reach the square before he could say what he wanted. She drew to a sudden halt and spoke indignantly:

"What nerve! One of our neighbors, acting like a fresh stranger!"

"Yes, you're right, I am a neighbor but I'm not behaving like a stranger. Can't neighbors talk to one another?"

Hamida frowned and said:

"No. A neighbor should protect a neighbor, not insult them."

"I never thought for one moment of insulting you, God forbid. I only want to talk with you. Is there any harm in that . . . ?"

"How can you say that? It's wrong for you to stop me in the street and expose me to a scandal."

Her words horrified him and he seemed stunned:

"Scandal? God forbid, Hamida. I have only the most honorable intentions towards you. I swear by the life of Hussain. You'll soon learn that if you only give me a chance. Listen to me. I want to talk to you about something important. Turn off towards Azhar Street so we can be away from prying eyes."

Hamida exclaimed in feigned horror:

"Be away from people? What a thing to suggest! You're right, you are a good neighbor!"

Abbas had now become a little braver as a result of her arguing with him and he demanded indignantly:

"What's a neighbor's crime anyway? Has he got to die without saying what he feels?"

"How pure your words are . . ."

He sighed peevishly, showing his regret that they were approaching the busy square:

"My intentions are completely pure. Don't rush off, Hamida, let's turn into Azhar Street. I have something important to tell you. You must listen. I'm sure you know what I want to say. Don't you feel anything? One's emotions are the best guide."

"You've gone far enough . . . No . . . No . . . Leave me alone."

"Hamida . . . I want to . . . I want you . . ."

"So you want to disgrace me before everyone?"

They had now reached Husain Square and she crossed over to the opposite pavement and hurried off. She then turned down towards Ghouriyya, smiling self-consciously. Hamida now knew what he wanted. It was just as he had said. She saw the spark of love in his eyes just as she had suspected it was there when he stared at her window. She knew his financial state was not impressive but his personality was submissive and humble. This should have pleased her dominating nature; instead she felt no interest. This puzzled her.

What, then, did she want? And who would satisfy her if this kind young man did not? She knew no answer to this, and she attributed her indifference to his poverty. It was a fact that her love to dominate was a result of her love to quarrel, not the reverse. She had always resisted peace and quiet and found no joy in easy victory. Thus her confused feelings filled her with perplexity and distress.

Abbas refrained from following her, fearing that he might be seen. He started back home, his heart overflowing with disappointment, but not despair.

He told himself as he made his way slowly, oblivious to all about him, that she had at least spoken to him, and at some length too. If she had wanted to stop him, she could easily have done so.

It was obvious she did not dislike him and perhaps she was acting like any girl would. It could have been modesty that made her hesitate to make friends with him. He felt drunk with joy from some magic potion he had never before tasted. Abbas was truly in love and he felt certain his love for her would last a thousand years.

Consequently he felt no sense of failure from today's encounter. When he turned into Sanadiqiyya, he saw Sheikh Darwish coming from Husain Mosque. They met at the end of the alley and Abbas moved to greet him. The old man, however, pointed his forefinger at him warningly and, gazing from behind his gold-rimmed spectacles, he said:

"Never go out without a hat! I warn you against going bareheaded in weather like this, in a world like this. Young men's brains are liable to dissolve into steam and fly off. This situation is well known in *alma'sah* and the meaning of this in English is tragedy and it's spelled: T-R-A-G-E-D-Y . . ."

6

r. Kirsha, the coffee-house owner, was occupied with an important matter; indeed rarely did a year go by without his involvement in similar matters, in spite of the trouble they caused him. The hashish robbed him of any will to resist. He was a poor man, however, unlike the majority of café proprietors, not because his business was unprofitable, but because he was a squanderer, wasting his profits and throwing his money about with nothing to show for it. In fact, he gave free rein to his desires and passions and especially to that one unwholesome weakness of his.

When the sun was nearly set, he left his coffee-house without telling Sankir of his intention. Dressed in his black cloak and leaning on his old stick, he moved slowly and heavily. His gloomy eyes, almost hidden beneath heavy lids, scarcely allowed him to see his course. His heart was throbbing violently. Strange as it seems, Mr. Kirsha had always lived a most irregular life, and he had rolled in its dirt so long that it appeared to him a perfectly normal one.

He was a narcotic peddler and accustomed to doing his business under a veil of darkness. Normal life had eluded him and he had become a prey to perversions. Thus his submission to his vices was complete; he neither regretted them nor was he repentant. He would complain about the government for punishing people like himself and would slander those who openly despised and scorned his other passion. He always said of the government: "It has legalized wine, which God forbade and has forbidden hashish which God allowed. It protects hot and stuffy taverns while it suppresses hashish dens which supply medicine for both the soul and the intellect." He frequently shook his head sadly and said: "What's wrong with hashish? It gives peace to the mind and comfort to life and apart from both these facts, it is an excellent aphrodisiac!"

Concerning his "other vice," he would say in his customary way: "You have your religion, I have mine!" Nevertheless, the frequency with which he indulged in his passions did not prevent his heart from throbbing violently when he arrived on the brink of each new erotic adventure.

He went slowly down Ghouriyya, allowing his thoughts to wander and asking himself, his heart filled with hope: "What will the evening bring me, I wonder?" In spite of his absorption in his thoughts, he was conscious of the shops on both sides and from time to time he returned the greetings of some of the shopkeepers he knew. He mistrusted such greetings for he never knew whether they were merely greetings or whether they had some sly and derogatory meaning behind them. People wouldn't live and let live and were always only too ready to slander with their avid and greedy mouths. They were forever talking about him and what good did their defamation do? None at all! It was as though he enjoyed their criticism and he continued doing as he wished.

He continued until he came up to the last shop on his left, close to al-Azhar. Now his heart beat faster still and he forgot the greetings of people and the unpleasant thoughts they inspired, while a faint glint of evil seemed to issue from his dim eyes. He was now near the shop, his mouth gaping and his lips drooping as he crossed its threshold.

It was a small shop, with an old man sitting in the center behind a little desk. Leaning against one of the shop's shelves, piled high with goods, was a youthful-looking lad who was the shop's salesman. As soon as he saw the customer he stood up straight, smiling as an alert salesman should. Kirsha's heavy brows rose and his eyes settled on the youth; then he greeted him gently. The youth returned his greeting in a friendly fashion and suddenly realized that this was the third time in three successive days that he had seen this man. He asked himself why the man had not bought what he wanted all at the same time. Mr. Kirsha spoke:

"Show me what socks you have . . ."

The youth brought out several types and spread them on the counter. Kirsha examined them, looking surreptitiously at the boy's face as he did so. The youth did not shy away from him and a faint smile crossed Kirsha's lips. He dragged out his examination as long as he politely could, then he spoke quietly:

"Don't be angry at me, my boy, my eyesight is weak. Now, you choose a pair for me which appeals to your good taste . . ."

He was silent a moment, gazing intently into his face. Then he went on, a smile on his drooping lips:

"Just like your handsome face . . ."

The good-looking boy showed him another pair, pretending to ignore the compliment. Kirsha said:

"Wrap up six pairs for me."

He waited while the lad wrapped the socks, then he suggested:

"You had better wrap up a dozen. I am not short of money, praise God."

The youth silently did as requested and muttered, as he handed him the parcel:

"You have made a good buy."

Mr. Kirsha smiled, or rather his mouth split open mechanically; this was accompanied by a slight twitching of his eyebrows. He said mischievously:

"Thanks to you, my boy," and then quietly: "praise be to God."

Kirsha, having paid for his parcel, left the shop just as excited as he had been when he entered. He turned towards Azhar Street, crossed slowly to its opposite side and stopped in the shade of a tree. Standing with one hand on his stick and the other gripping his package, his eyes remained fixed on the shop a fair distance away. The lad, his arms crossed on his chest, was now standing in the same position as when Kirsha entered the shop.

Kirsha gazed towards him, only able to make out a dim picture of the boy, but his memory and his imagination supplied what his weak sight could not distinguish. He told himself: "He knew what I meant, for sure." Then he recalled how gentle, humble and well-mannered he was and his ears recalled his voice as he had said: "You have made a good buy." Kirsha's heart froze in excitement at the thought and he sighed from deep within him.

He remained standing in his place for some time, burning with apprehension and excitement until at last he saw the shop close its doors. When this was done, the old shopkeeper and the lad parted, the former going off towards the gold market and the lad moving towards Azhar Street. Slowly Kirsha left his tree and walked in the direction taken by the youth. The boy saw him when he had crossed two-thirds of the street but showed no concern or interest and was about to pass him by without more ado when Kirsha came up to him and said politely:

"Good evening, my boy."

The lad looked at him, his eyes giving a suggestion of a faint smile, and mumbled:

"Good evening, sir."

Kirsha, forcing conversation, continued:

"Have you locked up the shop?"

The boy noticed that he was holding back, as though inviting him to slow down, but he continued his pace and said:

"Yes, sir."

Kirsha was forced to quicken his pace and they walked together on the pavement, the café owner never taking his eyes off the boy. He remarked:

"Your working hours are long, may God help you!"

The boy sighed and replied:

"What's the alternative? If you want to eat, you must tire yourself out . . ."

Kirsha was delighted that the lad was conversing with him and sensed that his friendliness was an auspicious sign. He exclaimed:

"May God reward you for your exertions, my boy . . ."

"Thank you, sir."

The café owner went on indignantly:

"Life's really one long trial, but it's very rare that one's exertions receive the reward they deserve. What a vast number of exploited working people there are in this world."

This statement struck a responsive chord in the boy and with conviction he agreed:

"You are right, sir. What a lot of exploited workers there are in this world."

"Patience is the key to joy. Yes, what a lot of people are exploited and what this means in simple terms is that there are a great number of exploiters. However, by the graciousness of God, the world's not entirely devoid of merciful people, all the same . . ."

"Where are these merciful people?"

He almost answered: "I am one of them myself," but he stopped himself and said reprovingly:

"Don't be slanderous, my boy. All is well with Muhammad's people." Then he changed his tone and asked: "Why are you going so fast? Are you in a hurry?"

"I must go home to change my clothes."

Kirsha asked him with interest:

"And after that?"

"I go off to the coffee-shop."

"Which one?"

"Ramadan coffee-shop."

At this Kirsha's smile was so broad that his gold teeth gleamed in the dark and he said temptingly:

"Why don't you honor our café?"

"Which one is that, sir?"

Kirsha's voice went hoarse as he replied:

"Kirsha's café in Midaq Alley. I am Mr. Kirsha myself."

Much impressed, the lad commented:

"I am honored, sir. That is a very well-known coffee-shop . . ."

"Will you come?"

"If God wishes."

Kirsha, with patience, commented:

"Everything is dependent on God's wishes. But do you really intend to come or are you just saying that to evade me?"

The boy laughed quietly and said:

"No, I really intend to come."

"Tonight then!"

When the lad made no reply, Kirsha said emphatically, his heart dancing with delight:

"Without fail . . ."

The boy muttered:

"With God's permission . . ."

Kirsha sighed audibly and asked:

"Where do you live?"

"Wikala Lane."

"We are almost neighbors. Are you married?"

"Of course not . . . I am with my family."

Kirsha commented politely:

"You seem to come from a good family. I can tell. A good jug pours forth good water. You must take great care to look after your future. You must not remain a shop salesman all your life."

A look of anxiety crossed the boy's handsome face as he asked:

"Can someone like me hope for anything better?"

"Have 'we' run out of ideas?" asked Kirsha scornfully. "Weren't all big men once small?"

"Oh yes, but it's not inevitable that small men become big."

Finishing the boy's statement, Kirsha added:

"Unless he has some luck! Let's remember today, the day when we got acquainted, as a day of great good fortune. Shall I expect you tonight?"

The boy hesitated a moment, then said, smiling:

"Only a fool refuses generosity!"

They shook hands at Mutawali gate and Kirsha made his way back, stumbling in the dark. The absentminded café owner was now fully awake and a warm feeling of happiness ran through him. As he passed the closed shop he gazed at it with passionate longing. He came back at last to the alley, its shops bolted and enveloped in darkness, except for the one light coming from the café.

In contrast to the cold outside air, the air in the café was warm from the heat of the pipe-smoke, the breath of the people sitting within it, and the glowing stove. The men sat around on sofas talking and sipping coffee, while the stomach of the radio belched forth its clamor. Everyone ignored it, as if it were a boring speaker addressing the deaf. Sankir was bustling with activity, never still and incessantly shouting. Kirsha made his way quietly to his seat behind the till, avoiding the customers' glances. Just at that moment Uncle Kamil was asking friends to persuade Abbas to give up the shroud he was holding for him, but they all agreed to refuse his request. Dr. Bushi spoke to Kamil:

"Don't worry about the clothing of the next world. A man spends much of his time on earth naked, but he can't cross the threshold of the grave naked, no matter how poor he may be."

The simple-hearted Kamil repeated his request and was repeatedly refused and ridiculed, until at last he remained silent in defeat. Abbas told his friends of his decision to work for the British Army. He listened to their comments and advice as they all approved of his plan and wished him good fortune and wealth. Radwan Husaini was engaged in one of his long conversations filled with exhortation and advice. He turned to the man talking with him and said:

"Never say you are bored. Boredom is disbelief in God. Boredom is an illness that destroys faith. Does it mean anything other than dissatisfaction with life? Life is a blessed gift from God Almighty, so how can a believer become bored or dissatisfied with it? You say you are dissatisfied with this or that, and I ask you from where did this or that originate? Doesn't everything originate with the Glorious God who in His kindness rights all wrongs? Never rebel against the work of the Creator! All of life has beauty and taste, although the bitterness of an evil soul will pollute the most appetizing tastes. Believe me, pain brings joy, despair has its pleasure, and death teaches a lesson. How can we be bored when the sky is blue, the earth green, and the flowers fragrant? How can we be depressed when hearts have a capacity for love and our souls have the power of faith? Seek refuge from the devil in God and never say you are bored . . ."

He took a sip from his cinnamon-flavored tea and then added as though expressing the doubts of his own conscience: "As for life's tragedies, our love will defeat them. Love is the most effective cure. In the crevices of disasters, happiness lies like a diamond in a mine, so let us instill in ourselves the wisdom of love."

His pinkish-red face glowed with benevolence and light, his reddish beard framing it like a halo around the moon. In comparison with his own towering tranquility, all about him seemed chaos and confusion. His expression was all purity and it spoke of his faith, love and aloofness from personal ambitions.

It was said of him that he lost his dignity the day he failed his examinations at Azhar University and that he despaired of immortality when he lost his children; thus, he found compensation for his losses by winning people's hearts with his love and generosity. No one doubted that he was sincere in his faith, in his love, and in his kindness. It was remarkable however that this gentle man was harsh and uncompromising in his own house. Some thought that having despaired of any authority on earth, Husaini imposed his influence on the only person who would submit to his will—his wife. Thus he satisfied his greed for power by inflicting tyranny on her.

However, we must not underestimate the power of the traditions of the time and the place. We must not forget that among this class the prevailing opinion was that women were best treated as children, above all for the sake of their own happiness. His wife, nevertheless, had nothing to complain of in his treatment of her. Apart from those wounds indelibly engraved on her heart by the deaths of her children, she considered herself a fortunate woman, proud of her husband and of her life.

Kirsha was both present and absent at the same time. Sitting gave him no peace for a single minute; he suffered the bitterness of victory in spiritless silence. Every few minutes he peered towards the alley entrance. He stared at the till, patient, motionless and telling himself: "He will come for sure. He will come just as those before him did."

He seemed to see the boy's face and looked towards the chair standing between him and Darwish's sofa and in his mind's eye saw the boy putting his trust in him. In times gone by he would never have invited such a boy to his coffee-shop, but now his vice was well-known to the alley inhabitants. Now Kirsha's mask was removed and he indulged his perversion openly. Raging scenes took place between him and his wife, providing rich gossip for people like Dr. Bushi and Umm Hamida. However, he did not care at all. The flames of one scandal scarcely died down before he would delight them with the fuel of other misdemeanors; it was as though he found pleasure in creating scandals. Thus he now sat in apprehension, peace unable to find a path to his tarnished soul. At last Dr. Bushi noticed his anxious state and said to Abbas:

"These are the signs of the hour!"

Now Sheikh Darwish emerged from his silence and recited two lines of ancient love poetry, muttering:

"Oh madam; love is worth millions. I have spent, madam, for love of you, 100,000 pounds, but this is just a paltry sum!"

At last Dr. Bushi saw Kirsha look intently at the entrance to the alley. Suddenly he saw him sit up straight and smile broadly. Bushi looked towards the coffee-house door and soon the face of the lad appeared, his innocent eyes gazing hesitantly at the people in the café.

7

he bakery is next to Kirsha's café, near Mrs. Saniya Afifi's house. It is an almost square building, its sides built unevenly. An oven occupies the left side and the wall is lined with shelves. Between the oven and the entrance is a bench on which the owners of the bakery, Husniya and her husband, Jaada, sleep. Darkness would envelop the spot day and night, were it not for the light issuing from the door of the oven.

In the wall facing the entrance, there is a small, wooden door which opens on to a grimy little outhouse, smelling of dirt and filth, for it has only one tiny window in the opposite wall overlooking the courtyard of an old house. About an arm's length from the window there is a lighted lamp, placed on a shelf, throwing a dim light on the place, with its dirt floor covered with various and indeterminate rubbish; the room looks like a garbage heap. The shelf supporting the lantern is long and stretches the entire wall; on it are bottles, both large and small, various instruments and a great number of bandages, making it look just like a pharmacist's shelf, were it not so extraordinarily dirty.

On the ground, almost directly beneath the little window, something is piled, no different from the floor of the room in color, filthiness or smell, but possessed of limbs, flesh, and blood, and which therefore, despite everything, deserves to be called a human being. It was Zaita, the man who rented this hole from Husniya the baker.

If you once saw Zaita you would never again forget him, so starkly simple is his appearance. He consists of a thin, black body, and a black gown. Black upon black, were it not for the slits shining with a terrifying whiteness which are his eyes. Zaita is not a Negro; he is an Egyptian, brown-skinned in color. Dirt mixed with the sweat of a lifetime has caked a thick layer of black over his body and over his gown, which also was not originally black. Black was the fate of everything within this hole.

He had scarcely anything to do with the alley in which he dwelt. Zaita visited none of its people nor did they visit him. He had no need for anyone nor anyone for him. Except, that is, for Dr. Bushi and the fathers who resorted to scaring their children with his image. His trade was known to all, a trade which gave him the right to the title of "Doctor," although he did not use it out of respect for Bushi. It was his profession to create cripples, not the usual, natural cripples, but artificial cripples of a new type.

People came to him who wanted to become beggars and, with his extraordinary craft, the tools of which were piled on the shelf, he would cripple each customer in a manner appropriate to his body. They came to him whole and left blind, rickety, hunchbacked, pigeon-breasted or with arms or legs cut off short. He gained his skill by working for a long time with a travelling circus. Zaita had, moreover, been connected with beggar circles since his boyhood, when he lived with his parents, who were beggars. He began by learning "make-up," an art taught in the circus, first as a pastime, then as a profession when his personal situation became worse.

One disadvantage of his work was that it began at night, or at midnight to be exact. It was, however, a trivial disadvantage to which he had become completely accustomed. During the day, he scarcely left his den and would sit cross-legged, eating or smoking or amusing himself by spying on the baker and his wife. He delighted in listening to their talk, or peeping through a hole in the door and watching the woman beating her husband, morning and night. When night fell he saw them overcome with friendliness towards each other and he would see the bakeress approach her ape-like husband and tease him and talk to him coyly. Zaita detested Jaada, despised him and considered him ugly. Apart from this, he envied him for the full-bodied woman God had given him as a wife, a really bovine woman, as he said. He often said of her that she was among women what Uncle Kamil was among men.

One reason why the people in the alley avoided him was his offensive odor, for water never found its way to either his face or body. He happily reciprocated the dislike people showed for him and he jumped with joy when he heard that someone had died. He would say, as though speaking to the dead person: "Now your time has come to taste the dirt, whose color and smell so much offend you on my body." No doubt he spent much time imagining tortures he could inflict on people and found a most satisfying pleasure in doing just this. He would imagine Jaada the baker as a target for tens of hatchets striking at him and leaving him a smashed heap. Or he would imagine Salim Alwan stretched on the ground while a steamroller ran over him again and again, his blood running down towards Sanadiqiyya. He would also imagine Radwan Husaini being pulled along by his reddish beard towards the flaming oven and being eventually pulled out as a bag of ashes. Or he might see Kirsha stretched beneath the wheels of a train crushing his limbs, later to be stuffed into a dirty basket and sold to dog-owners for food! There were similar punishments that he considered the very least people deserved.

When he set about his work of making cripples at their request, he was as cruel and deliberately vicious as he could be, cunningly employing all the secrets of his trade. When his victims cried out at his torture, his terrifying eyes gleamed with an insane light. Despite all this, beggars were the people dearest to him and he often wished that beggars formed the majority of mankind.

.   .   .

Zaita sat thus engrossed in the wanderings of his imagination, waiting for the time for work to arrive. About midnight he got up, blew out the lamp and a deep darkness took over. He then felt his way to the door and, opening it quietly, he made his way through the bakery into the alley. On his way he met Sheikh Darwish leaving the coffee-house. They often met in the middle of the night without exchanging a single word. For this reason, Sheikh Darwish had a particularly rich reward awaiting him in the Court of Investigation to try mankind which Zaita had set up in his imagination!

The cripple-maker crossed over to the Husain Mosque walking with short, deliberate steps.

As he walked, Zaita kept close to the walls of the houses. In spite of the blackness of the shadows, some lights still gleamed, thus someone approaching would almost collide with him before seeing his flashing eyes glinting in the dark like the metal clasp of a policeman's belt.

Walking in the street he felt revived, lively and happy. He only ever walked out here when no one but the beggars, who acknowledged his absolute sovereignty, were about. He crossed to Husain Square, turned towards the Green Gate and reached the ancient arch. As he swept his eyes over the heaps of beggars on both sides of him he was filled with delight. His joy was that of a powerful lord mixed with the delight of a merchant who sees profitable merchandise.

He approached the beggar nearest him who sat cross-legged, his head bent on his shoulders and snoring loudly. He stood for a moment before him, gazing intently as though to probe his sleep and determine whether it was genuine or feigned. Then he kicked the dishevelled head and the man stirred, but not in a startled manner, merely as though gentle ants had wakened him. He raised his head slowly, scratching his sides, back and head. His gaze fell on the figure looking down on him; he stared up for a moment and, despite his blindness, recognized him at once. The beggar sighed and a noise like a groan rose from his depths. He thrust his hand into his breast pocket and withdrew a small coin and placed it in Zaita's palm.

Zaita now turned to the next beggar, then the next and so on until he had completely encircled one wing of the arch. Then he turned to the other wing and, when he finished there, he went round the niches and alleys surrounding the mosque, so that not a single beggar escaped him. His enthusiasm at receiving his dues did not make him forget his duty to care for the cripples he created and he frequently asked this or that beggar: "How is your blindness, so and so?" Or perhaps: "How is your lameness?" They would answer him: "Praise be to God . . . praise be to God!"

Zaita now went around the mosque from the other direction and on his way bought a loaf of bread, some sweets and tobacco and returned to Midaq Alley. The silence was complete, only broken from time to time by a laugh or cough from the roof of Radwan Husaini's house, where one of Kirsha's hashish parties was in progress. Zaita made his way past the threshold of the bakery as quietly as he could, taking care not to waken the sleeping couple. He carefully pushed open his wooden door and closed it quietly behind him. The den was neither dark nor empty as he had left it; the lamp burned and on the ground beneath it sat three men.

Zaita made his way unconcernedly towards them; their presence neither surprised nor troubled him. He stared at them with piercing eyes and recognized Dr. Bushi. They all stood and Dr. Bushi, after a polite greeting, said:

"These are two poor men who asked me to seek your help for them."

Zaita, feigning boredom and complete disinterest, replied: "At a time like this, Doctor?"

The "doctor" placed his hand on Zaita's shoulder and said: "The night is a veil, and our Lord ordained the veil!"

Zaita protested, belching out air: "But I am tired now!"

Dr. Bushi replied hopefully: "You have never let me down."

The two men begged and pleaded. Zaita yielded, as if unwillingly, and placed his food and tobacco on the shelf. He stood facing them, staring hard and long in silence. Then he fixed his eyes on the taller of the two. He was a giant of a man and Zaita, amazed to see him there, asked:

"You are an ox of a man! Why do you want to become a beggar?"

The man answered falteringly:

"I am never successful at a job. I have tried all kinds of work, even being a beggar. My luck is bad and my mind is worse. I can never understand or remember anything."

Zaita commented spitefully:

"Then you should have been born rich!"

The man did not understand what he meant and attempted to win Zaita's pity by pretending to weep, saying spiritlessly:

"I have failed in everything. I even had no luck as a beggar. Everyone said I was strong and should work, that is when they didn't curse or shout at me. I don't know why."

Zaita nodded:

"Even that you can't grasp!"

"May God inspire you with some way to help me," the big man pleaded.

Zaita continued to examine him thoughtfully and, feeling his limbs, said decisively:

"You are really strong. Your limbs are all healthy. What do you eat?"

"Bread if I can get it, otherwise nothing."

"Yours is really a giant's body, there's no doubt about it. Do you realize what you would be like if you ate as God's animals eat, on whom He lavishes good things?"

The man replied simply:

"I don't know."

"Of course, of course. You don't know anything, we understand that. If you had had any sense you would be one of us. Listen, you oaf, there's nothing to be gained by my trying to twist your limbs."

A look of great melancholy came into the man's bullish face and he would have burst out weeping again if Zaita had not spoken:

"It would be very difficult for me to break an arm or a leg for you, no matter how hard I tried. Even then, you wouldn't gain anyone's

sympathy. Mules like you only arouse indignation. But don't
despair"—Dr. Bushi had been patiently waiting for this expression—
"there are other ways. I'll teach you the art of imbecility, for example.
You don't seem to lack any talent for that, so idiocy it will be. I'll teach
you some ballads in praise of the Prophet."

The huge man's face beamed with delight and he thanked Zaita
profusely. Zaita interrupted him:

"Why didn't you work as a highwayman?"

He replied indignantly:

"I am a poor fellow, but I am good and I don't want to harm
anyone. I like everyone."

Zaita commented contemptuously:

"Do you wish to convert me to that philosophy?"

He turned to the other man, who was short and frail, and said
delightedly:

"Good material, anyway."

The man smiled and said:

"Much praise to God."

"You were created to be a blind, squatting beggar."

The man seemed pleased:

"That is because of the bounty of our Lord."

Zaita shook his head and replied slowly:

"The operation is difficult and dangerous. Let me ask what you
would do if the worst happened. Supposing you were really to lose
your sight because of an accident or carelessness?"

The man hesitated, then replied unconcernedly:

"It would be a blessing from God! Have I ever gained anything by
my sight that I should be sorry to lose it?"

Zaita was pleased and commented:

"With a heart like yours you can really face up to the world."

"With God's permission, sir. I will be eternally grateful to you. I
will give you half what the good people give me."

Zaita shot a penetrating look at him and then said harshly:

"I am not interested in talk like that. I want only two milliemes a
day, besides the fee for the operation. I know, by the way, how to get
my rights if you are thinking of getting away without paying."

At this point Bushi reminded him:

"You didn't remember your share of the bread."

Zaita went on talking:

"Of course . . . of course. Now, let's get down to planning the work. The operation will be difficult and will test your powers of endurance. Hide the pain as best you can . . ."

Can you imagine what this thin and meager body would suffer under the pounding of Zaita's hands?

A satanical smile played about Zaita's faded lips . . .

8

_T_he company's premises in Midaq Alley produced a clamor which continued all day long. A number of workers carried out their jobs with only a short break for lunch, and there was a constant flow of goods in and out of the establishment, while large trucks rumbled noisily into Sanadiqiyya Street and those adjoining Ghouriyya and Azhar. There was also a steady stream of customers and tradesmen.

The company dealt with perfumes, wholesale and retail, and there was no doubt that the wartime cut in imports from India badly affected trade. However, the company managed to keep both its reputation and position and, indeed, the war had doubled its activities and profits. The wartime situation convinced Salim Alwan of the wisdom of trading in commodities which previously had not interested him, for example, tea. Thus he had become active in the black market and profited heavily from it.

Salim Alwan always sat at his big desk at the end of the corridor leading off the central courtyard within the company premises, around which were the warehouses. Thus his position was central and he could observe all the activities of the company; he could easily watch his employees, the workmen and the customers at the same time. For this reason he preferred his position to sitting alone in an office as most of his fellow businessmen did. He always maintained that a true businessman "must always keep his eyes open."

He really approached the absolute ideal of a man of business; he was expert in his trade and also able to motivate it into action. He was not one of the "new rich" the war produced. Mr. Alwan was, as he put it, "A merchant and son of a merchant." Previously, however, he was not considered rich; then the First World War had come along and he had emerged successful. This second war had so far been even more nourishing for his business and now he was very prosperous.

Salim Alwan was not without his worries; he felt he was fighting life without anyone to help him. True, his excellent health and vitality diminished these worries. However, he had to think of the future, when his life would end and the company would lose its director. It was unfortunate that not one of his three sons had come forward to help their father in his work. They were united in their efforts to avoid commerce and his attempts to dissuade them were useless. He had no other course—over fifty though he was—than to do the work himself.

No doubt he was responsible for this unhappy situation, for, in spite of his commercial mentality, he had always been kind and generous, at least in his own home and with his own family. His house was like a castle; handsome in appearance, with fine furniture and furnishings, and several servants. Moreover he had left his old house in Gamaliyya for a fine villa in Hilmiyya, raising his children in an atmosphere quite cut off from that of other merchants. The new area had an atmosphere which had no doubt instilled in them a contempt for merchants and trade. Unknown to their father, who was busy with his affairs, his sons had assimilated new ideals and standards, a result of their comfortable life and pleasant environment. When matters came to a head, they rebelled against his advice and even refused to enroll in the trade school, lest it be a snare for them. They had gone into law and medicine, and now one was a judge, the other a barrister, and the third was a doctor at Kasr al-Aini hospital.

In spite of this, Salim Alwan's life was a happy one, as was shown in his plump body, chubby, pinkish face and youthful vitality. His happiness stemmed from an inward contentment; his business was profitable, his health excellent, his family happy and his sons successful and contented in their chosen professions. Besides his sons, he had four daughters who were all happily married. Everything would have been perfect had he not occasionally had uneasy thoughts about the fate of his company.

In time, his sons became aware of their father's concern but they viewed the matter from quite another angle. They feared that the reins would some day slip from their father's fingers, or that he would hand them over to his sons and they would be helpless. And so his son Muhammad Salim Alwan, the judge, had suggested that he liquidate his company and enjoy a hard-earned rest. The father was quick to realize his son's true fears and did not attempt to hide his indignation. "Do you want to inherit what I have while I am still alive?" he had shouted.

His father's comment shocked the son, for he and his brothers had a genuine love for their father and none wanted to broach this delicate subject. However, the matter did not end there and they continued to point out—confident that they would now not incite his anger—that to buy land or build apartments would be better than keeping money in cash. Because he was perceptive in money matters, he realized the wisdom of their advice. He was well aware that his profitable business could perish in a reversal of good fortune. Alwan also knew that by buying real estate, for example, and registering it in the name of his sons or his wife, he would be able to get out of possible difficulties with a little money. He might even manage to keep quite a sum. He had heard of rich merchants who had ended up penniless or, worse, had committed suicide or died of grief.

Salim Alwan knew these things well and was aware his sons spoke wisely. He himself had already entertained such thoughts, but wartime conditions allowed him to plan no such action. That was clear and so the matter must be postponed; he would let it mature in his mind until he could accomplish it easily. But scarcely had he set aside this worry before his son, the judge, suggested that he should try and gain the title of "Bey." His son pointed out: "How is it you are not a bey when the country is full of "Beys" and "Pashas" who have neither your wealth, reputation nor position?"

This suggestion pleased him. Unlike more prudent merchants he was much impressed by social status and, in his simplicity, he wondered how he should set about acquiring the title. The matter became the concern of his entire ambitious family, and though they encouraged him they differed in the method to be pursued. One or two suggested he dabble in politics. The trouble was that Salim Alwan scarcely understood anything apart from the world of commerce, and his opinions and beliefs were hardly above those of Abbas the barber, for example. People like him would humbly prostrate themselves before the tomb of Husain, or pay homage to Sheikh Darwish. In short he was essentially ignorant. However, in many cases, politics demand little more than this. He would have considered this seriously, if his barrister son, Arif Salim Alwan, had not opposed the idea and said warningly:

"Politics would surely ruin us and the business. You will find yourself spending twice as much on the party as what you spend on yourself, your family and your business. Supposing you are put up for Parliament. As the price for an insecure seat the elections will swallow up thousands of pounds. Is Parliament in our country anything other than a man with a diseased heart which is ready to stop beating at any moment? And then, what party will you choose? If you choose any party other than the Wafd your business reputation will suffer, and if you choose the Wafd, a Prime Minister like Sidqi Pasha will destroy your business and scatter it to the winds."

Salim Alwan was very impressed by what his son said. He had faith in his educated sons and his determination to put politics aside was reinforced by his ignorance and indifference to that world. His only political awareness was of a few names, and some affection, or aversion for a few of these from the era of the nationalist hero Zaghloul. Some of his family advised him to contribute money to a charitable organization, and thus get his title of "Bey" as a reward.

This suggestion displeased him, for his business instincts were opposed to spending or giving money away. None of this conflicted with his well-known generosity because this was confined to himself and his household. However, he did not refuse point blank. A title was still attractive to him and he continued to want one for himself. Alwan had realized he would have to spend not less than five thousand pounds to get one. What then was he to do? He could not make up his mind, although he said no to his children. Despite this, he added the cost of his title to other inevitable expenses such as the business and the purchase of real estate. He was content to leave the whole matter to the future and whatever it might bring.

However important these concerns, they did not upset the serenity of a person's life, and especially not that of a man engrossed in work all day and in satisfying his natural desires at night. The truth was that when work absorbed him, he was unable to think of anything else. He could, for example, be seated at his desk giving his entire attention to a Jewish broker, so that a stranger would have thought Alwan a close friend of the man. He was, in fact, a veritable crouching tiger, willing to cringe and fawn until he mastered his adversary; and woe to anyone he *did* master! Experience had taught him that this gentleman and others like him were enemies with whom one must be friendly. They were, as he put it, useful devils.

If he made a contract for tea, which was certain to bring a good profit, he would sit twisting his moustaches and belching whenever an unpleasant thought struck him. The visitor would try, after the tea contract, to persuade him to buy some real estate—he already knew of Alwan's desire to do so—but the merchant had decided to postpone the matter until after the war and refused to listen to the broker. The visitor then would leave the office, satisfied with the one contract he had made.

At midday, it was Alwan's custom to have lunch in his pleasant room that contained a couch for his subsequent afternoon siesta. His lunch generally consisted of vegetables, potatoes and a bowl of husked green wheat. When he finished, he rested on his couch for an hour or two. During this time the activity in the company premises subsided and the whole alley became quieter too.

The bowl of husked grain had a story behind it, which the entire alley knew. It was both a food and a prescription which one of his senior employees prepared for him. For some time it had remained a secret between the two men, but, of course, no secret survived long in Midaq Alley. It consisted of a bowl of cooked green wheat, mixed with pieces of pigeon meat and ground nutmeg. He would have it for lunch, then drink tea every two hours afterwards. Its magic effect began at night and lasted for two full hours of sheer delight. The preparation had long remained a secret between him, his employee and Husniya, the baker's wife. The alley people who saw it thought it a harmless lunch. One commented: "May it prove wholesome and bring a cure," while others would mutter, "May it be full of poison, with God's permission!"

One day curiosity possessed Husniya and she decided to try the preparation on her husband, Jaada, the baker. She scooped out a large portion of the food in Alwan's dish and filled the empty space with plain green wheat. She was confident that Alwan had not noticed the substitution. Encouraged by the success of the experiment on her husband, she tried it again. However, Salim Alwan was not long in discovering what was happening. He could not help noticing the sudden change which had affected his nightly activities. At first he blamed the employee who prepared the dish. When he denied it, Salim Alwan became suspicious of Husniya, and he easily learned of the theft. He called Husniya and rebuked her. Furthermore he stopped sending his dish to her bakery; instead he sent it to the European bakery over on New Street.

The secret was now out and it spread until Umm Hamida knew of it. That was too much, of course, and soon all the inhabitants of the alley learned of it and, in the wink of an eye, they were all experimenting with it. At first Salim Alwan was angry when he heard his secret had spread, but he soon ceased to care. Although he had spent most of his life in the alley, he had never really belonged there. The truth was he cared for none of them. In fact, the only two to whom he ever raised his hand in greeting were Radwan Husaini and Sheikh Darwish.

For a time, the bowl of food almost became the staple diet of the whole alley, and had it not been for its costliness no one would have given it up. Kirsha, the café owner, Dr. Bushi and even Radwan Husaini tried it after verifying that it contained no ingredient prohibited by the sacred law. Salim Alwan ate it regularly. The truth was that he seemed to spend his whole life in a suspended state of excitement. Mornings he galloped to the office while his nights were devoid of the customary amusement for a man of his type. He frequented no coffee-house, club or bar and had absolutely nothing except his wife. It was for this reason that he indulged in his marital pleasures in a most immoderate fashion.

He woke up in the early afternoon, performed the ritual washing and said his prayers. Then he put on his gown and cloak and returned to his office, where he found his second cup of tea waiting for him. He sipped it slowly and with pleasure, belching so noisily that it produced an echo in the inner courtyard, and set about his afternoon with the same vigor as he had in the morning. However, from time to time, he looked as though something were disturbing him. He would turn towards the alley and consult his great golden watch, while his nose twitched uncontrollably.

When the sunlight reached the top of the alley wall, he turned his sprung chair and faced the road. Heavy minutes passed during which his eyes remained on the road. Then his eyes gleamed and he pricked up his ears at the sound of slippers on the slanting flagstones. Hamida passed quickly in front of the office door. Alwan twisted his moustaches carefully and turned his chair back to his desk, a look of pleasure in his eyes, though he felt somewhat uneasy.

It was only at this time of day that he got a chance to see her, except for the occasional glance he stole at her window when he would venture out in front of his office, pretending to calm his nerves by walking a bit. He was naturally eager to preserve his honor and dignity. After all, he was Salim Alwan, whereas she was only a poor girl and the alley overflowed with sharp tongues and roving eyes. He stopped his work and thoughtfully drummed the top of his desk with his forefinger. Yes, she was indeed poor and lowly, but unfortunately desire could not be denied, could it?

She was poor and humble, but what about her bronze-colored face, the look in her eyes and her lovely slender body? All these were qualities which far outweighed mere class differences. What was the point of being proud? He quite frankly desired that pretty face, that body of sensuality and those beautiful buttocks which were able to excite even a pious old man. She was, in fact, more precious than all the merchandise from India.

He had known her since she was a little girl. Often she had come to his shop to buy mascara, cosmetics and perfumes her mother needed. Alwan had seen her breasts develop from tiny bulges to medium size, and finally to their present protuberant form. He had observed her bottom while it was only a foundation, with no structure yet raised upon it. He had seen it become a slender rounded form, ripening to maturity and now, at last, it was a dome of perfect femininity and most attractive.

Salim Alwan continued to nourish his admiration until at last it grew into an all-consuming desire. He acknowledged this and no longer attempted to deny his true feelings. He often said to himself: "If only she were a widow like Mrs. Saniya Afifi." Indeed if she were a widow like Mrs. Afifi, he would have found a way long ago. However, since she was a virgin, the matter must be considered most carefully. Now he asked himself, as he had so often done in the past, what he could do to win her.

But, in the back of his mind lingered thoughts of his wife and family. His wife was a worthy woman, possessed of all a man could desire as far as femininity, motherhood, tenderness and household ability were concerned. In her youth she had been pretty and fertile and he could not make a single criticism of her. Apart from that, she came from a noble family, far above his own where ancestry and position were concerned. He had a sincere affection for her. In fact all he had against her was that her youth and vitality were gone and she could neither keep up with him nor bear his attentions. In comparison he seemed, with his extraordinary vitality, an eager youth unable to find in her the pleasures he yearned for.

The truth was that he did not know whether it was this that attracted him to Hamida, or whether it was his passion for her which made him more conscious of his wife's inadequacies. Whatever the reason, he felt an irresistible urge for new blood. He finally said to himself: "What's wrong with me? Why should I deprive myself of something made lawful by God?"

However, he was a respectable man and longed for people's esteem. The thought that he might be the center of gossip horrified him. He agreed with the saying, "Eat what you please, but wear what pleases others." So it was that he ate his bowl of wheat, but as for Hamida . . . ! Good Heavens!

If she had been from a noble family, he would not have hesitated a moment to ask for her hand. But how could Hamida become a fellow wife of his present wife, Mrs. Alwan? And how could Umm Hamida become his mother-in-law just as the late Mrs. Alifat had been? How on earth could Hamida become the wife of the father of Muhammad Salim Alwan the judge, Arif Salim Alwan the barrister and Dr. Hassan Salim Alwan? There were other things, too, no less serious than these, which he must give due consideration. There would have to be a new household set up and new expenses; these would probably double his previous expenses. There would also be new relatives entitled to an inheritance. This would probably destroy his close family unity and would cause ripples of discontent across its calm surface.

For what, he asked himself, would he undergo all these difficulties? The desire of a fifty-year-old man, a husband and father, for a girl in her twenties! None of this escaped him, for he was not the sort of man to overlook consideration of anything concerned with money or the proper conduct of his life. He continued turning all this over in his mind, bewildered and irresolute. His desire had now become one more worry to plague his life. It formed part of the chain of his unsolved problems: the management and future of his business, whether or not to buy real estate and build apartments and how to arrange for his title of "Bey." This desire, however, was both more compelling and more inspiring than his other problems.

When he was left alone, his mind kept turning over all these problems, and he could think. But whenever Hamida appeared before him or when he saw her through her window, his mind could concentrate on one thing only . . .

9

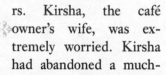rs. Kirsha, the café owner's wife, was extremely worried. Kirsha had abandoned a much-loved habit and could only have done so for a serious reason: he was enjoying his nightly pleasures outside his own house. Having invited his usual associates to come to his room on the roof at midnight, he remained with them until dawn.

The woman tossed her unhappy memories over in her mind, and the pain which so embittered her life returned. What could attract him to spend the night outside his own house? Was it the same old reason? That filthy disease? The dissolute fellow would probably say that it was just a change to relieve his boredom or else that he had only moved off to a better spot for the winter season. These lying excuses, however, would not satisfy her. She knew that everyone else knew. For these reasons then, she was extremely worried, and was firmly resolved to take a decisive action, whatever its consequences.

Mrs. Kirsha was a strong woman, although approaching fifty, and she had lost none of her courage, as often happens. She was one of those alley women renowned for their tempers—like Husniya the baker's wife and Umm Hamida—and she was particularly famous for the furious rows she had with her husband concerning his dirty habits. She was also well known for her large, broad, snub nose.

She had been a fertile wife and had produced six daughters and one son, Husain Kirsha. All her daughters were married and experiencing lives filled with troubles, even though they had refrained from divorce. A tragedy occurred to their youngest daughter which was the talk of the alley for a while. In the first year of her marriage, she had disappeared and gone to live with a man in Boulaq. The matter had ended by her being sent off to prison with him. This disgrace was a heavy burden on the family, but not the only one to afflict them. Kirsha himself had a problem, both old and new, and it seemed endless.

Mrs. Kirsha questioned Uncle Kamil and Sankir, the café waiter, until she learned of the boy who had begun to frequent the coffee-house being served most graciously by Kirsha himself. Secretly she watched the coffee-house visitors until she saw the boy and watched him sit at the café owner's right after receiving a warm welcome. It made her furious and she felt all the old wounds opening again. Mrs. Kirsha spent a tortured, sleepless night and was even worse when she awoke in the morning. She could not make up her mind on a definite course of action. In the past she had often had to battle over this matter, although without success, and so she did not hesitate to try again. She wavered slightly, however, not from fear of his anger, but because she did not want to cause a scandal for the gossips.

Husain Kirsha was getting ready for work and she approached him, breathless with anger. With extreme emotion she exclaimed:

"My boy, do you know that your father is preparing a new scandal for us?"

Husain knew at once what she meant, for her words could only mean one well-known thing. He was filled with scorn and his small eyes flashed in anger. What sort of life was this, never a single day free from hardship and scandals? Perhaps this was the reason he threw himself into the arms of the British Army. His new life had only doubled his dissatisfaction with his home, rather than reconciling

and calming him. He disliked his family, his house, and the entire
alley. Now what his mother said was only fuel to the flames that
already raged. He asked her, in a fury:

"What do you want from me? What have I to do with all that? I
interfered before and tried to reform him and we nearly came to
blows about it. Do you want me to try physical force on my own
father?"

His father's misconduct did not concern him in the least. All he
objected to were the scandals and disgrace his father caused and the
fiery quarrels and scenes at home. The "sin" itself did not bother him
in the slightest. Indeed, when news of it first reached him, he merely
shrugged his shoulders in indifference and said unconcernedly: "He
is a man and men don't care about anything!" Then he had come with
the others to feel irritation and indignation towards his father
when he learned his family was the subject of gossip and cruel
jokes. Originally, even, his relations with his father had been
strained, as always happens when two people of similar characters
clash head-on. They were both rude, ill-natured and bad-tempered.
When this trouble had first arisen, it had doubled their natural friction until they had become like enemies, sometimes fighting, sometimes declaring a truce; but their animosity towards each other never
died out.

Mrs. Kirsha did not know what to say, but she had no intention of
causing a new enmity to flare up between father and son. She permitted him to leave the flat, livid with anger, and spent a most unhappy
morning herself. She was not one to submit to defeat, despite the
great and frequent misery the years had brought her. Her mind was
made up to reform the sinful man, even though in doing so she might
expose herself to the gossips.

Mrs. Kirsha thought it best to convey her warning while her blood
was still up. She waited until midnight when the café customers left
and her husband was ready to lock up; then she called down to him
from her window. The man raised his head, obviously annoyed, and
shouted up inquiringly:

"What do you want, woman?"

Her voice came down to him:

"Come up, please, I have something important to tell you."

The café owner made a sign to his "boy" to wait for him where he was and slowly and heavily made his way up the stairs. He stood panting at the threshold of his flat and asked her harshly:

"What do you want? Couldn't you have waited until morning?"

The woman noticed his feet had come to a firm stop at the threshold and that he did not wish to cross it. It was as though he was reluctant to violate the privacy of someone else's home. Anger seethed within her and she stared hard at him, her eyes red from sleeplessness and rage. However, she did not want to show her anger too soon and said, stifling her anger:

"Do please come in!"

Kirsha wondered why she did not speak up if she really wanted to tell him something. At last he asked her roughly:

"What do you want? Speak up now!"

What an impatient fellow he was! He spent the long nights outside their home without being bored and yet he could not bear conversation with her for a couple of minutes. Nevertheless he was her husband in the sight of God, and of men, and the father of all her children. It was amazing that she could not, despite his bad treatment of her, hate him or despise him. He was her husband and her master, and she would spare no efforts to hold him and bring him back whenever the "sin" threatened to overtake him.

In fact, she was really proud of him, proud of his masculinity, of his position in the alley and of the influence he had over his associates. If it were not for this one abominable shortcoming of his, she would not have a single complaint against him. Yet here he was answering the call of the devil and wishing that she would finish what she had to say so that he could go off at once to him. Her anger increased and she said sharply:

"Come inside first . . . What are you doing standing there on the threshold like a stranger?"

Kirsha blew into the air with annoyance and disgust and crossed the threshold into the hall and asked in his husky voice:

"What do you want?"

His wife, closing the door behind them, said:

"Sit down for a little . . . What I have to say won't take long."

He looked at her suspiciously. What did the woman want to tell him? Was she going to try and stand in his way once again? He shouted at her:

"Speak up then! What are you wasting my time for?"

She asked sarcastically:

"Are you in a hurry then?"

"Don't you know that I am?"

"What is it that makes you so impatient?"

His suspicions increased and his heart filled with anger as he asked himself why he put up with this woman. His feelings towards her were disturbed and conflicting. Sometimes he disliked her and sometimes he loved her. Dislike, however, was always uppermost when the "sin" appealed to his senses and always increased when the woman attempted to come down on him. Deep inside he wished his wife were just "sensible" and would leave him to his own affairs.

The strange thing was that he always considered himself in the right and was astonished at her attempts to stand in his way without justification. Was it not his right to do as he wished? And was it not her duty to obey and be satisfied as long as her needs were satisfied and she was adequately provided for? She had become one of the necessities of his life, like sleep, hashish and his home, for good or bad and he never really considered dispensing with her. If he had wanted to, there would have been nothing to prevent him, but the fact was that she filled a need and looked after him well. In any case, he wanted her to be his wife. In spite of this and in the midst of his anger, he could not help asking himself why he put up with this woman. He shouted at her:

"Don't be stupid and speak up or else let me go . . ."

"Can't you think of a better way to address me than that?"

Kirsha flew into a rage:

"Now I know you have nothing really to say to me. You had better go off to sleep like sensible women do . . ."

"If only you would go off to sleep like sensible men do!"

Kirsha slapped his hands together and shouted:
"How can I go to sleep at this hour?"
"Why did God create night then?"
Her husband, astonished and furious, exclaimed:
"Since when have I gone to sleep at night? Am I ill, woman?"
She replied in a special tone of voice which she knew he would at once recognize and understand:
"Turn in repentance to God, and pray that He accepts your repentance even though it comes so late!"
He realized what she meant and his doubts gave way before certainty. However, he pretended not to understand and, bursting with anger said:
"What sin is there in staying up talking for which a man should repent?"
His deliberate failure to understand merely increased her fury and she shouted:
"Repent about the night-time and what goes on in it!"
Kirsha replied spitefully:
"Do you want me to give up my whole life?"
She shouted back, now completely overcome with anger:
"Your whole life?"
"That's right. Hashish is my life."
Her eyes flashed:
"And the other hashish?"
He answered sarcastically:
"I only burn one kind."
"It's me you burn! Why don't you have your parties in your usual place on the roof any more?"
"Why shouldn't I have my parties where I please? On the roof, in the government buildings, in Gamaliyya police station? What's it to do with you?"
"Why have you changed the place where you hold your parties?"
Her husband threw up his head and shouted:
"May God bear witness! I have managed to stay out of government courts so far and I am now lucky enough to find my own home a

permanent court-house!" He lowered his head and continued, "It's as though our house were under suspicion and there were investigators prowling around it all the time."

She added bitterly:

"Do you think that shameless youth is one of the investigators who have made you leave your home?"

Oh, so the insinuations were becoming declarations? His near-black face became even darker and he asked her, his voice showing his annoyance:

"What youth is that?"

"The immoral one. The one you yourself serve with tea as if you were a waiter, like Sankir!"

"There's nothing wrong in that. A coffee-house owner serves his customers just as the waiter does."

She asked scornfully, her voice trembling with anger:

"Why don't you serve Uncle Kamil, then? Why do you only serve the immoral one?"

"Wisdom says that one should take care of new customers!"

"Anyone can talk glibly, but your conduct is disgraceful and immoral."

He gestured towards her warningly with his hand and said:

"Hold your tongue, you imbecile!"

"Everyone around here is grown up and acts intelligently . . ."

He ground his teeth, swore and cursed but she took no notice of him and continued:

"Everyone around is grown up and acts intelligently, but your brain seems to have got smaller the bigger you got!"

"You are raving, woman, raving by the life of the Prophet's grandson Husain! May God recompense him for his cruel murder!"

Quivering with emotion, she shouted hoarsely:

"Men like you really deserve to be punished. You have brought disgrace on us again! Now we will have another nice scandal!"

"May God recompense him for his cruel murder! May God recompense him!"

Despair and anger got the better of her and she shouted out warningly:

"Today only four walls can hear us. Do you want the whole world to hear, tomorrow?"

Kirsha raised his heavy eyebrows and demanded:

"Are you threatening me?"

"I am and I am threatening your whole family! You know me!"

"It seems I'll have to smash that silly head of yours!"

"Ha-ha . . . The hashish and your immoral living haven't left an ounce of strength in your arms. You couldn't even raise your hand! It's come to an end, to an end, Kirsha!"

"It's your fault things are where they are. Isn't it always women who put men off women!"

"How sorry I am for a man who is past women altogether!"

"Why? I have fathered six daughters and one son . . . apart from abortions and miscarriages."

Umm Husain, quite beside herself with rage, shouted:

"Aren't you ashamed to mention your children? Doesn't even thinking of them keep you from your filthy behavior?"

Kirsha struck the wall hard with his fist, turned around and made for the door, saying:

"You're completely crazy."

She shouted after him:

"Has your patience run out? Are you longing for him because you had to wait? You'll see the results of your filthy behavior, you pig!"

Kirsha slammed the door hard behind him and the noise shattered the silence of the night. His wife stood wringing her hands in anger and desperation. Her heart overflowed with a desire for revenge.

10

bbas the barber gazed critically at his reflection in the mirror. Slowly a look of satisfaction came into his slightly protruding eyes. He had curled his hair nicely and carefully brushed away the dust from his suit.

He went outside his saloon and stood waiting. It was his favorite time of day, early evening, and the sky was clear and deep blue. There was a slight warmth in the air, brought on by a whole day of drizzle. The surface of the alley, which was only bathed two or three times a year, was wet; some of the hollows in Sanadiqiyya Street were still filled with thickly clouded clay-dust water.

Uncle Kamil was inside his little shop, asleep in his chair, and Abbas' face glowed with a smile of pleasure. The love deep down within him stirred and he sang quietly to himself:

"Will you, my heart, after your long wait delight.

Will you soon win your love and in her delight.

Your wounds will mend though you can't tell when.

Something will cure you, you'll never know how.

I've learned the maxim from men of experience.
That the key to happiness, O misery, is patience."
Uncle Kamil opened his eyes and yawned. Then he looked towards the young man, who laughed, standing in the door of the barber's shop. He made his way across the road to him, poked him in the ribs and said delightedly:
"We are in love and the whole world must laugh with us."
Uncle Kamil sighed and his high-pitched voice piped:
"Congratulations then, but please give me the shroud now before you sell it to get a dowry for your wife."
Abbas laughed and strolled leisurely out of the alley. He wore his grey suit, which was also his only one. A year ago he had reversed its cloth and darned a few holes and, because he took care to clean and press it, it appeared fairly neat. He glowed with excitement and self-confidence and he was experiencing that feeling of deep tension which normally precedes the revelation of the hidden desires of the heart. His love was a mixture of gentle affection, sincere devotion and hungry passion. He longed to feel the warmth of her body and experience the magical, mysterious intoxication of her eyes. Abbas had felt the joy of victory when he approached the girl on the street in Darasa and his fancy told him that her resistance was merely what all women pretend in answer to the call of desire.
His intoxication had lasted for days. Then it and his confidence had smouldered and died, and neither renewed themselves. Doubt stirred in him and he asked himself why he saw her resistance as proof of her love. Why shouldn't it be genuine opposition? Was it because she had not been cruel or rude? But then could one expect any worse treatment from a life-long neighbor?
Each morning he appeared in front of his shop ready to catch a glimpse of her if she should open the window to let the sun into her flat. Each evening he sat outside the coffee-house beneath her window, smoking a water pipe and glancing up time after time, hoping to see her lovely form moving behind the shutters of the closed window. He was not satisfied with this lonely vigil and had approached her a second time in Darasa. Again she had snubbed him. Again he had tried and failed.

So it was that he set out once more, filled with hope, confidence and his burning infatuation. He saw Hamida approaching with her companions and he turned to one side to let them pass. Slowly he followed them. He noticed that the girls looked at him with mischievous curiosity, and this pleased and flattered him. Abbas pursued them until the last girl had turned off at the end of the street. Then he quickened his step until he was within an arm's length of her. He smiled at her with a mixture of formal politeness and apprehension and muttered his prepared greeting:

"Good evening, Hamida . . ."

She had anticipated this encounter, but was plagued with doubts; she neither liked nor disliked him. Perhaps it was because he was the only young man in the alley suitable for her that she refrained from ignoring him or dealing with him with decisive cruelty. Hamida decided to excuse his crossing her path once again and satisfy herself with a mild rebuke, for if she had wanted to deal him a stunning blow she could have done so.

In spite of her limited experience in life, she was aware of the great gulf between this humble young man and her own greedy ambitions which could ignite her natural aggressiveness and turn it into uncontrollable savagery and violence. She would be wildly happy if she saw a look of defiance or self-confidence in anyone's eyes, but this look of simple humility in Abbas' eyes left her emotionless. She felt neither attraction nor aversion towards him. But he was the only suitable young man in the alley. Had it not been for her belief in marriage as her natural destiny she would not have hesitated to reject him cruelly. For these reasons she was pleased to encourage him so that she might eventually discover what he was really like and what he wanted. She hoped by this method to solve her own disturbing indecision.

Abbas was afraid she might remain silent until they came to the end of the street and so he muttered imploringly:

"Good evening . . ."

Her handsome bronze-colored face showed the trace of a smile and she slowed her walk, sighed in feigned annoyance and asked:

"What do you want?"

He saw her faint smile and took no notice of her apparent annoyance. He replied hopefully:

"Let's turn off into Azhar Street. It's quieter there and it's beginning to get dark."

She turned towards Azhar Street without a word. And he followed her, almost giddy with joy. The memory of his words, "It's quieter there and it's beginning to get dark," lingered in her mind and she realized that she dreaded the idea of anyone seeing them. The corner of her mouth twisted in a cruel smile. Morals were no part of her rebellious nature. She had grown up in an atmosphere almost entirely outside their shelter and without the restriction that they impose. Her own capricious nature and the fact that her mother was rarely home had only increased her indifference to them. She had always followed her own primitive nature, fighting and quarrelling with no concern for anything, least of all questions of morality.

Abbas now caught up with her and walked at her side. His voice expressed delight:

"That was very nice of you!"

Almost angrily, she replied:

"What do you want from me?"

The young man, doing his best to control his excitement, answered:

"Patience is a virtue, Hamida. Be kind to me. Don't be cruel."

She turned her head towards him, keeping it covered with a corner of her cloak, and said unkindly:

"Will you say what you want at once."

"Patience is a virtue ... I want ... I want everything that's good ..."

"You don't really have anything to say," she grumbled, "and we are still walking, getting further off our route. I can't be late getting back."

He was sorry they were wasting time and said regretfully:

"We'll start back soon. Don't be afraid and don't worry. We'll think of some excuse you can tell your mother. You think a lot about a few minutes, whereas I think about the whole of life, about our life together. This is what I'm concerned about. Don't you believe me? It's the thing I think and worry about most of all, by the life of Husain who blessed this fine quarter."

He was talking simply and sincerely and she found a new interest and pleasure in listening to him, even though he did not manage to stir her frigid heart. She tried to forget her painful indecision and gave him all her attention. She did not, however, know what to say and so just took refuge in silence. The young man was gaining confidence and he began to speak with emotion:

"Don't grudge me a few moments or repeat your strange question. You ask me what I want, Hamida. Don't you really know what I want to say? Why do I come up to you in the street? Why do my eyes follow you wherever you go? You have what you want, Hamida. Don't you read anything in my eyes? Don't they say that the heart of a believer is clear for all to see? What have you learned? Ask yourself. Ask anyone in Midaq Alley, they all know."

The girl frowned and muttered as though not aware what she was saying:

"You have disgraced me . . ."

These words horrified him and he exclaimed:

"There will be no disgrace in our life and I wish you only well. This mosque of Husain bears witness to what I say and what my intentions are. I love you. I have loved you for a long time. I love you more than your mother loves you. I swear this to you by my belief in Husain, in the grandfather of Husain and in the Lord of Husain . . ."

Hamida delighted in these words and her feelings of pride and vanity diminished her usual inclination towards violence and domination. She was experiencing the truth that strong words of love always please the ears, although they do not always appeal to the heart. They release the pent-up emotions.

However, her mind leaped uncontrollably from the present into the future and she asked herself what her life would be like under his protection, if his hopes were fulfilled. He was poor and what he earned was just enough to live on. He would take her from the second floor of Mrs. Saniya Afifi's house to the ground floor of Radwan Husaini's. The most she could expect from her mother would be a second-hand bed, a sofa and a few copper pots and pans. She would only have sweeping, cooking, washing and feeding children to look forward to. No doubt she could hope for no more than a patched dress to wear.

She shuddered as though she had seen some terrifying sight. Her inordinate desire for clothes stirred within her, as did her fierce dislike of children for which the alley women reproached her. All these emotions affected her as well as her painful state of indecision. Now she wondered if she had been right or wrong in agreeing to walk with him.

Meanwhile Abbas gazed at her in fascination. Desire, hope and her silent thoughtfulness increased his tension.

"Why are you silent, Hamida? One word would heal my heart and make the whole world change. One word is enough. Please speak to me, Hamida. Please break your silence."

She still remained silent and full of indecision. Abbas tried again: "One word would fill my spirit with hope and happiness. Perhaps you don't realize what my love for you has done to me. It has made me feel as I never felt before. It's made a new person of me. It's made me want to take life by the horns quite without fear. Do you know that? I have wakened from my stupor. Tomorrow you'll see me a new man . . ."

What did he mean? She raised her head questioningly, and his heart sang at her interest. He spoke full of confidence and pride:

"Yes, I am going to put my trust in God and try my luck like the others. I am going to work for the British Army and I might easily be as successful as your brother Husain!"

Her eyes gleamed with interest and she asked, almost as if unaware of what she said:

"Really? When will that be?"

He would have preferred her to say something romantic rather than financial. He longed to have her say that sweet word he wanted so to hear. However, he thought that her interest was merely a veil woven by her modesty to conceal an emotion similar to his own. His heart burst with joy and he said, smiling broadly:

"Very soon. I am going to Tell al-Kabir and I will start work there with a daily wage of 25 piasters. Everyone I have asked has said that this is only a small part of what people working for the army really get. I will do all I can to save as much as possible. When the war is over— and people say that will be a long time—I will come back here and open a new barber shop in New Street or Azhar Street and I will make a luxurious home for us together, if God wishes. Pray for me, Hamida . . ."

This was something unexpected that had not occurred to her. If he were successful he could certainly provide some of the things she craved. A disposition like hers, no matter how rebellious and un-manageable, could be pacified and tamed with money.

Abbas muttered reproachfully:

"Do you not want to pray for me?"

She answered in a quiet voice which sounded beautiful to his ears, although her voice was certainly not equal to her beauty:

"May God grant you success . . ."

Sighing happily, he replied:

"Amen. Answer her prayer, O God. The world will smile on us, with God's grace. If you are good to me, so is the whole world. I ask nothing of you except that you be happy."

Slowly she was emerging from her state of indecision. She had found a gleam of light in the darkness surrounding her, the gleam of glistening gold! Even if he did not interest or excite her perhaps that gleam of light she so wanted might come from him and answer her craving for power and wealth. After all, he was the only suitable young man in the alley. This could not be denied. Happiness filled her as she heard him say:

"Do you hear me, Hamida? All I ask is that you be happy."

A smile spread over her thin lips and she muttered:

"God grant you success . . ."

He continued, overcome with delight:

"It isn't necessary for us to wait until the end of the war! We will be the happiest two in the alley."

With a scowl she spat out:

"Midaq Alley!"

He looked at her in confusion but made no defense of the alley which he preferred to any place in the whole world. Abbas wondered whether she despised it, as her brother Husain did. They really had sucked from one breast then! Wishing to do all he could to erase the bad impression, he said:

"We will choose a place you like. There's Darasa, Gamaliyya, Bait al-Qadi—choose your home wherever you wish."

She listened in embarrassment to what he said and realized that her tongue had betrayed her in spite of herself. Hamida bit her lip and said disbelievingly:

"My house? What house do you mean? What have I got to do with all this?"

Full of reproach, he asked:

"How can you say that? Aren't you satisfied yet with torturing me? Don't you really know which house I mean? God forgive you, Hamida. I mean the house we will choose together—no, the house *you* will choose all by yourself. It will be your house, just yours and belong to no one else. As I told you, I am going away to earn money for this house. You prayed for success for me and now there is no backing out of the wonderful truth. We have reached an agreement, Hamida, and the matter is decided."

Had they really reached an agreement? Yes, they had! If not she would never have agreed to walk and talk with him and get involved in dreams about the future. Where was the harm in that for her? Was he not bound to be her young man anyway? Despite this she felt some apprehension and hesitancy. Was it true that she had become a different girl who had almost no power over herself any more?

When she reached this point in her thoughts, she felt his hand touch and grip hers, giving warmth to her cold fingers. Should she take her hand away and say: "No, I will have nothing to do with that sort of thing." However, she said and did nothing. They walked along together, her hand in his warm palm. She felt his fingers passionately press her hand and she heard him say:

"We will meet often . . . won't we?"

She refused to say a word. He tried again:

"We will meet often and plan things together. Then I will meet your mother. The agreement must be made before I leave."

She withdrew her palm from his hand and said anxiously:
"Our time is up and we have gone a long way . . . let's go back now."

They turned on their heels together and he laughed delightedly as some of the happiness which had ebbed in his heart returned. They walked off quickly and reached Ghouriyya Street, where they parted, she to go down it and he to turn towards Azhar Street back to the alley via Husain Street.

11

"Oh, God, grant me your forgiveness and mercy."

Mrs. Kirsha spoke this phrase as she entered the building where Radwan Husaini lived. She asked God's forgiveness and mercy for the despair, rage and exasperation that she was suffering. She was determined to reform her husband but seemed powerless to restrain him. In the end she had seen no way out but to consult Radwan Husaini. She hoped that, with his righteousness and venerability, he might succeed where she had failed. She had never before come to Husaini about her affairs. But now her despair and her concern for the gossips had forced her to knock hopefully on his virtuous door.

It was Husaini's wife who received her inside the house and they sat together for a while. Mrs. Husaini was in her mid-forties, an age many women highly respect and consider the peak of their maturity and femininity. This lady, however, was thin and worn. Her body and mind reflected fate's scars which had removed her children one after another from her arms. For this reason, she gave her quiet house an air of sadness and melancholy which even her husband's deep faith could not dispel. Her slimness and wistfulness contrasted with her strong and healthy husband, who beamed in contentment. She was a weak woman and her faith, although firmly rooted, was not able to diminish her steady decline. Mrs. Kirsha knew what she was like and unhesitatingly released her troubles, quite convinced that she would find a sympathetic audience. Mrs. Husaini eventually excused herself and went to find her husband. After a few minutes she returned and led the visitor to see him in his room.

Radwan Husaini was sitting on a rug saying his beads, an open brazier in front of him and a pot of tea by his side. His private room was small and neat, with an armchair in each corner and on the floor a Persian carpet. In the middle of the room stood a round table piled with yellowing books, above which a large gas lamp hung from the ceiling. He was dressed in a flowing grey gown and a black, woollen skull cap beneath which his white face, flecked with red, shone forth like a brilliant full moon. He spent a great deal of time in this room alone, reading, saying his beads, and meditating.

It was here too that he met with his friends, all men like himself learned in their religion. They would sit and exchange tales and traditions of the Prophet and discuss the opinions expressed in them. Radwan Husaini was not a scholar claiming to know all about holy law and Islam, nor was he unaware of his limitations. He was merely a sincere believer, pious and God-fearing. He captivated the minds of his scholarly friends with his generous heart, tolerance, compassion and mercifulness. All agreed he was truly a saintly man of God.

He stood to receive Mrs. Kirsha, his eyes modestly lowered. She came over to him, veiled in her outer gown, and gave him her hand wrapped in one of its corners, in order not to spoil his state of ritual cleanliness.

"Welcome to our much respected neighbor," he said, greeting her and offering her a seat.

She sat down in the armchair facing him while he squatted on the fur rug. Mrs. Kirsha invoked blessings upon him:

"May God honor you, sir, and grant you long life, with the generosity of the chosen Prophet."

He had already guessed the reason for her call and therefore refrained from making any inquiry concerning the health of her husband, which was the customary polite duty of a host. He knew, as did everyone else, of Kirsha's conduct and news had reached him of the disputes and quarrels which had broken out violently on previous occasions. Now he realized he was unfortunately to be involved in this ever-recurring dispute. Husaini submitted to the inevitable and met it with the same welcome he always gave to unpleasant affairs. He smiled graciously and encouraging her to speak out, said:

"I hope you are well."

The woman scarcely knew the meaning of hesitation, and shyness was not her weakness. She was, in fact, both fearless and shameless. Indeed there was only one more ungovernable woman in Midaq Alley and that was Husniya, the baker's wife. Mrs. Kirsha replied in her coarse voice:

"Radwan Husaini, sir, you are all goodness and kindness and there is no better man in the alley than yourself. For this reason I have come to ask for your help and to make a complaint against that lecherous man, my husband."

Her voice had now risen to a plaintive wail. Radwan Husaini merely smiled and said in a slightly sad tone:

"Let's hear all about it then, Mrs. Kirsha. I am listening."

Sighing heavily, she went on:

"May God reward you for being such a fine man. My husband knows no modesty and won't reform himself. Every time I think he has given up his sinful behavior he brings a new disgrace upon me. He is completely immoral and neither his age, his wife, nor his children can cure his lechery. Perhaps you may have heard about that brazen boy he has with him every evening in the coffee-shop? Well, that's our new disgrace."

A look of distress flickered in the man's clear eyes and he remained silent, thinking deeply. His own personal bereavement had not been able to penetrate his felicity, but now he sat silent and filled with sadness, praying that his own soul would be free of the devil and his wickedness. The woman took his apparent distress as an indication that her anger was justified and she growled:

"The brazen immoral fellow has disgraced us all. By God, if it were not for my age and the children, I would have left his house long ago and never returned. Do you approve of this disgusting business, Mr. Husaini? Do you approve of his filthy behavior? I have warned him but he takes no notice; I can do nothing else but come to you. I didn't want to bother you with this revolting news, but I have no choice. You are the most revered and respected man in the neighborhood and your orders are obeyed. You might be able to influence him where I and everyone else have failed. If I find he won't take your advice, then I will have to adopt other ways of dealing with him. Today, I am controlling my anger, but if I see there is no hope of reforming him, then I will send fire raging through the whole alley and the fuel for it will be his filthy body."

Radwan Husaini shot her a critical glance and said with his customary calmness:

"Cheer up, Mrs. Kirsha, and put your faith in God. Don't let your anger get the better of you. You are a good woman, as everyone well knows. Don't make yourself and your husband a subject for the tongues of the gossips. A really good wife acts as a close-fitting veil over all those things God might wish to keep concealed. Go back home in confidence and peace of mind and leave this matter to me. I will seek help from God."

Mrs. Kirsha, scarcely able to control her emotions, exclaimed:

"God reward you! God bring you happiness! God bless your goodness! You are a real refuge of safety. I will indeed leave this matter in your hands and wait. May God decide between me and that lecherous man . . ."

Radwan Husaini quieted her as best he could with words of comfort, but whenever he said anything nice, she replied by spitting forth a stream of curses on her husband and expanding on his disgraceful conduct. His patience nearly spent, he bade her a polite farewell, releasing a sigh of relief as he did so.

He returned to his room and sat thinking. How he wished he could have escaped being involved in this affair, but the damage was done now and he could not break his promise. He called his servant and asked him to fetch Kirsha. As he waited, the thought struck him that he was inviting to his home, for the very first time, a known profligate. In the past, only the poor or ascetic men of religion had been in this room with him.

Sighing deeply, he recited to himself the saying: "He who reforms a profligate does better than he who sits with a believer." But could he ever make the man reform? He shook his large head and recited the verse from the Koran: "You cannot lead aright whomever you wish; it is God who leads whomever He wishes." He sat wondering at the enormous power of the devil over mankind and how easily he makes man deviate from God's intent.

His train of thought was interrupted by the servant announcing the arrival of Kirsha. Looking tall and slim, Kirsha came in and gazed at Husaini from beneath his heavy eyebrows with a look of admiration and respect. He bowed low as they shook hands in greeting. Radwan Husaini greeted him and invited him to be seated. Kirsha sat down in the armchair occupied so short a time before by his wife; a cup of tea was poured for him. He felt completely at ease and confident, with not a trace of apprehension or fear and he had no idea why Husaini had invited him here. With all those who reach his state of confusion and promiscuity, prudence and intuition are likely to vanish.

Husaini read what was in the man's half-shut eyes, and, filled with quiet self-assurance, he politely commenced:

"You have honored our house with your presence, Mr. Kirsha."

The café owner raised his hands to his turban in salutation and said:

"May God reward you for your goodness, Mr. Husaini."

Husaini continued:

"Please don't be annoyed at me for inviting you here during your working hours, but I would like to talk to you as a brother about an important matter. Consequently I could think of no place more suitable than my home."

Kirsha bowed his head humbly and commented:

"I am at your command, Mr. Husaini."

Husaini was afraid that by avoiding the issue they would merely waste time and Kirsha would be kept from his work. He decided to tackle the matter straightaway and he lacked neither the courage nor the directness of speech to do so. In a serious, regretful tone of voice he began:

"I want to speak with you like a brother, or as brothers should speak if they have real love for one another. A truly sincere brother is one who, if he sees his brother falling would reach to catch him in his own arms, or who would help him up if he stumbled or one who would, if he thought it necessary, give his brother the benefit of some good advice."

Kirsha's peace of mind was shattered. Only now did he realize he had fallen into a trap. A look of panic appeared in his gloomy eyes and he muttered in embarrassment, scarcely aware of what he was saying:

"You are quite right, Mr. Husaini."

The man's obvious confusion and embarrassment did not restrain Husaini and he continued with a sternness somewhat modified by the look of modest sincerity in his eyes:

"My friend, I am going to tell you truthfully what I think and you must not be angry at my speaking out, for someone motivated as I am by friendship, sincerity and a desire to do good should not be looked upon with anger. The fact is that what I have seen of some of your habits has distressed me very much, for I do not think them at all worthy of you."

Kirsha frowned and said under his breath: "What's it got to do with you!" Feigning astonishment, however, he said out loud:

"Has my conduct really distressed you? God forbid!"

Husaini took no notice of the man's simulated surprise and continued:

"Satan finds the doors of youth an easy entrance and he slips in both secretly and openly to spread his havoc. We should do all we can to prevent the doors of youth opening to him and keep them tightly closed. Just think of elderly men to whom age has given the keys of respectability, what would be the situation if we were to see them deliberately opening these doors and calling out in invitation to the devil? This is what has distressed me, Mr. Kirsha."

Boys and elderly men! Doors and keys! A devil of devils! Why didn't he mind his own business and let others mind theirs? He shook his head in confusion and then said quietly:

"I don't understand at all, Mr. Husaini."

Husaini looked at him meaningfully and asked him in a tone not devoid of reproach:

"Really?"

Kirsha, beginning to feel both annoyance and fear, replied:

"Really."

Husaini was determined and went on:

"I thought you would realize what I meant. The truth is that I am referring to that dissolute youth . . ."

Kirsha's anger grew. However, like a mouse caught in a trap, he did his best to fight his way out from behind the bars and he asked in a voice which almost acknowledged his defeat:

"What youth is that, Mr. Husaini?"

Trying hard not to enrage Kirsha, he replied quietly:

"You know, Mr. Kirsha, I have not brought the matter up to offend you, nor to make you feel ashamed. God forbid! I just want to offer my advice for whatever good it will do. What is the point of denying it? Everyone knows and everyone is talking about it. This is really what has distressed me most of all: to find you the subject of scandal and gossip . . ."

Anger at last got the better of Kirsha and he slapped his thigh hard with his hand. He shouted hoarsely, his bottled up resentment flying out in a stream of spittle:

"What's wrong with people that they can't mind their own business and leave others to mind theirs? Do you really see everyone talking about it, Mr. Husaini? People have been like that ever since God created the earth and all that's on it. They criticize, not because they really disapprove, but just to belittle their fellow men. If they don't find anything to complain about, they invent something. Do you think they gossip because they are really upset and shocked? Certainly not! It is really envy which eats at their hearts!"

This opinion horrified Radwan Husaini and he commented in amazement:

"What a dreadful opinion that is! Do you think people envy that filthy practice?"

Kirsha burst out laughing and said spitefully:

"Have not a single doubt of the truth of what I said! They are a hopeless crowd. Wouldn't it do them more good to look into their own souls . . ." At this point he realized that he had admitted the accusation by making so little attempt to refute it. He continued: "Don't you know who that boy is? He is a poor boy whose poverty I am trying to alleviate by being charitable to him."

Husaini was annoyed at the man's equivocation and he shot him a glance as though to say: "Do you really expect me to believe that?"

"Mr. Kirsha," he said, "it seems you don't understand me. I am neither judging you nor reproaching you; we are both poor sinners in need of God's mercy and forgiveness. Don't deny it. If the boy is poor, then leave him in the care of his Creator. If you want to do good, the world is full of unfortunate people."

"Why can't I do good for this boy? It hurts me that you don't believe me. I am an innocent man."

Hiding his displeasure, Radwan Husaini looked at the near-black face before him and said pointedly:

"This boy is immoral and has an evil reputation and you have made a mistake in trying to deceive me. It would have been far better if you had taken my advice and told the truth in speaking with me."

Kirsha knew that Husaini was annoyed, although it did not show on his face. He took refuge in silence, bottled his anger and thought of leaving but Husaini was still talking:

"I am appealing to you for your own good and the good of your home. I will not despair of drawing you back to decent behavior. Give up this boy; he is just filth created by Satan. Turn in repentance to your Lord; He is full of mercy and forgiveness. Even if you were once a good man, you are now a sinner. Though you are successful now, you will eventually lose everything by wallowing in filth. You will end up lonely and penniless. What do you say?"

Kirsha had finally made up his mind to avoid being openly obstinate. He told himself that he was free to do as he wished and that no one, not even Radwan Husaini himself, had any authority over him. However, not for a moment did he consider making Husaini angrier, nor would he challenge him in any way. He lowered his eyebrows over his gloomy eyes and disguised his real feelings by saying:

"It is God's will."

Distress showed on Husaini's benevolent face and he said sharply:

"No, it is the will of the devil! Shame on you!"

Kirsha muttered:

"When God shows the true path!"

"If you don't obey the devil then God will lead you to your salvation. Leave this boy or let me get rid of him in peace."

This annoyed Kirsha and anxiety flooded him so that he could no longer disguise his feelings.

"No, Mr. Husaini, don't do that," he said in a determined tone of voice.

Husaini looked at him in disgust and scorn and said regretfully:

"Can't you see how wickedness prevents you finding salvation?"

"It's up to God to lead us."

Finally despairing of reforming him, Husaini said:

"For the last time I am asking you to leave him or let me get rid of him in peace."

Kirsha, leaning out from the edge of the sofa as if about to get up, insisted stubbornly:

"No, Mr. Husaini. I appeal to you to let this matter rest until God shows the path . . ."

Husaini was astonished at his insolent stubbornness and asked weakly:

"Doesn't your lust for this filthy conduct make you ashamed?"

Kirsha, tired of Husaini and his preaching, got up:

"All men do many things that are dirty and this is one of them. So leave me to find my own path. Don't be angry with me and please accept my apologies and regrets. What can a man do to control himself?"

Husaini smiled sadly and rose too, saying:

"A man can do anything if he wants to. You just don't understand what I said. The matter is in God's hands."

He extended his hand:

"Goodbye."

Scowling and muttering to himself, Kirsha left the flat, cursing people in general and particularly Midaq Alley and Radwan Husaini.

12

rs. Kirsha waited, patient and motionless, one day and then two days. She stood behind the shutters of her window overlooking the coffee-house and watched for the boy's arrival. She would see him swagger past during the day and then, at midnight, he would appear once again, this time with her husband, going off towards Ghouriyya. Her eyes would turn white in loathing and rage and she asked herself whether Radwan Husaini's advice had gone unheeded. She visited him once again and he shook his head sadly, saying:

"Leave him as he is until God works His inevitable will."

She had returned to her flat seething with anger and plotting her revenge. Mrs. Kirsha no longer worried about the slander of the gossips, and now she waited at her window for night to fall. Eventually the boy arrived and, wrapping herself in her cloak, she ran from the flat like a mad woman. She bounded down the stairs and, in a moment, was in front of the coffee-house. All the shops had closed and the alley people were gathered in the café as was their evening custom.

Kirsha himself was bent over the till, apparently in a daze. He did not notice her arrival. Her quick gaze fell on the lad, who was sipping tea. She passed in front of her husband, who did not raise his eyes, and approached the boy. With one blow of her hand she knocked the cup from his grasp and the tea fell into his lap. He jumped up screaming in fright and she shouted at him in a voice like thunder:

"Drink your tea then, you son of a whore!"

The eyes of all present, some people from the alley and some who did not know her, stared fixedly at the woman. Kirsha, who looked as though cold water had been hurled in his face, made a motion towards her as if to get up, but his wife pushed him in the chest, seating him once more. Mrs. Kirsha screeched into his face, her rage making her scarcely aware of what she said:

"Just you try and move, you filthy wretch!"

She turned once more towards the boy and went on:

"What has frightened you, you clever fellow? You woman in the clothes of a man! Would you like to tell me what brings you here?"

Kirsha was now standing behind the till, his anger having locked his tongue, his face pale with fury. She shouted in his face:

"If you are thinking of defending your 'friend,' then I will smash your bones to pieces in front of everyone!"

She moved threateningly towards the youth, who retreated until he reached Sheikh Darwish:

"Do you want to ruin my home, you rake and son of rakes!"

The youth, trembling violently, answered:

"Who are you? What have I done so as to . . ."

"Who am I? Don't you know me? I am your fellow-wife . . ."

She fell upon him, punching and slapping him forcefully. His tarboosh fell off and blood flowed from his nose. She then grasped his necktie and pulled it till his voice trailed off in a strangled gasp.

All the customers in the café sat stunned, gaping wide-eyed in amazement at the spectacle. They thoroughly enjoyed witnessing such a dramatic scene. Mrs. Kirsha's yelling soon brought Husniya the baker's wife racing to the spot, closely followed by her husband,

Jaada, his mouth open. Then, after a moment or two, Zaita the cripple-maker appeared; he remained standing a little way off, like a small devil the earth had belched forth. Soon all the windows of the alley's two houses were flung open, heads peering down at them. Kirsha watched the boy twisting and writhing in pain, trying to free his neck from the woman's strong grip. He charged towards them, literally foaming at the mouth like an enraged stallion. He grasped his wife's two arms, shouting in her face:

"Leave him alone, woman, you have caused enough scandal!"

Her husband's strong grip forced Mrs. Kirsha to release her rival. Her cloak fell to the ground and her blood was now boiling. Her voice rose in a shrill scream as she grasped her husband by the collar and yelled:

"Would you hit me to defend your friend, you animal? Bear witness, all you people, against this lecherous villain!"

The boy grasped this opportunity to escape and streaked from the coffee-house, scared out of his wits. The battle between Kirsha and his wife continued, she holding tightly to his collar and he trying to free himself from her grasp. At last Radwan Husaini came between them and ended their struggle. Mrs. Kirsha, panting for breath, wrapped herself in her cloak and, shouting in a voice loud enough to crumble the walls of the café, addressed her husband:

"You hashish addict! You nincompoop! You filthy lout! You sixty-year-old! You father of five and grandfather of twenty! You rotter! You dumb oaf! I feel like spitting in your dirty, nigger-black face!"

Mr. Kirsha, quivering with emotion, stared at her in a fury and yelled back:

"Hold your tongue, woman, and take away that lavatory of a mouth of yours; you're spraying us all with its filth!"

"Shut your mouth! You are the only lavatory around here, you scarecrow, you disgrace, you rat-bag!"

Shaking his fist at her, he shouted:

"Raving as usual! What's come over you, attacking my café customers like that?"

His wife gave a loud, hollow laugh:

"Customers of the café? I beg your pardon! I did not mean any harm to your café customers, I wished to attack your lordship's special customer!"

At this point Radwan Husaini interrupted her again and begged her to let the matter rest and go back home. However, Mrs. Kirsha, a new note of determination in her voice, refused, saying:

"I will never go back to the house of that filthy fellow as long as I live."

Husaini tried to insist and Uncle Kamil volunteered his help, saying in his angelic voice:

"Go home, Mrs. Kirsha. Go home, put your trust in God and take Mr. Husaini's advice."

Husaini tried to prevent her leaving the alley and only left his position when she entered the house, grumbling and giving vent to her indignation all the way. At that Zaita disappeared and Husniya, followed by her husband, left the scene. As they went off, she punched him in the back and said:

"You're always moaning about your bad luck and asking why you're the only husband who is beaten! Did you see how even your betters are beaten?"

The turmoil of the battle left a heavy silence. The onlookers exchanged amused glances of malicious delight. Dr. Bushi was the most amused and delighted of all. He shook his head and said in tones of mock sadness:

"There is neither might nor power, but in God. May God do what He can to patch things up."

Kirsha stood rooted to the spot where the battle took place. He now noticed that the boy had fled and he scowled in annoyance. Just as he was about to go and look for him, Radwan Husaini, who stood not far away, placed his hand on Kirsha's shoulder and said quietly:

"Sit down and rest, Mr. Kirsha."

Kirsha snorted in anger and slowly took a step back, saying to himself:

"The bitch! But it's really my own fault. I deserve even worse than that. What a fool a man is who doesn't use a stick on his wife!"

The voice of Uncle Kamil was once again heard as he said:

"Put your faith in God, everyone."

Kirsha flung himself back into his chair. Then indignation overcame him again and he began beating his forehead with his clenched fist and shouting:

"In the old days I was a murderous ruffian. Everyone in this district knew me for the criminal I was, swimming in blood. I am a criminal, a son of a dog, a beast, but do I deserve everyone's contempt because I reformed my evil ways?" He raised his head and went on: "Just you wait, you bitch! Tonight you are going to see the Kirsha of the old days!"

Radwan Husaini clapped his hands together as he sat stretched out on the sofa and addressed Kirsha:

"Put your faith in God, Mr. Kirsha. We want to drink our tea in peace and quiet."

Dr. Bushi turned to Abbas and whispered in his ear: "We must bring about a reconciliation between them."

"Between whom and whom?" the barber asked wickedly.

Dr. Bushi concealed his laugh as best he could, so that it issued like a hiss from his nose.

"Do you think he will come back to the café after what has happened?" he asked Abbas.

The barber pouted and replied:

"If he doesn't come back another one will."

The coffee-house had now taken on its usual atmosphere and everyone played games or chatted as before. The battle was almost forgotten and it would have left no trace had Kirsha not burst out once again, shouting and roaring like a trapped beast:

"No, no! I refuse to submit to the will of a woman. I am a man. I am free. I can do what I like! Let her leave the house if she wants to. Let her roam with the street beggars. I am a criminal. I am a cannibal!"

All of a sudden Sheikh Darwish raised his head and said, without looking towards Kirsha:

"O Kirsha, your wife is a strong woman. Indeed, she has a masculinity which many men lack. She is really a male, not a female. Why don't you love her, then?"

Kirsha directed his fiery eyes towards him and yelled into his face:

"Shut your mouth!"

At this, more than one of those present commented:

"Oh, even Sheikh Darwish now!"

Kirsha turned his back on the old man in silence and "Sheikh" Darwish went on:

"It's an old evil. In English they call it 'homosexuality' and it is spelled H-O-M-O-S-E-X-U-A-L-I-T-Y. But it is not love. True love is only for the descendants of Muhammad. Come, my Lady Zainab, granddaughter of the Prophet . . . come, Madam . . . I am weak, O Mother of weak ones."

13

ow his meetings in Azhar Street had changed life for Abbas! He was in love. A new fire burned within him, desire melting his nerves and intoxicating his brain. He felt gay and confident, like a carefree troubadour knight—or perhaps a tippler safe in a familiar bar.

They now met frequently and their conversations never failed to center around their future. Yes, they now planned their futures as one, and Hamida made no attempt to resist the idea, either in his presence, or away from him. She often asked herself whether any of her factory girl friends could hope for anyone better. She made a point of walking with him just at the time when they left work and she delighted in watching their curious glances and in seeing the impression he made on them. One day they asked her about the young man "whom they had seen with her" and she had replied:

"He is my fiancé. He owns a barber shop."

She asked herself which one of them would not consider herself lucky to become engaged to a café waiter or blacksmith's apprentice.

Indeed, he was the owner of a shop, definitely middle-class. Moreover, he wore a suit. She constantly made practical comparisons, but never allowed herself to be drawn into his magical world of dreams. Only occasionally and briefly was she emotionally moved and at these rare times she seemed to be truly in love.

On one such occasion he had wanted to kiss her and she had neither yielded nor refused. She longed to taste one of those kisses about which she had heard. He carefully noted the passers-by while he felt for her mouth in the darkness of the evening and then placed his lips on hers, trembling violently as he did so. His breath engulfed her and her eyes closed tightly in ecstasy.

When the time for him to leave approached, he was determined to become engaged to her. He chose Dr. Bushi as his ambassador to visit Umm Hamida. The dentist's profession gave him friendly access to all the homes in Midaq Alley. The woman was delighted to accept the young man, whom she saw as the alley's only suitable husband for her daughter. Indeed she had always thought of him as "the owner of a barber shop and a man of the world." However, she feared the opposition of her rebellious daughter and foresaw a long and difficult battle with her. So Umm Hamida was truly astonished when her daughter accepted the news with mild resignation and even pleasure. Her daughter's unexpected attitude caused her to shake her head and say:

"This is what happened through that window, behind my back!"

Abbas commissioned Uncle Kamil to make a splendid dish of nutcake and send it to Hamida's mother. He called on her accompanied by Uncle Kamil, his partner in his house and his life. Uncle Kamil had great difficulty in climbing the stairs and frequently had to stop gasping for breath to lean against the banister. At last, on the first landing, he commented jokingly to Abbas:

"Couldn't you have put off your engagement until you returned from the army?!"

Umm Hamida greeted them warmly and the three sat and chatted affably. Eventually Uncle Kamil announced:

"This is Abbas Hilu, born and bred in our alley and a son of yours and mine; he wants Hamida's hand in marriage."

Her mother smiled and said:

"Welcome to him indeed, the sweet boy. My daughter shall be his and it will be as though she had never left me."

Uncle Kamil went on talking about Abbas and his fine qualities, about Umm Hamida and her fine qualities and then he announced:

"The young man, may God grant him success, is going away soon and he will become better off. Then the matter of the marriage can be concluded to our satisfaction and his, with the permission of Almighty God."

Umm Hamida said a prayer for him and then turned jokingly to Uncle Kamil and asked:

"And you, Kamil, when are you intending to marry?"

Uncle Kamil laughed so heartily that his face went red as a ripe tomato. He patted his enormous belly and said:

"This impregnable castle of mine prevents that!"

They read the opening verses of the Koran, as was the custom at all engagement parties. Then refreshments were passed round.

The lovers' last meeting took place in Azhar Street two days after this. They walked together in silence. Abbas felt warm tears seeking a path to his eyes.

She asked him:

"Will you be away long?"

The young man answered sadly and quietly:

"My period of service will probably last a year or two, but I am sure I will get a chance to come back before that."

Suddenly feeling a deep tenderness for him, she whispered:

"What a long time that is."

Hearing this, his heart leaped with joy. Yet his voice heavy with sadness, he said:

"This is the last time we'll meet before I leave and God alone knows when we'll meet again. I'm in a state of bewilderment, halfway between sadness and happiness. I'm sad that I'm going far away from you, yet glad that this long path I've chosen is the only one leading to you. I leave my heart with you, in the alley. It refuses to travel with me. Tomorrow I'll be in Tell al-Kabir and every morning I'll think of the beloved window from which I first glimpsed you combing your lovely hair. How I'll long for that window and our walks along Azhar Street and Mouski. Oh Hamida, these are the thoughts that will break my heart to bits. Let me take away with me as vivid memories as I can. Put your hand in mine and hold it as tightly as I grip yours. Oh God, how sweet it is to feel your touch! It makes my heart pound. My heart is in your hand, my darling, my love, my Hamida! How beautiful your name is; to say it makes me wild with joy."

His loving and passionate words lulled her into a sort of dream. Her eyes took on a far-away look as she murmured:

"It was you who chose to go away."

Almost wailing in lament, he said:

"You are the cause, Hamida. It is because of you, you! I love our alley and I am deeply grateful to God for the livelihood He provides me from it. I don't want to leave the quarter of our beloved Husain to whom I pray morning and night. The trouble is I can't offer you a life here which is worthy of you and so I have no alternative but to leave. May God take my hand and lead us towards better circumstances . . ."

Deeply touched, Hamida replied:

"I'll pray for your success and will visit the tomb of our Lord Husain and ask him to watch over you and bring you success. Patience is a virtue and it's a blessing to travel."

He answered wistfully:

"Yes, travel is a blessing, but how sad that I'll be so far away from you."

She whispered softly:

"You won't be the only sad one . . ."

He turned abruptly towards her, delirious at her words, and lifted her hand until it touched his heart, whispering:

"Truly?"

By the dim light of a nearby shop his love-filled eyes saw her sweet smile of reply. At that moment he was aware only of her beloved face. Words streamed from his lips:

"How beautiful you are! How tender and kind you are! This is love. It is something rare and beautiful, Hamida. Without it, the whole world means nothing."

She had no notion of how to reply and so she took refuge in silence. Hamida was delighted to hear his words, which made her tremble with ecstasy and she wished they would continue forever. The strength and passion that Abbas felt was such that he scarcely knew what he was saying as he went on:

"This is love. It is all we have. It is enough and more than enough for our needs. It is everything. It means happiness when we are together and comfort when we are apart. It gives us a life that is far more than life itself."

He was silent a moment and then added:

"I leave you in the name of love. By its strength may I return with lots of money."

"A great deal of money, I pray to God," she murmured, almost unaware of what she said.

"With God's permission and by the grace of Husain. All those other girls will really envy you."

She smiled happily and agreed:

"Ah, how nice that would be!"

Before they knew it, they were at the end of the street and they laughed aloud in unison. Then they turned and he suddenly realized that their meeting was approaching its end. Thoughts of a dreaded farewell swam before him. Sadness enveloped him and halfway along the street he asked nervously:

"Where shall we say goodbye?"

She understood what he meant and her lips trembled. She asked half-heartedly:

"Here?"

However, he opposed the idea, explaining:

"We can't just snatch this farewell hurriedly, like thieves."

"Where do you suggest?"

"Go home a bit ahead of me and wait for me on the stairs."

She hurried off and he followed slowly. When he reached the alley, all the shops were closed and he made his way dreamily towards Mrs. Saniya Afifi's house. He moved cautiously up the pitch-black stairs, breathing as quietly as possible, walking with one hand on the banister and one groping into the shadows before him.

On the second landing his fingers touched her cloak. This caused his heart to leap with desire. He took her arm and drew himself gently towards her. His mouth searched desperately for hers, touching first her nose and then making its way down to her lips which were already parted in welcome. He was transported on a wave of ecstasy from which he did not recover until she gently drew herself from his arms and went upstairs. He whispered after her: "Goodbye."

Hamida herself had never before had such an emotional experience. For this one brief period in her life, she brimmed with emotion and affection, feeling that her life was forever bound to his.

That night Abbas visited Hamida's mother to say farewell. Then he went to the café, accompanied by his friend Husain Kirsha, to have their last coffee together before departure. Husain was happy and triumphant with the success of his suggestion, and he said to Abbas, his voice somewhat challenging:

"Say goodbye from now on to this wretched alley life. Now start to enjoy a real life."

Abbas smiled silently. He had not told his friend of his agony at leaving both the alley and the girl whom he loved so dearly. He sat between his two friends and tried to suppress his sadness saying goodbye to well-wishers and enjoying their kind words. Radwan Husaini, too, had blessed him and said a long prayer for him. He also advised him:

"Save what you can from your wages after buying the necessities. Don't be extravagant and keep off wine and pork. Never forget that you come from the alley, and it's here you will return."

Dr. Bushi said to him, laughing:

"If God wills, you will return here a rich man, and when you do we'll have to extract those rotten teeth of yours and give you a nice set of gold ones appropriate to your new position."

Abbas smiled his gratitude to the "doctor." It was he who had acted as ambassador to Hamida's mother, and it was he who had bought his shop fittings at a price that provided the necessary expenses for his journey. Uncle Kamil sat silently listening, his heart heavy with his friend's impending departure. He dreaded the loneliness which would set in the next day, when the friend whom he loved, and with whom he had shared so many long years of his life, would be gone. Every time anyone shook his friend's hand or said how sorry he was that he was leaving, Uncle Kamil's eyes filled with tears so that everyone around him laughed.

Sheikh Darwish recited the holy "Throne Verse" from the Koran in blessing and commented:

"You have now become a volunteer in the British Army and if you prove yourself a hero, then it's not unlikely that the King of England will carve you out a little kingdom and appoint you ruler in his place. The title for this in English is 'Viceroy' and it is spelled V-I-C-E-R-O-Y."

Early next morning Abbas left his house carrying his clothes tied in a bundle. The air was cold and moist and the only people in the alley yet awake were Husniya and Sankir, the café waiter. Abbas lifted his head towards the sacred window and saw it was closed tight. He stared at it with such a fierce longing that the dew on its shutters almost seemed to evaporate.

He continued slowly, lost in thought, until he reached the door of his shop. Abbas stood looking at it sadly as his gaze rested on a notice in large letters: "For Rent." His chest tightened and his eyes flooded with tears.

He increased his pace, as though fleeing from his emotions. And when he reached the end of the quarter, he felt as though his heart wanted to pound its way out of his body and return to the alley.

14

t was Husain Kirsha who persuaded Abbas to serve with the British Army, and so the young man had gone to Tell al-Kabir leaving no trace of himself in the alley. Why, even his shop had been taken over by an old barber. Husain now found himself completely unsettled and full of hostility for the alley and its inhabitants. For a long time he had expressed his disgust for the alley and tried to plan a new life for himself. However, he had never clearly conceived a course of action and consequently had never made a firm resolution to achieve his dreams. Now that the barber was gone, he found himself filled with a desperate determination to do something. It seemed insupportable to him that Abbas should have escaped from the filthy alley and that he should have remained.

Finally he decided to alter his life no matter what it cost him. One day, with his usual crude bluntness, he said to his mother:

"Listen to me. I have made a firm decision. I can't stand this life any more and I see no reason why I should!"

His mother was used to his rudeness and his customary curses about the alley and its inhabitants. She considered him (as she did his father) to be utterly stupid, and never took his silly ravings seriously. So she made no reply and merely muttered to herself:

"Oh God, please spare me this dreadful life!"

Husain, however, his small eyes flashing and his near-black face becoming slightly paler in his anger, continued:

"I can't bear this life any more and after today I am not going to!"

She was not a woman noted for patience. As she shouted at him, her voice clearly betrayed what Husain had inherited from her:

"What's wrong with you? What's wrong with you, you son of a villain?"

The young man answered disdainfully:

"I must get away from this alley."

"Have you gone mad, you son of a lunatic?" she shouted, staring at him in fury.

Husain folded his arms nonchalantly and replied:

"No, I have my senses back after a long period of lunacy. Now listen to what I say and believe me, I am not talking just for the sake of it. I mean every word. I have tied my clothes into a bundle and there's nothing left but to say goodbye. It's a filthy house, the alley stinks and the people here are all cattle!"

She gazed at him searchingly, trying to read his eyes. His evident determination made her frantic and she screamed:

"What are you saying?"

"It's a filthy house, the alley stinks and the people are cattle," he repeated, as though talking to himself.

She bowed sarcastically and said:

"Welcome to you, honored sir! Welcome to the son of Kirsha Pasha!"

"Kirsha Coal-Tar! Kirsha, the laughing-stock! Ugh, ugh. Don't you realize everyone has smelled out the scandal now? Everywhere I go people joke and sneer at me. They say: 'His sister ran away with someone and now his father is going to run away with someone else!'"

He stamped his foot on the floor so hard that the window glass rattled violently. He screamed in a rage:

"What's forcing me to put up with this life? I'm going off to get my clothes and I'm never coming back."

His mother struck her breast with her hand and commented:

"You really have gone out of your mind. The hashish addict has passed his madness on to you! I will go and call him to bring you back to your senses."

Husain shouted contemptuously:

"Go on then, call him! Call my father; call our Lord Husain himself! I am going . . . going . . ."

Sensing his obstinate determination, his mother went to his bedroom and saw a bundle of clothes, just as he had said. Now she was convinced and, full of despair, decided to call her husband, no matter what the consequences. Husain, her son, was the only comfort she had left in life and she never expected that he would desert her. She had hoped he would always remain at home, even after he married, whenever that might be. Unable to overcome her despondency, she set off in search of Kirsha, shouting and lamenting her bad luck.

"Why should anyone envy us? In spite of our great misfortunes! In spite of our disgraces! In spite of our misery!"

After a little while Kirsha appeared, grinding his teeth with anger:

"What do you want, a new scandal?" he roared at her. "Have you seen another new customer to whom I serve tea?"

Thrashing her hands in the air, she answered:

"It's about your son's disgraceful conduct! Catch him before he goes and leaves us. He is fed up with us!"

Kirsha brought the palms of his hands together violently and, shaking his head in anger and disgust, roared:

"You want me to leave my work just for that? You want me to climb a hundred stairs just for that? Oh, you miserable pair, why on earth should the government punish anyone who kills off people like you?"

Gazing first at the mother and then at the son, he continued:

"Our Lord has obviously afflicted me with both of you as some sort of punishment. What has your mother been saying?"

Husain remained silent. His mother, as quietly as her short patience permitted, explained:

"Don't lose your temper; this is an occasion which calls for wisdom and not temper. He has bundled his clothes and plans to go away and leave us . . ."

Scarcely believing his ears, Kirsha gazed at his son with angry scorn and asked:

"Have you gone out of your mind, you son of an old hag?"

His wife's nerves were so on edge that she could not restrain from shouting:

"I called you in to deal with him, not to call me names . . ."

Turning angrily towards her, he shouted:

"Were it not for your congenital insanity your son would not have gone off his head!"

"God forgive you. All right, so I'm a lunatic and so were my parents. Let's forget all about that. Just ask him what is on his mind."

Kirsha stared fixedly at his son and spat out his question, sending spray in all directions:

"Why don't you answer, you son of an old hag? Do you really intend to go away and leave us?"

Normally the young man would have been careful not to antagonize his father. He had, however, definitely made up his mind to leave his old way of life no matter what the price. Therefore he did not hesitate, especially since he considered his staying or leaving to be entirely within his own rights which no one could deny. He spoke quietly and with determination:

"Yes, Father!"

Controlling his anger, Kirsha asked:

"And what for?"

"I want to lead a different life," answered Husain after a little thought.

Kirsha gripped his chin and shook his head sarcastically:

"Yes I understand that. You want to lead a life more suitable to your position! All dogs like you, brought up deprived and starving, go mad when they get money in their pockets. Now that you have money from the British, it's only natural that you should want to lead another life, more appropriate to your lordship's position!"

Husain suppressed his rage and replied:

"I have never been a hungry dog, as you describe me, because I grew up in your house and your house has never known hunger, thanks be to God! All I want is to change my way of life and this is my undeniable right. There is absolutely no need for your anger and sarcasm."

Kirsha was stunned. His son had always enjoyed a free life and he had never asked what he did. Why should he want to start a new life elsewhere? Kirsha loved his son, in spite of quarrels between them. He loved him, but the circumstances and atmosphere had never allowed him to express his love. He always seemed overcome with rage, exasperation and a desire to curse. For a long time he had almost completely forgotten that he loved his only son and at this particular moment, when the young man was threatening to leave home, his love and sympathy vanished behind a veil of anger and exasperation. The matter seemed to him a battle in which he must engage. For these reasons he spoke to him in tones of bitter irony:

"You have your money to spend as you wish. You can go off and enjoy yourself with drunkards, hashish addicts or pimps. Have we ever asked you for a penny?"

"Never, never. I am not complaining about that."

In the same bitter tone his father now asked:

"And that covetous woman, your mother, never satisfied unless her eyes are feasting on filth, has she ever taken a penny from you?"

Blinking with embarrassment, Husain replied:

"I said I am not complaining about that. The whole point is that I want a different life. Why, many of my friends even live in houses that have electricity!"

"Electricity? So, it's for the sake of electricity that you want to leave home? Thanks be to God that your mother, for all her scandals, has at least kept our house safe from electricity!"

At this point Mrs. Kirsha broke her silence and wailed:

"He keeps humiliating me! Oh God, by the murderous wrongs done to Hassan and Husain . . ."

Her son went on:

"All my friends live the modern way. They have all become 'gentlemen' as they say in English."

Kirsha's mouth opened wide in amazement, his thick lips exploding to reveal his gold teeth:

"What did you say?" he asked.

Scowling, Husain made no reply. His father went on:

"Galman? What's that? A new type of hashish?"

"I mean a neat, clean person," he muttered.

"But you are dirty and so how can you expect to be clean . . . Oh galman!"

Husain was now thoroughly annoyed and replied emotionally:

"Father, I wish to live a new life. That is all there is to it. I want to marry a respectable girl!"

"The daughter of a galman!"

"A girl with respectable parents."

"Why don't you marry the daughter of a dog like your father did?"

"May God have mercy on you! My father was a learned, pious man," said Mrs. Kirsha, groaning in disgust.

Kirsha turned towards her and commented:

"A pious, learned man indeed! He recited the Koran at burials! Why, he would recite a whole chapter for a penny!"

"He knew the Koran by heart and that's all that counts!" she declared, pretending to be offended.

Kirsha now turned away from her and moved several steps towards his son, until they were only an arm's length apart. Kirsha said, in his terrifying voice:

"Well, we have had enough talking and I can't waste any more time on two lunatics. Do you really want to leave home?"

"Yes," answered Husain shortly, summoning all his courage.

Kirsha stood looking at him. Then he suddenly flew into a rage and slapped Husain hard in the face with the palm of his hand. His son caught the heavy blow and it shocked and enraged him. He backed away, shouting:

"Don't you hit me! Don't you touch me! You'll never see me after today!"

His father charged again, but his mother stood between them, taking the blows herself. Kirsha stopped striking out and yelled:

"Take your black face away from me! Never come back here again.

As far as I'm concerned, you have died and gone to hell!"

Husain went to his room, took his bundle and, with one jump, was down the stairs. Taking no notice of anything, he rushed through the alley and, before he passed into Sanadiqiyya Street, he spat violently. His voice quivering in anger, he yelled:

"Bah! God curse the alley and all who live in it."

15

rs. Saniya Afifi heard a knock on the door. She opened it and discovered, with indescribable pleasure, Umm Hamida's pock-marked face before her.

"Welcome, welcome to my dearest friend!" she cried as though from the bottom of her heart.

They embraced affectionately, or at least so it seemed, and Mrs. Afifi led her guest into her living-room and told the servant to make coffee. They sat side by side on a sofa and the hostess took out two cigarettes from her case, which they lit and sat smoking in pleasure.

Mrs. Afifi had suffered the pangs of waiting ever since Umm Hamida promised to try and find a husband for her. It was surprising that, having lived patiently for many years as a widow, she could now scarcely bear this period of waiting, short though it was. Throughout the interval, she had made frequent visits to the marriage-maker. The latter had never stopped making her promises and raising her hopes. Eventually she became sure the woman was deliberately delaying in order to extract a reward larger than that agreed upon. Despite this, Mrs. Afifi had been most generous and kind towards her, letting her off paying rent for her flat, giving her several of her own kerosene coupons, as well as her clothing ration, not to mention a dish of sweets she had commissioned Uncle Kamil to make for her.

Then the woman had announced her daughter Hamida's engagement to Abbas! Mrs. Afifi had done her best to appear delighted, although in fact the news had disturbed her greatly. Would she have to help equip the girl for her marriage before she could arrange her own trousseau? So it was that during the whole period she was apprehensive about Umm Hamida and yet tried always to be as friendly as possible to her.

She now sat at her side, stealing a glance at her from time to time, wondering what this visit would bring and whether it would be just more promises and high hopes or the good news she yearned to hear. Mrs. Afifi did her best to hide her anxiety by keeping the conversation going and so it was she, contrary to normal, who did most of the talking while Umm Hamida listened. She gossiped about Kirsha's scandal and his son's leaving home and criticized the disgraceful conduct of Mrs. Kirsha in trying to reform the lascivious habits of her husband. Then she drew the conversation around to Abbas and praised him highly:

"He really is a nice young man. I'm sure God will be good to him and allow him to provide a happy life for his bride who is worthy of nothing but the best."

Umm Hamida smiled at this and replied:

"First things first! I've come to see you today to tell you of your engagement, my bride!"

Mrs. Afifi's heart raced as she remembered how she had sensed that today's visit might be decisive. Her face reddened as its fading pulse quickened with a new youthfulness. However, she managed to restrain herself and said in mock bashfulness:

"What a shameful thing to say! What can you be thinking of, Umm Hamida!"

"I told you madam, that I have come to tell you of your engagement," her visitor reiterated, smiling in triumphant delight.

"Really! Oh, what a thing to happen! Yes, I do remember what we agreed on, but I can't help feeling very upset and even ashamed about it. Oh, what a shameful thing!"

Umm Hamida joined in the acting and protested vigorously: "God forbid that you should feel ashamed about something in no way wrong or sinful. You are going to get married in accordance with God's law and the practice of the Prophet."

Mrs. Afifi let out a sigh, like someone yielding gracefully against her will; what her visitor said about marriage had a delightful ring to her ears.

Umm Hamida took a deep puff from her cigarette, shook her head in confidence and satisfaction and said:

"A civil servant . . ."

Mrs. Afifi was amazed. She gazed in complete disbelief at her visitor. A civil servant! Civil servants were rare fruits in Midaq Alley. Quizzically, she asked:

"A civil servant?"

"Yes, that's right, a civil servant!"

"In the government?"

"In the government!"

Umm Hamida was silent a moment, enjoying the hour of victory. Then she went on:

"In the government, and, what's more, in the police department itself!"

"What sort of men are there in the department besides policemen and police officers?" she now asked, even more surprised.

Umm Hamida looked at her with all the superiority of knowledge over ignorance and pointed out:

"They have civil servants too. You ask me! I know the government and the jobs there, and all the ranks and salaries, too. Why, that's my job, Mrs. Afifi!"

"He must wear a suit, too!" exclaimed the widow, her surprise mixed with unbelievable delight.

"He wears jacket, trousers, a tarboosh and shoes!"

"May God reward you for your great worth."

"I choose good for good and make a point of knowing people's value. If he had been in anything lower than the ninth grade, I would not have chosen him at all."

"The ninth grade?" asked Mrs. Afifi, somewhat querulously.

"The government consists of grades. Each civil servant has a grade. The ninth is one of those grades. His is a grade. But it's not like all the other grades, oh no, my dear!"

"You really are a fine dear friend to me!" said Mrs. Afifi, her eyes shining with delight.

Umm Hamida expanded, her voice ringing with victory and confidence:

"He sits at a big desk piled almost to the roof with folders and papers. Coffee is forever coming in and going out, with visitors seeking his help and asking him questions. He sits there and rebukes some and curses others. Policemen are always coming in to greet him and all officers respect him . . ."

The widow smiled and her eyes took on a dreamy look as Umm Hamida continued:

"His salary is not a penny less than ten pounds."

Mrs. Afifi hardly believed her and sighing deeply, repeated:

"Ten pounds!"

"Oh, that's only a small part of what he gets," Umm Hamida pointed out simply; "a civil servant's salary is not all he makes. With a little cleverness he can make twice as much. And don't forget his cost of living allowance, marriage allowance, children's allowance . . ."

The widow gave a slightly nervous laugh and asked:

"My goodness Umm Hamida, what have I got to do with children!"

"Our Lord can accomplish all things . . ."

"We must give Him praise and thanks for His goodness in any case."

"By the way, he is thirty years of age."

"Good gracious, I am ten years older than he!" exclaimed the widow, as though unable to believe her visitor.

Umm Hamida was not unaware that the widow was deliberately forgetting ten years of her life, but she merely said in a somewhat reproachful tone:

"You are still a young woman, Mrs. Afifi! Anyhow, I told him you were in your forties and he was delighted to agree."

"He was really? What's his name?"

"Ahmad Effendi Talbat. He is the son of Hajji Talbat Issa who owns a grocer's shop in Umm Ghalam. He comes from a fine family and he can trace his ancestors back to Lord Husain himself."

"A good family indeed. I, too, as you know, come from a noble stock."

"Yes, I know, my dear. He is a man who associates only with the best people. If it weren't for that, he would have married long ago. Anyway, he doesn't approve of modern girls and says they have too little modesty. When I told him of your excellent qualities and your bashfulness and that you were a noble and wealthy lady, he was delighted and said that you were the perfect wife for him. However, he did ask for one thing which was quite correct. He asked to see your photo."

The widow fidgeted and her face blushed as she said:

"Why, I haven't had my picture taken for a long time."

"Don't you have an old photo?"

She nodded towards a picture on the bookcase in the middle of the room. Umm Hamida leaned over and examined it carefully. The photo must have been more than six years old, taken at a time when Mrs. Afifi still had some fullness and life in her. She looked at the picture then back at its subject:

"A very good likeness. Why, it might have been taken only yesterday."

"May God reward you generously," sighed Mrs. Afifi.

Umm Hamida put the photograph, with its frame, into her pocket and lit the cigarette offered her.

"Well, we've had a nice long talk," she said, exhaling the smoke slowly. "You must certainly have an idea of what he expects."

For the first time the widow now gazed at her with a look of apprehension and waited for her to continue. When she remained silent, Mrs. Saniya Afifi smiled wanly and asked:

"And what do you think he expects?"

Did she really not know? Did she think he wanted to marry her for her youth and beauty? Umm Hamida was a little angry at the thought. She ignored the question and substituted her own instead.

"I take it you have no objection to preparing your own trousseau?" Mrs. Afifi immediately understood what she meant—the man did not want to pay for a dowry and expected her to provide it. Ever since she had set her mind on getting married she had realized that this was likely to be the case. Moreover, Umm Hamida had hinted at this before and the widow did not intend to oppose the idea.

"May God help us," she said in a tone of humble resignation.

"Let us ask God for success and happiness," smiled Umm Hamida.

When she got up to leave the two women embraced affectionately. Mrs. Afifi accompanied her to the outer door of her flat and leaned on the banister as the match-maker descended the stairs. Just before she disappeared from sight, Mrs. Afifi called after her:

"Thank you very much indeed. Kiss Hamida for me."

Then she returned again to her flat, her spirits soaring with new hope. She sat down and attempted to recall everything that Umm Hamida had said, sentence by sentence, word for word. Mrs. Afifi was inclined to meanness but she would never allow this to stand in the way of her happiness. For a long time money had sweetened her loneliness; both what she kept in a bank and that which was carefully wrapped in neat bundles in her ivory casket. This money, however, would never compete with the fine man who was to become, with God's permission, her husband.

Would he be pleased with her photograph, she wondered. She flushed at the thought. She moved to the mirror where she stood turning her head right and left, until she felt she had found her most attractive position; here she stopped and murmured to herself: "May God veil me."

Then she returned to the sofa saying to herself: "Money covers all blemishes." Had not the match-maker told her she was well-off? And so she was! The fifties were not the years for despair and she still had a full ten years ahead of her. And many women of sixty could still be happy if only God were kind enough to keep them from illness. Why, marriage could certainly regenerate a faded figure, revitalize a listless body. She blinked suddenly and asked herself: "What will everyone be saying tomorrow?" She knew the answer and was aware that Umm Hamida would be in the foreground of those gossips. They would be saying that Mrs. Afifi had gone off her head. They would say she was old enough to be mother of this man of thirty, whom she was about to marry. She knew also they would delight in estimating what it had cost to repair the damage time had wrought on her. No doubt they would probably gossip about many other things which were too humiliating to imagine. Let them say what they liked. Had their evil tongues ever stopped slashing her all the time she was a widow? Mrs. Afifi shrugged and sighed:

"Oh, God, save me from the evil eye!"

Suddenly she was struck by a comforting thought which she immediately determined to act upon. That was to see Rabah, the old woman who lived at the Green Gate. She would ask for a good-luck charm and have her horoscope read. Now was the ideal time for both, she thought.

16

hat do I see? You are indeed a venerable man!"

Zaita made this pronouncement as he looked up into the face of an erect old man standing before him. To be sure, his cloak was in rags and his body emaciated but it was as the cripplemaker had said, he had a most venerable appearance. His head was large, his hair white and his face elongated. His eyes were peaceful and humble. His tall and distinguished bearing was that of a retired army officer.

Zaita sat scanning him closely by the light of his dim lamp. He spoke again:

"But you really look like such a dignified man; are you sure you want to become a beggar?"

"I am already a beggar, but not a successful one," answered the man quietly.

Zaita cleared his throat and spat on the floor, wiping his lips with the hem of his black shirt before he spoke:

"You are too frail to bear any great pressure on your limbs. In fact it's not advisable to perform an artificial deformity after the twenties. You seem to think that a crippled body is just as easy to make as a real one. As long as the bones remain soft, I can guarantee any beggar a permanent deformity, but you are an old man with not long to live. What do you want me to do for you?"

He sat thinking. Whenever Zaita thought deeply, his mouth opened wide and his tongue quivered and darted to and fro like the head of a snake. After a while he suddenly blinked his eyes and shouted:

"Dignity is the most precious type of deformity there is!"

"What do you mean, reverend sir?" asked the old man, somewhat perplexed. Zaita's face clouded with anger, as he shouted:

"Reverend sir! Have you ever heard me reciting at burials?"

His anger surprised the old man and he spread out his palms in a gesture begging forgiveness.

"Oh no, God forbid . . . I was only trying to show my respect for you."

Zaita spat twice and his voice took on a proud tone:

"The best doctors in Egypt can't do what I can. Did you know that making a person appear crippled is a thousand times more difficult than really crippling him? Why, to really cripple someone would be as easy for me as spitting in your face."

"Please don't be angry with me. God is most merciful and forgiving," pleaded the old man.

Zaita's irritation gradually subsided and he stared at the old man. At last he said, his voice still sounding somewhat unfriendly:

"I said that dignity is the most precious deformity."

"How do you mean, sir?"

"Your distinction will ensure you great success as a beggar."

"My distinction, sir?"

Zaita drew out half a cigarette from a mug on the shelf. He then returned the mug to its place and lit the cigarette through the open glass of the lamp. He took a long puff, his bright eyes narrowing, and said quietly:

"It isn't a deformity you need. No, what you need is even greater handsomeness and intelligence. Give your robe a good washing and somehow get yourself a second-hand tarboosh. Always move your body with grace and dignity. Casually approach people in coffee-houses and stand aside humbly. Extend your palm without saying a word. Speak only with your eyes. Don't you know the language of the eyes? People will look at you in amazement. They will say that surely you are someone from a noble family who has fallen on hard times. They will never believe that you are a professional beggar. Do you understand what I mean? Your venerability will earn for you double what the others make with their deformities . . ."

Zaita asked him to try out his new role on the spot. He stood watching him critically, smoking his cigarette. After a little thought, Zaita scowled and said:

"No doubt you've told yourself that there'll be no fee for me, since I've given you no deformity. You're free to do as you like, provided you beg in some other quarter, not here."

The old man protested his innocence and said in a hurt voice:

"How could I think of deceiving the man who has made my fortune for me?"

At that the meeting came to an end and Zaita led the old man to the street. He took him as far as the outer door of the bakery. On his way back, he noticed Husniya, the baker's wife, squatting alone on a mat. There was no trace of Jaada and Zaita always seized any oppor-tunity to chat with Husniya. He wished to be both on friendly terms with her and to express his secret admiration for her.

"Did you see that old man?" he asked.

"Someone wanting to be crippled, wasn't it?" she asked indifferently.

Zaita chuckled and told her the story. She laughed and cursed him for his devilish cunning. Then he moved towards the door leading into his den but stopped, turned, and asked her:

"Where's Jaada?"

"In the baths," the woman answered.

At first Zaita thought she was making sarcastic fun of him for his notorious filth, and he looked at her warily. However, he saw that she was serious. Now he realized that Jaada had gone to the baths in Gamaliyya, a thing he did twice yearly. That meant he would surely not be back before midnight. He told himself there was no harm in sitting down and chatting with Husniya for a while.

He was encouraged by the obvious delight she took in his story. He sat on the threshold of his door, leaning back and stretching his legs like two thin sticks of charcoal, deliberately ignoring Husniya's astonishment as he did so. As the owner of his small room, she had only exchanged greetings when he entered or left. Apart from that she treated him as she did everyone else in the alley. She never thought the landlady-tenant relationship would change. She had not the slightest notion that he made a point of observing the most intimate details of her life. In fact Zaita had found a hole in the wall, between his room and the bakery; this served his curiosity and provided substance for his lecherous dreams.

Slowly his intimate knowledge of her became like one of the family, watching her at work and at rest. It especially delighted Zaita to watch her beating her husband. She did this at his slightest mistake. Jaada's days seemed to be filled with mistakes, for which he was constantly pummeled. Indeed beatings were almost a part of his daily routine. Sometimes he would accept them in silence, and at other times he howled wildly and his fists swung in the air. He never failed to burn the bakery bread, and he regularly stole a little something which he secretly ate when his duties permitted. Sometimes he bought a special sweet cake from money he earned for delivering bread to the alley houses. He made no attempt to stop or conceal his daily petty crimes, consequently he could not prevent his wife's painful beatings.

Zaita marvelled at the man's servility, cowardice and stupidity. It was a bit surprising that Zaita should find him ugly and constantly scoff at his appearance: Jaada was extremely tall, with long arms, and his lower jaw jutted out. Long and often Zaita had envied him the pleasures of his formidable wife whom Zaita both admired and desired. As it was, he despised Jaada and often wished he could toss him in the oven with the dough. And so it seemed natural to Zaita to sit pleasantly with his wife in the absence of the cowardly baker. Now he sat quite lost in his fantasies that centered around Husniya.

Husniya rose, walked to where he sat and bellowed out:

140 · NAGUIB MAHFOUZ

"Why do you sit there like that?"

Zaita said a silent prayer: "Oh God, spare me her wrath," and then replied in a friendly manner:

"I'm your guest and a guest ought not be insulted."

"Why don't you crawl off and spare me your face?"

His yellowed fangs showed as he smiled and said seriously:

"A man can't spend his whole life among beggars and garbage. One must sometimes see nobler sights and people."

"Meaning you can inflict your revolting sight and filthy smell on others?" she asked. "Go away and lock the door behind you!"

"I know of more disgusting sights and filthier smells."

Husniya realized he was referring to her husband and her face paled as she asked menacingly:

"Just what do you mean by that, you snake?"

"Our charming friend, Jaada," answered Zaita, his courage causing him some surprise.

Husniya shouted at him in her terrifying voice:

"Be careful, you rat! If I hit you I'll split you in two!"

Zaita paid no attention to the danger looming before him and continued:

"I told you guests shouldn't be insulted. Anyway I criticize Jaada because I'm quite sure you have nothing but loathing for him, plus the fact that you beat him up at the slightest excuse."

"Why, his little fingernail is worth more than all of you!"

"Well, I know what you're worth—but as for Jaada . . ."

"Do you think you're better than he is?"

Zaita's annoyance was obvious. His mouth dropped in amazement, not because he thought he was better than Jaada, but because he thought the comparison was an unpardonable insult. How could he be compared to that lowest of all forms of animal life who had not a single vestige of civilization in his character or personality?

"What do you think, Husniya?"

"I told you what I think," she snapped.

"That animal?"

"He's a man," she shouted. "Not like some I know, you ugly devil . . ."

"That creature you treat like a stray dog? You call him a man?" She heard the jealousy in his voice and it pleased her. No, she wouldn't hit him, much as she longed to. Rather she decided to nourish his envy:

"That's something you can't understand. You'll die longing for the blows that fall on him."

"Probably a beating from you is too good for me," said Zaita invitingly.

"Yes, it's an honor you'll never really know, you worm!"

Zaita sat thinking a moment. Could she really like living with that animal? He had often asked himself this question but had always refused to believe it was so. After all what else could she do but defend him like a loyal wife. And he was still sure she was being less than fully frank. His greedy eyes stared at her ample and firm body, and his determination and stubbornness increased. His imagination worked furiously, his lecherous eyes glistened with the feverish fancies conjured up by the empty room.

As for Husniya, his jealousy delighted her and she was not in the least afraid of being alone with him. Her confidence lay in her own strength. She spoke to Zaita sarcastically:

"As for you, you chunk of earth . . . first, get all that filth off your body and then maybe you can speak to people."

She was not angry. If she had been nothing would have prevented her from giving him a beating. She was deliberately flirting with him and Zaita was quick to see that the opportunity should be seized.

"You can't even tell the difference between dust and gold-dust," he said, pleased with his joke.

"Do you deny that you're just a chunk of clay?" she asked.

"We are all clay," Zaita replied, shrugging his shoulders.

"Shame on you! You're just dirt on dirt, filth piled on filth and that's why you're only fit to disfigure people. You love to draw other people down to your own filthy level."

Zaita merely chuckled at this and his hopes increased.

"But I am the best of people, not the worst," he said. "Don't you realize that regular beggars don't earn a penny, whereas if I give them a deformity they can earn their weight in gold. It's a man's worth, not his appearance, that counts. Now as for our friend Jaada, why he's neither handsome nor worth anything."

"Are you going back to that again?" demanded Husniya threateningly.

Zaita thought it best to abandon the subject he had deliberately broached. He went on in the tone of a public speaker.

"And apart from that, all my customers are professional beggars. What would you have me do with them? Would you like me to pretty them up and set them loose in the streets at the mercy of their 'well-wishers'?"

"You're a real devil! You talk like one and look like one, too."

Zaita sighed audibly and as though meekly seeking sympathy said: "Nevertheless, I was once upon a time a king."

"A king of devils?" she asked.

In the same tone of humility Zaita replied:

"No, of mankind. Which of us is not at first welcomed into the world like a king of kings, to be later carried wherever ill-fortune decrees. This is one of nature's wisest treacheries. Were it to show us first what is in store for us, we would all refuse to leave the womb."

"What next, you son of a whore!"

Zaita continued, his self-assurance unwavering:

"And so I, too, was once a happy creature whom loving hands coddled and enfolded with tender care. Do you doubt that I was once a king?"

"Not for a moment, master!" Her tone was now sarcastic.

Intoxicated by the power of his oratory and filled with anticipation, Zaita went on:

"Moreover, my birth was considered a most fortunate blessing. My parents were both professional beggars. They hired a baby which my mother carried on their rounds and, when God gave them me, they had no need for other people's children. So they were delighted."

At this, Husniya burst into a resounding laugh. This increased Zaita's confidence and desire and he continued:

"Oh, what memories I have of my happy childhood! I still remember my resting place on the sidewalk. I would crawl on all fours until I reached the street curb. I'd rest at a spot where there was a mud hole.

All kinds of scum and insects floated on its surface. It was a beautiful
sight! The water was full of garbage and its shores consisted of
rubbish of all colors—tomato skins, fruit-stains, beans, filth and flies
floating all around it and falling in. I would lift my eyelids, weighted
down with flies, and I'd wallow about in that delightful summer
resort. I was the happiest person alive . . ."

"Oh, how lucky you were," commented Husniya sarcastically. Her
pleasure and the way she listened delighted him, and he went on, even
more encouraged:

"This is the secret of my love for what you call filth. Man is
capable of growing fond of anything, no matter how strange. That's
why I'm afraid for you, getting attached to that animal."

"Must we talk of that again?"

"Why not? Man has no reason to disregard what is right."

"It's obvious that you've given up this world."

"I once tasted peace and mercy as I told you, in the cradle."

Then he made a gesture with his hand towards his room and he
went on:

"And my heart tells me that I may have another joy to taste, in that
room of mine." He nodded towards it with a sly wink.

Husniya seethed at his impertinence. She leaned over and roared
in his face:

"Watch out, you bastard, you!"

"How can you expect a bastard to guard against the natural sins of
his unknown father?" he asked, trembling.

"And if I were to break your neck?"

"Who knows—perhaps that would be delightful too."

He got up suddenly and walked back a bit. He felt he had what he
wanted and that Husniya would do as he wished. A fit of violent
passion gripped him, and he drew off his filthy cloak and stood quite
naked. For several moments Husniya remained dumbfounded. Then
she seized a heavy mug lying near and hurled it at him as violently as
she could. It struck him in the stomach and, letting out a bellowing
howl, he fell to the floor, writhing in pain.

17

Salim Alwan was sitting as usual at his desk one day when Umm Hamida came in to buy some things. He always made a point of welcoming her, but on this occasion his normal formal politeness was not enough. He invited her to sit in an armchair near him and sent one of his employees to buy the perfume she wanted. His kindness delighted Umm Hamida and she thanked him and blessed him profusely. If the truth were known this kindness was not particularly spontaneous, for Mr. Alwan had made an unalterable decision.

It is, after all, difficult for a man to have to live with his mind in a constant turmoil of indecision. It disturbed him deeply to see his whole life clouded with problems that he could not solve. He was well aware, too, of the distress this caused his sons. Yet he had no idea how to use his accumulated wealth, especially since the gossips said its cash value was likely to drop after the war. As for the matter of his title, whenever he managed to dismiss the matter, it kept coming back like an abcess. Another worry was his relationship with his wife and his fear that his youth and vitality were vanishing. Last but not least of his concerns was this emotion and desire of his which caused him so much anguish.

Now he realized the time had come when he must solve at least one of his problems, although he still could not decide which one. Eventually he decided he would settle the one that consumed him the most. He believed that when that one was settled, the other worries would also come to an end.

However, he was not unaware of the consequences. He knew that once he solved that problem, no less dangerous ones could emerge. Yet this was purely a matter of passion. The difficulties which stood in the way of his dreams now seemed trivial and he firmly told himself: "My wife has ceased her life as a woman and I am not the sort to enter into adultery at my age. Nevertheless why should I be punished? Allah made things easy, why should we make them difficult?"

Thus he had made up his mind to satisfy his desires and there was no retreat. So it was that he had invited Umm Hamida to come and sit near him so that he could broach the vital matter to her. Mr. Alwan was still a bit apprehensive of speaking out, not because he felt any indecision or hesitancy, but because it was not easy to descend in one jump from his high position and suddenly bare his soul to a woman like Umm Hamida.

At that moment one of his employees entered carrying his famous green wheat and pigeon concoction on a tray. Umm Hamida saw it and a faint smile flickered across her lips which he did not fail to notice. Alwan seized his opportunity and opened the conversation by speaking of the bowl. He tried to forget his dignity and revered position, and said to her in a slightly hurt tone:

"No doubt this bowl of mine offends you?"

Umm Hamida was afraid that he had seen her smile and she replied hastily:

"Heaven forbid! Why should you think that?"

In the same tone, Alwan went on:

"It does cause me a lot of trouble . . ."

"Why should you say that?" asked Umm Hamida, having no idea what he meant.

Alwan, conscious that he was talking to a professional match-maker, said quietly:

"My wife doesn't approve of it . . ."

Umm Hamida was astonished at this and she recalled how all Midaq Alley was at one time wild for a bit of this food. So Alwan's wife was too puritanical, was she, and didn't approve of it? She repeated to herself the saying: "People with fine voices often have no ears to enjoy their singing." Smiling, she muttered, quite unabashed:

"That's very strange!"

Alwan shook his head in sad agreement. His wife had never approved of his eating this food, even when she was a young woman in the prime of life. She was of a conventional disposition and had a genuine dislike of any sort of abnormality. She had always tolerated her passionate and virile husband from fear and respect; in no way did she want to displease him. Nevertheless she did not hesitate to advise him to give up a habit which she felt would eventually have serious consequences to his health. As she grew older, her patience decreased and her sensitivity about the matter increased. She now complained quite openly and would even leave home, apparently to visit her children. But actually, she was fleeing her husband.

Salim Alwan had naturally been annoyed and had accused her of frigidity and of being sexually exhausted. Their life was filled with constant friction, and yet her husband did not alter his passionate habits nor show sympathy for her obvious weakness. He had come to consider her rebelliousness, as he called it, a good excuse to start a new married life.

Alwan shook his head sadly and muttered, sure that Umm Hamida would be quite aware of what he meant:

"I've warned her I might marry someone else, and with God's permission, I intend to . . ."

Umm Hamida's interest was genuinely aroused and her professional instincts stirred. She gazed at him like a merchant examining a particularly important customer. However, she merely said:

"You are thinking of going as far as that, Mr. Alwan?"

"I've been waiting for you to call for a long time and I was about to send someone to look for you. What's your opinion?"

Umm Hamida sighed, overcome with an indescribable delight. As she herself said later, she had merely gone to buy some perfume and had stumbled upon a treasure instead! She smiled and answered: "Well, Mr. Alwan, you are a very important person indeed. Men like you are rare these days. Whoever you choose will be a very lucky woman. I am entirely at your service; I have virgins and widows and divorcees, young and middle-aged, rich ones and poor ones. Choose whomever you like."

Alwan sat twisting his thick moustaches and feeling a little embarrassed. He turned towards her and said quietly, a smile on his lips:

"There's no need for you to bother to make a search. The woman I want is in your own house!"

"In my house?" muttered Umm Hamida stupidly, her eyes opening wide in astonishment.

Alwan enjoyed her surprise and went on:

"Yes, in your house; nowhere else. And of your own flesh and blood. I mean your daughter Hamida!"

She simply could not believe her ears. She sat dumbfounded. Yes, she had heard, from Hamida herself, that Mr. Alwan stared at her when she went out for walks; but to be attracted and to want marriage are two very different things. Who would ever believe that Mr. Salim Alwan, the owner of the company, wanted to marry Hamida?

"But we are not of your class, sir!" she said, her voice near hysteria.

Alwan replied politely:

"You are a good woman and I am attracted to your lovely daughter. That's all there is to it. Are only the rich worthy of one's choice? What need have I for money, when I have more than enough already?"

Umm Hamida's astonishment remained complete, as she sat listening to him. Then she suddenly remembered something she had quite forgotten until now. She realized that Hamida was engaged. She let out a cry which led Alwan to ask her:

"What's wrong?"

"Forgive me. I forgot that Hamida is engaged! Abbas Hilu asked her to marry him before he went to Tell al-Kabir!"

Alwan's face fell and he turned red with rage. As though speaking the name of some vile insect, he shouted:

"Abbas Hilu!"

"And we even recited the Koran to confirm it!" let out Umm Hamida in a wail of regret.

"That simpleton barber?" scowled Salim Alwan.

"He's working for the army to earn more money. He left after we confirmed the engagement."

Alwan's anger at his exploded dream, and at Abbas as the cause, increased and merged into one. He commented bitingly:

"Does that fool think the army is a blessing that will last forever? Really, I don't see why you bring up this story."

"Well, I just remembered it. We never dreamed of you doing us such a great honor and so I had no reason to refuse his offer. Don't be angry with me, Mr. Alwan. You're the kind of man who only has to issue a command when you want something. We had no idea we'd be so privileged. Please don't be angry with me. Why are you so angry?"

Salim Alwan relaxed the expression on his face as he realized that he was angrier than he should be, as if Abbas was the aggressor and not the person against whom he intended to aggress. However, he went on:

"Haven't I every right to be angry?" He paused suddenly and his face went pale. With deep emotion, he asked:

"And did the girl agree? I mean, does she want him?"

"Oh, my daughter had nothing to do with it," answered Umm Hamida quickly. "All that happened was that Abbas came to me one day, with Uncle Kamil, and then we recited the Koran to seal the engagement."

"It's fantastic the way these young men act. Why, they scarcely have a penny to their names, yet they see no reason why they shouldn't get married and populate the whole alley with children who get their food from garbage carts. Let's forget the whole matter."

"A very good idea indeed, sir. I'll go now and be back soon, with God's help."

Umm Hamida stood up and bowed low over his hand in farewell. She picked up her perfume and went out.

Salim Alwan remained seated and perplexed, his face full of gloom, the steely glint in his eyes reflecting his annoyance and anger. So his first step had resulted in his stumbling. He spat on the floor as though expelling Abbas himself. Imagine a simple penniless barber, trying to compete with him! He could hear the gossips now, with more than their usual venom, while his wife accused him of trying to abduct a girl hairdresser from a barber shop in Midaq Alley. Yes, that's what she would say, again and again, and everyone else would say the same. Eventually, the matter would reach his children, his friends and his enemies. He sat thinking of all this, although he never wavered for a moment. The battle had been fought before today and he had now set out to accomplish the matter, placing his trust in God. He sat twisting his moustaches and shaking his head in defeat. He would have Hamida and whatever people said would make no difference to him. Had they ever kept their tongues from gossiping about him before? Their filthy fable about his bowl of green wheat, for instance. Let them think what they liked. He would do as he pleased.

As for his family, well, his fortune was large enough to satisfy all of them and his new marriage would cost no more than a title would. His anger cooled now and his mood was much better; his thinking had greatly relieved his anxieties. He told himself that he must never forget that he was a man of flesh and blood, otherwise he would fail to do justice to himself and merely succumb to fears and worries, which would eventually devour him.

What good was his fortune if he were to deny himself what he wanted and what he could so easily have? Why should he be consumed with longing for a body that could be his at merely a nod of his head?

18

mm Hamida hurried back and on the short walk between her flat and Alwan's office her mind was filled with conflicting dreams. She found Hamida standing in the middle of the room combing her hair. The older woman eyed her closely as if seeing her for the first time. She saw her as the clever female who had managed to captivate a man of Alwan's respectability, age, and wealth. Umm Hamida was experiencing something very much like envy. She was aware that half the money this anticipated marriage would bring the girl would go to her, and that she would be amply rewarded for each blessing that fell on the girl. She could not, however, dispel this strange feeling which weighed down her happiness, and she asked herself: "How could fate offer this happiness to a girl who knew neither a father nor a mother?" Now she wondered: "Has Mr. Alwan never heard her awful voice as she screams at the neighbors? Has he never seen one of her tantrums?" Without taking her eyes off the girl, Umm Hamida made a clucking sound and commented:

"My, my, you were certainly born under a lucky star!"

Hamida stopped combing her shining black hair and laughingly asked:

"Why? What do you mean? Is there anything new?"

The match-maker took off her cloak and threw it on the settee. Then she said quietly, closely watching the girl's eyes to see the effect of what she would say:

"Yes, a new husband!"

The girl's eyes flashed in interest and surprise, as she asked:

"Are you serious?"

"A very important man, indeed, and not just a dreamer, you bitch."

Hamida's heart beat furiously and her eyes shone so that their whites flashed. She asked:

"Who is he?"

"You guess."

"Who?" the girl asked, bursting with curiosity. Shaking her head and making her eyebrows dance, the match-maker replied:

"Mr. Salim Alwan, in all his full majesty!"

Hamida gripped her comb so tightly that its teeth almost broke in her hand. She shouted:

"Salim Alwan, the owner of the company?"

"Himself. A man who has so much wealth that it can't be counted."

Hamida's face glowed with happiness and she muttered unconsciously, almost beside herself with amazement and happiness:

"What a shock!"

"What good news! It couldn't be sweeter. I wouldn't have believed it if he hadn't told me himself."

The girl stuck her comb in her hair and rushed over to her adoptive mother's side. Shaking her shoulders, she demanded:

"What did he say? Tell me everything—word for word."

She listened attentively as Umm Hamida told her what had happened. Her heart throbbed and her face flushed, her eyes glistening proudly. Here at last was the stroke of fortune she had always dreamed of. This at last was the man who could give her all the luxury and freedom from drudgery she prayed for. She could think of no cure for her hunger for power other than a great deal of money. She wanted the other things it would bring: dignity, beautiful clothes, and jewelry, pride and a whole new world of secure and happy people. Her mother stood surveying the girl and then asked:

"What do you think?"

Umm Hamida had no idea what she would reply. She was determined to have an argument with the girl, in any case. If she said: "Mr. Alwan" she would reply: "And Abbas?" and if Hamida were to say "Abbas," she would reply: "And are we going to part with Mr. Alwan?" As it happened Hamida replied, as if not believing she was being asked the question:

"What do I think?"

"Yes, what do you think? The matter isn't easy to decide. Have you forgotten that you are engaged? And that I confirmed it by reading the Koran with Abbas?"

A vicious look came into the girl's eyes and shattered her beauty. She shouted in full, angry scorn:

"That barber!"

Her mother was amazed at the speed with which Hamida decided the matter. It was almost as though the barber had never existed. Her old feelings that her daughter was ambitious and cruel were renewed. She never really doubted what the girl's choice would be, but she would have preferred at least a little thought. She had hoped the girl would hesitate and that she could then convince her. She had certainly not expected to hear Hamida pronounce the word "barber" with such cutting scorn. The foster mother went on, in a critical tone:

"Yes, the barber. Have you forgotten that he's your fiancé?"

No, she had not forgotten, but in this case, to forget and to remember were really one and the same. Was her mother going to stand in her way? The girl peered closely at her and saw that her criticism was a mere sham. She shook her shoulders indifferently:

"He must go."

"What will people say about us?"

"Let them say what they like . . ."

"I'll go and talk to Radwan Husaini."

Hamida blanched at mention of him and objected:

"What's he got to do with my personal affairs?"

"Our family has no other man to consult."

She did not wait for a reply but rose quickly, put on her cloak and left the flat, saying: "I'll ask his advice and come back at once." The girl gazed after her in disapproval. Noticing that she had not finished combing her hair, mechanically she stroked her head, her eyes showing that she was lost in a world of sweet dreams. She rose, stood looking through the window at the business premises across the street and then returned to her seat.

As her mother guessed, Hamida had not abandoned Abbas without some thought. Yes, at one time she had thought she was bound to Abbas forever, and she was happy in the thought. She expressed her love by kissing him and it pleased him to hear her speaking of the future as though they would share it together. She promised to visit the mosque of Husain to pray for him and had indeed done so; normally she only went there to pray that one of her enemies be punished after some quarrel or other. But now things were different. After all, was it not Abbas who had raised her status from that of an ordinary girl to that of an engaged young woman? Now Mrs. Kirsha could no longer pull her long hair and threaten:

"I'll cut this off, if ever anyone gets engaged to you!"

Nonetheless, she knew she was virtually napping in the mouth of a volcano, and at no time had she felt quite satisfied with the whole matter. There was a constant restlessness inside her. True, Abbas eased some of her longing but he was not really the man she dreamed of as a husband. She had been confused about him since they first met and she remained so. Her ideas about what her husband should be like were quite unformed, and Abbas had certainly failed to form them. She told herself that actually living with him might possibly make her happier than she could imagine. This thought was with her constantly. But thought is a double-edged blessing and she had found herself asking what kind of happiness he could really give her. Was she over-optimistic in her dreams? Abbas promised to return and open a shop in Mouski Street, but could a shopkeeper's life give her many more comforts than she had now?

These thoughts confused her and strengthened her fears that the barber was not the ideal husband for her. She realized that her indifference towards him would never permit their living together happily. But what was she to do? Had she not bound herself to him forever? Oh, God, why had she not learned a profession, as her friends had? If she knew how to do something, she could have waited and married when and whomever she wished, or perhaps she might never have married at all.

This then, was her state of mind when Salim Alwan asked her hand in marriage. And so it was that she could discard her first fiancé with no regrets because he had really been banished from her heart a long time before.

Her foster mother was not gone long. She soon returned from Radwan Husaini's house, her face reflecting the seriousness of the situation. Taking off her cloak, she puffed:

"He would not agree at all."

Then she told what had happened between her and Radwan, how he compared the two men, saying: "The barber is young and Mr. Alwan is old; the barber is of the same class as Hamida and Mr. Alwan is not. The marriage of a man like Alwan to a girl like your daughter is bound to bring problems which will make her unhappy." He had finished by saying: "Abbas is a good young man and he has left home to improve his condition because he's eager for this marriage. He is by far the better husband for Hamida. You must simply wait. If he comes back penniless, which God forbid, then it is clearly within your right to marry her to the man of your choice."

Hamida listened, her eyes flashing fire, then she shouted, her anger revealing the ugliness of her coarse voice:

"Radwan Husaini is, of course, one of God's saints, or that's what he thinks he is. When he gives an opinion he cares nothing for anyone's feelings, so long as he has the respect of saints like himself. My happiness doesn't interest him in the slightest! No doubt he was influenced by the Koran, as a man with a long beard like him is bound to be. Don't ask him about my marriage! If you ask anything, ask him to explain a verse or chapter of the Koran to you. Why, if he were as good as you think he is, God wouldn't have taken all his sons!"

"Is that the sort of thing to say about the finest man alive?" asked the stunned Umm Hamida.

The girl shouted back viciously:

"He's a fine man if you like. He's a saint if you like. He's even a prophet, but he's not going to interfere with my happiness!"

Umm Hamida was pained by the girl's disrespect for the man but not because she wanted to defend his opinion, with which she herself secretly disagreed. Prompted by a desire to anger the girl even more, she commented:

"But you are engaged to be married!"

"A girl is free until the marriage agreement is signed. Nothing has passed between us but words and a dish of sweets!" answered Hamida, laughing sarcastically.

"And the recitation of the Koran?"

"Forgiveness is honorable . . ."

"Punishment for abusing the Koran is harsh, you know."

"I don't give a damn!" snarled the girl.

Umm Hamida beat her breast and cried:

"You serpent's child, you!"

Hamida noticed traces of hidden approval in her foster mother's eyes and she cried, laughing:

"Go and marry him yourself, go on."

This pleased the woman and she clapped her hands together and snapped:

"It's just like you to sell a dish of sweets in exchange for the bowl of spiced green wheat."

"On the contrary, I've refused a young man and chosen an old one."

"There's plenty of fat on an old rooster!" roared her foster mother. She settled down comfortably on the settee and soon forgot her mock opposition to the girl. She took a cigarette from a case, lighted it and smoked it with a look of deep pleasure on her face. Hamida looked at her and burst forth angrily:

"By God I think you are twice as pleased as I with my new fiancé. You were just deliberately trying to make me mad! God damn you!"

The older woman stared at her and spoke slowly and meaningfully:

"When a man like Mr. Alwan marries a girl, he's really marrying her whole family, just as when the Nile overflows, it floods all Egypt. Do you understand what I mean? Or do you think you're going off to your new palace while I stay here under the care of Mrs. Saniya Afifi and others like her?"

Hamida, who was braiding her hair, burst into laughter and said with exaggerated pride:

"In care of Mrs. Saniya Afifi, and Mrs. Hamida Alwan!"

"Of course . . . of course, you street orphan, you daughter of an unknown father."

Hamida went on laughing:

"Unknown, that's right! Unknown! But many known fathers aren't worth that!" she said snapping her two fingers in her foster mother's face.

The next morning Umm Hamida cheerfully set out for Alwan's office to read the Koran and to confirm the engagement. She had not a care in the world. However, she did not find Mr. Alwan at his desk and when she inquired she was told that he would not be in that day. She returned home, her happiness replaced by a feeling of uneasiness. Halfway through the morning, the news spread through the alley that the previous night Salim Alwan had suffered a heart attack. He was now in bed, hovering between life and death.

A swift wave of sadness spread through the alley, but in Umm Hamida's house the news struck like a thunderbolt.

19

ne morning Midaq Alley awoke to a tumult of great noise and confusion. Men were setting up a pavilion in a vacant lot in Sanadiqiyya Street, opposite Midaq Alley. The sight distressed Uncle Kamil, who thought they were constructing a funeral pavilion. In his shrill, high voice he wailed: "We all belong to God and to Him will we return; Oh Almighty, Oh Omniscient One, Oh Master." He shouted to a youth passing in the street and asked him who had died.

"The pavilion isn't for a corpse, it's for an election campaign party!" answered the boy with a laugh.

Uncle Kamil shook his head and mumbled: "Saad and Adli again." He knew nothing of the world of politics, apart from a few names he had picked up without comprehending their significance. Oh yes, hanging in his shop was a huge picture of the politician Mustafa Nahas, but that was only because one day Abbas bought two pictures of the leader and one was hung in the barber's shop, the other he gave to Uncle Kamil. He saw no harm in hanging it in his shop and anyway such pictures were part of every shop's decor. Why, even in the grocer's in Sanadiqiyya Street there were two pictures of the nationalist leaders, one of Saad Zaghloul and the other of Mustafa Nahas. And in Kirsha's coffee-house there was a picture of the Khedive Abbas.

Piece by piece they continued building the pavilion; vertical struts were put up and ropes tied between them on which screens were hung. The floor was covered with sand, chairs were set up on both sides of a narrow middle passage leading to a raised stage inside the pavilion. Loudspeakers were on all the street corners between Husain Mosque and Ghouriyya Street. But the best thing of all was the wide open entrance to the pavilion which allowed the alley people to watch the spectacle from their houses. Above the stage was a picture of the Prime Minister and under it one of Farhat, the candidate, whom most people in the quarter knew. He was a merchant on Nahasin Street. Two boys walked about putting posters on the walls. On them was printed in brilliant colors:

"Elect your independent candidate, Ibrahim Farhat,

In accord with the original principles of Saad.

The days of tyranny and destitution are over.

Now is the time of justice and prosperity."

They tried to paste a poster on Uncle Kamil's shop but Abbas' departure had had a shattering effect on him and he prevented them firmly:

"Not here, my fine fellows. It would bring bad luck to cut off my livelihood."

"No, it could mean a fortune for you," said one of the boys. "If the candidate sees it today, he'll buy up your whole stock of sweets at double the value."

By mid-morning the work was completed and the area took on its usual quietness. This lasted until late afternoon when Ibrahim Farhat appeared to direct the operation. He was surrounded by his retinue. Although not stingy, he was a merchant who always made the most minute scrutiny of his budget, thus spending only what was absolutely necessary. A short, stocky man, he strutted at the head of the crowd, dressed in a flowing robe. His brown circular face, with its active eyes, surveyed everything as he walked. His stride expressed the man's pride and self-confidence and his eyes revealed his honest simplicity. His appearance indicated that his belly was of far greater importance than his head.

His arrival created a stir in the alley and the surroundings, for they all considered him the man of the moment, as it were, and hoped for considerable benefit from his bounty. Behind him were groups of boys, following a man in a suit who kept shouting in a voice of thunder: "Who will be our deputy?" The youths chanted: "Ibrahim Farhat." "Who is the son of this district?" and they yelled back, "Ibrahim Farhat," and so on. This continued until the street was full of youths, many of whom entered the pavilion. All this time the candidate acknowledged the shouts by raising his hands above his head.

Eventually he moved towards the alley, followed by his retinue, most of whom appeared to be weight-lifters from the local sports club. He approached the old barber who had taken over Abbas' place and held out his hand:

"Peace be upon you, brother Arab." He then bowed low in humble greeting and passed on to Uncle Kamil:

"Please don't bother to get up; please, for our Lord Husain's sake, remain seated. How are you? God is great, God is great. My, this sweetmeat of yours looks delicious, as everyone will know tonight."

He passed on greeting everyone, until he arrived at Kirsha's coffee-house. He saluted Kirsha and asked his companions to be seated. People streamed into the café from all sides, even Jaada the baker and Zaita the cripple-maker were there. The candidate surveyed the assembled multitude with delight and then turned to Kirsha:

"Please, serve everyone tea."

He smiled in reply to the thanks from all parts of the café, and then said to Kirsha:

"I hope the café will be able to supply the pavilion's needs."

"We are at your service, sir."

Kirsha's stiffness did not escape the candidate, who said politely:

"We are all sons of the same district, we are all brothers!"

Mr. Farhat had come to the coffee-house with the firm intention of winning over Kirsha. He had invited him to call some days previously, in the hope of gaining Kirsha's support and those other café owners and workmen over whom Kirsha had influence. Farhat had offered him fifteen pounds for his support. Kirsha had refused, protesting that he was just as good as al-Fawal, who owned another café and who had reportedly received twenty pounds. Eventually, Farhat persuaded him to accept the money and made a promise of more. They had parted with the candidate feeling apprehensive that Kirsha might rebel against him. Indeed, Kirsha was still annoyed with those "politicos" as he called them, and would continue to harbour his ill-will unless he was offered a substantial sum for his support.

Kirsha really came to life during political campaigns. In his youth he had distinguished himself in the field of politics. He had taken an active part in the rebellion of 1919 and was reputed to have planned the great fire which destroyed the Jewish Cigarette Trading Co. in Husain Square. He was one of the heroes in the fierce fighting between the revolutionaries on one side and the Armenians and Jews on the other. When the bloody revolt subsided he had found a new, though restricted outlet for his energies in the subsequent election battles. In the elections of 1924 and 1925 his work was much appreciated even though it was rumored that he accepted bribes from the government candidate while supporting the Wafd Party. He had hoped to play the same role in the Sidqi elections, to accept money while boycotting the elections. However, government eyes watched him and he was one of several who were taken to the election headquarters. Thus, for the first time, he was forcibly prevented from giving his support to the Wafd. His last contact with politics was in 1936; it was then he decided to divorce politics and wed commerce. Since then he merely observed politics as he watched other lucrative markets, and he became the supporter of whoever "paid most."

He excused this renunciation by pointing to the corruption in political life. He would say: "If money is the aim and object of those who squabble for power, then there is clearly no harm in money being the objective of the poor voters." Now he was content to be corrupt, absentminded and beset by his own passions. All the spirit of the old revolutionary was gone, except for those vague memories that returned occasionally when he huddled over his warm brazier. He had rejected respectable life and now he cared only for the pleasures of the flesh. All else was pointless, he would say. He no longer hated anyone, not the Jews nor the Armenians, nor even the British.

He had no favorites, either, and it was surprising then that at one time he felt a curious enthusiasm for this war in which he sided with the Germans. He often wondered about Hitler's plans and whether it was possible that the Führer might lose the war and whether the Russians would not be wise to accept the unilateral peace offered them. Kirsha thought of Hitler as the world's greatest bully; indeed, his admiration for him stemmed from what he heard of his cruelty and barbarity. He wished him success, viewing him like those mythical bravados of literature, Antar and Abu Sayyid.

Despite all this, Kirsha still enjoyed a position of some power in local politics. This was partly because he was the leader of all the café owners who had regular evening meetings, and therefore the leader of their employees and hangers-on. So it was that Mr. Farhat cultivated his friendship and spent an hour of his precious time sitting in his café to achieve this end.

From time to time he glanced at Kirsha and now he leaned towards the café owner's ear and whispered:

"Are you happy then, Mr. Kirsha?"

Kirsha's lips spread in a slight smile as he answered cautiously:

"Praise be to God. You are the very soul of goodness and generosity, Mr. Farhat."

"I will compensate you well for what you missed before."

This pleased Kirsha. He glanced into all the faces present, and commented:

"If God wills, you won't disappoint our high hopes of you . . ."

From all sides voices were raised in unison:

"Oh God forbid, Mr. Farhat. You're the man we will vote for."

The candidate smiled and broke into a peroration:

"I am, as you know, independent, but I will keep to the true principles of Saad Zaghloul. What good are the parties to us? Haven't you heard their constant, senseless bickering? They are like . . ." He almost said "the sons of whores," but he suddenly recalled he was now addressing such sons. He checked himself and continued: "Let's not talk in metaphors. I have chosen to remain independent of the parties, so that nothing will prevent me from telling the truth. I will never be the slave of a minister or a party leader. In Parliament, if God grants us victory, I will always speak in the name of the people of Midaq Alley, Ghouriyya and Sanadiqiyya. The days of empty talk and bribery are over, and we are entering a period when nothing will distract us from those matters of vital interest to you; such as increased clothing rations, sugar, kerosene, cooking oil, no more impure bread and lower meat prices."

Someone asked in all seriousness:

"Is it true you will provide these necessities tomorrow?"

"There's no question about it," answered the candidate in a confident tone. "This is the secret of the present revolution. Only yesterday I visited the Prime Minister . . ." (he realized he had said he was independent and went on) "he was receiving all types of candidates, and he told us that his period of office will be one of prosperous plenty."

He moistened his lips and went on:

"You will see miracle after miracle," he continued. "And don't forget there will be rewards for all, if I win."

"Rewards only after the election results?" asked Dr. Bushi.

The candidate, uneasy with this question, turned towards him and said hurriedly:

"And before the results are out, too."

Sheikh Darwish now emerged from his usual silent fold and spoke in a far-off voice:

"Just like a dowry; he will give both before and after; so it is with all of them, except you, Oh Madam of Madams. You bring no dowry, for my spirit drew you down from the heavens themselves."

The candidate swivelled angrily towards the old man, but when he saw Darwish in a cloak and neck-tie and with gold-rimmed spectacles, he realized that he was a saintly man of God. A smile appeared on Farhat's round face and he said politely:

"Welcome indeed to our reverend sir."

Darwish made no reply and retreated into his usual state of torpor. Then one of the candidate's supporters shouted: "You can do what you like, but we are going to swear by the Holy Book . . ."

More than one voice replied:

"Yes, that's right. We must . . ."

Mr. Farhat asked to see the voting cards of all present, and when he asked for Uncle Kamil's, the latter explained:

"I don't have one. I've never taken part in any election."

The candidate asked:

"Where is your birthplace?"

"I couldn't tell you," answered Kamil indifferently.

Everyone in the café burst out laughing and Farhat joined them, saying:

"I must fix that little matter with the Sheikh of the quarter."

A boy dressed in a loose-flowing robe entered the café carrying a pile of small posters, which he distributed to all. Many assumed they were election posters and accepted them to please the candidate. Mr. Farhat took one and found that it read:

"Something is missing from your married life. Take Sanatury potion. Sanatury potion: Prepared scientifically, it is completely free from injurious ingredients. It has the endorsement of the Ministry of Health under license 128. It will revitalize and rejuvenate you. It will transport you from old age to youth in just fifty minutes.

"How to use it: Put a grain in a glass of very sweet tea and you will find your vitality restored. Far stronger, weight for weight, than any other known stimulant. It flows like electricity through the veins. Get your jar from the distributor of this announcement, the price is only 30 millième. So cheap! Your happiness for just 30 millième! We welcome our customers' comments."

Once again the laughter in the café made the candidate feel a bit uneasy. One of his retinue volunteered to ease his embarrassment by shouting:

"This is a good sign." Then he whispered in Farhat's ear:

"Let's go. We have many more places to visit."

The candidate rose and addressed the café assembly:

"We leave you in God's care then. May we meet again. I hope God will fulfil all our hopes."

He hesitated at Sheikh Darwish's chair and with a hand on his shoulder, whispered:

"Please pray for me, Sheikh."

Emerging from his silence, Sheikh Darwish spread his hands wide in blessing and intoned:

"May the devil take you!"

Before the sun had set the pavilion was filled. The audience passed the news from one to the other that an important politician would deliver a major speech. It was also rumored that reciters and comedians would perform. Before long a man appeared on the stage and recited from the Koran. He was followed by a musical ensemble consisting of old men in tattered robes who played the national anthem. The music from the loudspeakers instantly attracted young people from the nearby alleys and they soon choked Sanadiqiyya Street.

Applause and voices filled the air and when the national anthem was finished, the musicians made no attempt to leave the stage. Indeed, it almost seemed that the candidates might make their speeches to the accompaniment of music. Several of them stamped hard on the stage floor until the throng was silent. Presently a well-known monologue reciter, dressed in his village costume, rose and instantly the crowd went wild with anticipation and delight. When the applause subsided, the performer delivered his monologue. He was followed by a half-naked woman dancer, whose undulations were accented by cries of "Mr. Ibrahim Farhat—a thousand times . . . a thousand times." The man in charge of the microphones and loudspeakers joined her shouts with: "Mr. Ibrahim Farhat is the very best deputy. Microphones by Bahlul are the finest microphones." The singing, dancing, and applause continued as the entire quarter joined in the celebrations.

When Hamida returned from her afternoon stroll she found the party in full swing. Like everyone else in the alley, she had thought it would be merely a political rally with long speeches delivered in almost incomprehensible classical Arabic. Her heart danced when she saw the merry scene. She quickly looked about for a spot where she could both watch the musicians and the dancing, the likes of which she had never seen. She pushed her way through the crowd until she finally reached the entrance to the alley. She moved close to the barber's shop and climbed on a big rock near its wall. From here she could see the stage perfectly.

Boys and girls pressed round her from all sides. There were also several women, some carrying children in their arms or on their shoulders. The sound of singing was mixed with applause, talking, shouting, laughing, and wailing. The spectacle captivated her and her black eyes sparkled with enchantment. A sweet, pearly smile played over her normally expressionless lips. She stood erect, wrapped in a cloak which allowed only her bronze face, the lower part of her legs, and some stray locks of her black hair to be seen. Her heart danced to the beat of the music, her blood surged hot and fast, and she was almost overcome with excitement. The man who recited the monologues made her shriek with childish delight; even the hostility she felt for the dancing-girl did not spoil her excitement.

She stood completely engrossed in the entertainment, quite unaware that it was growing dark. Suddenly a compulsion seized her and forced her to look over her left shoulder.

She turned from the reciter and moved her head until her eyes met those of a man staring at her with insolent intensity. Her eyes rested on his and then quickly turned back to the stage. However, she could no longer recapture her earlier interest. She was overcome by an intense desire to look toward the left once again. Confusion and panic gripped her as his eyes pierced her with that same shameless insolence; at the same time they seemed to smile at her in a curious way. She could not bear to look at him. Instead she turned her attention to the stage in angry exasperation. It was his odd smile that infuriated her, for it seemed to express both a smug self-confidence and a challenging defiance. She could feel her temper rising, and she longed to dig her fingernails into something, into his neck for example. She decided to ignore him, although she hated giving up so easily, especially when she still felt his rude eyes on her. Now her good mood was gone and in its place her fiery temper had arisen.

The man seemed thoroughly pleased with himself. Now she saw him making his way towards the stage, to a spot in the direct line of her vision. No doubt he deliberately intended to block her view. He stood still, his back towards her. He was tall and lean, with broad shoulders, his hair long, and his head bare. He wore a suit of a greenish color. His tidy appearance and European dress made him seem oddly out of place in the crowd. She was now consumed with curiosity. This man was obviously well-to-do and what could he be doing in Midaq Alley?

Now he looked backwards again and stared straight at her. His face was lean and elongated, his eyes almond-shaped and his eyebrows thick. His eyes reflected both cunning and boldness. Not content with his previous examination, his gaze now travelled from her worn slippers up to her hair. She stood motionless, waiting for his face to reveal its impression. Their eyes met and again his gleamed with that insolent look of confidence and victory. Her blood boiled. She wanted to humiliate him with loud curses in front of the whole crowd. Each time she felt this impulse she repressed it. Quite overcome with emotion, she stepped from the stone and fled towards the alley. The moment she passed through it and crossed the threshold of the house, she felt an urge to go back. However, the insolent image of him returned, and she abandoned the urge.

She climbed the stairs, filled with self-reproach for not teaching him manners. She went to her bedroom, removed her cloak and peered at the street through the closed shutters. There he was, standing at the entrance to the alley. He was looking beseechingly at each of the windows overlooking the alley.

She stood there delighted at his obvious confusion and wondering why she had been so outraged. It was obvious that he was educated, middle-class and totally different from his predecessors. Moreover, she must have definitely attracted him. As for that challenging look in his eyes, what a splendid battle it invited. Why should he feel this boundless self-confidence? Did he consider himself some sort of hero or prince? Meanwhile, he showed signs of giving up his search for her.

She hesitated and then, turning the catch, she opened the window a bit, carefully standing behind it as though watching the celebration in progress. He stood with his back to the alley and she was sure he would renew his search. And so he did; he peered from window to window until he noticed the gap in hers. His face lighted up and he stood like a statue. Suddenly that smile was there and his whole appearance took on an even stronger look of arrogance and conceit. She realized that by allowing herself to be seen, she had committed an irretrievable blunder. Now he moved up the alley with such quick determination that she was afraid he would enter her house.

Instead he turned into Kirsha's café where he sat between Kirsha and Sheikh Darwish, the very spot where Abbas used to watch her shadowy form behind the shutters. Hamida remained behind the window still watching the stage, although her mind was far from what was taking place on it. She felt his gaze on her like a powerful searchlight.

The man remained in his seat in the café until the political rally finished, and she closed her window. For as long as she lived, Hamida was never to forget this night.

20

rom that evening on, he came regularly to Midaq Alley. He would come in the late afternoon, sit smoking a narghile and sipping tea. His sudden appearance and his air of respectable tidiness caused much surprise in the coffee-house, but eventually their astonishment diminished as they grew accustomed to him. After all, there was nothing unusual in his frequenting a coffee-house that was open to any passer-by. Nevertheless he annoyed Kirsha by always settling his bill with large notes, sometimes as much as a whole pound. He delighted the waiter Sankir by giving him tips greater than he had ever received.

Hamida watched his daily coming and going, her eyes and heart filled with excitement and anticipation. At first, she refrained from her usual walk, because of her shabby clothing. It annoyed her that her usually fearless character was now forced into confinement and retreat by a total stranger. She was fascinated by the banknotes the man held out to Sankir, and quite naturally they made a strong impression on her. Money might be a dead tongue in other places, but in Midaq Alley it was very much a live language.

Although the stranger was careful to conceal his reason for frequenting the coffee-house, he did not hesitate to glance up at her window. When his mouth touched the water pipe he puffed his lips slightly. He would then send the smoke high into the air, as though dispatching a kiss to her behind the window. She watched this with mixed emotions of pleasure, outrage and flattery.

She told herself that she should go for her usual walk and if he approached her—and she knew he would—she would fling at him all the insults she could think of, and shatter his smug self-confidence. She would attack him so viciously that he would never forget her as long as he lived. This was the very least he deserved for his conceit and impudence. To hell with him! What made him think he could treat her like a common street-walker? No humiliation was too much for him. She longed to go now and publicly insult him before the whole coffee-house. But oh, if she only had a nice cloak.

He entered her life at a time when she was overcome with despair. Salim Alwan had collapsed near death after giving her a day-and-a-half of hope for the life she had always wanted, and now this had happened, after she had banished Abbas from her dreams. Because she now knew there was no hope of marrying Alwan, she renewed her engagement to the barber, even though she felt only scorn for him.

She refused to submit passively to her ill-fortune and slandered her mother, saying that she envied her and coveted Alwan's wealth, and that this was why God had changed her fortune. This, then, was her state of mind when the new man came into her life. His arrogance infuriated and fascinated her. Yet his respectable appearance and his handsome masculinity attracted her. She saw in him qualities she had never before known in a man; strength, money and a fighting disposition. Try as she did she could not sort out her feelings for him. She was attracted to him and yet she had an uncontrollable desire to choke him. Perhaps by taking a walk she would find escape from her confusion, maybe in the street she could challenge him as he had her. This way she could release her indignation and also obey her deep impulse to fight—and to be attracted.

One afternoon she dressed carefully, wrapped her cloak around her and left the flat in a carefree mood. Soon she was making her way unconcernedly up the alley. As she turned off into Sanadiqiyya Street the thought struck her that he would probably misinterpret her going out like this. Wouldn't his vanity tell him that she had left the house purposely to meet him? He did not know of her daily walks, and so many days had passed without him seeing her leave the house. Anyway, no doubt he would follow her and approach her in the street and she refused to care what he might think. She would welcome whatever his vanity told him, so long as it encouraged him. So she danced off to meet him, her heart poised for a skirmish of any sort.

Despite her leisurely pace, she soon reached New Street. She imagined him jumping from his seat in the coffee-house and hurrying towards Ghouriyya, his eyes searching everywhere for her. She could almost see him at her back, his tall body hurrying forward, while her eyes scarcely saw the confusion of people, cars and carts in the street. Could he have caught sight of her? Was he wearing that evil smile? Let him go to the devil to whom he belonged. The beast had no idea what was in store for him. She must be careful not to look back; for one backward glance could be worse than total defeat. Even now perhaps only a few steps separated them. Why was he taking so long? Would he just follow her, like a homeless dog? Or would he overtake her to let her see him? Perhaps he would walk by her side and begin talking to her.

She continued on her way alert and on edge. Her eyes watched everyone before her and those who might overtake her, just as her ears strained for the sound of approaching footsteps. Her apprehension was extreme, and she longed to glance backwards. However, her stubborn determination restrained her. Suddenly she saw her factory girl-friends approaching her. She emerged quickly from her confused state and released a smile. She greeted them and they asked why she had been away for several days. Hamida pretended illness. She walked along chatting and joking with them while her eyes scanned both sides of the street. Where could he be? Perhaps he could see her from where he could not be seen. The opportunity to teach him a lesson was obviously gone now. Could he be following along behind the girls? This time she could not restrain herself and she looked back, examining the street carefully. He was nowhere to be seen. Perhaps he was slow in leaving the café and had lost sight of her. Perhaps at this very moment he was searching the streets for her. When they approached Darasa Street, it occurred to her that he would probably appear here, suddenly, just as Abbas had done one day. Her hopes now brightened and her spirits rose as she said goodbye to her companions. She walked slowly homewards and turned her gaze everywhere in the street. But it was empty, or rather empty of the one she wanted. Her spirits dropped; she covered the last part of the way home feeling utterly defeated. As she made her way up the alley she stared at the coffee-house and gradually she could see Kirsha coming into sight, beginning with the hem of his cloak, then his left shoulder until at last his dream-filled head came into view. Then there he was, sitting clutching the stem of his water pipe. Her heart throbbed and the blood rushed to her face as she dashed into the house, scarcely able to see before her. She scarcely managed to reach her room before she hurled her cloak on the floor and flung herself in an armchair seething with rage.

Then who was it he came to see every evening? And why did he stare at her like that? And who were those secret kisses for, that he blew into the air? Could it be there was no connection between his coming there every evening and what she imagined? Were these thoughts of hers just misleading fancies? Or had he deliberately ignored her today, to teach her a lesson or to torture her. Was he playing cat and mouse? She felt an urge to hurl a water-pitcher down at his head. Her confusion and rage were extreme but now she definitely knew one thing—that she wanted him to follow her in the street.

But what would she do then? Give him hell! But why should she want to take out her humiliation on him? It was that smile of his that caused all the trouble. Yes, she knew she could meet that smile and others like it. Deep within her she burned to match her strength with his masculinity, courage, and conceit.

She remained seated in the armchair, her mood totally bestial. Then she turned to the window, looked at it and crept forward until she was behind it. She peeped out from the shutters, so that she could see and yet not be seen, shielded by the shade engulfing the room. There he was sitting smoking his water pipe in obvious peace and contentment. He appeared lost in a world all his own and his face showed no sign of that arrogant smile. She stared down at him filled with an anger that increased her humiliation.

Hamida remained there until her mother called her for supper and spent a restless night plotting her revenge. The following morning she was deeply depressed; she looked forward to the afternoon with apprehension. Before she had never doubted he would come, but today she felt uncertain. All day she watched the sunlight move across the street and creep slowly up the café wall. It seemed strange to fear he would not come. His usual time came but there was no sign of him. Minute by minute passed until it was now clear that he would not appear. This confirmed her suspicions that he had deliberately stayed away. She smiled and sighed in relief. There was no reason why she should feel relieved but her instinct told her that if he stayed away today, then there was no doubt that he had deliberately refrained from following her the day before. If such was the case she need not feel frustrated. On the contrary, he was obviously putting all his skill and cunning into the chase. He was still on the battlefield, even though he could not be seen. She was delighted and relieved with her analysis of the matter. Now she was once again ready for the contest, this time with a renewed determination.

She felt restless, and wrapped herself in her cloak and went out, not even bothering to check her appearance as she had the day before. The cool air of the street refreshed her, lightening the day's anxieties. She walked along muttering angrily: "What a fool I am! Why did I torture myself like that? To hell with him!"

She hurried on, met her friends and started back with them. They told her a member of their group would soon marry a young man named Zanfal, who worked in Saidham's grocery shop. One of the girls commented:

"You got engaged before her, but she'll probably marry before you."

This remark upset Hamida and she replied indignantly:

"My fiancé is away earning money so we can lead a good life."

She expressed this pride in her fiancé against her will. Then she recalled how God had struck down Salim Alwan, as He does everything useless. She felt that life was the only enemy she did not know how to deal with.

She said goodbye to her friends at the end of Darasa Street and turned to go back the way she came. Only a few yards away she saw him, standing on the sidewalk as if early for a rendezvous. She stared at him for a few seconds in a state of shock, then continued on her way in a daze. She was sure he had planned for this unexpected encounter. He was organizing things quietly in his own way, each time making certain of catching her in a state of complete confusion. She summoned all her scattered resources in an attempt to work up a rage. It infuriated her that she had not dressed carefully.

The air was quite still in the brown hues of the sunset and the street was now almost deserted. He stood still, waiting for her to come nearer, a humble expression on his face. When she approached him he spoke quietly:

"He who endures the bitterness of waiting, attains . . ."

Hamida did not hear the end of the sentence because he mumbled it without taking his eyes off hers. She said nothing and quickened her pace.

He walked along with her.

"Hello, hello," he said in a deep voice. "I almost went crazy yesterday. I couldn't run after you because of what people would think. Day after day I have waited for you to come out, and when the chance came without my being able to take it, I almost went mad."

All this time he looked at her tenderly with no trace of the expression that had enraged her. There was no hint of challenge or victory, instead his words were more like a lover's lament. What could she possibly do now? Should she ignore him and walk faster and thus perhaps end the whole affair? She could do this so easily but she got no encouragement from her heart. It was as though she had been waiting for this meeting since that first day she saw him. Now her feelings were those of a woman quite sure of herself.

As for the man, he played his part skilfully, weaving his words in a clever fashion. Fear had not deterred him the previous day. His instinct and experience told him the time was not right for pursuit just as today he knew that tenderness and humility were his best weapons.

"Slow down a little," he said coming abreast of her, "I've something to . . ."

"How dare you speak to me? You don't know me!" Her voice was shrill and angry now.

"We're old friends . . . These past few days I've seen you more than your neighbors have in years. I've thought more about you, more than those closest to you ever could. How can you say I don't know you?"

He spoke calmly and without hesitation. She listened carefully, doing her best to remember every word. Taking care to conceal the natural harshness in her voice, she now spoke in a modulated tone:

"Why are you following me?"

"Why am I following you?" he asked in mock surprise. "Why do I neglect my business and sit in the coffee-house looking up at your window? Why have I given up my whole world and gone to live in Midaq Alley? And why have I waited for so long?"

"I didn't ask you so you could answer with those stupid questions," she snapped. "I just don't like you following me and talking to me."

"Didn't you know that men follow beautiful women wherever they are? This is a basic principle of life. If a girl like you were not followed, then there's something wrong in the world; it would mean that the day of resurrection were indeed near."

At that she turned into an alley where her friends lived. She hoped they might see her being courted by this handsome man in a European suit. She could see the mosque square looming ahead in the distance:

"Go away," she said. "People know me here."

His gaze fixed on her told him she was enjoying every minute of this intrigue. A smile crossed his lips which, had she seen it, would have kindled her fighting spirit.

"But this isn't your quarter, nor are these people relatives of yours. You are completely different. You don't belong here at all."

His words pleased her more than anything anyone had ever said to her. He continued to speak:

"How can you live among these people? Who are they compared to you? You are a princess in a shabby cloak, while these peasants strut in their new finery . . ."

"What's it to do with you? Go away," she said angrily.

"I will never go away."

"What do you want?" she asked.

With extraordinary audacity, he answered:

"I want you, nothing but you." This directness almost made her stumble.

"I wish you were dead," she blurted out.

"God forgive you. Why are you angry? Aren't you on this earth to be taken? And I'm just the one to take you."

They passed several shops on their way when suddenly she turned to him and shouted:

"Don't walk another step, if you do . . ."

"You'll hit me?" he asked, with that sardonic smile.

"Indeed I will."

"We'll see. Now I must leave you, but I'll wait for you every day. I won't return to the café, so no one will be suspicious. But I'll wait for you every single day . . . every day. God be with you then. You're the loveliest creature God ever created."

She continued on her way in a trance-like state of ecstasy. "You are different." Yes, and what else had he said: "You don't belong here . . . Are you not on this earth to be taken . . . and I will do just that." And then he had asked: "You will hit me?" She hurried along scarcely aware of anything about her. When she reached her room she came to her senses a bit. She asked herself how she could walk and talk to a strange man without feeling the slightest shame. Yes, she had done just as she pleased. She laughed out loud. Then she recalled how she had wanted to dig her fingernails in his neck, and she felt sad for a moment. She made excuses to herself that he had spoken to her most politely, even showing more than common courtesy. Yet she sensed he was really a tiger waiting to pounce. She determined to withhold judgement till he revealed his true self. And then? How sorry she'd make him!

21

D r. Bushi was just about to leave his flat when Mrs. Afifi's maid arrived and asked him to come and see her mistress. The "doctor's" face clouded as he asked himself what she could want and whether it might mean an increase in his rent. He soon dismissed the thought. After all, how could Mrs. Afifi violate the military regulations that controlled rents for the duration of the war? He left the flat and climbed the stairs, scowling as he went.

Like all her tenants, Bushi disliked Mrs. Saniya Afifi and never missed a chance to criticize her miserliness. Once he had gone around saying that she had intended to build a wooden room on top of the building so she could live there and rent her own flat. Most of all he disliked her because he had not once been able to avoid paying his rent to her. She always sought out Radwan Husaini if she had any difficulty and Bushi intensely disliked having to go and see him. He tapped on the door, saying a silent prayer and asking God's mercy and forgiveness in preparation for the trial ahead.

Mrs. Afifi, exuding a strong scent, opened the door and invited him into the reception room. He accepted and sat down, drinking the coffee the servant brought. She quickly explained what she wanted:

"I called you in, Doctor, for you to examine my teeth."

A new interest gleamed in Bushi's eyes and he was overcome by this unexpected good fortune. For the first time in his life he felt friendly towards her as he asked:

"I hope you don't have a tooth hurting you?"

"Oh no, thanks be to God." Mrs. Afifi explained: "But I have lost some of my back teeth and a few of the others are a little rotten . . ."

Dr. Bushi's good mood increased as he recalled the alley rumor that Mrs. Afifi was soon to become a bride.

"Well now, the best thing for you is to have a new set."

"That's what I thought, but would it take very long?"

Dr. Bushi got up and went over to her:

"Open your mouth . . ."

She opened her mouth wide and he peered into it carefully. The few teeth he saw surprised and annoyed him. However, he knew he must tread carefully:

"Well now, we'll need several days to take out these teeth, and then we'll have to wait six months before putting in the plate. That way the gums dry out and meanwhile you can rest your mouth."

Mrs. Afifi raised her painted eyebrows in alarm; she was hoping to be married in two or three months. Anxiously she replied:

"No, no. I want a quick job. It must be done in a month."

"A month?" said Dr. Bushi. "Impossible!"

"All right, goodbye then," snapped Mrs. Afifi.

He deliberately let a moment or two pass and then spoke:

"There is a way, if you like."

She realized he was bargaining and it made her angry. However, she decided to overlook this as she needed him.

"What way is that?"

"I could make you a gold plate. It could be put in immediately after the extractions."

Panic gripped her as she contemplated the cost of a gold plate. She almost rejected the doctor's suggestion, but she couldn't put off the impending wedding. How could she possibly go to her bride-groom with her mouth in its present decayed state? How would she ever have the courage to smile at him? Moreover, everyone in the alley knew that Bushi's fees were reasonable and that he somehow got plates that he sold at ridiculously low prices. No one ever asked where he got them; people cared only that they were cheap.

"How much would a set cost?"

Dr. Bushi was not the slightest taken in by her apparent indif-ference. He replied:

"Ten pounds."

She had no idea of the actual cost of gold plates, but she put on a shocked expression of incredulity:

"Ten pounds!"

Bushi flew into a rage:

"Do you realize it would cost fifty pounds at those dentists who treat their skills as a trade. People like me are just unlucky fellows, that's all."

They set about bargaining, he doing his best to keep it up and she to bring it down. Eventually they agreed on a price of eight pounds and Bushi left the flat cursing the old woman for trying to pretend she was young.

These days Mrs. Saniya Afifi was seeing the world in a new light, just as the world was seeing a new Mrs. Afifi. Her happy hopes were near fulfilment and her loneliness was now merely a temporary guest that would soon depart. Nevertheless, her happiness depended upon expense and a very heavy one at that. She realized just how heavy when she browsed in the furniture shops in Azhar Street and in the clothing shops along Mouski. On and on she went, spending the money she had hoarded for so long. Moreover, she kept no account of what she spent. All this time Umm Hamida scarcely left her side and she relied greatly on the match-maker's considerable adroitness. She was indeed a priceless treasure and was certainly proving very expen-sive. Umm Hamida herself, mindful that her job would soon be finished, took great care not to let Mrs. Afifi out of her grip.

The widow's furniture and clothing were not the only expenses;

her house needed renovation and even the bride herself required a great deal of care, preparation and repair. One day Mrs. Afifi said to Umm Hamida, laughing hysterically in her state of apprehension:

"Oh, Umm Hamida, can't you see how my worries are turning my hair grey?"

Umm Hamida, aware that whatever had whitened her hair it was certainly not worry, replied:

"Oh, those worries will easily disappear with dye. You know, there's hardly a single woman who doesn't dye her hair these days."

The widow now laughed and sighed:

"Heaven bless you, you wonderful woman. Whatever would I have done with my life if it weren't for you."

Then she waited a little, stroked her breast and went on:

"My goodness, will that young bridegroom you've found me be pleased with this dry body of mine? I have neither breasts nor a behind to attract men with."

"Don't belittle yourself; don't you know that being slender is fashionable and a very nice fashion too! Anyway, if you like I'll give you some marvellous dishes to fatten you up in no time . . ." She shook her pock-marked head proudly and continued:

"Have no fears as long as Umm Hamida is with you. Umm Hamida is the magic key to unlock all secret doors for you. Tomorrow you'll see how good I am in the baths; we'll go there together."

So the days of preparation passed, full of endless activities, pleasures and hopes, dyeing of hair and collecting perfumes, extracting teeth and making a gold plate; and all of this was costing money. The widow, struggling to overcome her stinginess, tossed her savings in the path of that long-awaited day. She even gave money to the mosque of Husain and dispersed it liberally to the poor surrounding it. In addition, she donated forty candles to Saint Shaarani.

Umm Hamida was overcome with amazement at the widow's sudden generosity. She clasped her hands together and said to herself:

"Are men worth all this trouble? Long may your wisdom reign, Oh Lord, for it is You who have decreed that women worship men . . ."

22

ncle Kamil woke from his usual permanent daydream to the sound of a bell ringing. He opened his eyes and listened. Then he craned his neck until his head appeared outside the shop. He saw a familiar carriage standing at the entrance of the alley and rose slowly, saying to himself in pleased surprise: "My goodness, has Mr. Salim Alwan really come back?" The driver now hurried from his seat to the carriage door to help his master climb down. Salim Alwan leaned heavily on his arm and carefully rose from his seat. First the tassel of his fez appeared, followed by his bent body and finally he stood on the ground straightening his clothes. His illness had struck him in the middle of the winter and it had taken until early spring to cure him. The biting cold winter was now replaced by a gentle wave of warmth which seemed to make the whole world dance with joy. But then what cure had he really had? Mr. Alwan had come back a different man. His paunch which used to stretch his clothes had quite disappeared and his florid, well-filled face was now sunken. His cheekbones were quite visible, his cheeks hollow, his skin pallid. His eyes had lost their sparkle and he now seemed sullen and faded beneath his scowling eyebrows.

Because of his weak eyes Uncle Kamil did not notice how much Alwan had changed. However, when he came closer to him and saw how old and worn the man looked, Kamil was really shocked. He bent low over Alwan's hand in greeting to hide his emotion, and shouted in his shrill voice:

"Praise be to God for your safe return, Mr. Alwan. This is a happy day indeed. By God and Husain, without you the alley isn't worth an onion skin!"

Withdrawing his hand, Mr. Alwan replied:

"That's very kind of you, Uncle Kamil."

He went off walking slowly and leaning heavily on his stick, his driver following behind with Kamil waddling in the rear like an elephant. It was obvious that the ringing of the bell had announced Alwan's arrival, for soon the entrance to the business premises was filled with workers. Kirsha and Dr. Bushi came out of the coffee-house and everyone surrounded Alwan, muttering prayers and praises to God for his safe return. The driver of the carriage raised his voice, shouting:

"Make way please for Mr. Alwan. Let him sit down first and then you can greet him."

The crowd cleared a path for him and he entered frowning, his heart boiling over with resentment. He would have been perfectly happy never to see one of their faces again. He had scarcely settled into his seat at the desk before his employees started streaming in. He had no choice but to give them his hand to kiss, one after the other, repelled by each touch of their lips, and saying to himself all the time: "What wicked liars you are! You're the real cause of this whole calamity!" The employees left and Kirsha now came in to shake his hand, saying:

"Welcome indeed to the master of the quarter. A thousand thanks to God for your safe return."

Alwan thanked him. As for Dr. Bushi, he kissed Alwan's hand and recited in oratorical tones:

"Today our joy is fulfilled and today our hearts are put at rest. Today our prayers are granted and . . ."

Hiding his disgust, Alwan thanked him. The fact was that he really despised the dentist's little round face.

When he was at last left in peace, he heaved a sigh from his weak lungs and said in a scarcely audible voice: "Dogs . . . dogs, the lot of them. They have bitten me with their envy-filled eyes!" He sat doing his best to shake off the rage and scorn welling up in him. He was not left alone long, for Kamil Effendi Ibrahim, his manager, appeared and at once Alwan forgot everything except checking the company's books. Tersely, he commanded:

"The books."

As his manager was about to go off, Alwan stopped him suddenly as though remembering something important. Imperiously, Alwan ordered him:

"Tell everyone that from now on I never want to smell tobacco smoke"—the doctor had forbidden him to use it—"and tell Ismail that if I ask him for water he is to bring a cup half-filled with cold and half with hot water. Smoking is absolutely forbidden. Now bring the books quickly!"

The manager went off to announce the new orders, grumbling to himself, for he was a smoker. Soon he returned with the books, worried by the obvious changes the illness had wrought in Alwan. He realized he was in for a difficult time.

The manager sat opposite Mr. Alwan and opened the first ledger, spreading it out on the desk before him, and they began working. Salim Alwan was most meticulous in his handling of business matters, no matter how delicate. He now settled down to the auditing of the books, going through them one by one, sparing no details. Next he summoned some employees, to question them about their punctuality, comparing what they said with what was recorded in the ledgers.

All the time Kamil Effendi sat patiently, frowning; not for a moment did he think of complaining. The audit was not the only thing his thoughts were following. He was silently pondering the ban on smoking which had descended so unexpectedly. This would not merely prevent his smoking in the office: he would also lose those fine Turkish cigarettes Alwan used to give him. He sat looking inquisitively at the other man bent over the ledgers and thought to himself sadly and angrily:

"My God. How the man has changed! This is a complete stranger." He particularly marvelled at Alwan's moustache, still large and splendid even though his face had lost its previous lines and features, quite obliterated by his dangerous illness. His moustache was like a lofty palm tree towering in a desert. His irritation caused him to observe: "Who knows? Maybe he deserves what has happened to him. God never treats anyone unjustly."

After three hours of work, Alwan finished the audit and returned the books to his manager, looking at him strangely as he did so. His look implied that although his suspicions were not confirmed by the audit, they still remained as strong as ever. Alwan told himself: "I'll do the audit again and again until I find out what they are hiding. They are dogs, the lot of them. While they have all the dirty tricks of dogs, they have none of their faithfulness!" Then he addressed his manager aloud:

"Don't forget, Kamil Effendi, what I told you. About the smoking and the warm water."

Soon his business friends and acquaintances arrived to wish him well, some staying to transact business. Others commented that he should postpone returning to work because of his health, but Alwan answered drily:

"If I were too weak, I should not have come to the office."

As soon as he was left alone Alwan's vindictive thoughts returned and, as was usually the case with him these days, his anger enveloped everyone. For a long time he had told himself that everyone envied him, that they envied his health, business, his carriage and his bowl of baked green wheat, and he now cursed them all from the bottom of his heart. During his illness these thoughts had frequently recurred to him and even his wife was an object of his spite. One day as she sat by the side of his bed, he said, his voice quavering with weakness and anger:

"And you too, madam, you have had your share of that. For years you've been trying to subdue me by saying that my wheat-bowl days are over. Why, it's as if you also resent my good health. Well, now everything is over and you can be satisfied."

She was quite shocked by this and stood there not knowing what to say. He broke in again angrily, his ill-temper in no way subsided:

"They envied me . . . envied me. Even my wife, the mother of my children, envied me!"

Although the reins of wisdom had now clearly slipped from his hands, death had already appeared before him sometime previously. He would never again forget that terrifying hour when the crisis had struck. He was just dropping off to sleep when a painful chest constriction attacked him. He felt the need to take a deep breath but he was unable to either inhale or exhale. Whenever he tried the pain racked his entire body. The doctor arrived and he had taken the prescribed medicine only to lie hovering between life and death for some days. When he opened his eyes he had been able to vaguely see his wife, sons and daughters sitting about him, their eyes red from weeping. He had drifted in and out of that strange state in which a man loses all desire to use either his intellect or his body. The world appeared a dark dream of obscure and disconnected memories, none really clear and seeming to have no connection one with the other.

In those few brief moments when he regained a degree of consciousness, he had asked himself in a cold shudder: "Am I going to die?" Was he to die surrounded like this, by his whole family? But then a man usually departs from this life surrounded by the hands of his loved ones, though what good did it do to have them around when one must die anyway? At that thought he started to pray and to make a declaration of faith, but was too weak. This attempt to pray merely caused a bit of internal movement that allowed moisture into his dry mouth.

His deeply embedded faith had not made him forget the horrors of this hour and he had submitted his body to it in spite of himself. As for his spirit, it clung in terror and fear to the fringes of life, his tear-filled eyes calling out for help and relief. This period eventually ended, the danger receded and he recovered. Slowly he came back to life again and he hoped his health would completely return so that he could lead his old life again. However, the warnings and advice of his doctor completely destroyed his high hopes, for clearly he had only a little life left. Yes, he had escaped from death. But now he was another person whose body was delicate and whose mind was sick. As time went on his sickness of mind became worse and he became more and more testy and filled with hate. He was really astonished at this reversal in health and fortune and he asked himself what sin could Almighty God be punishing him for. His had been one of those hearts only too ready to find excuses for others' faults, always thinking the best of them and refusing to see their shortcomings. He had a really fierce love of life, had enjoyed his personal wealth and provided well for his family. He had also, as far as he could see, kept within the bounds of God's laws and had felt a deep contentment in his life. Then this dreadful blow had struck that almost destroyed his health and very nearly his sanity. What sin had he committed? He had committed no sin; it was his enemies who had brought him down. It was their envy which had caused this eternal injury! So it was that everything that had been sweet in his life had now become sour and a permanent scowl etched itself into his brow. The truth was that his bodily damage was trivial in comparison to that done to his nervous system.

Sitting there at his desk in the office, he asked himself whether all he had left in life was to sit there auditing his books. Life seemed to frown on him more darkly than he on it, as he sat there frozen like a statue. He had no idea how long he had been sitting there lost in his thoughts, when he heard a noise at the entrance. He looked up and saw Umm Hamida's pock-marked face making its way towards him. A strange look came into his eyes as he greeted her, listening with only a quarter of his attention to her greetings and blessings. He was occupied with old memories that did not concern her.

Was it not strange how he had forgotten Hamida, as though she had never existed? During his convalescence she had occasionally crossed his mind, but only briefly and without effect. His disappointment at not being able to have her was not nearly so strong as his desire for her and recently he had really quite forgotten her. It was as though she had been a small drop of the healthy blood that flowed in his veins and when his health had gone she had vanished with it.

The strange look now left his eyes and their usual sullenness returned. He thanked the woman for coming to see him and asked her to sit down. In fact her coming had amazed him and he felt something approaching hatred for Umm Hamida. He wondered what had brought her, whether she really wanted to pass on her good wishes or to satisfy herself about that other matter. However, the woman felt no ill-will towards him for she had long ago despaired of him.

Rather like an apology, Alwan addressed her:

"We wanted . . . but God wanted otherwise . . ."

She understood and said quickly:

"It's not your fault, Mr. Alwan, and we only pray to God for your health and well-being."

She then said goodbye and left. Alwan was now in a worse state and even more upset than when she had arrived. He noticed a package of mascara slip from the hands of one of his workers and his anger boiled over. He shouted at the man:

"This business is going to close soon, so are you looking for a new job?"

He stood there trembling with rage. He was reminded again of what his sons recently suggested, that he should liquidate the business and rest. His rage increased as he told himself that it was his money they were really after and not their concern about his health. Had they not made the same suggestion before, when he was in perfect health? It was his money they were after all right. He seemed to forget that he had rejected the idea of restricting his life to working in the office and amassing money he would never be able to spend. However, his stubbornness got the better of him, coupled with an ill-will towards everyone he knew, including his children and his wife. Before he recovered from his rage, he heard a voice calling out in sincere sympathy:

"Praise be to God for your safe return. Peace be upon you, my brother."

Alwan turned and saw Radwan Husaini's tall, broad form approaching, his face beaming with joy. Alwan's face too, seemed happier than before and he made as if to get up but Radwan placed a hand on his shoulder and said:

"By our Lord Husain, please stay rested."

They embraced affectionately. Radwan had several times visited Alwan's villa during his illness and when he had not been able to see the merchant, had always left his greetings and blessings. Radwan sat near Alwan and they began talking together in a polite and friendly fashion. Salim Alwan cried emotionally:

"It was a miracle that I recovered!"

In his quiet, deep voice, Radwan replied:

"All praise be to God. It was a miracle that you recovered, and it is a miracle that you still live. It's a miracle, as you may know, that any of us are alive. For man to live a single second needs a great miracle from the Divine Power. The life of any man is a succession of divine miracles and just think of the lives of everyone put together and the number of lives of all living creatures! Let us therefore thank God day and night. How insignificant our thanks are in the face of these divine blessings."

Alwan sat silently listening and then muttered sullenly:

"Illness is a really evil, dreadful thing."

"No doubt it seems so, but from another angle it can be considered a divine test and so in this respect it is good."

This philosophy did not please Alwan at all and suddenly he felt hostility for the man who expressed it. The good effect of his coming was now quite dissipated. He managed to prevent giving way to his emotion, however, and asked, still obviously discontented:

"What have I done to deserve this punishment? Can't you see that I have lost my health forever?"

Radwan Husaini stroked his beard and answered critically:

"What can we, with our shallow intelligence, expect to understand of His mighty wisdom? It is true that you are a good man, worthy and generous, and keep strictly to God's ordinances. However, don't forget that God put Job to the test and he was a prophet. Do not despair and do not be sad. Remain faithful and good will come of it . . ."

Alwan's emotional state only got worse and he asked angrily:

"Have you noticed how Kirsha still retains the strength and health of a mule?"

"You with your sickness are far better off than him with his health."

Fury overcame Alwan at this and he shot Radwan a fiery glance, shouting:

"You can talk in your peace and contentment and sermonize in your pious godliness, but you haven't suffered as I have and have lost nothing like I've lost."

Radwan remained looking down until the man finished his speech. Then he raised his head, a sweet smile playing on his lips, and looked at Alwan, deep and straight from his clear eyes. Immediately, Alwan's anger and emotional state subsided. It was as though he was remembering for the first time that he was talking to the most afflicted of God's worshippers. The merchant blinked his eyes and his pallid face flushed slightly. Then he said weakly:

"Please forgive me, my brother! I am tired and on edge."

Radwan, a smile still on his lips, commented:

"Oh, you are not to be blamed; may God give you peace and strength. Remember God often, for it is by doing so that our hearts learn contentment. Never let despair overcome your faith. True happiness denies us, exactly as we deny our faith."

Alwan gripped his chin hard and said, angry again:

"They envied me. They resented my fortune and my good health. They envied me, Radwan!"

"To be envious is worse than to be ill. It is distressing how many people envy their brothers' good luck and transient fortune. Do not despair and do not be sad, and make your peace with your most merciful and forgiving God."

They talked for a long time and then Radwan Husaini said good-bye and left. Alwan remained quiet for a while, but soon returned to his previous scowling ill-temper. He was tired of sitting so long, and rose, walking slowly to the door of the office. He stood at the entrance, his arms folded behind his back. The sun was still high in the sky and the air was warm and fresh. At that time of the day the alley was nearly empty, except for Sheikh Darwish who sat sunning himself in front of the coffee-house. Salim Alwan remained there a minute or two and, as he had always done in the old days, looked up towards the window. It was open and empty. He felt uncomfortable standing there and returned scowling to his chair.

23

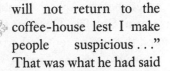will not return to the
coffee-house lest I make
people suspicious ..."
That was what he had said
when they had parted and Hamida, on the morning following their
meeting in Darasa Street, remembered his words. She felt full of life
and happy at the thought of him. She wondered whether she ought to
meet him today. Her heart immediately answered "yes," but she felt
obstinately "no, he must first come back to the coffee-house." And so
she refrained from going out at her usual time. She crouched behind
her window waiting to see what would happen.

The sun set and night spread its wings. Soon she saw the man
coming up the alley, his eyes fixed on the gap in the shutters of her
window. On his face she could see a slight smile of resignation as he
sat in his usual chair. As she watched him she felt the delights of
victory and revenge for the way he had punished her by appearing
unexpectedly in Mouski. Their eyes met and stayed fixed on one
another for a long time. She neither looked away nor moved. His
smile broadened and she smiled too, although she was unaware that

she did. What could he want? The question seemed idle to her, for she could see only one reason for his continuous pursuit of her. The same thing that Abbas wanted earlier and Salim Alwan too, before fate struck him down. Why shouldn't this fine young man be after the same goal? Why else would he say: "Are you not on this earth to be taken? And I am going to take you!" What could this possibly mean if not marriage? There seemed to be no obstacle in the way of her dreams, for her ungovernable vanity gave her a feeling of power and enormous self-confidence. So she remained looking out at him from behind the shutters, returning his intense looks without shyness or hesitation. His eyes spoke to her with depth and feeling, sharpening all her senses and igniting all her instincts. Perhaps it was this strange and deep feeling that she had experienced without even knowing it, when their eyes met that first time and he smiled at her victoriously. She was drawn to him as she had always been drawn by a challenge to battle. The truth was that his eyes revealed a great deal of herself. She had always wandered aimlessly through life and her confusion persisted before Abbas' humble gaze and the great wealth of Salim Alwan. She felt, however, that this man had been searching for her and this excitement and attraction drew her nearer to him. She felt drawn like the needle of a compass to the poles. She also knew that he was not just a penniless beggar who would make her endure want and poverty; his appearance and his banknotes proved that. Her eyes remained fixed on him reflecting desire and delight. She did not move from her position until he left the coffee-house, bidding her goodbye with a faint smile. Her eyes followed him as he went down the alley and she murmured as though in farewell: "Tomorrow."

On the following afternoon she left the house, her heart filled with anticipation, desire for battle and delight with life. She had scarcely left Sanadiqiyya Street when she saw him standing some distance away at the junction of Ghouriyya and New Street. A light gleamed in her eyes and she felt strange, obscure sensations stirring within her, that mixture of pleasure and a bestial desire to fight. She imagined he would follow her when she passed him until they were alone together in Darasa Street. So she went slowly on, feeling no anxiety or shyness and approached him as though she had not noticed he was there.

However, as she passed him something completely unexpected happened. He walked beside her and with indescribable boldness, stretched out his arm and gripped her hand. Paying no attention to the people walking by or standing about, he said quietly:

"Good evening, my darling."

She was taken unaware and tried vainly to release her hand but was afraid if she tried again she would attract too much attention and so she boiled with frustration. She was in a dilemma. If she were to release her anger there would be a disgraceful scandal and the whole affair would come to an end. If she were to give way, she would hate him because he had forced himself upon her and defeated her. Fury filled her as she hissed, trembling with emotion:

"What do you think you are doing? Let go of my hand at once!"

Walking at her side as though they were two friends out for a stroll together, he replied quietly:

"Patience, patience . . . friends shouldn't fight."

Seething with rage, she stuttered:

"But the people, the street . . ."

"Don't worry about the people of this street. They are all interested only in money. You wouldn't find a thing in their minds except bills. Come on, let's go over to a goldsmith's so that I can select something to match your beauty."

Her rage increased at his lack of concern and she said threateningly:

"Are you trying to show that nothing bothers you?"

"I didn't intend to annoy you," he replied quietly, still smiling. "I was just waiting for you so that we could walk together. Why are you angry?"

Still irritated, she replied:

"I hate your accosting me like this, and I warn you that if I lose my temper . . ."

Her face showed she was serious and so he asked hopefully:

"Promise me we can walk along together?"

"I won't promise anything. Let go of my hand."

He did so, but moved no further away from her and said, flattering her:

"Oh, what a stubborn self-willed person you are. Then take your hand, but we are not going to part company. That's true, isn't it?" "What a conceited oaf you are!" she spat out in rage.

He accepted the insult in smiling silence, and they walked away, with Hamida making no attempt to move away from him, aware of how she had lain in wait for him so recently in the hopes of walking with him along this very street. However, now her thoughts centered on the fact that she had forced him to let go of her hand. Perhaps if he were to try again, she would not prevent him; after all, hadn't she left her house for the sole purpose of meeting him? Anyway, it annoyed her that he should show more daring and self-confidence than she did and so she walked by his side, unconcerned about what passers-by might think. She could scarcely wait to see the envious astonishment his appearance would cause among the factory girls. The thought filled her with feelings of superiority and a desire for life and adventure.

The man spoke again:

"I would like to apologize for my rudeness, but really, what am I to do in the face of your stubbornness? You seem determined to punish me, when all I want is your sympathy for my sincere feelings towards you and my never-ending concern for you."

What could she say to him? She wanted to talk to him but she did not know how, especially since the last thing she had said had been an insulting rebuke. Now her thoughts were disturbed by the sight of her factory friends coming towards her. In mock confusion she exclaimed:

"Oh, my friends . . ."

He looked up and saw the girls approaching, staring at him with great curiosity. Disguising her delight, Hamida spoke again, her tone full of reproach:

"You have disgraced me!"

Pleased that she remained by his side speaking to him as one friend to another, he replied scornfully:

"Have nothing to do with them. Don't take any notice of them."

The girls were very close now, exchanging meaningful glances with Hamida, who recalled some of the adventures they had told her.

Whispering and giggling, the girls passed and the man continued with mischievous cunning:

"Are those your friends? No, you are not a bit like them, nor are they like you. It amazes me that they enjoy their freedom while you stay cooped up at home. How is it they can swagger about in nice clothes, while you have to wear this shabby black cloak? How can this be, my dear? Is it just fate? What a patient, tolerant girl you are!"

Her face went quite red and she seemed to be listening to her heart talking. Her eyes flashed the fire of the emotions burning within her. He went on, with complete confidence:

"Why, you are as beautiful as the stars."

She seized this opportunity to say something back to him. With all her natural boldness she smiled and asked, really not knowing what he meant:

"The 'stars'?"

He smiled gently and answered:

"Yes, don't you go to the cinema? They call beautiful film actresses 'stars.'"

She occasionally went to the Olympia cinema with her foster mother to see Egyptian films and now she understood what he meant. His words delighted her and her cheeks flushed.

Silence reigned for a few steps, then he asked:

"Tell me, what's your name?"

Without hesitation, she replied:

"Hamida."

"And this lovelorn fellow you see before you is called Ibrahim Faraj. In cases like ours, names are the last things known, usually exchanged only after the two people are quite sure they are really one. Isn't that so, my lovely friend?"

If only she were as skilful with words as she was in battle, for example. He was speaking tenderly but somehow she was unable to talk back that way. This annoyed her for, unlike some girls, she was not satisfied with a merely negative role. Her nature craved something more than waiting in humble silence. Since she found it so difficult to express her obscure feelings, her emotional stress increased and all she could do was stare at him. To add to her frustration they were approaching the end of the street. She had lost track of the time and suddenly ahead was Queen Farida Square. Hiding her regrets, she said:

"Now we will go back."

"Go back?" he answered in astonishment.

"This is the end of the road."

"But the world doesn't come to an end with Mouski Street," he protested. "Why can't we stroll around the square?"

"I don't want to be late as my mother will be worried."

"If you like we can take a taxi and cover a great distance in a few seconds," he pointed out temptingly.

A taxi! The word rang strangely in her ears. In her whole life she had only ridden in a horse-drawn carriage and the magic of the word *taxi* took time to die away. But how could she possibly ride in a taxi with a strange man? She was overcome by a powerful desire for adventure. She was amazed at her capacity for reckless adventures and it was difficult to say what most influenced her thoughts at this moment, whether it was the man who so stirred her, or the adventure itself. Perhaps the two were really one. She glanced at him looking cunningly in her direction, a trace of that infuriating smile of his on his lips. Her feelings changed abruptly:

"I don't want to be late."

Slightly disappointed, he asked, trying to appear sad:

"Are you afraid?"

"I'm not afraid of anything," she replied indignantly, her anger increasing.

His face lighted, as though now he understood many things. Gaily he said:

"I'll call a taxi."

She made no objection and fixed her gaze on the approaching taxi. It stopped and he opened the door for her. Her heart pounding and clutching her cloak she bent down and entered. The man followed her saying to himself delightedly: "We have saved ourselves two or three days' groundwork already." Hamida heard him say: "Sharif Pasha Street." Sharif Pasha! Not Midaq Alley, nor Sanadiqiyya, Ghouriyya or even Mouski, but Sharif Pasha Street! But why this particular street?

MIDAQ ALLEY • 197

"Where are you going?" she asked.

"We will have a little run round and then go back," he said, his shoulder touching hers.

The taxi started and she tried to forget everything for a while, even the man sitting so close to her. Her eyes were bewildered by the dazzling lights as a splendid, laughing new world appeared through the windows. The movement of the taxi had an effect on both her mind and body and a delightful feeling of intoxication stole over her. She seemed to be riding in an airplane, high, high above everything. Her eyes shone with delight and her mouth dropped open.

The taxi moved slowly, making its way through the sea of carriages, cars, streetcars and people. Her thoughts travelled with it. Now her will-power deserted her and her emotions were as intoxicated as her heart, her blood and all her feelings danced within her. She was suddenly aware of his voice whispering in her ear: "Just look at the fine ladies in their superb clothes!" Yes, they were swaying and dancing along like luminous stars . . . how beautiful they were, how wonderful.

Only now did she remember her own old cloak and slippers and her heart sank. She woke from her sweet dream as though at the sting of a scorpion. She bit her lips in annoyance and was overcome by a fighting spirit of rebelliousness. She noticed he had snuggled close to her and she began to sense the effect of his touch creeping over her. This enraged her and she pushed him away more forcibly than she intended. He glanced at her to see what was the matter and then took her hand and gently placed it between his own. He was encouraged by her permissiveness and searched for her lips with his mouth. She seemed to resist and drew her head back slightly. However, he did not find this a sufficient restraint and pressed his lips to hers. She trembled violently and felt an insane desire to bite his lips until they bled. The same insane desire, indeed, as whenever she got into a fight. However, he drew away before she could carry out her instinct. Rage burned within her, urging her to throw herself at him and dig her nails into his neck but suddenly she was soothed by his polite voice:

"This is Sharif Pasha Street . . . and that's my house a little way ahead. Would you like to see it?"

Her nerves on edge, she looked where he pointed and saw several blocks of skyscraper apartments and she had no idea which one he meant. He told the driver to stop and said to her:

"It's in this building . . ."

She could see a towering building with an entrance wider than Midaq Alley. Turning away from it in bewilderment, she asked almost inaudibly:

"Which floor is it on?"

"The first," he replied, smiling. "You won't suffer any hardship by condescending to visit it."

She shot him a critical, angry look and he went on:

"How quickly you get angry! Well, anyway, do let me ask you why it would be wrong. Have I not visited you many times since I first saw you? Why can't you visit me, just once?"

What did the man want? Did he think he had fallen on easy prey? Had the kiss which she had permitted given him an appetite for better, more dangerous things? Had his conceit and self-confidence blinded him? And was it love that made her lose her senses? Fury flamed within her and she gathered all her strength for the challenging battle ahead. She wished she could obey her instinct to go wherever he wished just to show him how mistaken he was and bring him back to his senses. Yes, her rebellious nature told her to plunge straight onto the battlefield. Could she possibly make the challenge and then refuse to accept it? What angered her were not the moral issues involved, nor her shyness; these could never infuriate her. No, what hurt was the slight to her pride and her belief in her own strength and her uncontrollable desire to use insulting language and have a good fight. Indeed, the desire for adventure which had led her to enter the taxi was still with her. The man looked at her closely, saying to himself thoughtfully:

"My darling girl is that dangerous type that explodes when touched. I must be very careful in handling her."

He spoke again, politely expressing his hope:

"I would very much like to offer you a glass of lemonade."

"Just as you wish," she muttered, looking at him in a stern and challenging fashion.

He stepped from the taxi, very pleased with himself. She followed boldly with apparent indifference and stood examining the building while he paid the driver. Her thoughts recalled the alley she had just left and she felt amazed at the unexpected adventure that brought her to this massive building. Whoever would believe it? What would Radwan Husaini say, for example, if he were to see her entering this apartment block? A smile played over her lips and she had a strange feeling that today was certain to be the happiest one in her whole life.

The man hurried to take her by the arm and they entered the building together. They walked up a wide staircase to the first floor and turned into a long corridor until they stopped at the door of an apartment on the right. The man drew out a key from his pocket and unlocked the door, saying to himself: "I've saved at least another day or two!" He pushed the door open wide for her and she went in, while he followed, locking the door behind them. She found herself in a long hall with rooms leading off on both sides and lit by a strong electric light. The apartment was not empty, for besides the light that was on when they entered she could hear sounds from behind one of the closed doors; people were talking, shrieking and singing inside.

Ibrahim Faraj went to the door opposite the entrance, pushed it open and asked her to come in. She found herself in a medium-sized room furnished with leather-covered couches somewhere between arm-chairs and sofas in shape. In the middle was an embroidered rug. Facing the door inside the room a mirror stretched to the ceiling above a long table with gold painted legs. He was delighted to see the look of amazement in the girl's eyes and he now spoke to her gently: "Do take off your cloak and sit down."

She chose a chair and, without taking off her cloak, leaned back enjoying the comfortable cushions. In a tone of warning, she murmured:

"I must not be too late . . ."

He went to an elegant table in the middle of the room on which a thermos flask stood and poured iced lemonade into two cups. He handed one to her, saying:

"Oh, the taxi will take you back in a couple of minutes."

They both drank and he then put the cups back on the table.

While he was doing this Hamida gazed at him closely. She appraised his tall, slim body and her eyes rested for a long time on his hands, noting with astonishment how beautiful they were. They were delicate and graceful; the long fingers gave an impression of strength as well as beauty. They had a strange effect on her, giving her a sensation she had never before experienced. He stood looking down at her, smiling gently as though trying to give her reassurance and courage. The fact was, however, that she felt no trace of fear, although her nerves were tingling with anticipation, apprehension and excitement. She remembered the voices she heard when they entered the apartment and she was amazed that she had forgotten them till now. She asked:

"What's all that noise in the apartment?"

Still standing facing her, he replied:

"Oh, some of the family. You will get to know them at the appropriate time. Why don't you take off your cloak?"

When he had invited her to his home, she thought he lived alone, and she was surprised that he brought her to a house with people in it. She ignored his last question and sat looking up at him calmly and challengingly. He did not repeat his request but came closer until his shoes touched her slippers. Then he leaned forward towards her, stretched out his hand to hers, gripped it and pulled her gently saying:

"Come, let's sit on the sofa."

She obeyed and they moved to sit side by side on a large sofa. All this time Hamida fought an inward battle for the attraction she felt for this man whom she loved against the hostility she felt for his thinking he could make fun of her. He moved slowly towards her until he was touching her. Then he put his arms around her waist and she submissively permitted this, not knowing when to start resisting him. He moved his right hand up to her chin and raised her mouth towards him, searching for it slowly and carefully with his own, as though he was thirsty, drawing water from a stream. Their lips met and they remained close together a long time, lost in a dream of love. He tried hard to summon all his strength and passion to his lips to accomplish what he wished. She was in a state of intoxication, though still alert and on her guard. She felt one of his hands leave her waist and travel up to her shoulder, lifting off her cloak. Her heart beat wildly and she drew her head away from him to replace the cloak in one nervous movement. She said harshly:

"Oh no . . ."

He looked at her in amazement to find her staring back with an expression of stubborn and defiant determination on her face. He smiled sheepishly, saying to himself: "Just as I thought, a difficult one. No, a very difficult one." He spoke quietly to her:

"Please, don't be angry with me, my darling. I forgot myself."

She turned her head away to hide her smile of triumph. However, the smile did not last long, for just then her eyes fell on her hands and she immediately noticed the immense contrast between his delicate hands and her own coarse ones. She felt overcome with shame. Finally, she said to him viciously:

"Why did you bring me here? This whole business is absurd!"

"This is the most wonderful thing I have ever done in my life," he insisted forcibly. "Why should you feel strange in my house? Is it not your house too?"

He gazed at her hair which could be seen under her cloak and, drawing his head close, kissed it saying:

"Oh God, how beautiful your hair is. It's the loveliest hair I have ever seen."

He said this sincerely, despite the smell of kerosene which filled his nose. His compliment delighted her, but she asked:

"How long will we stay here?"

"Until we know one another. Surely there must be many things we have to say to one another. Are you afraid? Impossible! I can see you aren't afraid of anything."

This pleased her so much she could have kissed him. He had been watching her closely and, having seen how his remark delighted her, said to himself: "Now I understand you, you tigress." He spoke out loud, his voice full of emotion:

"My heart has chosen you and my heart never lies. Nothing can separate two people brought together by love. You are mine and I am yours."

He drew his face towards her as though in supplication and she bent her neck towards him. They met in a violent kiss. He could feel the magical pressure of her lips pressing upon his so hard that they were almost crushed. He whispered in her ear:

"My darling . . . my darling . . ."

She sighed deeply and then turned away to regain her breath. He continued politely in a near whisper:

"This is where you belong. This is your home. No," he pointed to his chest, "this is where you belong."

She laughed shortly and said:

"You are reminding me that I must now go home."

He had, in fact, been following a planned course and he now said in disbelief:

"Which home? That house in the alley! What is there that so pleases you about that alley? Why are you going back there?"

"How can you ask me that?" she asked, laughing. "Isn't my home where my family is?"

"That's not your home nor is it your family," he insisted scornfully. "You are made of different stuff, my beloved. Why, it's nothing less than sinful for a lively, healthy, blooming body to live in a graveyard of decaying bones. Didn't you see all the beautiful women strolling along in their fine clothes? You are more beautiful and enchanting than any of them, so why shouldn't you strut about like them, wearing fine clothes and jewelry? God has sent me to you to restore your precious jewel of a self, your stolen rights. That's why I say this is your house."

His words played on her heart like the strings of a violin. Her mind had become almost numb, her eyelids half-closed, and a dreamy look came into her eyes. However, she was still capable of asking herself what he meant. All this her heart yearned for, but how to achieve these hopes and dreams? Why didn't he explain what he wanted and what his intentions were? He was certainly expressing all her hopes, dreams and desires as if she had stated them herself. His words revealed to her what had been obscure and hidden, giving form to it all so that she could almost see everything she desired before her eyes. There was only one thing he did not mention, nor even hint at, for that matter. She fixed her bold, beautiful eyes on him, and asked: "What exactly do you mean?"

The man realized he was now entering a difficult phase of his planned course. He gazed at her in a seductive and charming manner and said:

"I mean that you should stay in a house more suitable for you and that you should enjoy the finest things life has to offer."

"I don't understand," she said, laughing, in a state of bewildered confusion.

He gently smoothed her hair, taking refuge in silence while he collected his thoughts. Then he said:

"Perhaps you are wondering how I can possibly want you to stay in my house? Let me ask you in my turn, why you should go back to the alley? To wait, like all those other poor girls until one of the wretched alley men is kind enough to marry you, to enjoy your beauty in its bloom and your glorious youth and then cast you out in the garbage can? I know I'm not talking to one of those empty-headed girls. I know for sure that you are a very rare girl indeed. Your beauty is exquisite but it is only one of your many gifts. You are daring person-ified. When someone like you wants something you just have to say— so be it—and so it is."

Her color faded and the lines of her face were set. Angry now, she said:

"This is just flirting and you should not flirt with me. You started off joking and you now seem almost serious!"

"Flirting! Oh no, by God, I respect you too much for that. I never flirt when I should be serious, especially with someone like yourself who has filled me with respect, admiration and love. If my guess is right you have a big heart and will disregard all else to fill it. You cannot stand in its way. I need a partner in my life and you are the partner I want more than anyone else in the world."

"What partner?" she cried wildly. "If you're really serious, then what do you want? The path is obvious if you want to . . ."

She almost said "marry me" but stopped herself in time, looking at him with angry suspicion. He knew very well what she had

meant, and mocked her inwardly. However, he could see that there
was nothing to be gained by withdrawal at this stage and went on
speaking with theatrical fervour:

"I want a lover and partner with whom I can plunge headlong
through life, a life filled with gaiety, prosperity, dignity and happiness; not a life of household drudgery, pregnancy, children and filth. I
want a life for us like the film stars we were talking about earlier."

She opened her mouth in horrified amazement and an awful look
darkened her eyes as her face went white with rage. Fury overcame
her as she shouted, her back up straight:

"You are trying to corrupt me. What an evil, wicked seducer you
are!"

He smiled sarcastically and said:

"I am a man."

She interrupted, shouting:

"You are not a man; you are a pimp!"

He laughed out loud, asking:

"And are pimps not men too? Oh yes, my lovely young woman,
they are real men but not like others, I agree. Will ordinary men ever
give you anything but headaches? Why, pimps are stockbrokers of
happiness! But in any case, don't forget that I love you. Please don't let
anger finish our love. I'm inviting you to happiness, love and dignity.
If you were just a foolish girl I would have seduced you, but the fact is
that I respect you and have preferred to be sincere and truthful with
you. We are made from the same metal, you and I. God created us to
love and work with one another. If we join forces, then love, wealth
and dignity will be ours, but if we part there will be hardship, poverty
and humiliation—for one of us at any rate."

She remained staring at him, asking herself in confusion how
anyone could possibly be like this. Her breast heaved with outrage. It
was amazing how, hurt though she was, she still did not despise him
and had not ceased loving him for a single moment. Her emotional
stress became almost too much to bear and she stood up in one quick
violent movement, saying in angry indignation:

"I am not the sort of girl you think."

Doing his best to seem upset, he sighed audibly, although his businessman's confidence was undiminished. Full of regret, he commented:

"I can scarcely believe I could have been so disappointed in you. Oh God, are you one day to become one of those alley brides? Getting pregnant, having children, giving birth to children on the sidewalk, with flies everywhere, only beans to eat, your beauty fading away and getting fat? No, no, I don't want to believe that."

"That's enough!" she shrieked, unable to control herself any longer. She moved towards the door and he got up and caught her saying gently:

"Not so fast!"

However, he did not block her way. Instead he opened the door for her and they went out together.

She had arrived full of joy and fearless, and now she was leaving miserable and confused. They stood in front of the building while a boy brought them a taxi; then they got in, each by a separate door. It drove away swiftly. She was quite lost in thought. Sitting silently, he glanced at her and thought it wiser not to break the silence. So the journey passed until the taxi arrived half-way down the Mouski, where he ordered the driver to stop. She awoke at his voice and looked out. She moved as though to get out and he put his hand up to the door as if to open it for her, but hesitated and turning towards her, kissed her shoulder saying:

"I'll be waiting for you tomorrow."

She drew away from the door saying shortly and angrily:

"Oh no!"

Opening the door, he repeated:

"I'll be waiting for you tomorrow my darling, and you will come back to me."

Then, as she left the taxi, he said:

"Don't forget tomorrow. We will start a wonderful new life. I love you . . . I love you more than life itself."

He watched her as she walked quickly away, a sardonic smile on his lips. He told himself: "Delicious, no doubt about it. I'm quite sure I'm not wrong about her. She has got a natural gift for it . . . She's a whore by instinct. She's going to be a really priceless pearl."

24

hy were you late?" her
mother asked Hamida.

"Oh, Zainab invited
me over to her house and I
went with her," she replied, quite unconcerned.

Her mother then told her the news that they were soon to attend
the wedding of Mrs. Saniya Afifi. She also announced that the lady
was giving Hamida a dress so that she could attend the wedding
reception. The girl did her best to appear delighted and sat for a
whole hour listening to her mother's prattle. Then they had supper
and retired to the bedroom. Hamida slept on an old sofa while her
foster mother stretched out on a mattress on the floor.

The older woman was sound asleep in a few minutes, filling the
room with her snores, while Hamida lay staring at the closed window,
its shutters letting in a little light from the coffee-house below.
She lay there, recalling all the events of the bewildering day and she
remembered every single word and action that had taken place. She
relived it all over again, wondering how such fantastic adventures
could have happened to her. Despite her state of confusion, she was

happy and unafraid, her happiness fed by her satisfied vanity and her instinctive love for adventure. She remembered how, entering the alley, she had wished she had never seen the man but this thought found no echo in her heart. The truth was that she had learned more about herself in that one day than she had known in her whole life.

It was as if that man had crossed her path deliberately to uncover what was buried inside her, spreading it all before her eyes as though reflected by a mirror. She had said "no" when she left him, but she really had had no other choice. Anyway, what did her refusal mean exactly? Did it mean that she must keep hidden in her house waiting for the return of Abbas, the barber? Oh God, no! There was no longer any place for him in her life. His memory was erased and she would never let it return. All the barber could possibly give her was one of those wretched marriages and the inevitable pregnancies and children, giving birth to them on the sidewalks among the flies, and with all the other hateful ugliness of the picture she could see so clearly. Yes, she had no desire for motherhood as was the case with so many other girls she knew. In fact, the alley women were far from slandering her when they accused her of hardness and abnormality. What was she to do then? Her heart beat fast and she bit so hard on her lips that they almost bled. She knew what she wanted and what her soul yearned for. Before today she was in a state of uncertainty, but now the veil was lifted and her goal stood before her clearly.

It seemed extraordinary that, lying there, she saw no serious difficulty in choosing the path she would follow. There was simply her dull past and an exciting future. The truth was that without realizing she had chosen her path. She had chosen this man when she was in his arms in his flat. Outwardly she was angry while inwardly she danced with joy. Her face had gone pale with rage while her dreams and hopes breathed new life and happiness. Apart from this, she felt no scorn for him for a single instant; he had been, and still was, her life, her hope, her strength and her happiness. Her hate had only been aroused by his self-confidence, when he said the words: "You will come back to me!"

Yes, she would go back. But he would pay a high price for this conceit of his. Her love was neither worship nor submission, but rather a constant heated battle. How long she had suffocated in that house and in the alley! How she yearned for release into the light, to dignity and to power. Was there any other way of slipping the noose of the past except with this man who had lighted such a fire within her? But she would not go crawling to him, shouting "I am your slave forever. Do with me what you will." Her love was not like this. Neither would she speed off to him like a bullet and yell: "I am your lady mistress; submit to me!" No, she had no wish either to be or to have a passive lover. She would go to him, her heart filled with hopes and desires and say: "I have come with all my strength, so give me all of yours, too. Let us fight until death. Give me the dignity and happiness I long for." It was thanks to him that her path was now clear. How she hoped she would never lose it again, even though she had bought it with her very life.

Nevertheless, her night was not entirely free from thoughts that detracted from her resolution a little. She asked herself what people would be saying about her on the street the next day. Their answer came back in two words: "A whore!" Her mouth went dry at the thought and she remembered the quarrel she had once had with one of her factory girl friends, when she had shouted: "You streetwalker! Prostitute!" reproaching her for working like a man and wandering in the streets. What then would be said of her? The thought made her toss and turn in distress. However, nothing in the world could have altered her decision. She had made her choice with all her strength and it was the one she really wanted. She was sliding down her chosen route and all that blocked her way to the pit were a few pebbles.

Her thoughts suddenly turned to her mother and once again she heard her snoring, which she had been quite unaware of in the last long hour. She could imagine her state the next day when she would despair after her long period of waiting. Hamida remembered how the woman had sincerely loved her. So much so that she had only rarely felt a sense of not having a real mother. She recalled how she loved her too, despite their frequent quarrels. It was as if these feelings of affection were hidden deeply within her and only now beginning to move.

She told herself: "I have no father and no mother; he is all I really have in the world." Thus she managed to put the past behind her and set her thoughts on the future and what it might bring. Insomnia possessed her and her head and forehead burned with fatigue. She lay wishing that the torment would cease and that she could close her eyes and only open them in the light of tomorrow. She tried to kill all thoughts swarming in her mind. For a time she succeeded. However, the sound of voices coming from Kirsha's coffee-house disturbed her even more and she lay cursing them and accusing them of deliberately driving sleep from her.

"Sankir, change the water in the pipes!" That was the voice of that filthy hashish addict Kirsha. "Oh Sir, may our Lord give her her just desserts." That was that dumb brute, Uncle Kamil. "So what? Everything has its cause." That was that bleary-eyed, dirty Doctor Bushi. Suddenly, she had a vision of her lover in his usual seat between Kirsha and Sheikh Darwish, blowing kisses at her, and her heart throbbed violently. Her mind produced a picture of that apartment building and that luxurious room and she could hear his voice ringing in her ears, as he whispered: "You will come back to me . . ." Oh God, when would sleep have pity on her?

"Peace be upon you all, brothers." That was the voice of Radwan Husaini, who advised her mother to refuse the hand of Salim Alwan before he had been struck ill. What would he say tomorrow when the news reached him? Let him say what he liked; curses on all the alley people! Her insomnia became a wrestling match and almost a sickness as she lay there turning from side to back, to front. So the long night slowly passed, oppressive and exhausting. The decisive importance of tomorrow made her sleeplessness all the more painful.

A little before dawn a deep sleep settled over her but she woke again at daybreak. Suddenly her thoughts all rushed back to her, as though they had been awake long before she was. Now she felt no indecision and merely asked herself impatiently how long it would be before sunset. She told herself she was now merely a passing visitor in the alley, she was no longer part of it, nor it a part of her, just as her lover had said. She rose and opened the window, folded her mother's mattress and piled it into one corner. Then she swept the flat and washed the outer hall floor. She ate her breakfast alone, for her mother had left the house to attend to her endless affairs. Hamida then went to the kitchen and found a bowl of lentils which her mother had left her to cook for their lunch. She set about picking them over and washing them, lit the stove and stood talking to herself. "This is the last time I will do any cooking in this house . . . perhaps it's the last time in my life I will do any cooking. When will I ever eat lentils again?" It wasn't that she disliked lentils, but she knew they were the staple food of the poor. Not that she really knew anything about what rich people ate, except that it was meat and meat and meat.

Her mind set to work imagining her future food and how she would dress and adorn herself, her face beaming at the delightful dreamy thoughts. At noon she left the kitchen and took a bath. She combed her hair slowly and carefully and twisted it into a long thick pigtail that reached down to the lower part of her thighs. She put on her best clothes, but the shoddy appearance of her underwear embarrassed her and her bronze face turned red. She wondered how she could possibly go off to him as a bride dressed in clothes like these and her face went pale again at the thought. Hamida made up her mind not to give herself to him until she had changed these shabby clothes for pretty new ones. This idea appealed to her and all of a sudden she was filled with joy and passion.

She stood at the window, gazing down in farewell at the quarter where she had lived, her eyes moving quickly from spot to spot; the bakery, Kirsha's coffee-house, Uncle Kamil's shop, the barber's shop, Salim Alwan's business premises, and Radwan Husaini's house. Everywhere she looked memories flamed before her, like flares set alight by the matches of her imagination.

Surprising though it seems, Hamida stood there all this time cold and resolute, feeling not the slightest love or affection for either the alley or its inhabitants. The bonds of neighborliness and friendship were quite broken between her and the majority of the other women of the neighborhood; people like Mrs. Kirsha, who had suckled her, and Husniya. Even the wife of Radwan Husaini was not spared the sting of her tongue.

One day she learned the woman had described her as foul mouthed. Hamida watched closely until a day when Mrs. Husaini went to the roof of her house to hang her washing. Like a flash, Hamida climbed to her own roof, which adjoined the Husainis', and climbed to the intervening wall to confront her. She shouted in scornful sarcasm: "Oh, what a pity, Hamida, that you have such a foul mouth! You are unfit to live among the fine ladies of the alley, daughters of pashas that they are!" Mrs. Husaini preferred to keep her peace and took refuge in silence.

Hamida's eyes rested long on Alwan's office as she recalled how he had asked her to marry him and how she had remained drunk with dreams of riches, for a day and a half. How she had burned with regret at having to let him slip through her fingers! But then, what an amazing difference there could be between one man and another. Even though Salim Alwan had, with all his wealth, moved one side of her heart, this other man had moved it completely, so that he had almost plucked it whole. Her eyes moved on to the barber's shop and she remembered Abbas. She wondered what he would do when he came back one day and found no trace of her? At the thought of their last parting on the stairs, her heart almost stopped, and she wondered how on earth she could have given him her lips to kiss.

She turned on her heels and moved to the sofa, even more determined and resolute than before. At noon her foster mother returned and they ate lunch together. During the meal Umm Hamida said to her daughter: "I'm trying to arrange a wonderful marriage. If I can bring it off, then God will have made our future secure." Hamida asked indifferently about this marriage, not really paying any attention to what was said. Many times Umm Hamida had said this sort of thing and all it produced was a few pounds and some meat to eat.

When her mother lay down for a nap after lunch, Hamida sat on the sofa looking at her. This was the day she was to say goodbye forever; she would probably never again set eyes on her foster mother. For the first time she felt weak at the thought. Her heart went out to the woman who had sheltered and loved her and been the only mother she had known. Hamida wished she could at least kiss her goodbye.

Late afternoon came and she wrapped herself in her cloak and put on her slippers, her hands trembling with emotion, her heart thumping violently. There was nothing to do but leave her mother without saying a proper goodbye. She was unhappy at the thought as she looked at the woman lying blissfully unaware of what the next day would bring. It was time to leave and Hamida gazed at her mother and spoke:

"Goodbye, then . . ."

"Goodbye," Umm Hamida replied, "don't be late."

As she left that flat, her face showed strain and, disregarding all, she moved through the alley for the last time. From Sanadiqiyya, she walked into Ghouriyya and then turned off towards New Street. She walked at a measured pace. Eventually after some hesitation and apprehension she looked up and saw him waiting exactly where he had been the day before. Her cheeks burned as a strong wave of rebellion and anger swept through her. She longed to have her revenge on him and thus regain her peace of mind. She lowered her gaze but then wondered if he was now smiling in that insolent way of his. Nervously she lifted her eyes and found him quiet and serious, his almond-shaped eyes merely expressing hope and concern. Her anger subsided and she walked past him, expecting that he would speak or take her hand as he had done the previous day. Instead, he pretended to ignore her and she hurried on until a bend in the street hid her from sight. Then he slowly set out after her. Now she realized that he was being more cautious and treating the whole affair in a more serious manner. She walked on until she almost reached the end of New Street. Suddenly she stopped, as if she had just remembered something. She turned on her heels and started walking back and he followed her anxiously. He whispered:

"Why have you turned back?"

She hesitated, then said uneasily:

"The factory girls . . ."

Relieved at this reply, he suggested:

"Let's go into Azhar Street, no one will see us."

Still keeping their distance, they made their way in complete silence down Azhar Street. Hamida realized that, by saying what she did, she had announced her final surrender. They arrived at Queen Farida Square without saying a word. Because she did not know where to go now she stopped. She heard him call a taxi and suddenly he opened the door for her to enter. She raised a foot to step in and that one movement marked the dividing point between her two lives.

The car had scarcely begun to move when in a trembling voice he said with consummate skill:

"God only knows how much I have suffered, Hamida . . . I didn't sleep a single hour all last night. You, my darling, don't know what love is. Anyway, today I feel happy. No, I am almost mad with joy. How can I believe my eyes? Thank you, my love, thank you. I will make rivers of happiness flow beneath your feet. How magnificent diamonds will look around your neck! (He stroked it gently.) How beautiful gold will look on your arm! (He kissed it.) How marvellous lipstick will look on your lips! (He moved his head towards her trying to kiss her but she prevented him and he kissed her cheek instead.) Oh, what a shy temptress you are!"

After a moment he got his breath back and went on, a smile on his lips:

"Say farewell now to your days of hardship! From now on nothing will cause you discomfort . . . why, even your breasts will be held away from you by supports of silk!"

She was delighted to hear all this and felt not a trace of anger, even though she did blush. She yielded her body submissively to the movement of the taxi, carrying her away from her past life. The car stopped before the building which was to be her home. She stepped out and they walked quickly up to the apartment. It was just as it had been the day before, filled with voices coming from behind the closed doors. They went into the luxurious room and he said, laughing:

"Take off your cloak and we will both burn it."

Her face red, Hamida mumbled:

"I didn't bring my clothes with me."

"Well done," he shouted happily, "you'll need nothing from the past."

He sat her down in an armchair and walked to and fro across the room. Then he turned towards an elegant door beside a tall mirror and pushed it open, revealing a most attractive bedroom.

"Our room . . ." he said.

Hamida at once replied resolutely:

"Oh no . . . oh no . . . I am going to sleep here."

He looked at her piercingly and then replied resignedly:

"No, you will sleep inside and I will sleep here."

She made up her mind that she was not going to be taken like a sheep. She had no intention of submitting until she had satisfied her desire to be stubborn and difficult. It was obvious he sensed this, for he smiled ironically to express his resigned submission. Then he spoke with pride and delight:

"Yesterday, my darling, you called me a pimp. Now allow me to present my true self to you. Your lover is the headmaster of a school, and you will learn everything when the time comes."

25

alking to himself as he approached Midaq Alley, Husain Kirsha muttered: "This is the time when everyone meets in the coffee-house and they are all bound to see me. Even if my father is too blind to notice me, they will soon tell him I'm back." Night was drawing in now and the alley shops were all locked and silent, the only noise coming from the men chatting in Kirsha's café. The young man walked slowly and heavily, his face scowling and his spirits low. Close behind him followed a young woman, about his own age. Husain wore a shirt and trousers and carried a large suitcase just like the young man who followed him. The girl walked along daintily in a pretty dress, wearing neither coat nor cloak. She had an appealing air as she minced along, although something about her revealed her low class.

Husain made his way straight towards the house owned by Radwan Husaini and went in, followed by his two companions, without glancing at the café. They climbed the stairs to the third floor and Husain, now frowning intensely, knocked on the door of his parents'

home. He heard footsteps and then the door opened and his mother appeared. "Who is it?" she asked in her coarse voice, the darkness obscuring the figure before her. Her son answered quietly:

"It's me, Husain."

"Husain! My son!" shouted Mrs. Kirsha, unable to believe her ears. She rushed towards him, took him by the arms and kissed him, saying fervently:

"You have come back my son! Praise be to God . . . praise be to God who has brought you back to your senses and protected you from the devil's temptations. Come in, this is your home. (She laughed hysterically.) Do come in, you truant . . . what a lot of sleepless nights and worry you have given me."

Husain came in submissively, still scowling. Her enthusiastic welcome had done nothing to cheer him. As she moved to close the door behind him, Husain stopped her, making way for the couple who had been following him:

"I have some people with me. Come in Sayyida. You too, Abdu. This is my wife, Mother, and this is her brother."

His mother was stunned, and her eyes showed that she was more than a little annoyed. She stood gazing in astonishment at the newcomers and then overcame her feelings long enough to shake the hand extended to her. Unaware of what she was saying, she spoke to her son:

"So you got married, Husain! Welcome to the bride. But you married without letting us know! How could you have taken a bride without your parents being there, especially since they are still alive?"

Husain burst out:

"Satan is so clever! I was angry, rebellious and full of scorn . . . Everything is fate and chance!"

His mother took a lamp from the wall and led them into the reception room. She put the lamp on the sill of the closed window and stood gazing into the face of her son's wife.

The young woman said wistfully:

"It really made us sad that you couldn't be there, but there was nothing that could be done."

Her brother, too, expressed his regret. Mrs. Kirsha smiled, not yet recovered from her astonishment. She muttered:

"Welcome to you all."

She then turned to her son, upset at his obvious unhappiness. Now she realized for the first time that he had not uttered a single pleasant word since his arrival. Reproachfully, she commented:

"So at last you have remembered us."

Husain shook his head and answered gloomily:

"They have laid me off."

"Laid you off? Do you mean you are out of work?"

Before he could reply, their ears were assailed by a loud knocking on the door. Husain and his mother exchanged meaningful looks and then she left the room followed by her son, who closed the door after him. In the hall, Husain spoke:

"It must be my father."

"I think it is," she said anxiously. "Did he see you? I mean did he see you three, as you came in?"

Her son, instead of replying, opened the door and Kirsha came charging in. As soon as he saw his son his eyes shot sparks and his face contorted with rage:

"So it's you? They told me, but I couldn't believe it. Why have you come back?"

Husain replied quietly:

"There are guests in the house. Please come to your room where we can talk."

The young man moved quickly to his father's room and Kirsha followed, still fuming. Mrs. Kirsha joined them and lit the lamp, saying hopefully and warningly to her husband:

"Listen, my husband. Your son's wife and her brother are in the other room . . ."

The man's heavy eyebrows rose in astonishment and he bellowed:

"What are you saying, woman? Has he really got married?"

Husain, annoyed that his mother had released the news so abruptly and without introduction, thought it wisest to answer himself:

"Yes, Father, I am married."

Kirsha stood silently, grinding his teeth with rage. Not for a moment did he consider criticizing his son, for criticism would, in his opinion, imply a kind of affection. He determined to ignore the news. His voice full of rage and contempt he said:

"That doesn't interest me in the slightest. However, allow me to ask why you have returned to my house? Why are you now showing your face to me after God has given me a merciful relief from it?"

Husain took refuge in silence, bowing his head and frowning. His mother, attempting to pacify Kirsha, said in her shrill voice:

"They have laid him off."

Once again Husain inwardly criticized his mother for being too precipitate. As for Kirsha, what his wife said only increased his rage and he shouted in a voice so loud and threatening that his wife hurriedly shut the door:

"They've laid you off? Well, what next? And is my home an almshouse? Didn't you desert us, you hero? Didn't you bite me with your fangs, you son of a bitch? Why are you back now? Get out of my sight! Go back to your 'clean life' and your water and electricity. Go on. Hurry!"

Husain's mother spoke quietly:

"Please quiet down. Say a prayer for the Prophet . . ."

Kirsha turned towards her menacingly, his clenched fist raised, and yelled:

"Are you defending him, you daughter of the devils? You all need a good whipping and punishing in hell-fire. What do you want then, you mother of all evil? Do you think I should give shelter to him and his family? Have people told you I am some sort of pimp who gets money from everywhere without trouble or effort? Oh no! You might as well know the police are hovering around us; only yesterday they took four of my colleagues. Your future looks black, with God's permission!"

Mrs. Kirsha thought patience the best course to follow and so she said in a manner unusually gentle for her:

"Say a prayer for the Prophet and affirm your faith in the Oneness of God."

Kirsha shouted roughly:

"Am I to forget what he did?"

"Our son is headstrong and foolish," she replied, trying to pacify him. "The devil took a fancy to him and led him astray. You are the only person he has to turn to now."

"You're right," shouted her husband, full of angry scorn. "I'm the only person he can turn to, me, the one he curses when all seems well and crawls to when things get bad."

He turned and gazed hard and straight at Husain and asked reproachfully:

"Why did they fire you?"

Mrs. Kirsha sighed deeply. She knew instinctively that this question, despite the bitter tone, was a hopeful sign of reconciliation. Husain replied quietly, feeling the bitterness of complete defeat:

"They laid off many others besides. They say the war will end soon . . ."

"It may be finished on the battlefields, but it's only beginning in my own house! Why didn't you go to your wife's parents?"

"She has no one but her brother," answered Husain, looking down.

"Why didn't you go to him for help?"

"He has been laid off too."

Kirsha laughed sarcastically:

"Welcome! Welcome! It's only natural that you could find no other refuge for this fate-struck noble family, except my two-roomed house! Well done indeed! Well done . . . Didn't you save any money?"

Sighing, Husain replied sadly:

"No, I didn't."

"You've done well indeed. You lived like a king with electricity, water and entertainment and now you're back a beggar, just as you were when you left."

Husain answered indignantly:

"They said the war would never end and that Hitler would fight for decades and then eventually attack."

"But he hasn't attacked, instead he has disappeared, leaving the biggest fool alive empty-handed! His lordship is madam's brother?"

"That's the situation."

"Splendid . . . splendid. Your father is most honored. Get the house ready for them, Mrs. Kirsha, humble and inadequate though it is. I will improve the situation by installing running water and electricity. Why, I'll probably even buy Mr. Alwan's carriage for them."

Husain blew out air and said:

"That's enough, Father . . . that's enough . . ."

Kirsha looked at him almost apologetically and continued in a sarcastic tone:

"Don't be angry with me. Have I upset you? It was only a little joke. All glory and honor to you. Have mercy on these fine people down on their luck. Be more careful, Kirsha, and speak respectfully to these respectable people . . . Do take off your coats. As for you, Mrs. Kirsha, open up the treasure we keep in the lavatory and give the gentleman enough to make him rich and cheer him up."

Husain stifled his anger without saying a word and thus the storm passed. Mrs. Kirsha stood there saying to herself: "Oh Protector, protect us." Kirsha, in spite of his rage and sarcasm, had no intention of driving Husain away. All during this scene he was pleased at his son's return and delighted with his marriage. Eventually he simmered down and muttered:

"The matter is in God's hands. May God grant me peace from you all."

He turned to his son:

"What are your plans for the future?"

Realizing that he had survived the worst of the ordeal, Husain replied:

"I hope to find work and I still have my wife's jewelry."

His mother pricked up her ears at the word jewelry and she asked, almost automatically:

"Did you buy it for her?"

"I gave her some, her brother bought her the rest."

Turning towards his father, he went on:

"I'll find work and so will my brother-in-law Abdu. In any case, he will only be staying with us for a few days."

Mrs. Kirsha made use of the lull after the storm to address her husband:

"Come along then and meet your son's family."

She winked secretly at her son and Husain, with all the awkwardness of one who disliked being friendly or conciliatory, asked: "Would you honor me by meeting my family?"

Kirsha hesitated then said indignantly:

"How can you ask me to recognize this marriage to which I didn't give my blessing?"

When he heard no reply, he rose grumbling and his wife opened the door for him. They all moved into the other room, where introductions were made and Kirsha welcomed his son's wife and her brother. Their faces lit up at the welcome and the courtesies exchanged, their hearts concealing what they each really felt.

Kirsha remained apprehensive, not knowing whether his submission would prove wise or foolish. During the conversation his sleepy eyes settled on the bride's brother and he examined him carefully. At once he was overcome by a sudden interest which made him forget his irritation and hostility. He was young, bright and good-looking. Kirsha set about engaging him in conversation, moving as close as possible, his eyes wide with interest. He felt happy indeed and could sense a tremor of delight stirring deep within him. He opened his heart to the new family and bid them welcome, this time with genuine enthusiasm. Kirsha asked his son gently:

"Don't you have any luggage, Husain?"

"Just some bedroom furniture stored with neighbors," he replied.

"Go and get your things then!" Kirsha told him imperiously.

Some time later, when Husain sat talking with his mother and making plans, she suddenly turned to him and exclaimed:

"Do you know what's happened? Hamida has disappeared!"

Astonishment showed in his face as he asked:

"What do you mean?"

Making no attempt to conceal her scorn, Mrs. Kirsha replied:

"She went out as usual in the late afternoon the day before yesterday, and didn't come back again. Her mother went to all the houses in the neighborhood and to all her friends, searching for her, but it was no use. Then she went to the police station at Gamaliyya and to Kasr al-Aini hospital, but there was no trace of her."

"What do you think happened to her?"

His mother shook her head doubtfully but said with conviction:

"She has run away, you can bet your life! Some man has seduced her, taken possession of her senses and run off with her. She was pretty, but she was never any good."

26

amida opened her eyes, red with sleep, and saw a white, a pure white ceiling above her, in the middle of which hung a splendid electric light within a large red ball of transparent crystal. The sight astonished her, but only for a moment and then memories of the past night and of the new life rushed to her mind. She looked at the door and saw it was closed and noticed that the key was still where she had left it, on a table near her bed. As she had wished, she had slept alone while he slept alone in the outer room. Her lips spread in a smile and she threw back the soft coverlets from her body, revealing a nightdress trimmed with silk and velvet. What a deep chasm now separated her from her past life!

The windows were still closed, allowing a little of the sun's glare to penetrate and bathe the room in a soft, subdued light, showing that the morning was well advanced. Hamida was not surprised that she had slept so late, for insomnia had tormented her until just before dawn. She heard a quiet tap on the door and turned towards it in annoyance. Her gaze fixed on the door, she remained motionless and silent. Then she got out of bed and went to the dressing table, standing there in astonishment gazing at the mirrors surrounding it.

The knocking started again, this time more loudly. She shouted: "Who is it?" His deep voice answered: "Good morning. Why don't you open the door?" Looking into a mirror she saw that her hair was untidy, her eyes red and her eyelids heavy. Good heavens! Was there no water to wash her face? Couldn't he wait until she was ready to receive him? Now he was knocking impatiently but she paid no attention. She was recalling how upset she had been that first time in Darasa Street when he appeared unexpectedly and she had neglected to tidy herself properly. Today she was even more anxious and upset. She looked at the bottles of perfume on the dressing table but as this was the first time in her life she had seen them they could not solve her problem. She picked up an ivory comb and hurriedly ran it through her hair. With a corner of her nightdress she wiped her face, glanced again into the mirror and sighed in angry exasperation. Then she picked up the key and went to the door. She was annoyed at being inconvenienced like this and she shook her shoulders indifferently as she opened the door. They met face to face and he smiled pleasantly. He greeted her politely:

"Good morning, Titi! Why have you neglected me all this time? Do you want to spend all day, as well as all night away from me?"

Without saying a word she backed away from him. He followed her, the smile still on his lips. Then he asked:

"Why don't you say something, Titi?"

Titi! Was this some term of affection? Her mother had called her Hamadmad when she had wanted to tease her but what was this Titi business? She stared at him in disbelief and muttered:

"Titi?"

Taking her hands and covering them with kisses, he replied:

"That's your new name. Keep it and forget Hamida, for she has ceased to exist! Names, my darling, are not trivial things, to which we should attach no weight. Names are really everything. What is the world made up of, except names . . ."

She realized that he considered her name, like her old clothes, as something to be discarded and forgotten. Hamida saw nothing wrong in that; it didn't seem right that in Sharif Pasha she should be called what she had been called in Midaq Alley. After all her connections with the past were now cut forever, so why should she retain her name? Now, if only she could exchange her ugly hands for beautiful ones like his and trade her shrill and coarse voice for a nice soft one. But why had he chosen this strange name?

"It's a silly name; it doesn't mean anything."

"It's a beautiful name," he replied, laughing. "Part of its beauty is that it has no meaning and a word without meaning can mean almost anything. As a matter of fact it's an ancient name that will amuse Englishmen and Americans and one which their twisted tongues can easily pronounce."

A look of bewilderment and suspicion came into Hamida's eyes. He smiled and went on:

"My darling Titi . . . relax . . . you'll know everything in good time. Do you realize that tomorrow you will be a lady of dazzling beauty and fame? This house will perform that miracle. Did you think the heavens would rain down gold and diamonds? Oh no; they rain only bombs! Now get ready to meet the dressmaker. Excuse me, I just remembered something important. I must take you to our school. I am a headmaster, my darling, not a pimp as you called me yesterday. Wear this robe and put on these slippers."

He went to the dressing table and returned with a sparkling crystal bottle with a metal rim from which extended a red rubber tube. He pointed it at her and squeezed the bulb, spraying a heady perfume around her face. At first she trembled, then she inhaled deeply and relaxed, startled yet enjoying the sensation. He put the robe gently around her and brought her slippers to put on. Then he led her into the outer hall. They walked together to the first door on the right as he whispered:

"Try not to look shy or nervous. I know you're a brave girl and not afraid of anything."

His warning brought her to her senses; she stared hard at him then gave a shrug of indifference.

"This is the first class in the school," he continued, "the department of Oriental dancing."

He opened the door and they entered. She saw a medium-sized room with a polished wooden floor. It was almost empty except for a number of chairs stacked on the left and a large clothes-stand in one corner. Two girls sat on chairs next to one another and in the middle of the room stood a young man in a billowing white silk gown, with a sash tied around his waist. Their heads turned towards the new arrivals and they all smiled in greeting. Ibrahim Faraj called out in an authoritative tone that showed he was their master:

"Good morning . . . this is my friend Titi."

The two girls nodded their heads and the young man replied in a thin effeminate voice:

"Welcome, mademoiselle."

Titi returned the greeting in some bewilderment, staring hard at the odd young man. His modest, shy expression and crossed eyes made him appear younger than his thirty-odd years. He wore heavy make-up and his curly hair gleamed with Vaseline. Ibrahim Faraj smiled and introduced him to her:

"This is Susu, the dancing instructor."

Susu appeared to want to introduce himself in his own fashion for he winked at the seated girls and they began clapping in unison. The instructor then broke into a dance with astonishing grace and lightness. Every part of his body was in motion, from eyebrows to toes. All the time he gazed straight ahead with a languid expression on his face, smiling wantonly and exposing his gold teeth. Finally he ended his performance with an abrupt quiver. He straightened his back and the two girls stopped clapping. Thus the instructor's special welcome to the new girl was over. He turned to Ibrahim Faraj and asked:

"A new pupil?"

"I think so," he answered as he glanced at Titi.

"Has she ever danced before?"

"No, never."

Susu seemed delighted.

"That's marvellous, Mr. Ibrahim. If she doesn't know how to dance I can mould her as I wish. Girls who are taught the wrong dancing principles are very difficult to teach."

He looked at Titi, then turned his neck right and left and said challengingly:

"Or do you consider dancing just a game, my pet? I'm sorry, darling, but dancing is the art of all arts and those who master it are richly rewarded for their efforts. Look . . ."

He suddenly began making his waist shake with incredible speed. He stopped, then asked her gently:

"Why don't you take off your robe so I can see your body?"

Ibrahim Faraj interrupted him quickly:

"Not now . . . not now."

Susu pouted and asked:

"Are you shy with me, Titi? Why, I'm only your sister, Susu! Didn't you like my dance?"

She fought her embarrassment and tried to appear calm and indifferent.

"Your dance was marvellous, Susu," she said, smiling.

The instructor clapped his hands and executed a brief dance step.

"What a nice girl you are," he exclaimed. "Life's most beautiful thing is a kind word. Does anything else last? One buys a jar of Vaseline and one never knows whether it will be for oneself or for one's heirs!"

They left the room, or rather the "department," and went into the corridor again. He then led her to the next room feeling her eyes staring at him. They reached the door and he whispered, "The department of Western dancing."

Hamida followed him inside. She now knew that retreat was impossible and that the past was completely erased. She was resigned to her fate; nevertheless she wondered where happiness lay.

In size and decoration the room was similar to the previous one, except that it was alive with noise and movement. A phonograph played music that was both strange and unpleasant to her ears. The room was filled with girls dancing together, and a well-dressed young man stood at one side, watching them closely and making comments.

The two men exchanged greetings and the girls continued dancing, eyeing Hamida critically. Her eyes feasted on the room and the dancing girls, and she was dazzled by their beautiful clothes and skilled make-up. Now her feelings of longing and envy were mixed with those of humility. She turned towards Ibrahim Faraj and found him looking sedate and calm. His eyes radiated both superiority and power and his face broadened into a smile as he turned and asked:

"Do you like what you have seen?"

"Very much."

"Which type of dancing do you prefer?"

She smiled, but did not answer. They remained watching in silence and then left and went towards a third door. He had scarcely opened the door before she was staring wide-eyed in embarrassed amazement. In the middle of the room she saw a woman standing naked. Hamida stood frozen, unable to take her eyes off the spectacle. The naked woman stood looking at them calmly and boldly, her mouth parted slightly as though greeting them, or rather him. Then voices suddenly made her realize that there were other people in the room. To the left of the entrance door she saw a row of chairs, half of them occupied by beautiful girls either half-dressed or almost naked. Near the nude woman stood a man in a smart suit holding a pointer, its end resting on the tip of his shoes. Ibrahim Faraj noticed Hamida's confusion and reassuringly volunteered:

"This department teaches the principles of the English language . . . !"

Her look of utter bewilderment prompted him to make a gesture as though asking her to be patient. He then addressed the man holding the pointer:

"Go on with the class, Professor."

In a compliant tone the man announced:

"This is the recitation class."

Slowly he touched the naked woman's hair with the pointer. With a strange accent the woman spoke the word "hair." The pointer touched her forehead and she replied "forehead." He then moved on to her eyebrows, eyes, her mouth and then East and West and up and down. To each of his silent questions the woman uttered a strange word which Hamida had never heard before. Hamida asked herself how this woman could stand naked before all these people and how Ibrahim Faraj could look at her unclothed body with such calm indifference. Her uneasiness made her cheeks burn. She threw a quick glance at him and saw that he was nodding his approval of the intelligent pupil and murmuring: "Bravo ... bravo ..." Suddenly he turned to the instructor:

"Show me a little love-making."

The teacher approached the woman speaking in English, and she replied phrase by phrase in English until Ibrahim Faraj interrupted: "Very good. Very good indeed. And the other girls?"

Gesturing towards the girls sitting on the chairs:

"Oh, they're getting better," he replied. "I keep telling them they can't learn a language just by memorizing words and phrases. The only way to learn is by experience. The taverns and hotels are the best schools and my lessons merely clarify information which may be muddled."

Gazing over at his girls, Faraj agreed:

"You are right, quite right."

He nodded goodbye, took Hamida's arm and they left the room together, walking down the long corridor towards their two rooms. Hamida's jaw was set and her eyes reflected her mind's confusion. She felt an urge to explode, just to relieve her disturbed feelings. He kept silent until they were inside the room and then he spoke softly:

"Well, I'm pleased that you have seen the school and its departments. I suppose you thought the curriculum a rather difficult one? Now you have seen the school's pupils and all of them, without exception, are less intelligent, less beautiful than you."

She shot a stubborn, challenging glance at him and asked coldly: "Do you think I am going to do the same as they?"

He smiled and patted her on the shoulder. Then he spoke:

"No one has power over you and no one wants to force you into anything. You must make up your own mind. However, it is my duty to give you the facts and then the choice is yours. What luck that I found such an intelligent partner whom God has endowed with both determination and beauty. Today I tried to inspire your courage. Tomorrow, perhaps, you will give me inspiration. I know you quite well now. I can read your heart like a sheet of paper. I can say to you now in all confidence that you will agree to learn dancing and English and master everything in the shortest possible time. From the beginning I've been honest with you. I have refrained from lies and deception because I have quite honestly fallen in love with you. When we met, I knew you could never be mastered or deceived. Do what you like, my darling. Try the dancing or decide against it, be brave or not, stay or return. In any case, I have no power over you."

His speech was not without effectiveness for now Hamida felt all her cares gone and her nervous tension subsided. He drew close to her and took her hands between his, pressing them gently.

"You are the most marvellous piece of good fortune life has ever brought me . . . how fascinating you are . . . how beautiful . . ."

He stared piercingly into her eyes and raised her hands—still clenched together—to his mouth and kissed the tips of her fingers, two by two. Each time his lips touched her, she felt as if an electric shock had pierced her nerves. She released a long breath in a kind of passionate sigh. He put his arms around her and drew her slowly to him until he could feel her young full breasts almost digging into his chest. He stroked her back gently, his hands moving up and down while her face remained buried in his chest.

Eventually he whispered: "Your mouth," and she slowly lifted her head, her lips already parted. He pressed his lips to hers in a long hard kiss and her eyelids drooped as if she were overcome by sleep. Picking her up like a child, he carried her towards the bed, the slippers falling from her dangling feet. He put her down gently and bent over her, resting on his palms, gazing hard at her flushed face. Her eyes opened and met his as he smiled down gently at her. Her gaze remained steady and seductive. However, he was in full possession of himself; indeed his mind always moved faster than his emotions. He had decided on a particular course of action and he was not to be diverted from it. He got to his feet, restrained a sly smile and said:

"Gently, gently. American officers will gladly pay fifty pounds for virgins!"

She turned to him in astonishment, the languid look having quite disappeared from her eyes. A look of shock and harsh determination replaced it. She sat upright on the bed, then sprang to the floor with amazing speed and made for him like an enraged tigress. Now all her vicious instincts were roused as she slapped his face with such force that the blow crackled through the room. He stood motionless for some seconds and then the left side of his mouth formed a sardonic smile. With lightning speed he struck her right cheek as hard as he could. Then he slapped her left cheek just as violently. Her face went white and her lips trembled, her whole body quivering and out of control. She threw herself onto his chest, digging her clawed fingers into his neck. He made no attempt to defend himself. Instead, his full embrace almost crushed her. Her fingers gradually lost their hold and slipped from his neck, feeling for his shoulders. She clung to him, her head raised towards his face, her mouth open and trembling with passion . . .

27

he alley lay shrouded in darkness and silence. Even Kirsha's coffeehouse had closed and the customers gone their separate ways. At this late hour Zaita, the cripple-maker, slipped through the door of the bakery, making his rounds. He went down the alley to Sanadiqiyya and turned in the direction of the mosque of Husain, almost colliding with another figure coming towards him in the middle of the road. The man's face was barely visible in the dim starlight. Zaita called out:

"Dr. Bushi! . . . Where did you come from?"

Panting slightly, the "Doctor" replied quickly:

"I was coming to see you."

"You have some customers who want to be disfigured?"

In a near whisper, Bushi answered:

"It's more important than that. Abdul Hamid Talibi is dead!"

Zaita's eyes shone in the dark:

"When did he die? Has he been buried?"

"He was buried this evening."

"Do you know where his grave is?"

"Between Nasr Gate and the mountain road."

Zaita took him by the arm and walked with him in the direction he was going. To make sure of the situation he asked:

"Won't you lose your way in the dark?"

"Oh no I followed the burial procession and took particular note of the way. In any case, we both know the road well, we've often been on it in pitch-dark."

"And your tools?"

"They're in a safe place in front of the mosque."

"Is the tomb open or roofed?"

"At the entrance there is a room with a roof, but the grave itself is in an open courtyard."

In a faintly sarcastic tone, Zaita asked:

"Did you know the deceased?"

"Only slightly. He was a flour merchant in Mabida."

"Is it a full set or just a few?"

"A full set."

"Aren't you afraid his family might have taken it from his mouth before he was buried?"

"Oh no. They are country people and very pious. They would never do that."

Shaking his head sadly, Zaita commented:

"The days are over when people left the jewelry of their dead in the grave."

"Those were the days!" sighed Dr. Bushi.

They walked in darkness and silence as far as Gamaliyya, passing two policemen on the way, and then drew near Nasr Gate. Zaita took a half cigarette from his pocket. Dr. Bushi was horrified by the lighted match and reminded his companion:

"You couldn't have chosen a worse time to have a smoke."

Zaita paid no attention. He walked along, muttering as though to himself:

"There's no profit in the living and very few of the dead are any good!"

They walked through Nasr and turned along a narrow path lined on both sides with tombs, enshrouded in awesome silence and heavy gloom. After they had gone a third of the way down the path Zaita said: "Here's the mosque." Bushi looked about carefully, listening a moment or two, and then moved off towards the mosque, taking care not to make a sound. He examined the ground near a wall at the entrance, until he came across a large stone. From under the stone he lifted a small spade and a package containing a candle. He then rejoined his companion and they continued on their way. Suddenly he whispered: "The tomb is the fifth one before the desert path." They hurried on, Dr. Bushi gazing over at the graves to the left of the path, his heart pounding wildly. Presently he slowed down and whispered: "This is the tomb." Instead of stopping, however, Bushi hurried his friend along while giving instructions in a low monotone.

"The walls of the burial place overlooking this path are high and the path isn't safe. The best thing for us to do is to skirt through the graves from the desert side, and then climb over the back wall of the tomb to where the grave is in the open courtyard."

Zaita listened carefully and they walked in silence until they reached the desert path. Zaita suggested they rest on the roadside curb from where they could see the path. They sat side by side, their eyes searching the terrain. The darkness and desertion were complete. Behind them as far as the eye could see graves were scattered over the ground and although this adventure was not their first, Dr. Bushi's nerves and pounding heart were weighted with fear. Zaita remained quite calm. When he was sure the path was clear, he instructed the doctor:

"Leave the tools, go to the back and wait for me there."

Bushi rose quickly and crept between the graves, toward the wall. He kept close to it, feeling his way carefully along in the darkness that was broken only by starlight. He counted the walls until he reached the fifth. He stood still, looking about him like a thief; then he sat down cross-legged. His eyes could detect nothing suspicious nor did he hear a sound. However, his uneasiness increased and he grew more and more anxious. Soon he saw Zaita's shape appear a few arms' lengths away and he rose cautiously. Zaita eyed the wall for a moment and then whispered:

"Bend down so that I can get on your back."

Putting his hands on his knees, Bushi did as he was told and Zaita climbed on his back. He felt the wall, gripped the top and sprang up lightly and easily. He dropped the spade and the candle into the courtyard, extended his hand to Bushi and helped pull him to the top of the wall. Together they jumped down and stood at the base gasping for breath. Zaita picked up the spade and the package. Their eyes were now accustomed to the dark and they could see fairly well by the faint light from the stars. They could even see the courtyard quite clearly. There, not far from them, were two tombs, side by side, and on the other side of the courtyard they could see the door leading out to the road along which they had come. On each side of the door was a room and Zaita, pointing towards the two sepulchers, asked:

"Which one?"

"On your right . . ." whispered Bushi, his voice so low that the sound scarcely left his throat.

Without hesitating, Zaita went to the sepulcher, followed by Bushi, whose whole body was trembling. Zaita bent down and found the ground still cold and damp. He dug his spade carefully and gently into the earth and set to work, piling up the soil between his feet. This was not new to him and he worked briskly until he had uncovered the flagstones that formed a roof over the entrance to the vault of the sepulcher. He drew up the hem of his gown, gave it a good twist and tied it up round his waist. Then he grasped the edge of the first flagstone and pulled it up, straining with his muscles until it stood on edge. With Bushi's help, he drew it out and laid it on the ground. He then did the same with the second flagstone. The uncovered hole was now sufficient for the two of them to slip through and he started down the steps, muttering to the doctor:

"Follow me!"

Numb and shivering with fright, Dr. Bushi obeyed. On such occasions Bushi would sit on the middle step and light a candle which he placed on the bottom step. He would then close his eyes tight and bury his face between his knees. He hated going into tombs and he had often pleaded with Zaita to spare him the ordeal. However, his colleague always refused him and insisted he participate in each separate stage. He seemed to enjoy torturing Bushi in this way.

The wick of the candle was burning now, lighting the interior. Zaita stared stonily at the corpses laid out in their shrouds side by side throughout the length and breadth of the vault, their order symbolizing the sequence of history, the constant succession of time. The fearful silence of the place spoke loudly of eternal extinction, but brought no echo from Zaita. His gaze soon fixed on the new shroud near the entrance to the vault and he sat down beside it, cross-legged. He then stretched out his two cold hands, uncovered the head of the corpse and laid bare its lips. He drew out the teeth and put them in his pocket. Then he covered the head as he had found it and moved away from the corpse towards the entrance.

Dr. Bushi still sat with his head between his knees, the candle burning on the bottom step. Zaita looked at him scornfully and mumbled in sarcasm: "Wake up!" Bushi raised his trembling head and blew out the candle. He raced up the steps as though in retreat. Zaita followed him quickly but upon emerging from the vault he heard a fearsome scream and the doctor yelping like a kicked dog: "For God's sake have mercy!" Zaita stopped short and then rushed down the steps, icy with fear and not knowing what to do. He retreated backwards into the vault until his heel touched the corpse. He moved forward a step and stood glued to the floor, not knowing where to escape. He thought of lying down between the corpses but before he could make a move he was enveloped in a dazzling light that blinded him. A loud voice shouted out in an Upper Egyptian accent: "Up you come, or I'll fire on you."

In despair, he climbed the steps as ordered. He had completely forgotten the set of gold teeth in his pocket.

The news that Dr. Bushi and Zaita had been apprehended in the Talibi sepulcher reached the alley the next evening. Soon the story and all its details spread, and everyone heard it with a mixture of amazement and alarm. When Mrs. Saniya Afifi heard the news she was overcome with hysteria. Wailing in distress, she pulled the gold teeth from her mouth and flung them away, slapping hysterically at both cheeks. Then she fell down in a faint. Her new husband was in the bathtub and when he heard her screams, panic struck him. Throwing a robe over his wet body, he rushed wildly to her rescue.

28

ncle Kamil was sitting in his chair on the threshold of his shop, lost in a dream, his head resting on his chest. The fly-whisk lay in his lap. He was awakened by a tickling sensation on his bald head and he lifted his hand to brush off what he thought was a fly. His fingers touched a human hand. Angrily he seized it and groaned audibly, lifting his head to seek the prankster who had wakened him from his pleasant slumber. His gaze fell upon Abbas the barber and he could scarcely believe his eyes. He stared in blind confusion. Then his bloated red face beamed in delight and he made as if to get up. His young friend protested at this gesture and hugged him tightly, shouting emotionally:

"How are you, Uncle Kamil?"

"How are you Abbas?" the man replied in delight. "Welcome indeed. You made me very lonely by going away, you bastard!"

Abbas stood before him smiling while Uncle Kamil gazed at him tenderly. He was dressed in a smart white shirt and grey trousers. His head was bare and his curly hair gave him a decidedly appealing look. All in all he seemed extremely fit. Uncle Kamil looked him up and down admiringly and said in his high-pitched voice:

"My, my! Oh Johnny, you do look good!"

Abbas, obviously in the best of spirits, laughed heartily and replied:

"THANK YOU . . . from today on Sheikh Darwish is not the only one who can chatter away in English!"

The young man's eyes roved up and down his beloved alley and rested on his old shop. He could see its new owner shaving a customer and he stared longingly in greeting. Then his gaze lifted to the window. He found it closed just as it was when he had arrived. Abbas wondered whether she was home or not, and what she would do if she opened the shutter and saw him there. She would stare at him in delighted surprise while his eyes feasted on her dazzling beauty. This was going to be the happiest day of his life . . .

His attention was once again drawn to Uncle Kamil's voice asking:

"Have you quit your job?"

"Oh no, I've just taken a short holiday."

"Have you heard what happened to your friend Husain Kirsha? He left his father and got married. Then they sacked him and he came back home, dragging his wife and her brother along behind him."

Abbas looked sad.

"What rotten luck! They're sacking a lot of people these days. How did Mr. Kirsha welcome him home?"

"Oh, he's never stopped complaining. Anyway, the young man and his family are still in the house."

He sat quietly for perhaps half a minute and then, as though he had just remembered something important, said:

"Have you heard that Dr. Bushi and Zaita are in prison?"

Then he related how they had been captured in the Talibi sepulcher and been convicted of stealing a set of gold teeth. This news staggered Abbas. He would not have put it past Zaita to commit the most dreadful evil, but he was amazed that Dr. Bushi was a participant in this ghoulish crime. He recalled how Bushi had wanted to fit him with gold teeth when he returned from Tell al-Kabir. He shuddered in disgust.

Uncle Kamil continued:

"Mrs. Saniya Afifi has got married . . ."

He almost added: "Let's hope you do the same." But he stopped suddenly, recalling Hamida. In days to come he was often amazed at his frequent lapses of memory. However, Abbas noticed no change in Uncle Kamil as he was quite lost in his dreams. He stepped back a couple of paces and said:

"Well then, goodbye for now."

His friend was afraid the news might shock him terribly if it came too suddenly and he asked hurriedly:

"Where are you going?"

"To the coffee-house to see my friends," replied Abbas, moving along.

Uncle Kamil rose with some difficulty and shuffled off after his friend.

It was late in the afternoon and Kirsha and Sheikh Darwish were the only ones in the café. Abbas greeted Kirsha, who welcomed him, and he shook hands with Sheikh Darwish. The old man stared at him smilingly from behind his spectacles but did not speak. Uncle Kamil stood to one side, gloomily obsessed with thoughts about how he could broach the painful news. At last he spoke:

"How about coming back with me to the shop for a while?"

Abbas hesitated between accompanying his friend and making the visit he had dreamed of these past few months. However, he wanted to please Uncle Kamil and he saw no harm in staying with him. He accompanied him, hiding his impatience with small talk.

They sat down and Abbas talked cheerfully:

"You know, life in Tell al-Kabir is perfect. There's plenty of work and plenty of money. I haven't been flinging my money about, either. I've been quite content to live as I always have. Why, I've only smoked hashish occasionally, even though out there it's as common as air and water. By the way Uncle Kamil, I even bought this; look at it."

He drew a small box from his trouser pocket and opened it. Inside was a gold necklace with a small dangling heart. "It's Hamida's wedding present. Didn't you know? I want to get married while I'm on leave this time."

He expected his friend to comment, but Uncle Kamil only turned his eyes away and settled into a heavy silence. Abbas looked at him in alarm and for the first time noticed his friend's gloominess and worried expression. Uncle Kamil's face was not the kind that could camouflage his emotions. Abbas was alarmed now. He frowned, shut the box and returned it to his pocket. He sat staring at his friend, his happy mood extinguished by a strange emotion which he neither expected nor could account for. The gloomy look on his friend's face was so obvious now that he asked suspiciously:

"What's wrong, Uncle Kamil? You're not yourself. What's made you change like this? Why won't you look at me?"

The older man raised his head slowly and gazed sadly at him. He opened his mouth to speak but no words came. Abbas sensed disaster. He felt despair smothering the last traces of his high spirits and suffocating all his hopes. Now he shouted:

"What's wrong with you, Uncle Kamil? What are you trying to say? Something's on your mind. Don't torture me with your silence. Is it Hamida? Yes, by God, it's Hamida. Say it. Tell me. Tell me!"

Uncle Kamil moistened his lips and spoke almost in a whisper: "She's gone. She's not here any more. She's disappeared. No one knows what's happened to her."

Abbas listened to him in stunned silence. One by one the words engraved themselves on his brain. Thick clouds seemed to swirl over his mind and he seemed suddenly to have been transported into a whirling feverish world. In a quivering voice, he asked:

"I don't understand anything. What did you say? She's not here any more, she's disappeared? What do you mean?"

"Be brave, Abbas," Uncle Kamil said soothingly, "God knows how sorry I am and how grieved I was for you from the very first, but nothing can be done about it. Hamida has disappeared. No one knows anything. She didn't return after going out as usual, one afternoon. They searched everywhere for her, but without success. We tried the police station at Gamaliyya and Kasr al-Aini hospital, but we found no trace of her."

Abbas' face took on a vacant stare and he sat rigidly, not saying a word nor moving, not even blinking. There was no way out, no escape. Hadn't his instincts warned him of disaster? Yes, and now it was true. Could this be believed? What had the man said? Hamida had disappeared . . . Can a human being disappear, like a needle or a coin? If he had said she was dead or had got married then he could foresee an end to his agony. At any rate, despair is easier to accept than torturing doubt. Now what should he do? Even despair was a blessing he could not hope for. Suddenly inertia subsided and he felt a sudden surge of anger. Trembling all over, he glared at Uncle Kamil, and shrieked:

"So Hamida has disappeared, has she? And what did all of you do about it? You told the police and looked in the hospital? May God reward you for that.

"Then what? Then you all returned to work as if nothing had happened. Everything came to an end and you simply returned to your shop and her mother went knocking on brides' doors. Hamida's finished and I'm finished too. What do you say to that, eh? Tell me all you know. What do you know about her disappearance? How did she disappear and when?"

Uncle Kamil was visibly distressed by his friend's outburst of hostility and he replied sorrowfully:

"Nearly two months have passed since she disappeared, my son. It was a terrible thing and everyone was deeply shocked by it. God knows we spared no efforts in searching and inquiring after her, but it was no use."

Abbas slapped the palms of his hands together, his face flushed and his eyes bulging even more. Almost to himself he commented:

"Nearly two months! My God! that's a long time. There's no hope of finding her now. Is she dead? Did she drown? Was she abducted? Who can help me find out? What are people saying?"

Gazing at him with sad affection, Uncle Kamil replied:

"There were many theories and people finally concluded she must have had an accident. Nobody talks about it any more."

"Of course. Of course," the young man exclaimed angrily, "she's not the daughter of any of you and she has no close relatives. Even her mother isn't her real one. What do you think happened? In the past two months I've been dreaming away, happy as could be. Have you ever noticed how a man often dreams of happiness while disaster waits nearby to snatch it? Perhaps I was just having a quiet conversation with a friend, while she was being crushed under a wheel or drowning in the Nile . . . Two months! Oh, Hamida! . . . There is no power nor strength except in God."

Stamping his foot, he rose and made for the door: "Goodbye."

"Where are you going?"

"To see her mother," Abbas answered coldly.

Walking out with heavy dragging feet, Abbas recalled that he had arrived tingling with anticipation and joy; now he left crushed and broken. He bit his lips and his feet came to a halt. He turned and saw Uncle Kamil gazing after him, his eyes filled with tears. Suddenly Abbas rushed into the shop and threw himself on the older man's chest. They stood there whimpering, weeping and sobbing, like two small children.

Did he really have no suspicion of the truth of her disappearance? Did he experience none of the doubts and suspicions common to lovers in similar circumstances? The truth was that whenever a shadow of suspicion had crossed his mind he dismissed it immediately, refusing to harbour it an instant. By nature Abbas was trusting and always tended to think the best of people. He was tender-hearted and belonged to that minority who instinctively make excuses for others and accept the feeblest excuses for the most frightful deeds. Love had not changed his good nature except, perhaps, to make it even stronger; consequently the whisperings of doubt and suspicion within him went unheard. He had loved Hamida deeply and he felt completely secure and confident in this love. He truly believed this girl was perfection, in a world of which he had seen so little.

That same day he visited her mother but she told him nothing new, merely repeating tearfully what Uncle Kamil had said. She assured him that Hamida had never stopped thinking about him, anxiously waiting for his return. Her lies only made him feel sadder and he left her as heartbroken as he had arrived.

His leaden feet slowly led him out of the alley. Dusk was falling now; it was the time when, in days gone by, he would catch sight of his beloved going out for her evening stroll. He wondered aimlessly, unaware of what was going on about him, but seeming to see her form in its black gown, her large and beautiful eyes searching for him. He recalled their last farewell on the stairs and his heart seemed to stop dead.

Where was she? What had God done with her? Was she still alive or in a pauper's grave? Why had his heart had no warning all this time? How could this happen? And why?

The crowds in the street jolted him from his dreams and he stared around him. This was the Mouski, her favorite street. She loved the crowds and the shops. Everything was just the same as before, except for her. Now she was gone. It was almost as if she had never existed. He wanted to cry out all the tears in his swollen heart but he would not give way. His weeping in Uncle Kamil's arms had unknotted his nerves a bit. Now he only felt a deep, quiet sadness.

He wondered what he should do next. Should he go to the police stations and the hospital? What was the point? Should he walk the streets of the city calling out her name? Should he knock on the doors of all the houses one by one? Oh God, how weak and helpless he felt. Should he return to Tell al-Kabir and try to forget everything? But why go back? Why bear the additional strain of being away from home? Why go on working and saving money? Life without Hamida was an insupportable burden and completely without purpose. His enthusiasm for life was gone now, leaving him with nothing but a numbing indifference. His life seemed a bottomless void enclosed by a black despair. Through his love for her he had discovered the only meaning of his life. Now he saw no reason for living. He continued walking, bewildered and purposeless. Whether he knew it or not, life still had a hold on his consciousness, for he was quick to notice the factory girls coming towards him, returning from work. Before he knew it he had blocked their path. They stopped in surprise and immediately recognized him. Without hesitating, he spoke:

"Good evening, girls. Please don't be angry with me. You remember your friend Hamida?"

A vivacious pretty girl was quick to reply:

"Of course we remember her. She suddenly disappeared and we haven't seen her since!"

"Do you have any clues to her disappearance?" A different girl, with a look of spiteful cunning in her eyes answered him:

"We only know what we told her mother when she questioned us. We saw her several times with a well-dressed man in a suit, walking in the Mouski."

An icy shudder shook his whole body, as he asked:

"You say you saw her with a man in a suit?"

The cruel look now left the girl's eyes as they registered the young man's anguish. One girl spoke softly:

"Yes, that's right."

"And you told her mother that?"

"Yes."

He thanked them and walked away. He was certain they would talk about him all the way home. They would have a good laugh about the young fool who went to Tell al-Kabir to earn more money for his fiancée, who left him for a stranger who appealed to her more. What a fool he had been! Probably the whole quarter was gossiping about his stupidity. Now he knew that Uncle Kamil concealed the raw truth, just as Hamida's foster mother had done. In a state of complete confusion he told himself: "I was afraid this might happen!" Now, all he could remember were those very faint doubts.

Now he was moaning and muttering: "Oh God! How can I believe it? Has she really run off with another man? Who would ever believe it?" She was alive, then. They were wrong to look for her in the police stations and the hospital. They had not realized she was sleeping contentedly in the arms of the man she had run off with. But she had promised herself to him! Had she meant to deceive him all along? Or was she mistaken in thinking she was attracted to him . . . How did she meet the man in the suit? When did she fall in love with him? Why did she run off with him?

Abbas' face had now turned ghastly white and he felt cold all over. His eyes glowered darkly. Suddenly he raised his head, gazing at the houses in the street. He looked at their windows and asked himself: "In which one is she now lying at her lover's side?" The seeds of doubt were now gone and a burning anger mixed with hatred took its place. His heart was twisted by jealousy. Or was it disappointment? Conceit and pride are the fuel of jealousy and he had little of either. But he did have hopes and dreams and now they were shattered. Now he wanted revenge, even if it only meant spitting at her. In fact, revenge took such possession of him that he longed to knife her treacherous heart.

Now he knew the true meaning of her afternoon walks: she had been parading before the street wolves. Anyway, she must be in love with this man in the suit, otherwise how could she prostitute herself, rather than marry Abbas?

He bit his lip at the thought and turned back, tired from walking alone. His hand touched the box with the chain in his pocket, and he gave a hollow laugh that was more an angry scream. If only he could strangle her with the gold chain. He recalled his joy in the goldsmith's shop when he selected the gift. The memory flowed through him like a gentle spring breeze but, meeting the glare of his troubled heart it was transformed into a raging sirocco . . .

29

Salim Alwan had scarcely finished signing the contract on his desk, before the man sitting opposite him grasped his hand and said:

"Well done, indeed, Salim Bey. This is a great deal of money."

Salim sat watching the man as he passed through the office door. A profitable deal, indeed. He had sold his entire tea stock to this man. He made a good profit and lost a burdensome worry; especially since his health could no longer bear the strains of the black market. Despite all this, he still told himself angrily: "A great deal of money, yes, but with a curse on it. There seems to be a curse on everything in my life." It was true what people said, that only a faint shadow of the old Salim Alwan remained.

His nerves were slowly devouring him and he was forever thinking about death. In the old days he neither lacked faith nor was he a coward, but now his frayed nerves made him forget the comforts of faith. He still remembered how in his illness he had lain there in pain, his chest rising and falling with that lung pain, his eyes failing fast. At such times life seemed to flow out from every part of him and his spirit seemed to have parted from his body. Could this really have happened? Isn't it true a man goes mad if his fingernails are pulled out? What happens then, when his life and spirit are extracted?

He often wished God would give him the good fortune of those who die of a heart attack. They simply expire in the midst of talking, eating, standing, or sitting. It was as if they outwitted death completely by slipping off stealthily. Salim Alwan abandoned hope of this good fortune, for indeed his father and grandfather had both demonstrated to him the sort of death he might expect. He would probably linger in great agony on the point of death for half a day and this no doubt would turn his sons grey.

Who would ever believe that Salim Alwan—healthy and life-loving—would ever harbor such fears? But not only dying terrified him, for now his feverish attention was also drawn to death itself. He spent a good deal of time analysing all aspects of it.

His imagination and the culture from ages past told him that some of his senses remained after death. Didn't people say that the eyes of a dead person could still see his family staring down at him? After all he had seen death as clear as daylight before him and he had almost felt eternity enclose him. Indeed, he felt he was already in the darkness of the tomb, with all its eerie loneliness, with bones, shrouds, and its suffocating narrowness and the painful love and longing he would probably feel for the living world. He thought about all this, his heart contracting in painful melancholy, his hands and feet icy and his brow feverish. Neither did he forget the afterlife. The assessment of his life, the retribution . . . Oh God, what a vast chasm there was between death and paradise . . .

So it was he clung to the fringe of life, even though it gave him no pleasure. All that was left for him was to audit the accounts and make business deals.

After his convalescence he had made a point of having a serious consultation with his doctor. He assured Alwan that he was cured of his heart condition but advised him to take care and to live cautiously. Salim Alwan complained about his insomnia and tensions and the doctor advised a nerve specialist. Now he consulted a procession of

specialists in nerves, heart, chest and head. Thus his illness opened a
door to a world populated by germs, symptoms and diagnoses. It was
amazing for he had never believed in medicine or doctors. Now in his
troubled state his faith in them was entire.

His working and leisure hours were now almost completely sub-
merged in his private hell of anxieties. Indeed, he was always either in
a state of war with himself or with people. His employees saw the
transformation before their astonished eyes. His manager left after
twenty-five years of service and those few employees who remained
were disgruntled. The alley people thought he was half crazy and
Husniya once commented: "It was the bowl of green wheat that did
it." One day Uncle Kamil said, trying to humor him:

"Why don't you let me make you a special dish of sweets which,
with God's grace, will restore your health?"

But Salim Alwan became angry and exploded:

"Keep away from me, you devil! Have you gone mad, you blind
fool? It's animals like you whose insides stay healthy until the day of
rest."

After this, Uncle Kamil had nothing more to do with him.

As for his wife, she was an easy target for his outbursts and hatred
and he still attributed his ill health to her jealousy. One time he
rebuked her by shouting:

"You've had your vicious revenge on my health. You've seen me
crushed before your eyes. Now enjoy your peace, you viper."

His hostility towards her increased and eventually he wondered if
she had suspected his plans to marry Hamida. He knew there were
many eyes watching for this sort of thing, and no shortage of ready
tongues to tell the interested party. If she did suspect something,
wasn't it possible that she had put a curse on him that ruined his
health? His irrational state only convinced him that he was right. He
planned a course of revenge on her. Thus he was rude to her, and
reviled and insulted her as often as possible. However, she met all his
cruelty with polite and patient submissiveness. He yearned to reduce
her long-suffering silence to tears. On one occasion he told her
directly:

"I'm tired of living with you, and there's no reason why I should hide the fact that I'm planning to get married. I'm going to try my luck once more."

She believed him and her self-control was shattered. She fled to her children and told them of their father's decision. They were amazed and ashamed, and one day they visited him and suggested that, for his health's sake, he liquidate his business and devote his time to regaining his health. He was aware of what they feared and he rebuked them more sharply and bitterly than he had ever done before:

"My life is my own to spend as I wish. I'll work as long as I please. Please spare me your selfish opinions."

Then he laughed and went on, his lackluster eyes staring into their faces, one after the other:

"Did your mother tell you I plan to marry again? It's true. Your mother is trying to kill me and so I'm leaving her for a new woman who will show me a little mercy. If your number should be increased by my new marriage it won't matter because my fortune is large enough to satisfy all your desires."

Then he warned them he would have nothing more to do with them and that each must rely on his own resources as long as their father lived.

"As you can see, I can scarcely taste even the bitter medicines so why should others enjoy my wealth."

His older son asked:

"How can you speak to us like this? We are your devoted sons."

"From now on you're your mother's sons!"

He kept to his threat. From that time on he gave nothing to his sons and deprived his house of the luxurious fare for which it was known. He did this so that everyone, especially his wife, would share in the restrictions imposed upon him. Alwan also constantly referred to his proposed marriage. He found this a most effective weapon for weakening his wife's patience. His sons all felt a genuine sadness for their father's condition; when they met to discuss the matter, the eldest one spoke first:

"We must abide by his wishes until God works His inevitable will."

"Unless he seriously intends to get married," replied his lawyer son, "then most severe steps must be taken. We cannot leave him to be neglected by someone only interested in his money."

Hamida's disappearance had been a shattering blow to Salim Alwan. Although he had thought about her occasionally after his illness, she had not really been in the mainstream of his thoughts until she disappeared. This news, however, had roused his anxiety and he had followed with great concern all efforts to trace her. When the gossip reached him about her having run off with an unknown man, he was extremely upset. That very day he was in such a temper that no one dared go near him. In the evening he came home with shredded nerves and a pounding headache that kept him awake until dawn. His heart burst with resentment and revenge towards the fickle girl. He pictured her dangling from a scaffold, her tongue hanging out and her eyes bulging. When he heard of Abbas' return from Tell al-Kabir, his frenzy subsided for some obscure reason and he invited the young man to see him.

He seated Abbas close to him and chatted amiably, asking about his living conditions and avoiding any mention of the girl. Abbas was pleased with the man's kindness and thanked him profusely. Trusting in Alwan's sympathy completely Abbas told him everything, while the businessman gazed at him hollow-eyed.

Soon after Hamida's disappearance something happened which, although probably trivial, is still remembered in the annals of Midaq Alley.

Early one morning Salim Alwan was on his way to his office, when he met Sheikh Darwish going in the opposite direction. In the old days, Alwan had been very fond of Sheikh Darwish and had often demonstrated this by gifts. After his illness, however, Alwan had completely ignored the old man. When they met near the office, Sheikh Darwish shouted out, as though to himself:

"Hamida has disappeared."

This took Alwan by surprise and he assumed Sheikh Darwish was addressing him.

"What's that got to do with me?"

"And she didn't just disappear," Sheikh Darwish continued, "she ran away. And she didn't just run away; she ran away with a strange man. In English they call that an 'ELOPEMENT' and it's spelled E-L-O-P . . ."

Before he could finish Salim Alwan exploded:

"It's a cursed day for me when I see your face in the morning, you idiot! Get out of my sight, a curse of God on you!"

Sheikh Darwish stood as though bolted to the ground and then a look like that of a terrified child came into his eyes. He burst out weeping. Mr. Alwan continued on his way, leaving Sheikh Darwish standing alone. His voice now rose to a near-scream until it reached Kirsha, Uncle Kamil and the old barber; they all rushed up to him, asking what was wrong. They led him off to the coffee-house and sat him down in his armchair, doing their best to calm him. Kirsha ordered a glass of water and Uncle Kamil patted him on the shoulder, saying sympathetically:

"Put your faith in God, Sheikh Darwish. Oh God, keep us from evil. For you to weep is an omen of some misfortune to come . . . Oh God, give us grace!"

However, Sheikh Darwish kept on weeping and howling, his breath gasping and his limbs trembling. Then he shut his lips rigidly, pulled at his necktie and stamped the ground with his wooden clogs. The windows of the houses were opening now and heads stared down at the scene. Husniya was the first to appear in front of the shop. Eventually the wailing reached Salim Alwan in his office. He wished the old man would stop his wailing. In vain he tried to turn his attention to something else, but it seemed to Alwan that the whole world was weeping and wailing. If only he had not shouted at the saintly old man! If only he hadn't crossed his path! He could have taken no notice of him and just passed politely on.

Alwan groaned in self-reproach: "A person as sick as you would be better off making peace with God, instead of angering one of His holy men." He abandoned his pride and made his way to Kirsha's coffee-house. Taking no notice of the surprised looks, he approached the weeping old man and placed his hand gently on his shoulder:

"Forgive me, please, Sheikh Darwish."

30

bbas was hiding in Uncle Kamil's flat when there was a loud knock on the door. He opened it and found Husain Kirsha standing there, dressed in a shirt and trousers, his small eyes glinting as usual. Husain rushed at him in a frenzied greeting.

"Why haven't you come to see me? This is your second day back in the alley! How are you?"

Abbas held out his hand and smiled.

"How are you, Husain? Please don't be annoyed with me, I'm very tired. I didn't forget you and I was not trying to avoid you. Let's go out and have a chat."

They walked off together. Abbas had spent a sleepless night and a thoughtful morning. His head ached and his eyelids felt heavy. Scarcely a trace of the previous day's bitter mood remained and he now bore no thoughts of revenge. Instead, a deep sorrow and black despair had settled on him. Husain spoke:

"Did you know I left home soon after you went away?"

"Really?"

"Yes, I got married and started living a life of luxury and ease."

Forcing himself to express more interest than he felt, Abbas answered:

"Praise be to God . . . well done . . . splendid . . . splendid."

They had now walked as far as Ghouriyya and Husain stamped the ground with his foot and said resentfully:

"On the contrary, everything in life is filth and corruption! They laid me off. There was nothing to do but return to Midaq Alley. Have they fired you too?"

"No. I was given a short holiday," replied Abbas listlessly.

Husain tried to keep the jealous note from showing in his voice:

"I persuaded you to go away to work, and you resisted the idea. Remember? And there you are enjoying it while I'm out of a job."

Abbas was probably more aware than anyone else of his friend's jealous and spiteful nature. He replied:

"Things are ending for us too, so they tell us."

This cheered Husain a bit and he asked:

"How can the war end so quickly? Who would have believed it possible?"

Abbas shook his head. It made no difference to him whether the war continued or ended and whether he worked or not. He no longer cared about anything. It bored him to talk with his friend although he found it better than sitting alone thinking.

"How can it have ended so quickly?" asked Husain. "Everybody hoped Hitler would be able to prolong it indefinitely. It's our bad luck that's brought it to an end."

"You're right . . ."

Husain shouted furiously:

"What hopeless wretches we are. Our country is pitiful and so are the people. Why is it that the only time we find a little happiness is when the world is involved in a bloody war? Surely it's only the devil who has pity on us in this world!"

He stopped speaking as they made their way through the crowds coming from New Street. It was getting dark now.

"How I longed to be in combat," sighed Husain. "Just imagine what it would be like to be a heroic soldier, plunging from one glorious victory to the next. Imagine being in airplanes and tanks attacking and killing and then capturing the fleeing women; not to mention spending money, getting drunk and raising the devil. That's the life! Don't you wish you were a soldier?"

Everyone in the alley knew that Abbas was thrown into panic at the sound of a siren and he practically lived in the air-raid shelters. Be a combat soldier? He wished he had been born brave; he would have loved the life of a soldier, avenging himself on all those who had hurt him and spoiled his dream of happiness and a luxurious life. So he replied weakly, "Who wouldn't like that?"

He turned his attention to the street and this brought tormenting thoughts to his mind. Oh God, would time ever erase memories of the alley from his heart? Here was where she walked; here was where she breathed this very air. He could almost see her straight slim figure walking before him now. How could he ever forget? He frowned at the thoughts of longing for someone so unworthy of his love. His face set in a look of vicious cruelty as a blast of the previous day's feeling of betrayal returned to him. He would forget her. Otherwise his heart would burn itself out with fantasies of her resting blissfully in his rival's arms. He cursed his soft treacherous heart. It had plotted against both his spirit and his body in loving someone who loved neither of these. Now it yielded him only suffering and humiliation.

He was awakened from his reverie by the harsh voice of Husain: "Here's the Jewish quarter."

He brought Abbas to a stop with his hand and asked:

"Don't you know Vita's Bar? Didn't you ever get a liking for drink up there at Tell al-Kabir?"

"No I didn't."

"How on earth did you live among the British and not drink? What a fool you are. Alcohol refreshes and is good for the brain. Come on . . ."

He tucked Abbas' arm under his and led him into the Jewish quarter. Vita's Bar was not far from the entrance to the left and it looked more like a shop. It was square and medium in size with a long marble-topped table stretching the length of one side, behind which stood Mr. Vita. On the wall behind the bar was a long shelf lined with bottles. Near the entrance door stood a large barrel. On the bar stood two bowls of nuts and some glasses belonging to the customers who were standing drinking. They appeared to be cabdrivers and laborers, some barefooted and half-dressed, more like beggars. The rest of the tavern consisted of an area with a few scattered wooden benches. On these sat some market loafers along with those unable to stand, either because of their age or intoxication.

Husain led his friend to an empty table at the back of the tavern where they sat down. Abbas swung his eyes around the noisy, boisterous place in silent uneasiness, until they rested on a boy of about fourteen. He was short and excessively fat; his face and cloak were covered with mud and his feet were bare. He stood in the middle of a crowd drinking from a full glass, his head rolling drunkenly from side to side. Abbas' eyes bulged in astonishment and he drew Husain's attention to the youth. Husain's observation reflected no astonishment as he commented:

"Oh, that's Awkal. He sells newspapers all day and spends the evening drinking. He's still just a boy. But there aren't many grown men like him, don't you agree?"

Husain leaned his head towards Abbas and went on:

"A glass of wine provides a little pleasure for unemployed people like me. A month ago I was drinking whisky in Vince's Bar, but times have changed. It's all in the luck of the game."

He ordered two glasses of wine which the bartender brought along with a plate of bitter nuts. Abbas stared at his glass suspiciously and then spoke as if searching for comfort:

"They say it's bad for one."

"Are you afraid of it?" asked Husain, gripping his glass. "Let it kill you . . . In hell, my friend, nothing makes any difference. Your health."

They clinked glasses and Husain downed his drink in one swallow. Abbas pushed his away in disgust. It was as though a tongue of flame had fired his throat. He screwed up his face and muttered:

"Horrible. Bitter. Hot."

Husain laughed and spoke in a smug and superior tone:

"Be brave, my boy. Life is much more bitter than this drink and its effects far worse . . ."

He lifted Abbas' glass and placed it to his companion's lips, saying: "Drink up and don't spill it." Abbas drained his glass and breathed out in a shudder. He felt a burning sensation in his stomach that rapidly spread throughout his body. With revulsion and interest he followed its course, as it sped through his blood until it reached his head. The dark world seemed to have lightened a little now and Husain said to him sarcastically:

"Be satisfied with only two drinks today."

He ordered himself another glass and went on:

"I'm staying at my father's house. My wife and her brother are also there. But now my brother-in-law has a job at the arsenal and he leaves us today or tomorrow. My father wants me to run the coffee-house for three pounds a month. In other words, I'm supposed to work from dawn through half the night for only three pounds! But what can you say to a mad hashish addict? Now you can see why I'm beginning to hate the world. There's only one answer to it: either have a life that suits you or to hell with it."

Abbas was now enveloped in a cosy peacefulness which he found both surprising and delightful after his long day of gloomy thoughts.

"Didn't you save any money?" he asked Husain.

"No, not a penny. I was living in a nice clean flat in Wayliyya. It had electricity and running water. I had a servant who called me 'Sir,' and I went often to the cinema and the theatre. I won a lot and I lost a lot, but that's life. Our lives are getting shorter daily, so why keep money? Still, I suppose one needs money up until the end. I've only a few pounds left, apart from my wife's jewelry."

He clapped and ordered a third glass and continued:

"Worst of all, my wife vomited last week . . ."

Pretending concern at the news, Abbas said:

"Oh, that's nothing to worry about, I hope."

"Nothing to worry about, but not good either. It's one of the signs of pregnancy, so my mother says. It's almost as if the fetus could see the life awaiting it, and wants to take out its feelings on the mother."

Abbas could no longer follow him; he seemed to be talking too rapidly and foolishly. Suddenly, melancholy replaced the past hour of peacefulness. His companion noticed the change and spoke:

"What's up? You're not listening to me . . ."

"Order me another drink," replied Abbas abruptly.

Husain was delighted to do so. He then looked quizzically at Abbas and spoke with some hesitation:

"You're worried about something and I know what it is."

His companion's heart beat wildly and he replied quickly:

"Oh, it's nothing. Tell me about yourself. I'm listening."

"Hamida . . . ," said Husain with a note of contempt in his voice.

Abbas' heart now beat as if he had swallowed another glass of the liquid fire. He felt betrayed and preyed upon at the same time.

"Yes, Hamida. She ran away with some stranger." His voice was not quite steady.

"Don't be a fool and get too upset. Do you think life is any easier for men whose women don't run away from them?"

A calm settled on the young man and he said, almost unconsciously:

"What do you suppose she's doing now?"

"No doubt what any woman does who goes off with a man . . ." replied Husain with a laugh.

"You're making fun of me."

"Your misery is ridiculous. Tell me, when did you hear that she had disappeared? Yesterday evening? By now you should have forgotten all about her."

Just then Awkal, the drunken newsboy, did something which drew the attention of the seated men. He staggered towards the tavern entrance, and stood at the door; his eyes half-closed and his head bent back proudly. Suddenly he shouted:

"I'm Awkal, the smartest fellow alive, the master of all men; I get drunk and feel great. Now I'm off to my beloved. Does anyone have any objections? Newspapers—the *Ahram*, the *Misri*, the *Baakuuka* . . ."

The boy disappeared from view, leaving a roar of laughter behind him. As for Husain Kirsha, he spat fiercely on the spot where the lad had stood and let forth a torrent of blasphemy. Were the boy still within reach, he would have subjected him to physical violence, his hostility was so uncontrollable. He turned towards Abbas, who was gulping his second drink and said defiantly, as though he had forgotten what they were discussing:

"This is life. This is not a child's game. We've got to live it. Do you understand?"

Abbas paid no attention. He was busy telling himself:

"Hamida will never come back. She is gone forever. And what if she does come back? If I ever see her again I'll spit in her face. That would hurt more than killing her. As for the man, I'll break his neck."

Husain talked on:

"I left the alley forever, but Satan pulled me back to it. I know, I'll set fire to it. That's the only way to free myself from it."

"Our alley is wonderful," Abbas commented wistfully. "I never wanted anything more than to live in it peacefully."

"You're just a brainless sheep! You should be sacrificed at the feast of al-Adha. Why are you crying? You're working, aren't you? You have money in your pocket. You're thrifty; soon you'll have saved up a lot of money. Why are you complaining?"

"You complain more than I do, yet I never heard you say a 'Praise be to God' in your life."

His companion stared hard at him. This brought Abbas back to his senses. Now he spoke mildly:

"Well, that's not your fault. You have your religion, I have mine."

Husain laughed so loudly that the whole tavern seemed to shake. The wine now had a grip on his tongue.

"I'd do better as a bartender than in my father's coffee-house. I'll bet there are good profits here, and besides a bartender gets his liquor free."

Abbas smiled half-heartedly and he decided to use caution in what he said to his explosive companion. The alcohol soothed his nerves, but instead of blotting out his misery, now all his thoughts centered about it.

Suddenly Husain shouted:

"I've a marvellous idea! I'll adopt British nationality! In England everyone is equal. A pasha and a garbage collector's son are the same. In England a café owner's son could become Prime Minister . . ."

The notion attracted Abbas and he shouted:

"A great idea! I'll become British too . . ."

"Impossible," said Husain with a contemptuous curl to his lip. "You're weak-kneed. You'd better adopt Italian citizenship . . . Anyway, we'll both go off on the same ship . . . Let's go."

They paid their bill and left the tavern. Abbas turned to Husain:

"Well now, where to?"

31

Perhaps the only hour of her past life that Hamida missed was her late afternoon walk. Now she spent that hour standing before the huge gold-trimmed mirror in her room.

Having spent an hour painstakingly dressing and applying her make-up, she now looked like a woman who from birth had known only the luxuries of life. On her head she wore a white silk turban, under which her oiled and scented hair curled appealingly. She knew from long experience that her bronze skin was more attractive to the Allies, and so she left it its natural color. She applied violet tinted shadow to her eyelids and carefully waxed and separated her lashes, their silky ends curling upwards. Two graceful arches were drawn in place of her eyebrows. Her lips were painted a lush scarlet that accented her dazzling white teeth. Large lotus-shaped pearls dangled on chains from her ears. She wore a gold wristwatch and a jewel-studded crescent brooch was pinned to her turban. The low neck of her white dress revealed a pink undergarment, and her short skirt

drew attention to well-shaped legs. She wore flesh-colored silk stock-
ings for no reason except that they were expensive. Perfume wafted
from her palms, neck and armpits. Things had indeed changed for
Hamida!

From the very beginning Hamida chose her path of her own free will.
Experience had shown her that her future life would be gaiety and
pleasure mixed with pain and bitter disappointment. Hamida realized she had arrived at a critical point in her life. Now she stood
perplexed and not sure where to turn.

She knew from the first day what was expected of her. Her instinctive reaction was to rebel. This she had done, not in the hope of
breaking her lover's iron will, but simply for the love of the consequent
battle. When eventually she gave way to the eloquence of Ibrahim
Faraj, it was because she wished to do so. Hamida had entered into
her new life with no regrets. She had justified her lover's comment
that she was a "whore by instinct." Her natural talents made a stunning display; indeed in a short time she had thoroughly mastered the
principles of make-up and dress, even though at first everyone made
fun of her vulgar taste. She had now learned Oriental and Western
dancing, and she also showed a quick ear for learning the sexual
principles of the English language. It was not surprising that she had
become so successful. She was a favorite of the soldiers and her
savings were proof of her popularity.

Hamida had never known the life of a simple respectable girl. She
had no happy memories of the past and was now quite engrossed in
the enjoyable present. Her case was different from the majority of the
other girls who had been forced by necessity or circumstances into
their present life and were often tormented by remorse. Hamida's
dreams of clothes, jewelry, money and men were now fulfilled and
how she enjoyed all the power and authority they gave her.

One day she recalled how miserable she had been the first time
when Ibrahim Faraj said he did not want to marry her. She had asked
herself if she really wanted to marry him. The answer, in the negative,
had come immediately. Marriage would have confined her to the

home, exhausting herself with the duties of a wife, housekeeper and mother; all those tasks she knew she was not created for. She now saw how far-sighted he had been.

Despite this, Hamida still felt strangely restless and dissatisfied. Not entirely ruled by her sexual instincts, she longed for emotional power. It was perhaps because she knew she had not achieved control over her lover that her attachment to him increased, along with her feeling of resentment and disillusion.

This then, was her state of mind as she stood before the mirror. Suddenly she saw his reflection as he hurried towards her; his face wore the look of a merchant who was just about to engage in a profitable transaction. He no longer bore the tender look of a man pleased with his new conquest. It was true he had encountered no resistance to the seduction. Many times since then she recalled that for a full fortnight she was saturated in what she believed to be his full capacity for love. Then his commercial instincts overcame her lover and he gradually revealed himself as the sex merchant he was.

He himself had never known love and it seemed strange to the romantically inclined girl that his whole life should be built on this sentiment. Whenever a new girl fell into his net, he played the part of the ardent lover—until she succumbed; after that he continued to court her for a short time. From then on he had made sure of his influence by making her dependent upon him emotionally and financially; often he even threatened to expose her before the police. When his mission was accomplished he dropped his role of lover for that of the flesh-merchant.

Hamida concluded his sudden indifference to her was the result of his constantly being surrounded by girls eager for his attention. She was obsessed with mixed feelings of love, hostility and suspicion as she stood looking at his reflection in the mirror.

To give the impression that he was in a hurry, Ibrahim Faraj said quickly:

"Have you finished, my darling?"

She determined to show her disapproval of his preoccupation with her trade by ignoring him. She sadly recalled those days and nights when he only spoke of his love and admiration for her. Now he spoke only of the work and profit. It was this work together with the tyranny of her own emotions which now prevented her emancipation. She no longer had that freedom for which she had risked her whole life.

Hamida only felt a sense of powerful independence when she was soliciting on the streets or in a tavern. The rest of the time she was tortured by a sense of imprisonment and humiliation. If only she were sure of his affection; if only he knew the humiliation of loving her, then she could feel victorious. Hostility towards him was her only escape from her predicament.

Faraj was aware of her animosity, but he hoped she would become accustomed to his coldness so that she would offer a minimum of resistance to the separation he planned. He thought it best to move slowly before delivering the decisive blow.

"Come, my darling, time is money." His tone was gentle but business-like.

"When will you stop using those vulgar terms?" she asked, turning suddenly towards him.

"When will you, my darling, stop talking nonsense?"

"So now you think you can talk to me that way?" she shrieked.

Putting on a bored expression, he answered:

"That's right . . . are we off on that old subject again? Must I say 'I love you' every time we meet? Can't what we feel be love without interfering with our work by talking about it constantly? I wish your brains were as sharp as your tongue and that you would dedicate your life, as I do mine, to our work and put it before everything else."

She stood listening, her face pale, to his ice-cold words, without a trace of feeling. This was merely a repetition of what she had now heard countless times from him. She recalled how cleverly he had planned all this by first criticizing her. One day he had examined her hands and said:

"Why don't you take better care of your hands; let your nails grow and put polish on them. Your hands are a weak point, you know."

On another occasion he said after a stormy quarrel:

"Be careful. You have a serious flaw I've not noticed before—your voice, my darling. Scream from your mouth, not from your larynx. It's a most ugly sound. It must be worked on. Those traces of Midaq Alley must be removed. Remember, your clients now come to see you in the best section of Cairo."

These words had hurt and humiliated her more than any she had ever heard in her life. Whenever she brought up the matter of her love for him he would avoid a discussion and soothe her with flattery about her work. Recently he had even dropped his false show of affection and once he told her:

"Get to work, my dear, love is only a silly word."

Damn him! Indignantly she commented:

"You have no right to talk like that to me. You know perfectly well that I work hard and make more money for you than all the other girls put together. So just remember that! I'm fed up with all your cunning. Just tell me honestly whether you still love me or not."

Now, he told himself, was the time to tell her. His almond-shaped eyes looked intently into her face as his mind worked furiously. He decided to choose peace for the time being. Doing his best to humor her, he said:

"We're on that same old subject, as usual . . ."

"Tell me," exploded Hamida, "do you think I'll die of grief if you deny me your love?"

The time was not right. If only she had asked him that question when she returned from work in the early morning, that way he would have more scope to maneuver. Now if he told her the truth, he would risk losing the entire profits for the day.

"I love you, darling . . ." he said softly, moving towards her.

How filthy it sounded coming from him now. Utter mortification swept over her and she felt she would never be able to stop despising herself, even if he were to guarantee to come back to her arms. For a fleeting moment she felt that his love was something worth sacrificing the world for, but a feeling of spitefulness welled up quickly within her and she stepped a few paces nearer to him, her eyes glinting like the diamond brooch pinned to her turban. Determined to carry on the argument to its ultimate end, Hamida went on:

"So you really love me? Then let's get married!"

His eyes revealed his astonishment and he looked at her only half believing what he had heard.

"Would marriage change our situation?" he asked in reply.

"Yes it would. Let's get married and get out of this kind of life."

His patience quite exhausted, he made a firm decision. He would deal with this matter with the candor and severity it deserved and so carry out what had long been running through his mind, even though it would probably mean the loss of the night's profits. He broke into loud, sarcastic laughter and said:

"A brilliant idea my darling! We'll get married and live like lords. Ibrahim Faraj and his Wife and Children, Incorporated! But really, what is marriage? I seem to have forgotten all about it, just like the other social graces. Let me think for a moment . . . Marriage . . . is a very serious thing, I seem to remember. It unites a man and a woman. There is a marriage official, a religious contract and all kinds of rites . . . When did you learn that, Faraj? In the Koran or in school? I've forgotten where. Tell me my darling, are people still getting married?"

Hamida was now trembling from head to foot. Suddenly she could restrain herself no longer. In one swift leap she reached for his throat. He anticipated her sudden action and met her attack with complete calm. Seizing her arms, he forced them apart and then released her, the mocking smile still on his lips. Hamida raised her arm and slapped his face with all her strength. His smile faded and an evil, threatening look came into his eyes. She stared back at him challengingly, impatiently waiting for the battle to begin. He was well aware that to engage in physical combat with her would only mean a strengthening of the ties he wished to liquidate and so he withdrew without defending himself. He retreated a step, turned his back on her and walked off, saying:

"Please come to work, my darling."

Hamida refused to believe her eyes as she stood there looking at the door through which he had disappeared. She knew what his retreat meant. She was suddenly consumed with an irresistible urge to kill this man.

Hamida felt she must leave that house at once. Walking heavily towards the door, she realized that she was leaving that room, their room, for the last time. She turned around as though to say farewell to it. Suddenly she felt as though she would faint. Oh God! How had everything come to an end so quickly? This mirror, how often she had looked into it so full of happiness. And the bed that harbored so much love-making and so many dreams. That settee where she had often been in his arms, listening to his advice amidst caresses. There was the dressing-table with a picture of them both in evening dress. In one swift dash she fled from the room.

The hot air of the street almost scorched her and she could scarcely breathe. She walked along saying to herself: "I'll murder him!" That would be a consolation, if she didn't have to pay for his life with her own. She knew that her love would always remain a scar deep within her, but she was not the sort of woman love could actually destroy. This thought cheered her a little and she waved to the driver of a carriage she saw approaching. She climbed in, feeling an urgent need for more air and a rest.

She told the driver:

"Drive first to the Opera Square and then come back along Fuad I Street. And drive carefully, please."

She sat in the middle of the seat, leaning back comfortably with her legs crossed. Her brief silk dress revealed a portion of leg above her knees. She lit a cigarette and puffed it nervously, unaware of passers-by staring at the flesh she revealed.

Hamida sat completely engrossed in her thoughts. A variety of future hopes and dreams came to comfort her but it never occurred to her that she might discover a new love to make her forget this old one.

After some time she turned her attention to the road. The open carriage was now circling round in front of the Opera House and in the distance she caught sight of Queen Farida Square. Her thoughts flew from there up to the Mouski, New Street, Sanadiqiyya Street and Midaq Alley, and shadowy figures of men and women from the past flitted before her eyes. She wondered whether any one of them would recognize her if they were to see her now. Would they see Hamida underneath Titi? Why should she care, anyway? After all, she had no father or mother of her own. She finished the cigarette and threw it from the carriage.

Settling back, she enjoyed the ride until the carriage returned to Sharif Street and made its way towards the tavern where she worked. Just then she heard a shrill cry rend the air: "Hamida!" She turned in terror and saw Abbas the barber, only an arm's length away from her.

32

"Abbas!"

The young man was panting furiously because he had run behind the carriage all the way from Opera Square. He had dashed blindly, bumping into people, careless of the shoves, curses and pushes directed at him. He had been walking with Husain Kirsha, wandering aimlessly from Vita's tavern, until they reached Opera Square. It was here Husain saw the carriage with the beautiful woman inside.

He did not recognize Hamida. He had instinctively raised his eyebrows in approval of the passenger. In fact he drew his friend's attention to her. Abbas looked up at the approaching carriage and fixed his gaze on the young woman in it. She seemed lost in thought. She looked somehow familiar. So faintly familiar that his heart, more than his eyes, was the detector. In spite of his slightly drunken state he shouted "Stop!"

The carriage now turned and headed for Azbakiyya Gardens. Abbas dashed off in mad pursuit, leaving his friend shouting after him. Heavy traffic at the head of Fuad Street delayed him, but he kept his eyes fixed on the carriage. He set off again running as fast as he could, his strength failing. Finally he caught up with her just as she was about to enter the tavern and called out her name with a piercing shriek. She turned towards him and weakly gasped out his name. Instantly his doubts vanished. He stood before her gasping for breath, not trusting the image before his eyes. She too, was obviously overcome with what she saw. Suddenly she seemed conscious of the many people watching them. She controlled herself and signalling him, she walked quickly off towards a small street next to the tavern. Abbas followed her into the first door on the right, a flower shop. The proprietress greeted her, recognizing Hamida as a frequent customer. She returned the greeting and accompanied Abbas to the back of the shop. The shopkeeper sensed she wanted to be alone with her companion and seated herself discreetly behind a flower display, as though she were alone in the shop.

They now stood face to face. Abbas trembled with excitement and total bewilderment. What had drawn him to his mortal enemy? What could he hope for from his meeting? Why had he not let her pass unnoticed? Suddenly he had no opinion, no plans. While he was running, memories of Hamida's desertion barely kept his mind on the road. He simply ran in blind instinct until he finally gasped out her name. From then on he was like a sleepwalker, following her into the shop.

He could feel himself slowly returning to consciousness as he examined this strange woman before him. In vain he tried to find a trace of the girl he had once loved. Abbas was not so simple that he failed to grasp the truth of what he saw before him. Then, too, the rumors in Midaq Alley had forced him to expect the worst. However, nothing was as shattering as what he now saw. He was overcome with a sense of the futility of life. However, strangely enough he felt no inclination to harm her—nor even to humiliate her.

Hamida looked at him with a child-like confusion. His presence aroused no feelings of affection nor regret. She felt only contempt and animosity and silently cursed the bad luck that had thrown him in her path.

The silence was beginning to strain their nerves, and now Abbas, unable to bear it, spoke softly:

"Hamida! Is it really you? Oh God, how can I believe my eyes? How could you have left your home and your mother and ended up like this?"

Embarrassed, but not ashamed, Hamida answered:

"Don't ask me about anything. I've nothing to say to you. It's all the will of God. It can't be changed."

Her embarrassment and control had the opposite effect to what she expected. Now both his anger and hatred were aroused. His voice rose in a bellow that filled the shop:

"You filthy liar . . . Some degenerate like yourself seduced you and you ran off with him! The alley is full of filthy rumors about you, you know. And I can see them all reflected in your hard face and your cheap get-up . . ."

His sudden anger ignited her quick temper and now all embarrassment and fear dissolved within her. All this added to the day's agonies and now her face turned pale.

"Shut up!" she shouted. "Don't talk like a maniac! Do you think you scare me? What do you want from me, you nothing, you have no claim on me. Get out of my sight."

Before she finished his anger had subsided. He stared at her in confusion and in a trembling voice he muttered:

"How can you say such things? Aren't you . . . weren't you once my fiancée?"

She smiled and shrugged impatiently.

"Why bring up the past? It's over and done with."

"Yes, it's over and done with, but I want to know what went wrong between us. Didn't you accept my proposal? Didn't I go away for the sake of our future happiness together?"

She now felt no embarrassment or uneasiness with him and only asked herself impatiently: "When will he drop the subject? When will he understand? When will he go away?" She replied in a bored tone:

"I wanted one thing, and the fates wanted another . . ."

"What have you done to yourself? Why have you chosen this filthy life? What has blinded you? What pig abducted you from a pure life and dumped you in the sewers of prostitution?"

"This is my life," she said with firm impatience. "It's over between us and that's all there is to it. We're complete strangers now. I can't go back and you can't change me. Be careful what you say to me, because I'm in no condition to forgive you. I may be weak but I'm simply fleeing from my horrible destiny. Forget me, hate me if you want to, but leave me in peace."

This was indeed a total stranger. Where was the Hamida he had loved and who had loved him? Had she ever loved him? What about their kiss on the staircase? When they said farewell had she not promised to pray to the Lord Husain to look after him and answer their prayers? Who was this girl? Did she feel no regret? No trace of the old affection? A sigh of impotent despair weighted his words as he spoke:

"The more I listen to you, the less I understand you. I came back yesterday from Tell al-Kabir. I couldn't believe what they told me about you. Do you know what brought me back?" He showed her the box containing the necklace. "I bought this for you. I planned to marry you before I went back . . ."

As she gazed silently at the box, Abbas noticed her diamond brooch and pearl earrings. He withdrew his hand and put the box in his pocket. He asked her pointedly:

"Do you have any regrets about your new life?"

In a tone of mock sadness, she answered:

"You don't know how unhappy I am."

His eyes opened wide in suspicious surprise as he spoke:

"How terrible, Hamida! Why did you ever listen to the devil? Why did you hate your life here in the alley? How could you throw away a good life for . . ." here his voice thickened, "a shameless criminal? It's a dirty crime and there's no forgiveness for it."

"I'm paying for it with my flesh and blood." Her voice was low and melodramatic.

Abbas was now more bewildered, but he felt strangely pleased with the confession he had extracted. Hamida's hostility had not, however, subsided purely by chance. Her mind raced with devilish inspiration. It occurred to her that she could conscript Abbas against the man who was using her so heartlessly. He would become the instrument of her revenge while she remained apart from any unpleasant consequences. Now she spoke in her frailest voice:

"I'm a poor, miserable creature, Abbas. Don't be angry at what I said. My mental agony has almost made me lose my mind. You see me only as a low prostitute. But it's what you said, I was betrayed by a devil. I don't know why I gave in to him. I'm not trying to excuse myself, nor asking you to forgive me. I know I've sinned and now I'm paying for it. Forgive my temper and hate me as much as your pure heart will let you. I'm just putty in the hands of this horrible man. He sends me into the streets after having robbed me of the most precious thing I had. I loathe and despise him. He's responsible for all my misery and suffering. But it's too late now, how can I ever get away from him?"

The wounded look in her eyes made him forget the hysterical woman who had been capable of murdering him only a few minutes before. Her appeal had worked as she hoped it would.

"How awful, Hamida! Both of us are miserable because of that low bestial criminal. I'm sorry but what you did will always stand between us. We suffer but his life goes on. I won't be happy until I smash his head in . . ."

This pleased Hamida and she turned her head lest Abbas notice her delight. He had fallen into her trap even faster than she had hoped. She was especially pleased that he had said: "What you did will always stand between us." She felt relief that he did not want to forgive her. Above all she did not want that, neither did she want to be taken back.

"I can never forget that you abandoned me and that people saw you with him . . . It's over between us. The Hamida I loved no longer exists. But that monster must suffer. Where can I find him?"

"You can't find him today. Come next Sunday afternoon. He'll be in the bar at the top of this lane, the only Egyptian in the place. I'll look towards him when you signal me. What do you plan to do to him?" She spoke as though she feared the consequences for Abbas.

"I'll smash the filthy pimp's head."

Looking at him, she wondered if Abbas could possibly be capable of murder! She knew the answer but she hoped the encounter might at least bring Ibrahim Faraj before the law; thus she would have her revenge and freedom as well. This fantasy delighted Hamida. She sincerely hoped no harm would come to Abbas and she cautioned him gently:

"Be careful, won't you? Hit him and then drag him to the police station. Let the law handle him from there."

Abbas, however, was not listening. He mumbled, downcast and half to himself:

"We shouldn't suffer without him paying too. We're both finished. Why should that pimp get off free and laugh at us? I'll break his neck; I'll strangle him!"

Looking up at Hamida, he asked:

"And you, Hamida, what if I get this gangster out of your life?"

This was the question she dreaded. It could mean only that Abbas's affection for her might revive. With quiet determination, she answered:

"My ties with the old world are broken now. I'll sell my jewelry and take a respectable job; somewhere far away . . ."

Abbas stood thinking. His silence filled her with uneasiness, but eventually he bowed his head and said almost inaudibly:

"I can't find it in my heart to forgive you . . . I simply cannot . . . but please don't disappear until we see how all this ends."

The note of forgiveness in his voice unnerved her. She would have preferred that both Abbas and Ibrahim Faraj perish.

Anyhow, it would be easy to disappear if she wanted to, but not until she had been avenged. It would be so easy to go to Alexandria; Ibrahim had often talked about the city. She could be . . . free there, away from the parasites.

Her tone was now sweet and gentle:

"As you like, Abbas . . ."

His heart was geared for revenge but it also throbbed with deep affection for Hamida.

33

t was a day of joyful leave-taking. Radwan Husaini was loved and respected by everyone in the alley. Husaini had hoped God would choose him to make the holy pilgrimage to Mecca and Medina this year and so He had. Everyone knew this was the day Radwan Husaini would leave for Suez on his way to those holy lands and his house was filled with well-wishers, life-long friends and devout Muslims.

They clustered in his modest room which had so often echoed with their pious and friendly discussions. They chatted about the pilgrimage and their reminiscences of it, their voices rising from every corner of the room and mixing with a trail of smoke billowing up from the brazier. They told tales of the modern pilgrimage and those of bygone days and related holy traditions and beautiful verses concerning it. One man, with a melodious voice, chanted verses from the Holy Koran and then they all listened to a long and eloquent speech by Radwan Husaini that expressed his heart's goodness.

A pious friend wished him:

"A happy journey and safe return."

Husaini beamed and replied in his most gentle manner:

"Please my friend, don't remind me of my return. Anyone who visits God's house with a longing for home deserves to have God deny him reward, ignore his prayers and destroy his happiness. I will think of returning only when I have left the scene of the revelations on my way back to Egypt. And by 'returning' I mean going back on the pilgrimage again, with the help and permission of the All Merciful. If only I could spend the rest of my life in the Holy Land, seeing the ground which once was trod by the Prophet, the sky once filled with the angels singing and listening to the divine revelation coming down to earth and rising to the skies again with souls from the earth. There one's mind is filled only with the revelations of eternity. One throbs with love for God. There are the remedy and the cure. Oh my brother, I long for Mecca and its bright heavens. I long to hear the whispering of time at every corner, to walk down its streets and lose myself in its holy places. How I long to drink from the well of Zamzam and take the road of the Messenger on his Flight, followed by the multitudes of thirteen hundred years ago and those of today, too. I long to feel my heart grow chill when I visit the grave of the Prophet and pray in the Holy Garden. I can see myself now, my brothers, walking through the lanes of Mecca reciting verses from the Koran just as they were first revealed as if I were listening to a lesson given by the Almighty Being. What joy! I can see myself kneeling in the garden imagining the beloved face of the Prophet before me, just as it appears to me in my sleep. What joy! I can see myself prostrated low before the edifice and pleading for forgiveness. What peace I'll have! I see myself going to the well of Zamzam, saturating with water those wounds of passion and crying out for a cure—what divine peace! My brother, speak not of my return but pray with me to God to fulfil my hopes . . ."

His friend replied:

"May God fulfil your hopes and give you a long and happy life."

Radwan Husaini lifted his outstretched palm to his beard, his eyes glistening with joy and passion, and continued:

"A fine prayer! My love for the after-life does not turn me towards asceticism nor make me dissatisfied with life. You all know of my love for life, and why not? It is a part of the creation of the All Merciful who filled it with tears and with joys. Let, then, he who will give thought and thanks. I love life in all its colors and sounds, its nights and days, joys and sorrows, beginnings and ends. I love all things living and moving and still. It is all pure goodness. Evil is no more than the inability of the sick to see the good concealed in the crevices. The weak and sick suspect God's world. I believe that love of life is one half of worshipping and love of the afterlife is the other half. Therefore, too, I am shocked by the tears and suffering, rage and anger, spite and malice which weigh down the world, and the criticism with which, as well as all these, the weak and sick afflict it. Would they prefer their lives had not been created? Would they ever have loved if they had not been created from nonexistence? Are they really tempted to deny divine wisdom? I do not declare myself innocent. Once sorrow overcame me too and it ate away a piece of my heart. In the throes of my pain and sorrow I asked myself: Why did God not leave my child to enjoy his share of life and happiness? Did not He, the Glorious and Almighty, create the child? Why, then, should He not take him back when He wished? If God had wanted him to have life then the child would have remained on earth until His will was done. But He reclaimed my child in all the wisdom His will decreed. God does nothing that is not wise and wisdom is good. My Lord wished well of both me and the child. A feeling of joy overcame me when I realized that His wisdom was greater than my sorrow. I told myself: Oh God, You brought affliction upon me and put me to the test. I have come through the test with my faith still firm, certain of Your wisdom. Thank You, Oh God.

"It has since been my practice, that whenever anything afflicts me, I express my joyful thanks from the bottom of my heart. Why should I not do so?

"Whenever I pass over some test to the shores of peace and faith, I become more and more convinced of the wisdom with which He uses His power. In this way my afflictions always keep me in touch with His wisdom. Why, you could even imagine me as a child, playing in his own little world. God treated me severely to rebuke me; frightening me with His mock sternness to double my delight in His real and everlasting kindness. Lovers often put their loved ones to a test, and if they only realized that test is merely a trick and not serious, then their delight in their lovers would be increased. I have always believed that those afflicted on earth are the closest favorites of God. He lavishes love on them in secret, lying in wait for them not far off, to see whether they are really worthy of His love and mercy. All praise to God for because of his generosity I have been able to comfort those who thought me in need of consolation."

He drew his hand happily over his broad chest, feeling in so expressing himself, much the same contentment as a singer lost in the rhythm of a melody and elated with the power of his art. He continued with firm conviction:

"Some consider that such tragedies afflicting apparently blameless people are signs of a revengeful justice, the wisdom of which is beyond the understanding of most people. So you will hear them say that if the bereaved father, for example, thought deeply he would realize his loss was a just punishment for some sin either he or his forebears committed. Yet surely God is more just and merciful than to treat the innocent as the guilty. Yet you hear these people justify their opinion by God's Koranic description of Himself as 'mighty and revengeful.' But I tell you, gentlemen, that Almighty God has no need of revenge and only adopted this attribute to advise man to practise it. God had already stated that the affairs of this life should be settled only on the basis of reward and punishment. Dear and Almighty God's own essential attributes are wisdom and mercy."

"If I saw in the loss of my children a punishment or penalty I merit then I would agree with that philosophy and be censured. But I would still be depressed and dissatisfied and no doubt protest that an innocent child died for a weak man's sins. And is that forgiveness and mercy? And where is the tragedy in what reveals wisdom, goodness and joy?"

Radwan Husaini's opinions drew objections based on both the literal texts and the scholastic interpretations of Islam. Some present insisted that what seemed revenge was in fact mercy. Many of the other men were both more eloquent and erudite than Radwan but he had not really been inviting argument.

He had merely been expressing the love and joy welling up within him. He smiled, as innocent as a child, his face flushed and his eyes beaming and went on:

"Please forgive me, gentlemen. Permit me to disclose a hidden secret. Do you know what has prompted me to make the pilgrimage this year?"

Radwan Husaini was silent a moment, his clear eyes glistening with a brilliant light. Then he spoke, in reply to the interested looks in his direction:

"I don't deny that I always longed to make the pilgrimage but each time it was God's will that I put the matter off. Then, as you know, certain things happened here in the alley. The devil managed to ensnare three of our neighbors—a girl and two men. He led the two men to rob a tomb and then left them in prison. As for the girl, the devil led her to the well of sensuality and plunged her into the slime of depravity. All this nearly broke my heart. And I don't wish to disguise from you, gentlemen, my feelings of guilt, for one of the two men lived by mere crumbs of food. He ransacked the graves and decayed bones seeking something of value like a stray dog scratching for food from a garbage heap. His hunger made me think of my own well-fed body and I was overcome with shame and humility. I asked myself what had I done, after all God's goodness to me, to prevent his tragic plight. Had I not simply let the devil amuse himself with my neighbors while I remained lost in my own complacent joy? Cannot a good man unknowingly be an accomplice of the devil by keeping to himself? My conscience told me that I should seek forgiveness in the land of repentance and stay there as long as God wills. I will return with a pure heart and I will put my all to good works in God's kingdom . . ."

The holy men said prayers for him and happily continued their conversation.

.   .   .

After leaving his house, Radwan Husaini visited Kirsha's coffee-house to say farewell. He was surrounded by Kirsha, Uncle Kamil, Sheikh Darwish, Abbas the barber and Husain Kirsha. Husniya entered and kissed his hand, asking him to pay her respects to the holy land. Radwan Husaini addressed them all:

"The pilgrimage is a duty for all who can make it. One should perform it for oneself and for all those who cannot go."

Uncle Kamil said in his child-like voice:

"May peace and safety accompany you and perhaps you will bring us back some prayer beads from Mecca."

Husaini smiled and said:

"I won't be like that fellow who gave you a shroud and then laughed at you."

Uncle Kamil chuckled and would have pursued the matter had he not seen Abbas' somber face. Radwan Husaini had deliberately brought up this subject in the hope of getting through to the miserable Abbas. He turned to him sympathetically and said gently but firmly:

"Abbas, please listen to me like the nice sensible fellow you are. Take my advice. Go back to Tell al-Kabir today. Work hard and save your money for a new life, God willing. Don't worry about your past bad luck. You're still only in your late twenties and your disillusion is only a small part of what every man suffers in his lifetime. Why, you'll get over this just as a child gets over measles. Be brave, and act like a man. In later life you'll recall it with the smile of a conqueror. Go on, put your trust in patience and faith. Earn as much as possible and be as happy as a pious man convinced that God has chosen him to help those in need."

Abbas made no reply, but when he saw Radwan Husaini's eyes fixed on him, he smiled and said vaguely:

"Everything will pass just as though it never happened."

Radwan Husaini turned to Husain Kirsha, saying:

"Welcome to the cleverest fellow in our alley! I will pray to God to lead you where your prayers will be answered. God willing, I hope to find you in your father's place when I get back, just as he wants."

At this Sheikh Darwish emerged from his silence and said thoughtfully:

"Oh Radwan Husaini, remember me when you are in the ritual dress and tell the People of the House that their lover's passion has drained and drunk him dry. Tell them he has spent all his wealth and possessions in pursuit of a futile love. Complain to them of the treatment he has suffered from the Lady of Ladies."

Radwan Husaini left the coffee-house surrounded by his friends. He was now joined by two relatives who intended to travel with him as far as Suez. Husaini turned off into the alley's business premises and found Salim Alwan poring over his ledgers. He greeted him cheerfully:

"It's time for me to go; let me say farewell to you."

Alwan lifted his colorless face in surprise; he knew that Husaini was leaving but it did not interest him in the least. Radwan Husaini knew, as everyone else did, of Alwan's sad condition but he ignored his indifference and refused to leave the quarter before saying goodbye. Alwan now seemed a bit embarrassed by his indifference. Suddenly Radwan Husaini folded Alwan in his arms, kissed him and said a long prayer for him. Husaini then rose, saying:

"Let's pray to God that next year we can make the pilgrimage together."

"If God wills," muttered Salim Alwan mechanically.

They embraced once more and Radwan Husaini rejoined his friends. They all walked to the alley entrance where a carriage loaded with baggage was waiting. The traveler shook hands heartily with his well-wishers and he and his relatives got into the carriage. His friends watched it move slowly towards Ghouriyya Street and then turn into Azhar Street.

34

ncle Kamil told Abbas:
"No one can give you
better advice than Rad-
wan Husaini. Get yourself
ready, put your trust in God and go. I'll wait for you no matter how
long you're gone. You will return in triumph and be the most successful barber in the whole quarter."

Abbas sat on a chair in front of the sweet-shop not far from Uncle
Kamil, and silently listened to what his friend said. He had told no
one of his new secret. When Radwan Husaini lectured him he had
thought of telling him of his decision, but he had hesitated and when
the older man had turned to Husain Kirsha, Abbas changed his mind.
He had given the advice a good deal of thought.

However, it was the coming Sunday that now occupied his
thoughts. A night and a morning had passed since the unexpected
meeting in the flower-shop. Meanwhile he had carefully gone over
the incident time and time again, in his mind. He now knew that he
still loved the girl, even though she was clearly lost to him forever.
Most of all he longed to have revenge on his rival.

Uncle Kamil asked him anxiously:

"Tell me, what have you decided to do?"

"I'll stay here at least until next Sunday," replied Abbas, getting up. "Then everything will be in God's hands."

"It won't be too hard to forget if you really make the effort," Uncle Kamil commented sympathetically.

"You're right," said Abbas, about to leave. "Goodbye then!"

He walked off, intending to go to Vita's Bar, where he thought Husain had gone after saying farewell to Radwan Husaini. Abbas was still in a deeply troubled state. He looked forward to Sunday, but what would he do when it came? Would he plunge a knife in his rival's heart? Would he really be able to do it? Could his hand manage a murderous thrust? He shook his head doubtfully. All degrees of crime and violence sickened his peaceful nature.

What would he do when Sunday came? He yearned to see Husain Kirsha to tell him Hamida's story and ask his advice. He desperately needed help. Now, convinced of his weakness, he recalled Radwan Husaini's advice: "Go back to Tell al-Kabir today." Yes, why should he not give up the past and all its sadness and summon up his courage and stoicism and go off to work and to forget?

In a turmoil of indecision he entered Vita's Bar. There was Husain Kirsha soberly sipping red wine. Abbas greeted him and said emotionally:

"You've drunk enough. I need you for something. Come on with me."

Husain raised his eyebrows in annoyance as Abbas lifted him by the arm saying:

"Hurry, I need you badly."

Husain groaned, paid his bill and left the tavern with his friend. Abbas was determined to get his advice before the effect of drink overcame him.

When they were in Mouski Street he said to Husain as though in great relief:

"I've found Hamida, Husain . . ."

"Where?" asked Husain, his small eyes glinting with curiosity.

"You remember that woman in the carriage I chased yesterday? It was Hamida!"

Husain shouted in surprise:

"Are you drunk? What did you say?"

Very serious and full of emotion, Abbas repeated:

"Believe me. That was Hamida and I talked with her."

Still stunned, Husain asked:

"You expect me to refuse to believe my own eyes?"

Abbas told him of his conversation with the girl and finished by saying:

"That's what I wanted to tell you. There's no hope for Hamida now, she's lost forever, but I am not going to let that filthy gangster escape without punishment."

Husain gazed at him for a long time, trying to understand him. By nature he was foolhardy and reckless and it took him time to get over his astonishment. Then he commented scornfully:

"Hamida is the real culprit. Didn't she run off with him? Didn't she yield to him? How can you criticize him? A girl attracted him and he seduced her; he found her easy and he got what he wanted. He wanted to exploit her talents so he let her loose in the taverns. Why, he's a clever fellow. I only wish I could do the same to get out of my financial problems. Hamida's the real criminal, my friend."

Abbas understood his friend and realized without a doubt that Husain had no scruples about what his rival had done. Therefore he refrained from criticizing the man's morals and tried to arouse Husain's sense of injury by another way. He asked:

"But don't you think this fellow has insulted our honor, therefore he must be punished?"

The use of the word "honor" did not escape Husain's notice and he realized that Abbas referred to the near-brotherhood ties that bound them so closely. He suddenly recalled how his sister had been thrown into prison because of a similar scandal and the thought enraged him. He roared:

"That doesn't concern me. Hamida can go to the devil!"

He was not completely truthful in what he said. If he had had the culprit before him at that moment he would have sprung on him like a tiger and dug his claws deep. Abbas, however, believed him. In a slightly critical tone, he said to Husain:

"Doesn't it infuriate you that a man should do this to a girl from our alley? I agree with you that Hamida is to blame, so one can't really criticize the man. But still, isn't it an insult to us that we should avenge?"

"What a fool you are," shouted Husain indignantly. "You're not mad because of your honor, as you think. It's pure jealousy. If Hamida agreed to come back to you, you'd go off with her quite happily. How did you greet her, you poor sap? You argued and pleaded with her? Bravo! Well done! What a brave fellow you are indeed . . . Why didn't you murder her? If I were in your position I wouldn't have hesitated a minute. I'd have throttled her on the spot and then butchered her lover and disappeared . . . That's what you should have done, you fool!"

His near-black face took on a satanical look as he continued to bellow:

"I'm not saying this to escape doing my duty. This fellow should pay for his aggression. And he will! We'll keep the appointment you made and we'll beat him up. Then we'll wait for him in all his haunts and beat him up again, even if he has a gang with him. And we won't stop doing this until he pays us off, at a good price. That way we'll have revenge and profit from him at the same time!"

Abbas was delighted at this unexpected conclusion and said enthusiastically:

"What a great idea! You're a very clever fellow!"

Husain was pleased at this praise. He wondered how he could carry out his plan, spurred on by the anger inspired by his sense of honor, his natural aggressiveness and his greed for money. He muttered viciously: "Sunday isn't far off."

When they reached Queen Farida Square they stopped and Husain suggested:

"Let's go back to Vita's Bar."

Abbas hesitated and said:

"Wouldn't it be better to go to the tavern where we'll meet him on Sunday, so that you'll know where it is?"

Husain lingered a bit and then walked off with his friend, stepping out more quickly now. The sun was about to set; only a few light shadows were now being thrown by its light. The whole sky was quiet and inky-black, as it always was when the first shadows fell. The street lamps were lit and traffic flowed on, indifferent to the change between night and day. The whole surface of the earth seemed to echo and resound with ceaseless noise. Streetcars rumbled by, motor-horns blew, vendors shouted their wares and the street musicians blew their pipes, while people bustled all around. Coming in from the alley to this street was like a translation from sleep to noisy wakefulness.

Abbas felt elated and his bewilderment dispersed. Now, with the help of his brave and strong friend he could see his way clearly before him. As for Hamida, he was content to let the unknown circumstances decide things. He felt unable to settle anything himself, or perhaps he was simply afraid to make a final decision about her. He wanted to talk to his friend about this but took one look at Husain's black face and the words choked in his throat. They continued on their way until they reached the scene of Abbas' last dramatic encounter with Hamida. The barber nudged his friend and said:

"This is the flower-shop where we talked."

Husain looked silently at the shop and asked with interest:

"And where is the tavern?"

Abbas nodded to a nearby door and muttered:

"That must be it."

They walked slowly towards it, Husain's small sharp eyes looking carefully all around. As they walked by, Abbas looked inside the tavern and an extraordinary sight met his eyes. He let out a gasp and the muscles of his face set hard. From then on things happened so quickly that Husain was left in a daze. He saw Hamida sitting amidst a crowd of soldiers. One stood behind her pouring wine into a glass in her hand, leaning towards her slightly as she turned her head towards him. Her legs were stretched on the lap of another soldier sitting opposite her and there were others in uniform crowding around her, drinking boisterously. Abbas stood stunned. His anger foamed within him and blinded his vision and he quite forgot that he had any enemy other than her. He charged madly into the tavern roaring out in a thunderous voice:

"Hamida . . ."

The girl was struck with terror and her face went white with fear. She bellowed angrily in her coarse, harsh voice:

"Out! Get out of my sight!"

Her anger and shouting acted like gasoline on flames and Abbas' rage turned to sheer fury. His normal hesitancy and reserve disappeared as he felt all the sorrow, disappointment and despair he had suffered in the past three days boil up within him to burst forth in a mad frenzy. He noticed some empty beer glasses on the bar, took one and not really aware what he was doing, hurled it at her with all the force of the anger and despair within him. He acted so quickly that no one, neither the soldiers nor any of the tavern employees, could stop him and the glass struck her in the face. Blood poured in a stream from her nose, mouth and chin, mixing with the creams and powders on her face and running down on to her neck and dress. Her screams mingled with the enraged shouts of the drunks in the tavern and angry men fell on Abbas from all sides like wild animals. Blows, kicks and glasses flew in all directions.

Husain Kirsha stood at the bar door watching his friend pelted with blows from fists and feet, just like a ball and quite defenseless. Each time he was struck, he yelled: "Husain . . . Husain." His friend, however, who had never before in his life drawn back from a fight, remained glued to the ground, not knowing how he could cut his way to Abbas through all the angry soldiers. Rage swept over him and he began searching left and right to find some sharp object, some stick or knife. He failed and stood there impotently with the passers-by now gathered at the door staring at the battle taking place, their fists clenched and their eyes filled with horror.

35

he morning light filled the alley and rays from the sun fell on the upper walls of Alwan's office and the barber's shop. Sankir the young coffee-house waiter appeared and filled a bucket with water which he sprinkled on the ground. The alley was turning another of the pages of its monotonous life, its inhabitants greeting the morning with their usual cries. Uncle Kamil was extraordinarily active for this early hour, standing in front of a dish of sweetmeat, serving it out to boys from the elementary school and filling his pocket with the small coins they gave him.

Opposite him the old barber was stropping his razors and Jaada the baker went by bringing dough from houses nearby. Salim Alwan's employees were arriving now, opening doors and storerooms and disturbing the peace and quiet with their noise which would continue all day long. Kirsha was squatting behind his till dreaming, splitting something between his front teeth, chewing it and then washing it down with coffee. Near him sat Sheikh Darwish, silent and lost to the world. Early though it was, Mrs. Saniya Afifi appeared at her window, to say goodbye to her young husband as he made his way down the alley, off to work in the police department.

This was the normal pattern of life in the alley, disturbed only occasionally when one of its girls disappeared or one of its menfolk was swallowed by the prison. But soon such bubbles subsided into its lake-like surface, calm or stagnant, and by evening whatever might have happened in the morning was almost forgotten.

The early morning, then, found the alley enjoying its quiet and peaceful life as usual but at mid-morning Husain Kirsha arrived, his face filled with gloom and his eyes red with loss of sleep. He came slowly and heavily up the alley, went over to his father and threw himself into a chair facing him. Without a greeting he said hoarsely:

"Father, Abbas has been killed . . ."

Kirsha, who was just about to reprimand him for spending the whole night away from home, made no reply. He sat staring in astonishment at his son, shocked and motionless. Then, suddenly, in an annoyed tone, he demanded:

"What did you say?"

Husain, sitting staring fixedly ahead, replied huskily:

"Abbas has been killed! The British murdered him . . ."

He moistened his lips and repeated all Abbas had told him the previous day on their walk. His voice full of emotion, he said:

"He took me to show me a tavern that bitch had told him about. As we passed it he saw her in the midst of a crowd of soldiers. He went wild, lost his temper, charged inside, and hurled a glass into her face before I knew what he was doing. The soldiers got mad and dozens of them beat him till he fell down senseless."

He clenched his fists tight and, gnashing his teeth in angry hate, went on:

"It was hell . . . I couldn't help him. There were just too many damned soldiers . . . If only I could have gotten my hands on one of those damned soldiers."

" 'All power and strength are in God's hands,'" quoted Kirsha, slapping his hands together. "What did you do with him?"

"The police arrived too late and put a cordon around the tavern. But what good could that do? They carried his body off to Kasr al-Aini hospital and took the whore off for first-aid treatment."

"Was she killed?" asked Kirsha.

"I don't think so," answered Husain. "Too bad; he lost his life in vain."

"And the British?"

Husain replied sadly:

"We left them surrounded by the police, and who can expect any justice from them?"

Kirsha once again brought his hands together in a slap and quoted:

" 'We are all God's creatures and to Him must we return.' Do Abbas' relatives know the news? Go out and tell his Uncle Hassan in Khurunfush so that God will perform His will."

Husain got up and left the coffee-house. The news soon spread as Kirsha told his son's tale repeatedly to people who came to ask. Their tongues in turn circulated the story, along with many additions and variations.

Uncle Kamil staggered into the café in a dazed state and sat slumped in a chair staring straight ahead and mumbling. Suddenly he threw himself on the sofa and began weeping like a child. He could not believe it possible that the young man—who had teased him about buying a shroud—was no longer alive. When the news reached Hamida's mother she fled the house and streaked down the alley wailing out the news to everyone. Some said she wept for the killer and not the victim.

The person most deeply affected was Salim Alwan. His sorrow was not one of personal loss but more the fact that death had forced its way into the alley. Now all his old worries and fears were redoubled. Dark thoughts and sick fancies of the throes of death itself and of the grave all came back to him. Terror gripped him and he could no longer bear to sit still. He paced up and down in his office and walked into the alley to gaze mournfully at the shop which had been Abbas's for so many years. He had, due to the hot weather, been disregarding the doctor's orders to drink only warm water; but now he instructed that it always be served warm as before. He spent a full hour sitting in his darkened office trembling with fear and panic, his nerves shattered by Uncle Kamil's weeping . . .

This crisis too, like all the others, finally subsided and the alley returned to its usual state of indifference and forgetfulness. It continued, as was its custom, to weep in the morning when there was material for tears, and resound with laughter in the evening. And in the time between, doors and windows would creak as they were opened and then creak again as they were closed.

In this particular period no matter of note occurred, except that Mrs. Saniya Afifi decided to clear out the flat which Dr. Bushi had occupied before he went to jail and Uncle Kamil volunteered to carry Bushi's personal belongings and dental tools into his flat. In explanation it was said that Uncle Kamil preferred to share his dwelling with Bushi rather than continue to endure unaccustomed loneliness. No one blamed him and indeed they may well have considered the act a kindness on his part, for a term in prison was not the sort of thing to bring disgrace on a man in the alley.

During these days, too, people talked about Umm Hamida's renewal of contact with her foster daughter, who was well on the way to convalescence and recovery. They gossiped about how the mother seemed to be hoping to reap some of the profits of this ample treasure.

Then the interest of the alley was suddenly really aroused when a butcher and his family came to occupy Bushi's flat. The family consisted of the butcher, his wife, seven sons and an extremely beautiful daughter. Husain Kirsha said she was as lovely as a new moon.

When, however, the time for Radwan Husaini's return from the Hijaz came close, no one at all could think of anything but this. They hung up lanterns and flags and put a carpet of sand down over the street, all promising themselves a night of such joy and happiness that they would never forget it.

One day Sheikh Darwish saw Uncle Kamil joking with the old barber and, gazing up towards the roof of the coffee-house, he recited loudly:

" 'Man is named only to be forgotten and there's never a heart that doesn't change.' "

Uncle Kamil's face clouded over and went pale and his eyes brimmed with tears. Sheikh Darwish shrugged his shoulders indifferently and went on, his eyes still fixed on the ceiling:

" 'Let he who dies of love die sad; there's no good in any love without death.' "

Then he shuddered, sighed deeply and continued:

"Oh Lady of Ladies, Oh fulfiller of all needs . . . mercy . . . mercy, Oh People of the House! I will be patient so long as I live, for do not all things have their end? Oh yes, everything comes to its *nihaya.*

"And the word for this in English is 'end' and it is spelled: E N D . . ."

THE
THIEF
AND
THE
DOGS

INTRODUCTION

o writer of the modern Arab world has enjoyed a success in literature to approach that of Naguib Mahfouz. His work has become appreciated as a voluminous and sharply focused reflection of the Egyptian experience through the turbulent changes of the twentieth century. His fame within the Middle East is consequently unrivalled and the importance of his score of published works has been widely noted abroad. Many of his stories have previously appeared in English and other foreign languages and he has received honorary awards and degrees from Denmark, France and the Soviet Union. His achievements are all the more extraordinary for his having remained employed full-time for over thirty years in various departments of the Egyptian civil service, in which he reached administrative positions of importance before his retirement in 1972.

The work of Mahfouz, then, reveals many of the changes of aspiration and orientation of Egyptian intellectuals over the span of his lifetime. In the thirties, a time when Mahfouz was emerging from Cairo University with a degree in philosophy, Egyptians were struggling for equilibrium between the contradictory pulls of pride in Islam or in ancient Egypt. Their dilemma was compounded by their awareness of the attitude of foreigners towards their national heritage. They witnessed every day in the streets of Cairo the enthusiasm of archaeologists and tourists for the treasures of their ancient tombs and pyramids but they also knew of the glories of their heritage from Islam and the Arabs in religion, architecture, culture and, above all, language. And they were only too aware of the disdain of foreigners for the state of their contemporary government and society.

Mahfouz' dilemma in orientation lasted, however, only for the thirties, during which period he composed a rather strange medley of short stories dealing with the life of his own time and several works on the ancient history of his country. He translated an English text on ancient Egypt and wrote three historical novels depicting aspects of the lives and times of the pharaohs. In them his particular concern was for the relationships between rulers and the people and the uprising of the Egyptians against the Hyksos invaders, subjects of obvious interest to his readers critical of the despotic Egyptian monarchy under King Farouk, himself dominated by the strong British presence in the country. By the early forties, however, Mahfouz had abandoned his plan of constructing a massive series of novels based on ancient history and almost all his work since has related specifically to the Egypt that he has himself witnessed.

In that middle period of his work, then, he wrote a series of novels, first published obscurely and later to achieve great and continuing popularity, that dealt both with his own milieu, the Muslim middle-class of Cairo, and with that of the colorful characters of the conservative quarters of the ancient city. These were followed by his *Trilogy*, which caused a literary sensation in the late fifties and consequently drew attention back to his earlier works. A voluminous work, the *Trilogy* presents a detailed panorama of the life of three generations of a Cairo merchant-class family over the turbulent first half of this century. It is a fascinating study of the social, political, religious and philosophical strains experienced by his countrymen at that time of fast transition and the consequent effects on their personal relationships.

Following the 1952 Revolution of General Naguib and Colonel Nasser, Mahfouz wrote nothing for seven years. His 1959 *Awlad Haritna* (translated as *Children of Gebelawi*) was serialized in the daily newspaper *al-Ahram* and never since republished in Egypt. It is a pessimistic portrayal in allegorical form of man's struggle for comprehension and solution of the problems of his existence. Discouraged by the furor the novel caused in traditional and religious circles, Mahfouz again refrained from writing for some time, until the publication of this novel, *The Thief and the Dogs*, in 1961. It was well received and was followed by a stream of fine novels in the sixties that detailed with delicacy and great courage the crisis of identity and conscience suffered by Egyptian intellectuals during that period of pervasive malaise and dissatisfaction.

His more recent works, following the 1967 war with Israel, have been circumspect and philosophical and he has favored the short story and the short play for expression of his frequently allegorical themes. However, *al-Hubb Tahta al-Matar* (*Love in the Rain*) published in mid-1973 in book form only, without serialization in the widely read daily press, contrasted (and by implication criticized) the free and at times immoral life which continued in Cairo with the soldiers' endless waiting, in discomfort and fear of death, for the inevitable renewal of warfare with Israel.

The present novel, then, was first published in 1961 and both its subject treatment and style marked distinct changes from Mahfouz' earlier work. This is a psychological novel, impressionist rather than realist; it moves with the speed and economy of a detective story. Here Mahfouz uses the "stream of consciousness" technique for the first time to show the mental anguish of his central figure consumed by bitterness and a desire for revenge against the individuals and the society who have corrupted and betrayed him and brought about his inevitable damnation. It is a masterly work, swiftly giving the reader a keenly accurate vision of the workings of a sick and embittered mind doomed to self-destruction. And, as he inevitably comes to the protagonist's disillusionment and despair, the reader gains intimate and authentic impressions of the values and structures of Egyptian society of the period.

Trevor Le Gassick

1

nce more he breathed the air of freedom. But there was stifling dust in the air, almost unbearable heat, and no one was waiting for him; nothing but his blue suit and gym shoes.

As the prison gate and its unconfessable miseries receded, the world—streets belabored by the sun, careening cars, crowds of people moving or still—returned.

No one smiled or seemed happy. But who of these people could have suffered more than he had, with four years lost, taken from him by betrayal? And the hour was coming when he would confront them, when his rage would explode and burn, when those who had betrayed him would despair unto death, when treachery would pay for what it had done.

Nabawiyya. Ilish. Your two names merge in my mind. For years you will have been thinking about this day, never imagining, all the while, that the gates would ever actually open. You'll be watching now, but I won't fall into the trap. At the right moment, instead, I'll strike like Fate.

And Sana? What about Sana?

As the thought of her crossed his mind, the heat and the dust, the hatred and pain all disappeared, leaving only love to glow across a soul as clear as a rain-washed sky.

I wonder how much the little one even knows about her father? Nothing, I suppose. No more than this road does, these passers-by or this molten air.

She had never been out of his thoughts, where bit by bit she'd taken shape, like an image in a dream, for four long years. Would luck now give him some decent place to live, where such love could be equally shared, where he could take joy in being a winner again, where what Nabawiyya and Ilish had done would be no more than a memory, odious, but almost forgotten?

You must pull together all the cunning you possess, to culminate in a blow as powerful as your endurance behind prison walls. Here is a man—a man who can dive like a fish, fly like a hawk, scale walls like a rat, pierce solid doors like a bullet!

How will he look when he first sees you? How will his eyes meet yours? Have you forgotten, Ilish, how you used to rub against my legs like a dog? It was me, wasn't it, who taught you how to stand on your own two feet, who made a man of a cigarette-butt cadger? You've forgotten, Ilish, and you're not the only one: She's forgotten, too, that woman who sprang from filth, from vermin, from treachery and infidelity.

Through all this darkness only your face, Sana, smiles. When we meet I'll know how I stand. In a little while, as soon as I've covered the length of this road, gone past all these gloomy arcades, where people used to have fun. Onward and upward. But not to glory. I swear I hate you all.

The bars have shut down and only the side streets are open, where plots are hatched. From time to time he has to cross over a hole in the pavement set there like a snare and the wheels of tramcars growl and shriek like abuse. *Confused cries seem to seep from the curbside garbage. (I swear I hate you all.) Houses of temptation, their windows beckoning even when eyeless, walls scowling where plaster has fallen. And that strange lane, al-Sayrafi Lane, which brings back dark memories. Where the thief stole, then vanished, whisked away. (Woe to the traitors.) Where police who'd staked out the area had slithered in to surround you.*

The same little street where a year before you'd been carrying home flour to make sweetmeats for the Feast, that woman walking in front of you, carrying Sana in her swaddling clothes. Glorious days—how real they were, no one knows—the Feast, love, parenthood, crime. All mixed up with this spot.

The great mosques and, beyond them, the Citadel against the clear sky, then the road flowing into the square, where the green park lies under the hot sun and a dry breeze blows, refreshing despite the heat—the Citadel square, with all its burning recollections.

What's important now is to make your face relax, to pour a little cold water over your feelings, to appear friendly and conciliatory, to play the planned role well. He crossed the middle of the square, entered Imam Way, and walked along it until he came close to the three-story house at the end, where two little streets joined the main road. *This social visit will tell you what they've got up their sleeves. So study the road carefully, and what's on it. Those shops, for instance, where the men are staring at you, cowering like mice.*

"Said Mahran!" said a voice behind him. "How marvellous!"

He let the man catch up with him; they said hello to each other, hiding their real feelings under mutual grins. *So the bastard has friends. He'll know right away what all these greetings are about. You're probably peeking at us through the shutters now, Ilish, hiding like a woman.*

"I thank you, Mr. Bayaza."

People came up to them from the shops on both sides of the street; voices were loud and warm in congratulation and Said found himself surrounded by a crowd—his enemy's friends, no doubt—who tried to outdo one another in cordiality:

"Thank God you're back safe and sound."

"We congratulate ourselves, being your close friends!"

"We all said we wished you'd be released on the anniversary of the Revolution."

"I thank God and you, gentlemen," he said, staring at them with his brown, almond-shaped eyes.

Bayaza patted him on the shoulder. "Come into the shop and have a cold drink to celebrate."

"Later," he said quietly. "When I'm back."

"Back?"

One man shouts, directing his voice to the second story of the house: "Mr. Ilish! Mr. Ilish, come down and congratulate Said Mahran!" *No need to warn him, you black beetle! I've come in broad daylight. I know you've been watching.*

"Back from what?" said Bayaza.

"There's some business I have to settle."

"With whom?" said Bayaza.

"Have you forgotten I'm a father? And that my little girl's with Ilish?"

"No. But there's a solution to every disagreement. In the sacred law."

"And it's best to reach an understanding," said someone else.

"Said, you're fresh out of prison," a third man added in a conciliatory tone. "A wise man learns his lesson."

"Who said I'm here for anything other than to reach an understanding?"

In the second story of the building a window opened, Ilish leaned out, and they all looked up at him tensely. Before a word could be said, a big man wearing a striped garment and police boots came from the front door of the house. Said recognized Hasaballah, the detective, and pretended to be surprised.

"You shouldn't have disturbed yourself. I have only come to reach an amicable settlement," he said with feeling.

The detective came up and patted him all over, searching with practiced speed and skill. "Shut up, you cunning bastard. What did you say you wanted?"

"I've come to reach an understanding about the future of my daughter."

"As if you knew what understanding meant!"

"I do indeed, for my daughter's sake."

"You can always go to court."

Ilish shouted from above: "Let him come up. Come up all of you. You're all welcome." *Rally them round you, coward. I've only come to test the strength of your fortifications. When your hour arrives neither detective nor walls will do you any good.*

They all crowded into a sitting room and planted themselves in sofas and chairs. The windows were opened: flies rushed in with the light. Cigarette burns had made black spots in the sky-blue carpet and from a large photograph on the wall Ilish was staring, holding a thick stick with both his hands. The detective sat next to Said and began to play with his worry-beads.

Ilish Sidra came into the room, a loose garment swelling round his barrel-like body, his fat round face buttressed by a square chin. His huge nose had a broken bridge. "Thank the Lord you're back safe and sound!" he said, as if he had nothing to fear. But no one spoke, anxious looks passed back and forth, and the atmosphere was tense until Ilish went on talking: "What's over is done with, such things happen every day; unhappiness can occur, and long-established friendships often break up. But only shameful deeds can shame a man."

Conscious that his eyes were glittering, that he was slim and strong, Said felt like a tiger crouched to spring on an elephant. He found himself repeating Ilish's words: "Only shameful deeds can shame a man." Many eyes stared back at him; the detective's fingers stopped playing with his beads; realizing what was passing in their minds, he added as an afterthought, "I agree with every word you say."

"Come to the point," the detective broke in, "and stop beating about the bush."

"Which point?" Said said innocently.

"There's only one point to discuss, and that's your daughter."

And what about my wife and my fortune, you mangy dogs! I'll show you. Just wait. How I'd like to see now the look you'll have in your eyes. It would give me respect for beetles, scorpions, and worms, you vermin. Damn the man who lets himself be carried away by the melodious voice of woman. But Said nodded in agreement.

One of the sycophants said, "Your daughter is in safe hands with her mother. According to the law a six-year-old girl should stay with her mother. If you like, I could bring her to visit you every week."

Said raised his voice, deliberately, so that he could be heard outside the room: "According to the law she should be in my custody. In view of the various circumstances."

"What do you mean?" Ilish said, suddenly angry.

"Arguing will only give you a headache," said the detective, trying to placate him.

"I have committed no crime. It was partly fate and circumstances, partly my sense of duty and decency that drove me to do what I did. And I did it partly for the sake of the little girl."

A sense of duty and decency, indeed, you snake! Double treachery, betrayal, and infidelity! O, for the sledge hammer and the axe and the gallows rope! I wonder how Sana looks now. "I did not leave her in need," Said said, as calmly as he could, "She had my money, and plenty of it."

"You mean your loot," the detective roared, "the existence of which you denied in court!"

"All right, call it what you like. But where has it gone?"

"There wasn't a penny, believe me, friends!" Ilish protested loudly. "She was in a terrible predicament. I just did my duty."

"Then how have you been able to live in such comfort," Said challenged, "and spend so generously on others?"

"Are you God, that you should call me to account?"

"Peace, peace, shame the devil, Said," said one of Ilish's friends.

"I know you inside out, Said," the detective said slowly. "I can read your thoughts better than anyone. You will only destroy yourself. Just stick to the subject of the girl. That's the best thing for you."

Said looked down to hide his eyes, then smiled and said, in a tone of resignation, "You're quite right, officer."

"I know you inside out. But I'll go along with you. Out of consideration for the company here present. Bring the girl, someone. Wouldn't it be better to find out first what she thinks?"

"What do you mean, officer?"

"Said, I know you. You don't want the girl. And you can't keep her, because you'll have difficulty enough finding some accommodation for yourself. But it's only fair and kind to let you see her. Bring in the girl."

Bring in her mother, you mean. How I wish our eyes could meet, so I might behold one of the secrets of hell! O, for the axe and the sledge hammer!

Ilish went to fetch the girl. At the sound of returning footsteps Said's heart began to beat almost painfully and as he stared at the door, he bit the inside of his lips, anticipation and tenderness stifling all his rage.

After what seemed a thousand years, the girl appeared. She looked surprised. She was wearing a pretty white dress and white open slippers that showed henna-dyed toes. She gazed at him, her face dark, her black hair flowing over her forehead, while his soul devoured her. Bewildered, she looked around at all the other faces, then particularly at his, which was staring so intently. He was unable to take his eyes off her. As she felt herself being pushed towards him, she planted her feet in the carpet and leaned backward away from him. And suddenly he felt crushed by a sense of total loss.

It was as if, in spite of her almond-shaped eyes, her long face, and her slender, aquiline nose, she was not his own daughter. Where were the instinctive ties of blood and soul? Were they, too, treacherous, deceptive? And how could he, even so, resist the almost overwhelming desire to hug her to him for ever?

"This is your father, child," said the detective impatiently.

"Shake hands with Daddy," said Ilish, his face impassive.

She's like a mouse. What's she afraid of? Doesn't she know how much I love her? He stretched out his hand towards her, but instead of being able to say anything he had a fit of choking and had to swallow hard, managing only to smile at her tenderly, invitingly.

"No!" said Sana. She backed away, trying to steal out of the room, but a man standing behind stopped her. "Mummy!" she cried, but the man pushed her gently and then began to coax her, "Shake hands with Daddy." Everyone looked on with malicious interest.

Said knew now that prison lashings had not been as cruel as he used to think. "Come to me, Sana," he pleaded, unable to bear her refusal any longer, half-standing and drawing closer to her.

"No!" she shouted.

"I am your daddy." She raised her eyes to Ilish Sidra in bewilderment, but Said repeated emphatically: "I am your daddy, come to me." She shrank back even further. He pulled her towards him almost forcibly, then she screamed, and as he drew her closer, fought back, crying. He leaned forward to kiss her, disregarding his failure and disappointment, but his lips caught only a whirling arm. "I'm your daddy, don't be afraid. I'm your dad." The scent on her hair filled his mind with the memory of her mother; he felt his face go hard. The child struggled and wept more violently, and finally the detective intervened: "Easy, easy, the child does not know you."

Defeated, Said let her run away. "I will take her," he said angrily, sitting bolt upright.

A moment of silence passed, at the end of which Bayaza said, "Calm yourself first."

"She must come back to me."

"Let the judge decide that," the detective said sharply, then turned questioningly to Ilish. "Yes?"

"It has nothing to do with me. Her mother will never give her up, except in compliance with the law."

"Just as I pointed out at the beginning. There's no more to be said. It's up to a court of law."

Said felt that if once given vent, his rage would be unrestrainable and therefore with supreme effort managed to keep it under control, reminding himself of things he had almost forgotten. "Yes, the court of law," he said as calmly as he could.

"And as you can see, the girl is being very well looked after," said Bayaza.

"First find yourself an honest means of living," the detective said with an ironic smile.

Able now to control himself, Said said, "Yes, of course. All that's quite correct. No need to be upset. I'll reconsider the whole affair. The best thing would be to forget the past and start looking for a job to provide a suitable home for the child when the time comes."

During the surprised silence that followed this speech, glances were exchanged, some incredulous, some perhaps not. The detective gathered his worry-beads into his fist and asked, "Have we finished now?"

"Yes," Said answered. "I only want my books."

"Your books?"

"Yes."

"Most of them have been lost by Sana," Ilish said loudly, "but I'll bring you whatever is left." He disappeared for a few minutes and returned carrying a modest pile of books, which he deposited in the middle of the room.

Said leafed through them, picking up one volume after another. "Yes," he remarked sadly, "most of them have been lost."

"How did you acquire all this learning?" the detective said with a laugh, rising to signal the end of the meeting. "Did you steal reading matter as well?"

They all grinned except Said, who went out carrying his books.

2

e looked at the door, open as it always used to be, as he walked up Gabal Road towards it. Here enclosed by ridges of the Muqattam hills, was the Darasa quarter, the scene of so many pleasant memories. The sandy ground was dotted with animals, teeming with children. Said gazed delightedly at the little girls panting from both emotion and exhaustion. Men lolled around him in the shade of the hill, away from the declining sun.

At the threshold of the open door he paused, trying to remember when he'd crossed it last. The simplicity of the house, which could hardly be different from those of Adam's day, was striking. At the left corner of the big, open courtyard stood a tall palm tree with a crooked top; to the right an entrance corridor led by an open door—in this strange house no door was ever closed—to a single room. His heart beat fast, carrying him back to a distant, gentle time of childhood, dreams, a loving father, and his own innocent yearning. He recalled the men filling the courtyard, swaying with their chanting, God's praise echoing from the depths of their hearts. "Look and listen, learn and open your heart," his father used to say. Besides a joy like the joy of Paradise that was aroused in him by faith and dreams, there had also been the joy of singing and green tea. He wondered how Ali al-Junaydi was.

From inside the room he could hear a man concluding his prayers. Said smiled, slipped in carrying his books, and saw the Sheikh sitting cross-legged on the prayer carpet, absorbed in quiet recitation. The old room had hardly changed. The rush mats had been replaced by new ones, thanks to his disciples, but the Sheikh's sleeping mattress still lay close to the western wall, pierced by a window through which the rays of the declining sun were pouring down at Said's feet. The other walls of the room were half-covered with rows of books on shelves. The odor of incense lingered as if it were the same he remembered, never dissipated, from years ago. Putting down his load of books, he approached the Sheikh.

"Peace be upon you, my lord and master."

Having completed his recitation the Sheikh raised his head, disclosing a face that was emaciated but radiant with overflowing vitality; framed by a white beard like a halo, and surmounted by a white skull cap that nestled in thick locks of hair showing silvery at his temples. The Sheikh scrutinized him with eyes that had been viewing this world for eighty years and indeed had glimpsed the next, eyes that had not lost their appeal, acuteness, or charm. Said found himself bending over his hand to kiss it, suppressing tears of nostalgia for his father, his boyish hopes, the innocent purity of the distant past.

"Peace and God's compassion be upon you," said the Sheikh in a voice like Time.

What had his father's voice been like? He could see his father's face and his lips moving, and tried to make his eyes do the service of ears, but the voice had gone. And the disciples, the men chanting the mystical *dhikr*, "O master, the Prophet is at your gate!"—where were they now?

He sat down cross-legged on the rush mat before the Sheikh. "I am sitting without asking your permission," he said. "I remember that you prefer that." He sensed that the Sheikh was smiling, though on those lips concealed amidst the whiteness, no smile was visible. Did the Sheikh remember him? "Forgive my coming to your house like this. But there's nowhere else in the world for me to go."

The Sheikh's head drooped to his breast. "You seek the walls, not the heart," he whispered.

Said was baffled; not knowing what to say, he sighed, then quietly remarked, "I got out of jail today."

"Jail?" said the Sheikh, his eyes closed.

"Yes. You haven't seen me for more than ten years, and during that time strange things have happened to me. You've probably heard about them from some of your disciples who know me."

"Because I hear much I can hardly hear anything."

"In any case I didn't want to meet you under false pretences, so I'm telling you I came out of jail, only today."

The Sheikh slowly shook his head, then, opening his eyes, said, "You have not come out of jail." The voice was sorrowful.

Said smiled. This was the language of old times again, where words had a double meaning.

"Master, every jail is tolerable, except the government jail."

The Sheikh glanced at him with clear and lucid eyes, then muttered, "He says every jail is tolerable except the government jail."

Said smiled again, though he'd almost given up hope of being able to communicate, and asked, "Do you remember me?"

"Your concern is the present hour."

Fairly certain that he was remembered, Said asked for reassurance: "And do you remember my father, Mr. Mahran, God have mercy upon his soul?"

"May God have mercy upon all of us."

"What wonderful days those were!"

"Say that, if you can, about the present."

"But . . ."

"God have mercy upon us all."

"I was saying, I have just come out of jail today."

The Sheikh nodded his head, showing sudden vigor. "And as he was impaled on the stake he smiled and said: 'It was God's will that I should meet Him thus.'"

My father could understand you. But me you turned away from, treating me as if you were turning me out of your house. And even so I've come back here, of my own accord, to this atmosphere of incense and disquiet, because a man so desolate, with no roof over his head, cannot do otherwise.

"Master, I have come to you now when my own daughter has rejected me."

The Sheikh sighed. "God reveals his secrets to His tiniest creatures!"

"I thought that, if God had granted you long life, I should find your door open."

"And the door of Heaven? How have you found that?"

"But there is nowhere on earth for me to go. And my own daughter has rejected me."

"How like you she is!"

"In what way, Master?"

"You seek a roof, not an answer."

Said rested his head with its short, wiry hair on his dark, thin hand, and said: "My father used to seek you when he was in trouble, so I found myself . . ."

"You seek a roof and nothing else."

Convinced that the Sheikh knew who he was, Said felt uneasy but did not know why. "It's not only a roof," he said, "I want more than that. I would like to ask God to be pleased with me."

The Sheikh replied as if intoning. "The celestial Lady said: Aren't you ashamed to ask for His good pleasure while you are not well-pleased with Him?"

The open space outside resounded with the braying of a donkey, which ended in a throaty rattle like a sob. Somewhere a harsh voice was singing, "Where have luck and good fortune gone?" He remembered once when he'd been caught singing by his father "I Give You Three Guesses": his father had punched him gently and said, "Is this an appropriate song on our way to the blessed Sheikh?" He remembered how, in the midst of the chanting, his father had reeled in ecstasy, his eyes swimming, his voice hoarse, sweat pouring down his face, while he himself sat at the foot of the palm tree, watching the disciples by the light of a lantern, nibbling a fruit, rapt in curious bliss. All that was before he'd felt the first scalding drop of the draught of love.

The Sheikh's eyes were closed now, as if he were asleep, and Said had become so adjusted to the setting and atmosphere that he could no longer smell the incense. It occurred to him that habit is the root of laziness, boredom, and death, that habit had been responsible for his sufferings, the treachery, the ingratitude, and the waste of his life's hard toil. "Are the *dhikr* meetings still held here?" he asked, attempting to rouse the Sheikh.

But the Sheikh gave no answer. Even more uneasy now, Said asked a further question: "Aren't you going to welcome me here?"

The Sheikh opened his eyes and said, "Weak are the seeker and the sought."

"But you are the Master of the house."

"The Owner of the house welcomes you," the Sheikh said, suddenly jovial, "as He welcomes every creature and every thing." Encouraged, Said smiled, but the Sheikh added, as if it were an afterthought, "As for me, I am Master of nothing."

The sunlight on the rush mat had retreated now to the wall.

"In any case," said Said, "this house is my real home, as it always was a home for my father and for every supplicant. You, my Master, deserve all our gratitude."

" 'Lord, you know how incapable I am of doing You justice in thanking you, so please thank yourself on my account!' Thus spake one of the grateful."

"I am in need of a kind word," Said pleaded.

"Do not tell lies." The Sheikh spoke gently, then bowed his head, his beard fanning out over his chest, and seemed lost in thought.

Said waited, then shifted backwards to rest against one of the bookshelves, where for several minutes he sat contemplating the fine-looking old man, until finally impatience made him ask, "Is there anything I could do for you?"

The Sheikh did not bother to respond and a period of silence followed, during which Said watched a line of ants nimbly crawling along a fold in the mat. Suddenly the Sheikh said, "Take a copy of the Koran and read."

A little confused, Said explained apologetically, "I just got out of jail today, and I have not performed the prayer ablutions."

"Wash yourself now and read."

"My own daughter has rejected me. She was scared of me, as if I was the devil. And before that her mother was unfaithful to me."

"Wash and read," replied the Sheikh, gently.

"She committed adultery with one of my men, a layabout, a mere pupil of mine, utterly servile. She applied for divorce on grounds of my imprisonment and went and married him."

"Wash and read."

"And he took everything I owned, the money and the jewelry. He's a big man now, and all the local crooks have become followers and cronies of his."

"Wash and read."

"It wasn't thanks to any sweat by the police that I was arrested." Said went on, the veins in his forehead pulsing with anger. "No, it wasn't. I was sure of my safety, as usual. It was that dog who betrayed me, in collusion with her. Then disaster followed disaster until finally my daughter rejected me."

"Wash and read the verses: 'Say to them: if you love God, then follow me and God will love you' and 'I have chosen thee for Myself.' Also repeat the words: 'Love is acceptance, which means obeying His commands and refraining from what He has prohibited and contentment with what He decrees and ordains.'"

I could see my father listening and nodding his head with pleasure, looking at me with a smile as if saying: "Listen and learn." I had been happy then, hoping no one could see me, so I could climb the palm tree or throw up a stone to bring down a date, singing to myself along with those chanting men. Then one evening when I'd come back to the students' hostel in Gizeh I saw her coming towards me, holding a basket, pretty and charming, all the joys of heaven and torments of hell that I was fated to experience hidden within her.

What had it been about the chanting I'd liked, when they recited: "As soon as He appeared the beacon of faith shone" and: "I saw the crescent moon and the face of the beloved"? But the sun is not yet set. The last golden thread is receding from the window. A long night is waiting for me, the first night of freedom. I am alone with my freedom, or rather I'm in the company of the Sheikh, who is lost in heaven, repeating words that cannot be understood by someone approaching hell. What other refuge have I?

3

Flipping eagerly through the pages of *al-Zahra* until he found Rauf Ilwan's column, Said began to read while still only a few yards from the house where he'd spent the night, the house of Sheikh Ali al-Junaydi. But what was it that seemed to be inspiring Ilwan now? Said found only comments on women's fashions, on loudspeakers, and a reply to a complaint by an anonymous wife. Diverting enough, indeed, but what had become of the Rauf Ilwan he'd known? Said thought of the good old days at the students' hostel, and particularly of the wonderful enthusiasm that had radiated from a young peasant with shabby clothes, a big heart, and a direct and glittering style of writing. What was it that had happened in the world? What lay behind these strange and mysterious events? Did things happen that were similar to what took place in the Sayrafi alley? And how about Nabawiyya and Ilish and that dear little girl who rejected her father? I must see him, he thought. The Sheikh has given me a mat to sleep on, but I need money. *I must begin life afresh, Mr.*

Ilwan, and for that purpose you are no less important than Sheikh Ali. You are, in fact, the most important thing I have in this insecure world.

He walked on until he reached the *Zahra* offices in Maarif Square, stopping in front of an enormous building where his first thought was that it would be very difficult to break into. The rows of cars surrounding it were like guards along a prison; the rumble of printing presses behind the grille of the basement windows was like the low hum of men sleeping in a dormitory. He joined the stream of people entering the building, presented himself at the information desk and asked in his deep "public" voice for Mr. Rauf Ilwan. Staring back with some displeasure at the bold, almost impudent, look in his eyes, the reception clerk snapped, "Fourth floor." Said made for the lift at once, joining people among whom he looked rather out of place in his blue suit and gym shoes, the oddness emphasized by the glaring eyes on either side of his long aquiline nose. A girl caught his eye, which made him curse his ex-wife and her lover under his breath, promising them destruction.

From the corridor of the fourth floor he slipped into the secretary's office before an attendant had time to intercept him and found himself in a large rectangular room with one glass wall overlooking the street, but no place to sit. He heard the secretary talking to someone on the telephone, declaring that Mr. Rauf was at a meeting with the editor-in-chief and would not be back for at least two hours. Feeling alien and out of place, Said poised himself with bravado, staring at the other people in the room almost defiantly, remembering a time when he would have fixed his gaze on people like them as if he wished to cut their throats. What were such people like nowadays, he wondered.

Rauf was now a very important man, it seemed, a great man, as great as this room. It isn't a suitable place for reunion of old friends. Rauf won't be able to behave naturally here. There was a time when he'd been nothing more than a scribbler with the magazine *al-Nadhir*, tucked away in Sharia Muhammad Ali, a poor writer whose voice rang with demands for freedom. *I wonder what you're like now, Rauf. Will he have changed, like you, Nabawiyya? Will he disown me, as Sana has done? No, I must banish these evil thoughts. He's still a friend and mentor, a sword of freedom ever drawn, and he'll always be like that, despite this impressiveness, this plush office suite, and those puzzling articles. If this citadel will not allow me to embrace you, Rauf, I'll have to look in the telephone directory and find your home address.*

Seated on the damp grass along the river bank beside Sharia al-Nil, he waited. He waited even longer near a tree silhouetted by the light of an electric lamp. The crescent moon had gone down early, leaving stars to glitter in a sky profoundly black, and a soft breeze blew, distilled from the breath of the night after a day of stunning, searing summer. There he sat, with his arms clasped round his knees and his back to the river, his eyes fixed on villa number eighteen.

What a palace, he thought. It was open on three sides, and an extensive garden lay on the fourth. The trees stood around the white body of the building like whispering figures. A scene like this felt familiar, full of reminders of the good living he'd once enjoyed. How had Rauf managed it? By what means? And in such a short time! Not even thieves could dream of owning a thing like this: *I never used to look at a villa like this except when I was making plans to break into it. Is there really any hope of finding friendship in such a place now? You are indeed a mystery, Rauf Ilwan, and you must be made to reveal your secret.*

Wasn't it strange that Ilwan rhymed with Mahran? And that that dog Ilish should grab and wallow in the fruits of my lifetime's labor?

When a car stopped in front of the villa gate he sprang to his feet. As the porter opened the gate he darted across the road and stood before the car, bending a little so the driver could see him. When the man inside apparently failed to recognize him in the dark, Said roared "Mr. Rauf, I am Said Mahran." The man put his head close to the open window of the car and repeated his name, in obvious surprise, his low voice carefully modulated. Said could not read Rauf's expression, but the tone of voice was encouraging. After a moment of silence and inaction, the car door opened and Said heard him say, "Get in."

A good beginning, he thought. Rauf Ilwan was the same man he knew, despite the glass-filled office-suite and the lovely villa. The car went down a drive that curved like the shape of a violin, towards a flight of steps leading to the main entrance of the house.

"How are you, Said? When did you come out?"

"Yesterday."

"Yesterday?"

"Yes, I should have come to see you, but I had some things I had to attend to and I needed rest, so I spent the night at Sheikh Ali al-Jumaydi's. Remember him?"

"Sure. Your late father's Sheikh. I watched his meetings with you lots of times." They left the car and went into the reception hall.

"They were fun, weren't they?"

"Yes, and I used to get a big kick out of their singing."

A servant switched on the chandelier, and Said's eyes were dazzled by its size, its multitude of upturned bulbs, its stars and crescents. The light that spread throughout the room was caught in mirrors at the corners, reflecting the brilliance. Objets d'art on gilt stands were displayed as if they had been salvaged from the obscurity of history for that sole purpose. The ceiling, he saw looking up, was richly decorated, while all around him comfortable chairs and cushions were casually disposed among vividly patterned carpets. His eyes rested last on the face of Maitre Ilwan, now round and full, a face he had loved, whose features he had long ago learnt by heart, having gazed at it so often while listening to Rauf speak; and, stealing occasional glances at the objets d'art, Said went on examining that face while a servant drew back curtains and opened French windows to the verandah overlooking the garden, letting a breeze heavy with the perfume of blossomy trees flow into the room.

The mixture of light and scent was distracting, but Said observed that Ilwan's face had become cow-like in its fullness, and that despite his apparent friendliness and courtesy, there was something chilly about him, as well as an unfamiliar and rather disturbing suavity, a quality that could only have come from a touch of blue blood, despite Rauf's flat nose and heavy jaw. What refuge would be left if this only surviving support also collapsed?

Rauf sat near the French windows to the verandah on a sofa that was arranged with three easy chairs in a square around a luminous

pillar adorned with mythological figures. Said sat down, without
hesitation and without showing his anxiety.

Ilwan stretched out his long legs. "Did you look for me at the
paper?"

"Yes, but I saw it wasn't a suitable place for us to meet."

Rauf laughed, showing teeth stained black at the gums. "The
office is like a whirlpool, in constant motion. Have you been waiting
long here?"

"A lifetime!"

Rauf laughed again. "There was a time no doubt when you were
quite familiar with this street?"

"Of course." Said, too, laughed. "I've had clients here with whom
my business transactions have made their premises unforgettable.
The villa of Fadil Hasanain Pasha, for instance, where my visit netted
a thousand pounds, or the one that belongs to the film star Kawakib,
where I got a pair of superb diamond earrings."

The servant came in pushing a trolley laden with a bottle, two
glasses, a pretty little violet-colored ice bucket, a dish of apples
arranged in a pyramid, plates with hors d'oeuvres, and a silver water
jug.

Rauf gestured to the servant to withdraw, filled two glasses himself and offered one to Said, raising the other: "To freedom." While
Said emptied his glass in one gulp, Rauf took a sip then said, "And
how is your daughter? Oh, I forgot to ask you—why did you spend the
night at Sheikh Ali's?"

He doesn't know what happened, thought Said, but he still remembers my daughter. And he gave Rauf a cold-blooded account of
his misfortunes.

"So yesterday I paid a visit to al-Sayrafi Lane," he concluded.
"There I found a detective waiting for me, as I'd expected, and my
daughter disowned me and screamed in my face." He helped himself
to another whisky.

"This is a sad story. But your daughter isn't to blame. She can't
remember you now. Later on she'll grow to know and love you."

"I have no faith left in all her sex."

"That's how you feel now. But tomorrow, who knows how you'll feel? You'll change your opinion of your own accord. That's the way of the world."

The telephone rang. Rauf rose, picked up the receiver and listened for a moment. His face began to beam and he carried the telephone outside to the verandah, while Said's sharp eyes registered everything. It must be a woman. A smile like that, strolling into the dark, could only mean a woman. He wondered if Ilwan was still unmarried. Though they sat there cozily drinking and chatting, Said now sensed that this meeting would be exceedingly difficult to repeat. The feeling was unaccountable, like the whispered premonition of some still undiagnosed cancerous growth, but he trusted it, relying on instinct. A resident now in one of those streets that Said had only visited as a burglar, after all, this man may have felt obliged to welcome him, having actually changed so much that only a shadow of the old self remained. When Said heard Rauf's sudden laugh resounding on the verandah, he felt even less reassured. Calmly, however, he took an apple and began to munch it, pondering the extent to which his whole life had been no more than the mere acting out of ideas that had come from that man now chuckling into a telephone. What if Rauf should prove to have betrayed those ideas?

He would then have to pay dearly for it. On that score there was not the slightest doubt.

Rauf Ilwan came in from the verandah, replaced the telephone and sat down looking extremely pleased. "So. Congratulations on your freedom. Being free is precious indeed. It more than makes up for losing anything else, no matter how valuable." Helping himself to a slice of pastrami, Said nodded in agreement, but without real interest in what had just been said. "And now you've come out of prison to find a new world," Rauf went on, refilling both glasses while Said wolfed down the hors d'oeuvres.

Glancing at his companion, Said caught a look of disgust, quickly covered by a smile. You must be mad to think he was sincere in welcoming you. This is only superficial courtesy—doing the right thing—and will evaporate. Every kind of treachery pales beside this; what a void would then swallow up the entire world!

Rauf stretched his hand to a cigarette box adorned with Chinese characters, placed in a hollow in the illuminated pillar. "My dear Said," he said, taking a cigarette, "everything that used to spoil life's pleasures for us has now completely disappeared."

"The news astounded us in prison," Said said, his mouth full of food. "Who could have predicted such things?" He looked at Rauf, smiling. "No class war now?"

"Let there be a truce! Every struggle has its proper field of battle."

"And this magnificent drawing room," said Said, looking around him, "is like a parade-ground." He saw a cold look in his companion's eyes and regretted the words instantly. Why can't your tongue ever learn to be polite?

"What do you mean?" Rauf's voice was icy.

"I mean it's a model of sophisticated taste and—"

"Don't try to be evasive," said Rauf with narrowed eyes. "Out with it. I understand you perfectly, I know you better than anybody else."

Said attempted a disarming laugh, then said, "I meant no harm at all."

"Never forget that I live by the sweat of my brow."

"I haven't doubted that for a moment. Please don't be angry."

Rauf puffed hard on his cigarette but made no further comment.

Aware that he ought to stop eating, Said said apologetically, "I haven't quite got over the atmosphere of prison. I need some time to recover my good manners and learn polite conversation. Apart from the fact that my head's still spinning from that strange meeting, when my own daughter rejected me."

Rauf's Mephistophelean eyebrows lifted in what looked like silent forgiveness. When he saw Said's gaze wander from his face to the food, as if asking permission to resume eating, he said, "Help yourself," quite calmly.

Said attacked the rest of the dishes without hesitation, as if nothing had happened, until he'd wiped them clean. At this point Rauf said, a little quickly, as if he wished to end the meeting: "Things must now change completely. Have you thought about your future?"

Said lit a cigarette. "My past hasn't yet allowed me to consider the future."

"It occurs to me that there are more women in the world than men. So you mustn't let the infidelity of one lone female bother you. As for your daughter, she'll get to know you and love you one day. The important thing now is to look for a job."

Said eyed a statue of a Chinese god, a perfect embodiment of dignity and repose. "I learned tailoring in prison."

"So you want to set up a tailoring shop?" said Rauf with surprise.

"Certainly not," Said replied quietly.

"What then?"

Said looked at him. "In my whole life I've mastered only one trade."

"You're going back to burglary?" Rauf seemed almost alarmed.

"It's most rewarding, as you know."

"As I know! How the hell do I know?"

"Why are you so angry?" Said gave him a surprised look. "I meant as you know from my past. Isn't it so?"

Rauf lowered his eyes as if trying to assess the sincerity of Said's remark, clearly unable to maintain his bonhomie, and looking for a way to end the meeting. "Listen, Said. Things are no longer what they used to be. In the past you were both a thief and my friend, for reasons you well know. Now the situation has changed. If you go back to burglary you'll be a thief and nothing else."

Dashed by Rauf's unaccommodating frankness, Said sprang to his feet. Then he stifled his agitation, sat down again, and said quietly, "All right. Choose a job that's suitable for me."

"Any job, no matter what. You do the talking, I'll listen."

"I should be happy," Said began, without obvious irony, "to work as a journalist on your paper. I'm a well-educated man and an old disciple of yours. Under your supervision I've read countless books, and you often testified to my intelligence."

Rauf shook his head impatiently, his thick black hair glistening in the brilliant light. "This is no time for joking. You've never been a writer, and you came out of jail only yesterday. This fooling about is wasting my time."

"So I have to choose something menial?"

"No job is menial, as long as it's honest."

Said felt utterly reckless. He ran his eyes quickly over the whole of the smart drawing room, then said bitterly, "How marvellous it is for the rich to recommend poverty to us." Rauf's reaction was to look at his watch.

"I am sure I have taken too much of your time," Said said quietly.

"Yes," said Rauf, with all the blank directness of a July sun, "I'm loaded with work!"

"Thanks for your kindness and hospitality and for the supper," said Said, standing up.

Rauf took out his wallet and handed him two five-pound notes. "Take these to tide you over. Please forgive me for saying I'm over-loaded with work. You'll seldom find me free as I was tonight."

Said smiled, took the bank notes, shook his hand warmly and wished him well: "May God increase your good fortune."

4

 o this is the real Rauf Ilwan, the naked reality—a partial corpse not even decently underground. The other Rauf Ilwan has gone, disappeared, like yesterday, like the first day in the history of man—like Nabawiyya's love or Ilish's loyalty. I must not be deceived by appearances. His kind words are cunning, his smiles no more than a curl of the lips, his generosity a defensive flick of the fingers and only a sense of guilt moved him to let me cross the threshold of his house. You made me and now you reject me: Your ideas create their embodiment in my person and then you simply change them, leaving me lost—rootless, worthless, without hope—a betrayal so vile that if the whole Muqattam hill toppled over and buried it, I still would not be satisfied.

I wonder if you ever admit, even to yourself, that you betrayed me. Maybe you've deceived yourself as much as you try to deceive others. Hasn't your conscience bothered you even in the dark? I wish I could penetrate your soul as easily as I've penetrated your house, that house of mirrors and objets d'art, but I suppose I'd find nothing but betrayal there: Nabawiyya disguised as

Rauf, Rauf disguised as Nabawiyya, or Ilish Sidra in place of both—and betrayal would cry out to me that it was the lowest crime on earth. Their eyes behind my back must have traded anxious looks throbbing with lust, which carried them in a current crawling like death, like a cat creeping on its belly towards a bewildered sparrow. When their chance came, the last remnants of decency and indecision disappeared so that in a corner of the lane, even in my own house, Ilish Sidra finally said: "I'll tell the police. We'll get rid of him" and the child's mother was silent—the tongue that so often and so profusely told me "I love you, the best man in the world" was silent. And I found myself surrounded by police in Sayrafi Lane—though until then demons themselves with all their wiles had failed to trap me—their kicks and punches raining down on me.

You're just the same, Rauf—I don't know which of you is the most treacherous—except that your guilt is greater because of your intelligence and the past association between us: You pushed me into jail, while you leapt free, into that palace of lights and mirrors. You've forgotten your wise sayings about palaces and hovels, haven't you? I will never forget.

At the Abbas Bridge, sitting on a stone bench, he became aware for the first time of where he was.

"It's best to do it now," he said in a loud voice, as if addressing the dark, "before he's had time to get over the shock." I can't hold back, he thought. My profession will always be mine, a just and legitimate trade, especially when it's directed against its own philosopher. There'll be space enough in the world after I've punished the bastards to hide. If I could live without a past, ignoring Nabawiyya, Ilish, and Rauf, I'd be relieved of a great weight, a burden; I'd feel readier to win an easy life and a lot further from the rope. But unless I settle my account with them, life will have no taste because I shall not forget the past. For the simple reason that in my mind it's not a past, but the here and now. Tonight's adventure will be the best beginning for my programme of action. And it'll be a rich venture indeed.

The Nile flowed in black waves slashed sidelong by arrows of light from the reflected street lamps along its banks. The silence was soothing and total.

At the approach of dawn as the stars drew closer to earth, Said rose from his seat, stretched, and began to walk slowly back along the bank towards the place from which he'd come, avoiding the few still-lit lamps, slowing his steps even further when the house came in sight. Examining the street, the terrain, the walls of the big houses as well as the river bank, his eyes finally came to rest on the sleeping villa, guarded on all sides by trees like ghostly figures, where treachery dozed in a fine unmerited tranquillity. *It's going to be a rich venture, indeed, and one to provide an emphatic reply to the treachery of a lifetime.*

He crossed the street casually without a movement to either right or left, without looking wary. Then followed the hedge down a side street, scanning carefully ahead. When he was sure the street was empty he dodged into the hedge, forcing his way in amidst the jasmine and violets, and stood motionless: If there was a dog in the house—other than its owner, of course—it would now fill the universe with barking.

But not a whisper came out of the silence.

Rauf, your pupil is coming, to relieve you of a few worldly goods.

He climbed the hedge nimbly, his expert limbs agile as an ape's, undeterred by the thick, intertwining branches, the heavy foliage and flowers. Gripping the railings, he heaved his body up by main force over the sharp-pointed spikes, then lowered himself until his legs caught the branches inside the garden. Here he clung for a while regaining his breath, studying the terrain: a jungle of bushes, trees, and dark shadows. *I shall have to climb up to the roof and find a way to get in and down. I have no tools, no flashlight, no good knowledge of the house: Nabawiyya hasn't been here before me pretending to work for a while as a washerwoman or a maid; she's busy now with Ilish Sidra.*

Scowling in the dark, trying to chase these thoughts from his mind, he dropped lightly to the ground. Crawling up to the villa on all fours, he felt his way along a wall until he found a drain pipe. Then, gripping it like an acrobat, began to climb towards the roof. Part way up he spotted an open window, just out of reach, and decided instantly to try it. He steered one foot to the window ledge, and shifted his hands one at a time, to grip a cornice. Finally when he could stand with his whole weight, he slid inside, finding himself in what he guessed was the kitchen. The dense darkness was disturbing and he groped for the door. The darkness would be even thicker inside, but where else could he find Rauf's wallet or some of his objets d'art? He had to go on.

Slipping through the door, feeling along the wall with his hands, he had covered a considerable distance, almost deterred by the darkness, when he felt a slight draught touch his face. Puzzling where it could come from, he turned a corner and crept along the smooth wall, his arm stretched out, feeling ahead with his fingers. Suddenly they brushed some dangling beads which rustled slightly as he touched them, making him start. A curtain. He must now be near his goal. He thought of the box of matches in his pocket; instead of reaching for it he made a quiet little opening for himself in the hanging beads and slipped through, bringing the curtain back to position behind him slowly, to avoid making any sound. He took one step forward and bumped some object, perhaps a chair, which he edged away from, raising his head to look for a night light he hoped he would find. All he could see was a darkness that weighed down upon him like a nightmare. For a moment he thought again of lighting a match.

Suddenly he was assailed by light. It shone all around him, so powerful that it struck him with the force of a blow, making him shut his eyes. When he opened them again, Rauf Ilwan was standing only a couple of yards from him, wearing a long dressing-gown, which made him look like a giant, one hand tensed in a pocket, as if he was clutching a weapon. The cold look in his eyes chilled Said to the core, his tightly closed lips; nothing but deep hatred, hostility. The ensuing silence was suffocating, claustrophobic, denser than the walls of a prison. Abd Rabbuh the jailer would soon be jeering: "Back already?"

"Shall we call the police?" someone behind him said curtly. Said turned round and saw three servants standing in a row. "Wait outside," said Rauf, breaking the silence.

As the door opened and closed Said observed that it was made of wood in arabesque designs, its upper panel inlaid with an inscription, probably a proverb or a Koranic verse. He turned to face Rauf.

"It was idiotic of you to try your tricks on me; I know you. I can read you like an open book." Speechless, helpless, and resigned, still

328 • NAGUIB MAHFOUZ

recovering from the shock of surprise, Said had nevertheless an instinctive sense that he would not be handed back to the custody from which he'd been set free the day before. "I've been waiting for you, fully prepared. In fact I even drew up your plan of action. I'd hoped my expectation would be disappointed. But evidently no mistrust in you can prove groundless." Said lowered his eyes for a moment and became aware of the patterned parquet beneath the wax on the floor. Then he looked up, saying nothing. "It's no use. You'll always be worthless and you'll die a worthless death. The best thing I can do now is hand you over to the police." Said blinked, gulped, and lowered his eyes again.

"What have you come for?" Rauf demanded angrily. "You treat me as an enemy. You've forgotten my kindness, my charity. You feel nothing but malice and envy. I know your thoughts, as clearly as I know your actions."

His eyes still wandering over the floor, Said muttered, "I feel dizzy. Peculiar. It's been like that ever since I came out of jail."

"Liar! Don't try to deceive me. You thought I'd become one of the rich I used to attack. And with that in mind you wished to treat me—"

"It's not true."

"Then why did you break into my house? Why do you want to rob me?"

"I don't know," Said said, after a moment's hesitation. "I'm not in my proper state of mind. But you don't believe me."

"Of course I don't. You know you're lying. My good advice didn't persuade you. Your envy and arrogance were aroused, so you rushed in headlong as always, like a madman. Suit yourself, do what you like, but you'll find yourself in jail again."

"Please forgive me. My mind's the way it was in prison, the way it was even before that."

"There's no forgiving you. I can read your thoughts, everything that passes through your mind. I can see exactly what you think of me. And now it's time I delivered you to the police."

"Please don't."

"No? Don't you deserve it?"

"Yes, I do, but please don't."

"If I set eyes on you again," Rauf bellowed, "I'll squash you like an insect." Thus dismissed, Said was about to make a quick exit, but Rauf stopped him with a shout: "Give me back the money." Frozen for a second, Said slipped his hand into his pocket and brought out the two banknotes. Rauf took them and said, "Don't ever show me your face again."

Said walked back to the banks of the Nile, hardly believing his escape, though relief was spoiled by a sense of defeat and now in the damp breath of early daybreak, he wondered how he could have failed to take careful note of the room where he'd been caught, how all he'd noticed had been its decorated door and its waxed parquet. But the dawn shed dewy compassion giving momentary solace for the loss of everything, even the two banknotes, and he surrendered to it. Raising his head to the sky, he found himself awed by the dazzling brilliance of the stars at this hour just before sunrise.

5

hey stared at him incredulously, then everyone in the café rose at once to meet him. Led by the proprietor and his waiter, uttering a variety of colorful expressions of welcome, they formed a circle round him, embraced him, kissing him on the cheeks. Said Mahran shook hands with each of them, saying politely:

"Thanks, Mr. Tarzan. Thanks, friends."

"When was it?"

"Day before yesterday."

"There was supposed to be an amnesty. We were keeping our fingers crossed."

"Thank God I'm out."

"And the rest of them?"

"They're all well; their turn will come."

They exchanged news excitedly for a while, until Tarzan, the proprietor, led Said to his own sofa, asking the other men to go back to their places, and the cafe was quiet again. Nothing had changed.

Said felt he'd left it only yesterday: The round room with its brass fittings, the wooden chairs with their straw seats, were just the way they used to be. A handful of customers, some of whom he recognized, sat sipping tea and making deals. Through the open door out the big window opposite you could see the wasteland stretching into the distance, its thick darkness unrelieved by a single glimmer of light, its impressive silence broken only by occasional laughter borne in on the dry and refreshing breeze—forceful and clean, like the desert itself—that blew between the window and door.

Said took the glass of tea from the waiter, and raised it to his lips without waiting for it to cool, then turned to the proprietor: "How's business these days?"

Tarzan curled his lower lip. "There aren't many men you can rely upon nowadays," he said contemptuously.

"What do you mean? That's too bad."

"They're all lazy, like bureaucrats!"

Said grunted sympathetically. "At least a lazy man is better than a traitor. It was thanks to a traitor I had to go to jail, Mr. Tarzan."

"Really? You don't say!"

Said stared at him surprised. "Didn't you hear the story, then?" When Tarzan shook his head sympathetically, Said whispered in his ear, "I need a good revolver."

"If there's anything you need, I'm at your service."

Said patted him on the shoulder gratefully, then began to ask, with some embarrassment, "But I haven't—"

Tarzan interrupted, placing a thick finger on Said's lips, and said, "You don't need to apologize ever to anyone!"

Said savored the rest of his tea, then walked to the window and stood there, a strong, slim, straight-backed figure of medium height, and let the breeze belly out his jacket, gazing into the pitch-dark waste land that stretched away ahead of him. The stars overhead looked like grains of sand; and the café felt like an island in the midst of an ocean, or an aeroplane alone in the sky. Behind him, at the foot of the hillock on which the café stood, lighted cigarettes moved like nearer stars in the hands of those who sat there in the dark seeking fresh air. On the horizon to the west, the lights of Abbasiyya seemed very far away, their distance making one understand how deeply in the desert this café had been placed.

As Said stared out the window, he became aware of the voices of the men who sat outside, sprawled around the hillock, enjoying the desert breeze—the waiter was going down to them now, carrying a water pipe with glowing coals, from which sparks flew upward with a crackling noise—their lively conversations punctuated by bursts of laughter. He heard the voice of one young man, obviously enjoying a discussion, say, "Show me a single place on earth where there's any security."

Another one disagreed, "Here where we're sitting for instance. Aren't we enjoying peace and security now?"

"You see, you say 'now.' There's the calamity."

"But why do we curse our anxiety and fears? In the end don't they save us the trouble of thinking about the future?"

"So you're an enemy of peace and tranquillity."

"When all you have to think about is the hangman's rope round your neck, it's natural enough to fear tranquillity."

"Well, that's a private matter—you can settle it between yourself and the hangman."

"You're chattering away happily because here you're protected by the desert and the dark. But you'll have to go back to the city some-time soon. So what's the use?"

"The real tragedy is that our enemy is at the same time our friend."

"On the contrary, it's that our friend is also our enemy."

"No. It's that we're cowards. Why don't we admit it?"

"Maybe we are cowards. But how can you be brave in this age?"

"Courage is courage."

"And death is death."

"And darkness and the desert are all these things."

What a conversation! What did they mean? Somehow they're giving expression to my own situation, in a manner as shapeless and strange as the mysteries of that night. There was a time when I had youth, energy and conviction too—the time when I got arms for the national cause and not for the sake of murder. On the other side of this very hill young men, shabby, but pure in heart, used to train for battle. And their head was the present inhabitant of villa number 18. Training himself, training others, spelling out words of wisdom. "Said Mahran," he used to say to me, "a revolver is more important than a loaf of bread." "It's more important than the Sufi sessions you keep rushing off to the way your father did." One evening he asked me, "What does a man need in this country, Said?" and without waiting for an answer he said, "He needs a gun and a book: the gun will take care of the past, the book is for the future. Therefore you must train and read." I can still recall his face that night in the students' hostel, his guffaws of laughter, his words: "So you have stolen. You've actually dared to steal. Bravo! Using theft to relieve the exploiters of some of their guilt is absolutely legitimate, Said. Don't ever doubt it."

This open wasteland had borne witness to Said's own skill. Didn't it used to be said that he was Death Incarnate, that his shot never missed? He closed his eyes, relaxing, enjoying the fresh air, until suddenly he felt a hand on his shoulder. And looking around he saw Tarzan, holding out to him a revolver in his other hand.

"May it be fire for your enemy, God willing," Tarzan said to him.

Said took it. "How much is it, Mr. Tarzan?" he said, inspecting the action.

"It's a present from me."

"No, thank you, I can't accept that. All I ask is that you give me some time until I can afford to pay you."

"How many bullets do you need?"

They walked back to Tarzan's sofa. As they passed the open doorway, they heard a female laugh ringing outside. Tarzan chuckled, "It's Nur, remember her?"

Said looked into the darkness, but could see nothing. "Does she still come here?" he asked.

"Sometimes. She'll be pleased to see you."

"Has she caught anybody?"

"Of course. This time it's the son of the owner of a candy factory." They sat down and Tarzan called the waiter over: "Tell Nur— tactfully—to come here."

It would be nice to see her, to see what time had done to her. She'd hoped to gain his love, but failed. What love he'd had had been the exclusive property of that other unfaithful woman. He'd been made of stone. There's nothing more heart-breaking than loving someone like that. It had been like a nightingale singing to a rock, a breeze caressing sharp-pointed spikes. Even the presents she'd given he used to give away—to Nabawiyya or Ilish. He patted the gun in his pocket and clenched his teeth.

Nur appeared at the entrance. Unprepared, she stopped in amazement as soon as she saw Said, a few steps away from him. He smiled at her, but looked closely: She'd grown thinner, her face was disguised by heavy make-up, and she was wearing a sexy dress that not only showed her arms and legs, but was fitted so tightly to her body that it might have been stretched rubber. What it advertised was that she'd given up all claims to self-respect. So did her bobbed hair, ruffled by the breeze. She ran to him.

"Thank God you're safe," she said, as their hands met, giggling a little to hide her emotion, squeezing him and Tarzan.

"How are you, Nur?" he asked.

"As you can see," Tarzan said for her with a smile, "she's all light, like her name."

"I'm fine," she said. "And you? You look very healthy. Only what's wrong with your eyes? They remind me of how you used to look when you were angry."

"What do you mean?" he said with a grin.

"I don't know, it's hard to describe. Your eyes turn a sort of red and your lips start twitching!"

Said laughed. Then, with a touch of sadness, he said, "I suppose your friend will be coming soon to take you back?"

"Oh, he's dead drunk," she said, shaking her head, tossing the hair from her eyes.

"In any case, you're tied to him."

"Would you like me," she said with a sly smile, "to bury him in the sand?"

"No, not tonight. We'll meet again later. I'm told he's a real catch," he added, with a look of interest that did not escape her.

"He sure is. We'll go in his car to the Martyr's Tomb. He likes open spaces."

So he likes open spaces. Over near the Martyr's Tomb.

Her eyelashes fluttered, showing a pretty confusion that increased as her gaze met his. "You see," she said with a pout, "you never think of me."

"It's not true," he said. "You're very dear to me."

"You're only thinking about that poor fish."

Said smiled. "He forms a part of my thinking of you."

"I'll be ruined if they find out," she said with sudden seriousness. "His father's an influential man and he comes from a powerful family. Do you need money?"

"What I really need is a car," he said, standing up. "Try to be completely natural with him," he went on, gently pinching one of her cheeks. "Nothing will happen to frighten you and no one will suspect you. I'm not a kid. When this is done we'll see a lot more of each other than you ever thought possible."

6

He knew this stretch of ground. Avoiding the road next to the barracks, he set out across the desert to reach the Martyr's Tomb in the shortest time possible, heading for it as if he had a compass built into his head. As soon as he saw the tomb's big dome in the starlight he began looking for the spot where the car would be tucked away. Walking round the tomb, he scanned the ground as sharply as he could, but it was only when he reached its southern wall that the shape at a little distance became visible. He made for it without another thought, keeping his head low, crouching as he came closer to the car, until he could hear through the silence the sounds of love being made in whispers. *There'll be terror, now, he told himself, in the middle of pleasure, and joy will suddenly vanish but it's no fault of yours: chaos and confusion envelop us all like the vault of the sky. Didn't Rauf Ilwan used to say that our intentions were good, but we lacked order or discipline?*

The breathing inside the car had turned to panting. Almost crawling on his hands and knees, Said crept up until he could touch the door handle. He tightened his grip on the handle, and yanked open the door, shouting, "Don't move."

Two people cried out in shocked surprise and a pair of heads stared at him in terror. He waved the gun and said, "Don't move or I'll shoot. Get out."

"I beg you—" said Nur's voice.

Another voice, throaty, as if strained through sand and gravel, said, "What—what is it you want, please?"

"Get out."

Nur threw herself out of the car, grasping her clothes in one hand, followed by the young man, who stumbled as he struggled to insert his feet in his trousers. Said thrust the gun so menacingly close that the young man began to plead. "No. No. Please don't shoot," he said almost tearfully.

"The money," Said growled.

"In my jacket. In the car."

Said shoved Nur back to the car. "You get in."

Groaning with pain, she climbed in. "Please let me go, for God's sake let me go," she stammered.

"Give me the jacket." He snatched it from her, removed the wallet and threw the jacket in the man's face. "You have exactly one minute to save your skin." While the young man bolted off in the dark like a comet, Said flung himself into the driver's seat, switched on the engine and the car shot forward with a roar.

"I was really scared," Nur said as she dressed, "as if I hadn't really been expecting you."

"Let's have a drink," he said as soon as they reached the road, still hurtling forward. She handed him a bottle and he took a swig. He handed it back to her and she did the same.

"Poor man, his knees were shaking," she said.

"You're very kind-hearted. As for me, I don't particularly like factory owners."

"You don't like anybody, that's a fact," she said, sitting up and looking ahead. Said didn't feel like trying to charm her and said nothing.

"They'll see me with you!" she squealed when she saw that the car was approaching Abassiyya. The same thought had occurred to him, too, so he turned off into a side street that led towards Darasa and drove a little slower.

"I went to Tarzan's café to get a gun and try to arrange something with an old friend, a taxi driver. But now look how luck has sent me this car!"

"Don't you think I'm always useful?"

"Always. And you were fantastic too. Why don't you go on the stage?"

"In the beginning I was really scared."

"But later?"

"I hope I was convincing, so he won't suspect me."

"He was so out of his mind with fear he wasn't capable of suspecting anything."

"Why do you need a gun and a car?" she asked, putting her head close to his.

"They're the tools of the trade."

"Heaven! When did you come out of jail?"

"The day before yesterday."

"And you're already thinking of doing that again?"

"Have you ever found it easy to change your job?"

Staring ahead at the dark road, visible only in the car's headlights, Nur made no reply. At the turn, the hill of the Muqattam loomed nearer, like a chunk of the night more solid than the rest.

"Do you realize how sad I was," she said softly, "when I heard you'd been sent up?"

"No. How sad?"

"When will you stop being sarcastic?" She sounded a little annoyed.

"But I'm dead serious. And absolutely certain of the sincerity of your affection."

"You have no heart."

"They've got it locked up in prison, according to regulations!"

"You were heartless long before you ever went to jail."

Why does she harp on the subject of affection? She should talk to that treacherous woman, and the dogs, and the little girl who rejected me. "One day we'll succeed in finding it," he said.

"Where will you stay tonight? Does your wife know where you are?"

"I don't think so."

"Are you going home then?"

"I don't think so, not tonight in any case."

"Come to my place."

"Do you live alone?"

"Yes, in Sharia Najm al-Din beyond the cemetery at Bab al-Nasr."

"Number?"

"There's only one house in the street; it's over a sackcloth store and right behind it is the cemetery."

"What a great location!" Said laughed.

Nur laughed too. "No one knows me there and no one's ever visited me. You'll find it on the top floor." She waited for his reply, but he was busy watching the road, which began to narrow between the hill and the houses that came after Sheikh Ali al-Junaydi's place. At the top of Sharia Darasa he stopped the car and turned towards her.

"This is a good place for you to get out."

"Won't you come with me?"

"I'll come to you later on."

"But where are you going at this hour of night?"

"You go straight to the police station now. Tell them exactly what happened as if you had nothing to do with me and give them a description of a person completely different from me. Say he's fat, fair-skinned and has an old scar on his right cheek. Tell them I kidnapped you, robbed you, and raped you."

"Raped me?"

"In the desert at Zinhum," he went on, ignoring her exclamation, "and say I threw you out of the car and drove away."

"Are you really coming to see me?"

"Yes, that's a solemn promise. Will you be able to act as well in the police station as you did in the car?"

"I hope so."

"Goodbye then." And he drove away.

7

*o kill them both—
Nabawiyya and Ilish—at
the same time, would be a
triumph. Even better would
be to settle with Rauf Ilwan, too, then escape, go abroad if possible. But who'll
look after Sana? The thorn in my side. You always act impulsively, Said,
without thinking, but you mustn't rush this time; you must wait until you've
arranged things, then swoop like an eagle. But there's no point in delay either:
you're a hunted man—you became a hunted man as soon as they knew you
were coming out—and now, after the car incident, the search will be intensified. Only a few pounds in the wallet of the factory owner's son—another
stroke of bad luck. If you don't strike soon everything will collapse. Who'll look
after Sana, though? That thorn again. She rejected me but I still love her.
Should I spare your unfaithful mother for your sake, then? I must find the
answer right away.*

He was hovering on foot in the pitch-darkness surrounding the
house at the crossroads where two lanes met in Imam Way. The car
was parked at the top of the road, back towards the Citadel square.
Shops were closed, the road was deserted, and no one seemed to be

looking for him: at such an hour every creature took shelter, blind and unsuspecting, in his hole. Said could easily have taken further precautions, but he was not going to be diverted from his purpose, even if it meant Sana's having to live alone all her life. For treachery, Mr. Rauf, is an abomination.

He looked up at the windows of the house, his hand clutching the revolver in his pocket. Treachery is abominable, Ilish, and for the living to enjoy life it is imperative that criminal and vicious elements be eradicated. Keeping close to the wall, he approached the door then entered the house and cautiously climbed the pitch-dark stairs, passing the first floor, then the second to the third. Right. And there was the flat, the door, snugly closed on the most rotten intentions and desires. If he knocked, who would answer? Would it be Nabawiyya? Was the police detective perhaps lurking somewhere? There was hellfire for them both even if he had to break into the flat. He must act at once. It was not right that Ilish Sidra should stay alive for even one day while Said Mahran was a free man. *You'll get away without a scratch, just as easily as you have scores of times: you can scale an apartment building in seconds, jump unhurt from a third floor window—even fly if you wish!*

It seems you must knock on the door. But knocking might arouse suspicion, especially at this hour. Nabawiyya would fill the world with her screams, and bring some cowardly fools. That detective, too. So you'd better break the little glass pane in the door.

He'd had the idea in the car on the way and now he came back to it. He drew his gun and gave the glass one blow through the twisted bars that protected it. As the glass broke and the pieces scattered, it made a noise like a choked-off scream in the silent night. He flattened himself against the wall, next to the door and waited, his heart beating fast and his eyes peering into the darkness of the entrance hall where the gun was pointed. A man's voice, which he could recognize as Ilish Sidra's despite the throbbing noise in his temples, said "Who's there?" and a door to the left opened, giving a faint light by which he could just make out the figure of a man approaching cautiously. Said pressed the trigger and the gun roared like a demon in the night. The man cried out and began to fall, but another bullet struck him even before he hit the floor, where he lay like a sack. A woman shrieked for help—Nabawiyya's voice. "Your turn will come! There's no escape from me! I'm the devil himself!" he shouted as he turned to escape, leaping down the stairs so recklessly that he reached the bottom in seconds where he paused briefly to listen, then slipped out. Once outside he walked away calmly, keeping close to the wall, leaving behind him the sounds of windows opening and voices questioning and vague cries whose words he could not make out. When he reached the place at the top of the road where he'd parked the car, and had pulled open the door to get in, he spotted a policeman running from the square towards Imam Way. Ducking down, he hid on the floor of the car as the policeman ran on past towards the screaming, remaining still until the footsteps sounded far enough away, then he sat up behind the steering wheel and sped off. At the square he slowed down to a normal speed, the din still haunting his senses and settling at last within his nerves. He felt stunned. Confusion pervaded his whole being and he was only half-aware of what he did as he drove on. *A murderer! But there's still Rauf Ilwan, the high-class traitor, really much more important and dangerous than Ilish Sidra. A murderer! You are now one of those who commit murder; you have a new identity now and a new destiny! You used to take precious goods—now you take worthless lives!*

Your turn will come, Nabawiyya. There's no escape from me. I'm the devil himself. I've granted you life, thanks to Sana, but I've enclosed you in a punishment greater than death; fear of death, the unrelenting terror. As long as I live you'll never enjoy the taste of peace.

He came down Sharia Muhammad Ali, in a stupor, without a thought to where he was going. Many people would now have a murderer on their minds. The murderer must hide. He must take care to avoid the rope and the gallows. *You must never have the executioner asking what your last wish is, Said! Oh no. The government must be made to ask you this question, but on some better occasion!*

When he returned to full awareness he found he'd covered the last stretch of Sharia al-Gaish and was speeding towards Abbasiyya. Alarmed to find himself unexpectedly returning to a place of danger, he doubled his speed and in a few minutes reached Manshiyyat al-Bakri, where he stopped at the first street branching from the main road, quietly abandoned the car, and walked away without looking left or right, slowly, as if exercising his legs. He felt numbness then some sort of pain, as if in reaction to the great nervous effort he had made. *Nowhere is safe for you now. Or ever after. And Nur? It would be risky to go to her place tonight, of all nights, what with the investigations and suspicions that are bound to ensue. Darkness must extend from now on to all eternity.*

8

He pushed the Sheikh's door, met no resistance, entered, closed it behind him, and found himself in the open courtyard where the palm tree towered, as if stretched upwards into space as high as the watchful stars. What a superb place for hiding, he thought. The Sheikh's room was open at night, just as it was by day. There it stood, pitch-black, as if waiting for his return, and he walked towards it quietly. He heard the voice muttering but could only distinguish the word "Allah," "God!" It went on muttering as if the Sheikh were unaware or perhaps reluctant to acknowledge his presence.

Said withdrew into a corner at the left of the room close to his pile of books and flung himself down on the rush mat, still in his suit and shoes and carrying his revolver. He stretched out his legs, supporting his trunk on the palms of his hands, his head falling back in exhaustion. His head felt like a beehive, but there was nothing he could do.

You wish to recall the sound of the bullet and the screams of Nabawiyya, feeling happy again that you did not hear Sana scream. You'd better greet the

344

Sheikh, but your voice is too weak to say, "Peace be upon you!" There's this feeling of helplessness, as if you were drowning. And you thought you were going to sleep like a log as soon as your skin touched the floor!

How the righteous and God-fearing would have shuddered, turned away from him in fright—until recitation of the name of God had made them less particular, less hard of heart. When would this strange man go to sleep? But the strange old man now raised his voice and began to sing: "In my view, passion is nothing but ingratitude unless it issues from my witnesses." And in a voice that seemed to fill the room, he said: "The eyes of their hearts are open, but those in their heads are closed!" Said smiled in spite of himself. So that's why he is not aware of my presence. But then I too am not fully aware of my own self.

The call to the dawn prayers rose above the quiet waves of the night. It reminded him of a night he'd once spent sleepless until the same call to the dawn prayers, excited over some special joy promised for the following day. On that occasion, he'd got up as soon as he heard the call, happy at release from a night of torment, had looked out of the window at the blue dawn and the smiling sunrise, and had rubbed his hands in anticipation of whatever it was he'd been about to enjoy, something he had since completely forgotten. And therefore he loved the dawn, which he associated with the singing of the prayer-call, the deep blue sky, the smile of the approaching sunrise, and that unremembered joy.

It was dawn now, but he could not move from exhaustion, not even to shift his revolver. The Sheikh rose to perform his prayers. Showing no awareness of Said's presence he lit the oil lamp, spread out the prayer mat, took up his position on it, then suddenly asked, "Aren't you going to perform the dawn prayers?"

Said was so exhausted he was incapable of giving an answer and no sooner had the Sheikh begun his prayers than he dropped off to sleep.

He dreamed that he was in jail, being whipped despite his good conduct, screaming shamelessly, but not offering any resistance. They gave him milk to drink. Suddenly he saw little Sana, lashing Rauf Ilwan with a whip at the bottom of a staircase. He heard the sound of a Koranic recitation and had a conviction that someone had died, but found himself, a wanted man, somehow involved in a car chase! The car he was driving was incapable of speed—there was something wrong with its engine—and he had to begin shooting in every direction, when all at once Rauf Ilwan appeared from the radio in the dashboard, grabbed his wrist before Said was able to kill him, and tightened his grip so mercilessly that he was able to snatch the revolver. At this point Said Mahran said to him: "Kill me, if you wish, but my daughter is innocent. It wasn't she who whipped you at the bottom of the staircase. It was her mother, Nabawiyya, at the instigation of Ilish Sidra." Escaping his pursuers, Said then slipped into the circle of Sufi chanters gathered round Sheikh al-Junaydi, but the Sheikh denied him. "Who are you?" he asked. "How did you come to be with us?" He told him he was Said Mahran, son of Amm Mahran, his old disciple, and reminded him of the old days, but the Sheikh demanded his identity card. Said was surprised and objected that a Sufi disciple didn't need an identity card, that in the eyes of the mystical order the righteous and the sinner were alike. When the Sheikh replied that he did not like the righteous and wanted to see Said's identity card to make sure that Said was really a sinner, Said handed him the revolver, explaining that every missing bullet meant a murder, but the Sheikh insisted on seeing his card; the government instructions, he said, were stringent on this point. Said was astounded: why did the government interfere with the affairs of the order? he asked. The Sheikh informed him that it had all resulted from a suggestion by their great authority Rauf Ilwan, who had been nominated for the post of Supreme Sheikh. Stunned with amazement for the third time, Said protested that Rauf was nothing but a traitor, who only had criminal thoughts, and the Sheikh retorted that that was why he'd been recommended for this responsible position. He added that Rauf had promised to offer a new exegesis of the Holy Koran, giving all possible interpretations, so as to benefit each man according to his purchasing power; the money this beneficent move would bring in would be invested in setting up clubs for shooting, hunting, and committing suicide. Said declared that he was prepared to act as treasurer for the new Exegesis Administration and that Rauf Ilwan would no doubt testify to his integrity as one of his brightest former pupils. At that point the Sheikh intoned the opening chapter of the Koran, lanterns were suspended from the trunk of the palm tree, and a reciter chanted, "Blessed be ye, O people of Egypt, our lord Husayn is now yours."

When he opened his eyes the whole world looked red, empty and meaningless. The Sheikh sat in repose, everything about him, from his loose garment to his skull cap and beard, a shiny white, and at Said's first movement the Sheikh turned his gaze on him. Said sat up hurriedly and looked apologetic, assailed by memories that rushed into his mind like roaring flames.

"It is now late afternoon," said the Sheikh, "and you haven't had a bite of food."

Said looked first at the hole in the wall, then at the Sheikh and muttered absentmindedly, "Late afternoon!"

"Yes. I thought to myself: let him sleep. God presents His gifts as His will alone decides."

Said was suddenly troubled. He wondered if anybody had seen him asleep there all day. "I was aware of many people coming in," he lied, "while I was asleep."

"You were aware of nothing. But one man brought me my lunch, another came to sweep the place, water the cactus, tend the palm tree, and get the courtyard ready for God's loving worshippers."

"What time are they coming?" he said, a little worried.

"At sunset. When did you arrive?"

"At dawn."

The Sheikh sat silent for a while, stroking his beard, then said, "You are very wretched, my son!"

"Why?" said Said, anxious to know the answer.

"You've had a long sleep, but you know no rest. Just like a child laid under the fire of the blazing sun. Your burning heart yearns for shade, yet continues forward under the fire of the sun. Haven't you learned to walk yet?"

Said rubbed his bloodshot, almond-shaped eyes. "It's a disturbing thought, to be seen asleep by others."

"The world is unaware of him who is unaware of it," the Sheikh replied, showing no concern.

Said's hand passed lightly over the pocket where he kept the revolver. He wondered what the Sheikh would do if he were to point his gun at him. Would his maddening composure be shaken?

"Are you hungry?" the Sheikh asked.

"No."

"If it is true that man can be poor in God, so is it true man can be rich in Him," the Sheikh went on, his eyes almost smiling.

If, that is, the first proposition is indeed true! thought Said. "Well then, Master," he said lightly, "what would you have done if you'd been afflicted with a wife like mine and if your daughter had rejected you as mine has me?"

A look of pity appeared in the old man's clear eyes: "God's slave is owned by God alone!"

Cut off your tongue before it betrays you and confesses your crime! You wish to tell him everything. He probably doesn't need to be told. He may even have seen you fire the gun. And he may be able to see much more than that.

A voice outside the window hawked *The Sphinx.* Said got up at once, walked to the window, called the newspaper boy, handed him a small coin and returned with the paper to where he'd been sitting, forgetting all about the Sheikh, his eyes riveted to a huge black headline: *"Dastardly Murder in the Citadel Quarter!"* He devoured the lines beneath in a flash, not understanding anything. Was this another murder? His own picture was there and so were pictures of Nabawiyya and Ilish Sidra, but who was that blood-stained man? His own life story was staring at him, too, sensational doings blown in every direction like dust in a whirlwind—the story of a man who came out of prison to find his wife married to one of his underlings. But who was the blood-stained man? How had his bullet entered this stranger's chest? This victim was someone else, and Said was seeing him for the first time in his life. *You'd better start reading again.*

The same day he'd visited them with the detective and Ilish's friends, Ilish Sidra and Nabawiyya had moved out of their flat and another family had moved in, so the voice he'd heard had not been

Ilish Sidra's nor had the screams been Nabawiyya's. The body was
that of one Shaban Husain, the new tenant who'd worked in a haber-
dashery in Sharia Muhammad Ali. Said Mahran had come to murder
his wife and old friend, but had killed the new tenant instead. A
neighbor testified that he'd seen Said Mahran leaving the house after
the murder and that he'd shouted for the police, but that his voice had
been lost in the din that had filled the entire street.

A failure. It was insane. And pointless. The rope would be after
him now, while Ilish sat safe and secure. The truth was as clear as the
bottom of an open tomb.

He tore his eyes away from the paper and found the Sheikh staring
through the window at the sky, smiling. The smile for some reason or
other, frightened Said: he wished he could stand at the window and
look at exactly the same bit of sky the Sheikh was looking at so he
could see what it was that made him smile. But the wish was
unfulfilled.

Let the Sheikh smile and keep his secret, he thought. Before long
the disciples would be here and some of them who'd seen the picture
in the paper might recognize him; thousands and thousands would be
gaping at his picture now, in a mixture of terror and titillation. Said's
life was finished, spent to no purpose; he was a hunted man and would
be to the end of his days; he was alone, and would have to beware even
of his own reflection in a mirror—alive but without real life. Like a
mummy. He'd have to flee like a rat from one hole to another, threatened by poison, cats and the clubs of disgusted human beings, suffering all this while his enemies kicked up their heels.

The Sheikh turned to him, saying gently, "You are tired. Go and
wash your face."

"Yes," Said said irritably, folding up the paper. "I'll go—and
relieve you of the sight of my face."

With even greater gentleness, the Sheikh said, "This is your
home."

"True, but why shouldn't I have another place to shelter?"

The Sheikh bowed his head, replying, "If you had another you
would never have come to me."

You must go up the hill and stay there until dark. Avoid the light. Shelter in the dark. Hell, it's all a waste of time. You've killed Shaban Husain; I wonder who you are, Shaban. We never knew each other. Did you have children? Did you ever imagine that one day you would be killed for no reason—that you'd be killed because Nabawiyya Sulaiman married Ilish Sidra? That you'd be killed in error, but that Ilish, Nabawiyya, and Rauf would not be killed in justice? I, the murderer, understand nothing. Not even Sheikh al-Junaydi himself can understand anything. I've tried to solve part of the riddle, but have only succeeded in unearthing an even greater one. He sighed aloud.

"How tired you are," said the Sheikh.

"And it is your world that makes me tired!"

"That is what we sing of, sometimes," the Sheikh said placidly.

Said rose, then said, as he was about to go, "Farewell, my Master."

"Utterly meaningless words, whatever you intend by them," the Sheikh remonstrated. "Say rather: until we meet again."

9

od, it's dark! I'd be better off as a bat. Why is that smell of hot fat seeping out from under some door at this hour of night? When will Nur be back? Will she come alone? And can I stay in her flat long enough to be forgotten? You might perhaps be thinking you've got rid of me forever now, Rauf! But with this revolver, if I have any luck, I can do wonderful things. With this revolver I can awake those who are asleep. They're the root of the trouble: They're the ones who've made creatures like Nabawiyya, Ilish and Rauf Ilwan possible.

Something sounded like footsteps climbing the stairs. When he was sure he heard someone coming, he crouched and looked down through the banisters. A faint light was moving slowly along the wall. The light of a match, he thought. The footsteps came higher, heavy and slow. To let her know he was there and to avoid surprising her, he cleared his throat with a loud rasp.

"Who is it?" she said apprehensively.

Said leaned his head out between the banisters as far as he could and replied in a whisper, "Said Mahran."

She ran the rest of the way up and stopped in front of him out of breath. The match was almost dead. "It's you!" she said, breathless and happy, seizing his arm. "I'm sorry. Have you been waiting long?"

Opening the door to the flat, she led him in by the arm, switched on the light in a bare rectangular hall, then drew him into a reception room, square and somewhat larger, where she rushed to the window and flung it open wide to release the stifling air.

"It was midnight when I got here," he said, flinging himself down on one of two sofas, that stood face to face. "I've waited for ages."

She sat down opposite, moving a pile of scraps of cloth and dress cuttings. "You know what?" she said, "I'd given up hope. I didn't think you'd really come."

Their tired eyes met. "Even after my definite promise?" he said, hiding his frozen feelings with a smile. She smiled back faintly, without answering. Then she said, "Yesterday they kept questioning me at the police station over and over. They nearly killed me. Where's the car?"

"I thought I'd better dump it somewhere, even though I need it." He took off his jacket and tossed it down on the sofa next to him. His brown shirt was caked with sweat and dust. "They'll find it and give it back to its owner, as you'd expect of a government that favors some thieves more than others."

"What did you do with it yesterday?"

"Nothing whatever, in fact. Anyway, you'll know everything at the proper time." He gazed at the open window, took a deep breath, and said, "It must face north. Really fresh air."

"It's open country from here to Bab al-Nur. All around here is the cemetery."

"That's why the air isn't polluted," he said with a grin. *She's looking at you as if she could eat you up, but you only feel bored, annoyed. Why can't you stop brooding over your wounded pride and enjoy her?*

"I'm terribly sorry you had to wait so long on the landing."

"Well, I'm going to be your guest for quite some time," he said, giving her a strange, scrutinizing look.

She lifted her head, raised her chin and said happily, "Stay here all your life, if you like."

"Until I move over to the neighbors!" he said with another grin, pointing through the window. She seemed preoccupied. She didn't seem to hear his joke. "Won't your people ask about you?" she said.

"I have no people," he replied, looking down at his gym shoes.

"I mean your wife."

She means pain and fury and wasted bullets! What she wants is to hear a humiliating confession; she'll only find that a locked heart becomes increasingly difficult to unlock. But what is the point of lying when newsprint pages are screaming with sensation?

"I said I have no people." Now you're wondering what my words mean. Your face is beaming with happiness. But I hate this joy. And I can see now that your face has lost whatever bloom it had, particularly under the eyes.

"Divorced?" she asked.

"Yes. When I was in jail. But let's close the subject," he said, waving his hand impatiently.

"The bitch!" she said angrily. "A man like you deserves to be waited for, even if he's been sent up for life!"

How sly she is! But a man like me doesn't like to be pitied. Beware of sympathy! "The truth is that I neglected her far too much." What a waste for bullets to strike the innocent!

"Anyway, she isn't the kind of woman who deserves you."

True. Neither is any other woman. But Nabawiyya's still full of vitality, while you're hovering on the brink: one puff of wind would be enough to blow you out. You only arouse pity in me. "No one must know I am here."

Laughing, as if sure she possessed him for ever, she said, "Don't worry; I'll keep you hidden all right." Then, hopefully, she added, "But you've not done anything really serious, have you?"

He dismissed the question by shrugging nonchalantly.

She stood up and said, "I'll get some food for you. I do have food and drink. Do you remember how cold you used to be to me?"

"I had no time for love then."

She eyed him reproachfully. "Is anything more important than love? I often wondered if your heart wasn't made of stone. When you went to jail, no one grieved as much as I did."

"That's why I came to you instead of anybody else."

"But you only ran into me by chance," she said with a pout. "You might even have forgotten all about me!"

"Do you think I can't find anywhere else?" he said, framing his face into a scowl.

As if to head off an outburst, she came up close to him and took his cheeks between the palms of her hands. "The guards at the zoo won't let visitors tease the lion. I'd forgotten that. Please forgive me. But your face is burning and your beard is bristly. Why not have a cold shower?" His smile showed her he welcomed the idea. "Off you go to the bathroom then! When you come out you'll find some food ready. We'll eat in the bedroom, it's much nicer than this room. It looks out over the cemetery, too."

10

hat a lot of graves there are, laid out as far as the eye can see. Their head-stones are like hands raised in surrender, though they are beyond being threatened by anything. A city of silence and truth, where success and failure, murderer and victim come together, where thieves and policemen lie side by side in peace for the first and last time.

Nur's snoring seemed likely to end only when she awoke in late afternoon.

You'll stay in this prison until the police forget you. And will they ever really forget? The graves remind you that death cheats the living. They speak of betrayal; and thus they make you remember Nabawiyya, Ilish and Rauf, telling you that you yourself are dead, ever since that unseeing bullet was fired.

But you still have bullets of fire.

At the sound of Nur's yawning, loud, like a groan, he turned away from the window shutters towards the bed. Nur was sitting up, naked, her hair dishevelled, looking unrested and run-down. But she smiled as she said, "I dreamed you were far away and I was going out of my mind waiting for you."

"That was a dream," he observed grimly. "In fact you're the one who's going out and I'm the one who'll wait."

She went into the bathroom, emerged again drying her hair; and he followed her hands as they recreated her face in a new form, happy and young. She was, like himself, thirty years old, but she lied outright hoping to appear younger, adding to the multitude of sins and sillinesses which are openly committed. But theft unfortunately was not one of them.

"Don't forget the papers," he reminded her at the door.

When she'd gone he moved into the reception room and flung himself down on one of the sofas. Now he was alone in the full sense of the word, without even his books which he'd left with Sheikh Ali. He stared up at the cracked white ceiling, a dull echo of the threadbare carpet, killing time. The setting sun flashed through the open window, like a jewel being carried by a flight of doves from one point in time to the next.

Your coldness, Sana, was very disquieting. Like seeing these graves. I don't know if we'll meet again, where or when. You'll certainly never love me now. Not in this life, so full of badly-aimed bullets, desires gone astray. What's left behind is a dangling chain of regrets. The first link was the students' hostel on the road to Giza. Ilish didn't matter much, but Nabawiyya—she'd shaken him, torn him up by the roots. If only a deceit could be as plainly read in the face as fever or an infectious disease! Then beauty would never be false and many a man would be spared the ravages of deception.

That grocery near the students' hostel, where Nabawiyya used to come shopping, gripping her bowl. She was always so nicely dressed, much more neatly than the other servant girls, which was why she'd been known as the "Turkish Lady's maid": The rich, proud old Turkish woman, who lived alone, at the end of the road, in a house at the center of a big garden, insisted that everyone who had to do with her should be good-looking, clean, and well-dressed. So Nabawiyya always appeared with her hair neatly combed and braided in a long pigtail, wearing slippers. Her peasant's gown flowed around a sprightly and nimble body, and even those not bewitched by her agreed that she was a fine example of country beauty with her dark complexion, her round, full face, her brown eyes, her small chubby nose, and her lips moist with the juices of life. There was a small green tattoo mark on her chin like a beauty spot.

You used to stand at the entrance to the students' hostel and wait for her after work, staring up the street until her fine form with her adorable gait appeared in the distance. As she stepped closer and closer, you'd glow with anticipation. She was like some lovely melody, welcomed wherever she went. As she slipped in among the dozens of women standing at the grocer's your eyes would follow her drunk with ecstasy. She'd disappear and reemerge again, your desire and curiosity increasing all the time—so did your impulse to do something, no matter what, by word, gesture or invocation—and she'd move off on her way home, to disappear for the rest of the day and another whole night. And you'd let out a long, bitter sigh and your elation would subside, the birds on the roadside trees would cease their song and a cold autumn breeze would suddenly spring up from nowhere.

But then you notice that her form is reacting to your stare, that she's swaying coquettishly as she walks and you stand there no longer, but, with your natural impetuosity, hurry after her along the road. Then at the lone palm tree at the edge of the fields you bar her way. She's dumbfounded by your audacity, or pretends to be, and asks you indignantly who you might be. You reply in feigned surprise, "Who might I be? You really ask who I am? Don't you know? I'm known to every inch of your being!"

"I don't like ill-mannered people!" she snaps.

"Neither do I. I'm like you, I hate ill-mannered people. Oh, no. On the contrary, I admire good manners, beauty, and gentleness. And all of those things are you! You still don't know who I am? I must carry that basket for you and see you to the door of your house."

"I don't need your help," she says, "and don't ever stand in my way again!" With that she walks away, but with you at her side, encouraged by the faint smile slipping through her pretence of indignation, which you receive like the first cool breeze on a hot and sultry night. Then she had said: "Go back; you must! My mistress sits at the window and if you come one step more she'll see you."

"But I'm a very determined fellow," you reply, "and if you want me to go back, you'll have to come along with me. Just a few steps. Back to the palm

tree. You see, I've got to talk to you. And why shouldn't I? Aren't I respectable enough?"

She shakes her head vigorously, but she does slow down. Murmuring an angry protest, she does slow down, her neck arched like an angry cat's. She did slow down and I no longer doubt I've won, that Nabawiyya is not indifferent and knows very well how I stand sighing there at the students' hostel. You know that casual stares in the street will become something big in your life, in hers, and in the world at large too, which would grow larger as a result.

"Till tomorrow then," you say, stopping there, afraid for her, afraid of the biting tongue of the old Turk who lives like an enigma at the bottom of the street. So you return to the palm tree and climb it, quick as a monkey, out of sheer high spirits, then jump down again, from ten feet up, into a plot of green. Then you go back to the hostel, singing, in your deep voice, like a bull in ecstasy.

And later, when circumstances sent you to al-Zayyat Circus, to work that took you from quarter to quarter, village to village, you feared that "out of sight, out of mind" might well be applied to you and you asked her to marry you. Yes, you asked her to marry you, in the good old legal, traditional Muslim way, standing outside the university that you had—unfairly—been unable to enter, though so many fools did. There was no light in the street or the sky, just a big crescent moon over the horizon. Gazing shyly down at the ground, her forehead reflecting the pale moonlight, she seemed overjoyed. You told her about your good wages, your excellent prospects and your neat ground-floor flat in Darasa, on Jabal Road, near Sheikh Ali's house. "You'll get to know the godly Sheikh," you said, "when we marry. And we've got to have the wedding as soon as possible. After all, our love has lasted quite a while already. You'll have to leave the old lady now."

"I'm an orphan, you know. There's only my aunt at Sidi al-Arbain."

"That's fine."

Then you kissed her under the crescent moon. The wedding was so lovely that everyone talked about it for ever after. From Zayyat I got a wedding present of ten pounds. Ilish Sidra seemed absolutely overjoyed at it all as if it was his own wedding, playing the part of the faithful friend while he was really no friend at all. And the oddest thing of all is that you were taken in by him—you, clever old you, smart enough to scare the devil himself, you the hero and Ilish your willing slave, admiring, flattering, and doing everything to avoid upsetting you, happy to pick up the scraps of your labor, your smartness. You were sure you could have sent him and Nabawiyya off together alone, into the very deserts where our Lord Moses wandered, and that all the time he'd keep seeing you between himself and her and would never step out of line. How could she ever give up a lion and take to a dog? She's rotten to the core, rotten enough to deserve death and damnation. For sightless bullets not to stray, blindly missing their vile and evil targets, and hit innocent people, leaving others torn with remorse and rage and on the verge of insanity. Compelled to forget everything good in life, the way you used to play as a kid in the street, innocent first love, your wedding night, Sana's birth and seeing her little face, hearing her cry, carrying her in your arms for the first time. All the smiles you never counted—how you wish you'd counted them. And how she looked—you wish it was one of the things you've forgotten—when she was frightened, that screaming of hers that shook the ground and made springs and breezes dry up. All the good feelings that ever were.

The shadows are lengthening now. It's getting dark in the room and outside the window. The silence of the graves is more intense, but you can't switch on the light. The flat must look the way it always has when Nur is out. Your eyes will get used to the dark, the way they did to prison and all those ugly faces. And you can't start drinking, either, in case you bump into something or shout out loud. The flat must stay as silent as the grave; even the dead mustn't know you're here. God alone can tell how long you'll have to stay here and how patient in this jail. Just as He alone could tell you'd kill Shaban Husain and not Ilish Sidra.

Well, you'll have to go out sooner or later, to take a walk in the night, even if only to safe places. But let's postpone that until the police are worn out looking for you. And let's hope to God Shaban Husain isn't buried in one of these graves here; this run-down quarter could hardly stand the strain of such a painful irony of fate. Just keep cool, keep patient, until Nur comes back. You must not ask when Nur will come back. You'll have to put up with the dark, the silence, and the loneliness—for as long as the world refuses to change its naughty ways. Nur, poor girl, is caught in it too. What, after all, is her love for you but a bad habit, getting stuck on someone who's already dead of pain and anger, is put off by her affection no less than by her ageing looks, who doesn't really know what to do with her except maybe drink with her, toasting as it were, defeat and grief, and pity her for her worthy but hopeless efforts.

And in the end you can't even forget she's a woman. Like that slinking bitch, Nabawiyya, who'll be in mortal fear until the rope's safely installed around your neck or some rotten bullet is lodged in your heart. And the police will tell such lies that you'll be cut off forever from Sana. She'll never even know the truth of your love for her, as if that, too, was just a bullet that went astray.

Sleep came over Said Mahran and he dozed off for a while on the sofa, unaware that he had been dreaming in his sleep until he woke, to find himself in complete darkness, still alone in Nur's flat in Shari Najm al-Din where Ilish Sidra had not surprised him and had not fired a hail of bullets at him. He had no idea what time it was.

Suddenly he heard the rattle of a key in the lock and then the door being closed. A light in the hallway went on and filtered in above the door. Nur came in smiling, carrying a big parcel. She kissed him and said, "Let's have a feast! I've brought home a restaurant, a delicatessen and a patisserie all in one!"

"You've been drinking?" he said as he kissed her.

"I have to; it's part of my job. I'll take a bath, then come back. Here are the papers for you."

His eyes followed her as she left, then he buried himself in the newspapers, both morning and evening. There was nothing that was news to him, but there was clearly enormous interest in both the crime and its perpetrator, far more than he'd expected, especially in the *Zahra*, Rauf Ilwan's paper. It discussed at length his history as a burglar and the list of the exploits revealed at his trial, with stories about the great houses of the rich he had burglarized, comments on his character, his latent insanity, and an analysis of "the criminal boldness that finally led to bloodshed."

What enormous black headlines! Thousands upon thousands must be discussing his crimes at that moment, all amused at Nabawiyya's infidelity and laying bets as to what his fate would be. He was the very center of the news, the man of the hour, and the thought filled him with both apprehension and pride, conflicting emotions that were so intense they almost tore him apart. Meanwhile, so many other thoughts and ideas crowded in confusion into his mind, that a kind of intoxication seemed to engulf him. He felt sure he was about to do something truly extraordinary, even miraculous; and he wished he could somehow communicate with all the people outside, to tell them what was making him—there all alone in the silence—burst with emotion, to convince them that he'd win in the end, even if only after death.

He was quite alone, separate from everyone else. They didn't even know, did not comprehend the language of silence and solitude. They didn't understand that they themselves were silent and alone sometimes, and that the mirrors dimly reflecting their own images were in fact deceptive, making them falsely imagine they were seeing people unknown to themselves.

His mind's eye focussed on the photograph of Sana, with a sense of wonder, and he was deeply moved. Then in his imagination he conjured up all their pictures—his own wild-looking self, Nabawiyya, looking like a whore—coming back to the picture of Sana. She was smiling. Yes. Smiling. Because she could not see him and because she knew nothing. He scrutinized her intensely, overwhelmed by the sense that he'd failed, that the night out there through the window was sighing in some kind of sympathetic sadness, desperately wishing he could run away with her to some place known to no one else. He yearned to see her, if only as his last wish on earth before his execution.

He went over to the other sofa to pick up the scissors lying in a pile of pieces of fabric, then returned to snip the picture carefully out of the newspaper. By the time Nur emerged from the bathroom he felt calmer. When she called him, he went into the bedroom, wondering as he walked how she could have brought him all those news reports and know nothing of them herself.

She'd spent a lot of money. As he sat by her side on a sofa, facing the food-covered table, his mouth watered in craving and to show his pleasure he stroked her moist hair and murmured, "You know, there aren't many women like you."

She tied a red scarf around her head and began filling the glasses, smiling at the compliment. To see her sitting there, proud and confident of having him, if only for a while, made him feel somehow glad.

She was wearing no make-up over her light brown skin and she looked invigorated from her bath, like a dish of good food, somehow, modest and fresh.

"You can say things like that!" she said, giving him a quizzical stare. "Sometimes I almost think the police know more about kindness than you."

"No, do believe me, I'm happy being with you."

"Truly?"

"Yes. Truly. You're so kind, so good. I don't know why anyone could resist you."

"Wasn't I like that in the old days?"

No easy victory can ever make one forget a bloody defeat! "At that time, I just wasn't an affectionate person."

"And now?"

"Let's have a drink and enjoy ourselves," he said, picking up his glass.

They set about the food and drink with gusto, until she said, "How did you spend your time?"

"Between the shadows and the graves," he said, dipping a piece of meat in tahina. "Don't you have any family buried here?"

"No, all mine are buried in al-Balyana, God rest their souls."

Only the sounds of their eating and the clink of glasses and dishes on the tray broke the silence, until Said said, "I'm going to ask you to buy some cloth for me—something suitable for an officer's uniform."

"An army officer?"

"You didn't know I learned tailoring in jail?"

"But why do you want it?" she said uneasily.

"Ah, well, the time has come for me to do my military service."

"Don't you understand, I don't want to lose you again?"

"Don't worry about me at all," he said with extraordinary confidence. "If no one had given me away the police would never have caught me."

Nur sighed, still troubled.

"You're not in any danger yourself, are you?" Said asked, grinning, his mouth stuffed with food. "No highwayman's going to waylay you in the desert, right?"

They laughed together, and she leaned over and kissed him full on the lips. Their lips were equally sticky.

"The truth is," she said, "that to live at all we've got to be afraid of nothing."

"Not even death?" Said said, nodding towards the window.

"Please. Don't."

"Listen, I even forget that too when time brings me together with someone I love."

Astonished at the strength and tenacity of her affection, Said relaxed and let himself feel a mixture of compassion, respect and gratitude towards Nur.

A moth overhead made love to a naked light bulb in the dead of the night.

11

ot a day passes without the graveyard welcoming new guests. Why, it's as though there's nothing more left to do but crouch behind the shutters watching these endless progressions of death. It's the mourners who deserve one's sympathy, of course. They come in one weeping throng and then they go away drying their tears and talking, as if while they're here some force stronger than death itself has convinced them to stay alive.

That was how your own parents were buried: your father, Amm Mahran, the kindly concierge of the students' hostel, who died middle-aged after a hard but honest and satisfying life. You helped him in his work from your childhood on. For all the extreme simplicity, even poverty of their lives, the family enjoyed sitting together when the day's work was done in their ground-floor room at the entrance to the building, where Amm Mahran and his wife would chat together while their child played. His piety made him happy, and the students respected him well. The only entertainment he knew was making pilgrimage to the home of Sheikh Ali al-Junaydi, and it was through your father that you came to know the house. "Come along," he'd say, "and I'll

show you how to have more fun than playing in the fields. You'll see how sweet life can be, what it's like in an atmosphere of godliness. It'll give you a sense of peace and contentment, the finest thing you can achieve in life."

The Sheikh greeted you with that sweet and kindly look of his. And how enchanted you were by his fine white beard! "So this is your son you were telling me about," he said to your father. "There's a lot of intelligence in his eyes. His heart is as spotless as yours. You'll find he'll turn out, with God's will, a truly good man." Yes, you really adored Sheikh Ali al-Junaydi, attracted by the purity in his face and the love in his eyes. And those songs and chants of his had delighted you even before your heart was purified by love.

"Tell this boy what it's his duty to do," your father said to the Sheikh one day.

The Sheikh had gazed down at you and said, "We continue learning from the cradle to the grave, but at least start out, Said, by keeping close account of yourself and making sure that from whatever action you initiate some good comes to someone."

Yes, you certainly followed his counsel, as best you could though you only brought it to complete fulfillment when you took up burglary!

The days passed like dreams. And then your good father disappeared, suddenly gone, in a way that a boy simply could not comprehend, and that seemed to baffle even Sheikh Ali himself. How shocked you were that morning, shaking your head and rubbing your eyes to clear away the sleep, awakened by your mother's screams and tears in the little room at the entrance to the students' hostel! You wept with fear and frustration at your helplessness. That evening however, Rauf Ilwan, at that time a student in Law School, had shown how very capable he was. Yes, he was impressive all right, no matter what the circumstances, and you loved him as you did Sheikh Ali, perhaps even more. It was he who later worked hard to have you — or you and your mother, to be more precise — take over Father's job as custodian for the building. Yes, you took on responsibilities at an early age.

And then your mother died. You almost died yourself during your mother's illness, as Rauf Ilwan must surely remember, from that unforgettable day when she had hemorrhaged and you had rushed her to the nearest hospital, the Sabir hospital, standing like a castle on its beautiful grounds, where you found yourself and your mother in a reception hall at an entrance more luxurious than anything you could ever have imagined possible. The entire place seemed forbidding, even hostile, but you were in the direst need of help, immediate help.

As the famous doctor was coming out of a room, they mentioned his name and you raced towards him in your gallabeya and sandals, shouting, "My mother! The blood!"

The man had fixed you in a glassy, disapproving stare and had glanced where your mother was lying, stretched out in her filthy dress on a soft couch, a foreign nurse standing nearby, observing the scene. Then the doctor had simply disappeared, saying nothing. The nurse jabbered something in a language you did not understand, though you sensed she was expressing sympathy for your tragedy. At that point, for all your youth, you flew into a real adult's rage, screaming and cursing in protest, smashing a chair to the floor with a crash, so the veneer on its back broke into pieces. A horde of servants had appeared and you'd soon found yourself and your mother alone in the tree-lined road outside. A month later your mother had died in Kasr al-Aini hospital.

All the time she lay close to death she never released your hand, refusing to take her eyes off you. It was during that long month of illness, however, that you stole for the first time—from the country boy resident in the hostel, who'd accused you without any investigation and was beating you vigorously when Rauf Ilwan turned up and freed you, settling the matter without any further complications. You were a true human being then, Rauf, and you were my teacher too.

Alone with you, Rauf had said quietly, "Don't you worry. The fact is, I consider this theft perfectly justified. Only you'll find the police watching out for you, and the judge won't be lenient with you," he'd added ominously with bitter sarcasm, "however convincing your motives, because he, too, will be protecting himself. Isn't it justice," he'd shouted, "that what is taken by theft should be retrieved by theft? Here I am studying, away from home and family, suffering daily from hunger and deprivation!"

Where have all your principles gone now, Rauf? Dead, no doubt, like my father and my mother, and like my wife's fidelity.

You had no alternative but to leave the students' hostel and seek a living somewhere else. So you waited under the lone palm tree at the end of the green plot until Nabawiyya came and you sprang towards her, saying, "Don't be afraid. I must speak to you. I'm leaving to get a better job. I love you. Don't ever forget me. I love you and always will. And I'll prove I can make you happy and give you a respectable home." Yes, those had been times when sorrows could be forgotten, wounds could be healed, and hope could bring forth fruit from adversity.

All you graves out there, immersed in the gloom, don't jeer at my memories!

He sat up on the sofa, still in the dark, addressing Rauf Ilwan just as though he could see him standing in front of him. "You should have agreed to get me a job writing for your newspaper, you scoundrel. I'd have published our mutual reminiscences there, I'd have shut off your false light good and proper." Then he wondered aloud, "How am I going to stand it here in the dark till Nur comes back near dawn?"

Suddenly he was attacked by an irresistible urge to leave the house and take a walk in the dark. In an instant, his resistance crumbled, like a building ready to give way, collapsing; soon he was moving stealthily out of the house. He set off towards Masani Street and from there turned towards open wasteland.

Leaving his hideout made him all the more conscious of being hunted. He now knew how mice and foxes feel, slipping away on the run. Alone in the dark, he could see the city's lights glimmering in the distance, lying in wait for him. He quaffed his sense of being alone, until it intoxicated him, then walked on, winding up at last in his old seat next to Tarzan in the coffee-house. The only other person inside apart from the waiter was an arms smuggler, although outside, a little lower down, at the foot of the hill, there was considerable noise of people talking.

The waiter brought him some tea at once and then Tarzan leaned over. "Don't spend more than one night in the same place," he whispered.

The smuggler added his advice, "Move way up the Nile."

"But I don't know anyone up there," Said objected.

"You know," the smuggler went on, "I've heard many people express their admiration for you."

"And the police?" Tarzan said heatedly. "Do they admire him too?"

The smuggler laughed so hard that his whole body shook, as if he were mounted on a camel at the gallop. "Nothing impresses the police," he said at last, when he'd recovered his breath.

"Absolutely nothing," agreed Said.

"But what harm is there in stealing from the rich anyway?" the waiter asked with feeling.

Said beamed as if he were receiving a compliment at some public reception in his honor. "Yes," he said, "but the newspapers have tongues longer than a hangman's rope. And what good does being liked by the people do if the police loathe you?"

Suddenly Tarzan got up, moved to the window, stared outside, looking to left and right, then came back. "I thought I saw a face staring in at us," he reported, clearly worried.

Said's eyes glinted as they darted back and forth between window and door and the waiter went outside to investigate.

"You're always seeing things that aren't there," the smuggler said.

Enraged, Tarzan yelled at him. "Shut up! can't you? You seem to think a hangman's rope is some sort of a joke!"

Said left the coffee-house. Clutching the revolver in his pocket, walking off into the open darkness, he looked cautiously around him, listening as he went. His consciousness of fear, of being alone and hunted, was even stronger now and he knew he must not underestimate his enemies, fearful themselves, but so eager to catch him that they would not rest till they saw him a corpse, laid out and still.

As he neared the house in Sharia Najm al-Din he saw light in Nur's window. It gave him a sense of security for the first time since he'd left the coffee-house. He found her lying down and wanted to caress her, but it was obvious from her face that she was terribly tired. Her eyes were so red it was obvious that something was amiss. He sat down at her feet.

"Please tell me what's wrong, Nur," he said.

"I'm worn out," she said weakly. "I've vomited so much I'm exhausted."

"Was it drink?"

"I've been drinking all my life," she said, her eyes brimming with tears.

This was the first time Said had seen her cry and he was deeply moved. "What was the reason, then?" he said.

"They beat me!"

"The police?"

"No, some young louts, probably students, when I asked them to pay the bill."

Said was touched. "Why not wash your face," he said, "and drink some water?"

"A little later. I'm too tired now."

"The dogs!" Said muttered, tenderly caressing her leg.

"The fabric for the uniform," Nur said, pointing to a parcel on the other sofa. He made a gesture with his hand affectionately and in gratitude.

"I can't look very attractive for you tonight," she said almost apologetically.

"It's not your fault. Just wash your face and get some sleep."

Up in the graveyard heights a dog barked and Nur let out a long, audible sigh. "And she said, 'You have such a rosy future!'" she murmured sadly.

"Who?"

"A fortune-teller. She said there'd be security, peace of mind." Said stared out at the blackness of night, piled up outside the window, as she went on. "When will that ever be? It's been such a long wait, and all so useless. I have a girl-friend, a little older than me, who always says we'll become just bones or even worse than that, so that even dogs will loathe us." Her voice seemed to come from the very grave and so depressed Said that he could find nothing to reply. "Some fortune-teller!" she said. "When is she going to start telling the truth? Where is there any security? I just want to sleep safe and secure, wake up feeling good, and have a quiet, pleasant time. Is that so impossible—for him who raised the Seven Heavens?"

You too used to dream of a life like that, but it's all been spent climbing up drain pipes, jumping down from roofs, and being chased in the dark, with mis-aimed bullets killing innocent people.

"You need to get some sleep," he told her, thoroughly depressed.

"What I need is a promise," she said. "A promise from the fortune-teller. And that day will come."

"Good."

"You're treating me like a child," she said angrily.

"Never."

"That day really will come!"

12

Nur watched him as he tried on the uniform, staring at him in surprised delight, until he'd done up the last button. Then, after a moment or two, she said, "Do be sensible. I couldn't bear to lose you again."

"This was a good idea," Said said, displaying his work and examining his reflection in the mirror. "I suppose I'd better be satisfied with the rank of captain!"

By the next evening, however, she'd heard all about his recent dramatic adventure and seen pictures of him in a copy of a weekly magazine belonging to one of her transient male companions. She broke down in front of him. "You've killed someone!" she said, letting out the words with a wail of despair. "How terrible! Didn't I plead with you?"

"But it happened before we met," he said, caressing her.

She looked away. "You don't love me," she said wanly. "I know that. But at least we could have lived together until you did love me!"

"But we can still do that."

"What's the use," she said, almost crying, "when you've committed murder?"

"We can run away together," Said said with a reassuring grin. "It's easy."

"What are we waiting for then?"

"For the storm to blow over."

Nur stamped her foot in frustration. "But I've heard that there are troops blocking all the exits from Cairo, as if you were the first murderer ever!"

The newspapers! Said thought. All part of the secret war! But he hid his feelings and showed her only his outward calm. "I'll get away all right," he said, "as soon as I decide to. You'll see." Pretending a sudden rage, he gripped her by the hair and snarled: "Don't you know yet who Said Mahran is? All the papers are talking about him! You still don't believe in him? Listen to me; we'll live together forever. And you'll see what the fortune-teller told you come true!"

Next evening, escaping his loneliness and hoping for news, he slipped out again to Tarzan's coffee-house, but as soon as he appeared in the doorway Tarzan hurried over and took him out into the open, some distance off. "Please, don't be angry with me," he said apologetically. "Even my café is no longer safe for you."

"But I thought the storm had died down now," Said said, the darkness hiding his concern.

"No. It's getting worse all the time. Because of newspapers. Go into hiding. But forget about trying to get out of Cairo for a while."

"Don't the papers have anything to go on about but Said Mahran?"

"They made such a lot of noise to everyone about your past raids that they've got all the government forces in the area stirred up against you." Said got up to leave. "We can meet again—outside the café—any time you wish," Tarzan remarked as they said goodbye.

So Said went back to his hideout in Nur's house—the solitude, the dark, the waiting—where he suddenly found himself roaring, "It's you, Rauf, you're behind all this!" Almost all the papers had dropped his case, all, by this time, except *al-Zahra.* It was still busy raking up the past, goading the police; by trying so hard to kill him, in fact, it was making a national hero of him. Rauf Ilwan would never rest until the noose was round his neck and Rauf had all the forces of repression: the law.

And you. Does your ruined life have any meaning at all unless it is to kill your enemies—Ilish Sidra, whereabouts unknown, and Rauf Ilwan, in his mansion of steel? What meaning will there have been to your life if you fail to teach your enemies a lesson? No power on earth will prevent the punishing of the dogs! That's right! No power on earth!

"Rauf Ilwan," Said pleaded aloud, "tell me how it is that time can bring such terrible changes to people!" *Not just a revolutionary student, but revolution personified as a student. Your stirring voice, pitching itself downward towards my ears as I sat at my father's feet in the courtyard of the building, with a force to awaken the very soul. And you'd talk about princes and pashas, transforming those fine gentlemen with your magic into mere thieves. And to see you on the Mudiriyya Road, striding out among your men—the men you called your equals—as they munched their sugar cane in their flowing galabiyyas, when your voice would reach such a pitch that it seemed to flow right over the field and make the palm tree bow before it— unforgettable. Yes, there was a strange power in you that I found nowhere else, not even in Sheikh Ali al-Junaydi.*

That's how you were, Rauf. To you alone goes the credit for my father enrolling me in school. You'd roar with delighted laughter at my successes. "Do you see now?" you'd say to my father. "You didn't even want him to get an education. Just you look at those eyes of his; he's going to shake things to their foundations!" You taught me to love reading. You discussed everything with me, as if I were your equal. I was one of your listeners—at the foot of the same tree where the history of my love began—and the times themselves were listening to you too: "The people! Theft! The holy fire! The rich! Hunger! Justice!"

The day you were imprisoned you rose up in my eyes to the very sky, higher still when you protected me the first time I stole, when your remarks about theft gave me back my self-respect. Then there was the time you told me sadly, "There's no real point in isolated theft; there has to be organization." After that I never stopped either reading or robbing. It was you who gave me the names of people who deserved to be robbed, and it was in theft that I found my glory, my honor. And I was generous to many people, Ilish Sidra among them.

Said shouted in anger to the darkened room: "Are you really the same one? The Rauf Ilwan who owns a mansion? You're the fox behind the newspaper campaign. You too want to kill me, to murder your conscience and the past as well. But I won't die before I've killed you: you're the number one traitor. What nonsense life would turn out to be if I were myself killed tomorrow—in retribution for murdering a man I didn't even know! If there's going to be any meaning to life—and to death, too—I simply have to kill you. My last outburst of rage at the evil of the world. And all those things lying out there in the graveyard below the window will help me. As for the rest, I'll leave it to Sheikh Ali to solve the riddle."

Just when the call to the dawn prayers was announced he heard the door open and Nur came carrying some grilled meat, drinks and newspapers. She seemed quite happy, having apparently forgotten her two days of distress and depression; and her presence dispelled his own gloom and exhaustion, made him ready again to embrace what life had to offer: food, drink, and news. She kissed him and, for the first time, he responded spontaneously, with a sense of gratitude, knowing her now to be the person closest to him for as long as he might live. He wished she'd never leave.

He uncorked a bottle as usual, poured himself a glass, and drank it down in one gulp.

"Why didn't you get some sleep?" Nur said, peering close at his tired face.

Flipping through the newspapers, he made no reply.

"It must be torture to wait in the dark," she said, feeling sorry for him.

"How are things outside?" he asked, tossing the papers aside.

"Just like always." She undressed down to her slip and Said smelled powder moistened with sweat. "People are talking about you," she went on, "as if you were some storybook hero. But they don't have any idea what torture we go through."

"Most Egyptians neither fear nor dislike thieves," said Said as he bit into a piece of meat. Several minutes passed in silence while they ate, then he added: "But they do have an instinctive dislike for dogs."

"Well," said Nur with a smile, licking her fingertips, "I like dogs."

"I don't mean that kind of dog."

"Yes, I always had one at home until I saw the last one die. That made me cry a lot and so I decided not to have one again."

"That's right," said Said. "If love's going to cause problems just steer clear of it."

"You don't understand me. Or love me."

"Don't be like that," he said, pleading. "Can't you see the whole world is cruel enough and unjust enough as it is?"

Nur drank until she could hardly sit up. Her real name was Shalabiyya, she confessed. Then she told him tales of the old days in Balyana, of her childhood amid the quiet waters, of her youth and how she'd run away. "And my father was the umda," she said proudly, "the village headman."

"You mean the umda's servant!"

She frowned, but he went on. "Well, that's what you told me first."

Nur laughed so heartily that Said could see bits of parsley caught in her teeth. "Did I really say that?" she asked.

"Yes. And that's what turned Rauf Ilwan into a traitor."

She stared at him uncomprehendingly. "And who's Rauf Ilwan?"

"Don't lie to me," Said snarled. "A man who has to stay in the dark, waiting by himself, a man like that can't stand lies."

13

little after midnight, with a quarter moon shining faintly in the west, Said headed off across the wasteland. A hundred yards or so from the café he stopped, whistled three times and stood waiting, feeling that he had either to strike his blow or else go mad, hoping that Tarzan would have some information at last.

When Tarzan appeared, moving like a wave of darkness, they embraced and Said asked him, "What's new?"

"One of them's finally turned up," the stout man replied, out of breath from walking.

"Who?" Said asked anxiously.

"It's Bayaza," said Tarzan, still gripping his hand, "and he's in my place now, clinching a deal."

"So my waiting wasn't wasted. Do you know which way he's going?"

"He'll go back by Jabal Road."

"Thanks very much indeed, friend."

Said left quickly, making his way east, guided by the faint moonlight to the clump of trees around the wells. He moved on along the south side of the grove until he reached its tip, ending in the sands where the road up the mountain began. There he crouched behind a tree and waited.

A cool breeze sent a whisper through the grove. It was a desolate, lonely spot. Gripping his revolver hard, he pondered the chance that might now be at hand, to bear down on his enemy and achieve his long-awaited goal. And then death, a final resting place. "Ilish Sidra," he said aloud, heard only by the trees as they drank in the breeze, "and then Rauf Ilwan. Both in one night. After that let come what may."

Tense, impatient, he did not have long to wait for a figure to come hurrying in the dark from the direction of the café towards the tip of the woods. When there was only a yard or two left between the man and the road Said leaped out, leveling his revolver.

"Stop!" he roared.

The man stopped as if hit by a bolt of electricity, and stared at Said speechless.

"Bayaza, I know where you were, what you've been doing, how much cash you're carrying."

The man's breath came forth in a hiss and his arm made a slight, hesitant movement, a twitch. "The money's for my children," he gasped.

Said slapped him hard across the face, making him blink. "You still don't recognize me, Bayaza, you dog!"

"Who are you? I know your voice, but I can't believe," Bayaza said, then cried out, "Said Mahran!"

"Don't move! The first move you make, you're dead."

"You kill me! Why? We've no reason to be enemies."

"Well, here's one," muttered Said, stretching his hand to reach into the man's clothing, locating the heavy purse and ripping it loose.

"But that's my money. I'm not your enemy."

"Shut up. I've not got all I want yet."

"But we're old pals. That's something you should respect."

"If you want to live, tell me where Ilish Sidra is staying."

"I don't know," Bayaza replied emphatically. "No one knows."

Said slapped him again, harder than before. "I'll kill you if you don't tell me where he is," he shouted. "And you won't get your money back until I know you're telling the truth!"

"I don't know, I swear I don't know," Bayaza whispered.

"You liar!"

"I'll swear any oath you like!"

"You're telling me he's disappeared completely, dissolved like salt in water?"

"I really don't know. No one knows. He moved out right after your visit, afraid of what you might do. I'm telling the truth. He moved to Rod al-Farag."

"His address?"

"Wait, Said," he pleaded. "And after Shaban Husayn was killed he took his family away again. He didn't tell anyone where. He was scared, all right, and his wife was, too. And no one knows anything more about them."

"Bayaza!"

"I swear I'm telling the truth!" Said hit him again and the man groaned with pain and fear: "Why are you beating me, Said? God damn Sidra wherever he may be; is he my brother or my father that I would die on his account?"

At last, and reluctantly, Said believed him and began to lose hope of ever finding his enemy. If only he wasn't a hunted man, wanted for murder, he would bide his time, and wait patiently for the proper opportunity! But that misdirected shot of his had struck at the heart of his own most intense desire.

"You're being unfair to me," said Bayaza. When Said did not reply, he went on: "And what about my money? I never harmed you." He held a hand to the side of his face where Said had struck him. "And you've no right to take my money. We used to work together!"

"And you were always one of Sidra's buddies too."

"Yes, I was his friend and his partner, but that doesn't mean I'm your enemy. I had nothing to do with what he did to you."

The fight was over now and a retreat was the only course. "Well," Said told him, "I'm in need of some cash."

"Take what you like, then," said Bayaza.

Said was satisfied with ten pounds. The other man left, dazed as if he scarcely believed his escape, and Said found himself alone again in the desert, the light from the moon brighter now and the whispering of the trees harsher. So Ilish Sidra has slipped out of his clutches, escaped his due punishment, rescued his own treacherous self, adding one to the number of scot-free traitors. Rauf, the only hope I have left is in you, that you won't make me lose my life in vain.

14

y the time Said had returned to the flat, dressed in his officer's uniform, and left, it was well after one o'clock. He turned towards Abbasiyya Street, avoiding the lights and forcing himself to walk very naturally, then took a taxi to Gala'a bridge, passing an unpleasant number of policemen en route.

At the dock near the bridge he paid to hire a small rowboat for two hours and promptly set off in it south, towards Rauf Ilwan's house. It was a fine starry night, a cool breeze blowing, the quarter moon still visible in the clear sky above the trees along the river bank. Excited, full of energy, Said felt ready to spring into vigorous action. Ilish Sidra's escape was not a defeat, not as long as punishment was about to descend on Rauf Ilwan. For Rauf, after all, personified the highest standard of treachery from which people like Ilish and Nabawiyya and all the other traitors on earth sought inspiration.

"It's time to settle accounts, Rauf," he said, pulling the oars hard. "And if anyone but the police stood as judges between us, I'd teach you a lesson in front of everyone. They, the people, everyone — all the people except the real robbers—are on my side, and that's what will console me in my everlasting perdition. I am, in fact, your soul. You've sacrificed me. I lack organization, as you would put it. I now understand many of the things you used to say that I couldn't comprehend then. And the worst of it is that despite this support from millions of people I find myself driven away into dismal isolation, with no one to help. It's senseless all of it, a waste. No bullet could clear away its absurdity. But at least a bullet will be right, a bloody protest, something to comfort the living and the dead, to let them hold on to their last shred of hope."

At a point opposite the big house, he turned shorewards, rowed in to the bank, jumped out, pulled the boat up after him until its bow was well up on dry land, then climbed the bank up to the road, where, feeling calm and secure in his officer's uniform, he walked away. The road seemed empty and when he got to the house he saw no sign of guards, which both pleased and angered him. The house itself was shrouded in darkness except for a single light at the entrance, convincing him that the owner was not yet back, that forced entry was unnecessary, and that a number of other difficulties had been removed.

Walking quite casually, he turned down the street along the left side of the house and followed it to its end at Sharia Giza, then he turned along Sharia Giza and proceeded to the other street, passing along the right of the house, until he regained the riverside, examining everything along the way most carefully. Then he made his way over to a patch of ground shaded from the street lights by a tree, and stood waiting, his eyes fixed on the house, relaxing them only by gazing out from time to time at the dark surface of the river; his thoughts fled to Rauf's treachery, the deception that had crushed his life, the ruin that was facing him, the death blocking his path, all the things that made Rauf's death an absolute necessity. He watched each car with bated breath as it approached.

Finally one of them stopped before the gate of the house, which was promptly opened wide by the doorkeeper, and Said darted into the street to the left of the house, keeping close to the wall, stopping at a point opposite the entrance door, while the car moved slowly down the drive. It came to a halt in front of the entrance where the light that had been left on illuminated the whole entranceway. Said took out his revolver now and aimed it carefully as the car door opened and Rauf Ilwan got out.

"Rauf!" Said bellowed. As the man turned in shock towards the source of this shout, Said yelled again: "This is Said Mahran! Take that!"

But before he could fire, a shot from within the garden, whistling past him very close, disturbed his aim. He fired and ducked to escape the next shot, then raised his head in desperate determination, took aim and fired again.

All this happened in an instant. After one more wild, hasty shot, he sped away as fast as he could run towards the river, pushed the boat out into the water and leaped into it, rowing towards the opposite bank. Unknown sources deep within him released immediate reserves of physical strength, but his thoughts and emotions swirled as though caught in a whirlpool. He seemed to sense shots being fired, voices of people gathering and a sudden loss of power in some part of his body, but the distance between the river banks was small at that point and he reached the other side, quickly jumped ashore, leaving the boat to drift in the water, and climbed up to the street, clutching the gun in his pocket.

Despite his confused emotions, he proceeded carefully and calmly, looking neither to the right nor left. Aware of people rushing down to the water's edge behind him, of confused shouts from the direction of a bridge, and a shrill whistle piercing the night air, he expected a pursuer to accost him at any moment; and he was ready to put all his efforts either to bluffing his way out or entering one last battle. Before anything else could happen, however, a taxi cruised by. He hailed it and climbed in; the piercing pain he felt as soon as he sat back on the seat was nothing compared to the relief of being safe again.

He crept up to Nur's flat in complete darkness and stretched out on one of the sofas, still in his uniform. The pain returned now, and he identified its source, a little above his knee, where he put his hand and felt a sticky liquid with more sudden pain. Had he knocked against something? Or was it a bullet—when he'd been behind the wall perhaps, or running? Pressing fingers all around the wound, he made sure it was only a scratch; if it had been a bullet, it must have grazed him without penetrating.

He got up, took off his uniform, felt for his night shirt on the sofa and put it on. Then he walked around the flat testing out the leg, remembering how once he'd run right down Muhammad Ali Street with a bullet lodged in the leg. "Why, you're capable of miracles," he told himself. "You'll get away all right. With a little coffee powder this wound will bind up nicely."

But had he managed to kill Rauf Ilwan? And who had shot at him from inside the garden? *Let's hope you didn't hit some other poor innocent fellow like before. And Rauf must surely have been killed—your aim never misses, as you used to show in practice out in the desert beyond the hill. Yes, now you can write a letter to the papers: "Why I killed Rauf Ilwan." That will give back the meaning your life has lost: the bullet that killed Rauf Ilwan will at the same time have destroyed your sense of loss, of waste. A world without morals is like a universe without gravity. I want nothing, long for nothing more than to die a death that has some meaning to it.*

Nur came home worn out, carrying food and drink. She kissed him as usual and smiled a greeting, but her eyes suddenly fastened on his uniform trousers. She put her parcel on the sofa, picked them up and held them out to him.

"There's blood!" she said.

Said noticed it for the first time. "It's just a minor wound," he said, showing her his leg. "I hit it on the door of a taxi."

"You've been out in that uniform for some specific reason! There's no limit to your madness. You'll kill me with worry!"

"A little bit of coffee powder will cure this wound even before the sun rises."

"My soul rises, you mean! You are simply murdering me! Oh when will this nightmare end?"

In a burst of nervous energy Nur dressed the wound with powdered coffee, then bound it up with a cutting from fabric she was using to make a dress, complaining about her ill-fortune all the time she worked.

"Why don't you take a shower?" said Said. "It'll make you feel good."

"You don't know good from bad," she said, leaving the room.

By the time she came back to the bedroom, he had already drunk a third of a bottle of wine and his mood and nerves felt much improved.

"Drink up!" he said as she sat down. "After all, I'm here, all right, in a nice safe place, way out of sight of the police."

"I'm really very depressed," Nur whimpered, combing her wet hair.

"Who can determine the future anyway?" he said, taking a swallow.

"Only our own actions can."

"Nothing, absolutely nothing is certain. Except your being with me, and that's something I can't do without."

"So you say now!"

"And I've got more to say. Being with you, after being out there with bullets tearing after me, is like being in Paradise." Her long sigh in response was deep, as if in self-communion at night; and he went on: "You really are very good to me. I want you to know I'm grateful."

"But I'm so worried. All I want is for you to stay safe."

"We'll still have our opportunity."

"Escape! Put your mind to how we can escape."

"Yes, I will. But let's wait for the dogs to close their eyes awhile."

"But you go outside so carelessly. You're obsessed with killing your wife and this other man. You won't kill them. But you will bring about your own destruction."

"What did you hear in town?"

"The taxi-driver who brought me home was on your side. But he said you'd killed some poor innocent fellow."

Said grunted irritably and forestalled any expression of regret by taking another big swallow, gesturing at Nur to drink too. She raised the glass to her lips.

"What else did you hear?" he said.

"On the houseboat where I spent the evening one man said you act as a stimulant, a diversion to relieve people's boredom."

"And what did you reply?"

"Nothing at all," Nur said, pouting. "But I do defend you; and you don't look after yourself at all. You don't love me either. But to me you're more precious than my life itself; I've never in my whole life known happiness except in your arms. But you'd rather destroy yourself than love me." She was crying now, the glass still in her hand.

Said put his arm around her. "You'll find me true to my promise," he whispered. "We will escape and live together forever."

15

hat enormous headlines and dramatic photos! It was obviously the major news item. Rauf Ilwan had been interviewed and had said that Said Mahran had been a servant in the students' hostel when he'd lived there, that he'd felt very sorry for him, and that later, after his release from prison, Said had visited him to ask for help, so he'd given him some money to start a new life; that Said had tried to rob his house the very same night and that he, Rauf, had caught and scolded him, but let him go again out of compassion. And that then Said had come back to kill him!

The papers accused Said of being mad, craving for power and blood: his wife's infidelity had made him lose his mind, they said, and now he was killing at random. Rauf had apparently been untouched, but the unfortunate doorkeeper had fallen. Another poor innocent killed!

"Damnation!" cursed Said as he read the news.

The hue and cry was deafening now.

A huge reward was offered to anyone giving information of his whereabouts and articles warned people against any sympathy for him. Yes, he thought, you're the top story today, all right. *And you'll be the top story until you're dead. You're a source of fear and fascination—like some freak of nature—and all those people choking with boredom owe their pleasure to you. As for your gun, it's obvious that it will kill only the innocent. You'll be its last victim.*

"Is this madness, then?" he asked himself, choking on the question.

Yes, you always wanted to cause a real stir, even if you were only a clown. Your triumphant raids on the homes of the rich were like wine, intoxicating your pride-filled head. And those words of Rauf that you believed, even though he did not—it was they that really chopped off your head, that killed you dead!

He was alone in the night. There was still some wine in a bottle, which he drank down to the last drop. As he stood in the dark, enveloped in the silence of the neighboring graves, slightly giddy, he began to feel that he would indeed overcome all his difficulties, that he could disdain death. The sound of mysterious music within him delighted him.

"A mis-aimed bullet has made of me the man of the hour!" he declared to the dark.

Through the window shutters he looked over the cemetery, at the graves lying there quiet in the moonlight.

"Hey, all you judges out there, listen carefully to me," he said. "I've decided to offer my defense myself."

Back in the center of the room he took off his gown. The room was hot, the wine had raised his body heat. His wound throbbed beneath the bandage, but the pain convinced him it was beginning to heal.

"I'm not like the others," he said, staring into the dark, "who have stood on this stand before. You must give special consideration to the education of the accused. But the truth is, there's no difference between me and you except that I'm on the stand and you're not. And that difference is only incidental, of no real importance at all. But what's truly ridiculous is that the distinguished teacher of the accused is a treacherous scoundrel. You may well be astonished at this fact. It can happen, however, that the cord carrying current to a lamp is dirty, speckled with fly shit."

He turned to a sofa and lay down on it. In the distance he could hear a dog barking. *How can you ever convince your judges, when there is a personal animosity between you and them that has nothing to do with the so-called "public welfare"? They're kin to the scoundrel after all, whereas there's a whole century of time between you and them. You must then ask the victim to bear witness. You must assert that the treachery has become a silent conspiracy: "I did not kill the servant of Rauf Ilwan. How could I kill a man I did not know and who didn't know me? Rauf Ilwan's servant was killed because, quite simply, he was the servant of Rauf Ilwan. Yesterday his spirit visited me and I jumped to hide in shame, but he pointed out to me that millions of people are killed by mistake and without due cause."*

Yes, these words will glitter; they'll be crowned with a not-guilty verdict. You are sure of what you say. And apart from that, they will believe, deep down, that your profession is lawful, a profession of gentlemen at all times and everywhere, that the truly false values—yes!—are those that value your life in pennies and your death at a thousand pounds. The judge over on the left is winking at you; cheer up!

"I will always seek the head of Rauf Ilwan, even as a last request from the hangman, even before seeing my daughter. I am forced not to count my life in days. A hunted man only feeds on new excitements, which pour down upon him in the span of his solitude like rain."

The verdict will be no more cruel than Sana's cold shyness towards you. She killed you before the hangman could. And even the sympathy of the millions for you is voiceless, impotent, like the longings of the dead. Will they not forgive the gun its error, when it is their most elevated master?

"Whoever kills me will be killing the millions. I am the hope and the dream, the redemption of cowards; I am good principles, consolation, the tears that recall the weeper to humility. And the declaration that I'm mad must encompass all who are loving. Examine the causes of this insane occasion, then reach your judgement however you wish!"

His dizziness increased.

Then the verdict came down: that he was a great man, truly great in every sense of the word. His greatness might be momentarily shrouded in black, from a community of sympathy with all those graves out there, but the glory of his greatness would live on, even after death. Its fury was blessed by the force that flowed through the roots of plants, the cells of animals and the hearts of men.

Eventually sleep overtook him, though he only knew it when he awoke to find light filling the room and he saw Nur standing looking down at him. Her eyes were dead tired, her lower lip drooped and her shoulders slumped. She looked the very picture of despair. He knew in an instant what the trouble was; she'd heard about his latest exploit and it had shocked her deeply.

"You are even more cruel than I imagined," she said. "I just don't understand you. For heaven's sake have mercy and kill me, too." He sat up on the sofa, but made no reply. "You're busy thinking how to kill, not how to escape, and you'll be killed, too. Do you imagine you can defeat the whole government, with its troops filling the streets?"

"Sit down and let's discuss it calmly."

"How can I be calm? And what are we to discuss? Everything's over now. Just kill me too, for mercy's sake!"

"I don't ever want harm to come to you," he said quietly and in a tender tone of voice.

"I'll never believe a word you say. Why do you murder doorkeepers?"

"I didn't mean to harm him!" he said angrily.

"And the other one? Who is this Rauf Ilwan? What is your relationship with him? Was he involved with your wife?"

"What a ridiculous idea," he said, laughing so drily, it was like a cough. "No, there are other reasons. He's a traitor, too, but of another sort. I can't explain it all to you."

"But you can torture me to death."

"As I just said, sit down so we can talk calmly."

"You're still in love with your wife, that bitch, but you want to put me through hell all the same."

"Nur," he pleaded, "please don't torture me. I'm terribly depressed."

Nur stopped talking, affected by a distress she had never seen in him before. "I feel as if the most precious thing in my whole life is about to die," she said at last, sadly.

"That's just your imagination, your fear. Gamblers like me never admit to setbacks. I'll remind you of that sometime."

"When will that be?" she asked quietly.

"Oh, sooner than you think," Said replied, pretending boundless self-confidence.

He leaned towards her and pulled her down by the hand. He pressed his face against hers, his nose filling with the smell of wine and sweat. But he felt no disgust and kissed her with genuine tenderness.

16

awn was close, but Nur had not returned— though the waiting and all his worry had exhausted him, bouts of insomnia kept crushing against his brain—and now the warm darkness was splitting apart to reveal one flaming question: Was it possible that the promised reward was having some effect on Nur?

Suspicion had tainted his blood to the last drop now: he had visions of infidelity as pervasive as dust in a wind storm. He remembered how sure he was once that Nabawiyya belonged to him, when in reality she'd probably never loved him at all, even in the days of the lone palm tree at the edge of the field.

But surely Nur would never betray him, never turn him over to the police for the sake of payment. She had no interest now in such financial transactions. She was getting on in life. What she wanted was a sincere emotional relationship with someone. He ought to feel guilty for his suspicious thoughts.

The worry over Nur's absence persisted, nevertheless. It's your hunger, thirst, and all the waiting that's getting you down, he said to himself. *Just like that time you stood waiting beneath the palm tree, waiting for Nabawiyya, and she didn't come. You began prowling around the old Turkish woman's house, biting your finger-nails with impatience and so crazy with worry you almost knocked on her door. And what a quiver of joy when she did emerge—a feeling of complete exhilaration, spreading through you, lifting you up to the seventh heaven.*

It had been a time of tears and laughter, of uncontrolled emotion, a time of confidence, a time of boundless joy. Don't think about the palm tree days now. They're gone forever, cut off by blood, bullets and madness. Think only about what you've got to do now, waiting here, filled with bitterness, in this murderous stifling darkness.

He could only conclude that Nur did not want to come back, did not want to save him from the tortures of solitude in the dark, from hunger and thirst. At the height of a bout of remorse and despair, he at last fell asleep. When he opened his eyes again he saw daylight and felt the heat slipping through the shutters into the closed room. Worried and confused, he stepped quickly into the bedroom, to find it exactly as Nur had left it the day before, then roamed around the entire flat. Nur had not returned. Where, he wondered, could she have spent the night? What had prevented her return? And how long was he to be sentenced to this solitary confinement?

He was feeling distinct pangs of hunger now, despite his worries, and he went into the kitchen. On the unwashed plates there he found several scraps of bread, bits of meat sticking to bones, and some parsley. He consumed them all, ravenously gnawing on the bones like a dog, then spent the rest of the whole day wondering why she had not returned, wondering if she ever would. He would sit for a while, then wander about and sit again. His only distraction was gazing through the shutters out over the cemetery, watching the funerals and aimlessly counting the graves. Evening came, but Nur had still not returned.

There must be some sort of reason. Wherever could she be? He felt his worry, anger, and hunger tearing him apart. Nur was in trouble, there was no doubt of that, but somehow she simply had to free herself from her difficulty, whatever it was, and come back. Otherwise what would become of him? After midnight he quietly left the flat, and made his way over the waste ground to Tarzan's coffee-house. He whistled three times when he arrived at the spot they'd agreed on and waited until Tarzan came out.

"Be careful," said Tarzan, shaking his hand, "there are agents watching everywhere."

"I need some food!"

"You don't say! You're hungry then!"

"Yes. Nothing ever surprises you, does it?"

"I'll send the waiter to get you some meat. But I'm telling you it really is dangerous for you to go out."

"Oh, we had worse trouble in the old days, you and I."

"I don't think so. That last attack of yours has turned the whole world upside down on top of you."

"It's always been upside down."

"But it was disastrous of you to attack a man of importance!"

They parted and Said withdrew a little. After some time the food was brought him and he gulped it down, sitting on the sand beneath a moon now really full. He looked over at the light coming from Tarzan's café on the little hill and imagined the customers sitting there in the room chatting. No, he really did not like being alone. When he was with others his stature seemed to grow giant-like: he had a talent for friendship, leadership, even heroism. Without all that there was simply no spice to life. But had Nur come back yet? Would she return at all? Would he go back to find her there or would there be more of that murderous loneliness?

At last he got up, brushed the sand and dust from his trousers and walked off towards the grove, planning to go back to the flat by the path that wound around the south side of the Martyr's Tomb. Near the tip of the grove, at the spot where he'd waylaid Bayaza, the earth seemed to split open, emitting two figures who jumped out on either side of him.

"Stop where you are!" said one of them in a deep urbanized country accent.

"And let's see your identity card!" barked the other.

The former shone a flashlight into his face and Said lowered his head as though to protect his eyes, demanding angrily, "Who do you think you are? Come on, answer me!"

They were taken aback by his imperious tone; they'd now seen his uniform by the flashlight.

"I'm very sorry indeed, sir," the first man said. "In the shadow of the trees we couldn't see who you were."

"And who are you?" Said shouted, with even more anger in his voice.

"We're from the station at al-Waili, sir," they answered hastily.

The flashlight was turned off now, but Said had already seen something disturbing in the expression of the second man, who had been peering very quizzically at him, as though suddenly filled with doubt. Afraid he might lose control of the situation, Said moved decisively and with force, swinging a fist into both their bellies. They reeled back; and before they could recover he went at them both, fists flying, until he felt them fall unconscious, and dashed away as fast as he could go. At the corner of Najm al-Din Street he stopped to make sure no one was following, then he continued along it quietly to the flat.

Once there he found it as empty as when he'd left, with only more loneliness, boredom, and worry there to meet him. He took off his jacket and threw himself down on to a sofa in the dark. His own sad voice came to him audibly: "Nur, where are you?"

All was not well with her, that was obvious. Had the police arrested her? Had some louts attacked her? She was bound to be in some sort of trouble. Emotions and instincts told him that much; and that he would never see Nur again. The thought choked him with despair, not merely because he would soon lose a safe hiding place, but because he also knew he'd lost affection and companionship as well. He saw her there in the dark before him—Nur, with all her smiles and fun-making, her love and her unhappiness—and the terrible depression he felt made him aware that she had penetrated much deeper within him than he had imagined, that she had become a part of him, and that she should never have been separated from this life of his which was in shreds and tottering on the brink of an abyss. Closing his eyes in the darkness, he silently acknowledged that he did love her and that he would not hesitate to give his own life to bring her back safe. Then one thought made him growl in anger: "And yet would her destruction cause so much as a single ripple anywhere?"

No, definitely not. Not even a pretense of grief would be made for loss of Nur, who was only a woman with no protector, adrift on a sea of waves either indifferent or hostile. And Sana, too, might well find herself one day with no one who cared to look after her. These thoughts scared and angered him and he gripped his gun and pointed it in front of him in the dark, as though warning the unknown. In deep despair, delirious in the silence and dark, he began to sob; and sobbed until late in the night sleep finally overcame him.

It was daylight when he next opened his eyes, aware that someone's knocking on the door had awakened him. He jumped up in alarm and tip-toed to the front door of the flat, the knocking continuing all the time.

"Madame Nur! Madame Nur!" a woman's voice shouted.

Who was the woman and what could she want? He fetched his revolver from the other room. Now he heard a man's voice: "Well, maybe she's gone out."

"No," he heard the woman reply, "at this time of day she's home. And she's never been late with the rent before."

So it must be the landlady. The woman gave one last angry bang on the door and yelled: "Today's the fifth of the month and I'm not going to wait any longer!"

Then she and the man walked away, grumbling as they went.

Circumstances were after him now, as well as the police. The woman would certainly not wait long and would be sure to break into the flat by one means or the other. The best thing for him was to get out of the flat as soon as he possibly could.

But where was he to go?

17

ate in the afternoon and then again during the evening the landlady returned. "No, no, Madame Nur," she muttered as she finally left, "everything has to come to an end sometime, you know."

At midnight Said slipped out. Although his confidence in everything had gone, he was careful to walk very naturally and slowly, as if merely taking a stroll. More than once, when the thought struck him that people passing by or standing around might well be informers, he braced himself for one last desperate battle. After the encounter on the previous day, he had no doubts that the police would be in occupation of the whole area near Tarzan's café, so he moved off towards Jabal Road.

Hunger was tearing at his stomach now. On the road, it occurred to him that Sheikh Ali al-Junaydi's house might well provide a temporary place of refuge, while he thought out his next moves. It was only as he slipped into the courtyard of the silent house that he became aware that he had left his uniform in the sitting room of Nur's flat.

With that realization infuriating him, Said went on into the old man's room, where the lamplight showed the Sheikh sitting in the corner reserved for prayer, completely engrossed in a whispered monologue. Said walked over to the wall where he'd left his books and sat down, exhausted.

The Sheikh continued his quiet utterance until Said addressed him: "Good evening, Sheikh Ali."

The old man raised his hand to his head in response to the greeting, but did not break off his incantations.

"Sheikh, I'm really hungry," Said said.

The old man seemed to interrupt his chant, gazed at him vacantly, then nodded with his chin to a side table nearby where Said saw some bread and figs. He got up at once, went to the table, and consumed it all ravenously, then stood there looking at the Sheikh with unappeased eyes.

"Don't you have any money?" the Sheikh said quietly.

"Oh, yes."

"Why not go and buy yourself something to eat?"

Said then made his way quietly back to his seat. The Sheikh sat contemplating him for a while, then said, "When are you going to settle down, do you think?"

"Not on the face of this earth."

"That's why you're hungry, even though you've got money."

"So be it, then."

"As for me," the Sheikh commented, "I was just reciting some verses about life's sorrows. I was reciting in a joyful frame of mind."

"Yes. Well, you're certainly a happy Sheikh," Said said. "The scoundrels have got away," he went on angrily. "How can I settle down after that?"

"How many of them are there?"

"Three."

"What joy for the world if its scoundrels number only three."

"No, there are very many more, but my enemies are only three."

"Well then, no one has 'got away.'"

"I'm not responsible for the world, you know."

"Oh yes. You're responsible for both this world and the next!"

While Said puffed in exasperation, the Sheikh continued, "Patience is holy and through it things are blessed."

"But it's the guilty who succeed, while the innocent fail," Said commented glumly.

The Sheikh sighed, "When shall we succeed in achieving peace of mind beneath the doings of authority?"

"When authority becomes fair," Said replied.

"It is always fair."

Said shook his head angrily. "Yes," he muttered. "They've got away now all right, damn it." The Sheikh merely smiled without speaking. Said's voice changed its tone as he tried to alter the course of the conversation. "I'm going to sleep with my face towards the wall. I don't want any one who visits you to see me. I'm going to hide out here with you. Please protect me."

"Trusting God means entrusting one's lodging to God alone," the Sheikh said gently.

"Would you give me up?"

"Oh, no, God forbid."

"Would it be in your power, with all the grace with which you're endowed, to save me then?"

"You can save yourself, if you wish," came the Sheikh's reply.

"I will kill the others," Said whispered to himself, and aloud said, "Are you capable of straightening the shadow of something crooked?"

"I do not concern myself with shadows," the Sheikh replied softly.

Silence followed and light from the moon streamed more strongly through the window onto the ceiling. In a whisper the Sheikh began reciting a mystic chant:

"All beauty in creation stems from You."

Yes, Said told himself quietly, the Sheikh will always find something appropriate to say. *But this house of yours, dear sir, is not secure, though you yourself might be security personified. I've got to get away, no matter what the cost. And as for you, Nur, let's hope at least good luck will protect you, if you find neither justice nor mercy. But how did I forget that uniform? I wrapped it up deliberately intending to take it with me. How could I have forgotten it at the last moment? I've lost my touch. From all this sleeplessness, loneliness, dark and worry. They'll find that uniform. It might supply the first thread leading to you: they'll have dogs smelling it, fanning out in all directions to the very ends of the earth, sniffing and barking to complete a drama that will titillate newspaper readers.*

Suddenly the Sheikh spoke again in a melancholy tone of voice: "I asked you to raise up your face to the heavens, yet here you are announcing that you are going to turn it to the wall!"

"But don't you remember what I told you about the scoundrels?" Said demanded, gazing at him sadly.

" 'Remember the name of your Lord, if you forget.' "

Said lowered his gaze, feeling troubled, then wondered again how he could have forgotten the uniform as depression gripped him further.

"He was asked," the Sheikh said suddenly, as if addressing someone else, " 'Do you know of any incantation we can recite or potion we can use that might perhaps nullify a decree of God?' And he answered: 'Such would be a decree of God!' "

"What do you mean?" Said asked.

"Your father was never one to fail to understand my words," replied the old man, sighing sadly.

"Well," Said said irritably, "it is regrettable that I didn't find sufficient food in your home, just as it is unfortunate that I forgot the uniform. Also my mind does fail to comprehend you and I will turn my face to the wall. But I'm confident that I'm in the right."

Smiling sadly, the Sheikh said, "My Master stated: 'I gaze in the mirror many times each day fearing that my face might have turned black!' "

"You?!"

"No, my Master himself."

"How," Said asked scornfully, "could the scoundrels keep checking in the mirror every hour?"

The Sheikh bowed his head, reciting:

"All beauty in creation stems from You."

Said closed his eyes, saying to himself:

"I'm really tired, but I'll have no peace until I get that uniform back."

18

At last exhaustion con-
quered his will. He forgot
his determination to get
the uniform and fell
asleep, awaking a little before midday. Knowing he would have to wait
until nightfall to move, he spent the time setting out a plan for his
escape, fully aware that any major step would have to be put off for a
while, until the police relaxed their surveillance of the area near
Tarzan's café. Tarzan was the very pivot of the plan.

Some time after midnight he entered Najm al-Din Street. There
was light coming from a window of the flat. He stood staring up at it
in amazement; and when he finally believed what he saw, his heart
seemed to beat so loudly as almost to deafen him, while a wave of
elation roared over him sweeping him out of a nightmare world. Nur
was in the flat! Where had she been? Why had she been away? At least
she was back now. And she must be suffering the scorch of those same
hell-fires where he'd been burning, wondering where he was. He
knew she was back by that instinct of his that had never deceived him
and the strain of being on the run would now recede for a while,

perhaps for good. He would hold her tight in his arms, pouring out his eternal love for her.

Intoxicated with joy and assured of success he crept into the building and climbed the stairs, dreaming of one victory after another. There was no limit to what he could do. He would get away and settle down for a long time, then come back eventually and deal with those scoundrels.

A little out of breath, he came up to the door. *I love you, Nur. With all my heart I do love you, twice as much as you have loved me. In your breast I will bury all my misery, the treachery of those scoundrels and my daughter's alarm.* He knocked on the door.

It opened to reveal a man he had never seen before, a little man in his underclothes, who stared back at him in astonishment and said, "Yes; what can I do for you?"

The little man's look of inquiry soon gave way to one of confusion and then alarm. Dumbfounded, certain he'd recognized him, Said silenced him instantly, slamming one fist into his mouth and the other into his stomach. As he lowered the body quietly to the threshold, Said thought of entering to search for his uniform, but he couldn't be sure the flat was empty. Then from inside he heard a woman's voice calling, "Who was that at the door, dear?"

It was hopeless. Said turned and raced back down the stairs and out into the street, then made his way up Masani Street to Jabal Road, where he could see suspicious figures moving about. There he crouched at the base of a wall, carefully recommencing his walk only when the street was entirely empty. It was a little before dawn when he once again slipped into the Sheikh's house. The old man was in his corner, awake and waiting for the coming call to prayer. Said took off his outer clothes and stretched out on the mat, turning his head to the wall though he had little hope of falling asleep.

"Go to sleep, for sleep is prayer for people like you," the Sheikh said.

Said made no reply. The Sheikh quickly chanted the name of God, "Allah."

When the dawn prayer was called Said was still awake and later he heard the milkman on his round. He knew he'd fallen asleep only when he was disturbed by a nightmare and opened his eyes to see light from the dim lamp spreading through the room like a fog, which made him suppose he'd slept for an hour at most. He turned towards the Sheikh's bed and found it empty, then noticed near his pile of books some meat, figs, and a pitcher of water. He silently thanked the old man, wondering when he had brought the food.

Voices coming from outside the room surprised him. Creeping on all fours to the partly open door, he peeped through the crack and to his amazement saw a group of men who had come to pray, seated on mats, while a workman was busy lighting up a large oil lamp above the outer door. Suddenly he knew it was sunset, not dawn, as he had imagined.

In that case, he realized, he had slept through the whole day without realizing it, a really deep sleep indeed.

He decided to put off any further thought until after eating. He consumed the food and drank his fill, then dressed in his outdoor clothes and sat on the floor with his back against his books and his legs stretched straight out in front of him. His thoughts turned immediately to the uniform he'd forgotten, to the man who had opened the flat door to him, to Sana and Nur and Rauf and Nabawiyya and Ilish, to the informers, to Tarzan and to the car with which he would break through the cordon. His mind stormed. Clearly neither further patience nor hesitation was now in his interest. No matter what the danger, he had to contact Tarzan that night, even if it meant crawling to him over the desert sands. Tomorrow the police would be busy everywhere and those scoundrels would be out of their wits with fright.

Outside he heard someone clap his hands. The men's voices were suddenly silent and no other sounds could be heard. Sheikh Ali al-Junaydi chanted the word "Allah" three times and the others repeated the call, with a melody that brought the memory of the motion of the mystic dance to his mind once more. "Allah . . . Allah . . . Allah." As the speed grew the chant increased in tempo and pitch like the sound of a train racing ahead, continuing without interruption for a considerable time. Then it began gradually to lose its power, its rhythm slowing, hesitating, and finally sinking into silence. At that point a full, fine voice arose in a chanted melody:

"My time in vain is gone
And I have not succeeded.
For a meeting how I long,
But hope of peace is
    ended
When life is two days long;
One day of vexation
And one of separation."

Said could hear the other men murmuring sighs in appreciation all around and then another voice began a melody:

"Love enough to lay me down enthralled:
My passion before me, my fate behind."

This song was followed by more sighs of delight and more singing, until someone clapped hands again and they all began repeating at length the name of God—Allah.

As he listened Said allowed his mind to wander and the evening wore on. Memories came drifting by like clouds. He remembered how his father, Amm Mahran, had swayed with the chanters, while he, then a young boy, had sat near the palm tree observing the scene wide-eyed. From the shadows emerged fancies about the immortal soul, living under the protection of the Most Compassionate. Memories of hopes once bright shook off the dust of oblivion and flashed with life again: beneath that lone tree at the edge of the field tender words were whispered again in early-morning joy; little Sana sat again in his arms, speaking her first wonderful baby-words. Then hot winds blew from the depths of hell and a succession of blows were struck.

In the background the prayer-leader's chant and the congregation's sighs wailed on. When would peace come, when his time had passed in futility, when he had failed, and fate was on his trail? But that revolver of his lying ready in his pocket, that was something at least. It could still triumph over betrayal and corruption. For the first time the thief would give chase to the dogs.

Suddenly from beneath the window outside he heard an angry voice explode and a conversation:

"What a mess! Why, the whole quarter is blocked off!"

"It's worse than in the war!"

"That Said Mahran . . . !"

Said tensed, electrified, gripping the revolver so tightly that every muscle in his body strained. He stared in every direction. The area was crowded with people and was no doubt full of eager detectives. *I mustn't let things get ahead of me. They must now be examining the suit and the dogs will be there too. And meanwhile here I am, exposed. The desert road isn't safe, but the Valley of Death itself is only a few steps away. I can fight them there to the death.*

He got up and moved decisively towards the door. They were still engrossed in chanted prayers, the passage to the outer door was clear, and he passed through into the street, then turned off to the left, walking with studied calm, moving into the road to the cemetery.

The night was well-advanced, but there was no moon and the darkness made a black wall across his path. He plunged off among the tombs, into the maze of ruins, with nothing to guide him, stumbling as he walked, not knowing whether he was going forwards or backwards. Though no spark of hope glimmered within him, he felt he was bursting with incredible energy. The loud noises which were brought to him now on the warm wind made him wish he could hide inside a grave, but he knew he could not stop. He feared the dogs, but there was nothing at all he could do. There was nothing within his power to stop.

After some minutes he found himself at the last row of graves in front of a familiar scene: the northern entrance to the cemetery, connecting with Najm al-Din Street, which he recognized, and in the only building on it, Nur's flat. He located the window. It was open and light was streaming out. He focussed his gaze on it and saw a woman through the window. Her features were indistinct, but the shape of her head reminded him of Nur. His heart pumped hard at the thought. Had Nur returned? Or were his eyes deceiving him now, as his emotions had done before? The fact that he had been so completely deceived foretold the end was near. If that were Nur, he told himself, all he wanted was for her to care for Sana, if his time indeed had come. He decided to shout to her, disregarding the danger, to tell her what he wanted, but before a sound could emerge from his mouth he heard dogs beginning to bark in the distance, and the barking went on breaking the silence like a series of explosive shots.

Said started back in fright, darting in again between the tombs while the barking grew louder. He pressed his back against a tomb and took out his gun, staring out into the darkness resignedly. There it was. The dogs had come at last and there was no hope left. The scoundrels were safe, if only for a while. His life had made its last utterance, saying that it had all been in vain.

It was impossible to tell precisely where the barking came from; it was carried in on the air from all around. It was hopeless now to think of fleeing from the dark by running away into the dark. The scoundrels had indeed got away with it; his life was a proven failure. The barking and the commotion were very close now and soon, Said knew, all the malice and vengefulness he'd been running from would be breathed right into his face. He held his gun poised as the barking grew ever louder and closer. And suddenly there was blinding light over the whole area. He shut his eyes and crouched at the base of the tomb.

"Give yourself up," a triumphant voice shouted. "There's no point in resisting."

The ground shook now with the thud of heavy feet surrounding him and the light spread all around, like the sun.

"Give yourself up, Said," the voice said firmly.

He crouched closer still to the tomb, ready to open fire, turning his head in all directions.

"Surrender," came another shout, confident, reassuring and dignified, "and I promise you you'll be treated with all humanity."

Like the humanity of Rauf, Nabawiyya, Ilish and the dogs, no doubt?

"You're surrounded. The whole cemetery is surrounded. Think it over carefully, Said. Give yourself up."

Sure that the enormous and irregular multitude of tombs prevented them from actually seeing him, Said made no movement. He had decided on death.

"Can't you see there's no point in resistance?" the firm voice shouted.

It seemed to be nearer now than before and Said shouted back warningly:

"Any closer and I'll shoot."

"Very well, then. What do you want to do? Make your choice between death and coming to justice."

"Justice indeed!" Said yelled scornfully.

"You're being very stubborn. You've got one minute more."

His fear-tortured eyes could see the phantom of death now, stalking through the dark.

Sana had turned away from him in alarm, hopelessly.

He sensed surreptitious movement near, flared with rage, and opened fire. The bullets showered in, their whistle filling his ears, chips flying from tombs all around. He fired again, oblivious to danger now, and more bullets pelted in. "You dogs!" he raved in a frenzy of rage and more shots came in from all sides.

Suddenly the blinding light went out, and the firing stopped; there was darkness again and quiet fell. He, too, wasn't firing any more. Slowly the silence was spreading, until all the world seemed gripped in some strange stupefaction. He wondered . . . ? But the question and even its subject seemed to dissolve, leaving no traces. Perhaps, he thought, they had retreated, slipped away into the night. Why then he must have won!

The darkness was thicker now and he could see nothing at all, not even the outlines of the tombs, as if nothing wished to be seen. He was slipping away into endless depths, not knowing for himself position, place or purpose. As hard as he could, he tried to gain control of something, no matter what. To exert one last act of resistance. To capture one last recalcitrant memory. But finally because he had to succumb, he surrendered, not caring. Not caring at all now.

MIRAMAR

CONTENTS

INTRODUCTION

pen cities are the mothers of open societies, and their existence is especially essential to literature—which is why, I suppose, we cherish our illusions about them, and forgive them so many of their sins. In the case of Alexandria, that prototype cosmopolis and melter of antitheses, we can hardly be blamed. *Antony and Cleopatra,* Cavafy, E. M. Forster, Lawrence Durrell . . . there is a formidably distinguished list of foreign celebrants and from them we have taken an indelible image of the place. It is languorous, subtle, perverse, eternally *fin de siècle;* failure haunts it, yet a failure of such richness that it is a kind of victory. What we have conspicuously lacked, in this comfortable pigeon-holing, is a view from the inside, from modern Egypt herself. The one we are now granted may come as something of a shock to those who still see Alexandria through European eyes. Only the sense of failure remains . . . and perhaps not least in the announcement of the death of the old city of our communal literary dream.

Though Naguib Mahfouz is his country's most distinguished

novelist, with a formidable body of work behind him, it would be idle to pretend his name is familiar in the West. I am very sure it is not because he is not worth reading; but nor is it quite a case of mere insularity on our side. Cairo may be only a few hours' flight from London or Paris, but the cultural journey is much more complex and hazardous. Of all the world's considerable contemporary literature, that in Arabic must be easily the least known, which is one very good reason why the Arab mind remains something of a mystery to Westerners—and the more mysterious as it becomes more urban and sophisticated. In one way it is a misfortune that so many great English writers, such as Doughty and T. E. Lawrence, have concentrated on the Bedouin side of the story; very few of us have any clear picture at all of how twentieth century educated Islam lives, feels and thinks.

One obvious hurdle is the Arabic language itself. With its sharp distinction between spoken and literary forms, it is far from easy to translate into a pragmatic, almost purely vernacular language like English—with all its own time-honoured notions of the "right" style and method in fiction. The differences among the spoken dialects of Arabic are much greater than among those in English; yet an Algerian and an Iraqi writer, because of the literary *lingua franca*, have no difficulty in reading each other's work. This much wider potential readership helps explain why serious writers in Arabic have resisted all attempts to evolve a demotic written form; but in addition the "vulgar" forms of Arabic are principally languages of transaction, lacking the finesse and richness a novelist requires of his basic clay; and there are in any case purely technical problems, due to the nature of cursive script, in notating the vernacular. That does not mean a modern Arab writer cannot employ colloquial usages in certain areas. A translator has to allow for that—and then jump to the other historical extreme with all the echoes of al 'arabiyyat al fusha, the classical form fundamentally derived—despite a greatly enriched vocabulary —from the language of the Koran and the eighth century founding fathers of Arabic philology, al-Khalil and Sibawaih. These resonances are obviously nearly impossible to render in another tongue without descending to fustian and the mock-biblical.

Then stylistically Arabic has an odd conjunction of paucity of rhetorical device but great subtlety of syntax and grammar. A translator into English is faced with the constant problem of staying true to his text on the one hand and making some accommodation to English stylistic conventions on the other. To take two small examples, both ellipsis and repetition of words are favourite devices in Arabic . . . and in general the very reverse in English. Perhaps the problem is best grasped by analogy with other arts; by recalling the difficulty of transcribing Arabic music, or of "translating" the visual ellipsis and repetition characteristic of Islamic decorative technique into a European pictorial style.

This linguistic Iron Curtain has kept us miserably short of firsthand information about the very considerable changes that Egypt has undergone in this century; and that alone, quite apart from the novel's intrinsic merits, makes the publication of *Miramar* in English a most welcome thing. Though the book is set in Alexandria, it is essentially about Egypt itself and the normal conflicts—both public and personal—that have arisen during the successive revolutions of these last sixty years.

It is not for nothing that the better educated male characters in the story all revolve around the shrewd-naïve figure of the peasant-girl, Zohra. The fellahin (from *falaha*, to till) are the heart of Egypt, and the heart of all its problems of social progress and national identity. Their age-old exploitation haunts every Egyptian conscience, just as their frequently mulish adherence to tradition is the despair of every Egyptian liberal—though it must be added that very little in the last five millennia has shown the fellahin to be wrong in suspecting the motives of would-be world-changers descending on the Nile Valley. Their character was once described to me thus: "Among the women the sole interest is sex, which is related to food and money; among the men the major interest is money, which is related to sex and food. Their lives are brutal; they live on an eternal frontier, where each year makes its own tradition, and strength is all that counts, so far beyond the reach of what we regard as civilization as to seem surreal, though we have all met their tough sweetness before, in the Russian novelists."

That is clearly not quite the case with the heroine of *Miramar*. It is precisely her determination to emancipate herself that the men about her admire . . . or resent; and why they are perhaps best defined by their varying reactions to her, since she stands for Egypt itself. To Western readers the miseries of her situation may seem exaggerated, a shade "Victorian" and melodramatic. I can say only that the peasant nursemaid in the house where I stayed in Cairo in 1972 had had very closely similar experiences to those of Zohra. She too was trying to educate herself, against intense family opposition—and in spite of the fact that they appropriated all her wages for their own upkeep. Only a month before I met her she had been publicly beaten in the street by her brother for refusing an old man her father had ordered her to marry for flagrant reasons of self-profit. Wahiba knew just enough English to have the story of my novel *The French Lieutenant's Woman* explained to her; and I count it as one of the most touching compliments I have ever been paid that this unhappy and courageous girl exclaimed, when she had understood the main theme, "Oh it is my story, it is me."

The symbolic overtones of this kind of exploitation, so skilfully used by Naguib Mahfouz, do not need elaborating. But a brief reminder (more fully amplified in the notes) must be given of the political and historical background to *Miramar.*

The driving spirit behind modern Egyptian nationalism was Saad Zaghloul (1860–1927). His long opposition to both the Sultanate and the British Protectorate led eventually to his being deported to Malta in 1919, along with his leading supporters. The whole of Egypt rose in protest, and the exiles were finally allowed to send a *wafd,* or delegation, to the Versailles Peace Conference. Though they failed there, containing Wafdist agitation forced the Milner Commission to recommend termination of the Protectorate (though not a British "presence," which lasted until 1954) in 1922. The first elections in 1924 gave the Wafd Party, which on this occasion had massive support from otherwise very disparate sections of society, a huge majority. Saad Zaghloul became prime minister.

The history of the next three decades was one of continual political seesawing, with the much-needed internal social and economic reforms largely sacrificed to the land-owning interest, the enduring problem of Anglo-Egyptian relations, and party squabbles. The once solid Wafd Party itself split into factions. The 1952 arson and riots in Cairo helped bring about the *coup d'état* of July 23, carried out by a military junta headed (or more accurately, figureheaded) by General Mohammad Naguib. Both the monarchy and parliamentary government were abolished. Naguib gave way in 1954 to Colonel Nasser, who initiated the famous programme of social, educational and land reform—the Revolution, whose consequences are to be seen on every page of *Miramar*. The Revolution is now regarded in Egypt as an almost total failure; but then so was the French Revolution in France, at the same remove.

It must be remembered that politically the novel (published in 1967) is already dealing with past history. In the last decade Egypt has become far less of a socialist country than it appears in the pages that follow. Effective power now resides with a new urban bourgeoisie—the "New Class," of whom President Sadat himself is an example. Statistically the top twentieth of the nation, this class had been quick to exploit, in a thoroughly capitalist way, the inherent weaknesses of Nasserist socialism—the population explosion, the growth of consumer demand, the switch from a shortlived national to a much deeper-rooted personal aspiration. According to a report in *Time*, there were as many millionaires in Egypt in the 1970's as during King Farouk's reign.

Appearing just before the disastrous 1967 war with Israel, the novel was a courageous anticipation of a subsequent "loosening of tongues" or release of steam after the thirteen years of tight control of the press and the arts practised by the Nasser regime. Mahfouz had already, in 1959, incurred the wrath of al-Azhar University, the bastion of Muslim traditionalism, with a religious and social allegory *Awlad haratina*, or The Young Men In Our Alley, in which one of the characters is God, and Moses, Jesus and Muhammad also appear. Despite his very considerable prestige ("approaching pharaohdom" in the tart phrase of one Cairo critic), he was obliged to publish in Lebanon. In 1967 *Miramar*, with its far from kind view of the "centres of power" (*scilicet* the Arab Socialist Union), reflected perfectly the feelings many Egyptian intellectuals had held in private towards the political excesses and mistakes of the past decade.

However, Mahfouz is most certainly not some Egyptian equivalent of an English Tory. His disillusionment was far less with specific policies and theories of the Egyptian left than with the moral failure (best represented in his novel by the figure of Sarhan) of the Revolution in practice. What haunts his novel, indeed, is something deeper than disillusion: despair at the eternal and cruel dilemma of his country. Western concepts like "social equality" and "freedom of the individual" have little meaning in Egypt, where the legal system is exiguous and the judiciary have no power over the executive. In any case, the country allows exceptional social mobility. It has to, when almost everyone is engaged in a no-holds-barred struggle for personal economic survival. Mahfouz's view is therefore more akin to the stoical, pessimistic side of humanism, both European and Islamic. History and geography are the fundamental villains; or the nature of things. We are perhaps not too far removed from the spirit of the most famous of Cavafy's poems.

Now what's going to happen to us without barbarians?
Those people were a kind of solution.

Two classes suffered, the one economically, the other morally, during the attempt to found a Moslem socialism—the rich and the ambitious. The first, the hereditary landlords, are represented in the novel by Tolba Bey and Husni Allam, the blind reaction of one generation turned into the feckless nihilism of the next; and the second class, the ambitious, by Sarhan and Mansour—the one sunk in an amoral hypocrisy, a blend of Tartuffe and Uriah Heep, the other retreated into a sort of narcissistic no-man's land. This latter pair may, I think, be seen as inevitable victims of a world locked in battle over the frontier between social good and personal survival.

An excellent study of Egypt's economic problems* makes it clear

*Robert Mabro, *The Egyptian Economy 1952–1972*, Oxford University Press (1974).

why the country feels this conflict with peculiar acuteness. Egypt is poor in natural resources and consequently short of white-collar jobs, a situation not helped by the great expansion, admirable in itself, in educational facilities since 1954. On top of that, population growth has been steadily accelerating (it now stands at some 2.5% *per annum*) and combines politically "difficult" features of high density and youthful composition. Almost all major Egyptian institutions in both private and public sectors are painfully overstaffed, with lamentable effects on managerial efficiency and productivity. Qualifications mean very little; and influence, very nearly all, which explains the importance given to the marriage theme in *Miramar*. All that really happened in the Revolution was that wealth and influence were re-distributed among a new elite; the detritus of the old was despatched to the Pension Miramar.

It is against this background that the predicament of the three young men in *Miramar* should be read, and their egocentricity, their lostness, their duplicity, understood. But, of course, such victims of greater circumstance, torn between self-interest and self-contempt, exist everywhere today, both East and West; and although some of the outward signs of tension—the outbursts of inappropriate laughter, the sudden plunges into sincere respect and emotion—may be specifically Egyptian, the basic type is surely universal. If we set aside moral judgements, perhaps the most attractive of the younger men is the playboy, Husni. At least he is going down in style. His strange and memorable slogan, *ferekeeko*, is explained in the notes; and again, in one form or another, some very similar word or phrase has crept into almost every language in recent years. Again the keynote is despair— young blood defeated by the irremediable faults of a very old world.

One other fickle element, quite literally element, in *Miramar* requires a brief comment: that is the weather. The repeatedly evoked clouds, storms and rain certainly reflect a society in painful evolution, but one may guess that they are also emblematic of the unpredictability of history, of forces beyond human control. Rain may suggest hope and fertility in the West, but we are in a grimmer, more fatalistic world here. So is it with the remnants of the old cosmopolitan Alexandria; Egypt is beyond help from that direction, too, now.

. . .

Naguib Mahfouz* was born in 1912, by nine years the youngest sibling of a lower middle-class family in Cairo, which meant that he was effectively brought up as an only child. He showed early promise in his own language, as also in history and the sciences. At eighteen he encountered Darwin, and this led to a severe crisis of faith. He entered the King Fuad I (now Cairo) University in 1930 as a student of philosophy. The lectures were then given in English and French and Mahfouz had difficulty in following them. To remedy this he translated James Baikie's *Ancient Egypt.*

On graduation in 1934 Mahfouz considered an academic career, but two years later he opted for writing, in spite of the poor financial rewards. His first three books received no payment at all, and gained him a nickname—*al-Sabir,* or "the patient one." Like all Egyptian writers, he had to look elsewhere for a living. He began as a university secretary, and then between 1939 and 1954 was employed in the Ministry of Religious Affairs. His subsequent work in the civil service was to do with the arts, most latterly as Consultant for Cinema Affairs to the Ministry of Culture. He retired from this post in 1972.

He did not develop an interest in foreign literature before his student days. One very strong influence then was certainly that of the British social-realist novelists of the beginning of the century: Galsworthy, Wells and Arnold Bennett. He also read the Victorian novelists, though curiously the one writer, Dickens, who might appear to have sparked Mahfouz's own brilliant descriptions of the Cairo poor, seems never to have impressed him—indeed, he once confessed he had never managed to finish a Dickens story. His literary interests broadened very considerably over the years. In French he admires Balzac, Proust, Sartre and (no surprise to anyone who reads the second section of *Miramar)* Camus. Joyce, Huxley, Orwell,

---

*I owe this brief account to a monograph by Marsden Jones and Hamdi Sakkut: *Najib Mahfuz, a bio-bibliographical study.* I should also like to add here my thanks to Dr. John Rodenbeck of the American University in Cairo for much general help and advice throughout this introduction.

Faulkner and Hemingway are among his preferred writers in English. His knowledge of ancient Arabic literature is slight, and among his contemporaries in modern Arabic literature, the only clear influence is from Tawfiq al-Hakim.

His work can be broadly divided into three periods. He began with three historical (the so-called "pharaonic") novels, but then wrote a series on social themes, the masterpiece of which was the *Trilogy* (completed in 1957). This huge and partly autobiographical work revealed the struggles and convolutions of Egyptian society with a Balzacian breadth and degree of technical innovation unparalleled in any other writer of his time. Some critics have complained of over-richness and plot proliferation, but the achievement was considerable.

His second period, beginning in 1959, forsook social realism for metaphysical allegory, or man in society for man in time, and showed a much increased use of symbolism and the stream-of-consciousness technique, sometimes resulting in a language nearer to poetry than to prose. The third period, dating from *Miramar* in 1967, shows a synthesis of these two rather different previous stages in his growth. Mahfouz has also published seven collections of short stories—there have been four since 1969—whose themes and styles echo the development in his novels. In general the tendency on this side of his writing has been to abandon conventional realism.

Mahfouz is not without his critics in his own country, as I have already suggested. He may be something of a literary pharaoh; but at least he appears to be a refreshingly modest one. Philip Stewart records the following of a conversation with him.

"Mahfouz's reticence comes from a deep-seated humility which can be illustrated by his view of his own work. He is glad that his books are read and agrees that he is amongst Egypt's leading authors; but, when asked how he would rate his own books in relation to European literature, he said they were 'probably, like the rest of modern Arabic literature, fourth or fifth rate.' He suggested tentatively Shakespeare, James Joyce and Tolstoy as examples of first-rate writing, and Wells, Dickens, Thackeray, Shaw, Galsworthy, Huxley and D. H. Lawrence as second- or third-rate European writers. Asked for examples of even lesser European writers, he said he had never read any and was not interested to do so, adding that he did not suppose many Europeans would be interested in modern Arabic literature as it has produced only such writing. He supposes that the reason for this is that literature is formed by its social context and by the attitudes of its readers, and that, since Egypt is still undergoing the industrial and social revolution which Europe passed through a hundred and fifty years ago, Arabic literature must use the technique and subject-matter of the nineteenth century. While there is nothing startling about this view, it is remarkable that it should be held by Egypt's best-selling novelist."

Clearly it is not easy for Westerners to place a writer so adamantly self-disparaging (even if one suspects Koranic precept plays a part in the judgement), and the greater part of whose work remains untranslated and therefore unknown. But I think few will disagree that we are with *Miramar* in the hands of a considerable novelist, and one who knows his country's complex problems, and complex soul, profoundly. Work of this quality also explains why Egypt was long seen by other Arabs as the literary leader of their world.

Like all novels worth their salt, *Miramar* allows us the rare privilege of entering a national psychology, in a way that a thousand journalistic articles or television documentaries could not achieve; and perhaps more importantly, beyond that, we can encounter in it a racial temperament that has been widely misunderstood in the West. The sometimes bizarre emotional mobility of the younger characters, their disorientation, their sensibility, their strikingly Romantic (shades of Chateaubriand) addiction to despair and *Weltschmerz* . . . these things may seem rather remote from our general picture of the Egyptian character, at any rate as formed by our image of their more recent political leaders. But this is an active, and unimpeachably witnessed, view of what we too often see as a passive — or impassive — culture.

If it cannot dispel every illusion or ignorance we hold about Egypt, it represents a very considerable first step. I sincerely hope that the reader will share the pleasure and interest I have got from this very revealing, and very human, novel.

John Fowles
1978

1

AMIR WAGDI

lexandria. At last. Alexandria, Lady of the Dew.[1] Bloom of white nimbus. Bosom of radiance, wet with sky-water. Core of nostalgia steeped in honey and tears.

The massive old building confronts me once again. How could I fail to recognize it? I have always known it. And yet it regards me as if we had shared no past. Walls paintless from the damp, it commands and dominates the tongue of land, planted with palms and leafy acacias, that protrudes out into the Mediterranean to a point where in season you can hear shotguns cracking incessantly.[2]

My poor stooped body cannot stand up to the potent young breeze out here. Not any more.

Mariana, my dear Mariana, let us hope you're still where we could always find you. You must be. There's not much time left; the world is changing fast and my weak eyes under their thinning white brows can no longer comprehend what they see.

Alexandria, I am here.

On the fourth floor I ring the bell of the flat. The little judas

opens, showing Mariana's face. Much changed, my dear! It's dark on
the landing; she does not recognize me. Her white face and golden
hair gleam in the light from a window open somewhere behind her.

"Pension Miramar?"

"Yes, monsieur?"

"Do you have any vacant rooms?"

The door opens. The bronze statue of the Madonna receives me.
In the air of the place is a kind of fragrance that has haunted me.

We stand looking at each other. She is tall and slim, with her
golden hair, and seems to be in good health, though her shoulders are
a little bowed and the hair is obviously dyed. Veins show through the
skin of her hands and forearms; there are tell-tale wrinkles at the
corners of her mouth. You must be sixty-five at least, my dear. But
there is still something of the old glamour left. I wonder if you'll
remember me.

She looks me over. At first she examines me; then the blue eyes
blink. Ah, you remember! And my self comes back to me.

"Oh! It's you."

"Madame."

We shake hands warmly—"Goodness me! Amir Bey! Monsieur
Amir!"—and she laughs out loud with emotion (*the long feminine laugh
of the fishwives of Anfushi!*)[3] throwing all formality to the winds. Together we sit down on the ebony settee beneath the Madonna, our
reflections gleaming on the front of a glassed bookcase that has always
stood in this hall, if only as an ornament. I look round.

"The place hasn't changed a bit."

"Oh but it has," she protests. "It's been redecorated a number of
times. And there are many new things. The chandelier. The screen.
And the radio."

"I'm so glad to have found you here, Mariana. Thank Heaven
you're in good health."

"And so are you. Monsieur Amir—touch wood."

"I'm not at all well. I'm suffering from colitis and prostate trouble.
But God be thanked all the same!"

"Why have you come here now? The season's over."

"I've come to stay. How long is it since I saw you last?"

"Since . . . since . . . did you say 'to stay'?"

"Yes, my dear. I can't have seen you for some twenty years."

"It's true. You never turned up once during all that time."

"I was busy."

"I bet you came to Alexandria often enough."

"Sometimes. But I was too busy. You know what a journalist's life is like."

"I also know what men are like."

"My dear Mariana, *you* are Alexandria to me."

"You're married, of course."

"No. Not yet."

"And when will you marry, monsieur?" she asks teasingly.

"No wife, no family. And I've retired." I reply somewhat irritably. "I'm finished." She encourages me to go on with a wave of her hand. "I felt the call of my birthplace. Alexandria. And since I've no relations I've turned to the only friend the world has left me."

"It's nice to find a friend in such loneliness."

"Do you remember the good old days?"

"It's all gone," she says wistfully.

"But we have to go on living," I murmur.

When we start discussing the rent, however, she can still drive as hard a bargain as ever. The *pension* is all she has; she has had to take in winter guests, even if they are those awful students; and to get them she is forced to depend on middlemen and waiters in the hotels. She says it all with the sadness of humbled pride; and she puts me in number six, away from the sea front on the far side, at a reasonable rent, though I can retain my room in the summer only if I pay at the special summer rate for holiday makers.

We settle everything in a few minutes, including the obligatory breakfast. She proves as good a businesswoman as ever, notwithstanding sweet memories and all that. When I tell her I've left my luggage at the station, she laughs.

"You were not so sure you'd find Mariana. Now you'll stay here with me forever."

I look at my hand and think of the mummies in the Egyptian Museum.

. . .

My room is pleasant enough, quite as good as any of the seaward rooms I used to occupy in the past. I have all the furniture I need. Comfortable, old-fashioned chairs. But there is no place for the books; I'd better leave them in the box and take out only a few at a time. The light here is not very good, a sort of constant twilight. My window opens on to a big air-shaft and the service stairs are so close that I can hear alley-cats chasing up and down and cooks and chambermaids carrying on their affairs.

I make the round of all the rooms where I used to stay in summer; the pink, the violet and the blue, all vacant now. There was a time when I stayed in each a summer or more, and though the old mirrors, the rich carpets, the silver lamps and the cut glass chandeliers are gone, a certain faded elegance lingers still on the papered walls and in the high ceilings, which are adorned with cherubs.

Mariana sighs and I see her false teeth.

"Mine was a very select *pension.*"

"'Glory be to Him who remaineth.'"

"These days, my guests in winter are mostly students. And in summer I take just anybody."

"Amir Bey, will you please put in a good word for me?"

"Your Excellency," I said to the Pasha,[4] "the man is not very efficient, but he lost his son in the Cause and should be nominated for the seat."

He backed my proposal. God rest his soul. My great Master. He loved me and read everything I wrote with the keenest interest.

"You," he said to me once, "are the Nation's throbbing cur."

He said *cur* for *core,* God rest his soul, and it became a standing joke. A few old colleagues from the National Party heard the story and they'd always greet me with "Hello, you cur!" Those were the days— the glory of working for the Cause, independence, the Nation! Amir Wagdi was someone indeed—full of favors for friends, but a man to be feared and avoided by enemies.

In my room I reminisce, read, or sleep. In the hall I can talk to

Mariana or listen to the radio. If I need further entertainment there is
the Miramar Café downstairs. It is not likely that I should see anyone I
know, even in the Trianon.⁵ All my friends are gone. The good old
days are over.

Alexandria, I know you in winter: you empty your streets and your
squares at sunset, leaving them to solitude, wind and rain, while your
inner rooms are filled with chatter and warmth.

" '. . . that old man shrouding his mummified form in a black suit that
dates from the Flood.' None of your long-winded rhetoric, please!"
said that nonentity of an editor, so typical of these days. "Give us
something a jet-age traveller can read."

A jet-age traveller. What would you know, you fat moronic puppet? Writing is for men who can think and feel, not mindless
sensation-seekers out of nightclubs and bars. But these are bad times.
We are condemned to work with upstarts, clowns who no doubt got
their training in a circus and then turned to journalism as the appropriate place to display their tricks.

I sit in an armchair wearing my dressing-gown. Mariana reclines on
the ebony settee beneath the statue of the Madonna. Dance music is
being played on the European Programme. I would rather listen to
something different, but I hate to disturb her. She is completely
absorbed in the music, just as she always used to be, nodding her head
to its beat.

"We've always been friends, Mariana."

"Yes, always."

"But we never made love, not once."

"You went in for your plump countrywomen. Don't deny it."

"Except for that one incident. Do you remember?"

"Yes, you brought home a Frenchwoman and I insisted that you
sign the register as Monsieur and Madame Amir."

"I was discouraged by the multitude of your aristocratic
admirers."

She beams with pleasure. Mariana, let's hope I may be the first of us two to go; no more shifting quarters. There you are, a living proof that the past was no illusion, even from the days of my great Master down to the present moment.

"My dear sir, I'd like to say goodbye." He looked at me, as usual not bothering to disguise his impatience. *"At my age, I think I should retire."*

"We shall certainly miss you," he answered with ill-concealed relief, *"but I hope you'll have a good time."*

That was all. A page of the newspaper's history turned without a word of goodbye, a farewell party, or even a jet-age snippet at the bottom of a page. Nothing. The buggers! A man has no value to them at all unless he plays football or something.

As she sits there under the statue of the Madonna, I look at her and say, "Helen in her prime would not have looked as marvellous!"

She laughs. "Before you arrived, I used to sit here all alone waiting for someone, anyone I knew, to come through the door, I was always in dread of . . . of getting one of my kidney attacks."

"I'm sorry. But where are your people?"

"They've gone, every one of them." She purses her lips, showing her wrinkles. "I couldn't leave—where should I go? I was born here. I've never even seen Athens. And after all, who'd want to nationalize a little *pension* like this?"

"Let us be true to our word and devoted to our work and may love, not law, control man's dealings with man." Look at us now. It was a kindness of God to give you death when he did—with a couple of statues as your memorial.

"Egypt's your home. And there's no place like Alexandria."

The wind plays outside. The darkness steals up quietly. She rises, switches on two bulbs of the chandelier and returns to her seat.

"I was a lady," she says, "a lady in the full sense of the word."

"You're still a lady, Mariana."

"Do you still drink the way you used to?"

"Just one drink at dinner. I eat very little. That's why I can still move around."

"Monsieur Amir, I don't know how you can say there's no place like Alexandria. It's all changed. The streets nowadays are infested with *canaille.*"

"My dear, it had to be claimed by its people." I try to comfort her and she retorts sharply.

"But *we* created it."

"And you, do you still drink the way you did in the old days?"

"No! Not a drop. I've got kidney trouble."

"We should make two fine museum pieces. But promise me you won't go before I do."

"Monsieur Amir, the first revolution killed my first husband. The second took my money and drove out my people. Why?"

"You've got enough, thank God. *We* are your people[6] now. This sort of thing is happening everywhere."

"What a strange world."

"Can't you tune the radio to the Arabic station?"

"No. Only for Umm Kulthum."[7]

"As you wish, my dear."

"Tell me, why do people hurt one another? And why do we grow old?"

I smile, not saying a word. I look around at the walls, which are inscribed with Mariana's history. There is the Captain's portrait, in full dress, heavy-whiskered—her first husband, probably her first and only love, killed in the Revolution of 1919.[8] On the other wall, above the bookcases, is the portrait of her old mother, a teacher. At the opposite end of the hall, beyond the screen, is her second husband, a rich grocer, "The Caviar King," owner of the Ibrahimiyya Palace. One day he went bankrupt and killed himself.

"When did you start this business of the *pension?*"

"You mean, when was I forced to open a boarding-house? In 1925. A black year."

"*Here I am, almost a prisoner in my house, and the hypocrites line up to flatter the King.*"

"*All lies, your excellency.*"

"*I thought the Revolution had cured them of their weaknesses.*"

"*The true heart of the nation is on your side. Shall I read you tomorrow's editorial?*"

She sits there massaging her face with a piece of lemon.

"I was a lady, Monsieur Amir. Living the easy life and loving it. Lights, luxury, fine clothes and big parties. I would grace a salon with my presence. Like the sun."

"I saw you then."

"You saw me only as a landlady."

"But you were still like the sun."

"My guests did belong to the elite. But that has never consoled me for such a comedown."

"You're still a lady. In every sense."

She shakes her head. "What happened to all your old friends in the Wafd?"

"What was fated to happen."

"Why did you never marry, Monsieur Amir?"

"Sheer bad luck. I wish I had a family. And you as well!"

"Neither of my husbands could give me children."

More than likely it was you who couldn't conceive. A pity, my dear. Isn't the whole purpose of our existence to bring children into the world?

That big house in Khan Gaafir, which slowly turned into a hotel: it looked like a little castle, its old courtyard standing where a path now runs to Khan al-Khalili. The image of the place is engraved in my memory—the ancient houses around it, the old Club—and in my heart. *A memorial to the ecstasy of first love. Burning love. Broken. Frustrated.* The turban and the white beard and the cruel lips saying "No." Blindly, fanatically dealing the blow, killing love, whose power has been with us for a million years, since even before the birth of faith.

"Sir, may I ask for your daughter's hand?" Silence. Between us stood a cup of coffee, untouched. "I am a journalist. I have a good income. My father was the keeper of the Mosque of Sidi Abu al-Abbas al-Morsi."

"He was a pious man, God rest his soul," he said, taking up his prayer beads. "My son, you were one of us. You studied in al-Azhar⁹ once. But don't let us forget that you were expelled."

That old story, when would they forget it?

"Sir, that was a long time ago. They'd expel you for the least thing—for being young and full of spirit, for playing in an orchestra or just for asking innocent questions."

"Wise men accused you of a terrible crime."

"Who can judge a man's faith, when only God sees through our souls?"

"Those who take God's words for a guide."

God damn it! Who can be sure of his faith? To His prophets God revealed himself once, but we need to see Him even more: when we consider our place in this enormous house we call the world, our heads begin to reel.

Beware of idleness. I had better try walking on sunny mornings. How pleasant to spend a warm day at the Palma or the Swan, even if you are all on your own in the midst of so many families; the father reading his paper, the mother sewing, the children playing around them. Someone should invent a machine that would hold conversations with lonely people, a robot to partner us at backgammon or tric-trac. Or we should be given a brand new pair of eyes, so we could watch the plants of the earth or the colors of the sky.

I have lived long and seen so many eventful changes. I have often thought of writing it all down, as did my old friend Ahmed Shafiq Pasha, but I've put it off for so long that my strength of purpose has evaporated. Too late now! my hand is too weak, my memory cloudy and nothing is left of the old intention but the sense of frustration. At this point I may commend to ashes my "Azhar Memories," "Conversations with the Great Musicians Sheikh Ali Mahmoud, Zakariya Ahmad, and Sayyid Darwish," "The People's Party: Its Pros and Cons," "The Wafd and the Great Revolution." Party differences, which eventually drove me into cold and meaningless neutrality. The Muslim Brethren, whom I did not like, the Communists, whom I did not understand. The July Revolution and what it meant, taking all previous political currents unto itself. My love life and Sharia Muhammad Ali.[10] My determined stand against marriage.

Yes, my memoirs would make a wonderful book—if they were ever written.

I have paid a nostalgic visit to the Atheneus, Pastoroudis and the

Antoniadis and have sat for some time in the lobbies of the Cecil and the Windsor,[11] the places where pashas and foreign politicians used to meet in the old days, the best places to pick up news. I saw no one I knew, only a few foreigners, Westerners and orientals, and made my way home with two silent prayers: may God help me back to the fold of His Faith . . . and may I die on my feet!

A lovely portrait, throbbing with youth and life: a young woman, her right knee on a chair, her left foot resting lightly on the floor, her wrists poised on the back of the chair, bending forward facing the camera and smiling with a proud sense of her own beauty, the extravagant décolletage of her old-fashioned dress showing a graceful neck and marble-white bosom.

Mariana sits in her black coat and navy blue scarf, waiting to leave for her appointment with the doctor.

"You said you lost your money because of the Revolution?"

She raises her pencilled eyebrows. "Haven't you heard of the stock market crash?" She can see the questioning look in my eyes. "That's when I lost all the money I'd made during the Second World War. And believe me, it was made out of courage. I stayed on in Alexandria, when everyone else had run off to Cairo and the country. I wasn't afraid of the German air raids. I painted the windowpanes blue and drew the curtains and let them dance by candlelight. You never saw anything like the generosity of His Britannic Majesty's officers!"

After she leaves I sit on my own, staring into the eyes of her first husband, who stares from his gilt frame back at me. I wonder who killed you, and how? How many of my generation did you kill before you came to your end? The generation that outdid all others in the extent of its sacrifice. Those were the days. So many fallen.

This foreign singing never stops. It is the worst trial of my solitary existence. Returning from her doctor's, Mariana has had a hot bath. Now she sits in the hall wrapped in a white bathrobe, her dyed hair done up and covered all over with dozens of white-metal curlers. She turns the sound of the radio down to a whisper in order to start her own broadcast.

"Monsieur Amir, you must have plenty of money."

"Do you have any project in hand?" I ask cautiously.

"Not really, but at your age, and mine too—though there is such a big difference—our worst enemies are poverty and ill health."

"I've always had enough for my needs and I hope to die with an easy mind." I remain on my guard.

"I don't remember that you were ever a spendthrift."

I laugh. "I hope my savings may outlive me."

She waves her hand carelessly. "The doctor was very encouraging today. I promised him I'd throw off all my cares."

"That's good."

"So we must have some fun on New Year's Eve."

"Yes. If our hearts can bear it."

"Oh, those wonderful parties!" She wags her head, beaming with recollected pleasure. "These old memories stir up the embers," she says wistfully.

"You were loved by many great men."

"I was truly in love only once." She points to the Captain's portrait. "He was killed by one of those students. Fancy my slaving for them now! This used to be the *pension* for quality. I had a cook working for me, his assistant, a waiter, a laundress and two other servants. Now it's a charwoman, once a week."

"Many of the 'quality' would envy you now."

"Don't make fun of me, Monsieur Amir."

I say hesitantly: "They would. If they knew."

Her face grows grave and I laugh to cheer her up.

The Beneficent
Hath made known the Koran.
He hath created man.
He hath taught him utterance.

The sun and the moon are made punctual.
The stars and the trees adore
And the sky He hath uplifted; and He hath set
the measure.

Sunk deep in the big chair, my feet resting on a cushion, I am
reading the Sura of the Beneficent,[12] dear to my heart since my days
at al-Azhar. Outside is a heavy downpour, the rain drumming loudly
on the iron stairs in my air-shaft.

Everyone that is thereon will pass away;
There remaineth but the countenance of thy Lord of Might
and Glory.

I hear voices in the hall. Is it a guest or a new lodger? Mariana's
tones are too warm for a stranger—it must be an old friend. I hear
laughter, too, a hollow male voice. Who can it be?
  It is early in the afternoon and it is still raining hard, the clouds
decanting enough darkness into the room to make it seem like night. I
reach to turn on a lamp but as I press the switch the shutters gleam
with lightning and I hear rolling thunder.

O company of jinn and men, if ye have power to penetrate
all regions of the heavens and the earth, then penetrate them!
Ye will never penetrate them save with Our sanction.

He is thick-set, with pudgy cheeks, a double chin and blue eyes,
in spite of his dark skin. Unmistakably an aristocrat, a silent, proud
man. His hands move with calculated precision when he speaks.
Madame introduces him in the evening as Tolba Bey Marzuq: "He
was Undersecretary of State for the Ministry of Mortmain Endowments[13] and a great landowner."
  I have no need of further introduction. I had known him well
enough in my profession, from those years of political and party
conflicts. He was one of the King's henchmen and naturally an enemy
of the Wafd. I recall that his property had been put under sequestra-

tion a year ago, with all his resources confiscated, leaving only the usual allowance. Mariana is in her best mood. She speaks repeatedly of their old friendship. Her warmth is explained when she calls him her "old flame."

"I read a great deal, years ago, of what you used to write," he remarks. I laugh pointedly and so does he. "Yours was a good example of a fine pen serving a bad cause." He laughs again, but I will not let myself be drawn into an argument.

"Tolba Bey is an old graduate of the Jesuit schools," Madame says smugly. "We shall listen together to the French songs on the radio." She adds, opening her palms wide in welcome: "He's come to stay."

"That's nice."

"He had a thousand *feddans*.[14] Money was nothing to him," she says nostalgically. "A mere plaything."

"No more playing now." He is obviously piqued.

"Where is your daughter, Tolba Bey?"

"In Kuwait. Her husband's in business."

I'd heard that Tolba Bey had been under suspicion for some attempt to smuggle his money out of the country, but his explanation is simple. "I had to pay for a piece of momentary folly."

"Was there an investigation?"

"They wanted my money," he says contemptuously, "that's all."

Mariana scrutinizes him thoughtfully. "You've changed a great deal, Tolba Bey."

"I had a stroke," he says, smiling with the little mouth that is buried in his fat cheeks. "Almost knocked me off. But I'm all right now. I can even drink whisky, in moderation."

He dipped the bun in his tea, eating slowly, for he was obviously not used to his new set of teeth. We were alone at breakfast. A few days had brought us nearer to one another. The sense of companionship had got the better of the old political differences as well as the deeply rooted aversion of two opposed temperaments, though occasionally the buried differences would drift up to the surface, reawakening an ugly antagonism.

"Do you know what really caused all those misfortunes of ours?"

"What misfortunes?" I asked, taken by surprise.

"You old fox! You know perfectly well what I mean!" He raised his grey eyebrows. "They've abolished your party's name and following, just as they've confiscated our money."

"You've forgotten that I left the Wafd—and all party politics— after February Fourth."[15]

"No matter. They have stricken the pride of all our generation."

I had no inclination to argue. "All right. And so?"

"One man is responsible for this," he said deliberately, with a deep note of loathing. "This chain tightening round our necks. And strangely enough, hardly anyone mentions him."

"Who's that?"

"Saad Zaghloul."[16]

It was so preposterous that I laughed in his face.

"But he is!" he retorted sharply. "He started all these troubles. This class business. His impudence, his arguing the toss with the King and playing up to the masses was only the beginning. It was an evil seed he sowed. And now like a cancer it'll finish us, one and all."

There were only a few visitors at the Palma. Tolba Marzuq sat staring at the sluggish Nile water running in the Mahmoudiyya Canal.[17] I stretched out my legs and sat back in my chair, drinking in the pristine rays of the sun. We had left the windy sea-front for this quiet haven at the far end of the city. It was a pleasant spot among the dense foliage of flowers and trees, warm and sunny on fine days.

For all his aggressive bad temper, I could not help pitying him.

To have to start a bitter new life after sixty! He envied his daughter the bliss of exile, and he had strange dreams. He had no patience whatever with any social theory that could justify his personal misfortune as an historical necessity: any attempt against his property was a breach of the laws of God and Nature.

"You know, I almost decided to leave the *pension* when I learned that you were there."

"But why?"

"I chose the Miramar in the hope that apart from that foreign woman I'd have the place to myself."

Why had he changed his mind then?

"It seemed to me that I'd never heard of anyone over eighty playing Judas."

That amused me very much. Was there any reason to fear government agents?

"None, really. But I sometimes need to find consolation in just talking. And I can't live in the country." He went on with rising anger. "They've taken my house. And in Cairo the atmosphere is a constant humiliation. So I thought of my old mistress. I said to myself: 'She's lost her husband in one revolution—and her money in the other. We'll be a fit match for each other.'"

A little later, he congratulated me on my good health, in spite of my age, and tried to persuade me to go with him to a cinema or an indoor café. Suddenly he asked:

"Why has God stopped using his powers?" And when I did not understand. "Why? Floods, catastrophic storms . . ."

"Do you think the Flood could possibly have killed more people than the Hiroshima Bomb?"

"Cut out the Communist propaganda, you hypocrite! The Americans should have taken control of the whole world, when they had the secret of the atom bomb all to themselves. Their pussyfooting was a terrible mistake."

"And you cut out your nonsense. And tell me something: are you back on the old terms with Mariana again?"

"You must be mad," he snorted. "I'm too old. Broken by age and politics. I'd need a miracle for that sort of thing. And as for her, she's a woman only in the abstract. But what about you? Have you forgotten all your old escapades? The scandal-sheets of the thirties were full of them; your chasing every skirt—or rather *melaya*—in Sharia Muhammad Ali."[18]

I laughed, and made no comment.

"Have you returned to the Faith?" he asked.

"What about you? Sometimes I think you must find it hard to believe in anything."

"How can I deny God," he asked angrily, "when I am deep in His hell?"

"People like you were made for hell! Get out! God will never bless any of your work! Get out of this sanctified house, as Iblis[19] was turned out of God's grace!"

The clock in the hall struck midnight. The wind whistled in the air-shaft. I sat sunk in my warm armchair, too lazy to go to bed, thinking in my loneliness: "What good is remorse after eighty?" Abruptly, the door opened and Tolba Marzuq stood there without knocking.

"I beg your pardon. I saw the light. Thought you were still awake." I looked at him in surprise. It was obvious that he was drunk.

"Do you know how much I used to spend every month just on medicine," he asked, "on vitamins, hormones, perfume, creams—and so forth?" He jerked his head sideways at every item.

I waited for him to go on, until he closed his eyes, as though exhausted by the effort, then went out and shut the door.

The marquee was full of people; the surrounding square was like Judgement Day. Fireworks burst in the air, crackling light turning night into day, to declare the Prophet's Birth. The Rolls Royce drew up slowly and stopped before the marquee. The crowd, fellow members of the Dimirdashiyya,[20] rushed forward to receive Tolba Marzuq, the Undersecretary of State, as he stepped out—followers of the Way, who had contrived somehow to reconcile love for the Prophet with love for His British Excellency, the Resident. His Other Excellency, the owner of the Rolls Royce, saw me in the crowd and deliberately turned his back. And that night, Tolba, they said that you'd turned up just as you've turned up tonight—drunk. *And then the Master of Song was called to the middle of the tent to begin the evening with "O Ultimate Heaven." He sang on and on into the small hours until he finally gave us "Would that mine eyes might see you every day," and ravished us all.*

A wonderful memory; when it was exactly I can't remember, but it must have been before the death of my own great master, or I would not have enjoyed myself as I did.

I was sitting by myself in the *pension* when the bell rang. I opened the judas as Madame always did and met a pair of eyes that belonged to a pretty face, a sun-tanned face, framed in the black scarf of a *fellaha*,[21] with features full of character and an expectant look that went instantly to the heart.

"Who are you?"

"I'm Zohra," she said simply, as if she were somehow sure I'd know the name.

"And what can I do for you, Zohra?" I asked, smiling.

"I want Madame Mariana."

I opened the door and she came in, carrying a little bundle. She looked around enquiringly.

"Where is Madame?"

"She'll be here soon. Sit down."

She sat on the edge of a chair with her bundle on her knees. I went back to my seat. A strong graceful figure, a very charming young face. I tried to draw her into conversation.

"Your name is Zohra?"

"Yes, Zohra Salama."

"Where do you come from?"

"Zayadiyya, Behaira."[22]

"You have an appointment with Madame?"

"No. I just came to see her."

"She knows you, of course?"

"Oh yes."

I regarded her. She was attractive. I hadn't felt so good for ages.

"You've lived here long?"

"I've never lived in Alexandria, but I used to come here often with my father before he died."

"How did you come to know Madame?"

"Father used to sell her cheese and butter and chickens, and once in a while I'd come with him."

"I see. You've taken up your father's business?"

"No." She turned her gaze away towards the screen. I could see she did not want to say any more. Respecting her privacy, I refrained from questioning her further, liking her the more for her reserve and admiring her in silence.

I kissed her thin, leathery hand.

"With your blessings, I am now a man you can well be proud of. Come with me to Cairo," I said.

"God prosper you tenfold"—she looked at me tenderly—"But I can't leave my home. It's my whole life." A weary old house, its walls flaking, beaten by a wind that left salt on its stones and the smell of fish in heaps on the shore at Anfushi.

"But you're all alone here."

"The Creator of day and night is always with me."[23]

The bell rang and Zohra went and opened the door. "Zohra!" Mariana cried. "What a surprise!" The girl kissed her hand, her face beaming at the warm welcome. "It is good to see you. God rest your father's soul. You're married?"

"No!"

"Impossible!" Laughing, Mariana turned to me as she took Zohra inside. "Her father was a truly good man, Monsieur Amir."

I felt a surge of paternal tenderness towards the girl.

"Now I can relax," Madame informed Tolba and me that evening. "Zohra will help me."

I was seized by mixed feelings of pleasure and anxiety. "Has she come to work as a maid?"

"Yes—and why not? She'll be better off here anyway."

"But . . ."

"But what? She used to rent half a *feddan* and work it herself. What do you think of that?"

"Good. But why did she leave her village?"

Mariana gave me a long look before saying: "She ran away."

"Ran away?"

"Did they take her for a feudalist as well?" said Tolba, chuckling.

"Her grandfather wanted to marry her to an old man, who probably needed her as a nurse. You can guess the rest."

"But it's extremely serious for her," I said gravely. "The village won't forgive her."

"She has no one but her grandfather and a married elder sister."

"What if they find out that she's here?"

"They may. But what does it matter?"

"Aren't you afraid?"

"She's not a child, you know. What have I done? Taken her in, and given her some honest work." She said finally, with a note of determination: "Monsieur Amir, I shall stick to that girl."

"I shall cling to duty as long as I live. Might is not right. Let them do their utmost."

She showed her what to do and Zohra seemed to learn very quickly. Mariana was delighted.

"She's wonderful," she confided to me happily. "She's strong and intelligent, understands everything once I tell her. I'm in luck, really."

A little later, she consulted me. "What do you think? Five pounds a month above her board and clothes?"

I said it was fair, but begged Madame not to dress Zohra in modern city clothes.

"Why? You don't want her to go around in those peasant rags?"

"My dear, she's very good-looking. Think . . ."

"I'll keep my eyes open. And she's a good girl."

And so, after years of concealment under an ankle-length *gallabiyya*,24 Zohra appeared in a cotton dress cut to a size that did justice to her charming figure. Her hair was washed with kerosene, parted in the middle and hung down her back in two thick braids. Tolba gave her a lengthy stare, then whispered, "Next summer we'll probably find her in the Genevoise or the Monte Carlo."

"Oh, for God's sake," I said.

As he passed her on his way to the door, he asked her jokingly: "Do you have any French ancestors, Zohra?"

She looked after him doubtfully. It was clear she didn't like him. "He's only joking," I said when she turned to me. "Take it as a compliment." I added with a smile: "I too am one of your admirers." She smiled gently back. I was pleased to see that she liked and trusted me. I had been kind to her and we had become friends.

When Madame invited her, after she'd finished her work, to sit with us as we gathered around the radio, she would choose a seat near the screen, a little apart, and follow our conversation with grave attention. One evening, supposing that we had not heard it from Mariana, she told us her story.

"My brother-in-law wanted to take advantage of my situation, so I farmed my piece of land on my own."

"Wasn't it difficult for you, Zohra?"

"No, I'm strong, thank God. No one ever got the better of me in business. In the field or at the market."

Tolba laughed. "But men are interested in other things, too."

"I can stand up to them like a man, if it's called for."

I heartily approved of this attitude.

"She's not an innocent," added Mariana. "She used to go everywhere with her father. He was very fond of her."

"And I loved him more than anything," Zohra said wistfully. "All my grandfather wants is to exploit me."

Tolba would not let it pass. "If you could stand up to them like a man," he teased, "then why did you run away?"

Mariana broke in. "I have come to her assistance!"

"Come now, you know what villages are like, Tolba Bey," I said. "How they worship the grandfathers and their terrible conservatism. She either had to run away or stay and be two-faced."

She looked at me gratefully. She said, "I left my land behind."

Then Tolba remarked: "They'll say you ran away because you had a lover, or something of the sort."

She gave him an angry look and her face darkened like a Nile flood. She pointed her fore- and middle-fingers at him. "I'd stick these into the eyes of anyone who dared to say a thing like that."

"Zohra, can't you take a joke?" cried Mariana.

"He's only teasing you." I tried to soothe her, surprised at the force of her anger. "Where's your tact, my dear sir?" I asked Tolba. "It's been sequestrated!"

Her eyes are as brown as honey, her cheeks are rosy and rounded and her little chin is dimpled. A child. *Barely as old as my granddaughter. And her grandmother? Lost in the blink of an eye. Without even knowing love or marriage. Who was she? Impossible. Impossible even to remember what she looked like.* In my memory now are only the names of places: Bargawan, Darb al Ahmar, and the saintly shrine of Sidi Abu al Suud,[25] the healer of broken hearts.

"How long will you be staying here, sir?"

She used to bring coffee to my room every afternoon and I would make her stay until my desire to converse with her was satisfied.

"For good, Zohra."

"And your family?"

"I have no one but you, my dear." That made her laugh.

Her little hands were hard, her fingertips calloused, her feet large and flat. But her figure and face were lovely.

"I don't like him," she once whispered to me about the other lodger.

"He's an old, unfortunate man. Besides," I said charitably, "he's sick."

"He thinks he's still living in the days of the pashas. And he acts like one."

At her words my mind went spinning back round the whole circumference of the last hundred years.

"They refuse to visit the Minister of Justice because he's an effendi and not a pasha or a bey?"

"My dear sir, members of the bench have their self-esteem."

"It is because I am above all a fellah, and they are Circassians.[26] Listen. They have always jeered at me because I am a leader of the people. And my

answer has always been that I am proud to lead the rabble in their blue gallabiyyas. Mark this. They shall come, and with all due respect."

She even learned the foreign names of all the brands of whisky she bought us at the High-Life Grocery. "People stare and laugh when I ask for these." In the silence of my heart I blessed . . . her simplicity.

What a noise! The voices were familiar, but loud and sharp. I wondered what was happening outside.

As I got out of bed and put on my dressing-gown, the clock was striking five in the afternoon. Out in the hall I saw Tolba disappearing into his room, wringing his hands. Zohra was hunched in a chair, her face puckered, on the verge of tears. In front of her stood Mariana, obviously distressed.

"What's happening?"

"Zohra is so suspicious, Amir Bey."

"He asked me to massage him," the girl shot back roughly, reassured by my presence.

"You don't understand," Mariana put in. "You know he's an invalid. He needs massage for treatment. He used to go to Europe every year for the cure. You don't have to do anything you don't like."

"I never heard of such things," the girl said angrily. "I went into his room in good faith and there he was lying on his face almost naked."

"Calm down, Zohra. He's an old man, older than your father. You just don't understand. Go and wash your face and forget it."

Left to ourselves in the hall we sat on the ebony settee. Madame broke the heavy silence.

"It was his request and I don't believe he meant any harm."

"Mariana," I said significantly, "there's never an end to folly."

"Don't you trust him? You know he's an old man."

"They have their own kind of folly."

"I thought she could earn some good money, instead of his going off to pay a professional."

"You know she's a *fellaha*. And after all you've taken responsibility for her."

Tolba joined us, putting on an innocent air and remarking scornfully: "Once a peasant, always a peasant."

"Leave her alone," I said. "Let her die as God made her."

He was clearly offended. "She's a wildcat. Don't let that dress and Mariana's grey cardigan fool you. She's a savage."

Poor Zohra, how sorry I am for you. Now I know how lonely you must be. This *pension* is no place for you; and Mariana, your protectress, would have no qualms at eating you up on the first available occasion.

"God's wisdom!" said Tolba, after his first drink.

"Watch out, Tolba Bey," said Mariana, glad to change the subject. "Don't blaspheme."

"Tell me, my dear," he said, pointing to the little statue of the Madonna, "why did God allow His Son to die on the Cross?"

"To redeem us," she said gravely, "or we should have been damned."

"You mean we aren't damned anyway?" He threw back his head and laughed, looking in my direction for encouragement, but I ignored him. Then he nudged me with his elbow. "You must help me make it up with Zohra, you old fox!"

A new guest?

Something about the well-formed dark features gives away his peasant origin. He is solidly built, rather dark, with a strong, piercing look; about thirty years old, I should guess. Mariana motions him to take a seat at the breakfast table.

"Monsieur Sarhan al-Behairi," she says, introducing us, and asking him, if he doesn't mind, to tell us more about himself.

"Deputy Head Accountant at the Alexandria Textile Mills," he says with a strong country accent.

When he leaves, Mariana confides happily: "Another lodger, on the same terms."

Not more than a week later came Husni Allam, a little younger than Sarhan, also as a permanent resident. Big and husky, he carried himself like a wrestler. Mariana said he belonged to one of the old country families of Tanta.[27]

Then came Mansour Bahi, an announcer with the Alexandria Broadcasting Service, twenty-five years old. I was charmed by his delicate, fine features. There was something childish, perhaps even feminine, about his face. One could see at once that he was rather withdrawn, an introvert.

All the rooms were now occupied and Mariana was very happy. My heart, hungry for contact, warmed to the new arrivals. "It's good to have young people around. I hope they won't be bored with our decrepit company."

"Well, at least they're not students," said Mariana.

We did not get acquainted any further until the first Thursday of the Umm Kulthum season, when I learned from Mariana that they would join us in the evening to listen to the concert on the radio. How pleasant. An evening of youth and music.

They had ordered a kebab supper and a bottle of whisky. We gathered around the radio and Zohra waited on us, moving lightly. It was a cold night, but the wind was hushed. Zohra said the sky outside was so clear you could count the stars. Drinks were passed around and she sat apart, next to the screen, her eyes smiling. Only Tolba Marzuq was unable to put away all anxiety: a few days before he had confided to me: "This place is becoming a hell!" He was suspicious of strangers, certain that they knew his history and the circumstances of his ordeal, either from the papers or through Mansour Bahi.

Mariana had of course got all the information she could about the young men. "Monsieur Sarhan al-Behairi is one of the Behairi family." I had never heard the name before nor, obviously, had Tolba Marzuq. "A friend of his recommended the *pension* when he learned that Monsieur Sarhan wanted to give up his flat."

"And Husni Allam?"

"He's one of the Allams of Tanta." It seemed to me that Tolba knew the family, but he made no comment. "He has a hundred *feddans*," she added, as proudly as if she herself were the owner. "The Revolution hasn't touched him," she went on, as joyous as someone about to be rescued at sea. "He's come to Alexandria to start a business."

"Why don't you cultivate your land?" Sarhan asked him when he heard that piece of information.

"It's been let."

"You should say instead that you've never laid a hand on a hoe or a spade in your life!" mocked Sarhan. The three of them roared, but Husni's own laugh was loudest.

"As for this young man," said Mariana, indicating Mansour Bahi, "he's the brother of an old friend, one of the best police chiefs I've ever known in this city."

Tolba's cheeks turned pale.

"And before he left," Mariana went on, "he advised this young man to come and stay with me."

When the others were busy drinking, Tolba leaned over and whispered: "We've landed in a nest of spies."

"Antisocial behavior is out of date," I said. "Don't be silly."

Whereupon politics erupted into the gathering.

"But the country has changed beyond recognition," Sarhan was saying passionately, as he argued on behalf of the government's land reforms, his voice rising and falling in proportion to the amount of food he had in his mouth. "And the working class! I spend my life among them. You should come to the mill and see for yourselves."

Mansour Bahi (the quietest of the young men, though even so he would sometimes burst out laughing, just like the others) asked him, "Are you really in politics then?"

"Of course. I was a member of the Liberation Organization and then the National Union. Now I'm on the Committee of Twenty and I'm also an elected member of the Company Board,[28] representing the staff."

"Were you in politics before the Revolution?"

"No."

"I support the Revolution wholeheartedly," said Husni Allam. "My people consider me a rebel."

"Why not?" replied Mansour. "The Revolution hasn't touched you."

"That's not the reason. Even the poorer members of our class may not support it."

"My own conviction," Mansour remarked, "is that the Revolution has been more lenient with its enemies than it ought to have been."

Apparently Tolba thought that in the circumstances his silence might be held against him. "I've been badly hit," he started. "It would be sheer hypocrisy to deny that I've been hurt. But it would also be selfish to deny that what they have done was necessary!"

Mariana did not drink. She took some of the kebab and a glass of warm milk. "It's a pity Umm Kulthum starts so late," she complained, even though the young men were helping us pass the time in a very agreeable fashion while we waited.

Mansour Bahi turned and spoke suddenly to me. "I know a great deal of your brilliant past." I was overcome with a childish pleasure: to be able to recall my youth! "I often look through the back numbers of old newspapers for a programme I write." Delighted, I encouraged him to say more. "You go back a long way. You made a major contribution to the political currents of the past—the People's Party, the National Party. The Wafd, the Revolution."

I seized this opportunity and took him with me at once on a voyage back into history, leading him to events that should never have been forgotten. We reviewed the parties one by one, the pros and cons of the People's Party and the National Party; the Wafd and how it resolved long-standing contradictions—and why, after all that, I had shifted away into independence, why I supported the Revolution.

"But you weren't interested in the basic social problem."

"I grew up in al-Azhar. Naturally I sought a compromise, a marriage of East and West."

"But isn't it strange that you should have attacked both the Moslem Brotherhood and the Communists?"

"No. It was a puzzling period of conflicting opposites. Then came the Revolution, to absorb what was best in each."

"So your dilemma is solved now?"

I said yes, but in fact what was in my mind was only my private dilemma, which no party or revolution could solve, and I sent up a lonely prayer. Then the hour struck. And with it I gave up my distress to a sea of song, hoping it would help resolve the conflicts in my soul, entreating that it would instil peace and love and purge my anguish in melody, bringing the supreme pleasure of insight to my heart and mind, which would both soften and sweeten the bitter obduracy of life.

"Haven't you heard? The Cabinet met in the houseboat that belongs to Munira al-Mahdia, the prima donna."

It was almost dawn when I retired to my room. Tolba joined me there, to ask what I'd thought of his little speech.

"Wonderful." My voice sounded strange, for I had removed my false teeth.

"Do you think anyone believed me?"

"It doesn't matter."

"I'd better look for other accommodation."

"Nonsense."

"For me to hear people praise these murderous regulations is enough to bring on another stroke."

"You'd better get used to it."

"As you have?"

I smiled. "We've always been different, you know."

"I wish you terrible dreams," he remarked as he left.

"These young men are so attractive and well-to-do."

Mariana often expressed her satisfaction with her young lodgers. Zohra's chores multiplied, but she rose to it all with redoubled energy.

"I can't trust any of them," Tolba complained.

"Not even Husni Allam?" Mariana enquired.

But he did not seem to listen. "Sarhan al-Behairi is the most dangerous. He's made good under the Revolution. Let alone the

Behairi family, of which no one has ever heard. Everyone in the province of Behairi is a Behairi, anyway. Even Zohra is Zohra al-Behairi."

I laughed and so did Mariana. Zohra passed us on her way out, wearing Madame's grey cardigan and a blue scarf she had recently bought with her own money. She was as graceful as a wild flower.

"Mansour Bahi is very intelligent, don't you think?" I asked. "He doesn't talk much, but just goes quietly to work. A true child of the Revolution."

"Why should he or anyone else go along with the Revolution?"

"You speak as if there were no peasants, no workers, no youth in the land."

"The Revolution has stolen the property of a few and the liberty of all."

"You speak of liberty in the old sense," I said. "And when you were top dog you didn't even show respect for that!"

Leaving the bathroom, I caught sight of two figures in the dim passage, Zohra and Sarhan whispering to each other. At that moment he raised his voice to give her instructions about his laundry. I went to my room as if I hadn't noticed anything, but I was filled with anxiety. How could Zohra live in peace in a place full of young men? When she brought my afternoon coffee, I asked her where she spent her free afternoon on Sundays.

She beamed. "I go to the cinema."

"On your own?"

"With Madame."

"God keep you," I said gently.

She smiled. "You worry over me as if I were a child."

"You are a child, Zohra."

"No. When I have to, I can take care of myself as well as any man."

I set my old face nearer her pretty young one. "Zohra, these young men are always ready to play, but when it comes to serious intentions . . ." I snapped my fingers.

"My father told me all about that."

"I won't pretend I'm not very fond of you. So I'm concerned."
"I understand. I haven't met anyone like you since my father. I'm fond of you, too."

I had never heard the words said so sweetly, and they were words that, if it had not been for an accusation made in stupidity, and which no man alive had the right to make, I might have heard from the lips of dozens of children and grandchildren of my own. *That white transparent veil! The old woman nips out from the door in the little alley: "Come on, it has stopped raining." The girl in the white veil follows, stepping carefully on the slippery stones. Has time dimmed all the details of that beautiful face, leaving only the deep impression? I stand to one side and I whisper: "God be praised for creating such beauty." While my heart is still pounding, I say to myself: "Take the decision, put your trust in God! The sooner the better!"*

I am alone with Mariana, who sits beneath the Madonna, her blue eyes dark with thought. It has been raining steadily since noon, the clouds shaken by occasional rolls of thunder. Mariana speaks.

"Monsieur Amir, I smell something fishy!"
"What?" I ask warily.
"Zohra," she says; and then, after a pause, "Sarhan al-Behairi."
My heart contracts. "What do you mean?"
"You know exactly what I mean."
"But the girl . . ."
"I have an instinct about these things."
"My dear Mariana, she's a good honest girl."
"Maybe, but I don't like people going on behind my back!"
Of course. Either Zohra stays "honest" or she works for you. I know you through and through, old woman.

I have dreams, during my siesta, about 1919, that bloody uprising,[29] and the British soldiers afterwards forcing their way into the Azhar. I open my eyes with a brain full of shouting demonstrators, the smack of rifles and the thud of bullets. There are loud voices in the entrance hall. I put on my dressing-gown and hurry out. Others are there, watching, but Sarhan is adjusting his collar and tie with an angry sneer on his face. And there is Zohra, pale with anger, her breast heaving, her dress torn at the neckline, while Husni Allam in his dressing-gown is just going out the door with a strange woman who screams and curses—and who just before the door closes spits in Sarhan's face.

"My *pension* has a good name!" Mariana shouts, "I won't stand for this sort of thing. No, no, no!"

I am still half asleep. When there are only the three of us left, I ask Tolba Marzuq what happened.

"I haven't the faintest idea. I arrived on the scene only just before you did."

Mariana disappears into Sarhan's room; for an explanation no doubt.

"It seems the Behairi boy is quite a Don Juan."

"What makes you think so?"

"Didn't you see her spit in his face?"

"Who was she, anyway?"

"Just a woman." He grins. "Come for her runaway boyfriend, I suppose."

Zohra comes back, still upset. "I opened the door for Monsieur Sarhan," she tells us, though we haven't asked her anything, "and there was this woman following him. He didn't see her. Then they started fighting."

Mariana returns from Sarhan's room. "The girl was his fiancée. Or so I understand."

We all understand. But it is Tolba Marzuq who slyly puts the question:

"Then what's Zohra got to do with all this?"

"I tried to break it up and she turned on me."

"You've got a fine fist, Zohra!"

"Let's not speak of it any more," I beg them.

Bismallah al-Rahman al-Rahim.
Ta. Sin. Mim.

These are revelations of the Scripture that
maketh plain.
We narrate unto thee somewhat of the story
of Moses and Pharaoh with truth, for folk
who believe.
Lo! Pharaoh exalted himself in the earth and
made its people castes. A tribe among them
he oppressed, killing their sons and sparing
their women. Lo! he was of those who work corruption.
And We desired to show favour unto those who
were oppressed in the earth, and to make
them examples and to make them the inheritors.[30]

Someone is knocking. Mariana comes in smiling and sits on the backless stool where I sometimes rest my feet. The wind is howling in the air-shaft and I am swathed in my dressing-gown. The room is very quiet and dim, drowsing in a light that does not reveal the time of day.

"Haven't you heard?" She is stifling a laugh.

I close my book and put it on the bedside table. "Good news, my dear?"

"Zohra's going to school!"

I do not understand.

"Really. She's made up her mind. She asked permission to stay away for an hour in the afternoon. To take lessons."

"Amazing."

"She's arranged it with a schoolmistress who lives on the fifth floor. A young teacher who'll give her private lessons."

I repeat, "It's amazing."

"I didn't object, but I'm afraid she's going to spend all her wages on it."

"That's thoughtful of you, Mariana. But I'm really and truly amazed."

When Zohra brought me my afternoon coffee, I said, "You've been keeping secrets from me, you naughty child."

"I keep no secrets from you," she answered shyly.

"What about this decision to study? What made you think of it?"

"All girls go to school now. The streets are full of them."

"But you never thought of it before."

"It's your fault," she smiled. "You said I was much prettier than they are and there was no reason why they should read and write while I stayed illiterate." She went on looking up brightly at me.

"But that isn't all."

"What else is there?"

"Well ... there's our friend Sarhan al-Behairi." She blushed. "Learning to read and write is a wonderful idea. As for Sarhan ..."

"Yes?" she asked, when I hesitated.

"Young men are ambitious."

"We're all the children of Adam and Eve," she replied tartly.

"True, but ..."

"Times have changed. Haven't they?"

"Yes, they have. They have indeed. But young men haven't changed."

"When I learn to read and write," she said thoughtfully, "I'll try and learn some profession. Like dressmaking, perhaps."

I was afraid I might hurt her feelings if I said much more.

"Does he love you?" She lowered her eyes. "May God bless you and bring you happiness!"

From time to time I would help her with her lessons, that mysterious world of letters and figures. All the lodgers learned of her decision and discussed it at length. No one laughed at her, at least not to her face. They all liked her, I suppose, each in his own way.

Tolba Marzuq exercised his usual penetration. "The best solution to her problem would be a new lodger. A film producer or something. What do you think of that?"

I cursed his dirty mind.

Late one afternoon when I took my usual seat in the hall, I saw an unfamiliar girl sitting next to Zohra on the settee—obviously the teacher, good-looking and well dressed. She had agreed to come down to her pupil because there were visitors in her own flat. Mariana had of course put all the questions she could. Later she told us that the young lady lived with her parents and had a brother who worked in Saudi Arabia.

Afterwards the teacher came frequently to the *pension*. She said she was pleased with her new pupil's perseverance.

One afternoon, as she brought my coffee, Zohra seemed depressed. I asked her how she was.

"I'm as fit as a mule."

"And the lessons?"

"Nothing to complain of."

"Then it's our friend Behairi," I suggested with concern. For a moment neither of us said a word, as if we were listening to the rain. "I can't stand seeing you unhappy. You must tell me what's happened."

"I believe you," she said gratefully.

"What's wrong?"

"Well, I suppose luck just isn't on my side."

"I warned you from the first day."

"It's not that easy, you know." She looked miserably at me. "What can I do? I love him. What can I do?"

"Has he deceived you?"

"No! He loves me too. But he always speaks of obstacles."

"But when a man's in love . . ."

"He *does* love me! Yet he keeps talking about these obstacles."

"But they're not your fault. You have to be sure where you stand."

"What's the good of knowing what I should do when I couldn't bring myself to do it?"

"My dear Pasha, how could you?"

"I had no alternative. I needed the loan from the Agricultural Credit Bank. Their terms were very clear-cut. I had either to quit the Wafd or be ruined."

"But many have chosen that latter alternative."

"Shut up!" he shouted. "You don't own one square inch of land! You have neither son nor daughter! And even though I have been beaten and im-

prisoned at Kasr al-Nil Barracks,[31] my daughter is dearer to me than either this world or the next!"

"Come with me," Mariana whispered. "Zohra's people are here."

I went out with her. Zohra's sister and brother-in-law were there, the girl herself standing proudly in the middle of the room. The man was speaking.

"It's all right that you came to Madame. As for your running away, though . . ."

"You shamed us," her sister cut in, "all over Zayadiyya."

"It's none of anybody's business," said Zohra bitterly.

"If only your grandfather could be here!"

"I answer to no one, now my father's dead."

"How dare you! He only wanted to marry you to a good man!"

"He wanted to sell me."

"God forgive you. Come along! Get your things ready."

"I am *not* going back. Not even if the dead themselves come out of their graves." Her brother-in-law was about to speak, but she stopped him. "It's none of your business. I have a good job here." She pointed to Mariana. "I earn my living by honest work."

It struck me that they would have liked very much to tell her what they thought of Madame, the *pension*, and the statue of the Virgin, but felt themselves unable to.

"Zohra is the daughter of a man I respected," said Mariana. "I treat her as a daughter and she's welcome to stay if she likes." She looked at me, as if to prompt.

"Think, Zohra," I said, "and make your choice."

"I am *not* going back."

Their mission was a failure. As he left with his wife, however, the man said to Zohra, "You deserve to be killed!"

Afterwards we talked it over at length until Zohra said, "What do you really think I should do?"

"I wish you could go back to your village."

"Go back to misery?"

"I said '*I wish you could*' —that is, go back and be happy."

"I love the land and the village, but I hate that misery." And when Mariana went out of the room, she said sadly: "Here is where love is. Education. Cleanliness. And hope."

I could understand her feelings. I too had left the village with my father; and after that, like her, I had loved the village but could not bear to live there. I had educated myself, as she would like to do, and I had been wrongly accused and many people had said, as they had just said to her, that I should be killed. And like her again, I had been entranced by love, education, cleanliness, hope. May your fortune be better than mine, Zohra!

Autumn is wearing on to its end. But Alexandrian weather, which knows no rule, blesses us with a bright warm morning; Ramleh Square is radiant with sunlight pouring out of a pure azure sky. Mahmoud Abu al-Abbas, the newspaper-seller, smiles at me as I stand in front of his stall, which is adorned with the covers of magazines and books.

"Sir," he begins, while I suppose there's been some mistake in our account, for he stands there, tall and thickset, saying, "you live in the Pension Miramar?"

"Yes." I nod.

"I beg your pardon. But there is a girl called Zohra."

"Yes?" I am suddenly attentive.

"Where are her people?"

"Why do you ask?"

"I beg your pardon, but I want to propose to her."

I reflect for a moment. "Her people are in the country. I think she's quarrelled with them. Have you spoken to her about it?"

"She comes here to buy papers, but she doesn't encourage me to talk."

The same evening he paid Mariana a visit and asked for Zohra's hand. Mariana spoke to her, but the girl refused him on the spot.

"You've spoiled her, Mariana," commented Tolba when he heard the story. "Cleaning her up and dressing her in modern clothes won't do her much good. She mixes with fine young men and her head's turned. She'll come to no good. You mark my words."

When she came with my afternoon coffee, we discussed the matter.

"You should have given it more thought."

"But you know everything!" she protested.

"Still, there's no harm in considering a serious proposal."

She said reproachfully, "You think I'm too humble to hope for anything better, don't you?"

"No!" I flung out my hand. "I just think he'd make you a suitable husband, that's all."

"It'd be the same as going back to the village." I did not like that answer. "You see, I overheard him speaking to another newsboy once," she explained. "He hadn't noticed me standing there. He was saying: 'All women have one thing in common. They're cuddly little animals without brains or religion, and the only way to keep them from going wild is to leather them every day!'" She challenged me. "Am I to blame if I refuse such a man?"

I had nothing to say. And though I pretended to be disturbed, I felt an unbounded admiration for the girl. I thought to myself, *no more old men's advice*! Saad Zaghloul always used to listen to what they had to say, then followed the counsel of the young. God protect you, Zohra.

"Great things are happening right under your nose, old man," Tolba Marzuq said, grinning slyly. We were sitting alone in the *pension*, listening to the beating rain.

"What's the matter?" I expected bad news.

"The Don Juan from Behaira is preparing another coup." I showed concern for Zohra's sake. "He's changed his quarry. Aiming at something else, in fact."

"Forget your own pleasures for a minute and speak plainly."

"It's the teacher's turn now."

"Zohra's teacher?"

"Exactly! I caught surreptitious looks going back and forth above the diligent student's head. I'm quite an expert, you know."

"Papa Amir, watch out for a most entertaining comedy at the Miramar!"

"You're simply depraved."

I was determined not to believe a word of what he said. But I was worried. The same evening Husni Allam told us about a fight between Sarhan al-Behairi and Mahmoud Abu al-Abbas the newsagent in the square. They'd come to blows, and people had hardly been able to separate them. I knew at once what had been behind the quarrel.

"They hit each other until people had to force them apart," said Husni.

"Did you see them fight?" asked Tolba.

"No, but I knew about it shortly afterwards."

"Did they go to the police?" Mariana wanted to know.

"No, the whole thing ended in a lot of name-calling—and threats."

Sarhan said nothing about this incident and none of us made any reference to it. The thought of Sarhan and the teacher depressed me. Poor Zohra.

" 'And when are the fair ever faithful? My only comfort is tears!' " We clap and cheer for several encores and he sings until the break of dawn. I am full that night of youth and strength and food. Drink, too. But the heart, alone, endures its secret chagrin.

Deep in sleep, in the lost hours of night, I had dreamed of my father's death. I saw them carry the body out of the arcade of the mosque of Sidi Abu al-Abbas, where death had found him, and take him home. I was weeping and I could hear my mother's shrieks of mourning and they went on and on until I opened my eyes. Good God, what could be going on outside? Was it the same thing again? The pension had become a battlefield, though by the time I left my room everything was over.

When she saw me Mariana came running. "No! No! To hell with

the whole lot of them!" she cried when we were in my room. I looked at her out of heavy-lidded eyes and I listened to the story. She'd been awakened by the sound of a fight and gone out to find Sarhan al-Behairi and Husni Allam exchanging blows in the corridor.

"Husni Allam?"

"Yes, why not? They're all stark mad."

"But why?"

"Apparently something happened that I didn't see. I was asleep, too."

"What about the girl?"

"Zohra says Husni came home dead drunk and that he tried to . . ."

"No!"

"I believe her, Monsieur Amir," said Mariana.

"I do, too. But Husni didn't seem interested in her."

"But we can't notice everything, Monsieur Amir. Anyway, Sarhan woke up at the right time. Why must these things happen?" She massaged her throat, as if to rub off the pain of shouting. "No," she repeated, "to hell with them."

"Anyway," I said with annoyance, "Husni should go."

But she made no comment; she did not seem to like the idea and went out with a disturbed look on her face.

When Zohra came in the next afternoon we just looked at each other.

"I am sorry you've been through all this, Zohra."

"They're not gentlemen."

"The truth is you shouldn't be here."

"I can always defend myself. Which I've done."

"But they won't leave you in peace. Living here isn't the right thing for a good girl like you."

"There are rats everywhere. Even in our village."

I was confined to the *pension* for several days by cold, wind, and rain. Though we all kept to our rooms the elements seemed to follow us there: rain rattled at the windows, the walls shook with thunder, and lightning flashed ominously, while the wind howled like a jinn. When I finally went out, it was another Alexandria that received me, the fury past, calm again, giving itself to the clear golden rays of the sun. I looked out at the waves in their nonchalant succession, the little cloud-puffs dotted across the sky. Then I went and took my seat in the Trianon and ordered my *café au lait* as I used to in the good old days with Gharabli Pasha, Sheikh Darwish and Madame Lobraska— the only Frank I ever made love to, once upon a time when I was drowned in women. Tolba Marzuq sat with me for a while, then left for the lobby of the Windsor, where he was meeting an old friend. I saw Sarhan coming towards me. He shook my hand and sat down.

"I'm glad I've met you here," he said. "I must say goodbye. I may not see you when I check out this afternoon."

I was really surprised. "Are you leaving the *pension?*"

"Yes, I am. I'd have been really sorry to go without saying goodbye to you."

I thanked him for his kind thoughts and would have liked to ask him a few questions, but he gave me no chance. He waved to someone, shook my hand and left. What about Zohra? Depressed, disturbed, I sighed to myself.

He clutched at the bars as he listened to the verdict. Then he shouted at the top of his voice: "Proud of yourself, you bastards? Are you happy, Naima, you officers' whore?"[32]

I found Mariana, Tolba Marzuq, and Zohra in the hall. The atmosphere was heavy with gloom.

"That hypocrite Sarhan has shown his true colors."

"I met him at the Trianon and he said he's leaving," I muttered.

"In fact I turned him out. He assaulted her shamelessly," said Mariana, indicating Zohra with a motion of her head. "Then he announced that he's leaving to marry the schoolmistress upstairs."

I glanced at Tolba and he looked back with a mischievous smile. "So he's finally made up his mind to get married."

"I never really liked him," said Mariana. "I could see through him from the start. A young man of no principles. Monsieur Mansour Bahi tried to talk to him and they started fighting as well. I told him to get out on the spot."

I looked at Zohra. What a monstrous thing! The game was up and the villain had gone unpunished. I was gripped by an anger I hadn't felt since the bitter old days of political struggle.

"He's a swine," I told Zohra. "Don't waste any regrets on him."

When we were alone I told Tolba I wished she would marry Mahmoud Abu al-Abbas.

"What Mahmoud?" he said provocatively. "Can't you see that she's lost something irretrievable?" I protested, though I felt stunned. "You old fool! Can't you see what's been going on under your nose?"

"Zohra isn't like that!"

"God bless you for an innocent!" I hated him. But I couldn't help beginning to doubt the poor girl. "Madame was the first to draw my attention to their relationship. Though I could have guessed myself."

"She's a wicked woman," I said angrily.

"But Madame, you understand, is most eager to act as her protector—or exploiter."

"No. She won't. I'll see to that."

When she came into my room in the afternoon, the girl was terribly downcast. She begged me pathetically not to remind her of my earlier advice. I said I wouldn't—but what was she going to do?

"I hope you won't give up the lessons."

"No. I'll find another teacher." Her voice was joyless, but determined enough.

"If you need any help, I . . ."

She bent and kissed my shoulder, biting her underlip to hold back her tears. I stretched out my veined and leathery old hand until it rested on her young black hair.

"God bless you, Zohra."

That night I kept more or less to my room, giving in to a sense of complete malaise, so fatigued that I was unable to go out for some days thereafter. Mariana kept pressing me to pull my strength together. "We must celebrate the New Year," she urged. "Shall we go to the Monseigneur as Tolba Bey suggests, or shall we celebrate it here?"

"Here would be better, my dear."

I didn't really care. How often had I celebrated it at Sault's, Groppi's, Alf Laila and Lipton Gardens! And one year I'd spent it in the military prison at the Citadel.[33]

On the morning of the third day of my seclusion, Mariana rushed in, extremely upset. "Have you heard the news?" she panted, sinking into an armchair. "Sarhan al-Behairi's been murdered."

"What!"

"His body was found on the road to the Palma."

Tolba Marzuq came in nervously clutching a paper. "This is really dreadful news. It may cause a lot of trouble."

We looked at each other and thought of all the probabilities — his first fiancée, Husni Allam, Mansour Bahi, Mahmoud Abu al-Abbas — until Madame said: "Why, the murderer may be someone we've never heard of!"

"Why not?" I agreed. "We know hardly anything about the young man."

Madame was very anxious. "Oh! I wish they'd find the killer soon. I hope it's no one we know. I don't want to see the face of a policeman here."

"I hope so, too," sighed Tolba Marzuq — doubtless for the same reason.

Madame sighed. I asked about Zohra.

"The poor girl is terribly shocked."

"Could I possibly see her?"

"She's locked herself in her room. Totally broken down."

We went on discussing the murder but could come to no conclusion. I closed my eyes and heard the words sing in my head:

Everyone that is thereon will pass away; There remaineth but the countenance of the Lord of Might and Glory. Which is it, of the favors of your Lord, that ye deny?[34]

2

HUSNI ALLAM

erekeeko,[35] don't put the blame on me. *The face of the sea is dark, mottled, blue from stifled wrath; there is unappeased rage in the ceaseless hammering of the waves.* Revolution? Why not? To put you where you belong, you progeny of whores, to take all your money and push your noses in the mud. Sure, I'm one of you. And I know it. That, unfortunately, is something that can't be changed. "No education," she said, "and a hazardous hundred *feddans.*" That's what Miss Blue-Eyes[36] said, as she slammed the door in my face and sat down behind to wait for the next prospective stud-bull to come along.

From my balcony at the Cecil I cannot see the Corniche unless I lean out over the railing. It's like being on a ship. The sea sprawls right below me. *A great blue mass, heaving, locked in as far as the fort of Sultan Qaitbay by the Corniche wall and the giant stone jetty-arm*[37] *thrusting into the sea. Frustrated, caged. These waves slopping dully landwards have a sullen blue-black look that continually promises fury.* The sea. Its guts churn with flotsam and secret death.

My room has a formal air, like our family house in Tanta. It bores me. The glory of having land is over. What we have now is the heyday of an educated rabble.

Good. Revolution, so be it! Let it cut you all down to the ground. I'm through with you, you scraps of tattered time! Don't blame me, *Ferekeeko!*

"How bored I am in this grand hotel of yours!" I say to Muhammad the Nubian waiter as he serves me breakfast in my room. A long-standing habit of mine, to be liberal and courteous to servants. Who knows, anyway? I might need them some day.

"Will you stay in Alexandria long, sir?"

"Yes, a very long time."

"Don't you think in that case that a *pension* would be more suitable, sir?"

I looked at him enquiringly.

"I know a more interesting and less expensive guest-house, sir. But this is just between us." Pleasant, serviceable and treacherous, employed by one master, secretly serving another. Like so many of my dear countrymen. All right. I suppose a *pension* would be more accommodating, a more suitable place for planning a new business. The only reason I've come to the Cecil is old habit—and, let's face it, ineradicable pride.

The little judas swings open. A very pretty face. Too pretty for a servant, much too pretty for a lady. A really beautiful girl. Who will no doubt fall in love with me at first sight.

"Yes?"

A *fellaha*! How strange. At that moment, as far as I'm concerned, the Cecil could sink beneath the black waves of the sea.

"I've been sent by Muhammad Kamil at the Cecil."

She shows me to a seat in the hall and goes inside. Meanwhile I get the feel of the place by looking at the photographs on the walls. An English officer? So. And that beauty leaning over the back of a chair?

Who could she be? She is lovely, exciting. She must be an antique, though. The style of her dress leaves little doubt that she went to school with the Virgin Mary.

A brilliant, gilded old lady comes in. The landlady, of course—a typical old retired French procuress. Or maybe (let's hope!) not quite yet retired. That photograph must be a portrait of her before time did her in. Things are falling into place. It would appear that the Nubian has interpreted my boredom at the Cecil in his own way. Fine! A little preliminary diversion is always good for thinking out new plans.

"Do you have any vacant rooms, Madame?"

"You were staying at the Cecil?" She is clearly very impressed, and wishes she were forty years younger. "How long would you like to stay?"

"A month, at least. Who knows? Maybe a year."

"There are special terms for the summer."

"That's all right."

"Are you a student?"

"No. A gentleman of property."

She brings out the register. "Your name, please?"

"Husni Allam." With no education, a hazardous hundred *feddans*, and lucky enough to know nothing at all about the thing our singers call love.

A good room, *violet wallpaper. The sea-view stretches as far as the eye can see, a clear blue. The curtains flutter in the autumn breeze. There is a scattered flock of clouds in the sky.* And as she makes the bed, spreading sheets and a counterpane. I study the form of the *fellaha:* a well-knit, shapely body, with obvious good points. If my guess is right, she hasn't run into pregnancy or abortion yet. I'd better wait, though, until I get to know the place a little better.

"What's your name, sweetheart?"

"Zohra," she answers stolidly.

"Bless him that named thee!" She thanks me with a grave nod. "Are there any other guests in the place?"

"Two gentlemen and a young man like your honor."

"What's your nickname?"

"My name is Zohra." Polite, not at all encouraging. Too serious, that's clear. She would enhance the interior decoration of any flat I might rent in the future, though. Certainly she's more beautiful than my idiotic kinswoman, who has decided to choose a husband with the guidance of the Revolutionary Charter.[38] *Ferekeeko,* don't blame me.

"Are you serious?"

"But of course, darling!"

"You don't even know what love is."

"I want to get married, you see."

"But I don't think you could possibly fall in love."

"Here I am proposing to you. Doesn't that mean I love you? I'm marriageable," I say, trying to keep any anger in check. *"No?"*

"What value does land have," she says after a moment's hesitation, *"these days?"* It serves me right for getting myself into such a degrading situation.

"Think it over," I say as I go out. *"Take your time."*

At breakfast I get to know the other guests. Amir Wagdi, a retired journalist—I reckon he must be eighty at least, quite tall, thin, but in very good health. There's nothing left for death to devour—a wrinkled face, sunken eyes, and sharp bones. The very sight of the man makes me detest him. I wonder how he can survive while generations of the young go on dying every day.

Tolba Marzuq is no stranger to me. I remember my uncle saying something sympathetic about the sequestration of his property, though naturally I don't bring it up. We follow all such events, the news of sequestration and confiscation, with avid interest; like the action of a horror film.

"One of the Allams of Tanta?" he asks and I nod, with secret smugness. "I used to know your father. An excellent farmer." Turning to Amir Wagdi, who is leaving the table, he laughs and says, "He wasn't under the influence of those comedians of yours for long, God rest his soul. I mean the Wafdists," he adds when he sees that I don't understand the joke.

"For all I know, he was a Wafdist," I answer with indifference. "At the same time the whole country was."

"That's right. I believe you have some brothers and sisters?"

"My brother is consul in Italy and my sister's married to our ambassador in Ethiopia."

"And you?" His mouth twitches.

I hate him so intensely at that moment that I wish he would drown or burn. But I put on an air of not caring.

"Nothing."

"Don't you farm your land?"

"No, it's been let. But I'm thinking of starting up a new business."

The third lodger has been listening attentively to our conversation; so has Madame. His name is Sarhan al-Behairi, Deputy Head of the Accounts Department at the Alexandria Textile Mills.

"What sort of business?"

"I haven't made up my mind."

"Why don't you look for a government post? It's more secure."

I detest him too. He has a hint of a country accent, like the smell of cooking that lingers in a badly washed pan. Would blue-eyed Mervat, I wonder, brand this mule "uneducated," though? I doubt it. If he has the insolence to ask about my lack of a degree I'll dash this cup of tea in Dream-Boy Behairi's[39] face.

"Where did you get all this zeal for their Revolution?"

"I believe in it, sir."

"I don't believe you."

"You should."

"Mervat's refusal," he says with a chuckle, *"would appear to have driven you out of your mind."*

I am irritated. "Getting married was just a passing thought."

He is angry, too. "You've got your father's obstinacy. God rest his soul. But none of his good sense."

Something urges me to attack the Revolution in the person of this Sarhan, who is clearly an opportunist, but I manage to give way.

"Why don't you tell us about your project?" the old lady asks.

"I still haven't made up my mind."

"You're well-off then?"

I give her a self-confident smile but make no reply. And her interest in me is obviously thereby doubled.

I leave the *pension* at the same time as Sarhan. We take the lift down together, his smiling eyes clearly inviting me to some sort of *rapprochement*, and my anger at him subsides a little. "A government job is, generally speaking," he says, half-consciously correcting his earlier *gaffe*, "more secure. A private business, however, if chosen carefully . . ." The lift is there before he can finish his sentence, but his ingratiating tone needs no further explanation. He goes to the tram stop and I go to the garages, passing the Miramar Café. I remember sitting there with my uncle in the old days before the deluge. He used to come late in the afternoon to smoke the *nargilah*[40] sitting there wrapped in his cloak, like a king in disguise, in the midst of a group of senators and country notables. Yes, those were the days. He deserved what he got, though, and then some.

I drive around in my Ford, aimless except to satisfy a craving for speed. *I'd better keep up the acquaintance with this Sarhan al-Behairi; I may find him useful some day. He has experience, and friends in the city.*

I drive fast along the Corniche—Mazarita, Chatby, Ibrahimiyya, and beyond. *My nerves have been racked and they respond gratefully to the car's speed as it slashes through the cold refreshing air under a cloudy sky. The blue-sea-edged Corniche is sharp, clear-cut, scrubbed clean of the clamour and smell of summer holiday-makers.* Tanta old girl, I'll never go back to you again, except of course to cash money or sell some land! To hell with you and your memories!

I turn off at Siyouf and cut over to the boulevard running towards Abu Qir[41]—the royal road—driving faster and faster as my spirits and confidence rise. And where, I wonder sadly, are the Frenchwomen? Where is beauty? Where is all that solid gold? I go into the Metro Cinema for the matinée and chat up a girl at the buffet in the interval. We lunch at Omar Khayyam,[42] then have a short siesta in her little flat at Ibrahimiya. By the time I get back to the *pension* at dusk, I have completely forgotten her name.

There is no one in the entrance hall. I take a shower and the cold water somehow reminds me of the pretty *fellaha*. Back in my room I order a cup of tea, just to talk to her. I give her a piece of chocolate.

She hesitates a little before taking it and I press her. "Why not? We're all one family here."

I look her over frankly, with pleasure, and she stares back unabashed, not even looking down. Is she cunning or is she afraid?

"Are there many like you in the country?"

"Plenty." She ignores my obvious intention.

"But surely not as pretty as you?"

She thanks me for the chocolate and leaves the room. Cunning? Or scared? Well, I don't need her now. And it's only her privilege to play a little hard to get, and her due as well for me to confess that she's very beautiful. *Ferekeeko*, don't blame me!

I stare at Madame's old photograph until she asks delightedly, "Do you like it?" She tells me the story of her first and second marriages. "How do you find me now?"

"As lovely as ever." I look at her veined wrists and muddy complexion.

"I've aged before my time. It's my bad health," she says with resignation. Then all of a sudden, veering over to a new subject: "But is it wise to risk your money on a new business?"

"Why not?"

"What if the government confiscates it?"

"There are such things as safe projects." Guessing that she might have contemplated hauling her own money out from under the floorboards, I add playfully, "Wouldn't it be wonderful if we were partners?"

"Me?" She laughs with pretended surprise. "But I can hardly live on what I get from the *pension*."

We are joined by the ancient journalist, closely wrapped up in a warm dressing-gown, and surprisingly cheerful, despite his disgusting longevity. Qalawoon, the Doddering Sultan.[43]

"The young seek adventure, the old long for security," he says, as if to comment on both his lot and mine.

I wish him good health.

"Have you come to Alexandria to start that project you mentioned?"

"Yes."

"And are you serious about it?"

"Well, I'm sick of doing nothing."

Chanting, he quotes the old verse: "Youth, leisure and worldly goods oft prove a man's undoing." But I despise poetry, as much as I despise being told about university degrees. And what I feel towards them is the ineffable superiority of a Turcoman horseman who finds himself living among sedentary trash. Of course the winds of fortune have soured some of them enough to give them a fair amount of polish, the same winds that at the moment are blowing my class's candle out. That's just what they're like, in fact, these revolutions— like some sort of freak of nature: like hurricanes, tornadoes. *I resemble someone trying to drive a car with an exhausted battery.*

A new face comes out from behind the screen, a young man I haven't met before, heading for the door. Madame invites him to sit down, introducing him as "Monsieur Mansour Bahi."

He works at the Alexandria Broadcasting Station. Another of those degrees. A handsome face, delicate features; rather effeminate, though. Another polished plebeian, whose diffidence tempts me to punch him in the face.

When the fellow has gone I ask Madame whether he is a resident or a transient guest.

"A resident, my dear," she says proudly. "I don't take transient guests."

Zohra comes back from the market, her plastic shopping bag heavy with groceries. I look after her greedily. The town is full of women, but this girl excites me. Is it my fault, *Ferekeeko?*

"So you've fallen in love, after all?"

"Not really, Aunt, but she's a fine girl. She's my cousin, and I want to get married."

"At any rate, you're a young man after any girl's heart."

.   .   .

The evening of Umm Kulthum's concert is a magnificent occasion, even at the Pension Miramar; we drink, laugh and talk of many things, including politics. But even strong drink cannot get the better of fear.

Amir Wagdi rambles on about the glory of his own past, deeds for which his own conscience must serve, alas, as the only witness; the old wreck wants to convince us that he was formerly a hero. So no one is commonplace in this damned world. And everyone sings the praises of the Revolution. Even Tolba Marzuq. So do I. Take care, I say to myself. Sarhan is an opportunist and Mansour is probably an informer. Even the ancient scribbler . . . who knows? Madame herself is probably required to keep her eyes open, in the service of security.

When Zohra comes with a bottle of soda-water I ask her: "And you, Zohra, do you like the Revolution?"

"Oh, you should see the portrait[44] hanging on the wall in her room," says Madame. Tacit permission for me to creep into the girl's room some night?

The whisky draws us together in a sort of familiarity, but I know it won't last, that there will never be any real friendship between me and Sarhan and Mansour; at most a transitory intimacy that will soon evaporate, just like the girl I picked up at the Metro. I remind myself that I should find some business to use up my energy and fill my time. Otherwise, who knows? I might do something stupid. Or commit some crime — a crime worthy of myself.

What is clear is that if getting married means risking another *no*, I'd prefer to remain a bachelor. And since it's impossible for me to find a suitable wife in this "Progressive Society," I'll permit myself to look upon all womankind as my personal harem. To fill the vacancy in my future home, I'll simply find a first-class maid. Right. A maid like Zohra, and why not Zohra herself. She'll certainly accept; she'll be grateful for the chance to play the lady without the trouble of child-bearing, nursing, and all that. She's beautiful. And she'll put up with my whims, my other love affairs. How could a girl from her background do anything else? Life isn't so bad, after all, and there's plenty of fun to be wrung out of it yet.

Sarhan tells us so many jokes that we are exhausted. Even Mansour bursts out laughing, then draws back into his shell. "Listen! Read this! A death sentence. Will the English do nothing about it? Will they let the Communists take over?"

The singing starts and they listen greedily to the wireless. I grow tense. As usual, sure, I can follow a verse or two, but I quickly get bored and distracted. There they sit, wrapped up in the music, and all I feel is terrible isolation. I'm astonished to notice that Madame is as fond of Umm Kulthum as any of them. "I've listened to her for so many years," she explains when she observes my surprise.

Tolba Marzuq is listening intently. "Thank God they didn't confiscate my ears, too," he whispers to me.

As for the Doddering Sultan, he's closed his eyes, also listening. Or having a quiet snooze.

Then I steal a look at Zohra on her seat near the screen. Very charming. But is she listening too? What's she thinking? What's she hoping? Is she being tossed around by life like the rest of us? She goes away for a moment. They are all drunk with rapture, absorbed in the music. I go after her, through the passage to the washroom and playfully pull her braid, whispering: "The only thing lovelier than the music is your face."

She steps back firmly. I try to take her into my arms, but stop short at her frigid look.

"I've waited so long, Zohra!"

With a light step, she turns away and goes back to her seat in the hall. All right, suit yourself! There are dozens like you at the big house in Tanta, you fool. Or do you think my education is lacking something too, you yokel?

I go back to the group of listeners, disguising my anger with exaggerated applause for the concert I am not following. I have a sudden impulse to speak out for once, to tell them what I really think of it, but I don't. In the interval they all scatter and I take the opportunity to leave the house.

I drive to Cleopatra:[45] it's cold and windy but I'm on fire with the whisky. I go to the house of a Maltese madame where I used to go on summer nights. She's surprised to see me out of season and it's past midnight.

"I have no one here," she says. "And I can't get you a woman now." She stands in front of me in her nightgown, past fifty, fat and flabby; but a woman still, though the down on her upper lip is like a moustache.

I push her into the bedroom.

"What are you doing?" she says with surprise. "I'm not ready."

"It doesn't matter."

I laugh. Nothing matters!

Later we spend another hour talking. When she hears about my business plans, she says, "People are selling out and leaving."

I yawn. "I'm not starting a factory or a company."

"Then look for some foreigner who wants to leave and buy his business."

"Not a bad idea, but I must think it over."

On the way back it rains heavily and I can hardly see my way through the windshield. I'm in a rotten mood. I know I've just been wasting my time.

Pretty, in spite of the smell of cooking.

"Two pieces of sugar, please." To stir the sugar for me she has to stay a little longer in my room. "You were hard on me, Zohra."

"No, you went too far."

"I wanted to tell you how much I admire you."

"I'm just here to work," she says coldly.

"Of course."

"You don't seem to be convinced."

"You misunderstand me."

"You're a gentleman. Please be reasonable."

"I shall love you forever," I call out after her as she leaves the room.

.   .   .

Come with me on a strange trip. A terrible day: my brother scolding, my uncle thundering: "School! School!" *Let us wander in the country lanes, a long strange trip, north and south, night and day. We'll stop at every village for food and drink.* "I'm over twenty-one!"

"I've seen you together."[46] I see you together in the passage to the bathroom. It's Dream-Boy Sarhan. He gently pinches your cheek. You do not raise your head in protest. Your charming face is lit by a happy smile. Your braided hair sways skittishly, the way things do in a cornfield. So the peasant has got in first. That's all right, just as long as we observe absolute equality of opportunity, even if he winds up with two evenings when I get only one.

Climbing into the Ford, I laugh and laugh. *Ferekeeko*, don't blame me.

I give Tolba Marzuq a lift to the Trianon and he asks me to have a drink with him. Sarhan is there with another man. We exchange a passing nod. When Tolba asks me how I spend my time, I tell him that I drive around making plans for my new business.

"Have you any business experience?"

"No."

"Then don't throw your money away."

"But I've made up my mind."

"You should get yourself a wife. You'd learn to be more cautious with your money."

I can hardly control my anger. "I'm determined to stay a bachelor and get on with a project."

"A smart boy," he says, indicating Sarhan. "A friend of mine works at the same firm. They speak of him there as a zealous revolutionary. That's enough, isn't it?"

"Don't you think he's a phoney?"

"We live in a jungle. Beasts of prey are fighting over the loot—our property!" I find a secret satisfaction in listening to him. "Under those uniforms," he continues, "they're mad for luxury."

"But you can't deny there have been a few reforms?" I am feeling comfortable in our privacy.

His mouth twitches. "All meant for the diversion of this ignorant mob, who don't have the head for it all. We're at the mercy of the Uniforms."

Sarhan joins me as I leave the tea-room. I give him a lift to the *pension.* He's a friendly bastard. And though I heartily detest him, I'd rather stay on good terms. He may come in useful some day.

"A fine conquest." I nudge him with my elbow. He shows a puzzled smile. "Zohra." He raises his thick eyebrows in surprise, then lowers them in virtual confession. "You're an open-handed country boy. Don't grudge me a share."

"To tell the truth," he says humorlessly, "I don't understand you."

"Let's be frank, just between friends—is it her you pay or Madame?"

"No, no!" he protests. "It's not the way you think."

"What way should I think, then?"

"She's a good girl. She's not like that, believe me."

"All right! Okay! I seem to have mistaken a private vehicle for some form of public transport."

Don't worry yourself over trifles, *Ferekeeko!*

I've made a mistake, all right. I've taken the New Age for my friend when it's really my enemy. But never mind—I'm happy in my freedom. So what if my class has left me to the waves and the boat sinking? How marvellous to be loyal to nothing, to be free, completely free, free of claims from class, country, or any duty whatever. And all I know of faith is that God is merciful and compassionate. *Ferekeeko,* don't blame me!

A terrible commotion, unheard of at a place like the *pension.* Just woken from my siesta, I run out into the hall to see what's happening. A fight in the entry way, which I watch from behind a screen. It's rather entertaining: a strange woman holding our friend Behairi by the throat, cursing and flailing him, with Zohra standing there nervously, trying to pull them apart. The woman suddenly turns on her, but Zohra is a magnificent fighter and punches her twice, banging the stranger each time into the wall. She's a lovely girl, Zohra, but as tough as an old boot.

I stay behind the screen for a while, the best seat in the house, then when other doors open behind me, I emerge from behind the screen and take the strange woman firmly by the wrist. I pull her gently out, apologizing and trying to calm her down. She is seething with anger, swearing nonstop, and doesn't seem to know I'm there.

Not bad as women go. I stop her when we get to the second floor. "Wait a bit! You should tidy yourself up before you go out." She smoothes her hair, takes out a hairpin and pins up a tear on her dress. I give her my handkerchief—it's scented—to wipe her face. "My car's at the door. I can take you home if you'll let me."

She looks at me for the first time. I am in my pajamas and dressing-gown. She thanks me. In the car I ask her where she wants me to take her.

"Mazarita," she replies in a hoarse voice.

The sky is clouded and it is dark soon, sooner than one would have expected. I try to draw her into conversation.

"You shouldn't get so worked up."

"The filthy bastard!" she hisses.

"He seems to be a nice country boy."

She says again, "Filthy bastard."

"Your fiancé?" I enjoy my own sarcasm.

She doesn't answer. She is still burning with rage. Really not bad, as women go, and on fire somewhere, that's for sure. We stop in front of a building on Sharia Lido. "You're a decent man," she says as she opens the door of the car.

"Are you sure you're all right? I don't want to leave you unless you're recovered."

"I'm all right, thank you."

"Then it's goodbye, is it?"

"I work at the Genevoise," she says, giving me her hand.

I start the car wanting to know more about her. Same old story, I suppose, a runaway boyfriend and the usual fracas. Now that he's met Zohra he's started a new romance. The woman is passable. I may need her some night. But why did I take the trouble to drive her home? Stupid! *Ferekeeko*, don't blame me!

By the time I get back to the *pension* I've forgotten her.

My car eats up the tarmac of crazed streets, lampposts and eucalyptus trees flying past in the opposite direction. Pure speed revives the heart, sweeping boredom away, while the wind howls like a maniac rattling the branches and the leaves of trees, and rain beats down, washing the fields bright green. From Qaitbay to Abu Qir, from the harbour to Siyouf, from the heart to the farthest limbs of the city, wherever there are roads, I wander with my car.

Time has passed and I've taken no serious steps as far as business is concerned. Then it occurs to me to conduct a systematic investigation of certain familiar centers of radiation. I pay a visit to an old procuress at Chatby; she brings me a girl who isn't bad to begin the day with. I have lunch with another madame in the neighborhood of the Sporting Club, who provides me an Armenian woman somewhat above the average.

And then my Sidi Gabir[47] madame presents me with a lovely piece (Italian mother, Syrian father) whom I insist on taking out in my car. She plays shy a little, says she's worried about the possibility of a storm, but I tell her I wish it would rain, I want it to. All the while I make love to her in the car, she keeps looking at the gathering clouds and saying: "What if it starts to rain?"

And finally, there on the open country road to Abu Qir, it begins to pour, just as I've been hoping it would. The place is deserted. I shut the windows and watch the deluge, the dancing boughs, the endlessly stretching landscape. The Italo-Syrian beauty at my side is in a panic.

"You're crazy."

"Just think," I say, trying to calm her down, "The two of us, naked in a car, but safe and sound all the same, kissing each other to the clap of thunder and the sound of the driving rain!"

"This is impossible," she says.

"But just think. Wouldn't you like, from this snug little shelter in the midst of cosmic rage, to stick your tongue out at the entire world?"

"Impossible," she says. "Impossible."

"Yes, but it will happen. Any minute now, my love." I drink straight from the bottle. And the more the thunder claps the more I ask for, begging the sky to pour down its whole hoard of rain.

"But the car may break down!" says my beauty.

"Amen!"

"It will be dark soon!"

"Let it be dark forever."

"You're crazy! Crazy!"

"*Ferekeeko*," I shout into the storm, "do not blame me!"

At breakfast I hear about Zohra's strange new resolution. The *fellaha* wants an education! Many comments, much joking, but everyone is generally encouraging. My old wound gives a twinge. Nobody looked after me when I grew up; I ran wild. I had no regrets then, but I've found out since, too late, that time is no friend. And now here's a *fellaha* who wants to learn to read. Madame explains the girl's situation and why she left her home village, all of which shows that she is not one of Madame's disciples. She may even be a virgin, unless Sarhan the Dream-Boy doesn't care for virgins.

"I thought Zohra was . . ." I say to Madame slyly, with an eloquent gesture.

"No, no," she assures me.

I change the subject abruptly. "I wonder if you've thought of any business we could share?"

The cunning old girl asks, "Where would I get the money?"

"What would happen if occasionally I brought a friend or two here?"

"I'm sorry." She shakes her head. "The house is full. And if I let one of you do that, wouldn't I have to let the others too? But you know, I could give you an address if you like."

When I see Zohra in the hall, I congratulate her on her decision. "Work hard! I'll soon need a secretary for my business." She smiles happily, looking very pretty. I still want the girl, even knowing beforehand that I'd be sick of her in a week. It's a week I need, though.

I drive round the city. The weather is too mild for my mood. For top speed I go to the desert road, drive for an hour at seventy-five miles an hour, then turn back. I have lunch at the Pam Pam[48] and pick up a girl as she is leaving a hairdresser's.

I go home to the *pension* around dusk. Zohra is sitting in the living-room with a girl I do not know, obviously the teacher. I sit down with Madame, occasionally stealing a look at the teacher. Not bad. Somewhat hunched about the shoulders, but not too noticeably. A little snub nose. Quite attractive, in fact. It's a pity a girl like her won't go in for a quick night of love. It would have to be a lengthy romance and, what's more, she'd probably look forward to wedlock, unpatriotically ignoring the Revolution's call for population control.

Madame introduces me, complete with my hundred *feddans*, business plans and all. I appreciate her tact; she's an old hand. After that I make a point of driving in the direction of her school in Moharrem Bey.[49] It works. I see her one afternoon at a bus stop; I stop the car and invite her in. She hesitates for a moment, but the sky is cloudy and threatening. All the way home I complain of loneliness in Alexandria. I need someone to consult on my business . . .

"I do think we should meet again," I say at the door.

"Drop in by all means. My father would be delighted to meet you."

Now, *Ferekeeko*, the truth is, I am quite an eligible match, young and rich. If I want to be safe in the company of these college girls I'll have to wear a fake wedding ring!

That evening I have nothing to do. I drop in on the Maltese madame at Cleopatra and ask her to call in as many of her girls as she can. I have a wonderful time—a wild evening, studded with delightful follies unheard of since the days of our great Haroun al-Rashid.

·　　·　　·

"I can't be hard on him. He never saw his mother. His father died when he was six." He was speaking calmly, but my brother was trembling with rage.

I am holed up with skeletons. I hate old Qalawoon. The day I see his face in the morning is always a bad day. Tolba Marzuq asks about the progress of my plans. I catch a whiff of incense in the hall and look interrogatively at him.

"It's Madame. You should have seen her make the round of the rooms with the incense-burner."

"So you like Umm Kulthum and use incense to keep off the evil eye. Very Egyptian for a Greek." Mine hostess gives me a fleeting smile. She is absorbed in listening to a Greek song on the radio. "I'm looking for some foreigner who'd be ready to sell out. So many of them are leaving just now."

"A good idea. What do you think, Mariana?"

"Yes. Wait a moment! I think the proprietor of the Miramar Café means to sell out." She speaks quickly, turning back to the song.

"What does it say?"

"It's about a young girl. She is describing to her mother the sort of man she'd like to marry." Her old face grimaces coyly. I look at the Captain's portrait and her ancient photograph. "I could have been a lady to this day."

"You are. A perfect lady."

"I mean lady of the big house in Ibrahimiya."

"You mustn't waste your time," says the Doddering Caliph. "Take up some business."

I curse him under my breath.

It is bitterly cold outside and I have a date with my Italo-Syrian beauty at the madame's house in Sidi Gabir. *Ferekeeko*, don't blame me!

At breakfast I hear that Zohra's sister and her brother-in-law have paid a stormy visit to the *pension*.

"She has made up her mind to stay here for good." Madame says that with deep satisfaction. "Thank god they didn't strangle her!"

"Apparently you Behairis are weaklings," I say to Sarhan.

"What do you mean, weaklings?"

"The close proximity of your province to Alexandria has obviously weakened its native traditions."

"We are more civilized than other provinces. That's all."

I give Tolba Marzuq a lift to the Windsor Hotel, where he is to meet an old friend. I like the old man and respect him deeply. To me he is the image of a venerable monarch who has been dethroned, but still keeps his personal dignity. I joke.

"Don't you think the *fellaha* should have gone home with her people?"

"She shouldn't have run away in the first place."

"I mean she must have had some strong reason for not going back, even if she wished to."

"You mean the Behairi lad?"

"Not particularly, though I'm sure he's partly responsible."

"Who knows?" He smiles. "He may be innocent after all. Maybe when she ran away from home it was some other fellow."

The news that she has rejected Mahmoud Abu al-Abbas adds to my wonder. Before applying to Madame for the hand of her maid, the fellow had consulted me.

I stop at his stall the next day knowing that he will open the subject. We exchange significant looks.

"That's modern girls for you!"

"The fool! She won't get another offer in a hurry."

"You'll marry a better girl some day. Actually, I don't believe the *pension* is a very suitable place for getting yourself a wife."

"I thought she was decent and well-behaved."

"I haven't said anything to the contrary, but . . ."

"Yes?"

"Why should you care, now that you're through with it all?"

"I have to find out why she turned me down."

"She's in love with Sarhan al-Behairi. If that's any help to you."
"The idiot! Would Mr. Sarhan marry her?"
"I said love. Not marriage."
I've detested this Dream-Boy from the start. My dislike has sometimes been overcome by his friendliness, but only momentarily. All this has nothing to do with Zohra; she's not that important. Maybe it's his bumbling tactlessness that annoys me so much. Or is it just that way he has of singing the glory of the Revolution on every possible occasion? I have to hold my tongue, unwillingly acquiescing in these hymns of praise, but one day I burst out: "All right, we all believe in the Revolution, but the past wasn't a total blank!"
"Yes, it was," he insists.
"The Corniche was there, and so was the University of Alexandria."
"The Corniche wasn't for the people, nor was the University. Why should you have a hundred *feddans* of your own," he asks with a smile, without malice, "when my whole family holds only ten?"
"Why should you have ten, when millions of peasants haven't even got a job?"

"I won't believe a word of what you say. You're just mad because Mervat turned you down. And you don't believe any of this rubbish about socialism and equality. It's simply power. If you have power you have everything. And meanwhile there's no harm in preaching socialism and equality to others. Have you actually seen any of that gang walking around in poverty lately, like our lord Omar?"[50]

A little while later I get wind of a lovely fight between the newsboy Mahmoud Abu al-Abbas and Sarhan al-Behairi, our hero from onion country. He says nothing about it, however, and I respect his silence. When we are alone in the living-room one evening I even consult him on my plans.
"Don't take up that café business," he urges. "You're a man of good family, you must think of something more suitable."

"Such as?"

"Now that I think of it, well, why not a poultry and dairy farm? There's a lot of money in that. We could rent a plot of land in Semouha. I have experience, friends. I might even come in as a partner, if I could get the capital."

Alexandria. How small it becomes when you look at it from behind the wheel of my madcap car. I can cut through it like the wind but it keeps turning itself, in spite of me, into a tin of sardines. Night follows day in dogged stupidity, nothing ever happens. Dawn after dawn the sky gets up and dresses itself, the weather does its usual tricks, and the women arrive in all colors, shapes and sizes. But nothing ever happens. The universe is really dead, you know. These are only the ultimate twitches before rigor mortis sets in.

I remember the Genevoise. One facade to the Corniche, bravely defying the sea and the season, but the actual entrance is through a narrow side street. Inside there's a stage at one end of the hall and a dance-floor in the middle. The walls, ceiling and lamps are a dirty red—a jinn's hide-out—and one look at the girls and the clientele is enough to tell you the place is a brothel.

Behairi's girl is performing an authentic belly-dance, with a fair amount of obscenity. I ask her to my table. At first she doesn't recognize me, then she apologizes for her conduct the day we met and explains that after such a lapse of time she'd stopped expecting me. She says her name is Safeya Barakat. God knows what her real name is. She is, in fact, better looking than the teacher; a little fat, though, and there's a distinctly professional look about her plump face.

I drink so much that I almost pass out. I invite her into my car and take her to Sharia Lido in Mazarita. On the way I try to make love but she says she's sorry, she has the curse. I go back to the *pension* in a deplorable condition, deeply disappointed. Zohra is just leaving the bathroom in her shift. I block her way with open arms.

"Go away," she says firmly.

I beckon her to my room.

"Leave me alone!" She threatens me.

Excited with drink and desire, I throw myself at her. She fights me off, beating my chest with her fists so fiercely that I'm enraged and go berserk. I start hitting her savagely, determined to shove her or drag her into my room. Then I feel a hand on my shoulder and hear Sarhan. He is breathing hard.

"Husni, have you gone mad?"

I push him away firmly, but his grip on my shoulder tightens.

"Go into the bathroom," he says, "and stick a finger down your throat. You'll feel better if you get it out of your system."

I turn on him suddenly and hit him in the face. He reels, then hits back in a rage. Then Madame comes in, pulling on her dressing-gown.

"What's the matter?" she asks anxiously, her voice rising. "No, no, gentlemen, you'll wreck the place! I won't stand for it! I won't stand for it!" She says the words furiously, breaking us apart.

Cherubs float or dance on the ceiling. Rain beats on the window and the waves make a deafening barrage. I close my eyes; my head aches badly. I yawn and I curse everything. I curse as I realize that I have slept in my coat and shoes. I curse again as the events of the awful night come back to me in a rush.

Madame enters and stands looking down at me as I try lethargically to get up. "You're late," she says reproachfully, taking the big chair. "You shouldn't drink so much." Our eyes meet and she smiles. "You're my favorite lodger, but please don't drink so much."

"I'm sorry," I say after a while, staring at the cherubs overhead. "I should apologize to Zohra."

"Good! But promise you'll conduct yourself as a gentleman of your family should."

"Give her my apology, then."

After that I cut Sarhan completely, though I manage with some difficulty to conciliate Zohra. But I must admit that I miss Sarhan's company. The other fellow, Mansour Bahi, I hardly know. We usually exchange bare civilities at breakfast and then settle back to loathe each other cordially in silence. I can't help despising him, with his arrogant effeminate introversion and his vulgar, acquired *politesse.* What a shock his voice on the radio gives me now. You'd think it was the voice of a fine orator, a hero. What a fraud. Curious. No one at the *pension* likes him except the Doddering Sultan. The old man must be an ex-pervert.

Maybe I shouldn't leave the room, but some sort of auspicious event is taking place outside. Could it be in Behairi's room? Yes. A little disagreement? A quarrel, a fight in fact, between the Behairi Romeo and the Behairi Juliet. What can it be? Has she submitted a request that he repair his technical oversight and make her an honest woman? And is he shirking the responsibility, as he did with Safeya? Delicious! I'd better stay in. I never thought there was so much entertainment in store for me in this place. Listen carefully, *Ferekeeko,* and enjoy it all.

"It's none of your business! Yes, I'll marry anyone I like! I'll marry Aleya!"

Ya Sayyid! Ya Badawi! Aleya! The schoolmistress! Has Dream-Boy accepted that standing invitation she offers everyone to visit her *en famille?* So he's switched his affections from the scholar to the teacher! *Ferekeeko,* be my witness! Long live the Revolution! Long live the July Ordinances![51] Alexandria, what a lovely day!

Here is Madame's voice, remonstrating in pidgin Arabic; and the great newscaster himself in the flesh, having condescended to interest himself in the affairs of the commonalty. He's sure to find a solution to this rustic imbroglio. *A moi!* Welcome the fray! Action, *Ferekeeko!* Never let events forestall you.

I hear the story later from mine hostess. "I have given him notice to leave," she says angrily. "I shouldn't have accepted him in the first place."

I praise her protective attitude towards Zohra and enquire after the girl.

"She's not well. She keeps to her room."

"The old story. It keeps coming round like the four seasons of the year. The Behairi must be glad to leave. He's been promoted to the fifth floor. Who knows where his extraordinary talents will take him from there?"

"The proprietor downstairs is thinking seriously of selling the Miramar Café," Madame ventures.

"I am ready to talk," I say with aplomb.

I go out with every intention of painting the town red. *Ferekeeko,* don't blame me.

She is deathly pale, with a new look of defeat about her, the light gone from her hazel eyes. She pours my tea and makes for the door, but I beg her to stay. The wind is blowing outside and clouds are gathering. The room suddenly darkens.

"Zohra, you always have to take the good with the bad. The world's full of wicked people. But there's still a lot of kindness in it." She isn't listening. She doesn't seem to care about anything. "Take me, for instance. I was fed up with life at home. That's why I'm here." Not a word. She isn't interested. "I tell you, nothing lasts forever, neither sorrow nor joy. We have to go on living. When hard luck leads us down a closed path, we have to look for another. That's all."

"Everything's all right. I regret nothing."

"But Zohra, you're sad, miserable. You have every reason to be. But you must find a way out. You've got to." She can hardly control herself. Her face, distorted with grief, looks ugly for a second. "Listen to me, I've something to tell you. Think it over, take your time. I'll be going into business soon—and I'll give you a good job." She doesn't seem to trust me. "This place is hopeless. A girl like you and a pack of wolves!" It's obvious that she doesn't take a word of what I'm saying seriously. "You'll be safe with me. A good job and a fine life."

She mumbles something I can't hear, takes the tray and leaves the room.

I lose my temper, angry at her and at myself to the point of loathing. Being able to play upon the starved passions of frustrated men appears to have blinded mademoiselle to her own true value— curse the land that gave you birth! And sourly I say: "*Ferekeeko!* Don't put the blame on me!"

. . .

I spend an evening within the dingy red walls of the Genevoise, guzzling with Safeya, and later she takes me home to her flat, where I pour my drunken troubles into her ears. When I mention my plan for buying a business, she sits up.

"There's a wonderful opening for you!" She lights a cigarette and speaks more deliberately. "The Genevoise. The owner wants to sell out."

"But it's seedy. And depressing."

"Think of the situation: on the Corniche, near the center of town. It will make a marvellous restaurant and nightclub. It brings in good money even now, and it's sure to bring in more once we've done it over." She goes on: "Look, you're a man of family. The police won't meddle with you in a hurry. And I've got masses of experience in this sort of business. The summer season's a sure thing and so's the rest of the year, thanks to the Libyans. Petro-dollars!"

"All right. Arrange a meeting with the boss." It's as if I'm in a trance.

"Good! And I'll be responsible for the female staff. Now," she suggests, kissing me, "why don't you come and live here with me?"

"Why not? But you've got to have one thing clear if we mean to get along together. I don't believe in love. I don't even know what it is."

I get back to the *pension* at about ten o'clock in the morning and in the porter's hall I run into Sarhan. We ignore each other, waiting for the lift without a word. Is he paying a visit, I wonder, to his future in-laws? Suddenly he speaks to me:

"I know very well you were behind the trouble with Mahmoud Abu al-Abbas." I turn a cold shoulder, deliberately cutting him. "He told me," he goes on. "Anyway, it was a rotten thing for you to do."

He is getting excited and I'm furious already.

"Shut up, you son of a bitch!"

We close, slugging each other until the porters separate us.

"I'll teach you something," he shouts, "you just wait!"

"Come on then. It would give me a big kick to relieve you of your dirty rotten life."

It's early evening and Madame and Tolba Bey are sitting in the living-room listening to the radio.

"Come on," says the lady, "give us your advice. Where shall we spend New Year's Eve? *He* thinks we should go to the Monseigneur. But Amir Bey says we should stay at home."

"Where is Amir Bey?"

"In bed, with a cold."

"Then let him stay in bed and let's go to the Monseigneur. We'll have a really good time drinking till morning."

I tell her later, "You know, I've found it at last."

"What?"

"The business investment I've been looking for."

She is obviously disappointed at the news. "Don't be in too much of a hurry," she advises. "You must think it over."

"I've had enough of thinking."

"The Miramar Café is a better investment." She hesitates. "And I was thinking seriously of coming in as a partner."

"I may have plans later to expand the business." I grin, suddenly possessed by the desire to enjoy my New Year's Eve to the full.

I go to see the proprietor of the Genevoise in his office, where we agree as to preliminaries. He invites me to come to his house in Camp de César[52] after closing time. Safeya is there to take part in discussing the details, and they both suggest that I spend New Year's Eve at the Genevoise: we can come back later to the Frenchman's house or go somewhere else. In any case I'm delighted at the idea of being rid of the old people's party.

I meet strange looks at breakfast. Madame and Tolba Bey have something queer about their faces. Old Qalawoon is keeping to his room, so is Mansour Bahi, and there's no sign of Zohra. My table-companions are silent, but their expressions suggest something ominous.

"Have you heard the news?" Tolba finally blurts out. "Sarhan al-Behairi was found dead last night. On the deserted road that goes to the Palma."

"Dead?"

"Murdered, perhaps!"

"But . . ."

"Here's the paper," Madame interrupts. "It's terrible. I think there'll be trouble."

I remember our fighting in the porter's hall and am seized with depression. Will I get into trouble? I say stupidly: "I wonder who did it?"

"That is the question," says Madame.

"I suppose they'll make enquiries about his enemies," one of the old men says.

"Among us, as it so happens," I observe ironically, "he certainly had no friends."

"He may have had other enemies."

"Sooner or later they'll find out the truth. God's will be done!" I feel barely recovered from the impact of the news. Then I ask about Zohra.

"She's in her room," says Madame. "In terrible shape."

I'd meant to give Madame notice of my leaving but decide to postpone it for the moment. When he sees that I'm on the point of going out, Tolba warns me:

"We'll probably be summoned for the investigation."

"I'll be there all right," I say at the door. "Let them call us."

I ought to clear my head, with a wild drive from one end of Alexandria to the other. *White clouds sail slowly above my head, almost within reach, drenched with colors; the air is light and sharp.* This is the last day of the old year and my lust for a hectic roaring time goes up a thousand per cent. Let them live or die, who cares? I know what I'm going to do. And as I put my car in gear, I tell my reflection in the mirror: "*Ferekeeko,* don't blame me."

3

MANSOUR BAHI

o I'm to stay prisoner here in Alexandria, to spend the rest of my life trying to justify myself." With that I said goodbye to my brother and went straight to the Pension Miramar. The judas opened, showing the face of an old woman, fine-featured in spite of her age.

"Madame Mariana?"

"Yes?"

"I'm Mansour Bahi."

She opened the door wide. "Welcome. Your brother spoke to me on the phone. Make yourself at home."

We waited at the door for the porter to bring up my two suitcases. She invited me to take a seat and sat down herself under a statue of the Madonna.

"Your brother is a very distinguished police officer indeed. He used to stay here occasionally before his marriage. Before he was transferred to Cairo. After working here for so many years!" She is

491

very friendly, but examines me closely all the same. "You live with your brother?"

"Yes."

"Are you a student?"

"No. I work at the Alexandria Broadcasting Service."

"But you come from Cairo, originally?"

"Yes, I do."

"Well, make yourself at home and don't mention the rent."

I laughed incredulously, but I'd already guessed she would give me a room for nothing, if I wished. Marvellous. The rank breath of corruption everywhere. But who am I to throw stones?

"How long will you stay?"

"Indefinitely."

"Good. You'll pay a moderate rent and I won't raise it in summer."

"Thank you, but my brother let me know what I ought to do. In summer I shall pay at the summer rate."

She tactfully changed the subject. "You're not married, are you?"

"No."

"When do you think you might get married?"

"I haven't thought about it yet. Not now anyway."

"What do you think about then?"

She laughed. So did I, without wanting to.

The doorbell rang and a girl came in with a big parcel of groceries. Very attractive. The housemaid, obviously. Madame spoke to her. Zohra. She was the same age as my friends at the University and that was where she should have been, not running errands for the old lady.

Madame showed me two rooms overlooking the sea. "This side is not very suitable for winter," she murmured apologetically, "but all the other rooms are taken."

"I like winter," I answered casually.

I stood alone on the balcony. The sea lay there under me, a beautiful clear aquamarine, little wavelets sparkling in the sun; a light cool wind caressed my face and there were a few white clouds in the sky. I felt almost overwhelmed with melancholy.

Then I heard someone move behind me in the room. It was

Zohra, making up the bed with fresh sheets, intent on her work, not looking in my direction. I watched her carefully, and was soon aware of her *fellaha* beauty. "Thank you, Zohra." My tone was sociable, and she gave me a pleasant smile. I asked her for a cup of coffee, which she came back with in a few minutes. "Wait until I finish, please." I put the saucer on the parapet and sipped my coffee while she stood waiting on the threshold, looking absently at the sea. "Do you like nature?" She didn't answer, as if she didn't understand my question. I wondered what she thought about. As the daughter of this good earth, I thought, her instincts are probably vibrating for the prime creative act of nature.

"I have a lot of books in this trunk," I said, trying to make conversation. "And there's no bookcase in this room."

She looked round at the pieces of furniture. "Keep them in the trunk?"

I smiled at her simplicity. "Have you been here long?"

"No."

"You . . . like the place?"

"Yes."

"Don't the men annoy you?"

She shrugged.

"They can be quite dangerous, you know."

She took away the cup. As she finally left the room, she said, "I'm not scared." I admired her self-assurance.

Then I went back to my own sense of frustration, my habitual thoughts, brooding on how things are, how they should be, drifting into my usual depression.

I examined the furniture again. I'll have to buy a little bookcase, I thought, but the little table standing between the wardrobe and the chaise-longue would do for writing.

I worked for some hours at the Studio recording my weekly programme, had lunch at Petro's in Sharia Safeya Zaghloul, then went to Ala Kaifak in Ramleh Square for my coffee, where I sat watching the square, busy under an overcast sky.

Raincoats were at the ready and people were hurrying by. All at once my heart gave a thump. That man there—Fawzi! I leaned forward, my forehead touching the window. Was it Fawzi? No. Of course not, not Fawzi, just a very close resemblance. (And then Doreya came to mind—by the law of association, as they say. Though she was always there, in fact, by her own law. Yes. Doreya.) But supposing it were Fawzi and our eyes met? Old friends would naturally have to greet each other with open arms. He was my mentor, after all, my professor. Then let me embrace him fervently, in spite of the thorns. He's seen me. Here he comes.

I asked him to sit down to a cup of coffee. Politeness demanded no less.

"I'm delighted to see you. What brings you to Alexandria at this time of the year?"

"A family visit."

Which meant that he was here on Party business,[53] but was keeping the fact from me—as he should.

"Well, I hope you have a pleasant stay."

"It's been two years since we saw you last. Not since you graduated, in fact."

"Yes. You know I was posted to Alexandria."

"I mean that you seem to have deserted us completely."

"I had some troubles."

"Perhaps it was wise to quit working for a cause so uncongenial to you."

"And perhaps it's wise to stop working for a cause you no longer have any faith in," I retorted, blindly, defensively, full of pride.

He paused, weighing his words as he always did. "They say your brother . . ."

"I'm over twenty-one," I said irritably.

"I'm sorry. I've annoyed you, have I?" He laughed.

My nerves were on edge. (Doreya!) A light shower began and I wished it would come down in torrents, clearing the square and leaving it deserted. (My love, don't believe them! Some old sage once said that in order to convince each other of the truth we may sometimes have to tell lies.) I looked at my dangerous friend.

"Don't you care about anything at all?" he asked me.

I almost laughed out loud. "As long as I'm alive, I must care about something."

"Such as?"

"Can't you see that I've shaved and arranged my tie neatly?"

"And what else?" he said gravely.

"Have you seen the new film at the Metro?"

"Good idea. Let's go and see a capitalist film!"

Madame paid a courtesy visit to my room. "Is there anything you need? Anything I can do for you? *Do* tell me! Your brother was always very frank with me. And so gallant—a real friend in need! And so big! A giant—but you're so finely built yourself—and strong, too! Consider the Pension Miramar your home. Think of me as a friend, a real friend in every sense of the word."

It wasn't courtesy that brought her, but the chance to fulfil herself in an orgy of verbal self-expression. She gave me her life story: her early well-to-do youth, her first love and marriage to an English captain, her second marriage to the Caviar King, the big house at Ibrahimiya, the comedown. Not an ordinary comedown, though: hers was the Pension of Quality, of the Pashas and Beys, of the good old days of World War II.

She invited me to tell her in exchange everything about myself. She gushed questions—a strange, tiresome, entertaining woman, a fading female. But even though I was seeing her only as an old ruin clinging to the rag-ends of life, it was still quite possible to imagine her—I could picture it all in the light of the old stories of autocrats and famous beauties—as the queen of brilliant *salons*.

At breakfast I was introduced to the other guests. What a weird assortment! But I needed a pastime, and if I could get the better of my introversion, I thought, I could find some companionship here. Why not? But let's not even think about Amir Wagdi and Tolba Marzuq; they belong to a dying generation. Then, I wondered, what about Sarhan or Husni? In Sarhan's eyes there was a native compatibility. He seemed sympathetic, in spite of his awful voice. But what were his interests? By contrast, Husni simply got on my nerves—that at least was my first impression of him. He was arrogantly taciturn and reserved and I didn't like his massive build, his big haughty head or the way he sat enthroned, sprawling in his chair like a lord, but a lord without any real sovereignty or substance. I presumed he'd feel at conversational ease only with someone he knew to be even more stupid and trifling than himself. He who deserts his monastery, I reminded myself, must be content with the company of the profane. And as usual my introversion got the better of me: They will say . . . They will think . . .

Reasoning like that had once made me lose the chance of a lifetime.

I was surprised one morning to see Sarhan al-Behairi come into my office at the studio. Beaming like an old friend, he shook my hand warmly.

"Just passing by. I thought I'd drop in to see you and have a cup of coffee with you." I said he was welcome, of course, and ordered the coffee. "Some day I'll want to pick your brain about the secrets of broadcasting."

With pleasure, I thought, you past master at loafing⁵⁴ I've never had the luck to be able to enjoy. He talked about his work at the Alexandria Mills, his membership in its board of directors and its ASU Base Unit.⁵⁵

"How wonderfully active you are! You're a splendid example to the uncommitted."

He gave me a long searching look. "It's our path towards building a new world."

"Did you believe in socialism before the Revolution?"

"Actually, my conviction was born with the Revolution."

I was aching to query this conviction of his, but thought the better of it. We were soon discussing the *pension*.

"A most interesting group," he said. "One never gets enough of their company."

"What about Husni Allam?" I asked cautiously.

"A nice chap, too."

"He seems like the Sphinx to me."

"Not really. He's a nice chap. He's got a natural talent for pleasure." We smiled at each other. Unwittingly he had given me the key to his own character rather than to Allam's. "He's a man of property, with no fixed profession. He probably has no degree. Remember that," he cautioned. "He has a hundred *feddans*, so he's entrenched in the front lines of the old regime. And without a degree. I suppose you can guess the rest."

"Why does he live in Alexandria?"

"He knows what's what. He's looking for some business."

"He'd better wipe that arrogant look off his face or he'll frighten away his customers."

I asked Sarhan why he lived in a *pension* even though he had been so long in Alexandria. He answered, but not spontaneously.

"I preferred a busy guest-house to a flat on my own in town."

The evening of the Umm Kulthum concert, an evening of drinking and music, during which many a hidden soul was bared. Naturally it was Sarhan al-Behairi, who probably contributed least to the expense, who was mainly responsible for bringing us together.

I stole a few looks at Tolba Marzuq. No one guessed what he meant to me: old recollections, dreams of bloodshed, of classes in conflict, books and pamphlets studied in secret meetings, a whole edifice of ideas. I was appalled at his flabbiness and humility, the compulsive movements of his cheeks, his abject cowering in his seat, his hypocritical playing up to the Revolution, as if he were not descended from men who had amassed their power from the flesh and blood of the people. It was his turn to play the flattering fool, now that his withered glory had left us with a nation of parasites. And Husni is just a wing of this broken eagle, I thought, which still flutters with life, and may manage at any moment to limp into some grotesque sort of flight.

"*I tell you all the old class barriers have been wiped out.*"

"*No. They've only given place to other ones. You'll see.*"

Sarhan was the soul of the group, infusing us with constant hilarity. He was kind-hearted, candid. Why not? Ambitious, to be sure, since his was basically an opportunist's interpretation of the Revolution.

Of them all, however, I soon found that Amir Wagdi was the most fascinating and the most worthy of affection and esteem. He was the Amir Wagdi whose articles I had reread for my radio programme; "Generations of Revolutionaries." I had been taken by his progressive but contradictory ideas and charmed by his style, which had developed from conventional rhyming prose[56] into a relatively simple but powerful idiom charged with occasional grandeur. My recognizing him and his writings pleased him so much that I could sense how injured he felt by callous neglect. It touched me deeply. He seized the opportunity like a drowning man clutching at a straw and gave me the story of his life, his long fight for the Nationalist cause, the political waves he had struggled against, the great heroes in whom he had believed.

"And what about Saad Zaghloul? The older generation worshipped him."

"What good are such idols? He stabbed the true workers' revolution to death at its birth."

Why did Tolba Marzuq give me such furtive looks? I caught his eye in the mirror of the hat-stand, suspicious, hostile. I poured him a drink and asked his opinion of Amir Wagdi's glimpses of history.

"Thank you," he said, as if to excuse himself. "Let bygones be bygones. Let's listen to the music."

Zohra served us admirably, but she rarely smiled at our jokes. When she sat next to the folding screen she watched us at a distance, her limpid eyes saying nothing. She was serving Husni Allam when he asked, "And you, Zohra, how do you like the Revolution?"

She blushed and turned away from our boisterousness, while Madame answered for her at length. But Husni had apparently wanted to draw her into the conversation; I could see that he was annoyed by Madam's interruption. "She likes it instinctively," I told him. He didn't seem to hear me, though, or perhaps he just ignored me, the pig. Before the end of the concert he disappeared and Zohra said he'd gone out.

I really admired Amir Wagdi, sitting up so late, and thoroughly enjoying the singing and the music. It was almost dawn when we got up to go to bed.

"Was there ever in your day a voice like Umm Kulthum's?"

"No." He smiled. "It's the only thing today for which the past can provide no equal."

I asked her to sit down, but she just stood there leaning against the wardrobe and gazing with me out through the window at a cloud-laden horizon. She was waiting for me to finish my cup of tea. I usually gave her a biscuit or a piece of cake from a small store I kept in my room, which she accepted in token of a growing friendship. I was pleased that her innocence made her sensitive to the admiration and respect I felt for her.

It began to rain. The small drops streamed down the windowpanes, transforming the world outside. I asked her about her village and she chatted with me. I guessed why she was driven from home, but said lightly, "If you'd stayed at home, you'd have been married by now."

Then she told me a terrible story about her grandfather and the old man they would have forced her to marry. She concluded, "And so I ran away."

I was disturbed. "But what will people say?"

"I don't care anyway. It's better than what I escaped from."

My admiration for her grew. But I pitied her for her loneliness, even though she stood there full of self-confidence. Rain stippled the windowpanes with water and mist, making the world almost disappear.

What was it? A bomb? A rocket? A flash of insanity? No, just a car, with that idiot Husni Allam at the wheel. What made him drive so

insanely? Only he knew. But there was a girl with him. (Looks like
Sonya. Is it Sonya?) Oh well, Sonya or not, the hell with him.

A little later I sat at my desk. Then one of my office colleagues
came up to me. "Your friends were arrested yesterday," he whispered.
I was stunned for a minute and couldn't say anything in reply. "They
say it's because . . ."

I cut him short. "That's not important."

"There are rumors . . ."

"I said it's not important."

He leaned on my desk. "Your brother was wise."

"Yes, very wise." I sighed with exasperation. Husni Allam must be
at the end of the world by now, I thought, and Sonya must be trembling with fear and desire.

"Not another word from you! I'm getting you out of this hole."

"I'm not a child any more."

"You sent your mother to her grave."

"I thought we'd agreed not to rake up the past."

*"But I see it in the present. You'll come with me to Alexandria even if I
have to carry you there by force."*

"I beg your pardon! You forget I'm a grown man."

"You're a fool. Did you think we didn't know? We know everything." He
looked hard at me. *"You conceited idiot! What do you take them for?
Heroes?"* He grunted. *"I know them better than you do. You're coming with
me, whether you like it or not."*

She opened the door herself. My heart was hammering; my mouth
had gone dry and my head was in a daze. In the dark corridor her face
shone white and pale. She stared at me stonily, without recognition.
Then her eyes widened in surprise.

She whispered, "Mr. Mansour."

She stood aside and I went in.

"How are you, Doreya?"

She led the way to the sitting-room, where everything around her seemed to reflect her own profound unhappiness. We both sat down. His portrait faced us from the opposite wall, looking out at us from a black frame. He was holding a camera, which he seemed to aim at the two of us together. We looked at each other.

"When did you come back?"

"I came straight from the station."

"You heard . . . ?"

"Yes, at the office. I took the two o'clock train." I looked at his photograph. The smell of his tobacco still hung about the room. "Did they get them all?"

"I think so."

"Where did they take them?"

"I've no idea." Her hair was untidy and her face was pale. She looked wilted, heavy-eyed from anxiety.

"And you?"

"As you see."

The fact that she was on her own, with no money or resources — he'd been an associate professor of economics, but had no savings — was all too clear.

"Doreya, you're an old friend, and so is he. My best friend . . . in spite of everything." I gathered my courage and went on. "I have a good job and income. And I have no one to support, you know."

She shook her head. "But you know I can't . . ."

I wouldn't let her go on. "I didn't think you'd refuse a little help from an old friend."

"I'll find a job."

"Yes, all right, but that will take time."

Nothing had changed in the room. His room, as I'd always known it in the past: the big studio sofa and the bookshelves laden with books, the tape-recorder, the record-player, the television set and the radio, the camera and the film equipment, the albums. (Where's the photograph we had taken at the Auberge in Fayoum?[57] He must have smashed it in a moment of anger.) My eyes met hers, then we both looked away, thinking the same thoughts, touched by the same memories. Past, present and future seemed to meet in a dark road, fearful and unknown.

"Have you any plans?"

"I haven't had time to think."

"You didn't think of writing to me."

"No."

"But it must have occurred to you I might turn up."

No reply. She left the room and came back with the tea tray. I lighted her cigarette and we sat smoking in silence, while an old unrecollected aroma came stealing back to me. And at last what had to be said was said.

"I suppose you know that I tried to come back and couldn't?" She made no comment. "I didn't get much encouragement, to put it mildly."

She murmured, "Let's forget it. Please."

"Even Fawzi would have nothing to do with me."

"I said forget it."

"Doreya, I know what they said. That I wanted to come back to spy for my brother."

She pleaded. "Can't you leave it alone? Can't you see I'm unhappy enough as I am?"

I looked down. "You know exactly how I feel."

"I'm very grateful."

I felt stung. "I mean the feeling I have that I should have been with them!"

She said sadly, "It's no good your torturing yourself."

"I wish—I wish you'd tell me frankly what you think of me."

"I've received you here in my house—*his* house, if you like." She spoke in a low voice, after a tense silence. "That's enough, I should think."

I sighed with relief, though I wasn't fully reassured: I knew I'd be right back in the old hell. But it was no time for explanations.

"I'll come to see you occasionally. And please write to me if ever you need help."

I was very fatigued from travelling, so I stayed in the *pension* and joined the group around the radio. Luckily they were my favourites,

Amir Wagdi, Madame, and Zohra. I was preoccupied with my own thoughts, not listening to their conversation, until I heard Madame addressing me.

"You always seem so far away from us all."

"The intelligent ones are always like that," said Amir Wagdi, looking at me gently. "Have you ever thought of bringing out some of the material of your programmes in book form?"

"I'm thinking of writing a programme," I threw out carelessly, "about the history of betrayal in Egypt."

"Betrayal!" The old man laughed. "What an enormous subject. You must come to me. I'll help you. I'll give you all the necessary references and recollections."

"I love you. You love me. Why don't you let me talk to him?"

"You're out of your mind."

"He's a rational man. He'll understand and he'll forgive."

"Can't you see? He loves me and he considers you his best friend."

"But he hates falsehood. I understand him perfectly."

"A programme on betrayal—what a programme that would be! But mind you, write a book in the end or you'll soon be forgotten, as I've been. The only man who survived without writing down his thoughts was Socrates."

Madame was listening to a Greek song that she herself had requested on the radio. About a virgin listing the qualities of the man of her dreams, or so she says. The sight of her as she listened silently, with her eyes closed, was touching, a tragicomic image of the irrepressible desire to live.

"It was Plato, a disciple, who gave him immortality," Amir Wagdi went on. "But isn't it strange that he should have chosen the poisoned cup when he had the chance to escape?"

"Yes." I added bitterly, "And to do so even though he had no sense of guilt."

"And yet how numerous are the people now who in comparison with Socrates don't even seem to belong to the same species!"

My bitterness bordered on insanity. "They're betrayers. All of them."

"There are facts and there are legends. Life is an enigma, my boy."

"But your generation believed. You had faith."

"Faith. Doubt." He chuckled. "They are like day and night."

"May I ask what you mean?"

"I mean that they are inseparable." After a moment of silence, he said, "And what is your generation like, my boy?"

"What counts is what you do, not what you think," I answered impatiently. "And therefore I'm really no more than an idea."

"Do? Think? What's all this about?" Madame smiled in bemusement.

The old man smiled too. "Sometimes a tired thinker may come to the conclusion that the best things in the world are a good meal and a pretty woman."

Madame crowed, "Bravo! Bravo!"

Zohra laughed. It did me good to hear her laugh for the first time. Then there was a moment of silence, during which we listened to the wind howling outside, driving at the walls and the closed windows.

I felt myself lapsing into anxious depression. "I'm sure the ideal is to believe and put your beliefs in action. To have nothing to believe in is to be lost forever. But to believe in something and none the less sit there paralysed is sheer hell."

"I agree. You should have seen Saad Zaghloul in his old age, defying banishment and death."

I looked at Zohra, the lonely exile. She sat there full of hope and self-confidence. I envied her.

The following week I paid Doreya another visit. The place looked as neat and well kept as in the old days and she seemed to be taking care of herself, but of course she was still alone—without hope and without an occupation to fill her time.

"I hope my visits don't disturb you."

"At least they make me feel that I'm still alive."

Her voice was lifeless. It almost broke my heart, for it made me imagine the barrenness and poverty of her existence. I longed to be able to tell her something of what I felt, but memories silenced me. We agreed that she should get a job. But how? Her having only a B.A. in classics didn't make it easy.

"Don't shut yourself up in this house."

"I have thought of that, but I've made no move yet."

"If I could only see you every day."

She smiled. "It would be better," she said, after thinking a moment, "if we could meet away from here."

I was not very happy at the idea, but I could see that she was right. So I agreed.

Our third meeting in Cairo was at the zoo. Except for a changed expression in her eyes, from which all the joyfulness had gone, the beautiful radiant face that day looked the same as ever. We walked for a while along the fence that shut off the grounds from the road leading up to the gates of the University—that highway of memories, unforgettable, shared.

"You know you're inflicting too much on yourself?"

"But you can't imagine how happy this makes me!" Should I have said that? "Loneliness is terrible, Doreya. It's the worst evil anyone can suffer." The world-weary tone I used was probably calculated.

"I haven't been to the zoo since our student days."

"I'm lonely as well," I said, persisting. "I know what it's like."

She now had the look of a cornered animal. I was upset. My feelings were growing more twisted, more tangled, but I couldn't control myself any longer. When our eyes met it seemed to me that she flinched.

"It's wretched that I should be walking here in the fresh air, while he's . . . in there." Then she noticed that I was very quiet. "What's the matter?"

"I can't get over this sense of guilt."

"I'm afraid my company will only add to your pain."

"No. It's just that this accursed feeling feeds and thrives on despair."

"We can try to find some comfort in seeing each other."

"And despair ends in recklessness. Which can only add to the trouble."

"What do you mean?"

"I mean . . . I mean . . . Would you forgive me if I couldn't help myself . . . and told you . . . that I love you now as I loved you in the past?"

I'd done it. Madness. What could I gain by it? Like someone who in order to put out the fire that's burning his clothes dives headlong into a watery abyss.

"Mansour!" The note of reproach in her voice was like a slap across the face.

"Forgive me." My voice sounded weak. "I can't imagine how I spoke out. But believe me, I can never find happiness, or even try to."

As I took the train back to Alexandria I reminded myself that a man could show more courage in letters.

I woke up to a terrible noise, which for all I knew might have been a projection of my own troubles. But the noise outside was of a quite different kind. I left my room in time to catch the last scene of a battle and I could see from their faces that Sarhan, Zohra and another woman had been either its heroes or its victims. But who was the woman? And what did Zohra have to do with it all?

When Zohra brought my afternoon cup of tea she told me all about what had happened; how the woman had rushed in after Sarhan on his return to the *pension*, how they'd fought, and how she'd become involved as she tried to separate them.

"But who's the woman, Zohra?"

"I don't know."

"I heard Madame say she'd been Sarhan's fiancée."

She considered the idea for some time. "Maybe."

"But why should she hit you?"

"I said I was trying to separate them."

"That's no reason why she should turn on you."

"Well, it just happened."

I looked at her kindly. "Is there anything between you and . . . ?"

She wouldn't answer. "There's nothing wrong in that. I'm asking you as a friend." She nodded in reply. "So you're engaged and keep it a secret from me?"

"No!" she said emphatically, shaking her head.

"Ah! You haven't announced your engagement yet?" Her silence worried me. "Then when will it be announced?"

"All in good time." She seemed confident.

I was still worried. "But he deserted this other woman."

She said naively, "Because he doesn't love her."

"Then why did they get engaged?"

She looked at me for a moment, then took courage. "She wasn't really his fiancée. She's a fallen woman."

"That doesn't alter his fickleness." My own words sounded pathetic and odd in my ears; and immediately my thoughts were shot with poison. I cursed Sarhan, whom I hated as I hated myself.

A few days later she came in at the same time in the afternoon and cried out gaily, "Mr. Mansour, shall I tell you something?"

I looked up expecting to hear something of her relationship with Sarhan.

"I'm going to learn to read and write." I did not understand. "I've made arrangements with one of the neighbors—Miss Aleya Muhammad, the teacher. She's going to give me lessons."

"Really?"

"Yes, we've arranged it all."

"That's wonderful, Zohra. How did you think of that?"

"I won't stay ignorant forever. And then I have something else in mind."

"What?"

"That I'll learn some craft or trade, of course."

"Good, Zohra. Excellent." I admired her very much. I was happy for her, and pondered these feelings in my room after she'd gone.

It was raining heavily outside and the sea seemed to rage in a strange broken language. It didn't take long for the elation I'd felt a few minutes earlier to cool, condensing back into the stagnant shape of my habitual moodiness. Thus rising at once recalls falling, strength recalls weakness, innocence recalls depravity, hope recalls despair.

For the second time, I had found in Sarhan the perfect object on which to project my anger. I cursed him.

We chose a table under a eucalyptus tree in the little café on the Nile bank, where the afternoon sun was feebly pursuing the biting cold of a Cairo winter. Avoiding my eyes all the time, she said, "I shouldn't have come."

"But you have," I answered reassuringly. "So that's decided."

"Nothing is decided, believe me."

I looked at her. I had to take the plunge. "I'm sure your coming . . ."

"No. It's just that I wouldn't stay alone with your letters."

"There's nothing new in my letters."

"But you've written them to someone who just doesn't exist." I touched her hand lying on the table in proof, as it were, that she did exist. She took her hand away. "They're four years late."

"But they tell you things that have nothing to do with time or place."

"Can't you see that I'm weak and miserable!"

"Well so am I. Our friends see me as a spy. I see myself as a renegade, a traitor. I have no one but you."

"Some comfort."

"There's nothing left for me otherwise. Except madness or death."

She sighed as if it hurt. "I betrayed him in my mind a long time ago."

"No. You were a classic example of false loyalty."

"Another way of putting it."

"We suffer for no real cause," I explained angrily. "That's the tragedy." We watched the Nile, its lead-colored wavelets almost still. Behind the table my hand stole to hers and held it tenderly. I pressed it a little, ignoring her feeble attempts at resistance. I whispered, "We mustn't let morbid thoughts overcome us."

"We're falling," she said sadly. "Faster than I could have imagined."

"Never mind. We'll come out of it as pure as gold."

But I wanted to fall all the way, wanted to hit the bottom, as if to bear witness by my very self that the end-all of mankind's greed for happiness is Hell.

At the station in Cairo I ran into an old friend, a journalist who was sympathetic to progressive causes, but was careful never to dabble in politics. We sat together in the station café. I was waiting for my train and he was waiting for someone arriving from the Canal Zone.

"I must say I'm glad I ran into you like this. I really wanted to see you." Marvellous. What did he want? I hadn't seen him since I'd gone to Alexandria. "What brings you to Cairo?" I stared at him. He knew, of course, that I'd be startled at the question. "Excuse my being so frank," he went on, "but I must plead our old friendship. It's rumored that you come here for Mrs. Fawzi."

I wasn't as upset as he expected. Doreya and I had guessed that there'd be talk.

I said coldly, "She needs a friend, you know."

"I also know—"

"That I was in love with her once." I made the interruption as if I didn't care.

"What about Fawzi?"

"He's greater than they think."

He was obviously troubled. "As a friend of yours, I'm not very happy at what I hear people say."

"Tell me what you've heard." He was silent and I added nervously, "That I'm a spy, that I ran away at the right moment, and that now I'm sneaking back to my old friend's house?"

"I only meant to . . ."

"Do *you* believe it?"

"No, no. If you think that for a moment, I won't forgive you."

On my way back to Alexandria I wondered if I deserved to live. What other solution was there, after all, to so many contradictions? Why shouldn't death provide the answer—a final word? I wanted to sit for a while in the Trianon, but when I saw Husni Allam and Sarhan al-Behairi inside talking, I decided against it. Colored clouds driven by fresh gusts of wind raced over my head as I turned away. Along the

Corniche, when the waves were rising high and cold spray was flying over the road, I walked defiantly, wishing I had something valuable in my hands, so I could smash it to bits. I said to myself that only a disaster, huge in scale, something in the order of a colossal earthquake, could bring back harmony.

Zohra brought in my tea. "My people came to fetch me back," she said, "but I refused to go." She spoke proudly, sure of my interest in her. And I was interested, in spite of my low spirits at the time.

"Well done!"

"Even good old Amir Bey advised me to go back home."

"He's afraid you'll be in trouble, that's all."

"But you're not smiling the way you always do." She said that after she had looked at me for a while and I tried to grin at her in reply. "I understand," she said.

"You understand?"

"Yes. Your going away every week and your brooding." At that I couldn't help smiling. "I hope I'll be able to offer you congratulations and best wishes very soon!"

"May God give ear to what you say, Zohra." We exchanged glances and she made a movement with her hands as if to lift me into happiness. "But someone keeps spoiling things for me."

"Who's that?"

"Someone who betrayed his faith."

She threw up her hands in horror.

"And betrayed his friend and master."

"Oh!"

"But he's in love. Do you suppose that could help him earn a pardon for his crime?"

She was still horrified. "It's wicked to have no faith. A treacherous man's love is as rotten and unhealthy as he is."

I buried myself in my work, but when I could no longer bear the stress of my shattered nerves, I would make the trip to Cairo, where I found a kind of happiness. But what kind was it? When she stopped resisting and finally surrendered herself, it's true, I was overjoyed. But afterwards I was torn by anxiety, obsessed with the morbid idea that love was the road to death and that my own excesses would destroy me.

"I'd loved you for a long time," I said to her once. "You remember that, don't you? Then came the shock of hearing about your engagement."

"You've always been so diffident," she said, with a regret that seemed to apply to both past and present. "And that's why you're sometimes misunderstood. It was because of his strength of character that I accepted Fawzi. You know. He's an admirable man."

The place was full of lovers.

"Are we happy?"

She looked up in surprise. "Mansour, what a question!"

"I mean, perhaps you don't like becoming the talk of the town."

"I don't care. As for Fawzi . . ." She was going to repeat to me what I'd often told her about his tolerance, his great heart and so on, but she stopped short. I hated hearing the old story. I changed the subject.

"Doreya, did you ever suspect me the way they did?" She frowned. She had often warned me not to bring up the subject, but I couldn't help myself. "After all, it would only have been natural . . ."

"For God's sake, why do you torture yourself?"

I said with a smile, "I often wonder why you should have thought differently."

"The fact is, it's not in you to betray anyone." She was annoyed.

"What's a traitor like? Certainly I'm weak or I wouldn't have given in to my brother. And it's the weak who are most likely to betray."

She took my hand in hers. "Please, don't torment yourself. Think of us."

She had no idea that her love itself had now become one of my torments.

Madame came into my room and I knew I was in for some news. She flitted around with her gossip like a butterfly. "Haven't you heard,

Monsieur Mansour? Mahmoud Abu al-Abbas has proposed to Zohra but she's refused him. It's madness, monsieur!"

"She doesn't love him," I said simply.

"She's set her heart in the wrong direction." She gave me a wink. I was possessed by a strange idea about Sarhan al-Behairi. I found myself wishing that in fact he'd really desert her so that I could punish him as I'd been longing to.

"Please speak to her," whispered the old lady. "She'll listen to you. She's fond of you."

She's fond of me! I could hardly keep my temper in hand. The old cow! ("*She comes from a good family, but she's no saint. Her business has its demands. If I hadn't helped her, her flat and her money would have been confiscated long ago.*")

A wild wind was driving rain against the windows and the roar of the waves was shaking me to the heart. I didn't hear Zohra come in. She set the cup of tea before me on the table. I was glad to see her. I thought she might be able to rouse me out of my dark melancholy. We smiled at one another and I gave her her biscuit.

"There. You've refused another offer." I laughed, but she just looked at me cautiously. "To tell you the truth, Zohra, I'd recommend Mahmoud rather than Sarhan."

She frowned. "That's because you don't know him."

"Do you really know the other fellow as well as you should?"

"You all think it would be beneath him to marry me."

"But we're your friends. You shouldn't say that."

"That Mahmoud thinks a woman is like an old shoe."

I laughed when she told me an anecdote about Mahmoud. "You can stand up to him all right." But she was in love with Sarhan. She'd go on until he married her or ditched her. "Zohra, I respect your philosophy and the way you act. Let me look forward to wishing you every happiness soon."

.   .   .

A rush of urgent work held me up one week, I couldn't go to Cairo, and Doreya telephoned, complaining of her loneliness. When we met the following week she said anxiously, "Now it's my turn to chase you."

I kissed her hand as we entered a private room at the Florida. I explained my week's absence and gave her my news. Her nerves were on edge, and she smoked all the time. I was in no better shape.

"I've tried to drown myself in work, but I always come back to the surface in spite of myself, with a strange voice telling me that I've forgotten something important. And from time to time I really have forgotten things. In my room or in the office."

"But I'm all by myself," she pleaded. "I can't stand it any more."

"We're at a dead end. And we don't lift a finger to help ourselves."

"What can we do?"

I pondered a little. The alternatives were very logical. But built on what kind of premises? I felt completely distraught. "It just stands to simple reason: we should either separate or try to get you your divorce." I said it challengingly, as if I were looking for even more trouble than I already had.

Her grey eyes widened in fascination as well as fear, quite possibly because she was not as repelled by this idea as she was actually allured by its brutality.

"Divorce!"

"Yes." I said quietly, "Then we could start all over again."

"That would be mad."

"But natural. And ethical, if you like."

She leaned her forehead on her hand and fell quiet, defeated.

"You see, you won't do a thing! Tell me," I said after a pause, "what would Fawzi do if he were in my place?"

"You know he loves me," she said weakly.

"But he wouldn't hold you, if he knew you loved *me*."

"Don't you think this is all just theoretical?"

"But I know Fawzi and what I've said is a fact."

"Think. Imagine what he'd say."

"That you deserted him when he went to prison? Is that it? That's not so important. You're leaving Fawzi himself, not what he stands for." I could see him lying back on the studio sofa, watching me with his almond-shaped black eyes, smoking his pipe, discussing all kinds of problems, but never once doubting the security of his own marriage.

"What are you thinking?"

"Life gives nothing except to those who are strong enough to take." I took her hand in mine. "How about a drink? We've had enough thinking."

I was almost stunned with anger. I'd heard of Husni Allam's attack on Zohra and was seething with rage. Sitting in the drawing-room with Amir Wagdi and Madame, I couldn't hear any of their talk except as a sort of incessant buzzing. I'd also heard about a fight between Husni and Sarhan and I sat there wishing they'd fought to the death, the two of them. I longed to teach Husni a lesson, though I knew I stood no chance against him, which made me hate him to the point of madness.

As Madame left the room, I awoke at once from my dreams of fighting and death. Amir Wagdi was watching me, and I suddenly had the odd notion that this old man could have been a good friend of my father or my grandfather.

"What are you dreaming of?"

All I could say was, "I think I have no future."

He smiled gently. He knew all about it; he'd been through it all. "Youth doesn't favour contentment," he said. "That's all. Really."

"I've been so engulfed in the past that I've come to feel and believe that there is no future."

His smile vanished and he spoke in earnest. "Perhaps there was some shock, some lapse, or some bad luck in your case. But you're someone who undoubtedly deserves to live."

It was repugnant to me to discuss my troubles with him, even the real ones. I changed the tack. "And what about your own dreams, sir?"

He chuckled. "Literal or figurative? If you mean literal, I must tell you that old men sleep so lightly that they can hardly dream. Figuratively, my dream is a gentle death."

"Is there more than one kind?"

"The happiest death for a man is after a pleasant evening to go to sleep and simply never wake up."

I was charmed by the old man's conversation. "Do you believe there'll be life for you after death?"

"Yes." He laughed. "If you publish the material of your programme in a book."

I liked the weather in Alexandria. It suited me. Not just the days of clear blue and golden sun; I also liked the occasional spells of storm, when the clouds thickened, making dark mountains in the sky, the face of morning glooming into dusk. The roads of the sky would be suddenly hushed into ominous silence. A gust of wind would circulate, like a warning cry or an orator clearing his throat; a branch would start dancing, a skirt would lift—and then it would pounce wildly, thundering as far as the horizon. The sea would rage high, foam breaking on the very curbs of the streets. Thunder would bellow its ecstasies out of an unknown world; lightning would coruscate, dazzling eyesight, electrifying the heart. The rain pouring down would hug earth and sky in a wet embrace, elements mixing their warring natures to grapple and heave as if a new world were about to be born.

Only after that would sweet peace fall on the city. The darkness would lift and Alexandria would show a face made serene by her ablutions—sparkling roads, spots of fresh dark green, a clean breeze, warm sunshine—in a tranquil awakening.

I watched the storm from behind the glass of my window panes until it finally cleared. This drama of the elements touched a sympathetic chord in my inmost heart. I had a premonition that forecast, in terms still incomprehensible to me, my personal destiny.

When the clock had moved round to strike the hour I stopped my ears against any further sense of time.

But strange sounds invaded the quiet of the room. An argument? A fight? (There's enough going on in this *pension* to keep a whole continent amused.) Something told me that as usual it concerned Zohra. A door opened noisily and the voices were now clear: Zohra and Sarhan. I leaped to my door. Face to face, with Madame in the middle, they were standing in the hall.

"That's none of your business," Sarhan was shouting. "I'll marry as I like. I'll marry Aleya."

Zohra was fuming with anger, furious at the way she'd been used, at the collapse of her hopes. So the bastard had had what he'd been after and wanted to run away. I went up to him, took him by the hand and led him into my room. His pajamas were torn and his lips were bleeding.

"She's a wild beast!"

I tried to calm him down, but he wouldn't stop.

"Can you imagine? Her Highness wants to marry me!" I tried to quiet him, but he still went on. "The crazy bitch!"

I'd had enough of his shouting. "Why does she want to marry you?"

"Ask her! Ask her!"

"I'm asking you."

He looked at me, listening for the first time.

"Why? There must be some reason behind such a request." Then he asked guardedly, "What are you getting at?"

I shouted, "I'm getting at the fact that you're a bastard."

"What did you say?"

I spat in his face. "There," I shouted. "I spit on you and the like of you. Traitors!"

We crashed together, pounding each other until Madame ran in to separate us. "Please, please," she pleaded, "I'm fed up with all this. Settle your quarrels outside, not in my house. Please." She took him out of the room.

My heart heavy and my mind distracted, I went to my office at the studios. A woman was sitting near my desk. It was Doreya. I couldn't speak for a moment, then my head cleared. "Doreya! What a surprise!"

I smiled. I had to smile. I was supposed to be very glad to see her. I took her hand and pressed it. And indeed a sudden joy came over me, scattering the worry and fear that had been gnawing at my vitals.

She looked up at me, her face very pale.

"I might have waited for a day or two until we met, but I couldn't stand it any more. I rang you and you weren't there."

I fetched a chair and sat down facing her, with an incomprehensible anxiety beginning to creep over me.

"Let's hope it's good news, Doreya."

"I got a message from Fawzi," she said, looking down. "Through an old friend, a journalist." My heart sank. *That* journalist. No good news here, certainly. "He's freed me to do what I like with my future."

My heart was pounding and though everything was clear I insisted on a detailed explanation. Strangely enough, I was excited, but curiously enough, I was far from happy. I kept asking, "What does he mean?"

"He knows about us. Obviously."

"But how?"

We looked at each other. I felt myself not just involved, but enmeshed in something, enchained to a point where the fact that her news had not brought me happiness or relief in the least could only make me wonder. *What's the matter?* I asked myself. Then, "Do you think he's angry?"

She sounded a little impatient when she spoke: "Well, he's acted as you expected him to." I bowed my head. "So now I want to know what you think."

Yes, of course. Now all she wanted was my green light, and everything to go her way. I was to build her the nest I'd always longed and pleaded for. My dreams were about to come true.

But it had dawned on me that I wasn't pleased with the prospect. Not at all pleased, in fact, but worried by it, feeling neither shame nor regret for our relationship or her situation, but something that had to do with myself alone. Could I ever be happy? And supposing that I couldn't bring myself to fight for my own personal happiness? In that case what position should I take?

"Whenever you start thinking and stop responding," she said in a rather exasperated tone, "you make me feel so unwanted—so hopelessly alone."

I needed more time to consider the situation. Meanwhile my anxiety had reached the point where I simply couldn't respond to her feelings or bother to disguise my indifference. All at once, almost as if the spell had been broken by a sudden physical blow, I was free of her power, and over my anxious and frightened soul there now swept a black, subversive wave of cruel aversion. I must have gone mad.

"Why don't you speak?" she asked sharply.

I replied in a terribly calm voice. "Doreya. This kind offer of his. Don't accept it." She stared full in my face, dazed, unbelieving. Sadistically, I ignored her look of angry misery. "Don't hesitate."

"Is it you saying this?"

"Yes."

"It's ridiculous. I can't understand."

I said desperately, "We'll try to understand later."

"You can't leave me like this, without any explanation!"

"I have no explanation."

Her deep grey eyes shot me a furious look. "I'm beginning to think you're mentally deranged."

"I deserve that."

"Were you playing with me? All the time?"

"Doreya!"

"Tell me the truth. Was it all a lie?"

"No!"

"Then has your love for me died so suddenly?"

"No! No!"

"You can't be serious!"

"I have nothing to say. To tell the truth, I hate myself. Never get too close to a man who hates himself."

Her staring eyes reflected her inner collapse. Contemptuously, she looked away. She was silent for a while, as if she didn't know what to do with herself. "I've been a fool. I'll have to pay for it now." She muttered, as if she were talking to herself, "I could never really rely on you. How could I have forgotten that? You've just used me, with your insane impulsiveness. That's it. You're mad."

Like a guilty but penitent child, I bore her anger meekly, and to end the scene I simply said nothing, ignoring her raging looks, her fingers tapping on the edge of my desk, her sighs as she tried to catch her breath. I would not meet her eyes. I was dead to everything. Her voice came at me, urgently.

"Have you nothing to say?"

I was immovable.

She got up, pushing back her chair, and I stood as well. She went out and I followed her outside. As we crossed the street she hurried on ahead of me. It was all too obvious that she didn't want my company.

I stopped and followed her with my eyes, as if I were watching a dream, a dream that grew larger and larger until at last it pushed reality out of sight beyond the horizon. I stood there looking after her, watching her loved and familiar figure as she walked away; and even then, even at such an absurd moment, it was clear to me that this broken creature I watched disappearing into oblivion was my first and probably my last and only love. With that disappearance I felt the beginning of my own downhill slide. And in spite of my suffering, a curious ease came over me.

The sea stretched out a smooth blue surface (where was that mad tempest of yesterday?), the sun as it went down touched the edges of the light clouds with fire (where were yesterday's mountains of gloom?), and the evening air played with the tips of the palm trees lining the Silsila (where were those wild, earth-shaking winds?).

I looked at Zohra's pale face, the dried tears on her cheeks, her broken look. It seemed to me that I was looking in a mirror; or rather, that this was life facing me in all its ruthless primitiveness, with its intimations of pure possibility, its thorny indomitability, and its vain beguiling hopes—those qualities manifest in the power of its eternal spirit, which maintains its attraction for both the ambitious and the desperate and offers to each his proper food. Here was Zohra, robbed of both honor and pride. Yes, I was looking into a mirror.

"I don't want to hear anything," she warned. "No reproaches, no remarks."

"Just as you like." I had not yet recovered from my experience with Doreya; I had not had time to analyze and understand it and I was still charged with it to the point of losing my mind. I knew the storm was near at hand, that I hadn't reached the catastrophe of the drama yet. I couldn't remain silent.

"It may all be for the best," I said sympathetically. But she didn't answer. "What are your plans for the future?"

"I am alive, as you see."

"What about your dreams?"

"I'll go on." She sounded determined, but where was her spirit?

"You'll get over it. You'll marry and have children."

"I'd just better stay away from men, that's all," she said sourly. And I laughed, for the first time in ages. She knew nothing of the tempest in my own soul or the madness stalking me.

Suddenly a notion flashed through my brain. Or was it really so new and so sudden? For it must have had deep roots in my mind, of which I'd been unconscious. Something really tempting—strange, mad, and original. For all I knew, it might be the end of my quest, the cure to my chronic troubles. I looked at her tenderly. And I said, "Zohra, I can't bear to see you so unhappy."

She smiled her thanks with reluctance. I was carried away on a wave of emotion. "Zohra! Look up! Hold on to your strength, the way you used to. Tell me, when shall I see you smiling happily again?" She looked down and smiled again. Another surge of emotion carried me higher still. Here she was, lonely, dishonored, deserted. "Zohra, you probably don't know how dear you are to me." I said, "Zohra, marry me."

She turned suddenly, startled, unbelieving, and opened her lips to speak but couldn't make a sound. I went on, still under the influence of my insanity. "Please take me, Zohra! I mean it."

"No!"

"Let's get married as soon as we can!"

Her fingers moved nervously and she said, "You're in love with another woman."

"There was no love. You just imagined it. Please answer me."

She took a deep breath, watching my face suspiciously. "It's kind and decent on your part. Your pity's got the better of you. Thank you. But I can't accept. And you don't mean it. Please don't mention it again."

"You refuse me?"

"Thank you very much. But just forget it."

"Believe me. I mean it. Give me a promise, a hope and I'll wait."

"No." She spoke firmly, obviously not believing a word of what I'd said. "Thank you for all your kindness. I really appreciate it, but I can't accept it. Go back to your girl. If there's anything wrong, it must be her fault and you'll soon forgive her."

"Zohra, please believe me."

"No! Stop it. Please!" She sounded adamantly firm, but her eyes showed how tired she was. And as if she couldn't bear the situation any longer, she thanked me with a nod of her head and left the room.

Rebounding back into emptiness, I looked around like a drowning man. When would the earthquake come? When would the storm begin to blow? What had I said? And how could I possibly have said it? Why? Was there some mysterious double who put words in my mouth at his will? How could I put a stop to it all?

How can I put a stop to it? I repeated the question obsessively as I left the room.

In the hall Sarhan was on the telephone. His suitcase stood near the door, announcing his final departure. I looked with loathing at the back of his head, bent to the receiver, hating him with an intensity that seemed inevitable. He occupied a greater place in my life than I had imagined. What would I do with my life if he disappeared altogether? How would I find him again? I would be unable to keep myself from following him, tracking him down: *Sarhan is the poisoned cup that would cure me.*

"Good!" he shouted down the receiver. "Eight o'clock! I'll wait for you at the Swan!"

It was a date. He was giving me a direction and a goal. His self-assured voice drew me to destruction, commanding me to follow him. He would serve me, deliver me.

·   ·   ·

I went to the Atheneus and thought of writing a letter to Doreya, but my agitation got the better of everything, my will, my mind.

At the Swan, I took a seat in the furthest corner of the inner hall, like an emigrant packed, ready, awaiting his departure, who has completely washed his hands of the city and all its cares. My brain began to clear. I drank two cognacs, my eyes riveted on the entrance.

At a quarter to eight my quarry arrived, in the company of Tolba Marzuq. Had he been the man on the phone? When had this chance friendship started? They sat down on the other side of the hall. I watched them drink their cognac. I remembered that I had agreed at breakfast to Tolba Marzuq's suggestion that we spend New Year's Eve at the Monseigneur. I had promised to celebrate the New Year! I watched them from my corner, drinking, talking, laughing.

I take care not to let him see me, but he gets a glimpse of me in the mirror. I ignore him and go out cursing. The road is completely deserted. And then I hear his shoes creaking behind me. I slow my pace until he almost catches up with me. We have gone quite a distance down the deserted road. He comes up to me and slackens his stride, not wishing to expose his defenceless back to me.

"You've been following me! I spotted you from the start."

I say curtly, "Yes."

"Why?" he asks warily.

"To kill you," I say, taking the scissors out of my coat.

His eyes stare at the scissors. "You must be crazy."

We put ourselves on guard, braced, ready to attack or defend.

"You're not her keeper, are you?"

"It's not just for Zohra. Not just for Zohra."

"What is it then?"

"For life. My life. I have no life if I don't kill you."

"But you'll be killed too. Can't you see that?"

I am completely detached. The emigrant feeling comes over me again and I delight in it.

"How did you know where I was?" he asks without warning.

"I heard you talking on the phone at the pension."

"And made up your mind to kill me?"

"Yes."

"You never thought of that before?" I flinch and make no reply, but do not back down. "You don't really want to kill me?"
"I do. And I will."
"Supposing you hadn't seen me or heard me when I was on the phone?"
"I did see and I did hear. And I'm going to kill you."
"But why?"
I flinch again. But my desire to kill him grows stronger and stronger. "That's why!" I cry, stabbing at him. "Take this. And this!"

As he talked to Tolba Marzuq I heard Sarhan laugh. He left the table a number of times, but always eventually returned to his seat. I cursed Tolba Marzuq, his coming had spoiled everything. But after an hour or so he left. Sarhan stayed alone at the table, and I grew impatient for the moment of my deliverance.

He went on drinking, but kept looking anxiously towards the entrance. Was he waiting for someone else? Would I miss my opportunity forever? The waiter called him to the telephone. In a few moments he came back frowning, looking, in fact, completely dejected. He did not sit down, but paid his bill and left. I watched him through the glass screen and saw him go to the bar. More drink? I waited until he went out and then I followed him slowly.

When I came out of the door, he had already crossed the road. I drew my coat close against the biting breeze. A light mist hung around the street lamps. The road was deserted and, except for the sound of the wind in the undergrowth on either side, absolutely quiet. I followed him cautiously, keeping close to the wall. But he was so completely oblivious of everything around, so absorbed in a world of his own, that he had even forgotten to put on the coat he was carrying over his arm. What was it? He'd been laughing and talking all the time. Why the sudden change? As for me, I was obsessed by one thought alone, my sole salvation.

He turned up the lonely country lane that led to the Palma, dark and empty, completely without life at that hour. *Where is he going?* I thought. *What Fate delivers him to me in this way?* For fear of losing him I hurried, keeping close to the railings of the parks, for it was pitch-dark. *I must make ready to strike,* I said to myself. But he suddenly stopped. *Something will happen, someone will come.* I was trembling all over. *I have to wait.* He made a strange sound. A word? A signal? He was vomiting. He moved slowly forward for a short distance, then fell. Stone drunk! He had drunk too much! I listened carefully, but nothing happened. Creeping closer, I almost stumbled over him in the dark. I bent over him, trying to call out his name, but the words stuck in my throat. I touched his body and his face but he did not move. He was completely unconscious. *He'll die without fear or pain,* I thought, *the death old Amir Wagdi wishes for.* I shook him gently, but he would not move. I shook him harder, violently, but there was no way of waking him up. I stood up angrily and pushed my hand into my coat pocket for the scissors.

Nothing. I looked in every pocket. Had I forgotten to take the scissors? I had been extremely upset, desperate, when Madame came in to consult me about celebrating New Year's Eve. Yes, I'd left the room without taking what I'd come for.

I was furious at myself and at this drunk enjoying an oblivion he didn't deserve. I kicked him in the ribs once, twice, brutally, then I was kicking him like a lunatic, everywhere, until my anger and excitement were spent and I fell back panting against the iron railing, saying to myself, *I've finished him. I've finished him!* I was nauseated, barely able to breathe, obsessed by the thoughts of my own madness.

I was insane. A madman behaving madly in the dark. And there was Doreya, gazing into my eyes, disappearing among the crowd in the street.

I walked back to the *pension,* imagining Zohra sleeping, a heavy oppressive sleep. Then I took a sleeping pill and threw myself on the bed.

He was shoving me with a hand on my shoulder. My brother. I shouted back at him. "You've broken me for good!"

4

SARHAN AL-BEHAIRI

he High-Life Grocery. What a brilliant spectacle for the gourmet and the epicure—bright lights playing over jars of *hors d'oeuvres*, pots of pickles, and tins of sweets, the cold meat and smoked fish, the bottles and flasks of all shapes sparkling with wines from every corner of the earth. Willy nilly, my feet want to stop in front of every Greek grocery in the city.

This time, as the ripe autumn breeze brings a heady aroma wafting into my nostrils I stand there watching a *fellaha* at the counter and thinking: Blessed be the land that fed those cheeks and those breasts of yours![58] I'd seen her as I was scrutinizing the prices on the wine bottles in the window: my eyes passed over the barrel of olives, slipped through a space between a Haig and a Dewar's, hopped across the ham slicer, and lit on the profile of her nut-brown face, which was tilted up towards the grocer with his big Balkan mustachios. She carried a straw bag full of groceries and the tip of a bottle of Johnny Walker was just peeping out at one corner.

I stood in her way as she left the shop. Our eyes met, mine smiling with admiration but hers severely questioning, then I followed close behind her, paying tribute to her country beauty. At the Corniche we were met by squalls of autumn wind, tinged with the faltering rays of the sun. She walked on in quick straight steps and when she turned in at the entrance to the Miramar building she looked back quickly: honey-brown eyes, exquisite but rigidly noncommittal.

I remembered the cotton-picking season at home.

I'd almost forgotten her when I saw her again at the end of the week. She was buying the papers at Mahmoud's stall.

"What a lovely morning!"

It was Mahmoud who responded to my greeting, but she glanced at me and I looked her straight in the eyes, staring like a hawk, mesmerically. She hurried away, but in my senses the way she moved had already laid a charge.

"You lucky devil!" I said to Mahmoud, who laughed innocently. "Where does she come from?"

"She works in the Pension Miramar," he said indifferently.

I paid back some money I'd borrowed from him to send home and walked round the fountain waiting for Engineer Ali Bakir.

What a sweet *fellaha*, absolutely delicious: there she goes, pulling my vitals after her. The whole world delighted me — the excitement of my own desires, the softness of the sunlight, with the multitude of faces I saw waiting around me. And I remembered again the cotton-picking season at home.

Ali Bakir turned up about ten. I took him to my flat in Sharia Lido in Mazarita. Safeya was ready and we went to the Metro cinema. At one in the afternoon we came out. They went straight on to the flat, while I went to the High-Life to get a bottle of Cyprus wine.

At the counter shopping, as my fantastic dream-like good luck would have it, stood the *fellaha*, again. Something made her sense that I was behind her: she turned her head, met my smiling face, and looked away. In a mirror in the middle of the wine bottles, though, I caught a glimpse of a smile forming on her rose-pink lips. Like a daydreamer I could see myself living in the *pension*, wallowing in the warmth of her love. She had crept into my soul, stirring my heart the way it had been stirred only once before, in college. That bright and candid smile, like the sun! A peasant girl, away from home, alien in that *pension*, like a faithful dog astray, looking for its master.

"If it weren't broad daylight I'd drive you home," I said as we went out of the shop side by side.

"*You* don't underrate yourself!" She wasn't really being angry. As I made my way back to our place, I had sweet visions of the country, of virgin love.

Ali Bakir was sitting cross-legged on a cushion. Safeya was cooking in the kitchen. I threw myself down next to Ali and set the bottle before him. "It's an inferno. That's the latest scientific definition of the current price situation."

He laid his hand on my arm. "I suppose you've managed to get your family through the usual school-opening crisis?"[59]

"Yes, but not without suffering for it." I had told him that I'd given up the rent from my share of the inheritance to my mother and brothers, but four *feddans* couldn't go far.

"You're still young," he said encouragingly. "You have a brilliant future before you."

But I was bored with that kind of talk. "Let's stay with the present, if you don't mind. What's life worth without your own villa, your own car, and your own woman?"

He laughed in agreement, but Safeya heard me as she was bringing in the tray and shot me a searing look.

"He's got everything he needs," she said to the engineer. "But he's a hard-hearted son of a bitch."

I retreated. "The fact is I have nothing but the woman."

"We've been living together for over a year," she said in her nagging fashion. "I thought I'd teach him to be careful with money, but he's taught me how to throw it away."

We ate and drank. Then we slept. In the evening the three of us went out, Safeya to the Genevoise, Ali Bakir and I to the Café de la Paix.

"Does she still hope she can marry you?" he asked as we sipped our coffee.

"She's out of her mind. What can you expect from a nut?"

"I'm worried . . ."

"She's got her head in the clouds. Besides, I'm sick of her."

Through the glass window we looked out at a sunny evening. I felt Ali Bakir's eyes turned on me, but I ignored them. I knew what was coming.

"Now let's get serious," he suddenly said.

I looked at him. We were facing each other. It was too late. There was no way out.

"Right. Let's get serious."

"Fine. The plan's been thoroughly gone over from beginning to end." He was unnervingly calm.

My heart contracted. I looked at him, surrendering, drawn on even though full of misgivings.

"Now I'm the superintendent. You're responsible for the accounts and books. The lorry-driver is safe and so is the guard. Nothing is left but for the four of us to get together and swear on the Koran."

I laughed out loud. He looked at me, surprised, then realized how ridiculous what he'd just said was.

"All right." He laughed in return. "Even so, we'll take an oath. The goods are up for grabs. You can imagine what a lorry load of yarn can make on the black market. It's a safe operation and we can repeat it four times a month."

What he said made me thoughtful and I let my mind drift.

"Believe me," he went on, "there's no other way. Doing it legally is running after nothing. You get a promotion or a bonus now and then. So what! You can't afford anything. How much does an egg cost? How much do you have to pay for a suit? Even for food! And you're talking about a car, a villa and a woman. All right. Buy all that. Look, you were elected to the ASU Base Unit and to the Board of Directors. What did it all come to? You volunteered to arbitrate for the workers and solve their problems. Did they give you anything? Did they open the doors of Heaven for you? Prices are going up, salaries are going down. And life is going by. Great! There's something wrong somewhere! How did it happen? Are we being used for guinea pigs? Baby, just turn my face to the wall!"[60]

"When do we start?" My own voice sounded strange in my ears. "We won't start for another month or two. We have to plan all the details very, very carefully. Afterwards you'll live the life of good old Haroun al-Rashid."

I still felt very edgy, even though I'd really given in to him long before.

"Eh? What do you say?" He looked me sharply in the eye.

I burst out laughing. I laughed until the tears came; and he sat there, his cold face set, eyes fixed on me all the while. I leaned across the table. "Okay," I whispered, "chum!"

He shook me by the hand and left. As I sat there alone I was torn by all kinds of ideas. I remembered an incident with Mahmoud Abu al-Abbas, a few days before.

"*Ustad*,"[61] he said, "I'll soon be needing your help and experience."

"What for?"

"God willing, I'll buy Panayoti's restaurant when he sells out and leaves."

I was astounded. Had he made enough money out of the newsstand to buy a little restaurant? "What can I do for you? All I know about food is that we eat it."

"No. Just teach me how to keep the books."

I promised finally to help him.

The thought crossed my mind that I might sell the few *feddans* I had and come in as his partner. "You'll probably need a partner," I said.

But he obviously disliked the idea. "No, I prefer to work on my own. I'd rather keep it a small business and not attract the attention of the government."

I'd been to the headquarters of the Socialist Union where I'd listened to a talk on the black market, followed by a discussion. As I was leaving the hall at the end of the meeting, I heard someone call my name. I stopped, looked around, and saw Rafat Amin making his way towards me in the crowd. I hadn't seen him since we'd been together at college. We shook hands cordially and pushed through the throng together out to the road. He said he'd attended the meeting because he too was a member of the Base Unit of the Socialist Union, at the Amalgamated Metallurgies. It was a pleasant evening, so we walked in the direction of the Corniche. When we finally found ourselves alone in the street, we burst out laughing at the same time, for no apparent reason, but because of memories we shared, memories we couldn't forget or ignore—the number of meetings we'd been to where we'd clapped and cheered together. We'd both been members of Wafdist Student Committees. *Do you remember? Sure! Who can forget those days?* Then we were in opposition to the State. Now we *are* the State!

"I can't imagine that you of all people should have turned your back on your precious Wafdism!" he said, laughing all over again.

"And what about you? You couldn't have been a loyal Wafdist. Tit for tat and you started it."

"But you! *Are* you a real socialist?" he asked, nudging me with his elbow.

"Of course."

"Why, if you don't mind telling me?"

"Even the blind can see the achievements of the Revolution."

"But you're not blind, are you?"

"I mean it," I said seriously.

"So you're a revolutionary socialist?"

"Certainly."

"Congratulations. Now tell me where we can spend the evening."

I took him to the Genevoise. At midnight I wanted to wait for Safeya, but she said she was going out with a Libyan customer.

I was just coming out of the Strand Cinema when I saw the pretty *fellaha* coming down Safeya Zaghloul Street in the company of an old Greek woman. Dark, soft, with bewitching eyes and a ripe figure. The pavement was crowded. A cool salt-laden breeze was blowing; and a halo of clean carded cotton covered the dome of the sky, giving the air a purity and softness that perched on the heart like happiness itself. The two women threaded their way through the crowd. I stepped back to make way for them, greeting the girl with a slight nod and a flicker of my eyelids. Cautiously, she smiled. Good, I said to myself. A cautious smile, there's something in that. I was so pleased; it was like the sweet taste of green beans in my mouth, virgin-fresh, just picked out of the green fields.

I looked at her face at dusk as I drank my coffee. Her eyes were red and swollen after a long sleep, her thick lips slack. Looking her worst, as usual in the early evening, she didn't know what I had in store for her.

"Safeya?" I put as much sorrow in my tone as I could. She looked up. "I'm in a fix. There's a stupid situation we have to face together." She shot me a wary glance and gestured to me to explain. "We'll have to change our way of life. I mean living together in the same flat." She frowned and looked up, ready for a fight. "It's a catastrophe. Especially in light of the housing shortage. But one of my colleagues gave me a hint yesterday. You must remember, surely, that I told you about the Administrative Survey? They pry into everything, they've been asking questions. I'm sure you care about my career as much as I do."

"But we've been living together for a year and a half," she protested.

"They've been the happiest days of my life. We might have gone on forever without anybody knowing. But . . ." I looked into my empty cup as if I were reading my fortune ". . . but I'm out of luck. It seems I'll just have to go back to living on my own in a messy bachelor flat. I may even have to live in some dirty little hotel or noisy *pension.*"

"There *is* a way!" she hissed. "You *know* there is. Only you're an ungrateful bastard!"

"I've been honest. I told you from the beginning: I'm not the marrying kind. I'll always love you, but God didn't design me for marriage."

"Because he made you without a heart."

"In that case there's no use in going over all this again."

She looked me deep in the eyes. "You want to leave me?"

"Safeya, stop it. If that were the case, I'd have said it right out a long time ago."

She was terribly upset; and her grimaces added to the ugliness of her face at the moment. I wished she'd hate me and let me go my own way.

We're through, I thought. I said to myself that on Judgement Day we'd balance each other in the scales. *We've shared everything except her presents to me on special occasions, which I couldn't return because of my commitments at home. Other men exploit their mistresses shamelessly. True, I'm not used to spending money on women. In any case I expect a final battle. I've been through all this before. I really fell in love once at college, but I'd arrived on the scene too late. It would have been a wonderful match—a beautiful girl with a great future, the daughter of a rich doctor, rolling in money from his patients. But what's the use of that now? It's too late. Anyway, I've fallen again. Yes, I think I love the* fellaha, *though it's just a physical attraction, I suppose, like the one that led me to Safeya at the Genevoise.*

"I'd like a room for a long stay."

Her inquisitive blue eyes gleam with satisfaction. She leans back on the sofa under a statue of the Madonna, an air about her of faded gentility, her peroxide hair suggesting a desperate clinging to the past. She haggles shamelessly over the price of a room and insists that I should pay a higher price when summer comes.

"But have you just arrived in Alexandria?"

It isn't simply a passing question, but one in a series of enquiries. I respond by giving her an account of my work, my age, my home town and my marital status.

As we are talking the *fellaha* comes in. She blushes and looks down, taking in the situation at a glance. Madame doesn't notice the girl's confusion or her heightened color. By the time she shows me the room, the last vacant one overlooking the street, we're like two old friends.

I like the room and sit comfortably in the big armchair. I can hear
her call the girl, so I get to know her name without asking. She comes
in shortly to make up the bed with fresh sheets and blankets. I watch
her happily, examining her closely, at my ease, the hair, the fine
features of the face, and the tall figure. My God! What a beauty!
Bewitching! And she has character too! She tries to steal a look at me,
but I am on the alert. I smile at her confusion.

"I am so happy, Zohra!" She goes on with her work as if she hasn't
heard. "God bless you! You've reminded me of my home in the
country." She smiles. "Let me introduce myself. Sarhan al-Behairi at
your service."

"A Behairi?" she asks.

"From Farquasa in Behaira."

"I'm from Zayadiyya," she says, biting off a smile.

"Fancy that!" I exclaim happily, as if the fact that we come from
the same province is a good omen for love.

She has finished her work and is going out, but I beg her:
"Please stay a little. I have so much to tell you."

She shakes her head with innocent coquetry and leaves. I am
pleased with her refusing me; I consider it something special. She
couldn't have treated an ordinary lodger so. All I have to do now is put
out my hand and pluck. Her body looks innocent, though; and I don't
know if she'd be willing or not.

I love her and can't do without her. I wish we were together
somewhere, away from this *pension*, which must be full of tiresome,
inquisitive fools.

At breakfast I am introduced to two strange old men. One of
them, Amir Wagdi, is so old he's an actual mummy, but he's a merry
old fellow. They say he's an ex-journalist. The other is Tolba Marzuq,
whose name sounds vaguely familiar. He's under sequestration. I
don't know what brings him to the *pension*, but I'm keenly interested
in him from the start; anything out of the ordinary is interesting, a
criminal, a madman, someone under a sentence or under sequestration. He keeps his eyes on his cup, avoiding my looks. Out of caution,
I wonder, or pride? I stare at him with mixed feelings, a sense of

triumph over his class mixed with pity for his individual plight. But I'm strangely alarmed at the thought of the state confiscating property. After all, it could happen to anyone.

Amir Wagdi compliments me on being an economist. "The state now depends mainly on economists and engineers," he says courteously. But the thought of Ali Bakir grips and depresses me. "In my time it was the eloquent speech-makers who carried the day." I laugh sarcastically, but the old man is hurt. Apparently he has merely stated it as a fact and not as a piece of criticism, but he goes on to defend his generation. "My son," he protests, "it was our task to wake the people after a long sleep. You need words, words for that. Not economics or engineering."

"Your generation has honorably fulfilled its duty," I say by way of apology, "or we wouldn't be able to do ours."

Tolba Marzuq, the other old man, says nothing throughout the entire conversation.

My heart has recovered an innocence as youthful as this beautiful morning, the clear blue sea, and the blessed warmth of the sun. A kind of vigour seems to sing in my blood: my love for life expands with every breath I take. I work well at the plant, then have lunch with Safeya in my old flat. She gives me a penetrating look and I put on the mask of depression. I complain of my loneliness at the *pension*. "I don't think I can stand it for long, darling. I've asked a house-agent to try and get me a flat." I hear the old song about being an ungrateful bastard. In bed with her after lunch, I wonder when I'll be released from this hard labor.

Later back at the *pension* I see Zohra carrying a cup of coffee to Amir Wagdi's room. The clock strikes five, so I order a cup of tea. She comes in blooming like a flower or a song, a melody of black hair, dark skin and delectable eyes. I touch her hand as she gives the cup.

"I am a prisoner in this room," I whisper, "for your sake."

She frowns to disguise her excitement and turns away.

"I love you!" I call out after her. "Don't forget that ever."

The next afternoon she responds to my attempts at drawing her into conversation. I want all the information about her I can get.

"What brought you here from Zayadiyya?"

"I had to make a living," she says in her homely country accent. She tells about her people, her running away from home and finding refuge with Madame, an old client of her father.

"But she's a foreigner. And the *pension* is almost a market place, you know."

"I have worked in the fields," she replies proudly, "and in the markets."

The girl is no fool. But should I take her story at its face value? Village girls who run away from home have usually left something behind.

"It all happened," I say, dazzled by her, "so that we might meet in this *pension.*"

She looks at me curiously and not unsuspiciously, but cannot disguise her liking for me.

"I love you! I can't stop telling you that over and over again, Zohra."

"That's enough," she murmurs.

"No! I won't stop it until I hear the same words from your lips, and have you safe in my arms."

"Is that what you're up to?"

"Yes. Otherwise I can find no pleasure in life."

She is not angry or upset, but leaves me with an untroubled face. I congratulate myself. And I find myself feeling my old longing for marriage overflowing like water over a fountain's rim. I wish with all my heart I could, Zohra, but . . . if . . . damn all those stupid deadly obvious facts and figures!

Two new guests come to stay at the Miramar, Husni Allam and Mansour Bahi. I look forward to making their acquaintance. I have a sort of hunting instinct that makes me want to add new friends or acquaintances to my bag indefatigably.

Husni Allam comes from an old family of Tanta. A gentleman of property. He has a hundred *feddans*, is handsome, tall and powerfully built, just what we'd all love to be. I may hate his class in the abstract, but I'm fascinated by any of them, if I'm lucky enough to keep him company. It's easy to imagine the kind of life Husni leads in spite of everything. If he's as open-handed as he ought to be, we'll have lots of good nights out together.

Mansour Bahi is quite different, a broadcaster at the Alexandria Broadcasting Service and the brother of a really big man in the police. Which is good—could be useful in fact—but he's very introverted; he has very delicate features and is as innocent as a child, but cold as a statue. Where's the key to his character? How could I find out what his real feelings are? I get so many applications for help from people from home looking for jobs here that I could do with an extra friend or two. Besides, a high police official can come in useful in lots of situations.

I grab her. I wait until she sets the cup of tea on the table, then grab her by the arm. She loses her balance and falls into my lap as I sit down in the big armchair. I take her in my arms and kiss the curve of her cheek—all I can see of her face—a quick, hungry, hurried kiss. She disentangles herself, her strong hands pushing me off, then jumps up and moves swiftly away. I look at her expectantly and smile. Her expression softens like the sea on a mellow autumn morning. I beckon her nearer, but she won't come nearer. And yet she doesn't run away. Mad with desire I leap up and take her again in my arms. She hardly resists. Our lips meet in a long hungry kiss, the smell of her hair filling my nostrils. "Come to me tonight," I whisper.

She looks hard at me. "What do you want?"

"I want *you*, Zohra." Her eyes are serious as she stands there in front of me. "Will you come?"

"What do you want from me?" she asks sharply. The way she says it sobers me a little.

"We'll talk," I reply lamely, "and make love."

"But we're doing that now."

"Yes, but there's too much haste, too much fear. That spoils everything."

"I don't trust you."

"But you don't understand me, Zohra!"

She tosses her head skeptically. But in spite of all that, she walks out of the room smiling.

I'm miserable. If only she came from some important family or had education or money. I let out a stream of curses.

I thought I'd spend the evening of Umm Kulthum's concert at Ali Bakir's, to listen to the music in the kind of quiet that it requires, and Rafat Amin has also invited me to his place. But after some reflection I opt for the *pension*, to consolidate my relations with the other lodgers.

There's a big tray of shish kebab and I need a quick drink or two to prepare myself for the attack. I speak at length of the glory of the Beheiry family, and of the importance of my post as Deputy Accountant, not for mere boasting's sake but to prepare them for the signs of wealth I'll be showing when Ali Bakir's plans come through. But they will talk politics; there is no avoiding the subject. Have you heard? What do you think? To tell you the truth . . . and so on and so on. I can see that for them I represent the Revolution,[62] though Mansour might come in for a share. We all praise the Revolution, of course, and drink to its future.

I catch a glimpse of Zohra. She's the one who's all in favour of the Revolution. I remember how she prayed for it one day in my hearing, and how touched I was at the sincerity and fervent innocence of her prayer.

Does Mansour Bahi, I wonder, have his doubts about my sincerity? My friend, can't you see that here I am, a natural enemy of the enemies of the Revolution, and that it's been a very good thing for me?

"*Well, they've closed as many doors as they've opened.*"

"*Think of the masses.*"

"*All right. But what about the greedy ones who are living in the lap of luxury?*"

"*People like that are the real enemies of the Revolution. You shouldn't judge by their example.*"

I am sincerely fond of Madame Mariana; not just because she loves our music, but because I like her quick wit and her stories of the past, which she repeats with true unquenchable Greek nostalgia. And through those reminiscences, her old love stories and her weakness for the easy life, I can easily identify her with myself: her people are basically nomads, content to find a home wherever they can find happiness.

Amir Wagdi is a most interesting piece of antiquity. Discovered by Professor Mansour Bahi—a monument to a fascinating period of our history of which (alas!) we know very little.

When Tolba Mazuq joins in our praise of the Revolution, I can only salute this delectable hypocrisy, thinking how true it is that mankind is up to its ears, for all its conquests and inventions, in folly and stupidity.

It strikes me that it would be a good idea in general to bring a few enemies together from time to time and make them spend a long evening drinking and enjoying good music in each other's company.

"So you don't believe in Heaven and Hell?"

"Heaven is any place where you live in dignity and peace. Hell is simply the opposite."

When Mansour laughs at one of my jokes he's like a charming child. I begin to have hopes that I may soon find out what really makes him tick, and that by the end of this musical evening we'll have become fast friends.

As for Husni Allam—long live Husni Allam! He has single-handedly donated two bottles of Dewar's to this evening's entertainment and is sitting square in his seat like a country squire, filling our glasses, laughing uproariously. When he suddenly disappears at midnight, the evening suffers something of a blow.

I cannot enjoy the singing the way I usually do, nor do I join in singing any of the verses of Umm Kulthum's songs. All my potential for ecstasy is focused on Zohra and whether she moves about serving us or sits in smiling wonder by the screen to watch us laugh and drink, a rich current seems to flow secretly between us. Our eyes meet stealthily, often, and though far apart, we secretly embrace and exchange lovers' kisses and torments.

.   .   .

I must have seen that man before. He was walking to the Trianon from the direction of Saad Zaghloul Street, while I was coming from the Square. It was Tolba Marzuq. I'd never seen him in his outdoor clothes, the thick coat, the dark red tarboosh and the scarf. I shook his hand respectfully and pressed him to take a cup of coffee. We sat behind the closed glass doors on the sea-front side of the café. The wind was playing with the crests of the palms that circled the statue of Saad Zaghloul. The sky was covered with light clouds, their fringes lambent at the touch of the sun.

We exchanged a few commonplaces. I did my best to show him deep respect and sympathy. He can't be completely broke, I thought. There must be a way of getting his confidence. He may want to make an investment, but is afraid to show that he's got any money left. I led the conversation around to the rising cost of living.

"A young man like me can't possibly depend on a government salary to get by."

"What can he do?"

"I am thinking," I said in a low confessional voice, "of starting some business."

"Where would you get the money?"

"I'd sell a few *feddans* and find a partner." I put on an innocent smile.

"But are you allowed to go into business and keep your government job?"

"No!" I said with a smile. "The business would have to be a secret."

He wished me lots of luck, then spread out his paper as if he'd entirely forgotten I was there. *Maybe he really has nothing left. Or is it just a manoeuvre?* Anyway I lost all hope of getting anything out of him.

Pointing to a red headline about some news of East Germany, he said suddenly, "I suppose you've heard about how poor *they* are, particularly when compared with West Germany." I agreed. He was talking domestic politics now, using the language of foreign affairs. "Russia has nothing to offer her satellites. But the United States . . ."

"We've had really valuable aid from Russia, though."

"That's different," he said hastily. "We are not a Russian satellite." He was on his guard. I regretted what I'd said. "Russia and the United States both wish to dominate the world," he went on. "Our stand of non-alignment is really the best policy and the wisest." I'd lost him and I knew I couldn't get him back soon. I was sorry about that.

"In fact, if it hadn't been for the July Revolution the country would have been overwhelmed by bloodshed."

He nodded his tarboosh in assent. "God is great. His wisdom be praised, which alone has saved us!"

"Where've you been? Why, we haven't seen Your Highness for three days! So you've finally remembered me! But then why should you remember something you've thrown away? Didn't I say you were an ungrateful bastard? Don't give me any of your silly excuses. Don't tell me about your fantastically important work. Even a minister of state wouldn't neglect his mistress the way you've been neglecting me."

I smile complacently as I pour wine in our glasses, keeping down my loathing. I can't stand her and now that she's playing the dictator, I've simply got to get rid of her—free myself from her once and for all.

Every worry in the world goes away when I see Zohra bring in my cup of tea.

We hold each other in a long embrace. I kiss her mouth, her cheeks, her forehead and her neck, then with deeper awareness I relish her lips as she presses them against mine. She draws back a little, sighing, then says, "I think sometimes that they all know."

"Let them!" I am reckless with the ecstasy of love.

"*You* don't care, but . . ."

"I only care for one thing, Zohra." I look at her so that my eyes can tell her how I really feel. I plead. "Let's live together. Away from here."

"Where?" she asks suspiciously.

"In a home of our own."

She waits for me to go on but when I add nothing to my proposal, her eyes cloud with disappointment. "What do you mean?"

"You love me as I love you."

"I love you," she says in a low voice, "but you don't really love me."

"Zohra!"

"You look down on me, just the way they all do."

"I love you. God is my witness," I say with total sincerity. "I love you with all my heart."

She muses sadly for a moment. "Do you consider me your equal as a human being?"

"Why, of course." She shakes her head. I understand what she's getting at. "There are problems one can't solve."

She still shakes her head, looking upset now. "I had to face problems at home, but I didn't give in."

I hadn't imagined she was so proud. I feel desire driving me to the brink of an abyss, I even let my foot slip over the edge, and at the last second try to save myself, as it were, by throwing all my weight backwards. I take her hand in mine, kiss its back, its palm, and whisper in her ear, "I love you, Zohra!"

When I look at Husni Allam's strong and handsome face I always think of wonderful nights on the town. When I hear that he's come to Alexandria to start a business, though, my attitude towards him changes immediately. Tolba Marzuq is only a phantom and I'd better drop him. But Husni is a man determined to work, to achieve something, and what I must do is find myself a part to play in his project. It's not just a question of work or success: he might save me at the last moment from Ali Bakir's God-forsaken plans. The pity of it is that Husni is so mercurial you can hardly catch hold of him. He talks about his projected business once or twice, but he's always daydreaming, dashing around in his car, driving at a ridiculous speed—and always with some woman or other in the seat beside him.

"A man of the world," I advise him, "doesn't spend his time just fooling around."

"How does he spend it?" he asks with amusement.

"Well," I say earnestly, "he studies a plan, considers all the angles, then goes into action."

"Fine, but I prefer to do my studying and considering while I'm playing. We're living on the eve of Doomsday." And he roars with laughter.

My God! I moan inwardly in despair. *I want to make good and help someone else do the same. What shall I do?*

It was a terrible fight. She fired her insults at me and I exploded in anger.

"Can't you forget it for once? Is it Judgement Day already?"

The insults flew back and forth between us, we bombarded each other with curses, and Mahmoud Abu al-Abbas stood there dumbfounded. He had gone with me to her flat for his third lesson in arithmetic and bookkeeping. I got up determined to leave and he followed me out. At the gate of the building, I asked him to go and tell her I wasn't coming back.

I went to the Miramar but didn't realize that she had followed me until I was at the door of the flat, when I felt a hand on the back of my neck and heard Safeya shouting, "You think you can throw me over like that? What do you take me for? A kid? A toy?"

I struggled to get away from her, but she was already inside the door.

"Go away!" I hissed, struggling for breath. "You're disturbing the lodgers. Everyone's asleep."

"You think you can rob me and get away with it!" she screamed. "I've fed you and clothed you and now you want to run away from me, you pig!"

I slapped her, she slapped me back and we wound up in a scuffle. Zohra tried to break it up, but couldn't. "Please stop that," she said to Safeya. "This is a respectable house."

It didn't do any good. She threatened. "Will you go? Or shall I call the police?"

Safeya stepped back and looked at Zohra in surprise. Then she looked from Zohra to me, drew herself up and said, "A servant. How dare you . . . ?"

Before she could finish, Zohra slapped her across the mouth. Safeya hit back, but the girl was too strong for her and hit her until she almost collapsed. Everybody was awake, doors were opened and steps came along the corridor. Husni Allam was there first. He took Safeya by the hand and led her out.

I went to my room, blind with rage. Madame followed me there, very upset. I apologized to her, but she wanted to know who the woman was. I had to tell a lie in order to save face.

"She was my fiancée and I've broken the engagement."

"Her behavior shows you were right to break with her," she said, shaking her head. "But please settle accounts with her somewhere else. I live on the good name of my *pension*."

When Zohra came in, her face still carried traces of the fight. I thanked her and apologized for what she had suffered. We exchanged anguished looks and I had to explain.

"I left her for you."

"Who is she?" she asked curtly.

"A loose woman! I knew her a long time ago. But that's all over and done with. I had to tell Madame she'd been my fiancée."

I kissed her cheek lightly, grateful, regretful.

Outside the wind roars. Inside, even though it's still only early afternoon, my room exudes evening. My mind pictures the dense clouds outside and the mounting waves of the sea. Zohra comes in and switches on the light. I haven't seen her since yesterday and I've been in torment waiting for her.

"Let's go away, Zohra," I plead. She sets the cup on the table and looks at me with biting reproach. "We'll live together forever. Forever."

"And there won't be any problems then?" she asks sarcastically.

I answer with shameful frankness. "The problems I was referring to are created by marriage."

She mutters, "I should be sorry I ever fell in love with you."

"Please don't say that. Please try to understand. I love you—I can't live without you. But marriage would cause difficulties for me, with my family and at work too. It would ruin my career and that would inevitably threaten the home we make together. What can I do?"

She says even more angrily, "I didn't realize I could bring you so much calamity."

"It's not you! It's people's stupidity. These rigid barriers, these stinking facts! What can I do?"

"What can you do indeed?" she says, her eyes narrow with rage. "Turn me into a woman like the one from yesterday?"

"Zohra!" I say desperately. "If you loved me as much as I love you, you'd understand me better."

"I do love you," she says acidly. "It's a mistake I can't help."

"Love is stronger than everything. Everything."

"Everything except your problems," she says contemptuously.

We look at each other, feverish and desperate, furious and inflexible. If it wasn't for my fear and my strength of will, I might give in. I think quickly, in a flash. "Zohra, there are compromises. There's the Islamic marriage in its pure original form." Curiosity replaces anger in her eyes. I really know very little about the subject, but I go on. "We marry as the first Muslims used to marry."

"How was that?"

"I solemnly declare in the company of us two that I take you for my wife, according to the commandments of God and the doctrines of His Prophet."

"With no witnesses?"

"God is our witness."

"Everyone else around us behaves as if they didn't believe in His existence." She shakes her head stubbornly. "No."

She's really mulish. It hasn't been as easy as I expected. There's no persuading her. If she consents to live with me, I'm ready to give up the prospect of marriage, including my plans of advancement through a suitable match. I've thought of leaving the *pension* as a first step to getting her out of my mind, but I can't. We haven't quarrelled; she still brings in my tea as usual, and lets me kiss her or take her in my arms.

One afternoon I am stunned to see her sitting in the hall bent over a primary reader, deciphering the letters. I look at her incredulously. Madame is at her place under the statue of the Virgin. Amir Wagdi is in the armchair.

"Look at our scholar, Monsieur Sarhan," exclaims Madame, smiling. "She's made an arrangement for private lessons with a neighbor, a teacher. What do you think of that?"

I am about to laugh at Madame's teasing irony when suddenly I feel genuinely impressed. "Bravo, Zohra! Good for you."

The old man watches me with clouded eyes. I am all at once afraid of him, I don't know why. I go out.

I am deeply moved. Some inner voice tells me that I have been taking the girl's feelings too lightly and that God will not look kindly on me. But I can't come to terms with the idea of marrying her. Love is only an emotion and you can cope with it one way or another, but marriage is an institution, a corporation not unlike the company I work for, with its own accepted laws and regulations. What's the good of going into it, if it doesn't give me a push up the social ladder? And if the bride has no career, how can we compete in the rat race, socially or otherwise? My problem is that I've fallen in love with a girl whose credentials are insufficient for that sort of thing. But if she'd accept my love without conditions I'd give up the ideal I've always had of marriage altogether.

"You've got a lot of will power, Zohra," I say later, to give her her due. "But it's a pity you're tiring yourself out and wasting all your wages."

"I won't stay illiterate all my life," she says proudly, standing on the other side of the table.

"What good will it do you?"

"I'll learn some profession. And I won't be a servant any more."

That stabs me to the heart. I sit there tongue-tied.

"Some of my people came to fetch me home today," she says in a new voice.

I look at her, smiling to hide my anxiety, but she ignores my expression. "What did you tell them?"

"We settled it. I'll go back next month."

I cry out in extreme anxiety. "Seriously! You're going back to the old man!"

"No. He's married now." She drops her voice. "There's someone else."

I catch her by the hand. "Let's go away together. Tomorrow," I beg. "Today if you like . . ."

"I said I was going home next month."

"Zohra! Have a heart."

"That's one solution, without problems."

"But you love me!"

"Love and marriage are two different things," she answers angrily. "Isn't that what you said?"

But her lips soon give her away; I detect the shadow of a smile. "Zohra, you devil, you've been joking." I am tremendously relieved.

Madame comes in, drinking tea out of a cup in her hand. She sits on the bed and tells me the story of Zohra's refusing to go back home with her relations.

"Don't you think it would have been better for her to go back home?" I suggest slyly.

Madame smiles that knowing smile of a procuress. "Her true relations are here, Monsieur Sarhan."

I avoid her eyes, completely ignoring the implication of her remark, but guessing that a little bird has carried gossip about us from one room to another. She probably thinks worse of us than we deserve, but I'm pleased at the idea of my imaginary conquest. Zohra's obstinacy will not give an inch, though, and I ask myself when I shall have the courage to get out of the *pension*.

It's the usual afternoon scene: Madame sitting close to the radio, almost leaning her head against the set, listening to some foreign song, and Amir Wagdi helping Zohra with her lessons. Then the bell rings. It's Zohra's teacher.

"I do hope you'll excuse me. We have visitors upstairs. If you don't mind, I'd rather give the lesson down here."

Very courteous indeed. We make her welcome. She's quite good-looking; she is also smartly dressed, a career girl. I watch her teach Zohra and I find myself comparing the two of them, simplicity and ignorance, beauty and poverty on the one hand, with education, elegance, and a career on the other. If only Zohra could have found herself in this other girl's world, with all its potentialities.

To satisfy her perpetual curiosity, Madame intrudes on the lesson and we soon learn the lady's name, particulars of her family, even to the detail about the brother working in Saudi Arabia.

"Do you think he might send us some special goods on request?" I find myself asking her. She would enquire, she says.

I leave the *pension* for the Café de la Paix to meet Engineer Ali Bakir.

"Every step is carefully laid out," he says confidently. "It's in the bag." Good! So let's take the leap and make our earthly sojourn worthwhile after all. "I met Safeya Barakat at the Délices. Have you really ditched her?"

"To hell with her!"

Looking shrewdly at me, he laughs. "But have you really left her for a . . . ?"

"How can you believe her? Since when was she somebody anyone could believe?"

For a moment or two he seems to assess me closely. Then he says, "I hope you understand that this deal of ours is the kind of thing you don't talk about, not even to your wife or your own son."

"God forgive you! What do you take me for?"

Wonderful! A look to flatter any male's ego. She didn't smile, didn't bat an eyelid. She just suddenly turned her eyes away from Zohra and her book and landed a look on me. As a rule I might encounter scores of such eyes and never turn a hair. But hers carried some kind of spark, transmitting a message that was quite complete.

So I've changed my route and sit down behind the glass panes of the Miramar Café, watching the clouds and waiting, not with any clear end in view, not warmed by any touch of emotion, but out of sheer curiosity born of boredom and despair, a simple craving for an adventure of any kind. Actually, she isn't at all the kind of girl that grabs me, but that look she gave me was as welcome as an invitation to a picnic on an otherwise empty weekend.

She passes by the front of the café, her hands deep in the pockets of her grey overcoat. I follow her at a distance, then at the Atheneus come up to her. She has bought some sweets and is standing there debating which way to go. I say hello and invite her to a cup of tea. She says she's been thinking of sitting down for a while in the tea-room, so we might as well. We drink our tea and eat two pieces of pastry. Our conversation is cursory but not without interest, in part because of the useful information I gather about her family and her work. In any case it makes me ask for another date, when we meet in the café at the Amir Cinema, then go in together to see the film. It's up to me from then on to decide what kind of affair it's going to be.

I don't find her worth a great deal of effort. And yet when she invites me to meet her family, I accept. I realize that she's looking for a husband and I weigh it all up cold-bloodedly—her salary and what she makes out of private lessons. And always in my mind is the increasing hopelessness of my relationship with Zohra.

When I meet the family I find a new attraction: they own a fair-sized tenement house in Karmouz.[63] I find myself actually taking it all seriously, not out of love for the girl or greed for wealth—theirs is only moderate, after all—but simply to satisfy the longing I've had for a prosperous marriage. But what about Zohra? Is it conceivable that I could find consolation for having abandoned Zohra in marriage to a woman I don't love? Perhaps. But can I really fight down a passion so fixed, so deeply entrenched in my heart?

I had bought the paper and was turning away when Mahmoud made a signal to me to wait a little while he served another customer. When he'd finished, he turned to me.

"*Ustad*, I'm going to propose to Zohra."

To cover my dismay, I grinned at him. "Congratulations! Have you settled it with her?"

"Almost." He seemed very sanguine.

My heart beat painfully. "What do you mean by 'almost'?"

"Well, she's a regular customer, comes here every day. I haven't proposed to her in so many words, but I understand women pretty well." I hated him. "What do you think of her character, sir?"

"Very good. As a matter of fact."

"Until I can meet her people, I'll try to speak for her through Madame."

I wished him luck and walked away. I'd gone only two steps when he caught up with me. "What do you know about her quarrel with her family?"

"Who told you about that?"

"Amir Bey, the old gentleman."

"All I know is that she's extremely stubborn and proud."

"Oh? Well, I know the answer to that one," he boasted. Then he laughed.

When he did propose he was refused. I was delighted, but it added to my sense of guilt and responsibility. I was torn by love and anxiety, and for the time being Aleya's image seemed to recede and grow fainter in the background. It was with pleading tenderness that I took Zohra's wrists.

"Zohra! Save me! Let's go away at once," I begged.

But she disengaged herself roughly. "Stop that. I hate to hear it."

It's no good, I thought. *She loves me, but won't give in without marriage: and I love her, but cannot accept that bond. And both positions, hers and mine, have nothing to do with love that should annihilate mind and will.*

Aleya's father, al-Sayyid Muhammad, invited me to lunch with them and I accepted. At the end of the week I invited the whole family to dinner at Pastoroudis'. After we had sat down in the restaurant, the weather changed; the wind whistled dismally and the rain came down in torrents. I tried to convince myself that Aleya was an excellent girl and that it would be a fine match. *She's good-looking, very well dressed, educated, with a good salary. What more can you want? If she hadn't liked me . . . but why am I so reserved? She certainly loves me. If she wants a husband, she certainly wants a lover. What have I got out of love anyway? The heaven it promises is only an illusion.* Outside the storm raged, almost as if it intended to uproot the city. The sense of warmth and security indoors seemed only to be enhanced. *Now I've introduced myself to this respectable family, without any definite plans or sincere intentions. I haven't even got any money. I should let them know the situation, tell them about my commitments to my family—and leave it up to them.* The conversation soon led to the subject of "marriage" in general.

"In my day," said Aleya's father, "we used to marry early and have the pleasure of seeing our children grow to manhood in our lifetime."

"Those were the days," I said, shaking my head sadly. "Our times are as hard as stone."

He leaned towards me. "A good man is a fortune in himself," he whispered. "Honest people should make things easy for him."

His face was distorted with rage. I'd been only two steps from his stall when he'd noticed me and his whole expression had changed violently. Looking daggers, he muttered something sarcastic without bothering to give me the paper I took every day.

"Why didn't you tell me you were her lover?"

His impudence startled me. I shouted, "You're out of your mind!"

"Coward!"

I lost my temper. I slapped his face with the back of my hand, and he slapped me. Then we grappled blindly, punching each other until passers-by tore us apart and we separated trading insults and curses. For some time afterwards I walked without seeing where I was going, wondering who could have slipped that idea into his empty head.

A long time passed before I saw him again. I had gone into Panayoti's restaurant for a light supper, saw him sitting at the proprietor's place in front of the cash desk, and was on the point of going out again when he leaped up from his seat, embraced me, and kissed my head.[64] He insisted on serving me supper on the house, apologized for his past offence and informed me it was Husni Allam who had told him such a lie.

"My dear, please don't let Zohra know anything about us."

We were sitting at the Palma beside the Mahmoudiyya Canala, enjoying the warmth of the sun. Her regular contact with Zohra worried me. Aleya knew nothing about Zohra's real motive for taking lessons and Zohra had no notion that her teacher had stolen her man.

"Why?" she asked, suspiciously.

"She's a terrible gossip. We don't want any gossip at this stage of our engagement."

"But our engagement will be known sooner or later."

I tried being blunt. "Sometimes I think she has a special fancy for me."

She smiled wanly. "Maybe she has reasons for it."

"All the lodgers tease her occasionally. I've done the same. That's all."

Our relationship had developed considerably and Aleya had come to love me. I didn't care whether she believed me or not; I just wanted her to be on her guard with Zohra. Reason had finally got the better of love. It was up to me now to announce the engagement. But I still hesitated, putting it off under the pretext that I had to apply to my family and invite them down from the village to play their traditional role.

Every day my feelings towards Zohra became more painfully tense. I couldn't bear the thought of letting her down so shamefully. I burned with remorse for my treachery. *If only she would give in, I told myself, I'd be faithful forever.*

What's that? Thunder? An earthquake? Or a demonstration? Has anything fallen in my room? I put my head out from under the bedclothes. It was pitch-dark; and I was myself. *Yes, this is my bed, and this is my room at the Pension Miramar. But what's that? God, it's Zohra! She's calling for help!* I ran out and saw her by the nightlight struggling desperately with Husni Allam.

I guessed the reason for the scene at once and tried to save her

without too much scandal and without spoiling my relationship with
Husni. I laid my hand gently on his arm. "Husni."

But he didn't hear me. I caught him by the shoulder and said
aloud, "Husni, are you out of your mind?"

He shrugged me off violently, but I clutched him by both shoulders and said firmly, "Go into the bathroom and stick your finger
down your throat."

He turned on me and hit me on the forehead. Mad with anger, I
hit him back and we didn't stop until Madame came out. She treated
the aggressor too leniently. I understood the old woman perfectly. *She
was like me, hoping to get something out of his famous business project. The
door is closed in my face now,* I thought, *and she's ready to blame me for his
sake.*

A few days later I caught sight of him leaving the Genevoise, at
about one in the morning, in the company of Safeya Barakat, and I
remembered the day he had taken her out of the *pension. They're birds
of a feather, those two,* I thought, *impulsive dreamers. I suppose they'll live
together on love and dreams.*

I had spent the evening at George's Bar with Ali Bakir and Rafat
Amin. It was a clear night and we walked on the Corniche, braced by
the wine and the weather. Rafat Amin's only subject, especially when
he was drunk, was the Wafd. And Ali Bakir, I soon realized, hardly
knew the difference between the Wafd and the National Sporting
Club. Personally I don't care for politics, in spite of my considerable
political activity. So when Rafat Amin went on and on about the Wafd
in a thick drunken voice, I asked him ironically, "Can't you tell when
something is dead and buried?"

"Praise the Revolution all you like," he roared in a voice that
echoed through the deserted streets. "I can't gainsay its overwhelming power. But I believe that when the Wafd died, the Egyptian
masses died too."

It was then that I saw Husni and Safeya making for the Corniche,
like two ambling bears. I pointed them out at a distance and said with
a laugh, "There are your Wafdist masses, mobilized, ready, prepared
to carry their gallant struggle far on into the night."

Before I left Ali Bakir whispered in my ear. "We'll soon give the go-ahead."

They were all asleep when I got back to the *pension*. I could see a light under Mansour Bahi's door. I knocked and went in. I had no motive for this late visit; it was the wine. He looked up at me in surprise. He was sitting in his armchair and I took a seat near him.

"Excuse me," I said. "I'm drunk."

"Evidently."

"I have failed in fact to make a friend of you." I smiled apologetically. "You're such an introvert."

"It takes all sorts to make a world." He was polite, but not encouraging.

"I suppose you're preoccupied with the problems of your own thinking?"

He replied enigmatically. "My own thinking is the problem."

"Blessed are we, the empty-headed." I laughed.

"Oh come on. You're the center of ceaseless mental activity."

"Really?"

"Yes. Your political life, your revolutionary ideas. Your numerous conquests."

I was struck by the last phrase, but I was too drunk to take it seriously. I understood I wasn't welcome, so I shook him by the hand and left.

When Zohra comes into my room with the tea-tray, I forget all my plans and give myself up to love. But her face is hard, pale and angry.

"Zohra, what's the matter?" I ask with concern.

"If I didn't know that God's wisdom was above everything, I'd lose my faith."

"What's wrong? Is it some new trouble?"

"I saw the two of you with my own eyes." She spits the words out contemptuously.

I know who she means and my heart falls. I ask desperately, "You mean . . ."

"The teacher," she says with savage hatred. "That whore, that man-hunter."

I laugh. I have to, affecting the kind of careless laughter we use to face unjustified anger.

"If you mean your teacher, I just met her by chance and did her a courtesy."

"Liar," she cuts in savagely. "It was *not* by chance. She told me about it today."

"No!"

"The bitch admitted she'd been going out with you. Her parents weren't at all surprised. They were surprised at my asking questions."

I am dumb, unable to say a word to appease her. She cries out in enraged disgust.

"Why does God make sneaks like you?"

I'm shattered, defeated. "Zohra!" I beg from the depth of my despair. "There's no reason to behave like this. I only turned to her in desperation. Please reconsider it, Zohra. We've got to get out of here."

She doesn't seem to hear a word I say.

"What can I do? I have no claims on you. You filthy swine. To hell with you!" She spits in my face.

In spite of my shameful situation, I'm suddenly furious. I shout, "Zohra!"—she spits at me again—"Get out of my sight, or I'll smash your head to bits." I am blind with rage. She leaps at me, slapping my face with unbelievable strength. I shoot up out of my chair in fury and seize her wrist, but she tears away violently and slaps me again. Losing all control, I hit her savagely and she hits back more strongly than I could ever have imagined. Then Madame comes running in, protesting in outlandish gibberish, and takes Zohra away.

"It's none of your business!" I scream after her. "I'll marry whomever I like. I'll marry Aleya."

Mansour Bahi comes and takes me to his room. I can't remember afterwards how the conversation went, but I remember his impudence and I remember that I found myself involved in another fight. His behavior came as a complete surprise to me. I hadn't suspected that he was in love with Zohra too. It explained his strange aloofness with me. Madame arrives on the scene and decides to make a scapegoat of me, the old whore. She says the *pension* has lost its peace since I came to stay, that I've turned it into a public market, with vulgar fighting and rioting.

"Find yourself another place to stay!" she says in a shrill voice.

I have nothing to stay for; out of obstinate pride, however, I insist on staying until the next day, since I've paid the rent in advance.

I go out and wander aimlessly in the streets under a cloudy sky, pregnant with rain. I look in the shop windows brilliant with New Year gifts and stare listlessly at old Santa Claus. Then I go to Pedro's to meet Ali Bakir.

"I hope you've taken care of the alibis," he says. "We start tomorrow at dawn."

Early in the morning I go to work thinking, "The dawn is over; the die is cast." I am tense, impatient for news. I ring the plant and ask for Ali Bakir, but they tell me he's on his morning round. Good. Everything has gone according to plan and he's doing his routine work as usual. Too excited to work, I leave the office early. As I pass by Broadcasting House, I see Mansour and a pretty girl going out together. *Who can it be? His fiancée? His mistress? Will Zohra find herself on the shelf a second time?* At the thought of Zohra I am depressed, which makes me realize that I'm not cured of love for her yet. It's been the only true emotion that ever beat in my wayward heart.

I pay a visit to Aleya Muhammad and her family, who give me a very cool welcome. I'd intended to invent a few lies, but her father bursts out angrily.

"Imagine a housemaid taking us to task like that!"

It's lunchtime, but no one asks me to stay and I leave their flat without any hope of putting things right. Not that I really care. *In a few hours I'll be rich and sure to find a splendid wife.* I have lunch at Panayoti's—Abu al-Abbas's now—then move on to Ali Bakir's house, but he isn't at home and by the time I get to the *pension* I am frantic for news. I pack my suitcase and take it to the entrance hall. From there I ring Ali Bakir and when I hear his voice over the receiver I am immensely relieved.

556 · NAGUIB MAHFOUZ

"Hello."

"This is Sarhan. Greetings. How are things?"

"Everything's fine. I haven't talked with the driver yet."

"When do we know?"

"Let's meet at eight o'clock, at the Swan."

I leave the Pension Miramar and check in at the Pension Eva. Aimless after that, I wander from one café to another, drinking all the time, throwing my money away, drowning my anxiety and the pain of my love-tormented heart in drink, and vowing that my family will enjoy prosperity they've never dreamed of since my father died. A little before eight I arrive at the Swan. I am annoyed to run into Tolba Marzuq at the entrance, but I shake his hand, pretending I'm glad to see him.

"What brings you here?" he says.

"A date."

"Well. Let me buy you a drink. We'll sit together until your friend comes." We sit in the winter lounge. "Cognac?" he asks me, his hollow voice reverberating in his jowls. I am drunk already, but thirsty for more. We drink, talking, laughing.

"Do you think they'd let me go to Kuwait to visit my daughter?" he suddenly asks.

"I expect so. Do you want to make a new start?"

"No. But my son-in-law—he's also my nephew—has become very rich."

"You're probably thinking of emigrating."

There is a cautious look in his eyes. "No. I just want to see my daughter."

I draw my head near his. "Shall I tell you something that should comfort you?"

"What's that?"

"Some people don't like the Revolution. But look at it this way: what other system could we have in its place? If you think clearly, you'll realize that it has to be either the Communists or the Muslim Brotherhood. Which of those lots would you prefer to the Revolution?"

"Neither," he replies hastily.

I smile in triumph. "Exactly. Let that be your comfort."

It is time. But Ali Bakir has not shown up. I wait in agony for another half hour, then I telephone his flat, but get no answer. He's probably on his way. *So what's keeping him? Can't he understand what this delay is doing to me?*

Tolba Marzuq looks at his watch. "It's time for me to go." He shakes me by the hand and leaves.

I cannot stop drinking. Finally a waiter calls me to the telephone. I run to the booth and take up the receiver, my heart thumping.

"Hello! Ali, why haven't you come?"

"Listen, Sarhan, it's gone badly wrong."

His words are all mixed up with the alcohol blurring my brain, everything seems to be spinning around me.

"What's that you're saying?"

"We're lost!"

"But how? Tell me everything."

"What difference does it make? The driver wanted the whole lot for himself. They got him and he's going to give everything away. He's probably done it already."

"What do we do? What are you going to do?" My mouth has gone dry.

"We're finished. I'm going to do what the devil tells me."

He rings off.

I'm trembling, shaking so badly that I can hardly stay on my feet. I think of running away, but the waiter is watching me. I go back to the table. But I can't sit down. I drink off what's left in my glass, pay my bill and walk out. But terror—suffocating, hopeless—is closing in on me. I can't fight it. I head for the bar, order a whole bottle and find myself drinking madly, while the barman watches in alarm, glass after glass, gulping it down without a pause or a word or a look around me. Then I'm looking up at him.

"A razor, please."

The barman smiles, but does not move.

I say it again. "A razor, please!"

He hesitates a little, but when he sees the look in my face he calls a waiter, who comes back from somewhere with a used blade. Thanks.

I put it in my pocket. Now I'm turning away from the bar and walking out towards the front door; I'm reeling. Not from drunkenness. From desperation. Haste. I'm crossing the road, and I wish I had the strength left in me to run.

I have no hope. No hope.

5

AMIR WAGDI

y peace had been destroyed by all these incidents. I had taken asylum in Mariana's *pension* hoping to live quietly in my old age and to find consolation in my memories for the unbearably cruel disappointment of the last years of my career. It had not occurred to me that it would turn into an arena of brutal conflict, ending with violence and even murder.

When a little energy had welled up in me again, I joined Mariana and Tolba Marzuq for our usual gathering in the hall. I wished to see Zohra, but Mariana's hysterics and Tolba's scowls prohibited it. I didn't wish to bring her into such an atmosphere which would be intensified by her woes and would not respect them. I understood that Husni Allam had gone out at his usual hour. He had been upset by the terrible news for a while, but soon seemed to forget it altogether. Mansour Bahi, on the other hand, behaving quite unlike his usual self, was still in bed asleep.

"Here's a miserable ending to the year," complained Mariana. "I wonder what the New Year has in store for us."

"A lot of trouble, no doubt!" said Tolba irritably.

"As long as we're not to blame . . ." I muttered.

He snapped, "You're protected by your old age."

We heard Mansour's door open; he was on his way to the bathroom. Half an hour later he went back to his room. A little after that he came out from behind the screen, his eyes clouded. Madame told him his breakfast was ready, but he refused it with a shake of his head, not saying a word. It upset us all to see him in this condition. Madame was the first to speak.

"Won't you sit down, Monsieur Mansour? Are you all right?"

"Quite all right." He still stood. "I've overslept, that's all."

Madame pointed to the newspaper spread out on the sofa.

"Haven't you heard the news?" He didn't seem interested. "Sarhan al-Behairi was found dead on the road to the Palma."

He gazed into her eyes, showing no surprise or alarm, just staring at her, as if he had not heard or did not understand. Or perhaps he was more seriously ill than we had imagined. Mariana offered him the paper. He looked at it blankly for a while, then read in silence. We were all watching him. Then he looked up.

"Yes, he was found dead—murdered."

"Do sit down," I said. "You're tired."

"I'm all right," he replied coldly, probably not fully conscious of what he was saying.

"You can see we're rather worried," remarked Mariana.

He looked from one face to another.

"Why?"

"Well, we're afraid the police will come. It will be very upsetting."

"They won't come."

"But the police, don't you know . . ." began Tolba Marzuq.

"I killed Sarhan al-Behairi," said Mansour. Then, before we had understood what he said, he walked to the door, opened it, and looked back at us. "I'm going to the police myself."

He closed the door behind him. We looked at one another in amazement and for a moment were all struck dumb.

"He's mad," said Mariana, panic-stricken.

"No, he's sick," I said.

"Maybe Sarhan did kill him," said Tolba Marzuq after a pause.

"That timid, well-behaved young man?"

"He's certainly sick," I said, feeling sorry for the boy.

"But why should he kill him?" wondered Mariana.

"Why should he confess that he did it?" wondered Tolba in his turn.

"I'll never forget his face," said Mariana. "Something has touched his brain."

Tolba went on with his theorizing. "He was the last one to fight with Sarhan."

I protested that everyone had fought with him.

"There lies the cause," he said, pointing to Zohra's room.

I began to be angry. "But he's the only one who hasn't shown any special interest in her."

"That doesn't necessarily mean that he wasn't in love with her, or that he didn't wish to take revenge on a rival."

"My dear sir, Sarhan left her."

"Yes, he left her. But he took her heart and her honor."

"Do shut up. Don't accuse people like that."

"Will he really go to the police?" said Mariana.

We went on talking heatedly until we were exhausted and finally I called a halt.

"That's enough," I said. "We'll submit to what Providence decrees."

Or as darkness on a vast, abysmal sea.
There covereth him a wave, above which is a wave, above
    which is a cloud.
Layer upon layer of darkness.
When he holdeth out his hand he scarce can see it.
And he for whom Allah hath not appointed light, for him
    there is no light.

Hast thou not seen that Allah, He it is Whom all who are in the
heavens and the earth praise, and the birds in their flight?
Of each He knoweth verily the worship and the praise; and
Allah is Aware of what they do.

And unto Allah belongeth the sovereignty of the heavens and
the earth, and unto Allah is the journeying.[65]

My eyes soon grew tired of reading. As I left my room it struck
four. Mariana was writing in the hall.

"It's the first time I've spent such a depressing New Year's Eve,"
she said. "It's like a funeral."

"No more of that, please," said Tolba Marzuq.

"It's like a curse on the place," she went on angrily. "Zohra must
go. She'll have to earn her living somewhere else."

I felt stabbed. "But Mariana, what's she done? She's just unlucky.
It's not her fault. She's turned to you in her trouble."

"She's brought bad luck with her."

"Why don't *we* celebrate the New Year?" said Tolba, snapping his
fingers as if he'd found a bright idea.

"*We?*" I said. "How ridiculous!"

But he ignored me.

"Get ready, my dear," he said to Mariana. "We'll go out together
as we planned."

"But my nerves, Monsieur Tolba, my nerves . . ."

"That's why I'm taking you out."

And as far as they were concerned, everything was suddenly
transformed.

Husni Allam came in and announced his intention of moving out
of the *pension*. When we told him about Mansour Bahi's strange
confession, he was genuinely surprised. He talked it over for a while,
then shrugged his broad shoulders, went and packed his suitcase, said
goodbye, and left.

"We're back on our own, as we started," I commented sadly when
I saw him go.

Tolba said merrily, "Thank God for that!"

And suddenly they were bubbling with energy and excitement and there were no traces of anxiety left. Mariana was decked out as she would have been in the old days. She wore a dark blue evening gown that set off the whiteness of her skin, a black coat with a real fur collar and gilded shoes; and she had put on diamond earrings and a string of pearls. Covering the signs of age with make-up, she seemed to have reverted to the days of her famous beauty. As she stood in the hall, theatrically posed, we looked at each other. And she laughed with joy, like a young girl.

"I'll wait for you," she said to Tolba as she went out, "at the hairdresser's."

I was all by myself, with nothing to keep me company but the howling of the wind. I called for Zohra. I had to call her three times before she finally appeared from behind the screen. She stood there, looking inexpressibly sad and broken, until it seemed to me as if she had actually become bent and shrunken. I pointed to the sofa. Without a word she crossed the room and sat down, under the statue of the Madonna. She folded her arms and looked down at the floor. My heart was so filled with tenderness and compassion for her that tears, too feeble at this late period in my life to give me the relief of weeping, sprang to my eyes.

"Why do you sit there alone, as if you were without friends? Listen. I'm an old man, very old, as you see. I stumbled in my life three or four times. When that happened, I would cry 'It's all over!' and wish I could kill myself. But here I am, as you see, at an age that very few live to. And all that's left of those terrible times of despair are vague memories, without odour, taste or significance. They might have happened to someone else."

She listened without response.

"Let's leave grief to time, which wears away iron and stone. You must think of your future. The truth is, Madame doesn't want you to stay."

"I don't care!"

"What are your plans for the future?"

"Just what they were," she said, looking at the floor. "Until I get what I want."

I sensed a strength of will in her that reassured me. "It's right that you should go on with your plan of learning a profession. But how will you live?"

"I'm offered work at every turn." She spoke with both confidence and defiance.

"What about your village?" I said gently, trying to be persuasive. "Won't you consider going home?"

"No. They don't think well of me."

"What about Mahmoud Abu al-Abbas?" I was almost begging her. "He has his faults, but you're strong. You could certainly reform him."

"He's no better than anyone at home."

I gave up. "I'd so like to see you happy and well, Zohra." I sighed. "I'm very fond of you and I know you like me. And I hope you'll come to me if you're ever in trouble or need." She looked at me with affectionate gratitude. "However painful your past experience has been life will still be the same. You'll still go on looking for the one man who can make you happy." She lowered her head and sighed. "And you will find the man who is worthy of you. He's there now, somewhere. Perhaps he's been waiting for the right happy moment to meet you."

She murmured something I couldn't understand, but I had the feeling that what she had said was right.

"Life is still good," I said. "And it will always be so."

We sat together for a while, between harmony and silence. After some time, she excused herself and went to her room.

I had fallen asleep in my chair and woke up at the sound of the door opening. Mariana and Tolba came in singing. They were drunk. Tolba shouted, "What are you doing up so late, old man?"

"What's the time?" I asked, yawning, rather startled.

"We are two hours into the New Year," said Mariana in a blurred, intoxicated voice. The man pulled her after him to his room, kissing her, and she followed after a half-hearted show of resistance. The door closed behind them. I sat looking at it as if in a dream.

Madame did not come to the table and after setting breakfast Zohra left Tolba and me alone. He had a hangover.

"Lovely morning," I said, pulling his leg. "And congratulations."

He ignored me for some time, then murmured, "It's your evil eye!" But he soon burst out laughing. "It was such a flop, a double fiasco—ludicrous and humiliating at the same time."

I pretended not to understand.

"You know what I mean, you old fox!"

"Mariana?"

He could not help laughing again. "We tried everything you could imagine. In vain. When she took off her clothes she looked like a wax mummy. 'What in the world have we sunk to now?' I said to myself."

"You must have been out of your mind."

"Then she had a kidney attack. Started crying, if you can imagine. Said I was mutilating her!"

After breakfast he followed me into my room and sat down facing me.

"I think I'll go to Kuwait soon. Our departed friend prophesied I would."

"Departed friend?"

"Sarhan al-Behairi." He gave a short laugh. "He tried to reconcile me to the Revolution with the most curious argument. He assured me that the only alternatives to the Revolution were either the Communists or the Brothers. And he thought he'd covered it all!"

I could not see that he hadn't. "But that's the truth."

"There *is* a third alternative," he said mockingly.

"What's that?"

"America."

"You want the United States to govern us?"

"Through a moderate right wing." He mused. "Why not?"

I'd had enough of Tolba's dreams.

"Go to Kuwait, before you lose your mind completely!"

The papers have carried news of the crime—strange, contradictory news. Mansour Bahi confessed to having committed the murder, but could not convince anyone as to his motives. He said he had killed Sarhan because in his opinion Sarhan deserved such a punishment. Why had he deserved it? Because of conduct and qualities bad in themselves, but by no means peculiar to Sarhan. Then why had Mansour chosen him? By mere chance; he might have picked someone else. Those were his answers. Who would have been convinced by such talk? Could the boy be really deranged or was he only pretending?

The post-mortem report stated the cause of death to be a razor cut across the arteries of the left wrist, not a beating with a shoe, as the alleged murderer had claimed. It appeared that most probably it had been a suicide. Then, when the relationship between the victim and the incident of the lorry of stolen yarn came out, the hypothesis of suicide was confirmed.

We wonder what sentence Mansour will get. He will probably be released soon to pick up his life again. But with what heart? Or what reason? "He's an excellent young man," I think sadly, "but he suffers from some secret malady of which he must be cured."

And then there's Zohra, looking, except for a touch of sadness, just as she did when I first saw her. These days that have passed have given her more depth than all the preceding years of her life. I take the cup from her, disguising my old man's heavy-heartedness with a smile.

She says casually, "I'm leaving tomorrow morning."

I have tried to persuade Madame to keep her, but she has refused. For her part, Zohra has told me that she wouldn't stay even if Madame changed her mind. "I am going to a better place," she says—and believes it.

"God bless you!"

She gives me a tender smile. "And I shall never forget you as long as I live."

I motion to her to bring her face nearer to me and kiss her on both cheeks. "Thank you, Zohra."

Then I whisper in her ear.

"Remember that you haven't wasted your time here. If you've come to know what is not good for you, you may also think of it all as having been a sort of magical way of finding out what is truly good for you."

And as often happens, when my heart is too full, I turn to the Sura of the Beneficent, and recite:

The Beneficent
Hath made known the Koran.
He hath created man.
He hath taught him utterance.
The sun and the moon are made punctual.
The stars and the trees adore.
And the sky He hath uplifted; and He hath set the measure,
That ye exceed not the measure,
But observe the measure strictly, nor fall short thereof.
And the earth hath He appointed for His creatures,
Wherein are fruit and sheathed palm trees,
Husked grain and scented herb.
Which is it, of the favours of your Lord, that ye deny?[66]

NOTES

1. *Lady of the Dew.* Literally, "beautiful dew drop," an epithet identified with Princess Qatr al-Nada (Beautiful Dew Drop), the pampered daughter of Sultan Khumaraweyh ibn Ahmed ibn Tulun (864–905). Khumaraweyh's court was renowned for its luxury—the Sultan took his siesta in a garden of gold and silver fruit trees, floating at the center of a pool of quicksilver on a leather air-mattress tethered by silver cords to silver mooring-posts, guarded by a blue-eyed lion—and Qatr al-Nada's wedding journey from the Egyptian capital to Baghdad as the bride of the Caliph was an event of dazzling splendour, unparalleled until the heyday of the Fatimids, a century or so later.

2. *The massive old building . . . tongue of land . . . shotguns cracking incessantly.* The actual approximate site of the author's imagined building, with the fictional Pension Miramar on its fourth floor and a fictional Café Miramar on the groundfloor, is occupied at present by a busy place of entertainment (*cf.* the fictional Genevoise) that specializes in the diversions traditionally enjoyed by visiting seamen and bears (no doubt by coincidence) the same name as the novel. The nearby tongue of land is the Silsila (the Chain), a breakwater protecting the eastern entrance to the Eastern Harbour. At the

seaward tip of the Silsila stands the Tiro Club, which used to offer its customers not only food and drink, but also trap-shooting over the water.

3. *Anfushi.* Amir Wagdi is reminded by Mariana's laugh of the district where he was born, a fishing community at the seaward extremity of the peninsula separating the Eastern and Western Harbours, where his father was keeper of the major mosque. See Notes 9 and 23.

4. *the Pasha.* A fictional character based in part upon the historic character of Saad Pasha Zaghloul (1860–1927), the great nationalist statesman, Minister of Education (1910), Minister of Justice (1912), founder of the Wafd, leader of the 1919 Revolution (see Note 8), and Prime Minister (1924–1927). See Notes 8, 16, 26. Despite retrospective attacks on his character from both the right and the left, Saad's memory remains revered throughout Egypt. Among many very human traits was the fact that he could not differentiate in speech between Arabic consonants *qaf* and *kaf,* which made possible a confusion between *qalb* (heart) and *kalb* (dog), represented here by "core" and "cur." With important exceptions, through which Mahfouz suggests the subsequent moral decline of the Wafd, the words attributed throughout the novel to the Pasha could have been spoken by Saad.

5. *the Trianon.* A fashionable tea-room near the Cecil Hotel (see Note 11), formerly the meeting place of officials and politicians.

6. *your people.* Amir Wagdi refers, of course, not just to Mariana's family or friends but to the Greeks of Alexandria, the ethnic descendants of its founders, most of whom left the country after the July Revolution.

7. *Umm Kulthum.* The most famous and most adored of Egypt's female singers (1899–1975), whose concerts on the first Thursday of each winter month between 1937 and the 1970's were broadcast from Cairo over all the Arab world.

8. *The first revolution . . . the second . . . the Revolution of 1919.* Using the war against the Central Powers as their excuse, the British had deposed the Khedive Abbas Hilmi in 1914 and established a Protectorate, effectively suspending meanwhile the parliamentary powers of the Legislative Assembly. Immediately after the Armistice a delegation (in Arabic, *wafd*) led by

Saad Zaghloul approached the British authorities to demand complete independence. Rebuffed in Cairo and refused permission to travel to London or Paris, where the Egyptian case might, they hoped, have been argued more effectively, the Wafd then organized a campaign for support that led to the arrest and deportation of Saad and three other notables. Demonstrations of protest over this event broke out on 9 March 1919; and on 10 and 11 March—events that Amir Wagdi participated in and remembers well—they spread to al-Azhar (see Note 9), where British soldiers killed or wounded a number of students. Almost instantly the whole country rose. More than 800 Egyptians were killed during the next three weeks, at the end of which the British capitulated on the issue of Saad's arrest. After three more years of continual struggle, Whitehall allowed the establishment of a monarchy under Fuad I and with it a limited amount of sovereignty, though the Occupation itself was in effect to continue for another thirty years, during which the Wafd became the dominant political party in Egypt. Like Amir Wagdi, however, the old Wafd has no heirs. The second revolution, the July Revolution led by Gamal Abdul Nasser in 1952, put an end to the monarchy and the Wafd as well as the Occupation.

9. *Khan Gaafar . . . Khan al-Khalili . . . the Club . . . the turban . . . al-Azhar.*
Khan Gaafar is a street in the heart of the Gamaliyya, the vivid medieval quarter where Mahfouz himself (like the Khedive Ismail) was born, and of which in his famous Trilogy he has made the most extensive artistic record. A large portion of the Gamaliyya is covered by the Khan al-Khalili, a bazaar area since the fourteenth century and well known to tourists as "the Mouski," a name properly applied to an adjacent area in the neighboring district of the Ghuriyya. The Club was a cinema (al-Club al-Misri) that flourished in the Gamaliyya from the First World War onward; like Feshawi's, a nine-hundred-year-old coffee-house recently half-demolished to make room for a parking lot, it was one of the centers of the cultural florescence that took place in the Gamaliyya during the twenties and thirties, when the district was still essentially middle-class, as exemplified in Amir Wagdi's prospective father-in-law. The turban of the prospective father-in-law indicates in this instance a sheikh trained at al-Azhar (The Resplendent), Cairo's thousand-year-old teaching mosque which stands in the Ghuriyya, a stone's throw away from Khan Gaafar, and is now a university, the international center of Islamic learning. As keeper of the Mosque of Sidi Abu al-Abbas al-Morsi, the principal sea-front mosque of Alexandria, Amir Wagdi's

father would also presumably have been Azhar-trained. (Sidi Abu al-Abbas al-Morsi, who died in the fourteenth century, is the patron saint, as it were, of Alexandria's sailors and fishermen; the Mosque is an eighteenth-century Turkish-style building that replaces an earlier structure and overlooks the Eastern Harbour from Anfushi. (See Note 3.) The reason for Amir Wagdi's expulsion from al-Azhar is not clear but it very likely involved "the least thing." Taha Husain, whose classic *Stream of Days* (1939) is a description of student life at al-Azhar during precisely the same era when Amir Wagdi must have been there (*circa* 1905), tells us that the order for his own expulsion arose from a private remark to the effect that a single ambiguous statement ascribed to a general who died in 714 might conceivably be insufficient to convict that general posthumously of heresy. Reinstated through the influence of two powerful politicians, one of whom declared that he had committed a "sin," Taha Husain later left al-Azhar and the world of the turban for what he calls "the world of the tarboosh," the world of secular thought and religious reform, symbolized in the then-modernist headgear that had been introduced from Turkey and that only three decades later, after the July Revolution, would come to be associated with reactionary old gentlemen like Tolba Marzuq. Saad Zaghloul himself, Amir Wagdi's "master," made the same transition at an earlier date.

10. *Ahmed Shafiq . . . Sharia Muhammad Ali.* Ahmed Shafiq (1860–1940) chronicled the history of the Wafd. Sheikh Ali Mahmoud (1902–1949) was famous as the developer of a style of Koranic recitation and Zakariyya Ahmad (1890–1961) was a renowned composer. Both were identified with the cultural life of the Gamaliyya. Sayyid Darwish (1893–1923), the finest singer of modern Egypt before Umm Kulthum (see Note 7), has given his name to the foremost of Cairo's concert halls and his songs are not only sung with undiminished success but have recently been stunningly adapted to contemporary tastes by Muhammad Nuh. The People's Party and the Nationalist Party were rivals of the Wafd. The Muslim Brotherhood, which like the Communist Party was banned after the July Revolution, espoused the idea of a state founded on theocratic principles. Sharia Muhammad Ali (*Sharia* means "street") built by the Khedive Ismail (*regnavit* 1863–1879) in imitation of the Rue de Rivoli and named for his despotic grandfather, leads from Azbakiyya, the site of the Cairo Opera House (mysteriously destroyed by fire in 1971), to the foot of the Citadel (see Note 33) and continues to be identified with musicians, dancers, and women of negotiable virtue. More

especially identified with the latter was an area spreading a kilometre or so to the north and east of Azbakiyya known as the Wasaa (the Open Land) where both local and imported services were formerly available in accommodation ranging from luxurious licenced houses to one-room hovels (see Note 32).

11. *the Atheneus, Pastoroudis', and the Antoniadis . . . the Cecil and the Windsor.* The Atheneus and Pastoroudis' are Greek restaurants. The Antoniadis is a park near the Mahmoudiyya Canal (see Note 17). The Cecil and the Windsor were the leading hotels in Alexandria and had the status of institutions.

12. *the Sura of the Beneficent.* Al-Surat al-Rahman, Koran LV. (Pickthal translation, George Allen & Unwin.)

13. *Undersecretary of State for the Ministry of Mortmain Endowments.* Not without symbolic significance in the context of the novel, this post was formerly one of the most lucrative and powerful in the Egyptian government, since it involved administering, as a "government within a government," the funds and property bequeathed by the Faithful to Islam, accounting for an enormous amount of capital, especially in the form of urban real-estate. Tolba Marzuq's character resembles in part that of one of the actual early Undersecretaries in this ministry, where Naguib Mahfouz himself was employed for several years.

14. *feddans.* A *feddan* is very nearly equivalent to an acre. At the time covered by the novel, legal land reforms instituted under the Nasser regime had reduced holdings by individuals first to two hundred, then to a hundred *feddans,* and they were later to be cut further, with compensation to the former owners. Many holdings were seized outright, however, along with houses, flats, cars, bank accounts, jewelry, furs, books, furniture, and other personal property, in actions that were described as sequestrations and have since been declared illegal. It should be understood that Tolba Marzuq's thousand *feddans* represented first-class agricultural land in a country where the *per capita* share of cultivable land was half an acre and is now two-tenths of an acre, and that such a holding would have been quite sufficient to maintain a millionaire. Land reforms would have reduced it to a hundred *feddans,* but apparently everything Tolba possessed has been placed under sequestration, including even this legal post-reform acreage.

15. *February Fourth.* On 4 February 1942, in the midst of the Second World War, the British drew up a tank battalion in front of Abdine Palace and forcibly installed a Wafd ministry that was presumed to be pro-Allied in its sympathies, thus reducing the Egyptian government openly to puppet status, damaging the moral prestige of the Wafd itself—the party originally identified with constitutionalism and nationalist aspirations—virtually beyond restitution, and laying the ground for the July Revolution ten years later. It is significant that Amir Wagdi, with his humane, high-minded, old-fashioned patriotism, should have abandoned—or been abandoned by—Egyptian politics.

16. *Saad Zaghloul.* See Notes 4 and 8.

17. *the Palma . . . the Mahmoudiyya Canal.* The Palma is a tea-garden situated rather remotely from the center of the city on the Mahmoudiyya Canal, which links Alexandria with the Nile and defines the southern and western edges of the city proper.

18. *melaya . . . Sharia Muhammad Ali.* The *melaya* is the black shawl or drapery traditionally used by Egyptian women as an outer garment or overcoat. For the significance of Sharia Muhammad Ali, see Note 10.

19. *Iblis.* The Koranic name of Satan. See Note 9, on *the turban.*

20. *the Prophet's Birth . . . the Dimirdashiyya.* The birthday of the Prophet is celebrated as a holiday in most Muslim countries. In Cairo a notable part of the celebration is a procession of the Sufi sects, one of the best endowed of which was the Dimirdashiyya, headed by a pasha of the Dimirdash family. Amir Wagdi's remarks reflect the opinion that this sect nurtured collaborationist tendencies.

21. *fellaha.* A farm-woman or peasant.

22. *Behaira.* The agricultural province adjoining Alexandria famous for its onions and other market produce.

23. *I kissed . . . with me.* "She" is Amir Wagdi's widowed mother, living alone at Anfushi. See Note 3.

24. *gallabiyya.* The typical long cotton gown of Egypt, made fashionable recently in the West as a "caftan."

25. *Bargawan, Darb Al Ahmar . . . Sidi Abu al Suud.* Bargawan, named for a tenth-century vizier, is in the neighborhood of the Gamaliyya. The Darb Al Ahmar quarter takes its name from its major street, which is lined with fourteenth-century buildings and runs north-easterly from the Gate of the Vizier at the Citadel (see Note 33) to Bab Zuweila, the southern gate of the Fatimid royal enclosure in which the districts of the Gamaliyya and the Ghuriyya lie and for which the whole of Cairo is named. The shrine of Sidi Abu al Suud stands in Fustat, at the southern outskirts of modern Cairo, on what is now Sharia Salah Salem.

26. *Minister of Justice . . . effendi . . . Circassians.* See Note 5 on *the Pasha.* The conversation recorded here takes place before the Pasha had been elevated to that rank. As used in Egypt the Turkish title *effendi* (master) was freely applied as a mode of address to the clerical class and is now virtually equivalent to "sir" or "mister." *Pasha* or *bey,* titles bestowed before 1914 by the Ottoman Sultan, came to signify wealth and social status rather than simply political power. From the Mamluk period until after 1919 the ruling class in Egypt, the class of the *pashas* and *beys,* was largely Turco-Circassian in origin. Turkish remained the court language until the accession of Farouk—whose first language was English—in 1936.

27. *Tanta.* A city in the Delta between Cairo and Alexandria, capital of the province of Gharbiyya.

28. *Liberation Organization . . . Company Board.* The Organizations listed by Sarhan are all parts of the apparatus set up by the July Revolution. See Note 55.

29. *1919, that bloody uprising.* The uprising following Saad's arrest. See Note 8.

30. *Bismillah . . . inheritors.* Koran XXVIII. 1–6 (The Sura of the Narration).

31. *My dear Pasha . . . Kasr al-Nil Barracks.* The conversation here takes a symbolic turn to define the Pasha's (and the Wafd's) later character as opposed to the ideals for which Saad Zaghloul and the original Wafd had stood. The Agricultural Credit Bank was founded four years after Saad Zaghloul's death, reputedly with the aim of ruining Wafdist landowners, and still exists. The Kasr al-Nil Barracks do not. Reserved by the British for the use of Guards regiments and therefore, not surprisingly, occupying the most luxurious site in Cairo (though also notoriously vermin-ridden), they have been replaced by Madan al-Tahrir (Liberation Square), the Arab League and Arab Socialist Union Secretariats, and the Nile Hilton Hotel.

32. *He clutched . . . officer's whore.* Amir Bey recalls a famous police episode of some forty years earlier, the sentencing of the notorious Ibrahim el-Gharby, the King of the Wasaa (see Note 10) — an enormously obese Nubian transvestite who controlled the entire Cairene traffic in women during the second decade of the century — who amassed not only a fortune but also considerable social and political influence, was exiled to the country, and later died in prison, leaving his inheritance to a younger and more brutal generation. The political overtones behind this reminiscence should not be missed.

33. *Sault's, Groppi's, Alf Laila, and Lipton Gardens . . . the Citadel.* Sault's, Groppi's, and Lipton Gardens were tea-gardens in the area between Shepheard's Hotel (burned in 1952) and the Kasr al-Nil Barracks (see Note 31). Groppi's still exists; the others have disappeared as the area has changed its character. The Citadel is a complex of buildings that dates back in its origins to Saladin. Overlooking Cairo from the Muqattam Hills east of the Nile, it has served as headquarters for military rule intermittently from that time down to the present. The nineteenth-century Turkish mosque that surmounts it contributes a picturesque if rather spurious "oriental" highlight to the Cairo skyline; the small palace nearby was burned in 1972.

34. *Everyone . . . deny?* Koran LV. 25–27 (The Sura of the Beneficent). These verses have frequently been said to summarize the Arab view of what the West calls "history" and are often quoted — being inscribed, for example, on the tomb in Cairo of one of the Abbasid Caliphs, the sixth in that long line of luxuriously maintained but impotent figureheads.

35. *Ferekeeko.* A slang nomen of no certain lexical origin, modish among the alienated young of the early 1960's, approximately equivalent to *man* in "Man, dig that!" or "Watch your head, man!" An index to both period and social class, the word is so distant from colloquial, classical, or literary Arabic as to suggest in itself a certain amount of conscious social rebellion.

36. *progeny of whores . . . feddans . . . Miss Blue-Eyes.* The possession of a hundred *feddans* (see Note 14) would suffice in itself to define Husni's social position, for in an Egyptian context they could only represent the remains of a larger holding reduced in the course of the July Revolution's land reforms. They would also suffice to keep him living comfortably. His own remarks, as well as his cousin Mervat's blue eyes and Turkish name, point to the fact that Husni, like Tolba Marzuq, belongs to the remnants of the Turco-Circassian elite (see Note 26), many of whom traced their descent from Circassian concubines, girls who were either purchased or acquired as gifts and who were frequently passed on, slightly used, to friends, colleagues or clients of the original husband or owner.

37. *fort of Sultan Qaitbay . . . giant stone jetty-arm.* Like Amir Wagdi, Husni Allam looks out over the Eastern Harbour, which the Corniche, sweeping along the shore from right to left, shapes into a crescent that terminates two kilometres away across the harbour at Anfushi in a little peninsula surmounted by the fort of Sultan Qaitbay (d. 1495), situated on the site of the ancient Pharos. Near at hand to the right and running out perpendicular to the Corniche, almost closing the arc of the crescent, is the breakwater of the Silsila. (See Note 2.)

38. *the Revolutionary Charter.* Promulgated in February 1962, the Charter described "the socialist situation" as "inevitable" and defined the Arab Socialist Union as the major political instrument for guiding the Revolution into such a situation. (See Note 55.)

39. *Dream-Boy Behairi.* Husni puns on Sarhan's name, which means "dreamer," and suggests both the strength of his charm and the weakness of his moral vision.

40. *nargilah.* The hubble-bubble or water pipe.

41. *Mazarita, Chatby, Ibrahimiyya . . . Siyouf . . . the boulevard to Abu Qir.* The Pension Miramar stands in Mazarita, just within the Eastern Harbour. Immediately to the east, outside the harbour along the Corniche, is the district of Chatby; beyond lie Ibrahimiyya, the Sporting Club district, Cleopatra, Camp de César, Sidi Gabir, and Siyouf.

42. *Omar Khayyam.* An Alexandrian restaurant.

43. *Qalawoon, the Doddering Sultan.* One of the ablest, most successful and long-lived (1220–1290) of the notoriously short-lived Mamluk Sultans, founder of a hospital that has served the Gamaliyya continuously down to the present time, Qalawoon died while on his way at the age of seventy to lead a siege against Acre. His name is Mongol in origin and may have an absurd ring in Arabic, which the editors have tried to suggest in their transliteration, but Husni's allusion in referring to Amir Wagdi by the name is intended as ironic on other grounds which the editors have attempted to clarify with the epithet "Doddering Sultan." There is an additional irony, however, given Amir Wagdi's lamented childlessness, in that Qalawoon founded a dynasty lasting nearly a hundred years.

44. *the portrait.* A portrait of Gamal Abdul Nasser (1918–1970), leader of the July Revolution.

45. *Cleopatra.* See Note 41.

46. *I've seen you together.* A piquant allusion on Husni's part to a song popular in the early 1960's that began: "Don't lie to me—I've seen you together."

47. *Qaitbay . . . Abu Qir . . . Siyouf . . . Chatby . . . Sidi Gabir.* (See Note 41.)

48. *Pam Pam.* A restaurant and nightclub near the Corniche.

49. *Moharrem Bey.* An inland district.

50. *our lord Omar.* The second of the four Orthodox Caliphs who immediately succeeded the Prophet as heads of Islam, renowned for his piety, abstemiousness, and common sense.

51. *Ya Sayyid! Ya Badawi!* . . . *July Ordinances!* Repeating a homely banality that originally had the character of a pious ejaculation, Husni Allam invokes the name of Sayyid al-Badawi (d. 1275), a Muslim saint whose shrine in Tanta attracts crowds of a million or more during his annual *moulid.* Such an invocation ordinarily suggests astonishment tinged with some degree of moral sentiment and can thus be turned, as it is in Egypt and certainly is in this instance, to ironic effect. The July Ordinances of 1961 introduced socialism into Egypt, virtually creating a *coup d'état,* and may be compared in their rather different aims and effects with the July Ordinances promulgated in France in 1830.

52. *Camp de César.* See Note 41.

53. *Party business.* It should be understood that Mansour's friend Fawzi is a Communist, that the Communist Party has been outlawed by the regime, that Mansour has been forced by his brother to leave it, but has retained essential loyalty to it, and that his schizoid behavior arises from this loyalty.

54. *loafing.* The original refers to Sarhan as a *habitué* of the *mastaba,* a low seat formerly found in front of shops or important houses, especially in villages, where men customarily gathered to gossip, talk politics, or discuss business. The *mastaba* is now often nostalgically identified with the supposed leisurely pace of traditional or country life, especially by urbanites, the *mastabas* of Cairo having been summarily removed as long ago as the 1840's by order of that energetic Prince, Muhammad Ali, in the interests of improving the flow of traffic.

55. *board of directors* . . . *ASU Base Unit.* In accord with socialist measures that began to be implemented in 1961 and included the Charter (see Note 38), industrial and office workers were given twenty-five per cent of the shares in their firm's profits and seats on their firm's board of directors. Scores of firms, including the entire banking and commercial network of the cotton industry, were nationalized, and the ASU (the Arab Socialist Union) became the sole instrument of popular democracy, with theoretical powers of direction at all levels. Sarhan represents the workers on the board of directors of the Alexandria Yarn Mills, but as an important and up-and-coming member of the ASU he is also, in effect, a member of the political body to which that board must answer. He has thus made a place for himself

580 • NAGUIB MAHFOUZ

in what a capitalist would be tempted to define as four very different interest groups—government, stockholders, management, and labour—though it is obvious that Sarhan is the last person likely to be concerned by the multitudinous possibilities in such a situation for conflict of interest.

56. *conventional rhyming prose.* In Arabic, *saj'*, a prose mode that dates to earliest literary history among the Arabs and was consecrated by its association with the Koran, surviving all the way down to the present century, rhyme becoming in fact the primary rhetorical feature of consciously literary prose. The closest stylistic analogy to *saj'* in English is probably the short-lived euphuism identified with John Lyly (d. 1606) which may have been influenced by Arabic indirectly through North's translation of Guevara.

57. *the Auberge in Fayoum.* A formerly fashionable country resort south of Cairo.

58. *Blessed . . . of yours.* Sarhan does not say these words aloud, though the Egyptian, like the Spaniard or Latin-American with his *piropo* (Blessed be the land where the tree grew from which they took the wood to make your cradle!), has a ready stock of flowery or provocative phrases to fire at passing girls, and can also improvise. A Cairo traffic policeman has been known to bring a thousand cars crashing to a halt in order to allow the unimpeded passage of a particular beauty, while declaiming a dozen lines or so made up on the spot to rhyme with the favored girl's name.

59. *school-opening crisis.* For a family like Sarhan's finding the money for shoes and clothing alone would have meant a considerable sacrifice, in which he would naturally be expected to share.

60. *the wall.* Ali Bakir's sardonic humor here hinges on the fact that the direction of prayer, indicated in a mosque by the *qibla* niche in one wall, is also the direction in which one turns the face of the dead at burial.

61. *Ustad.* Literally, "professor," this word is used as the polite mode of addressing the presumably educated.

62. *the Revolution.* See notes 8, 38, and 55.

63. *Karmouz.* An inland slum district backing on the Mahmoudiyya Canal.

64. *kissed my head.* Implying the desire for forgiveness and reconciliation, this typical gesture creates a tableau bearing an accrbic political symbolism that should not be lost.

65. *Or as darkness . . . the journeying.* Koran XXIV. 40–42 (The Sura of Light).

66. *The Beneficent . . . deny?* Koran LV. 1–13. See Notes 12 and 34.